Kyle Achilles Series, Book 1

Pushing Brilliance

Tim Tigner

**If something strikes you as unrealistic,
kindly consider taking another look at reality.**
(Links are included after each novel to help you get started.)

**This one's for mom. She's been pushing me to be brilliant for
nearly five decades. Most people would have given up by now, but
not Gwen Tigner. Love you, mom.**

Copyright © 2018 Tim Tigner
All rights reserved.
ISBN: 9781729391389

For more information on this novel or Tim Tigner's other thrillers,
please visit timtigner.com

PUSHING BRILLIANCE

PART 1: AUDACITY

Chapter 1

The Kremlin

HOW DO YOU PITCH an audacious plan to the most powerful man in the world? Grigori Barsukov was about to find out.

Technically, the President of Russia was an old friend — although the last time they'd met, his old friend had punched him in the face. That was thirty years ago, but the memory remained fresh, and Grigori's nose still skewed to the right.

Back then, he and President Vladimir Korovin wore KGB lieutenant stars. Now both were clothed in the finest Italian suits. But his former roommate also sported the confidence of one who wielded unrivaled power, and the temper of a man ruthless enough to obtain it.

The world had spun on a different axis when they'd worked together, an east-west axis, running from Moscow to Washington. Now everything revolved around the West. America was the sole superpower.

Grigori could change that.

He could lever Russia back into a pole position.

But only if his old rival would risk joining him — way out on a limb.

As Grigori's footfalls fell into cadence with the boots of his escorts, he coughed twice, attempting to relax the lump in his throat. It didn't work. When the hardwood turned to red carpet, he willed his palms to stop sweating. They didn't listen. Then the big double doors rose before him and it was too late to do anything but take a deep breath, and hope for the best.

The presidential guards each took a single step to the side, then opened their doors with crisp efficiency and a click of their heels. Across the office, a gilded double-headed eagle peered down from atop the dark wood paneling, but the lone living occupant of the Kremlin's inner sanctum did not look up.

President Vladimir Korovin was studying photographs.

Grigori stopped three steps in as the doors were closed behind him, unsure of the proper next move. He wondered if everyone felt this way the first time. Should he stand at attention until acknowledged? Take a seat by the wall?

He strolled to the nearest window, leaned his left shoulder up against the frame, and looked out at the Moscow River. Thirty seconds ticked by with nothing but the sound of shifting photos behind him. *Was it possible that Korovin still held a grudge?*

Desperate to break the ice without looking like a complete fool, he said, "This is much nicer than the view from our academy dorm room."

Korovin said nothing.

Grigori felt his forehead tickle. Drops of sweat were forming, getting ready to roll. As the first broke free, he heard the stack of photos being squared, and then at long last, the familiar voice. It posed a very unfamiliar question: "Ever see a crocodile catch a rabbit?"

Grigori whirled about to meet the Russian President's gaze. "What?"

Korovin waved the stack of photos. His eyes were the same cornflower blue Grigori remembered, but their youthful verve had yielded to something darker. "I recently returned from Venezuela. Nicolas took me crocodile hunting. Of course, we didn't have all day to spend on sport, so our guides cheated. They put rabbits on the riverbank, on the wide strip of dried mud between the water and the tall grass. Kind of like teeing up golf balls. Spaced them out so the critters couldn't see each other and gave each its own pile of alfalfa while we watched in silence from an electric boat." Korovin was clearly enjoying the telling of his intriguing tale. He gestured with broad sweeps as he spoke, but kept his eyes locked on Grigori.

"Nicolas told me these rabbits were brought in special from the hill country, where they'd survived a thousand generations amidst foxes and coyotes. When you put them on the riverbank, however, they're completely clueless. It's not their turf, so they stay where they're dropped, noses quivering, ears scanning, eating alfalfa and watching the wall of vegetation in front of them while crocodiles swim up silently from behind.

"The crocodiles were being fooled like the rabbits, of course. Eyes front, focused on food. Oblivious." Korovin shook his head as though bewildered. "Evolution somehow turned a cold-blooded reptile into a warm white furball, but kept both of the creature's brains the same. Hard to fathom. Anyway, the capture was quite a sight.

"Thing about a crocodile is, it's a log one moment and a set of snapping jaws the next, with nothing but a furious blur in between. One second the rabbit is chewing alfalfa, the next second the rabbit *is* alfalfa. Not because it's too slow or too stupid ... but because it's out of its element."

Grigori resisted the urge to swallow.

"When it comes to eating," Korovin continued, "crocs are like storybook monsters. They swallow their food whole. Unlike their legless cousins, however, they want it dead first. So once they've trapped dinner in their maw, they drag it underwater to drown it. This means the rabbit is usually alive and uninjured in the croc's mouth for a while — unsure what the hell just happened, but pretty damn certain it's not good."

The president leaned back in his chair, placing his feet on the desk and his hands behind his head. He was having fun.

Grigori felt like the rabbit.

"That's when Nicolas had us shoot the crocs. After they clamped down around the rabbits, but before they dragged 'em under. That became the goal, to get the rabbit back alive."

Grigori nodded appreciatively. "Gives a new meaning to the phrase, *catch and release*."

Korovin continued as if Grigori hadn't spoken. "The trick was putting a bullet directly into the croc's tiny brain, preferably the medulla oblongata, right there where the spine meets the skull. Otherwise the croc would thrash around or go under before you could get off the kill shot, and the rabbit was toast.

"It was good sport, and an experience worth replicating. But we don't have crocodiles anywhere near Moscow, so I've been trying to come up with an equally engaging distraction for my honored guests. Any ideas?"

Grigori felt like he'd been brought in from the hills. The story hadn't helped the lump in his throat either. He managed to say, "Let me give it some thought."

Korovin just looked at him expectantly.

Comprehension struck after an uncomfortable silence. "What happened to the rabbits?"

Korovin returned his feet to the floor, and leaned forward in his chair. "Good question. I was curious to see that myself. I put my first survivor back on the riverbank beside a fresh pile of alfalfa. It ran for the tall grass as if I'd lit its tail on fire. That rabbit had learned life's most important lesson."

Grigori bit. "What's that?"

"Doesn't matter where you are. Doesn't matter if you're a crocodile or a rabbit. You best look around, because you're never safe.

"Now, what have you brought me, Grigori?"

Grigori breathed deeply, forcing the reptiles from his mind. He pictured his future atop a corporate tower, an oligarch on a golden throne. Then he spoke with all the gravitas of a wedding vow. "I brought you a plan, Mister President."

Chapter 2

Brillyanc

PRESIDENT KOROVIN REPEATED Grigori's assertion aloud. "You brought me a plan." He paused for a long second, as though tasting the words.

Grigori felt like he was looking up from the Colosseum floor after a gladiator fight. Would the emperor's thumb point up, or down?

Korovin was savoring the power. Finally, the president gestured toward the chess table abutting his desk, and Grigori's heart resumed beating.

The magnificent antique before which Grigori took a seat was handcrafted of the same highly polished hardwood as Korovin's desk, probably by a French craftsman now centuries dead. Korovin took the opposing chair and pulled a chess clock from his drawer. Setting it on the table, he pressed the button that activated Grigori's timer. "Give me the three-minute version."

Grigori wasn't a competitive chess player, but like any Russian who had risen through government ranks, he was familiar with the sport.

Chess clocks have two timers controlled by seesawing buttons. When one's up, the other's down, and vice versa. After each move, a player slaps his button, stopping his timer and setting his opponent's in motion. If a timer runs out, a little red plastic flag drops, and that player loses. Game over. There's the door. Thank you for playing.

Grigori planted his elbows on the table, leaned forward, and made his opening move. "While my business is oil and gas, my hobby is investing in startups. The heads of Russia's major research centers all know I'm a so-called *angel investor*, so they send me their best early-stage projects. I get everything from social media software, to solar power projects, to electric cars.

"A few years ago, I met a couple of brilliant biomedical researchers out of Kazan State Medical University. They had applied modern analytical tools to the data collected during tens of thousands of medical experiments performed on political prisoners during Stalin's reign. They were looking for factors that accelerated the human metabolism — and they found them. Long story short, a hundred million rubles later I've got a drug compound whose strategic potential

I think you'll appreciate."

Grigori slapped his button, pausing his timer and setting the president's clock in motion. It was a risky move. If Korovin wasn't intrigued, Grigori wouldn't get to finish his pitch. But Grigori was confident that his old roommate was hooked. Now he would have to admit as much if he wanted to hear the rest.

The right side of the president's mouth contracted back a couple millimeters. A crocodile smile. He slapped the clock. "Go on."

"The human metabolism converts food and drink into the fuel and building blocks our bodies require. It's an exceptionally complex process that varies greatly from individual to individual, and within individuals over time. Metabolic differences mean some people naturally burn more fat, build more muscle, enjoy more energy, and think more clearly than others. This is obvious from the locker room to the boardroom to the battlefield. The doctors in Kazan focused on the mental aspects of metabolism, on factors that improved clarity of thought–"

Korovin interrupted, "Are you implying that my metabolism impacts my IQ?"

"Sounds a little funny at first, I know, but think about your own experience. Don't you think better after coffee than after vodka? After salad than fries? After a jog and a hot shower than an afternoon at a desk? All those actions impact the mental horsepower you enjoy at any given moment. What my doctors did was figure out what the body needs to optimize cognitive function."

"Something other than healthy food and sufficient rest?"

Perceptive question, Grigori thought. "Picture your metabolism like a funnel, with raw materials such as food and rest going in the top, cognitive power coming out the bottom, and dozens of complex metabolic processes in between."

"Okay," Korovin said, eager to engage in a battle of wits.

"Rather than following in the footsteps of others by attempting to modify one of the many metabolic processes, the doctors in Kazan took an entirely different approach, a brilliant approach. They figured out how to widen the narrow end of the funnel."

"So, bottom line, the brain gets more fuel?"

"Generally speaking, yes."

"With what result? Will every day be like my best day?"

"No," Grigori said, relishing the moment. "Every day will be better than your best day."

Korovin cocked his head. "How much better?"

Who's the rabbit now? "Twenty IQ points."

"Twenty points?"

"Tests show that's the average gain, and that it applies across the scale, regardless of base IQ. But it's most interesting at the high end."

Another few millimeters of smile. "Why is the high end the most interesting?"

"Take a person with an IQ of 140. Give him Brillyanc — that's the drug's name — and he'll score 160. May not sound like a big deal, but roughly speaking, those 20 points take his IQ from 1 in 200, to 1 in 20,000. Suddenly, instead of being the smartest guy in the room, he's the smartest guy in his discipline."

Korovin leaned forward and locked on Grigori's eyes. "Every ambitious scientist, executive, lawyer ... and politician would give his left nut for that competitive advantage. Hell, his left and right."

Grigori nodded.

"And it really works?"

"It really works."

Korovin reached out and leveled the buttons, stopping both timers and pausing to think, his left hand still resting on the clock. "So your plan is to give Russians an intelligence edge over foreign competition? Kind of analogous to what you and I used to do, all those years ago."

Grigori shook his head. "No, that's not my plan."

The edges of the cornflower eyes contracted ever so slightly. "Why not?"

"Let's just say, widening the funnel does more than raise IQ."

Korovin frowned and leaned back, taking a moment to digest this twist. "Why have you brought this to me, Grigori?"

"As I said, Mister President, I have a plan I think you're going to like."

Chapter 3

2 Years Later

WHILE THE MELODIC CLINK of a silver spoon on Waterford crystal quieted the banquet's fifty guests and halted the jazz trio playing in the corner, Achilles leaned toward his brother and whispered, "Who's the speaker?"

Colin swallowed his last bite of steak. "Sometimes I forget you're from a different world. That's Vaughn Vondreesen. He's the venture capitalist who recruited dad to Vitalis."

Achilles really was from a different world, Colin mused. Whereas Colin and his father were entrepreneurial physicians, Achilles was a spy. Well, he used to be a spy. Currently, he was unemployed. Funny thought, that. An unemployed spy. *How did spies get jobs?*

"He looks like George Clooney," Achilles said.

"And he's just as charming. Even has a British accent from his Oxford days." Colin gave his younger brother one of those some-guys-have-all-the-luck nods. "They say Vondreesen is as powerful in Silicon Valley as Clooney is in Hollywood."

The brothers were at a four-top table in the back of a stylish Santa Barbara restaurant named Bouchon. Colin was seated beside his girlfriend, Katya. Achilles sat next to an empty chair. As the honoree's immediate family, custom would have seated them at the head table, but they'd ceded the seats to their father's favored colleagues. The businessmen had all driven down from Silicon Valley for the night, whereas the family would be dining together for another week.

As if on cue, Vondreesen began, his regal intonation instantly silencing the crowd. "We're here tonight in Santa Barbara's finest restaurant, with Silicon Valley's finest executives, to celebrate the sixtieth birthday of the finest man I've ever known, and alas, his retirement."

Applause erupted, and everyone stood. After a minute of heartfelt clapping, the guests returned to their seats and Vondreesen continued. "Let me tell you a few things you might not know about John ..."

Achilles again leaned toward his brother. "What's going on?"

"What do you mean?" Colin asked, knowing full well what he meant.

"You're nervous about something."

The brothers had no secrets. Achilles was just eighteen months younger, but their boyhood rivalry had long ago given way to brotherly love. As they'd grown, their careers and personalities had evolved as differently as the flower from the leaf. But with common roots and seed, they generally shared one mind. "No worries. I'll tell you later."

"And they say I'm the mysterious one," Achilles replied.

"What's mysterious?" Katya asked, more interested in their discussion than Vondreesen's speech.

Colin flashed Achilles a warning with his eyes, possibly confirming a suspicion but figuring that was better than the alternative.

"From my perspective," Katya continued, "The only mystery tonight is why Achilles hasn't been flirting with Sophie."

"Who's Sophie?" Colin asked.

"Our waitress," Katya said. "She's been eying Achilles all night."

"It's the clothes," Achilles said. "She thinks I'm a rebel."

"It's not the James Dean wardrobe," Katya said. "Trust me." While she spoke, Katya beckoned for Sophie to come over.

Katya was the love of Colin's life. He had fallen for her at first sight, and a year later she still electrified him every time she walked into a room. She was beautiful and brilliant, bold and brave, compassionate and kind. He was utterly, completely, and blissfully bewitched. In other words, he loved her dearly.

When the waitress arrived, Katya caught her eye. "Achilles here was just wondering where you're studying."

Sophie's face turned a cute combination of coy and confused. "Did she call you by your last name?"

"She did. I've always gone by Achilles."

"What's your first name?"

"It's a secret."

Sophie's expression indicated that she wasn't sure if Achilles was joking or not, but she moved on. "Okay. Now that we've kinda cleared that up, what makes you think I'm a student?"

"That was actually Katya's question."

"Oh," Sophie said, sounding wounded.

"I already know you study marine biology at UCSB," Achilles said.

Sophie and Katya both did double takes at that. Colin smiled.

"How do you know that?" Sophie asked.

"Is he right?" Katya asked.

"He's right," Colin said. "I don't know how he knows, but trust me, he knows." Colin beckoned Sophie closer. It was his turn to whisper. "Achilles used to work for the CIA." He met her widening eyes with a reassuring nod.

A round of applause broke the moment. Vondreesen had completed his toast. As a lawyerly-looking guest launched into his kind remarks, Sophie grabbed the empty seat next to Achilles and asked, "How did you know that about me? Do you have some facial recognition phone app? Were you *practicing tradecraft* on me?"

"Practicing tradecraft?" Achilles raised his eyebrows.

"I read Ludlum and Flynn," she replied, mock challenge in her voice.

"Well, Sophie, since you read Ludlum and Flynn, you can appreciate that I was conducting a basic threat assessment."

Sophie brought her hands to her proud chest, fingers splayed. "Surely I don't look threatening?"

"You were obviously concealing something over there on the side table, among the menus. Given the way you went back to it whenever you had a spare minute, I figured it was a book rather than a bomb. Either some fantastic fiction like Ludlum or Flynn, or perhaps a textbook, but I've learned not to assume. So I checked it out."

Colin was pleased to see Sophie's flirtatious reaction. He was happy to be out of the dating game, but still enjoyed it as a spectator sport. And his brother could use a good time.

"I have a chemistry test Monday," Sophie said. "That's a chemistry textbook. How'd you know I'm a marine biology student?"

Achilles held up both hands. They were big as a quarterback's, and calloused from thousands of hours climbing rocks. Very manly. He held his fingers wide and then brought them together like the overlapping circles of a Venn diagram. "Graduate level chemistry classes and scuba diving have a pretty limited overlap."

"Scuba diving? What makes you think I'm a scuba diver?"

"The tan lines on your face and wrists indicate you frequently wear a wetsuit with a hoodie."

"Maybe I surf, or dive as a hobby." Sophie was obviously enjoying the mental joust. "This is Santa Barbara, after all."

"It's scuba. Surfers don't typically wear wetsuit hoodies. Hobby doesn't fit either. You're working your way through graduate school as a waitress, and you're busy and diligent enough to risk sneaking a textbook to work on a Saturday night, so you don't have the kind of free time those tan lines would imply if coming from a hobby."

Rather than respond, Sophie studied Achilles for a moment. "Are you sailing later tonight, or in the morning?"

"Late morning. After brunch."

Colin looked Sophie's way and cleared his throat. She checked her watch and stood. "Time for dessert."

Katya threw a *you're welcome* look in Achilles' direction, followed by a toothy grin. She had a big beautiful mouth that used to remind Colin of the actress Anne Hathaway. Now Anne's smile reminded him of Katya. Apparently Katya was quite pleased with her good deed. Or maybe she wanted Achilles off the yacht for the night. Perhaps she sensed what was coming.

Chapter 4

A Cold Reception

TIME LIES. It masquerades in symmetrical guise, using clocks and calendars as accomplices. They cloak it in perfect uniformity, regular as hatch marks on a ruler, stretching forward and backward without variance of size or scale or import. As anyone who has lived even a little knows, this is a grand deception.

I was about to be served with the most pivotal of days, and the longest of my thirty-one years. The day that would forever split my life into *before* and *after*. But of course, I didn't know. We never do. Time only lets us look in one direction. So I had no clue what was to follow that knock at my hotel room door.

"Who is it, Achilles?" Sophie asked.

Turning my head from the peephole, I called back, "Are you in some kind of trouble?"

"I don't think so," she said, sitting up without covering up and sending my waking body in an altogether different direction from my brain. "Why? Who's at the door, the police?" She was joking, but she'd nailed it.

"Yeah."

That brought the sheet right up, but it didn't elicit panic. The deduction became pretty basic at that point. They were here for me.

I addressed the door. "Give me twenty seconds to get some clothes on, officers."

I pulled on my jeans and t-shirt, tied my shoes, and donned my leather jacket. Sixteen seconds. I gave Sophie a reassuring smile, and mouthed, "Sorry." Then I cracked the door in twenty flat.

"Kyle Achilles?"

"That's right."

"We need you to come with us, please."

I checked the authenticity of the officers' footwear and then their proffered credentials. "Okay."

I turned back to Sophie. "Looks like I'll have to give you a rain check on breakfast."

Her mouth said, "I understand. It was nice meeting you." Her face said she was unsure what to make of this and didn't necessarily want to find out.

That made two of us.

I knew she'd be okay a few seconds later when I heard her shout through the door, "So it's *Kyle*."

From outside, the Santa Barbara Police Department looked more like a Spanish mansion than a government office, right down to the lush manicured garden. White stucco walls and red-tiled roofs, with lots of arches and gables and a shady colonnade. Clearly the locals were proud of their heritage and their wealth.

Officer Williams swiped open the door to Interview Room One. Once he'd ushered me inside, he turned to leave. "Detective Frost will be with you shortly."

"Can I get some coffee? Big and black."

Williams replied, "Sure thing," but his tone was ambiguous and I couldn't see his face. As the lock clicked, leaving me in isolation, the implication of Officer Williams' words struck me. I was expecting some kind of CIA inquiry or debriefing, having just resurfaced back in the US for the first time since resigning a year earlier. But Langley wouldn't involve a police detective. They'd videoconference or send a local agent.

My empty stomach twitched a warning.

I looked at my watch: 10:49 a.m. My family would be polishing off their mimosas right about now at whatever local gem had earned the best Sunday brunch reviews. I had until 1:00 p.m. to get back to the *Emerging Sea* if we were going to stick to the schedule. Dad was big on schedules, as was Colin. Martha and Katya seemed considerably more relaxed, although I was still getting to know them.

I started to pull out my phone to call my dad, but remembered that my cell's battery had died without the usual overnight recharge. I was debating pounding on the door and asking for a phone when it opened and a mid-fifties bureaucrat walked in. He had more hair sprouting from his ears than above them, like a continuation of his mustache, and his paunch was bigger than a bag of bagels. To be working here looking like that, this guy had to be either very good or well-connected.

"I'm detective Frost." He took a seat across from me without offering either his hand or coffee. Well-connected it was.

"You don't appear to have brought coffee."

"What?"

"Williams said he'd send some coffee."

"Maybe later." Frost pulled a reporter's notebook from his back pocket, flipped past several penned pages to a blank one, and readied a cheap plastic pen.

Chapter 5

Revelations

MY STOMACH DROPPED with Detective Frost's first question. This was definitely not a CIA debriefing. "What brings you to Santa Barbara?"

I knew it would be pointless to press Frost for information before he was ready to give it. Interrogations didn't work that way — and that's exactly what this was beginning to feel like. About what, I hadn't the faintest idea. "I'm just passing through. I'm in the midst of a two-week cruise from San Francisco to San Diego with my family."

"How many are sailing with you?"

"Five, including me. My father, his wife, my brother, and his fiancée." Hoping to speed things along, I added, "We're celebrating my father's sixtieth birthday and retirement. Yesterday was his actual birthday, so last night we had the formal party right here in your fine city."

"Private cruise?"

"That's right. We're breaking in my father's new yacht." I would normally have said *boat* even though the *Emerging Sea* was clearly a yacht, because using *my* and *yacht* in the same sentence isn't in my nature, but here at the SBPD they were clearly used to bowing to *haves* while dealing with *have-nots*. I was hungry and budding a caffeine-withdrawal headache, so I was ready for a little less dealing and a little more bowing.

"When did you arrive?" Frost asked, flipping the page and continuing to write.

"We docked around 4:00 yesterday afternoon, and plan to set sail two hours from now." I tapped the face of my Timex.

"And what did you do after docking?"

"Once the ladies were ready, we went straight to Bouchon for the party."

"Bouchon," he repeated back. "That's very nice. How long did the ladies take to get ready?"

"An hour or so."

"Meanwhile the guys were doing what?"

"We put the yacht in order, and then got dressed ourselves."

"Did you go to the party, at Bouchon, dressed like that?"

"I did."

My answer seemed to disappoint Frost. Truth was, I'd been living out of a backpack for the last year, wandering Europe from rock-face to rock-face, climbing hard and contemplating life. Thirty-one might be a bit old for that, but I had my reasons.

The necessity of packing light had led to an appreciation for a simple wardrobe. By sticking with white t-shirts over cargo shorts or jeans, along with climber's approach shoes and a black leather jacket when required by circumstance or weather, I freed my backpack and my mind for more important things. Of course, this had made me the only person at Dad's retirement bash not in formal attire, but nobody, least of all my father, had seemed to mind. It was a California crowd, after all.

"And how late were you there?" Frost asked.

"Until about 1:00 this morning."

"And where did you go then?"

"Right next door to the hotel where your colleagues found me."

"Why not back to the yacht?"

"I met someone at the party, and opted for a little privacy."

"Do you do that kind of thing often?"

"Not often enough."

"You're being evasive."

You're being rude. "I only recall one other such occasion. That was about four months ago in Greece. Coincidentally, her name was Sophie too."

Frost jotted something, then closed his notebook and leaned forward. "Tell me about your brother's fiancée."

I didn't lean in to match Frost's posture, but rather stayed right where I was with my right leg crossed over my left knee. I was intrigued by his pivot but didn't want to show it. "Katya's Russian, like our mother. She's a doctoral candidate in mathematics at Moscow State University. They just got engaged last night over dessert, in fact. Made the night a triple celebration."

Frost wet his lips. "She's beautiful."

Katya had a classic Slavic face, as in the kind Czars paid Dutch Masters to paint. Perfectly proportioned features perched between high cheekbones. Thick honey-blonde hair framing a broad jaw, lithe neck, and lean shoulders. Beautiful was an understatement. Katya was spectacular. "She is. Smart too. I'm happy for Colin. They're good together."

"What's your relationship with her?"

"My relationship? I don't have one. Is this about Katya?"

Frost stood up and then leaned forward, placing both his fists on the table. I wasn't sure if he was going for hemorrhoid relief or the alpha-gorilla look. "If you don't have a relationship with her, then why did she spend last night in your stateroom?"

I kept my face passive, but inside was shocked, as much by Frost's apparent knowledge as by the fact itself. Every other night she'd been in Colin's bed. What had changed? "I wouldn't know, since I wasn't there. I was in a hotel. As we've already established."

"Doesn't Katya's behavior strike you as odd, spending her engagement night apart from her fiancé?"

"I've never been engaged, so I can't speak to that. But I have heard my brother snore after he's been drinking, so I can appreciate her wanting to seek a quieter refuge — afterwards."

"When did you first meet Katya?"

I wondered if it was always so frustrating on this side of the table, or if Frost just had a knack for irritation. "Your use of *first* implies a pattern. There is no pattern. Before leaving on the cruise last Sunday we'd only met one other time."

"Would you mind telling me where and when?"

I was starting to mind a lot of things, but I didn't want Frost to know it. "In Moscow. A little over a year ago. I was there on business. My brother was working there and dating Katya. He was crazy about her and brought her along when we hooked up for dinner."

"Are you telling me you had no contact with Katya between those meetings?"

"That's right."

"You sure?"

"Yes, I'm sure."

"That's not what she says. But we'll come back to that later."

"Wait a minute. Katya's here?"

Frost gave me a smug smile. "In the next room, speaking to my colleague."

I stood up. Put my own fists on the table. "It's time you told me what this is all about, detective."

"Sit down."

"I'll sit down when I'm ready."

"It's for your own good." Frost's timbre changed as he spoke. "There's something I need to tell you."

Chapter 6

Icebergs

FOR THE FIRST HALF of the movie *Titanic*, everyone is cruising along enjoying life, certain that tomorrow holds as much promise as today. Then they hit the iceberg, and their world turns upside down. Frost's voice sounded like ice ripping through the hull of my life. He sat down and I followed suit as a shiver ran up my spine.

Frost cleared his throat before he spoke. "I'm sorry to tell you that your brother, father, and stepmother all passed away this morning. Carbon monoxide poisoning appears to have been the cause."

I stared at Frost's mustached mouth with its coarse salt and pepper hair and crooked teeth.

Tears started streaming.

My jaw lost its grounding.

I couldn't speak. Couldn't process the news. Just hours ago we'd all been having the time of our lives. My father had worked his tail off for forty years and finally received the big payoff. Now he and Martha were set to spend the next forty years living the dream. And Colin ... that was ... unfathomable. He was the conservative Achilles. The responsible bookish older brother. A single grade ahead in school but six steps ahead in life, with a prestigious MD, a great girl, and a boundless horizon. A black body bag didn't fit in the frame.

"Katya called 911 at 6:00 a.m. after finding your brother, and then your parents," Frost continued. "A patrolman was there by 6:06, the paramedics by 6:08, and my partner and I by 6:45. The paramedics pronounced them dead on the scene. Are you familiar with carbon monoxide poisoning?"

I nodded once, my mind stuck on Colin. My self-identity was always evolving, but *brother* had been a constant from day one. Though half a world apart and as different as water and wine, Colin and I had been riding the river of life as a two-man team. Now I was completely alone, and reeling.

Frost continued speaking, but I wasn't really listening. "It's easy to diagnose as a cause of death because a fatal dose turns the cheeks cherry red. We see it a few times a year between suicides and accidents. Such a—"

The professional part of my brain suddenly kicked in like a safety light during a power outage. I interrupted Frost. "Why wasn't Katya killed as well?"

"We've been looking into that along with the source of the gas. Well, the source was the yacht's engine, obviously, so rather we're investigating how the gas circumvented the exhaust system and safeguards. Technicians are still on the scene. As for Katya's survival, we're working on that too. She's younger, slept in a different room, and got up early to work at the dining table. Apparently she has an important presentation coming up. Do you know anything about that?"

"She's scheduled to defend her doctoral dissertation in a few weeks, after five years of work. She's very nervous about it. It's in mathematics. Apparently people frequently fail the first time. Some never pass."

"Doctoral dissertation. In mathematics, no less. So she's practical? Clever?"

"She's brilliant." As the words came out of my mouth, Frost's line of reasoning came together in my head like a clap of thunder. I knew what he was up to. I felt my sea of grief becoming a swell of anger, but before my numbed mind computed my next move, someone knocked on the door.

Frost got up and stepped out into the corridor. When the heavy lock clicked behind him, I found myself facing the worst day of my life.

I took one deep breath, then another, counting down from six as I exhaled. My mind was racing, my pulse was pounding, my heart was broken. I knew how to rein in the physiological reactions. Controlling those had been a professional requirement. The grief, however, threatened to topple the cart.

I couldn't let that happen.

Not now.

Not until Frost believed in my innocence.

Chapter 7

Four Bags

TO RETURN REASON to the driver's seat, I had to relegate emotion to the back. To accomplish this, I did as I was trained. I painted my grief as a big gray blanket on the canvas of my mind, heavy and coarse and damp with tears. I folded it in half and half again until it was a manageable size. Then, reverently and temporarily, I set it aside.

Sometime later I heard the lock click. The door opened, and a very different detective walked in. She was ship-shape and petite and a good ten years younger than Frost. A huge and pleasant contrast.

The first thought to cross my refocused mind was that she too had to be either pretty darn good or well connected to get a plum detective job with her demographic profile. My second thought was that she hadn't brought me coffee either. Rather she was carrying a black backpack by the top handle as though it were a briefcase. She set it down on the floor and came around the table to introduce herself with an extended hand and a courteous smile. "I'm detective Flurry."

Her greeting surprised me. Not her words, but her actions. When I rose to shake her hand, I was a full foot taller and twice her size. Her hand disappeared into mine like a baseball into a glove. I could have tossed her like a ball too, literally pulling her in with my right while hoisting her over my head with my left, and sending her sailing with no more effort than a Sunday morning yawn. The contrast put me in a psychologically dominant position at a time when traditional police tactics called for the opposite. I watched her eyes closely as we shook, but she gave absolutely no sign of discomfort.

I liked her immediately. Decided to test my instincts.

"Why start with a lie?" I asked. "Aren't you supposed to be establishing trust?"

"Pardon?"

"Santa Barbara's population is only what, a hundred thousand? I'd be surprised if there were more than two detectives in the crimes-against-persons unit. You're telling me the two happen to be named Frost and Flurry?"

"You should find that reassuring."

"How so?" I asked.

"The names are real."

I chewed on that for half a second. "So you have a daily reminder that coincidences do happen."

She smiled.

One point for Flurry.

"I'd like you to take a look at something for me. Four things, actually." She unzipped her backpack and extracted a bunch of clear plastic bags. Evidence bags. She pulled them onto her lap where I couldn't see them. Setting the first on the table, she said, "Look, but don't touch."

The bag appeared empty.

Flurry studied me while I studied it.

I looked back up at her with a blank expression. She didn't comment either. She just dealt the second bag as if it were a poker card, watching me all the time for a reaction. It appeared empty at first too, but this one was less crumpled and the room's fluorescent light hit it at a different angle. I saw that it contained a piece of clear packing tape. I tilted my head to reexamine the first and then saw that it contained tape too.

I allowed my face to show my confusion.

The third bag was a bit more interesting, but still not very. It held an empty tube of superglue rolled up like a toothpaste tube to extract every last drop.

I said, "Three strikes."

She said nothing.

The fourth and final bag presented something very different. Something I definitely had seen before. That was when the worst day of my life became the worst day imaginable.

Flurry picked up on my reaction immediately. She finally asked a question that I could answer. "Recognize this?"

I said, "I'd like to speak to an attorney now."

Chapter 8

Emerging Sea

WHEN I INVOKED my right to counsel, Flurry didn't sigh and shake her head and slowly get up to leave the interrogation room. She didn't pull out her radio and inform Frost. Instead she said, "I believe your attorney just arrived."

That solved one mystery, but created another. Now I knew why she'd rushed to get my reaction to the evidence. She wanted to be sure she got it before I lawyered up. Another sound tactical move by an impressive detective. But I had no idea how my lawyer could have arrived. I didn't have a lawyer. I didn't know a single lawyer in the state of California. My best guess was that Katya was ahead of me, but that seemed a stretch for a foreigner just in from Moscow.

The door opened as if on cue and two men in dark suits and bright ties walked in. I recognized both from Bouchon. The first was Vaughn Vondreesen, the uber-charismatic guest and master of ceremonies. The second had also given a toast. He was handsome as well, but a mere mortal, and I didn't know his name. He spoke first. "Detective, I'm Casey McCallum, Mr. Achilles' attorney. Kindly give us the room and complete privacy." He motioned toward the camera on the ceiling.

As soon as the door clicked behind Flurry and the blinking red diode went out, Vondreesen closed the gap between us. "Casey's the best criminal defense attorney in the Bay Area. The minute I heard what happened to your family I took the liberty of asking him to stick around. Just in case." He put a hand on each of my shoulders. "I'm so sorry for your loss. Your father was the best man I knew."

Vondreesen radiated energy from his hands and eyes in a way that I found both comforting and disconcerting. Casey had a similar energetic vibe about him. Perhaps it came with being a captain of Silicon Valley. Perhaps it was a prerequisite. In any case, I was encouraged to know that it would be working for me against the aggressive detectives in the Santa Barbara Police Department.

Vondreesen lowered his arms with a final reassuring shoulder squeeze and I stepped forward to offer Casey my hand. "Thank you for coming. Your presence and Vaughn's prescience are most welcome."

Casey shook my hand reassuringly and then got right to it, a quality I was glad to find in a man who was undoubtedly charging my father's estate an astronomical hourly rate. "What have they told you?"

"They haven't told me anything, directly. But given the fact that they've been questioning rather than consoling me, they're clearly leaning toward a homicide ruling. Just before you walked in, Detective Flurry confronted me with four evidence bags. The first two contained pieces of clear packing tape. The third held an empty tube of superglue. They meant nothing to me. The fourth, however, contained a piece of PVC pipe with collars at both ends. I'd seen it last Sunday. As soon as she showed it to me I stopped talking and asked for counsel."

"Always a smart move. Where did you see it last Sunday?"

"When I first boarded the *Emerging Sea* I found it on my bunk along with a full tube of superglue and a roll of packing tape. Right there in the crease where the bedspread meets the pillow. I gave it a once-over, then put all three items in a drawer. Didn't think about them again until Flurry pulled out the piece of PVC. The moment I saw it, the darkest day of my life became midnight black, because I understood two things." I held up my fingers to count them off. "One, my family didn't die in an accident. They were murdered. And two, I'm being set up to take the fall."

Chapter 9

Deep Freeze

CASEY'S FACE reflected serious concern. He clearly shared my conclusion. But figuring out who was setting me up, and why, would have to wait. First, we had to deal with the evidence against me.

Casey wasted no time with sugarcoating or sentimentality. "So the police have your fingerprints on what we assume will be the piece of exhaust pipe that was loosened to release the carbon monoxide into the yacht's bedrooms. And if that proves to be true, then no doubt the tape and superglue will also be linked to the crime and covered with your prints. Have they fingerprinted you?"

I held up my hands in a reflexive but pointless display. "No need. My prints are already in the system."

Vondreesen chimed in for the first time. "Tell Casey about your professional background. He was a Marine, way back. I'm sure he'll appreciate it."

I looked at Casey who nodded. "Please."

"I used to work in the CIA's Special Operations Group."

"Used to?"

"I left a year ago, after five years of service."

"And what do you do now?"

Casey's question was simple, my answer anything but. "I've been traveling in Europe. Climbing rocks and contemplating life while trying to figure out what I want to do with the rest of mine."

"You're not currently employed?"

"No."

"And you don't have a family of your own?"

"No."

"But you've got family money. A recent development, from what I understand?"

I acknowledged what we both knew was coming. This was not going to look good. "My father was a physician in the Air Force. Not a highly paid position, but he enjoyed it and put in his twenty. Then he spent the last fifteen years working in biotech, kind of a continuation of his military specialty. Ten of those years were with a company that got acquired last year for half a billion. His net from stock options as their chief medical officer was around ten million dollars. He was going to retire then, but as I gather you know, Vaughn talked him into joining another start-up, Vitalis Pharmaceuticals."

Casey didn't comment.

"My stepmother wasn't wild about him giving up retirement, so as a compromise he bought the *Emerging Sea* and agreed to take her on a month-long cruise in conjunction with his sixtieth birthday. Then, as is so often the case in Silicon Valley, Vitalis folded and the birthday bash became a retirement party as well."

"And now you'll be inheriting an estate worth at least ten million?"

I knew the smart move was to come clean right away. While Casey watched, I double-checked that the camera was still off before replying. "I haven't seen the wills, but would expect to be the primary surviving beneficiary. Martha had no children. As for the money, I helped my father move it overseas, so I know your estimation is accurate."

"You helped him move it? Overseas?"

"A certain amount of know-how came with my CIA job."

"That won't look good if they find out, but at least it puts the money out of the court's reach for the moment. Can you access it?"

"I can."

Casey ran a hand through his thick gray hair, front to back, then massaged his neck for a second. "What exactly does the CIA's Special Operations Group do?"

"We're essentially the military arm of the State Department. We quietly attend to America's overseas interests."

"Military arm," Casey repeated. "Would I then be right to assume that in addition to banking, you have a lot of practical knowledge when it comes to mechanical things like engines and weapons of all kinds, including explosives and toxins?"

"That also went with the territory."

"How about investigations? Did your work involve those?"

"It did."

"Therefore you understand the challenge we're up against?"

"Ten million worth of motive, plus means, opportunity, and presumably compelling physical evidence. They're also exploring my relationship with my brother's fiancée Katya, in case there's a jealousy or a collusion angle."

Casey's face looked nearly as grim as I felt. He was exceptionally good at projecting empathy. He had to be. His income rose with the misfortune of others, but he could never let that calculation show. His acting skills would serve me well with a jury, if it ever came to that.

There was a sharp double rap on the door and then Frost walked in, followed by Flurry. Two more uniformed officers remained in the hall. Frost spoke clearly and officially, without preamble. "Kyle Achilles, you're under arrest for the murders of John Achilles, Martha Achilles, and Colin Achilles."

Chapter 10

Batter Up

ASSISTANT DISTRICT ATTORNEY Patrick Kilpatrick studied the two detectives seated across the table from him. They were far from a matched set. Frost was old-school. A middle-aged white male who knew how to work the system and benefited from being married to the mayor's cousin. He had the same rumpled appearance as television's Lt. Colombo, but from what Kilpatrick had seen during the years they'd worked together, little of Colombo's deductive power and none of his charm.

Flurry, on the other hand, looked nothing like a classic television detective. She was petite, vivacious, and Latina. This would be the first case he worked with her, and he was curious to see what she brought to the table. From what he'd heard, she was quick-witted and diligent, but garnered the resentment of many of her peers for a rapid rise they attributed more to her minority status than to her competence.

"I'm familiar with the evidence gathered and facts of the case," Kilpatrick began, "but I need to know more about the players. I understand we have a potential PR complication there? Our prime suspect won an Olympic medal?"

Frost's head whipped up from his notes. "A bronze medal. In a minor sport. No big deal."

Kilpatrick shifted his gaze to the junior officer. "Detective Flurry, why don't you tell me who we're dealing with."

Flurry began speaking from memory. This immediately differentiated her from Frost, who couldn't think without staring at his notes. "Kyle Achilles is the son of an Air Force physician and a Russian Olympic gymnast. His only sibling was the brother who died with his father during the incident in question. Achilles went–"

"Wait a minute," Kilpatrick interrupted. "Didn't his mother die on the yacht as well?"

"That was his stepmother. I'm not sure what happened to his real mother."

"Huh. Go on."

"Achilles went to the University of Colorado, where he was a star skier. Apparently he was also an excellent marksman, as he made the Olympic biathlon team and eventually won bronze in Vancouver. Somehow he caught the attention of the CIA, and he ended up in their Special Operations Group, where he worked for five years before resigning suddenly, a year ago."

"Forget the past," Frost said, his tone dismissive. "Look at the present. At the time his multimillionaire father was murdered — along with the only other people who stood to inherit his fortune — Achilles was an exceptionally capable and highly trained but unemployed killer."

"That's one way to look at it," Flurry said.

"You have a better way?" Frost asked.

"Let's keep focused," Kilpatrick said. "What else do we know about him? What's he been doing since he left the CIA?"

"He hasn't earned a dime," Frost said.

"He's been traveling around Europe, competing in rock-climbing competitions," Flurry said.

"He's a bum," Frost said.

"He's an American hero who decided to take his college graduation trip a decade late," Flurry said.

"Climbing rocks?" Kilpatrick asked.

"It's his hobby," Flurry said. "According to a magazine profile, he poured his frustrations into rock climbing after a lower-back injury ended his biathlon career. They do a lot of climbing in Colorado, along with skiing and shooting. Apparently he's gotten pretty good at free-soloing. He set a couple of speed records in Greece."

"Free soloing?" Kilpatrick asked.

"That's the technical term for what you or I might call monkey-style. No ropes, tools, or safety equipment. Just special shoes and chalk for your hands."

"How do you know so much about it?" Frost asked.

"My college boyfriend was really into free-soloing — until it killed him."

Kilpatrick exhaled, pushed back from the table, and stood to pace. "What about the woman we found him with?"

"I checked her out," Frost said. "Sophie Gramercy is a UCSB graduate student who waitresses evenings at Bouchon. She's clean. They only just met at the party."

"And the Russian girl, the brother's fiancée?"

"Katya Kozara was our only other suspect," Flurry said. "But whereas Kyle Achilles stands to inherit over ten million dollars from the death of his family, Katya loses. She'd just gotten engaged to Colin Achilles at that party, just set herself up to be an American doctor's wife. She would have been in line to eventually share in that ten-million-dollar inheritance, but now she's getting nothing."

"No chance Kyle and Katya were working together?"

"It doesn't look that way. In any case, we appear to have a very solid case against him — clear motive, clear means, clear opportunity — so we'd rather not complicate it."

Kilpatrick stopped pacing to survey Frost. "Do you agree with that?"

"Not entirely. I think you should put the Russian before the grand jury as well. They probably won't indict her, but that will give us the chance to learn everything she knows. As soon as we kick her loose, she'll fly back to Russia and we'll never see her again."

Kilpatrick picked up a bat that Barry Bonds had autographed for him, and began swinging at the air. "Okay. Sounds like we've got our man and our plan. I happen to know Achilles' attorney. He's from the Bay Area, and he's top-notch. The best around. So I need you to keep on it until you've got all the facts buttoned down tight. I don't want any surprises." Kilpatrick brought the bat down on the desk like a judge's gavel.

"The DA is watching this one closely. A triple homicide at the yacht club makes for a very high-profile case with tourists and taxpayers alike, so she's ordered me to get a conviction. Whatever it takes."

Chapter 11

6 Months Later

804, 805, 806–

"Man, why you keep doing that? Looks painful."

I didn't pause, but redirected my focus across the hall long enough to appraise the new guy. He was pacing his cell like a caged panther. 812, 813, 814. He could have been straight from an NFL defensive line. Mid-twenties. A fit 300 pounds on a 6'6" frame. No visible gang tattoos. Conservative haircut. Healthy complexion. Reasonably intelligent, lucid eyes. 821, 822, 823. I'd worked with many a man who looked like him, and called more than one my friend. "A guy's got to do something, right?"

"You're not just passing time," NFL said, his voice thick and slow. "Nobody does a thousand sit-ups hanging by his toes jus' to pass the time. You're training for something."

"Domestic violence?"

"What?"

"You kill your girlfriend?"

"No, man. She's fine. It was an accident, but her old man's a cop. When a guy's my size, people make assumptions, you know?"

I understood, but I didn't reply immediately. This was fast approaching the longest conversation I'd had with a fellow inmate during the six months I'd been awaiting trial at Santa Barbara County Jail. On the hunter-gatherer spectrum, I was much more spear than basket. So rather than wasting time getting to know my fellow inmates, I was treating my time awaiting trial as though the SBCJ was a training camp.

While Casey's investigators were out looking for an alternative man and motive to wave before my jury, I was keeping to myself and getting into the best climbing shape of my life. 860, 861, 862.

I was also exercising my brain in a way I'd never done before. In *Moonwalking with Einstein*, I'd read that a person could win the US Memory Championship by practicing an hour a day for a year. Sounded pretty cool to me — not to mention therapeutic. I'd found that I could force myself to block out virtually any amount of physical or emotional pain if focused on a compelling goal.

While I wasn't planning on being in jail for a whole year, I could easily dedicate an hour a day to *each* of the competition's categories. After six months, I was up to 49 random words and 147 random digits. I was also getting competitive with memorizing decks of cards, my favorite.

At the moment however, I was focused on my physical routine — and my new neighbor. NFL was about as close to Miss Manners as they came in this place. 888, 889, 890. Since the endorphins were flowing and the inverted sit-ups were just the beginning of my routine, I answered his question. "I'm a climber. As in rock. Lots of core strength required. Can't be wimping out when you're a hundred meters up a cliff face and the wind starts—"

The distinctive double snick of an extending steel baton cut me off like a guillotine. I cursed my lack of vigilance even as I released my toes and twisted to absorb the fall to the concrete floor with my left deltoid rather than my skull.

The baton whistled and then cracked across my feet, creating a wave of pain powerful enough to loosen my dental work. "Hands and feet are to remain inside the cell at all times." Officer Grissel sneered down at me, exposing brown teeth.

My feet were screaming, but I clenched my jaw against the surging pain and building rage. Without responding, I rolled into a handstand and started doing pushups with my back to him. 1, 2, 3. I kept doing them until Grissel moved on. Then I piked down and into a cross-legged position to inspect the damage.

"Anything broken?" NFL asked.

"I got my toes clear of the bar in time. Might have been ugly otherwise. Could have ended my vacation plans then and there."

"Vacation plans? What you in here for?"

"Triple homicide. But I got a good lawyer."

NFL grunted at that. "They all like that here?" he asked, doing a head tilt in the direction of Grissel's departure.

"Grissel's the worst, and he doesn't like me very much. He confuses rank with superiority, and I've never done too well with that type. Plus I think he's suffering from a constant toothache." I rolled back into the handstand and continued my workout routine. "You smell that breath?" 18, 19, 20.

"Like he gargles with sewage."

NFL went back to pacing. Every once in a while he'd stop and watch me, shaking his head with his massive arms crossed. I figured we both targeted a thousand in our workouts, but whereas mine were reps, his were pounds.

I was in my fifth set of pushups when I heard approaching footsteps. They weren't Grissel's. Grissel was my height, and these belonged to someone considerably shorter in stature. I flipped back onto my feet and received an emphatic reminder of the foul guard's handiwork. I'd be leaving the burpees and jumping jacks out of my routine for a day or three.

Officer Hicks' mop of dirty blonde hair came into view. "You've got a visitor, Achilles. Your attorney."

I slipped into my shoes and stepped to the door without wincing audibly. Hicks unlocked it and escorted me toward the south holding cell block gate.

NFL called after me. "Give your attorney my name! Marcus Fry! Tell him I can pay!"

Chapter 12

Cui Bono

WITH MARCUS'S PLEAS echoing behind us, Officer Hicks prompted me down a long windowless corridor, through another gate, and finally into the visitation area. I'd learned that jails differ from prisons in a few key ways. They're designed for relatively short stays while inmates await trial. So, even though this one had room for 640 occupants, it didn't have all the amenities of a prison. There was no library, or gymnasium, or even a contact visitation room. I had to use a handset to speak to my visitors through the thick plexiglass window that separated us.

Not that I had many visitors.

Other than Casey, my only visitor had been Sergeant Dix, a Special Forces master sergeant. My CIA recruiter had enlisted Dix as part of the training program he'd designed to bring me up to par with the SOG's other recruits, most of whom hailed from elite military units. Dix and I had grown close over the course of a very intense year, and had kept in touch the way guys tend to do, which is to say very occasionally, or whenever it was important.

I didn't know Casey nearly as well as I knew Dix. My first battle beside him was still a couple of weeks away. But even without that familiarity, I could tell from the look in his bright eyes that the news wasn't going to be good.

Casey picked up his handset, and I picked up my handset, and he launched right into it. "The investigators still haven't come up with anything solid to support our *other man* defense."

As my heart sank ever deeper, he began counting off fingers.

"No witnesses who saw suspicious activity around the yacht.

"No witnesses who saw other people on the yacht.

"No credible reason to believe such a person exists.

"No unexplained fingerprints."

"They did, however, independently confirm that the section of PVC with your fingerprints on it exactly matches the rest of the PVC pipe connected to the motor. Your prints are on the original."

I wanted to pound my head against the plexiglass. This had been going on for months now. Lots of activity, no progress. Casey's investigators were like hamsters spinning wheels. Now we were virtually out of time. "Any good news? Anything at all?" I asked.

"There are traces of talcum powder on the packing tape used to cover the carbon monoxide detectors. That supports our assertion that the real killer used gloves while applying it, latex gloves in this case. But frankly, that's a lot more circumstantial than what the prosecution has, which is your actual fingerprints."

"Anything else?"

"I'm afraid so. As you know *Cui Bono* is the starting point of every murder investigation. *Who benefits* is also the question to which every juror will demand a satisfactory answer. Your inheritance gives the prosecution a ten-million-dollar motive, whereas the defense is broke. You're the only person who profits financially from your parents' death. Your brother's too, for that matter." Casey's expression was grim.

"As for other potential motives, we couldn't find anyone with a major grievance against any of the victims. None of the three appear to have been involved in anything that would make someone want to silence them. I trust you haven't thought of anything in either of those regards since the last time we spoke?"

"No, I haven't."

"Without some variant of those motives in play, we're left with homicidal mania and jealousy. Katya is beautiful enough that I could easily spin the jealousy motive, and her being from Russia would do a lot to open up the jury's imagination. But for that to work, you need to identify the individual. She swears there is nobody out there in a jealous fervor. My investigators kept her under tight surveillance in Russia and confirmed that she is not seeing or being stalked by anyone. She's back from Moscow, by the way. Arrived last weekend to start her post-doc at Stanford."

Katya had written me a couple of times. Long, despondent, tear-soaked letters written late at night. They were full of sorrow over shattered dreams and wistful memories of Colin. They'd also brought me up to date on her career progression. "Couldn't we say it's the police's job to find the stalker, not ours? Muddy the waters of reasonable doubt?"

"We could, but that would likely backfire. Assistant District Attorney Kilpatrick is pretty sharp. He'd position you at the top of that suspect list. They have you on tape lying to the police about having contact with her."

"It wasn't really contact. All I did was reply to an email she sent with a question about Colin. It slipped my mind in the interrogation room."

"But you see how they could spin the headline? Lying to the police about your history with her. Plus they could say the engagement was what threw you over the edge. It dashed your hopes. They'll say you were upset, infatuated, and intoxicated. Better we don't go there."

"What you're telling me is that with less than three weeks left until my trial you have nothing for me, other than a half million dollars in legal fees?"

"Actually I have Plan B all teed up and ready to go."

"Maybe you should have started with that."

The rebuke slid off Casey like water off a duck. "Kilpatrick owes me a few favors. I called them in, applied some leverage, played up your medaled Olympian status, and got him to agree to a sweetheart deal based on an alternative scenario."

"What alternative scenario?"

"Something got stuck in the exhaust pipe. Say a rat crawled in and died. You removed the dead rodent, but then didn't sufficiently reattach the piping."

"That's quite a scenario."

"As I said, he owes me."

"What about the tape over the carbon monoxide detectors, the portholes superglued shut, and all the other adjustments that had to be made to override the yacht's safety systems?"

"Those will be considered circumstantial and disregarded."

Casey was beginning to look like a miracle worker after all. "So what's the deal?"

"He'll drop the charges from the top end of the scale all the way to the bottom. From three counts of murder in the first degree, to three counts of involuntary manslaughter."

"And the number?"

"Involuntary manslaughter carries a sentence of one to four. I got you two."

"Two years?"

"Two years each, with consecutive sentences. Six years total."

Six years. I shuddered at the thought of what six years in captivity would do to me. "And I'd be a felon, convicted of killing his family."

Casey said nothing.

I'd run a million deal scenarios through my mind, fighting pride and weighing time. Figuring out where to draw the scrimmage line wasn't the hardest thing I'd ever done. But it was close. "Tell Kilpatrick I'll take my chances with the jury."

Chapter 13

The Fourth Man

FORTY-FOUR HOURS elapsed between the time Casey delivered his bad news and the moment I received my next message. It wasn't what most people would consider to be good news either. In fact, it would probably top the nightmare list for many. But my circumstances were special, in more ways than one, so I was happy to be the recipient.

It was Saturday morning, two weeks and two days from the start of my trial. I'd come to learn that like on the outside, jailhouse moods were best on weekend mornings. The inmates had visitation to look forward to, and the guards had a slightly more relaxed attitude without the warden around.

My message arrived in a shower bay. Three mountains of muscle cornered me the moment I was alone.

"Hello, pretty boy," the middle one said, identifying himself as their leader. "I heard you was lookin' for comp'ny."

These guys weren't going to be winning any genius awards, but they weren't complete fools either. They were going for the misdirect, trying to make me think rape rather than murder. It was a sound battlefield tactic. All war is based on deception, after all. But then I wasn't deceived. And despite outward appearances, I had the advantage.

I hadn't been granted bail while awaiting trial due to the nature of the crime, and the surfeit of compelling evidence. It also didn't help that I'd been trained to disappear. But I hadn't been convicted either. No one here had. This was jail, not prison. The three message boys had hope of seeing freedom someday soon.

They had a lot to lose.

Therefore, they would be highly motivated to make my death look accidental.

That gave me an advantage, because I didn't care about appearances.

Three on one would seem to most to be a lopsided fight, especially if all involved were of similar size and stature. I stand 6' 2" and weigh 220 pounds, which puts me an inch and 5 pounds below the average NFL quarterback, but still north of 19 out of 20 American males. The heights of the three facing me were also in that 1 of 20 range, but they'd register closer to 280 on the meat scale. More like defensive ends than quarterbacks. Advantage attackers. However, unlike football, where the rules of the game amplify the laws of physics, combat puts myriad additional factors into play. Among those applicable at the moment were tactics, technique, and attitude. I knew I had them on tactics and technique. The laws of probability made that a lock. Their need for *accidental* also tipped the scale. Advantage Achilles.

"You heard right." I sauntered toward the leader, acting all peaches and cream. "I've got six months of lonely all pent up inside."

As attacker one digested this unexpected twist in the conversation, I dropped to my right knee and drove my right fist up and into his exposed testicles like a battering ram on a castle door. I packed the blow with six months of pent-up rage, powering it with my shoulders and back, and punching it through as if I was reaching for the stars.

It was devastating.

As my fist lifted him up and back, I could hear his ancestors cursing the termination of their bloodline. My objective was to disable one of them before any knew the battle had even begun, and in that I succeeded with style points to spare.

But I was still two-thirds of the way from home.

As the eunuch heaved forward and vomited, I spun up and around to my right, where I delivered a rapid triple combination to the second slab of beef. First plowing my right elbow into his solar plexus and robbing him of his ability to breathe, then delivering a stunning backhand to the bridge of his nose. Finally, I whipped back around to yank his head downward into my lifting knee. *Oomph! Crack! Crunch!*

The crunch was gruesome. A ten-pound head colliding at speed with a ten-pound knee spelled all kinds of jeopardy for the two-ounce nose caught between. The sound alone sent a shudder down my spine.

I'd expected the third attacker to pause and assess the situation that was so rapidly veering from plan. But he didn't. The starting whistle had blown and so he jumped into play. He dove at me like people who weigh 280 pounds are inclined to do.

I couldn't get out of the way in time.

As my knee finished off number two, number three took me to the tiled floor. Hard.

Getting me on the ground worked in three's favor. My remaining opponent's only advantage was his weight, and a floor fight played to it. The bad news for him was that I'm not a football. There was no ref, and no whistle. He didn't know what to do next. He didn't know whether to try to hold me until one of his buddies recovered enough to help out, or to try to get on top and pummel me to death.

His moment of hesitation gave me all I needed, because I did know what to do.

For five long, hard, happy years, my government had sent me into kill-or-be-killed situations with enemies who did not hesitate. They didn't flinch or pause or think twice. They gave homicide no more forethought than insecticide. I hadn't become numb, but I had learned to postpone the self-recrimination until after the fact, after I'd done what needed doing to survive.

I reached down and grabbed the back of my third assailant's shaved head with my left and then I drove my right thumb into his left eye socket as if I was trying to ram a cork into a bottle. No hesitation. No half-measure. Full-on engagement powered by fury and frustration.

He spasmed and went limp. He'd likely lose the eye, but that was preferable to what he'd planned for me.

Attacker two remained motionless where he dropped, but the eunuch was struggling to regain his footing. Extricating myself from the muddle, I leapt up, grabbed him with both hands, and whacked his head into the wall with enough force to knock him out for hours. He hit with a nasty crack and collapsed like a fat sack of flour.

I moved beneath one of the running showerheads to rinse the vomit and gore from my bare flesh while giving the scene a quick survey. One thing wasn't quite right. I repositioned number two a bit, smearing his right thumb with the bloody goo oozing from number three's left eye socket.

Satisfied that there was no physical evidence to contradict the story that a trio had gone at it and beat each other senseless, I went for the fourth guy.

There had to be a fourth guy. He'd be just around the corner of our shower bay, leaning one shoulder against the wall, trying to look casual to any passing guard while he kept everyone else out. He'd surely have heard the scuffle behind him despite the running showers, but he wouldn't have been able to look without defeating the purpose of his mission. I'd probably find him snickering as he pictured the scene.

I moved quickly but quietly across the tile to the corner. Crept to within inches of where I was sure he'd be leaning. My plan was to step out, reach around, grab him by the throat and wrist, and pull him back around the corner where I could reason with him privately. Make him see the mutual advantage of not having seen or heard anything to contradict the three-way tussle story, lest it become a four-way.

I slipped around the corner, arms poised to pounce, and froze in place. The man before me wore a guard's uniform. It was Grissel.

Chapter 14

The Visitor

I DUCKED BACK into the shower bay and pulled my clothes on without pausing to towel off. For six months I'd held in a torrent of grief and a swarm of frustrations, but my cork had popped along with number three's eye. I wanted to grab Grissel by his big ears and head-butt him full on the nose. I wanted to feel his cartilage crushing and hear his nose cracking and see his blood spurting. Grissel's sworn duty was to protect me, but he had tried to kill me instead.

I closed my eyes and counted to three before stepping out directly behind him. "There are two ways to deal with this."

Grissel whipped around, his face showing surprise before flashing anger and then fear.

I kept my inner beast caged, but gave him a glimpse of the animal within. As he swallowed dry, I said, "Either both of us were here, or neither of us were here."

I walked past him without another word. I could almost hear his mind whirring behind me. Pride fighting fear, curiosity battling with self-preservation. I did hear his decision. I heard him walk away.

With Grissel off guard duty, an inmate would discover the bodies momentarily. I didn't want to be in the area when that happened. I hustled back to my cell and began flipping through my thick stack of playing cards.

"Why you spend so much time jus' looking at those?" Marcus asked, leaning against his bars.

"Really want to know?"

"Yeah, man. Ain't like I got no pressin' engagement."

"Pull out your deck. I'll show you."

Marcus did.

"Hold up the cards one at a time and show them to me, fast as you can. Just put them back down in the same order."

"Fast as I can?"

"The faster the better."

The toilet-sink combo unit was near the bars, so Marcus used it as a makeshift table. Holding the deck in his hand, he began flipping up cards one at a time, and discarding them in a pile on the sink's rim.

"Faster."

Marcus shook his head, but began flashing them at a rate of about one a second. Within a minute, he was done. " 'kay. Now what?"

"Four of clubs, six of spades, five of spades, nine of diamonds, jack of hearts … I was on the thirty-forth card, and Marcus's eyes were big as boiled eggs, when my ears triggered a warning. A guard was walking my way with a purposeful stride. It didn't sound like Grissel.

Hicks came into view. "You've got a visitor."

"My attorney?"

"She doesn't look like an attorney to me." The guard spoke with the inflection men use among themselves when referencing attractive women. I didn't know him well enough to tell if it was a ruse. Hicks was a new hire. He might be leading me to a closet where Grissel would be waiting with another crew.

I had no choice but to follow.

Hicks did usher me to the visitation room, where I spotted my visitor the moment he opened the door. About two-thirds of the way down the row of twenty stations, glowing like a lighthouse beacon on a stormy shore, was Katya.

She was wearing the same slim-cut toffee-colored suit she'd worn to the party and her preliminary hearing. In the courtroom I'd figured it was the only suit in her travel bag. Now I suspected it was the only one she owned. There was no need for it here, however. Most jailhouse visitors wore clothes anyone could buy at a truck stop or ball game. She must have associated jail with court and dressed accordingly. I guessed she was regretting the decision, given that she was also using three white tissues to shield her hand, chin, and ear from whatever might be growing on the handset's speaker.

I picked up my handset without taking protective measures. Between growing up with a military physician, and countless missions in hazardous places, I'd developed an immune system tougher than a buzzard's stomach. And I was eager to talk. Katya and I hadn't spoken since the day of our preliminary hearings, when I was indicted and she was released. She'd flown straight back to Moscow and her doctoral defense. I'd moved into cell 412.

"Hello, Achilles."

She wore a smile, but I could see worry in her amber eyes. "I heard you were back from Moscow. Congratulations. Do I call you Doctor now?"

"Maybe Professor someday. I see you're still waiting for your trial. It's been so long."

"My attorney delayed it as long as possible to give us more time to investigate. But we're only a couple of weeks out now."

She paused there, not sure what to say. I thought I understood her predicament. Talking about my case could easily suck up the entire 45 minutes visitors were allotted, but I suspected she hadn't driven five hours from Stanford for that. "What can I do for you?"

"It's so incongruous, you and this place. Colin loved to talk about you as *the guy who could do anything*. But here, they let you do nothing. I feel like a fool now for coming. I had a very different image in my mind." She shook her head, and looked down.

My mind stuck on her comment. I didn't know my brother had talked like that about me. I didn't know he'd talked about me at all.

Katya flicked something off the countertop with a long, elegant finger. "Clearly I didn't think things through. Forget about me. What can I do for you? I guess I should have brought you some cookies. Or, I don't know, a TV."

"Tell me what's worrying you. The best thing you could do for me is give me someone else's problems to worry about."

She looked back up and her eyes melted a bit. "I think someone's trying to kill me."

Chapter 15

Terminate Her

SOMEONE WAS TRYING to kill me too, but I wasn't about to tell Katya. I had a couple of competing theories playing out in my head. Her arrival fit both of them.

I met her eye, then made a point of glancing to the left and right. "Tell me about it, *po Russkie*." In Russian.

Katya nodded her understanding. "Two days ago I was coming out of the math department when a big guy sitting in the courtyard made me nervous. It wasn't how he was dressed that first drew my eye — Stanford attracts all types — but rather his disposition. Even sitting there drinking coffee he radiated a predatory, soldierly vibe. Seemed to be directing it at me, although with his wraparound sunglasses I couldn't be sure."

"What did he look like?"

"He was even bigger than you. Chiseled face with a military-style haircut. Dressed in a black suit. He'd have looked like a Secret Service agent except that he was wearing a black t-shirt rather than a white shirt and tie."

Looking at Katya through the thick plexiglass, I couldn't help but admire the way her mind worked, her mathematical precision. She'd thought about this. Reduced it down.

Katya was one of those people who surprised everyone she met, because she confounded expectations. When someone's that beautiful, you expect her to play to it. Lots of mirror time, and selfie shots, and coquettish behavior. I was beginning to understand why she didn't behave that way, why her behavior didn't even acknowledge her physical status. Colin had pointed it out, but I hadn't latched on. Her mind was her best feature. "Then what happened?"

"I crossed the courtyard, heading for the parking garage. He got up and followed me. Not right behind, but close enough that a three-second sprint would put him on top of me. I've been followed before, in Moscow. Stalked even. But those instances were always a lone guy half acting out some sexual fantasy. Sometimes not so subtly. Nothing serious ever happened, but those experiences prompted me to take some self-defense courses. I learned how to avoid and escape those situations, and how to make use of my fists, elbows, knees, and teeth." She mimicked a few moves.

"I was preparing myself to jump into my car and lock the door and hit the horn when I saw a second guy. Same huge size. Same serious outfit. Same soldierly vibe." She rattled off the facts like premises in a proof.

"He was sitting in a black Escalade, which he'd parked facing my car from across the aisle. The moment I saw him, I changed direction and walked over toward a group of guys who had piled out of a Honda. There were five of them, Ultimate Frisbee players in their late teens. I told them my concern and one of them launched a Frisbee right at the head of the suit who was following me. It was a great throw, fast and straight. The suit saw it, stopped and leaned his head just far enough to the right for it to sail past within an inch of his ear. He was almost robotic. Then the Escalade started up and pulled around and he got in and they drove off."

Scary as that sounded, I was certain there was more to come. She'd used the word *kill*, and we weren't there yet. "Did you get a license plate?"

"Only subconsciously. Enough to recognize it later when I saw a black Escalade parked near the entrance to my cul-de-sac. When the familiar letter pattern registered I felt my heart turn to ice. I kept driving, right past my apartment complex. I wanted to get lost in a crowd, so I drove to the mall, got a hot tea, and sat in the food court, thinking about my options."

"What did you conclude?"

"I concluded that I wasn't a random target, a young body picked from the crowd at Stanford to be raped, or sold into prostitution, or whatever. And they weren't spying on me. These guys were definitely more *Terminator* than *Bond*. From there, I reduced my predicament down to two root conditions: either they were trying to harm me, or they weren't. If they weren't, then there were no mistakes to be made. If they were, and I made a mistake, then I'd either be hurting or dead. So the only logical move was to assume the worst, that a couple of professionals were trying to kill me, and act accordingly. Make sense?"

I couldn't speak to her psychological health, but her logic was bulletproof. "You've got a remarkably cool head. What'd you do next?"

"The first thing I did was make sure I'd stay alive in the short-term. The second thing I did was try to figure out how to stay alive in the long-term." She paused there to look me in the eye.

"And that plan involves me. Even though I'm locked up in jail 300 miles from Palo Alto."

Katya shrugged and smiled meekly. "I've only been in the US for a week. The only other people I know are mathematicians. Hardly a rough-and-ready crowd. And I don't know any of them well. You, on the other hand, are almost family. I also happen to know that you are very well-trained to deal with situations like these. I suspect that you can do more from behind bars than 99% of people could do on the outside."

"What's your backup plan?" My question was analytical — reflecting her preferred style — but I immediately regretted it.

Katya deflated. "No choice really. I can't afford to hire bodyguards, and that's not my style anyway. I'll have to leave Stanford. Give up on my dream and go back to Russia."

"Well, then you're in luck." I locked my eyes on hers, leaned in, and mouthed the next sentence. "I'm about to break out of jail."

Chapter 16

Windbreakers

THEY CAME FOR ME at midnight. Grissel and a squirrelly guard with hairy ears named Willis.

Stopping before my cell, Grissel flicked open his baton and swished it through the air like a pirate testing a sword. "On your feet!"

The smell of his breath hit me with physical force. I'd almost have preferred the baton. I tried not to inhale while I slid on my sneakers and stood.

Willis dangled a set of handcuffs from his index finger like balls on a string, so I backed up to the door with my hands behind me as per prison protocol. He snapped them on with vigor and then unlocked my cell door while Grissel stood tapping the business end of his baton against the flat of his left palm. One way or the other, I knew I'd never see cell 412 again.

"Good luck, man," Marcus called, from across the corridor.

Grissel stayed about five feet behind me while we walked, far enough to remain out of kicking range, yet close enough to keep my skull within the baton's strike zone. I'd never traversed the jailhouse at night before. The darkness seemed to amplify the sounds and smells of bodily emissions, bringing the walls in even closer.

At the far end of my cellblock, we passed through a gate I'd never used to a hallway I'd never tread. The rhythmic smack of the guards' boots became the dominant sound until a lock buzzed and a steel door swung — and I found myself in a room occupied by two navy blue windbreakers adorned with bright yellow lettering. FBI.

The shortest but broadest of the two special agents turned to study my face, comparing it to a photo he had clipped to a fresh brown folder. "Kyle Achilles?" His bright white teeth flashed in sharp contrast with his shiny ebony skin as he spoke, drawing my gaze.

"Yes."

He pivoted left to face the window that partitioned our room from the control booth. This was one no-nonsense pro. High-speed, low-drag, and squared away, as my peers used to say. He signed a document that was waiting on the partition ledge, then pushed it through the receiving slot.

I stole a glimpse. It was a transfer of custody order, signed by a federal judge named Bartholomew Cooley.

"We've got him from here," the lead special agent said. "You can take the cuffs off. We brought our own."

Willis uncuffed me.

The guard behind the glass had me sign for my belongings.

The taller FBI agent then cuffed me again, hands in front this time so I could carry the paper grocery bag that held my watch, wallet, and clothes.

There was no more fanfare. A few buzzes and clicks later, we were outside in the crisp California air, walking towards a black Suburban with government plates.

They put me in the back.

The lead agent slid in beside me.

The taller one sat behind the wheel. He keyed the ignition, snicked the selector into drive, and pressed the gas, making it real.

I was out.

We turned north on Calle Real and the driver pressed the accelerator with enthusiasm. In less than a minute, the perimeter lights of the Santa Barbara Community Jail were out of sight.

I held up my arms. "I think it's safe to uncuff me now."

Sergeant Dix turned and gave me a big grin. "I kinda like it this way."

He unlocked me anyway.

"You do a pretty good special agent impersonation."

"Not my first time wearing blue. Just my first time without sanction." Dix's bonhomie morphed to a more serious tone. "Your girl came through. She called not more than a minute after I hung up with you. Don't know if that means you can trust her, but it's a good sign."

I agreed. "Did you come up with a passport for her?"

Special Forces units routinely generated false identities for their operatives. This was tightly controlled, of course, but Dix was a clever senior NCO, so he knew how to work the system and he had the connections to do it. Still, whereas he'd had months to prepare the other aspects of my backup plan, Katya was a late addition.

"Yep. Here you go." He handed me a hefty manila envelope. "In case you do travel together, we made her Kate Yates to match your Kyle alias. Couples attract less attention, as you know. You've got matching Indiana driver's licenses and credit cards too."

"How about the Russian travel visas?"

"Yep. Belorussian too, so you'll have a bolt hole."

"I like your thinking."

"Not my first rodeo. Is Russia your contingency plan?"

"More like a working theory. Why's the envelope so heavy?"

"Used a little of your money to pick up a couple of clean iPhones."

"Outstanding, sergeant. What did you tell Katya about tonight?"

"Operationally, she's in the dark. She just knows to expect you around now."

"Perfect. Where is she?"

"She's in a hotel over between the airport and the university. About 10 minutes from here. Key's in the envelope. Room 229. I'll drop you off, but then we've got to run. Ortega needs to return the SUV to his brother, and then we're wheels-up out of Vandenberg at 02:00. Best we get back to Bragg before we're missed."

I opened the paper bag and began changing into my civilian clothes. "I see you switched to the new Sig."

"You noticed that, huh?"

"Yeah. Been meaning to try it out myself."

"I suppose you'd like to field-test mine?" Dix's teeth flashed in the dark.

"Thanks. You can keep the belt and holster. I'm sure it will fit in my pocket."

"I can keep my belt and holster? That's mighty kind of you."

The P320 did indeed slide easily into my jacket pocket, but then, like all my clothes, it was extra large. "How's life back at Bragg?" I asked.

"Same as always. Lots more practicing than doing. I was glad you finally green-lighted this op. For more reasons than one. It's good to see you. Why'd you wait so long? I was expecting to pull you out months ago."

"I wanted to exhaust my traditional options before going unconventional."

"You mean you thought your lawyer might work some magic? From what you told me, he didn't have a chance. Course, if I were him, I might have taken my time to tell you that as well. What's he charging you? Five hundred an hour? A thousand?"

"Enough to bring tears to your eyes, my friend."

Dix and I spent the rest of the short drive catching up in the quasi-awkward way old friends who rarely see each other do. Then Ortega pulled into a parking space near a side door to the UCSB Summer Inn, and our reunion ended. We all shook hands and I thanked them again.

"Consider yourself freed," Dix replied, referencing the Special Forces motto.

I had one foot out the door when I turned back to my old friend. "Who's Judge Cooley?"

"Just somebody Winks invented for the occasion," Dix replied, referring to Herald Winkle, the computer genius we'd worked with at the CIA. "He sends his best, by the way. As for old Bartholomew, he'll disappear from the DOJ database later tonight. I suggest you do the same."

I whipped off a salute. "Thanks. But I've got other plans."

Chapter 17

Telltale Tea

I KNOCKED on Katya's door and announced myself, knowing she'd be nervous. With anyone else, I'd have used the key to slip quietly inside, but with Katya that would have felt like a violation.

Ours was an unusual relationship, simultaneously intimate and awkward. The total number of hours we'd spent conversing could be counted on fingers and toes, but circumstances had rendered us closer to each other than to anyone else on the planet.

Katya opened the door and I stepped into a room that smelled of honeysuckle in bloom. Quite a treat for a nose that had just endured six months in lockup. The picture of a steaming tub with tiny bubbles and bare shoulders popped into my mind. I forced it right back out. She'd nearly been my brother's wife.

Katya threw the bolt and slid the chain, then turned to look at me with warm, wide eyes. "Did you really break out of jail?"

I paused for a second, reflecting on the fact that my résumé had a new bullet point, and aware of how atypical a career had to be for *successful jailbreak* to be a selling point. "I had a lot of help."

"Were those guys from the Special Operations Group?"

"For their sake, it's better if we don't get specific."

"Did you … have to hurt anybody? To get out, I mean?"

Katya was clearly wound up tight and starved for information, which was easy enough to understand. I didn't mind talking. My tongue was due for some exercise. "There are two ways to break out of prison. You can either outsmart the engineers and guards, or you can outsmart the bureaucrats. We outsmarted the bureaucrats. We used uniforms, forged papers, and a very talented hacker who had access to the Department of Justice network. So no bullets were required."

"You tricked the guards?"

"We played to their weakness."

"Sounds risky."

"Fortune favors the bold. And the deck was rigged in our favor. A prison guard's entire world revolves around the chain of command. Blindly following orders is programmed into their autonomic nervous systems, like breathing. Once the hackers and forgers did their thing, all my guys had to do was look the part and exude authority."

Katya gave me a look that said she grasped the theory, if not much more. "I'm sorry if I offended you. I certainly appreciate it."

"No worries. I understand. People hear 'Special Operations' and they think snipers and explosives. We use those too, but only when that's the smartest way to complete a mission."

Katya double-checked the door lock.

"How are you feeling?"

"I'm a bit overwhelmed by recent developments, but I'm feeling a lot better, now that you're here."

If Katya had been anyone but my brother's fiancée, I'd have given her a big hug at that moment. As it was, I kept a healthy distance. "Glad to be of service. Now, we should get going."

"Going? It's one o'clock in the morning. Where are we going? Oh, are the police looking for you?"

"No. At this point, as far as my jailers know, I've become the FBI's problem. But there's a different clock counting down my fate, and it's very short on time."

She didn't press me to clarify, and three minutes later I was driving her Ford north on the 101.

"Where are we going?" Katya asked.

"Back to Palo Alto."

"Are your friends meeting us there?"

"No. They need to be back home before anyone notices they were gone. And we won't need them anyway."

As I activated the cruise control, she asked the question I'd been anticipating. "If you could have broken out of jail at any time, why did you wait? Don't get me wrong, I'm profoundly grateful, but as we mathematicians like to say, the equation doesn't appear to balance."

The truth was, I'd have broken out just to save Katya. I owed that to Colin. But she didn't need to know that. "I broke out the moment the benefits of doing so outweighed the benefits of staying in. Helping you added weight to the escape side, but I'd already green-lighted the plan. Good thing I did too."

"How so?"

"Three inmates tried to crack my skull in the shower this morning, with the help of a bent guard. It was a contracted kill, a coordinated assassination attempt."

"Assassination? Why? What could anyone gain by killing you?"

I liked how her mind jumped right to the unsolved part of the problem. "I need coffee. Please grab an iPhone out of the manila envelope in the glovebox and find us a diner that's open 24 hours."

She did. Denny's was just one exit and two right turns away.

As the waitress filled my cup with coffee, I said, "Please keep it coming."

Wendy said, "Sure thing, sugar."

Mid-fifties and working the graveyard shift at Denny's and our waitress still had a good attitude. I admired people like her. Wondered momentarily about her source of joy — a hobby or a granddaughter that offset the grind.

Katya tried her tea, and then looked at me expectantly.

I dove right in, answering the question she'd asked in the car. "There is exactly one person with something to gain by killing me. It's the same person who killed my family and framed me for it."

Katya processed that faster than most people over thirty can recall their age. "That doesn't make sense. If he'd wanted you dead, he'd have killed you at the same time. The frame was clearly part of the killer's calculation."

"You're thinking like a mathematician. I admire that, but this isn't like solving a mathematical proof."

Katya wrinkled her nose. "You don't think the rules of logic apply to investigations? Sherlock Holmes would disagree."

"That's not what I said. Logic is exactly what I'm using. But not a mathematician's logic."

"Mathematics is the purest form of logic."

"Purest, perhaps. But this isn't a pure situation." I paused, but didn't take my eyes off hers while I stole a sip of coffee. "It's evolving."

Her face flushed a bit as comprehension dawned. "Of course. It's game theory, not algebra. Do you have any suspects?"

"I have two. One for each motive."

"And what are those motives?"

"The first motive is money."

"What money?"

"My father's money."

"But you got it all."

"I did, for now. Whether or not I get to keep it is a different question. Someone could be playing a long game. Someone with the ability to predict the result of a complicated series of events ... the solution to a long equation."

I studied Katya's face as I spoke. I liked coffee as much as the next guy and more than most, but we were in Denny's rather than her car for one reason: so that I could study her face at this moment. Katya didn't go through the usual feigned surprise or delayed reaction that the rules of etiquette call for when polite discussion turns accusatory. Perhaps that was because it was 2:00 a.m. at Denny's and not 4:00 p.m. at Harrod's, but I took it as a sign of her character.

"How could I benefit financially? Colin and I weren't married. We were barely engaged."

"In Russia, that would be the end of it. But as everyone knows, the US has a very special legal environment. People sue for things here. It's practically a national sport. First, you get the murders pinned on me. Then you sue the estate for damages. You were almost killed. Certainly traumatized. A jury would likely be very sympathetic, especially with the money coming from a convicted murderer."

Chapter 18

Motives

KATYA DIGESTED my accusation in silence, intermittently sipping her tea and flicking her fingernails off the pad of her left thumb. One, two three, four. One, two, three, four. She probably ran a thousand iterations through that big brain of hers before she looked up. "What's the second potential motive? The one that isn't money."

I'd seen what I wanted to see. "Let's hit the road. I'll tell you in the car."

I paid at the counter while Katya visited the restroom. Using Kyle Yates's new credit card, I tipped Wendy more than the cost of our beverages. It felt good to be back in society. Signing the check, it occurred to me that coffee at Denny's had been my first purchase as a rich man, legal fees aside. Alas, the money would likely all be gone before the credit card bill came due.

Katya took the driver's seat this time. As she moved it forward I racked the passenger seat all the way back. I still couldn't fully stretch out my legs, but wasn't complaining. This was the most comfortable I'd been for months. Not that there wasn't tension. In fact, I thought I detected a bit of anger in the way Katya handled the steering and pressed the gas as we navigated back onto the highway, but I had no comparison. She'd never driven me before.

Once Katya had engaged the cruise control, she turned my way. "Why did you tell me that? If you suspect me, wouldn't the smart tactical move be feigning ignorance?"

"You just answered your own question, but on top of that, it was a tactical decision. The odds of my making a mistake go up considerably if I have to split my attention between two investigations. And I can't afford any mistakes. Plus, I don't have time to play it subtle, which isn't really my style anyway."

"What do you mean, you don't have time?"

"You'll see."

"Anyone ever tell you that you're cryptic?"

"Cryptic used to be my job description."

Katya kept quiet for a few miles.

I felt her relaxing.

"Why did you quit? You never really told me. The first time we met, when you were on that case in Moscow, you seemed so happy."

I didn't want to add that emotional maelstrom to the mix I was already feeling. "That's a long story for another time."

"There you are being cryptic again."

I said nothing.

A minute later, she asked her next question. "What's the second motive?"

"It's a bit more nebulous than the first. Let me tell you what I'm thinking. You can tell me if my deduction passes muster."

That pepped her right up. "Okay."

"Watch your speed."

"Sorry."

"Let's begin with the reason for framing me. In this scenario, that would be misdirecting the police investigation."

Katya was all over that theory. Clearly, she'd given it some thought while I was in jail. "Wouldn't it be better if they weren't investigating anybody at all? They could accomplish that by making the murders appear to be an accident. Surely that would be simpler. We should be looking for the simplest explanation. Occam's razor."

"You're right. And you've just hit on the key. The best way to avoid a serious investigation would have been to make the murders look like an accident. So that's what they would have done — if they could have."

"You're implying they couldn't?"

"Exactly. They couldn't. But *why* couldn't they? More specifically, what would make it difficult to credibly stage the murder as an accident?"

Katya turned from the road to look at me. "You've obviously run the permutations. What did you conclude?"

"I figure they needed to kill more than one person. They needed to kill at least two of the three, one of which had to be my brother."

"Why did one have to be Colin?"

"Because it would have been easy to stage an accident killing my father and mother. They're always together. A hit and run car crash would have been quick, and clean, and credible."

"There could be a hit and run with Colin in the car too."

"Sure, if Colin was with them on any kind of a regular, predictable basis. But he was in Moscow. The sixtieth birthday cruise, however, was tightly scheduled well in advance. There were plane tickets on both ends, and a detailed itinerary in the middle. Two weeks' worth. It also provided a controlled and isolated environment. Perfect for a planned murder."

I gave her a second to think that through.

"I've never heard of a fatal yacht crash."

"Exactly. So what kind of accidents can you have on a yacht? Not a lot of pirates off the coast of California. You're left with poison and explosions."

She mulled that over as a black Lamborghini screamed past at twice our speed like the shadow of an airplane. "Suppose that's true. Suppose they implemented a scenario that framed you, with inheritance as the obvious motive. Why? What was their motive? How did they benefit?"

"That's the rub, and it's driving me crazy."

Chapter 19

Invisible Enemies

DURING MY DISCUSSION with Katya, I began to feel something unexpected: a great sense of relief. The district attorney, the detectives, and the actual perpetrators were all still out to get me, but talking to Katya made me feel better. As they say, a problem shared is a problem halved.

I was no longer waging this war alone.

Sure, back in jail, I had Casey. But when the meter's running at an obscene rate, you don't really feel like a team. And while Dix had been beyond great, he was also remote, and our contact infrequent. Interaction feels different live, and when people are truly in it together, as Katya and I were now.

I looked over at my unlikely comrade in arms, seated behind the wheel of her little red Ford, and continued presenting my analysis under this new light. "I can't come up with a direct financial motive for the killings. Therefore I've concluded that there must be some *indirect* benefit."

"Indirect benefit. What could that be?"

"My best and only guess is that it's a *business* benefit. Colin and my father both worked at the same startup."

Katya shook her head. "But it wasn't making any money. The product was still in clinical trials when it folded."

"True, but startup valuations are based on expectations of future earnings. With pharmaceutical companies, I'm sure nine-figure valuations aren't uncommon."

"Do you know what Vitalis was valued at?"

"I have no idea, but with a big name like Vondreesen involved in the financing, it had to be significant."

Katya's expression told me she wasn't impressed with my deduction. "It really doesn't matter. The company folded a couple of months before the ... incident. Vitalis's valuation dropped to zero. Your father retired and Colin got a new job."

"I know. That's why I'm stuck."

"If there's a business benefit behind this, it could just as easily be Colin's new job. He talked about it with your father, doctor to doctor, businessman to businessman."

"I know. You're right. I've got a lot of investigating to do. That's another reason I needed to be out of jail."

Katya chewed on that for a while.

I started to doze.

"There's a third option, a third motive."

That woke me up. "I'm all ears."

"You started this conversation by saying that the reason for framing you was to misdirect the police investigation, but what if that's wrong? What if everything was done for revenge against you? I suspect you made some cunning enemies during your government career?"

"You're right. I left that one off the list. It had been at the top for months. In my cell I cranked out hundreds of thousands of sit-ups and pull-ups and leg-lifts and crunches while working up my list of suspects and how to get at them. But that motive faded the moment someone ordered a hit on me. It vanished when they also went after you."

"Why?"

"Because they were winning. My case was looking hopeless. And because killing you doesn't fit that scenario at all."

She was quick processing that one too. "You're right. I agree."

"Somebody has a business interest they're trying to protect, Katya. A business interest that my father and brother somehow threatened. A business interest that's still vulnerable."

"And you plan to expose them?"

"I plan to destroy them. These people killed my family. When I get done with them, they will–" I stopped myself there, remembering that I wasn't talking to Dix or one of the guys. "They'll regret it, for a second or two."

Katya didn't seem put off by this glimpse of my inner animal, reminding me of where she'd come from and what she'd been through growing up in Moscow during perestroika.

"Where are we going to start?" she asked.

Her use of the plural pronoun rang sweet in my ears. "We're going to start with one of the things that changed. We're going to start with the guys who are trying to kill you."

Chapter 20

Cul-de-sac

I FELT LIKE I'd spotted the Loch Ness Monster. It was two hours after sunset, but the East Palo Alto rooftop was still warming us from below when a black Escalade entered the cul-de-sac, running dark. A shiny black hole in the calm California night. Katya inhaled sharply beside me as we watched it glide to a stop beside a red curb.

The driver kept the motor running.

"What are they doing?" she whispered.

"They're counting the windows to be sure your light is on. They'll get excited in a second when the oscillating fan shifts the curtains. After two days of reporting failure, you can be sure they're eager for good news and redemption."

The Escalade rolled forward, lights still off. It drove quietly past the entrance to Katya's apartment building before backing into a visitor's spot. This time, the driver cut the engine. The passenger pushed a button on the ceiling before they opened the doors, killing the cabin light. Katya had told me they were disciplined. Apparently they were also meticulous.

I smiled. If I was right, their professionalism would soon be working in my favor.

Both the goons' heads crested the Escalade when they stood. I put them at 6'4" or 6'5" — Katya had been right, they were taller than me. Her mind hadn't exaggerated despite the fear and stress. I tucked that observation away for future reference.

They weren't wearing wraparound sunglasses, but otherwise the pair matched her description. Black suits and buzz cuts, or as she'd put it, Secret Service agents with t-shirts rather than ties. I saw no evidence of firearms, and knew their mission wouldn't require them. Against Katya's relatively fragile frame, 500 pounds of beef would more than suffice. I watched them turn and walk toward Katya's building, without locking their car.

"Will you be okay up here alone for a few minutes?" I asked Katya.

"I'll be fine. Will you? I'm worried about you." She inclined her head toward the giant receding figures. "Maybe we should call the police?"

"No worries. These guys won't know what hit them until it's too late."

Rolling to my left, I pulled out my iPhone and tapped the only stored contact. As Katya's phone began to vibrate, I dropped over the side of the two-story building and lowered myself to the ground using nothing but handholds, a technique climbers called *campusing* because of the campus boards widely used to practice climbing with only hands.

I was halfway across the parking lot when Katya's whispered words came across my wireless earpiece. "You didn't tell me your plan."

"The general plan is to disable one of them and question the other. I was planning to strike when they exited your apartment. Whack one and push the other back inside. But now I think I'll wait to jump them in their car. More private, and the confinement will work to my advantage." As we spoke, I slipped in the driver's side door and ducked behind the second-row passenger seat. "Let me know when you see them coming."

I pulled on a black balaclava. I'd swapped my habitual white tee for a long-sleeved black one, and with the headgear was now sufficiently shadow-like. "When they find your place empty, they might wait inside to ambush you, but my guess is that they'll come back to the car to wait for your return."

"Why is that your guess?"

"It gives them more control and options if you don't come home alone."

We lapsed into silence.

The most recent twelve months aside, my entire adult life had been one competitive mission after another. First with the Olympic biathlon team, then with the CIA's Special Operations Group. Observation and assault. Measures and countermeasures. Winners and losers. This was what I knew. My comfort zone.

Katya, on the other hand, had spent her adult life immersed in probability theory. Distribution functions and stochastic processes and the theorems of Kolmogorov and Cardano. No doubt she found my tools and techniques as foreign and intimidating as I'd find the equations in her notebooks.

"How did you end up at the CIA?" she asked, burning off nervous energy.

I played with the release lever on the bucket seat before me as I formulated my response. It flipped the seat forward, first pancaking it and then rolling the whole assembly against the front passenger seat. It was quick and quiet, yielding sufficient room to operate.

I decided to answer Katya's question with a question. "Suppose you tripped and hit your head, and lost your ability to solve equations. What would you do?"

"I don't know." Her voice was wrought with emotion. "I'd be devastated. Mathematics is my life. Oh, I see. That's essentially what happened to you with the Olympics. But I don't see the connection, except that biathletes and spies both need to be sharpshooters."

Boy was she quick. Her mind hummed like a Gatling gun. "The connection was indirect. Not wanting to become bitter after my injury, I funneled all my energy and frustrations into rock climbing. I went straight for free-soloing, tackling cliffs like they were battlefields, and I was my ancient namesake. I was reckless. But with my Olympic conditioning, I quickly set a couple of speed records. Nothing newsworthy anywhere outside Colorado or climbing circles, but enough to make the local papers. The top guy at the Special Operations Group, Granger, was visiting the Air Force Academy when he saw an article and got curious. He ended up recruiting me. Kinda made me his pet project and brought in top guns like Dix for my training, since I didn't have a Special Forces background. I was very fortunate."

"So why did you leave? Wait! Here they come!"

"Both of them?"

"Both."

"Okay. Please mute your microphone. If bad becomes worse, call 911 and give them the Escalade's license plate number."

Chapter 21

Bad Connection

EARLIER IN THE DAY, I'd hit a military surplus store to stock up for our little operation. My purchases included the black tee and balaclava I now wore, plus a sap — a heavy little flexible club designed for knockout blows to the head.

As the assassins approached, I readied Dix's new Sig in my left hand, palmed the sap in my right, and rehearsed the combat sequence in my head.

The driver was the first to reach his door. He slid in and started the car. His partner hopped in a second later, rocking the whole car.

"*Zdec budem zhdat?* We going to wait here?" the driver asked in Russian.

"*Ona machinu znayet.* She knows the car. *Luche sprachemsya.* Better to hide."

The driver flipped the selector and pulled out slowly. I hoped Katya had heard them so she wouldn't panic. The seatbelt reminder began to chime. *Listen to it, guys*, I willed them. *Buckle up. Strap yourselves in.* The passenger complied but the driver ignored the chime's warning. He circled the cul-de-sac, looking for an inconspicuous parking place with the right vantage point. I didn't dare raise my head to look, but the map in my mind had them driving a route similar to the one Katya and I had used that morning when searching for their Escalade.

The passenger pointed. "Look, her car's in its spot. She must be at a neighbor's. Or maybe the gym. This dump have a gym?"

"I don't know."

I decided not to wait to find out what would happen next. I wanted the driver busy driving and the passenger strapped in. I brought my right hand across my body, preparing it for a backhanded knockout sap strike to the side of the passenger's skull. Still holding the Sig in my left, I readied my middle finger on the seat lever. I pictured the two giant enforcers attacking Katya, pummeling her tiny frame with their massive arms. Rabid dogs with a rag doll, begging to be put down. I felt my muscles twitch and my adrenaline rise and then I flipped the seat lever.

I rocketed forward, swinging the sap as I flew. Whether the move took a quarter of a second or a half, it proved to be all the time they needed to react. These were no ordinary men. They weren't rent-a-cops or mob enforcers or strip mall martial artists. They had combat-hardened reflexes as quick and true as those of any elite soldier I'd known. And their eyes, their piercing, intelligent eyes were so unexpected that their gaze nearly stopped me in my tracks.

But it didn't.

I adapted instead.

Ratcheted it up.

The passenger spun fast enough that the sap struck him between the eyes. The driver was faster still. He had his Glock out and sweeping in my direction before the sap's sickening crack had fully registered on my ears.

From there on it was a race.

I was bringing my Sig up from below.

He was bringing his Glock around from the front.

I still had a three-foot arc to traverse.

He only had two.

It didn't matter how much faster his gun would be lined up with my head than my gun with his. Ten seconds or a tenth of a second, the end result would be the same.

He was leaning forward, giving his shoulder room to move.

I was leaning left, forcing his arc to extend.

I was straining and groaning and willing my muscles to move faster than they'd ever moved before. But I couldn't move my whole body faster than he could move his arm.

He was going to win.

My whole reason for being collapsed down to completing a single task. My brain didn't need to think. My heart didn't need to beat. My lungs didn't need to breathe. For that one split second of time, the only thing I had to do was prevent that arm from traversing those three feet.

The Escalade is a luxury vehicle. It's high on polish and full on feature, kind on the eye and cruel on the wallet. The driver's seat is designed to make its occupant feel like a million bucks. It's wrapped in rich leather, coddling the captain, while a tough plastic shell defends his backside from kicking kids and clumsy cargo. Inside, the driver's seat is packed with framing tubes and motion systems, heating elements and cooling fans. Wires and rods and cushions and sensors. It's a miracle of modern engineering.

A nine millimeter parabellum, while an engineering marvel in its own right, is a far less sophisticated artifact. A quarter ounce of lead wearing a full metal jacket, it escapes the barrel of a Sig P320 at 1,300 feet per second. Minimal weight, but tremendous velocity, and spec'd to punch through 14 inches of hog muscle. I didn't know how 14 inches of pork compared to an Escalade seat, but I was about to find out.

I didn't wait for the headshot. I didn't even wait to clear the seat. I started squeezing the trigger as soon as there was flesh in the flight path. Bang. Bang. Bang. Buttocks. Kidney. Heart. The driver's arm dropped, head slumped, and body rolled — lifeless, onto the door.

Glancing beyond the windshield, I saw that while I'd stopped the driver, I'd failed to halt the car. We were now seconds from colliding with a parked pickup and attracting attention.

I dove for the selector switch and slammed it into park with my right while I swung the Sig back at the passenger with my left. My eyes met his, but they weren't looking back. He wasn't dazed, he was dead.

I'd killed them both.

That was a problem. Dead men tell no tales.

Chapter 22

Travel Plans

I PUT AN ARM around Katya's shoulders as she averted her eyes from the fresh corpses of her would-be killers. She was shivering, but her mind wasn't shaken.

"What are we going to do now?" Her query was analytical, not accusatory, and it nailed the big question on the head. We'd just lost our only leads.

I was amazed by her resilience. She was a 28-year-old academic, not a homicide detective. "Are you all right? I know this isn't your comfort zone."

"I may not have been in jail, but I've been out of my comfort zone since I found Colin's body. Then these killers came for me. Twice. You saved my life. So while I may not be all right, I am a lot better with them gone. But, now that we don't have anyone to question, I am quite anxious to learn what's next?"

I was happy to keep the analytical side of her mind occupied. "We've got a tactical decision, and a strategic decision."

She gave me a lay-it-on-me wag of her chin.

"Tactically, we have to decide what to do with the bodies. Leave them or hide them."

"Why would you hide them?"

"To confuse the enemy. Always a good move." I paused there to help the point stick, like Granger always did. "Put yourself in your assailants' shoes for a minute. They've been reporting failure for nearly a week now. Odds are their boss is pretty upset. Odds are he's not the warm-and-fuzzy type. Life and death situation like this, I'm guessing he threatened them. Applied a bit of stick. So if they disappear now, he won't be certain if they were killed — or they ran."

Katya took a second to process our unusual problem. "Where would you hide them?"

"We could dumpster the bodies and leave the Escalade to be stolen. Or we could cover the bodies with a blanket in the back of the Escalade and leave it in long-term parking at the airport."

While Katya wrapped her big brain around our body-disposal options — a first for her, I'm guessing — a car entered the cul-de-sac, headlights blazing.

We were in her Ford, parked in her assigned spot like a couple at the end of a date. But the corpses were exposed. They were bleeding out where they'd died, in the front seats of a car badly parked in a fire lane. If anybody bothered to look, they'd be on 911 before their screaming stopped. Whatever we decided to do, we had to do it quickly.

"You also referenced a strategic decision?"

My brain had bridged that gap while Katya was contemplating. "I think I just figured that out. We should head for the airport. And since we're going there anyway–"

"We have our plan for the bodies." Katya's voice was upbeat, given the circumstances.

"Right. Let's run inside so you can change into jeans and throw your travel essentials into your backpack. If you'll give me your two worst blankets, some window cleaner, and a roll of paper towels, I'll get to work down here."

"Slow down, Achilles. You're being cryptic again."

"I don't mean to be. I'm just excited. I found the common thread connecting your assailants with the death of my family. It's just a thread, but it's enough for us to start unraveling this thing."

"But we didn't learn anything from the hit men. You killed them before question one."

"That was my first reaction too. But then I realized that I was overlooking the obvious." I wanted to let her figure it out. She'd feel better if she did.

The dim light from a streetlamp filtered through the windshield onto Katya's contemplative face. I watched her mind working it. She seemed to appreciate the mental exercise and momentary distraction. After a few blank seconds, I threw her a prompt. "Remember our discussion last night about motive?"

She nodded. "You concluded that your father and Colin were killed to gain some unknown business benefit. You convinced me that no other motive explained the incident."

"Right. Now think about the hit men. What do they have in common with a business interest my brother and father shared?"

"We didn't learn anything from the hit men. At least I didn't. Did you see something?"

"It wasn't what I saw. It was what we heard."

Katya was clearly frustrated that she couldn't grasp it, but I knew that she would. She began thinking out loud. "They were talking about what to do. Where to wait for me. They saw my car and figured I was at a neighbor's house or the gym. Nothing about themselves or their boss …" Her voice trailed off, then I saw her get it. "Russian. They were speaking Russian. Your father and brother had business in Russia."

"Can't be a coincidence. Do you happen to know who Colin worked with?"

"The company folded."

"The company may no longer exist, but hopefully some of the former employees still do. Did you know any of them?"

She thought about that for a moment, her face delightfully animated. "I didn't move in with him until after Vitalis closed, so I don't know much about it at all. I do know that he was the only company employee in Russia. As a startup they outsourced everything. His focus as chief medical officer was the clinical trial, and for that he worked with a contract research organization based out of the Sechenov Medical School. The *Clinical Connection* or something like that. It's over near Moscow State University. The only person Colin ever mentioned was the clinical coordinator, Dr. Tarasova. Tanya Tarasova. She called him more than once. I can look up the office number and ask for her."

"Excellent. When we get to the airport, give her a call and make an appointment."

"We're going to Moscow? That's the flight we have to catch?"

"You got it."

Chapter 23

Bad Call

NINETY MINUTES LATER the assassins' Escalade was in a distant corner of SFO's long-term lot, Dix's disassembled Sig was on its way home compliments of an express mail drop box, and Kyle and Kate Yates were ticketed for Moscow via Frankfurt. They were already calling our flight when we cleared security.

I pointed Katya toward our gate. "Why don't you see if you can get through to Dr. Tarasova before boarding. I have another call to make, but I want to use a payphone."

"Moscow as well?"

"No, local."

"At eleven o'clock on a Sunday night? This part of the strategic plan?"

"Just the first move. The second call will be the big one. I'll make that from Frankfurt during our layover. Go ahead and board as soon as you're done with Tarasova. No sense making it easy for anyone watching the video surveillance of my call to figure out we're together."

"I should have guessed," Katya said, with the hint of a smile.

One tough girl.

I ran to the other international wing and began stuffing quarters into a pay phone that wasn't under direct surveillance from a security camera.

My call was answered on the second ring. "Santa Barbara Police Department."

"ADA Kilpatrick, please."

"I'm sorry, the District Attorney's office is closed right now."

"I'm sure it is. I need to get ADA Kilpatrick an urgent message. Can you do that for me?"

"I can try."

I dictated the message, then added, "Please be sure to tell him the number from which I called."

Ten hours and nine time zones later, I picked up a different pay phone. I fed this one with euros while Katya stood by my side. I didn't dial the SBPD directly, but rather a CIA relay. With that trick, the caller ID would show up as *Unknown* even if I dialed the White House or the

Hoover Building.

"Santa Barbara District Attorney's Office."

"ADA Kilpatrick, please. He's expecting my call."

"Hold on."

Katya leaned up and in to hear.

"Mister Achilles?"

"Morning Mister Kilpatrick. Do you have Casey McCallum and Detective Flurry with you?"

"We're all here, as is Detective Frost," Casey said. "And anxious for your, ah, update."

"Thank you for getting together on short notice. I appreciate your time, and will get right to the point. I'm calling to arrange for bail."

As we listened to silence, I pictured the faces of the three senior officers of the court, first looking at each other and then staring into space. The brooding eyes and furrowed brows of professionals who just moments ago had thought they'd already heard it all.

Kilpatrick broke the silence. "Your request for bail was denied some six months ago, Mister Achilles. I'm about to have a bench warrant issued for your arrest. I would have done so already if your attorney hadn't convinced me that you could be made to see reason."

"I thought it might be in everyone's best interests if you reconsidered my bail request."

"I don't see how granting you bail would be in anyone's interest but yours."

Patrick Kilpatrick was a boy-faced redhead, with freckles and sad eyes that seemed to reflect all the misery he'd witnessed in the course of prosecuting cases of domestic violence, child abuse, murder, and rape. I could picture those eyes now, dark tranquil pools concealing the shark within. "Well, first of all, if I'm not out on bail, then the nightly news will carry a story that makes your boss look bad, Mister Kilpatrick. Secondly, compared to the alternative, it's a win-win situation. If I show up for my trial, then no one looks incompetent. If I don't show up, then I'm just another bail-skip, and the city gets a fat payout. No news story there."

"Are you planning to show up for your trial?"

"Absolutely — if I get bail. There's no other reason to ask for it, given the circumstances."

"Then why did you break out? You'd already been in jail for six months. What's the big deal about two weeks more?"

"It wasn't a question of time. It was a question of necessity. It became clear that I was going to have to conduct my own investigation in order to prove my innocence."

"That's what you're currently doing, investigating?"

"Exactly. And that's why I wanted Detective Flurry on the phone. I may need some help."

"Detective Frost and I have already concluded our investigation," Flurry said.

"Yes, but I got the feeling your gut was at odds with the evidence against me. I thought you'd want the chance to help get it right."

Before Flurry could answer, Kilpatrick said, "I don't think we can go for this. There's no precedent for it. Without precedent, the DA would be out on a limb."

My stomach dropped.

I needed bail.

Without bail, my odds of walking away free and clear plummeted from low to near zero. Precedent or not, granting bail in these conditions seemed like a no-brainer to me. I suppose I should have known better after working for the CIA. Risk aversion was a way of life for people counting on government paychecks and pensions. But I'd felt certain that with elected officials like the DA involved, the desire to CYA would trump all. "Check with your boss, Kilpatrick," I said, trying to sound more upbeat than I felt. "I'll call you back tomorrow."

Chapter 24

Tricky Situation

FROST SLAPPED HIS NOTEBOOK against his palm the moment Casey left the conference room. "I really want to nail this bastard. First he manipulates the system to make us look incompetent, then he tries to use that very fact to blackmail us. Fuck him and his special request."

Kilpatrick rose from the table, but the detectives remained seated. By now, they both knew that the ADA literally liked to think on his feet. Anyone visiting his office figured that out pretty quickly. Kilpatrick had stacked old Martindale-Hubbell law directories under the legs of his desk, raising it an additional eighteen inches so that he could stand while working. If anyone commented, he'd note that each volume included the name of at least one attorney he'd trampled in court.

Kilpatrick began pacing with his bat. "I think we're all agreed on the goal, as you so eloquently put it, detective. Let's make sure we don't underestimate Achilles again. As I see it, we have two options for putting him back in jail. We can either find him, or we can trick him."

Flurry scooted forward in her chair. "What do you mean by trick him?"

"The use of deceptive tactics in situations like these is sanctioned. Let's think about what we could tell him the next time he calls to lead him into a trap. Detective Flurry, why don't you focus on that."

"Okay."

Frost looked up from his notebook. "Shall I focus on finding him?"

Kilpatrick shook his head without turning his gaze from the garden outside the window. "I don't want any attention drawn to this situation. It's too politically sensitive. That means no BOLO's or other forms of outside involvement. Given that, and the fact that Achilles has almost certainly fled the jurisdiction, and most likely the country, there's nothing you can do. Our hands are tied, for now."

"What about the jailbreak? Shall I look into that?" Frost asked.

"Not yet. Same reason. For now, besides the perpetrator and his attorney, we're the only people who know that there's been a jailbreak. I'd like to keep it that way until he's back behind bars, or ..." Kilpatrick drifted off into thought.

Frost and Flurry sat in silence, watching and waiting until the ADA spun back around. When he did, there was excitement plastered across his ruddy cheeks.

"Achilles inherited about ten million dollars, right?"

Flurry was faster off the mark. "He did. I moved to seize it, but his father kept it overseas, and Achilles was smart enough to have it moved again before we could get to it. It's gone."

"So let's get him to bring it back."

Frost chuffed. "You mean as bail? All of it? No way he's going to do that. The guy's in the wind with ten million in the bank. He'd be a fool to take that deal."

Kilpatrick swung his bat in slow motion at an imaginary target. "Let me worry about the negotiation. Meanwhile, let's figure out how to catch him quietly, on our own. If we apprehend him now, we've got a lock on an escape conviction. With that, the triple homicide conviction will be virtually guaranteed. He'll go away for life."

PART 2: CONNECTIONS

Chapter 25

Déjà Vu

WE REGISTERED our fresh passports at a big old hotel near Katya's former dormitory. Perched in the woody Sparrow Hills, the Korston Hotel overlooks a big bend in the Moscow river and many of the city's most notable landmarks. It also transports visitors through time and space.

Walking through the Korston's lobby doors, tourists exchange views of Moscow State University's iconic stone spires and the legendary gardens of Gorky Park, for those of old Las Vegas. Red carpets, colored lights, and cocktail lounges abound — all designed to put people in a playful mood. A round-the-clock buffet keeps clientele inside and fueled while noisy slot machines and chatty prostitutes drain their pockets. Hardly my definition of paradise, but to each his own.

Katya and I skipped the glamour and glitz and headed straight for our room, aiming for power naps amidst piles of pseudo-silk pillows.

I woke after forty minutes, and hit the shower. It was my first since the prison attack and I welcomed it like vindication. I listened to half of Adele's latest album under the hot torrent of a large showerhead, part of it performing maintenance, all of it enjoying a simple pleasure six-months denied.

Exiting the bathroom wrapped in a towel and surrounded by a refreshing cloud of steam, I walked into a trap I thought I'd avoided. I found myself flanked by two enormous black suits, both wearing wraparound shades.

To the left, a gorilla with a shaved head held Katya's throat in his fist. He looked ready to crush it like an empty beer can. Straight ahead, a brute with a wicked scar covering half his left cheek held a Glock pointed at my heart. Rock steady. *The G43 slimline subcompact*, I noted reflexively. Ideal for concealed carry. A considered purchase. A professional shooter. And the same model used by the boys in Palo Alto.

Scar pointed to the pile of clothes outside the bathroom door. "*Odevaicya*. Get dressed."

I played out the next ten minutes like a fast-forward movie, scrambling to find a place to splice an escape into the film. The pressure points were the hand on Katya's throat, and the finger on the Glock's trigger. I needed a situation that would enable me to neutralize both long enough to work some magic.

Our hotel room was no good. They'd established advantageous

positions and had space to maneuver.

The doorway was better. A pinch point that split their attention.

The hallway was bad. They'd be behind us with straight shots, unless we were lucky enough to run into a crowd. I wasn't feeling lucky.

The descent was the first situation that held promise. Ten flights of elevator or stairs. Holding someone by the throat on an elevator was risky, since they didn't know how often the doors would open, or who'd be there when it did. For that reason, I figured they'd go for the stairs. Nobody used those. Plus, they were more isolated and controlled.

They'd exit us into a waiting vehicle, probably through an exit that avoided the lobby. That would take us through back hallways, and potentially past fire extinguishers, cleaning carts, and maintenance supplies. All were potentially useful, but none were predictable.

I needed something I could rely on. Something in my control. Once we were in the car, or truck, or van, then rope, or handcuffs, or duct tape would come into play, and our odds of escape would plummet.

I had to act before we got that far.

I had to come up with a plan before we left the room.

In my mind, I backed up to the stairwell and pictured it as a battlefield. A jungle of concrete walls and metal rails slathered in gray paint. Twenty flights of tripping points and sharp turns, of rigid corners and precipitous drops.

I made my decision.

Raising my hands slowly, I put quiver in my voice. "Don't shoot. Don't shoot me. I'll give you whatever you want."

"*Odevaicya*," Scar repeated, the right side of his mouth drawing back in a sneer.

I pulled my t-shirt on first, followed by my jeans and leather jacket. I was consciously fumbling in fear on the outside while my mind raced, surreptitiously searching for weapons or tools. The floor was bare, and there were no tabletop trinkets within range. I settled my mind on the Bic pen I'd used to complete our customs forms. A simple yellow cylinder in my back jeans pocket, next to the paperclips I always carried as makeshift tools. I tied my shoes and stood slowly, shoulders slumped, palming the pen out of sight while dangling my arms like broken wings.

Scar gestured toward the door with his gun. "Let's go."

Chapter 26

Making a Point

WHEN CONFRONTED with superior numbers, the first rule is split the opposing force. Divide and conquer.

I beckoned to Katya with my head, urging her to go first and allowing my eyes to flash lucidity as they met hers. I wanted her to know I was on my game. I wanted her prepared.

She started walking as though there wasn't a fist wrapped around her throat. The gorilla slid his grip to her shoulder, covering it like a baseball mitt as she led us out of the room.

"To the right," Gorilla said, steering her toward the stairs. The hallway was empty. Not so much as a maid's cart to be seen. Two steps in front of me, Gorilla had his paw on Katya's shoulder. Two steps behind me, Scar had his Glock leveled on my center of mass. He'd literally be shooting from the hip, firing through his suit coat pocket, but at that range, a drunk blind man couldn't miss.

At the stairwell entry, Gorilla swapped his left hand to Katya's shoulder so he could use his right to open the fire door, which was no doubt held closed from the inside by a heavy pneumatic spring. We accordianned back together as a foursome and I followed the leading couple through.

I reached up with my left hand to prop the door for Scar, glancing over my left shoulder as people in polite company do. Of course, people in polite company don't have guns pointed at each other's backs, so Scar was left with a dilemma. Should he pull his gun hand out to prop the door, or should he let me hold it while he walked through, or should he reach awkwardly across with his left?

I was ready for all three.

He went with option one, pulling the gun from his pocket and using the butt to prop the door. He had four inches and fifty pounds on me, and three minutes prior had heard me quiver with fright. Hardly high-tension for him. Just another day on the brute-squad job.

My left hand followed my gaze, rocketing up from my waist to grab his right wrist from below, pushing it up while my fingers clamped down like emergency brakes. The moment they locked on, I sprang up and back with my legs, pulling Scar off balance and on top of me.

He began squeezing the trigger as he toppled forward, his sunglasses flying from his face. Once, twice. Crack! Crack!

We went airborne, nose to nose, with concrete chips flying and the echoes of gunshots reverberating.

I brought my rigid right arm around, pen now clenched like an icepick in my fist, eager to extinguish the confident gleam in his eyes. Ignoring the threat of the rising concrete floor, I put my back and shoulder into the swing, driving the exposed inch straight into his left ear canal. This stunned him, but it didn't put him down. His grip on the gun remained firm as we smacked down on my left side.

If Gorilla also had a gun, this was the moment where I'd meet my maker. I hadn't seen a telltale bulge on his breast or ankle or in the hollow of his back, but that was far from definitive with slimline automatics against that much bulk. In any case, it was out of my hands, so I put it out of my mind.

I used Scar's moment of shock to wrap my legs around one of his, taking knees out of play and gaining some control. Our arms began a desperate two-front tug-of-war. My right hand kept pressure on the pen puncturing his ear, as Scar struggled with savage fury to pull it out the way it had gone in. Meanwhile my left hand battled his right for control of the gun. I couldn't pull the trigger, but he couldn't aim.

I looked up and back, over my head, and along my arm.

I saw Gorilla making the decision to abandon Katya and go for Scar's gun.

Then I witnessed the bravest act I'd ever seen.

The strongest muscle in the human body isn't the arm's biceps brachii or the thigh's rectus femoris. Pound for pound, the jaw's masseter muscle takes the prize. Delivering up to 270 pounds of force through dense mandibular bone and teeth designed to cut and grind, it powers nature's original weapon, and it functions with equal ferocity whether the object encountered is dead or alive.

Katya twisted her long slender neck down to the left and clamped the full breadth of her jaw around Gorilla's left hand. The move was amazing, both for its accuracy and its speed, like a chameleon catching a fly. She must have been rehearsing it in her head. Must have spent the walk screwing her courage tight and preparing for that strike.

And that wasn't all.

While maintaining the grip with her teeth, Katya swung her fist down and back between her tormentor's legs, making audible contact and eliciting a tortured groan. The combination blow momentarily knocked Gorilla out of commission, and saved both our lives.

Or at least it postponed our deaths by a few auspicious seconds.

I pushed my left arm up while vising my thighs in and down, leaving Scar's shoulder with minimal leverage so I could direct the gun. I didn't need it pointed anywhere in particular. I just needed it clear of Katya.

With her safe for a second, I focused on the pen. Scar was desperate to pull it out. I was determined to drive it in. But I didn't have the room. The pen was only five and a half inches long, and my fist was covering four. We were at a stalemate, but one that wouldn't last. Katya's bite had bought us the ability to keep fighting, but Gorilla would knock her aside and get to Scar's gun in a heartbeat or two.

I rolled, torquing to the right with everything I had, as if swinging for survival on the face of a cliff. I pulled Scar on top of me and then over, all the way from my left side to my right. A hundred-eighty-degree roll of five hundred furious pounds. The instant my right side hit the bottom I released my left hand from around Scar's wrist, and prepared it to deliver a powerful palm strike to his upturned ear.

His gun hand now freed, Scar began swinging the Glock toward my head.

I was in a race all over again. The second in as many days. Two lives in the balance, milliseconds on the clock.

As Scar's Glock neared the completion of the arc that would end my life, my left palm pummeled his exposed ear with a powerful thud, driving his head down on the pen like a hammer on an inverted nail.

His head hit the floor.

The Bic disappeared.

The lights went out.

Once again, I'd beaten my rival to the punch by the breadth of a hair.

Scar fired wide as he spasmed in death. Somewhere in the back of my brain I registered that there would be three rounds left if he'd started with a full load, four if he kept one in the chamber. I reached and rolled and took it down to two. Gorilla took my round in the heart and collapsed like a duck blown out of the air. His body hit the stairs and slid to the next landing, lifeless and limp, his head thunking surrender on each bloody step.

Chapter 27

Wheels Turning

I LEAPT to my feet and wrapped my arms around Katya, pulling her to my chest. "You were amazing," I whispered. "You saved us both."

She was trembling like a baby in an ice bath.

I guided her across our landing to the upward staircase and sat her down on the second step. "Just close your eyes and breathe deep for a couple of seconds."

She nodded weakly, maintaining a thousand-yard stare rather than closing her eyes.

I picked up the Glock and zipped down the adjacent stairs, sticking to the right to avoid leaving footprints in the smeared and spattered blood. Rummaging through Gorilla's pockets, I found nothing but a wad of rubles and a slim ceramic lock-blade knife. No papers. No identification. No phone. I pocketed the plunder along with the Glock and bounded back up to search Scar. A Mercedes key, more rubles, and a folded sheet of paper. I was curious, but it could wait.

I extended my hand to Katya. "Okay. Let's go."

We didn't have a key to our room, but a couple of warm smiles and a hundred-ruble note convinced a gray-haired janitor to let us in. I didn't like leaving impressions, but figured our secret was safe with his generation. Stalin had taught them to keep their heads down and tongues tight.

I spoke the moment our door closed. "Let's gather our things and go. An investigation is going to erupt the moment someone uses those stairs, and we need to be gone by then."

I retrieved our passports, wallets, and phones from under the mattress while Katya stuffed her clothes and our toiletries into her backpack. We left the Korston without checking out, as people often do. The morning maid would find that the bed had been slept in and the shower used, so there would be nothing to draw suspicion to Mr. and Mrs. Yates.

"Metro?" Katya asked, as we traded the dim hotel lobby for afternoon sunlight.

I held up a finger. "Maybe. Wait here. I'll be back in thirty seconds."

I headed toward the hotel's back parking lot.

Katya began to follow. "Talk to me, Achilles. Tell me what's going on."

I stopped and turned. "They had a car, and I've got the key. We may as well use it. Plus, it may yield clues. These guys didn't have cell phones or wallets on them."

She stared at me. "What if they have a driver waiting in the car? He'll shoot you on sight."

"That's why I asked you to wait. You have to trust me, Katya. I promise to explain everything once we're clear. I just don't want to stop to do that now. We're too exposed here."

Her mouth started to tremble, and I knew I'd screwed up. I had to get better at working with an amateur partner. "I don't think anyone will be in the car. It's much more common to work in twos than threes. And if there were a getaway driver, then why would Scar have a key? Besides, I have a gun now too. By asking you to wait, I'm just being cautious. Make sense?"

She nodded.

"I'll be right back. Okay?"

"Okay."

I made a mental note to work some decompression into our schedule. As soon as possible. Next stop.

Rounding the back corner of the building, I saw an old beer truck parked before the delivery door, and beyond it a likely candidate. A shiny new Mercedes van sat backed up to the employee entrance. The beer truck rumbled to life as I approached, and pulled out after its loud transmission clanked into gear. The bearded driver paid me no attention in his side mirror.

The Mercedes was a white panel van emblazoned with the blue logo of the GasEx corporation. I walked around it as though it were my own, visually confirming that it was empty while listening intently. Satisfied, I returned to the driver's door, yanked it open, and hopped in with my Glock covering the cargo area. Nothing there but a large stainless-steel storage box and an ominous packet of heavy duty cable ties.

I located the cover for the fuse box under the steering column, popped it open, and extracted the fuse for the entertainment console. Starting the engine, I confirmed that there was no power to the GPS system, and drove to pick up Katya.

"Won't they be able to track us?" Katya asked, as we rolled over the Metro Bridge into central Moscow.

"If they use LoJack, then yes. But they're more likely to use GPS, if anything at all, and I've disabled that."

"And if it is LoJacked?"

"They won't get around to tracking it for hours. How about dinner? We'll eat and see if anyone shows up looking for it."

I followed Katya's guidance to a neighborhood a couple of kilometers south of the Kremlin, stopping along the way to purchase a couple of movie posters and a roll of packing tape. We parked strategically in a courtyard near the Frunzenskaya Embankment, and covered the GasEx logos with the posters. Ours was now just another of the thousands of panel vans in the city that twenty-million Russians called home.

"Do you think the van really belongs to the GasEx Corporation?" Katya asked, as we walked the Moscow River embankment. "Or is that camouflage?"

"Camouflage seems more likely to me. I can't imagine how an oil and gas behemoth could be connected to Vitalis Pharmaceuticals, but it might be genuine. A big part of our problem is that we have no idea what we're up against. I'm beginning to get the feeling that this is big. Very big."

"What do you mean by that?"

"The murder of my family was the biggest event of my life, with framing me for it a close second. So I naturally assumed that it was a big event for the perpetrator too, and I've been looking at this like a murder investigation. But what if it wasn't? What if I got the scale wrong? What if Colin, and Martha, and my father were just three victims in a war?"

Chapter 28

A Thousand Words

WE STROLLED in contemplative silence toward the shadow of the Crimean Bridge, as the dark waters of the Moscow River rippled past. Ahead on our left, the sign for a Georgian restaurant Katya favored glowed like the light at the end of a long tunnel.

Opening Guria's arched pinewood door for her, I saw heavy pinewood tables with matching chairs, forest-green curtains, and a bit of Georgian bric-a-brac. The decor was nothing special, but the smells were divine. Roasting meats and melting cheeses and spices I knew I'd love but couldn't identify. The dining room was packed with jovial patrons sucking down juicy dumplings and dark red wine, toasting to health, and looking for love. We got lucky with a table, and a motherly waitress in a green apron and headscarf was soon with us.

"I'm thinking we should get it all," I said to Katya so the waitress could hear. "Pork and lamb shashlik, khinkali, and khachapuri, with beans and greens. Does that sound good to you?"

"Sounds great." Katya's voice was noticeably less tense than the last time she'd spoken.

"Wine?" the waitress asked.

"Borjomi," I said, referencing the famous Georgian sparkling water.

The waitress gave me a spirited look that said I'd earned a B-plus.

I pulled up an iPhone app and found a couple of private apartments in the area advertising as B&B's. Got the thumbs up from Katya and made note of the addresses as the Borjomi and khachapuri arrived. I stuck my nose out over the steam, closed my eyes, and inhaled deeply. Freshly baked bread browned just so, rimming a buttery puddle of melted cheese. Hard to beat that.

I put a slice on each of our plates and raised my effervescent glass. Katya raised hers back at me in the Georgian tradition. "Survival of the fittest. It's nature's primary rule. Adapt and flourish, or freeze and perish. In my line of work, I've seen a lot of it, but I've never seen anyone adapt like you, Katya. Colin was right, you are amazing."

She blushed and clinked my glass.

"I'll never forget the image of you biting that guy. It was so perfect, but so out of character. How did you ... what made ... where did that ferocity come from?"

"Remember that self-defense course I told you about the day I visited you in jail?"

"Sure."

"The instructor primed us to change our character when threatened with physical violence. He showed us some pretty scary surveillance videos of attempted rapes so that we wouldn't have any illusions about what attackers would be willing to do to us. Then he conditioned us to react to *rape* as a trigger word, a word that would instantly recall those horrible images and evoke that fighting mentality. He made us shout it as we practiced his defensive techniques, both as a means of attracting help, and to act as a psychological trigger. So I screamed *RAPE* in my head, and bore my teeth."

"Wow. I'll remember that one. And if I ever meet your teacher, I'll be buying him a couple of drinks."

"I must say, I never thought I'd need to use it."

I raised my glass. "Let's hope you never do again."

As the dumplings and shashlik arrived, I asked, "Have you heard back from Dr. Tarasova?"

"Nope. But I left a message saying that I'd stop by first thing in the morning. They open at nine. What is it you expect her to tell us?"

That was the big question. We were only at the beginning of a complex international investigation, an investigation I had less than two weeks to solve. If we failed, I'd likely spend the rest of my life in jail. It was going to be tight, intense, and apparently very dangerous.

"We have a general motive we need to make specific. To do that we need to learn about Vitalis's business. We don't know what its product was supposed to do, or why it failed. As their clinical coordinator, Dr. Tarasova should have a pretty good understanding of the basics, but I doubt they told her more than that."

Katya cocked her head. "Why would they hide things from her?"

I used a finger to wipe a thin string of cheese from Katya's chin. "Pharmaceutical companies are very secretive before patents issue and products launch. There's so much competition, with billions potentially on the line. But at a minimum, she'll know what Vitalis's product was supposed to do, for whom, and how. She'd have to know that to recruit patients."

Katya pushed her plate back and leaned in. "And she'd have to know why they cancelled the trial."

"Not necessarily. The lab results would likely have gone straight to Colin as the chief medical officer. All part of the secrecy thing. How much Tarasova knows really depends on whether Colin regarded her as a partner or a contractor."

"I got the impression he thought of her as a partner. He was very collegial with her on the phone. I could tell that he liked and respected her."

"Great. The more she knows, the easier it will be for us to figure out what was worth killing for."

My poor choice of words put a shadow on our conversation, and we turned our focus back to the food. As we finished off the last of the dumplings, Katya asked, "How did they find us at the hotel?"

I set the paper I'd snatched from Scar onto the table, still folded closed into quarters. "How do you think? Work it like an equation. You have the result. What are the predicates?"

She gave me an appraising smile, her eyes aglow. "Thank you."

"For what?"

"For understanding me." She blushed a bit. "The most basic predicate is that they were looking for us, which is disturbing news."

"It's a good sign actually, given our race against the clock. It will be easier to find them if they're also looking for us."

"Do you think they followed us from California, or picked us up here?"

"There wasn't time for anyone to follow us. We went straight from your place to SFO and onto a plane, so they picked us up here."

"But no one knew we were going to that hotel."

"Right ..."

Katya chewed on that for a second. "So they spotted us at the airport?"

"That's my hypothesis. If I'm right, the paper I took off our assailants will back it up." I slid the folded white sheet across the table to Katya. She opened it up, exposing a printout of four pictures. It was a format I was familiar with, the kind generated by facial recognition programs and used during stakeouts. It displayed a full frontal shot and a profile shot for two people, complete with calibration marks. The background was familiar too. It was the Santa Barbara County Superior Court. We were looking at our own faces.

Chapter 29

Knock Knock

I SET ASIDE my breakfast plate and stood to go. "I think you should wait here while I talk to Tarasova. This is going to be dangerous."

Katya shot me a glance that reflected a feisty combination of anger and fear. "The last time you left me alone in a hotel room I ended up with a gorilla at my throat. And that was just for a trip to the shower."

"This is different."

"How is it different? You promised me you weren't going to be cryptic."

She was right. "Do you want the long answer?"

"I would love the long answer."

To signal my commitment to acting partner-like, I moved from the breakfast table to the couch that had served as my bed. Plunking down onto the coarse green fabric, I signaled her to join me. "My work at the CIA revolved around the neutralization of very bad guys. As my employers put it when talking to their congressional overseers, these were 'individuals actively engaged in actions sufficiently hostile to the American people or government to warrant targeted covert action.' Do you follow?"

"Are you saying you hunted down the CIA's equivalent of the FBI's most wanted list?"

"Pretty much, although my list was unpublished. Too sensitive. For that reason, my work was not officially sanctioned either, so if I got caught doing something unsavory on foreign soil, there was always the chance I'd be on my own."

"You volunteered for that?"

"I jumped at the chance. It was exciting, meaningful work. And special operatives don't think about the downside any more than policemen or firemen or soldiers do. I suppose that's a testosterone thing."

"Uh-huh. I trust that *neutralize* is a euphemism?"

"For lead therapy?"

Katya elbowed me.

"Actually, the more beneficial and interesting operations involved turning the perpetrator into an asset. That was my specialty. Of course we had to locate them first. Given that these were people working very hard to stay hidden, I had to get creative. The secret to my success was becoming adept at arranging circumstances that would bring our targets to a predictable place within a predictable window. Rather than hunting them, I'd figure out a way to draw them to me. The corollary to this, as you would say, is that I've become well-attuned to not acting predictably."

I paused there to let Katya digest.

She didn't take long. "And going to the clinical trial site is predictable."

"Very. Assuming we're right, and all this is somehow related to Vitalis."

"Well then *we'll* just have to be extra careful."

I wasn't about to challenge her informed decision. For all I knew, she'd be the one saving the day again.

We arrived at the medical school campus promptly at nine o'clock and ostensibly undetected. We'd camouflaged ourselves within a group walking from the metro, so I was pretty sure we hadn't been spotted. Yet.

Tarasova's building bordered a construction site on one side and the Palace of Youth's park on the other. Number 28 was a long, eight-story structure clad with white tile and adorned with wraparound balconies on the higher floors. Lots of places to put a spotter, but I didn't see any. Speaking loud enough to be heard over the rattle and hum of earth-moving equipment, I said, "Nice building."

Katya had apparently been thinking the same thing. "The medical school's lucky to have it. I'm sure that renting it out to commercial enterprises helps to keep their lights on."

Speaking of keeping the lights on, a sign on the elevator door recommended using the stairs on account of frequent electrical outages. A result of the neighboring construction. A couple of students approached and bravely pressed the up button while we read. "Which floor?" I asked Katya.

"Top one, of course. The eighth."

"Feel like some exercise?"

I felt my stomach squirming as we began to climb. If this visit wasn't successful, I wasn't sure what we'd do next, but I did know that losing momentum could be deadly. Speaking of which, I slid my hand into my jacket pocket and around the butt of Scar's Glock.

My focus shifted to Katya, who was breezing up the stairs as though she did a thousand a day. It occurred to me that I had no idea what she did to keep so fit. I'd have to ask. After 126 stairs, the Clinical Connection's office door opened to reveal a typical medical practice.

Except that nobody was there.

Chapter 30

Sirens

I SLIPPED THE GLOCK back into my pocket as we entered the Clinical Connection. The small reception area was outfitted with soft chairs, a rack of well-thumbed magazines about pop stars and fast cars, and a reception counter beside the door that led to all the action. There were no patients, and no receptionist. It was quiet as midnight.

"Hello," I called. Once. Twice.

Footsteps broke the silence, high heels double-clicking across hard floors. A moment later, a matronly woman appeared wearing gray wool slacks and a white lab coat. Her nameplate read Perova. "Yeah?" she asked, as though picking up a call from a telemarketer.

"We're here to see Dr. Tarasova."

"She's not here. If she was, you'd be talking to her, and I'd still be working."

"We had an appointment," Katya pressed.

Perova frowned. "Really? She wrapped everything up last week."

"Last week?"

"The Vitalis trial. That's why you're here to see Dr. Tarasova, right? I don't see you on the calendar. What are your names?"

I leaned forward on an elbow and spoke softly. "When do you expect her?"

Perova gave me an appraising glance. "I don't know. She was here earlier. She's supposed to be here now. We have a lot of cleanup to do."

"Would you please double-check?" Katya asked. "Maybe she's on the phone."

Perova practically rolled her eyes, but whirled and clattered off.

Katya and I exchanged surprised glances the moment Perova turned. "Last week? The company folded eight months ago."

I thought about it. "Maybe there's some Ministry of Health regulation requiring follow-up visits, regardless."

Katya shrugged.

The office was quiet enough that we could hear Perova's progression as she moved from room to room. I leaned over the counter and looked around. Nothing notable. In fact, not much at all. Looked like a bare-bones operation. "They're not very busy. I wonder how many trials the

Clinical Connection has going?"

"Don't know, but the elevator situation can't help."

The footsteps signaled Perova's return a few seconds before her head appeared. "I told you. She's not here. What time was your appointment?"

"I left her a message requesting one first thing this morning, but didn't hear back," Katya said.

"Well, that's hardly the same thing as having an appointment, is it? I need to get back to my work now. Apparently I'm the only one working today."

Katya smiled sympathetically. "We'll check back in a bit. I saw a Coffee Mania back by the metro. Can we bring you something? Cappuccino and a pastry, perhaps?"

Perova seemed shocked by the offer. "This is a clinic. No food or beverage allowed."

I liked Katya's idea. I was feeling the jet lag. Ready for that second cup. I gestured toward the elevator. "What's the deal? Is it safe?"

"We've had patients get stuck. Don't get me started."

"That can't be good for business."

Perova snorted. "Especially if you're running an incontinence trial. We're moving. That's why it's so quiet around here. All the action is at the new office."

"Is Vitalis there now too?" Katya asked.

"Didn't I just tell you that they wrapped up last week?" Perova wheeled about without waiting for an answer.

"You did."

We took Perova's advice and used the stairs, which wrapped around the elevator shaft. "How did Colin explain Vitalis folding?" I asked.

"He didn't want to talk about it. I remember him staring at some paperwork and shaking his head while repeating 'game over' as though he couldn't believe it."

"Yeah, I also got that impression and didn't want to press, especially on the phone. Now I wish I had. Would you say Colin was surprised, or just disappointed?"

"He was more than surprised. He was shocked and devastated. One day he was on top of the world, certain he had the best thing since penicillin, the next he was unemployed."

Noise echoed up the stairwell from below, disrupting our discussion and growing louder as we descended. The clamor of a crowd was being augmented by the two-tone wail of an approaching ambulance.

Emerging into the front lobby, we found it packed with people facing the street. I took Katya's hand and guided us toward the exit and the epicenter of the excitement, brushing shoulders and making holes. A few steps revealed a couple of police cars parked in V-formation, their lights flashing red and blue. I went up on my toes, using my height to beat the crowd.

"What do you see?" Katya asked.

"Three uniformed officers, circled up and looking at the ground. A fourth studying the sky, shielding his eyes against the reflection of the rising sun." I nudged us closer, glancing skyward like the fourth cop, then back at the ground.

"What?" Katya persisted.

I tightened my grip on her hand and started plowing us through the crowd toward the approaching siren and the main road, cataloguing cars and faces as we walked, my senses on high alert. "Someone fell from the roof. Brunette in her mid-thirties. Landed on her back. She was wearing a white lab coat. I couldn't see her whole name tag, but it started with *Tar.*"

Chapter 31

The Rocket

CLEAR OF THE GAWKING CROWD, we continued walking briskly, digesting the latest turn of events in silence, not sure where to go. As we neared Komsomolskiy Prospect, Katya spoke, her voice showing strain. "Are you certain the dead woman was Tarasova?"

"You can do the math. What are the odds of having a last name starting with Tar?"

"Any chance it was a suicide? Maybe from guilt over complaisance in whatever killed Colin. Perhaps my call triggered it?"

I wanted to ease Katya's mind, but noise from the approaching ambulance made conversation awkward. As the siren passed us racing toward the scene, and the Doppler effect changed the *ah ah* to *oh oh*, a white panel van rolled past in the other direction, a blue GasEx logo on its side.

Our matching van was still a kilometer away, so I released Katya's hand and spun around to face the oncoming traffic. I stuck my arm out to flag any driver willing to work as a cab and began waving. To my great relief, a maroon Lada 5 pulled right over.

"Change of plans?" Katya asked as I ushered her inside. "Tired of walking?"

Speaking rapid Russian to the Lada's young driver, I said, "We're following the white van that just turned right on Komsomolskiy. I've got a hundred dollars US for you if you can stick behind it."

"You got it!" he said, accelerating after his target. "Where's it going?"

"That's what I want to find out." I extracted a Benjamin from my wallet so he could see that I meant business. "But I don't want the van's driver to know he's being followed. Think you can manage that?"

"Depends where he goes." The driver repositioned his rearview mirror to study Katya and me. "This car is about as anonymous as they come. We should be fine as long as it stays on busy streets. And they're all busy at this hour."

As we crossed the Moscow River on the same long bridge we'd driven the evening before, I turned to face Katya and spoke in English. "No chance at all."

She took a second to pair the answer with her suicide question.

"How can you be sure?"

"First of all, a GasEx van just left the scene. Secondly, I saw the passenger and driver."

Her expression ran a gamut of emotions before stopping on fear. "Black suits?"

"With black t-shirts and sunglasses."

"It looks like GasEx is where we're heading," the driver said in English, pointing to the distinctive skyscraper now visible on the horizon. GasEx's Moscow headquarters looked like the Washington Monument, but made of blue glass and with auxiliary towers running up each of the four corners, giving it an X-shaped footprint. The glass pyramid at the top reminded me of the entrance to the Louvre Museum.

"They call it Barsukov's Rocket," the driver said.

"I get the rocket part. But who's Barsukov?"

"The new chairman of GasEx," Katya and the driver replied in unison.

"Why don't I know that? The name's not familiar."

"He stays behind the scenes," Katya said. "The CEO, Antipin, is the public face. He's much more presentable. I'm sure you've heard of him."

"Arkady Antipin, sure. Looks like a cross between a sweet grandfather and an elder statesman. Trustworthy and competent. What makes Barsukov unpresentable?"

The driver hopped on my question. "He's got dark, deep-set eyes and a face they say is allergic to smiling."

Katya nodded. "I can confirm that. He spoke at MSU last year. Part of his victory lap after landing the chairmanship. He hosted a recruiting dinner afterwards for PhD candidates in STEM disciplines, and I was seated at his table. He's incredibly smart and very smooth, but inherently creepy. When you look into his eyes you see a crocodile's soul."

I found my curiosity growing the closer we came to his monumental headquarters. "Seems an odd choice for a chairmanship appointment."

"They say he's an old KGB friend of President Korovin's," the driver said. "Do you want me to try to follow the van onto the GasEx complex if it turns in?"

A friend of the president's. "Oh yes."

Chapter 32

Evil Eye

KATYA TURNED to me as we neared the GasEx gate. "Isn't it risky, going in unprepared?"

"The way things are going, standing still is risky too. We won't do anything rash, but at the very least, we'll see which building they enter."

She put on a brave smile.

I wondered if I should try to hide her away in some suburban hotel until this was over. I doubted she'd go for that, but resolved to ask her later.

The fence that surrounded the GasEx complex rolled by to our right, black iron spears, tightly spaced, with a deep lawn beyond. Modern high-security of the sort used by Bel-Air estates, and G7 embassies. Closer now, we could see a circle of smaller buildings and flagpoles surrounding The Rocket, again reminding me of the Washington Monument atop the National Mall.

A couple of cars ahead, the white van's turn signal began to blink right. I watched it roll to a stop before a card reader in the employee lane. A black sleeve extended a blue card, and the iron gate swung open in response.

While we waited behind a black Mercedes S550 in the visitor's lane, I rolled down my window. "I'll do the talking."

I felt Katya tense beside me as our turn came and we stopped before a beefy guard in a black suit. His appearance and demeanor were similar to that of our friends, but rather than sunglasses and a black t-shirt, he wore a black collar shirt with a blue tie the same hue as the GasEx logo.

My eyes moved to his left hand as he greeted us. It held something similar to a laser pointer. A metallic cylinder with an eye. He directed it at each of us for a second. I didn't recognize it until the damage was done.

In English, I said, "Good morning. We're tourists and stockholders and were just curious and attracted by your beautiful building. Do you have a museum or anything like that?"

"I'm sorry, sir," he replied in perfect English. "You're welcome to visit in June during the annual stockholders' meeting, but otherwise the grounds are closed to visitors. However, I'm sure that if you reached out to investor relations, a tour could be arranged." He produced a business card from his breast pocket. "Here's their contact information." He turned to the driver and gestured while saying, "You can exit to the left."

"Where to?" the driver asked once we were facing the street again.

"The nearest metro. As fast as you can get us there."

"Sixty seconds fast enough?"

"Why'd you give up so easily?" Katya asked, disappointment evident. "I thought you'd planned to finesse our way in."

"That was before we were fucked."

The driver turned to look at me as Katya said, "What are you talking about?"

"I was stupid. Should have anticipated."

"What?"

"First thing the guard did was take our pictures. No doubt they went directly into a facial recognition program, probably the same one that processed the courtroom photos. They've got a bead on us now. And worse, they know we've got a bead on them. We need to disappear, fast."

I turned to the driver. "You'll be fine if you keep a low profile and stick to a slim version of the truth. If asked, tell them we flagged you down on Komsomolskiy Prospect and paid you a hundred rubles to drive us to GasEx. Then you dropped us at the metro when we couldn't get in. That's it. We didn't say anything during the drive, and for God's sake don't mention following a van. Keep it boring and they'll get bored with you. Sorry for the hassle. Here's an extra hundred bucks."

The driver sighed somber resignation and a couple of seconds later pulled to the curb near the entrance to Kaluzhskaya metro station.

We made for the escalator without another word.

Once we were underground, Katya asked, "What now?"

I grabbed her hand and increased our pace. "It's time to deploy a secret weapon."

Chapter 33

Dim

GRIGORI BARSUKOV had his feet on his office desk and a cigar in his mouth when he got the news. He was celebrating. It was thirty months to the hour since he'd walked the lonely Kremlin corridor and made his initial pitch to President Korovin.

He'd been a bundle of nerves walking into the meeting. He could admit that to himself now. The president's hunting allegory had nearly pushed him over the edge. But he'd hung in there, steeled his will, and kept his eye on the prize.

They'd met three more times. The first had just been an update on the Brillyanc rollout, but the second and third had been much more. At the second meeting, Grigori revealed an unexpected twist. A tantalizing, delicious, unbelievable twist. At the third, they'd agreed on an audacious plan to exploit it.

Now Grigori was sitting on a chair made from the hide of the very crocodile Vladimir had referenced in their initial meeting. A gift from the big man himself. A daily reminder of who had given him his position, and who could pluck him from it. But Grigori chose to regard the chair as a symbol of his own strength and guile. Evidence of the type of tactics that prevailed in a predatory world.

The modern chime of his private elevator struck a chord dissonant with the Beethoven symphony playing in the background. Then the brushed-aluminum doors opened to reveal his head of security.

From the outside, Grigori's office/apartment looked like the entrance to the Louvre Museum, except that it was perched thirty-stories up, atop GasEx's Moscow headquarters, rather than in a Parisian palace courtyard. The pyramid forming the walls of Grigori's office consisted of 576 panes of a special blue glass, the clarity or opacity of which Grigori could control electronically from a tablet. His power to block out the sun with the flick of a wrist was a little godlike, as of course was the Olympus-like view from atop his 'rocket.'

Grigori had one of his technical people write a program that kept the window pattern arranged so that the sun spotlighted anyone exiting the elevator. This gave Grigori a physical and psychological advantage in the crucial first seconds of every meeting. This time, the spotlight told him Pyotr was about to ruin his day.

"Achilles just showed up at the front gate," Pyotr said, removing his wraparound shades now that he was clear of the sun. "He's with Katya and a guy we have yet to identify. Probably a cabbie, but my guys are checking as we speak."

"Excellent. Do you need my help disposing of the bodies?"

Pyotr's big bald head reddened. "We don't have them. They turned around at the gate, after their images were captured, but before the facial recognition program alerted us to the match."

Grigori drummed his fingers audibly on the back of the tablet. "Not so excellent. In fact, that's pretty much the opposite of excellent, wouldn't you say? Now we need to worry about what brought them here. Coming to Moscow was one thing. That was a logical move given the data available to them. Any competent investigator would have done the same. But coming here, to my property specifically? Well, that presents an entirely different deck of cards. That indicates significant progress. Which indicates the existence of a trail. Which indicates a breach in security. Which indicates incompetence. Wouldn't you say?"

Pyotr's whole head flushed red again. "Yes, sir. We're trying to identify the trail, even as we search for them. It's not the Clinical Connection. We retrieved all the records and eliminated the doctor before they arrived."

"That's too bad."

"Sir?"

"There aren't a lot of trails to cover. Not here in Moscow anyway. If it's not the clinical people, that leaves your guys. Doesn't it?"

Pyotr just blinked.

"We assume they got your guys in California. We know they got your guys in the hotel. Maybe your guys talked?"

"They wouldn't talk."

"Then how do you explain Achilles showing up on my doorstep?"

"I can't."

"If you're this stupid after Brillyanc, I don't know how you survived before it."

"Yes, sir."

"Put guys at the airports and train stations. Good guys. Brillyanc guys. Sooner or later, they're bound to flee. I'm going to call in some outside help to try and make it sooner."

"Yes, sir. We only have eight Brillyanc guys left, but there are three airports and nine train stations."

"Prioritize. Improvise. Get your own butt out in the field. I don't want to call in help. It increases my exposure and makes me look weak."

"Yes, sir."

"And Pyotr?"

"Sir?"

"You're only understaffed because you're down four to Achilles. If he makes it five, I'm going to make it six. Are we clear?"

A few more blinks. "Yes, sir."

His celebratory mood ruined by the incompetence of others, Grigori grabbed a special cell phone and headed for the terrace door. He had an important call to make.

Chapter 34

Pets

GRIGORI'S OFFICE SUITE had three points of egress. All biometrically controlled. All locking down at night — leaving him safe as an eaglet in a nest. The first was the private elevator that had just swooshed closed behind Pyotr. The second was the entrance to his residence — a sliding slab of granite resembling a square of sandy beach still wet from a wave. The third exit led to the roof, or more accurately, a circumferential terrace.

Surrounding the pyramid to a depth of three meters, the limestone terrace provided a hundred-meter circuit for walking off frustrations, as well as access to his helipad, which topped the south tower. It was Grigori's refuge, retreat, and secret weapon.

Grigori pressed his palm against a plate embedded in one of the big glass triangles. A powerful electric motor engaged with a whir and a whoosh and lifted the heavy window up and out along its hinge, creating a doorway that measured two meters on each of its three sides. Cool April air blasted in and blew ash from Grigori's cigar back onto the granite tile behind his feet, where it disappeared into a mélange of earth tones. Ignoring it, he stepped through, bringing the phone to his ear. "Call Kazan."

With his left hand, he side-pitched his spent cigar out and over the edge like he was skipping a stone. He followed it, all the way to the edge so he could watch the cigar's thirty-story plummet.

There was no rail, no ridge, no barrier of any kind between him and five seconds of free fall. A single solid gust would send him to Splatsville. But life on a tightrope had made Grigori immune to heights. The metaphorical had translated into the physical via nervous system fatigue. He'd run out of fear. A discovery he routinely used to his advantage during negotiations and power plays. Nothing like a casual walk inches from the edge to establish an alpha position.

Grigori had come to enjoy life on the edge. Aided by toys and girls, of course. Fantastic toys, like the new Ansat helicopter parked a few steps to his left. And breathtaking girls, like those downtown at Angels on Fire.

His call connected before the cigar landed. "This is Doctor Galkin."

"Mikhail, it's Grigori. I'm looking for good news."

"Afternoon, Grigori. I've got good news. Very good news. Two vectors have proven viable. They'll be available with time to spare."

The cigar crashed onto a mature bloom, scattering red tulip petals across green grass like drops of blood. "Redundancy and time to spare. That's impressive. I've got a role for you running my security if biotechnology ever begins to bore you."

"Pardon me?"

"Never mind. Long story. I greatly appreciate your competence. A ten-million-ruble bonus will be headed your way."

"Thank you. Thank you very much, Grigori."

"You're welcome. Now, when can I expect my new pets?"

Chapter 35

Behind the Curtain

WE TOOK THE METRO back to central Moscow, and then walked to our stolen van. As I keyed the ignition, Katya pointed to the storage container bolted to the floor behind us. "Aren't we going to see what's in the big metal box first?"

I hit the gas. "I wish we could. It's basically a safe. I know the brand, and unfortunately we're not going to be able to get in without either the combination or special equipment."

"Couldn't you shoot it open?"

"No. The steel is much too thick for that, and the lock incorporates multiple deadbolts."

"Power tools?"

"I like your attitude, but it would take a lot of time, make a lot of noise, and require some serious equipment."

"What do you think's in there?"

"The guys that attacked us didn't have wallets with them, and only one was armed, so at a minimum I figure we'll find ID and key cards and another weapon."

She percolated on that for a second. "Where are we going?"

I didn't want to worry her, but she had a right to know. "If the car is LoJacked, they'll pounce once we start moving. I want to go just far enough to either draw them out, or be sure they're never coming. We'll stash the van someplace similar, a couple of kilometers from here. I'll show you something interesting while we watch for them from safety."

"Why not forget the van? We can take taxis."

"Investigations are about stirring things up. Plus the van is a ticket into the complex, if we ever get our hands on those IDs."

As we pulled off the embankment road onto side streets, Katya returned to the discussion of motives. "Did you figure out what an energy company has to do with a pharmaceutical company? I can't think of a single connection."

"Yes and no. Both are high-risk, high-reward. Pharmaceutical development is often compared to energy exploration. Both require massive upfront investment with no guarantee of any return at all. Both also rely heavily on lobbyists to maintain favorable tax and legislative environments. But I don't see how any of those similarities could play into our situation."

"What are you thinking then?"

"I'm thinking that it's an indirect connection, as per last night's big-picture discussion. And I'm thinking that if the connection isn't at the industry level, it's at the individual level."

I could almost hear Katya's brain working that idea as we drove the next few blocks. Police cars were all over the place, but no other GasEx vans were in sight. We crossed Komsomolskiy and drove toward the famous New Maiden Convent and Cemetery. After a quick lap to check for tails, I parked within sight of both the convent and the hotel Randevu. An interesting choice of name, given its pious neighbor.

I paid cash for a room that overlooked the van while Katya talked the manager into letting us rent his laser printer for an hour. Then I went to work on my iPhone while Katya maintained lookout.

By this point, I was ready to trust Katya with my life. But my next move involved a different kind of trust. The CIA had given me access to some very sensitive tools. I needed to make use of those tools now, and there was no way to do so without making Katya aware of their existence. She was too smart to attempt to fool, and there was no mundane explanation for the magic I was about to work.

I whirled the desk chair around to face the bed. Katya had kicked off her shoes and shed her sweater and was lying chest down in skinny jeans and a caramel-colored cotton shirt. She'd propped her chest up on a pillow and had her bare feet crossed in the air. All she was doing was watching the van through the open balcony blinds, but she looked as sexy as anything I'd ever seen in my life. She glanced over, studied my face, and then grew an inquisitive half-smile. "What?"

I dove right into the deep end of business. "When I worked for that other government agency, they didn't give us special computers. Those would have marked and encumbered us. Instead, they gave us protocols for accessing hidden websites from any connected device."

Katya pulled herself up into a cross-legged position that made it easy for her to rotate her head back and forth between me and the street. "What kind of websites?" she asked, her intonation reminding me of the excitement I'd felt when Granger pulled back the curtain for me.

"Some are portals to access databases we can query. Others are operation-specific repositories. The operation-specific ones are deleted as soon as the mission wraps up, but the portals are permanent. I'm logged into one of them now."

I wasn't going to tell her that this particular portal queried both Interpol and the equivalent of the FBI for most of the industrialized world, including Russia's FSB. I'd never actually been told that was what it did, but I figured that was the only way it could work its magic. "And here she is: Tatiana Tarasova, MD, born in Moscow on October 10,

1980, residing at ... married to ... graduating from ... home phone ... work phone ... cell phone. There we go! Now, I'll take Tarasova's phone numbers to another portal, identify the one she used to call my brother's cell, and then get us a printout of the other numbers she called from that phone."

Two minutes later, I'd identified Tarasova's cell phone as the one she'd used to call Colin, and we were in business. Five minutes after that, the printer was spitting out records of Dr. Tarasova's cell phone calls for the past twelve months.

"What are you going to do with that information?"

"We'll use it to identify other Vitalis patients. Then we'll pick a few to interview."

I set to work turning numbers into names, and names into profiles. Katya went to work analyzing the results, looking for patterns and attempting to identify individuals whose backgrounds indicated that they'd be knowledgeable about pharmacology. A few dozen candidates into it, she yelled, "Bingo!"

Chapter 36

Clinical Connection

"BINGO?" I repeated back to Katya, wondering what could have elicited so much excitement.

"Saba Mamaladze is on the list. We're classmates. He's still in the doctoral program at MSU. Brilliant mathematician, and a good guy."

"You sure it's the same Saba Mamaladze?" I couldn't keep a straight face while repeating the melodic name. "What kind of a name is that?"

"It's Georgian. And yes, Achilles, I'm sure."

"You know him socially?"

"Sure do. I've been to his dorm room many times. He lived in the same building, the next entrance over. Should I give him a call, tell him we'll be stopping by?"

"No. That would be poor operational security."

"You told me you were going to work on the cryptic thing."

"It's best that we don't let anyone know that we're coming. We don't know who may be listening. We called Tarasova in advance, and she ended up dead before we could speak to her. There may or may not be causality there, but let's not take that chance with your friend." Not wanting her to dwell on that topic, I hastened to add, "I want to go back to the Clinical Connection on the way. We might as well come clean with Perova and see what we can get out of her."

"You think she'll be receptive?"

"I'm not sure about receptive, but I think we can get her talking if we give her a bit of information."

"What are you planning to tell her?"

"The truth."

No one had paid any attention to the van while we were at the Hotel Randevu, so I was comfortable that it wasn't being tracked. Still, we parked a few blocks from the medical school to be safe, and approached cautiously on foot.

I rang the bell in the empty reception room. "We're back."

We got the sound of high heels in response. They were moving slower than before. Perova's face, already visibly shaken by the morning's events, turned even paler at the sight of us.

"We know what happened," I said, saving her the pain of breaking the news. "And I have a confession to make. We're not patients, we're investigators. My brother was Dr. Tarasova's contact at Vitalis Pharmaceuticals, Dr. Colin Achilles."

Perova pursed her freshly painted lips, not sure what to make of all that. Finally, she composed herself. "I don't know your brother. I wasn't involved with the trial. Vitalis was all Dr. Tarasova."

"We were coming to talk to Dr. Tarasova this morning because my brother was murdered. We think it was related to his work. Katya was his fiancée," I added, inclining my head in Katya's direction. "Now Tarasova is dead too."

Perova's red eyes grew wide. "Oh my God! Am I in danger?"

"We're not certain what to think at this point."

"But the police said there was no evidence of foul play." Perova's tempo was quick and her voice high. "I told them I didn't think Dr. Tarasova was suicidal, but they said it was often completely unexpected. Do you think she was killed by the same person who killed your brother?"

"That's our theory. What can you tell us about the Vitalis trial? We thought Vitalis had ceased operations months ago around the time of my brother's death, so we were surprised this morning when you said the clinical trial had concluded last week."

"It did wrap up last week." Perova took a seat behind the counter. "The last patients were in Friday."

Katya and I exchanged glances.

"What can you tell us about the product?" Katya asked.

"The only thing I know is that the codename was *Brilliance* — spelled with y-a-n-c to be cute or something." She rolled her eyes.

"All our clients are secretive, but Vitalis was over the top. Dr. Tarasova was the only person who knew anything. She had to do everything herself, from briefing the patients, to running their labs, to hooking up their IVs."

"IVs?" Katya asked.

"Yes, Brillyanc is a parenteral delivered once every three months during a six-hour infusion. We've never had anything else like it. Dr. Tarasova had a good setup for it though, with comfortable chairs and snacks and personal televisions. And the patients were all upscale, well dressed, and educated. Usually we get the opposite here. That's why I immediately associated you with the Vitalis trial this morning."

"What about records?" I asked.

"Everything was managed electronically. Dr. Tarasova had a laptop for her own use and a tablet for patient input. The police were looking for both of them this morning, but neither is here."

"Isn't that strange?" Katya asked. "Surely she'd have brought her laptop to work today."

"Ordinarily, yes. But she didn't have a project to work on, so maybe she didn't bother. The metro is so crowded these days, the less baggage you have the better. Today she was supposed to be helping me out, preparing for the move."

"Who else has been asking questions today?" I asked.

"The police were here most of the morning, followed by a couple of investigators. They left just before you got here."

"Did they ask the same questions?" Katya asked.

"More or less. They wanted to know who Tanya discussed her work with, and what I knew about it. Like I told you, the answers were *nobody* and *not much*."

"Did you see identification?" I asked. "For the investigators."

"No, but it was obvious who they were. Very police-like."

"Big guys?"

"Yes, with square jaws, bright eyes, short haircuts, and black suits."

Chapter 37

Connecting the Dots

SABA MAMALADZE had thick, curly black hair, lively eyes, and a nose that belonged on an eagle. He wore faded jeans, a yellow polo shirt, and a smile that wouldn't quit — at least around Katya. He hugged her for a good five seconds while saying, "It's so good to see you, so good." Releasing her, he stepped back like a tailor admiring a suit. "Once you left for Palo Alto, I figured I wouldn't see you again unless I managed to score a post-doc at Stanford for myself. Speaking of which, I'm still counting on your help with that, you know."

"Stanford would be lucky to get you, Saba. When the time comes, let me know and I'll be sure the right people pay attention to your application."

Saba put his hands on his hips. "Well, aren't you a peach. So what does bring you back? Get a craving for Max's dumplings?"

Katya turned to me. "Max is Saba's roommate. He's also Georgian, and his family owns the best restaurant in Tbilisi. Every once in a while, when he's overly stressed out, he'll spend a day making dumplings. Hundreds of them. The best you ever tasted. So Saba and I do our best to keep him stressed."

"The secret is the meat." A convivial voice spoke from the hallway. "I use three kinds, but I'm not going to tell you which."

We all turned to see another beaming Georgian face. "How are you, Katya?"

Max had a slim, academic build similar to Saba's. He also wore faded jeans and a big grin shaded beneath a prominent nose, but his polo was royal blue, to match his intelligent eyes.

"I'm okay. You're looking great, Max. So are you, Saba. Have you guys adopted a new exercise routine or something? I want your secret."

The Georgians exchanged knowing glances.

"Who's your friend?" Max asked Katya.

"Guys, this is Achilles. He's Colin's younger brother."

The jovial Georgian faces turned solemn at the mention of Colin's name. Obviously they'd heard the news. We took turns shaking hands.

"To what do we owe the pleasure of your company?" Max asked. "Assuming it's not my dumplings."

"We had a few questions for Saba. And we brought a little something to loosen his tongue." Katya turned toward me.

I held up the bottle of Georgian wine we'd picked up on the way over. After Perova's mention of black suits, I figured a good bottle would satisfy both etiquette and Katya's nerves.

"Khvanchkara!" Saba accepted the precious bottle of semisweet red with smiling eyes. "Ooh la la. I'll get four glasses."

While Saba Mamaladze was obviously naturally exuberant — how could he not be with a name like that — he was clearly very fond of Katya. Watching the trio's interaction I had the feeling Max was even more fond of her. Max rolled two desk chairs over by their old Ikea couch and then grabbed a stool from the kitchenette for us to use as a drink table.

Feeling Katya relax beside me, I realized that I'd never seen her with friends before. I kicked myself for not thinking to suggest something like this earlier, given all she'd been through in the past couple of days. Katya was holding up as well as most professionals, so I had to work to keep in mind that she was a civilian swept up in circumstance.

"What questions did you have for me?" Saba asked, pouring the rich red.

"I just learned that you were participating in Colin's clinical trial. I want to learn more about it."

Saba exchanged a glance with Max again like they were an old married couple. "I didn't know Brillyanc was Colin's. I'm sorry, this is a bit awkward given the circumstances and all. What are you trying to find out?"

"We're investigating Colin's death, and as part of that we want to learn everything we can about Brillyanc. We didn't even know the drug's name until an hour ago."

"I thought he died in a boating accident," Saba said, his voice suddenly slow, deliberate, and tense. "Carbon monoxide poisoning."

"That's right. We don't think Brillyanc killed him. No need for you to worry about that. But the carbon monoxide poisoning wasn't accidental, so we're looking for motives."

Max said, "I heard they'd arrested Colin's brother for that." He turned to me, connecting the dots.

"It wasn't me. But to prove that I need to find out who it really was. Right now, our only evidence points to the company where my brother and father worked. We know next to nothing about it. So when we learned that you were part of the Vitalis trial, we came right over. Will you please tell us what you know about Vitalis and Brillyanc?"

"Of course. We both will. Max was in the trial too."

Chapter 38

Priceless

OUR FIRST BREAK, I thought, as Max confirmed that he'd also been in the clinical trial. If I was remembering correctly, Katya had said Max was getting his PhD in biochemistry.

Katya brought her hand to her chest. "I saw your name, but there must be ten thousand Max Ivanov's in Moscow, so I read right over it. When I hit Mamaladze however…"

"Please start with the basics," I said, eager to dive in. "Other than the intriguing name, we don't know anything about the drug."

Saba set down his wine glass, and began. "They told us it was a 'metabolic enhancement product.' Those were the words they used. When we pressed them for details, they told us we'd notice improvements in the way we felt. They refused to get more specific because of the placebo effect, and because individual metabolisms vary greatly."

Katya and I nodded along, not wanting to disrupt the flow.

"Of course, our primary concern was side effects. But they told us there weren't any related to the product itself, just those related to the delivery, to being hooked up to an IV for six hours."

"And that was all little stuff," Max added. "Like redness and swelling around the puncture site, headache, and nausea. The typical panoply of minor maladies you find on most medications if you read the fine print."

"But Max, being Max, ran his own tests. He did blood work on both of us before and during the trial."

"What did you test?" I asked Max.

"I tested the typical annual-physical parameters: a complete blood count and chemistry panel, fibrinogen, hemoglobin, hormones, and PSA. None of them changed significantly for either of us. If anything, they trended slightly better."

"What did change was our mental clarity," Saba continued, lifting his refilled wine glass as if in a toast to the medical gods. "It's been every student's dream. I started breezing through my research, digesting everything I read on the first pass. I actually began stopping by Dr. Abramov's office to discuss *Annals of Mathematics* articles with him. Just for fun. Can you imagine that, Katya? Well actually I'm sure *you* can, you were always his darling. But can you imagine *me* doing that?"

"You were always your own harshest critic, Saba. Are you sure it isn't the placebo effect? Perhaps brought on by the name?"

"If it is, it's the best placebo effect ever. My dissertation is done. I wrapped it up last week, a full half-year ahead of schedule." In reaction to Katya's surprised expression, he added, "I know I didn't mention it the last time I saw you. Things were going so unbelievably well, I was afraid to jinx it."

Max set his wine glass down. "My results were similar. I'll be finishing my dissertation months ahead of schedule as well, and my adviser has been a lot more complimentary than he was before I started."

"How long have you been taking it?" I asked.

"Eighteen months. It's been fantastic. Frankly, I'm worried about what's going to happen now that we're off it. One more dose and I'd have been set, dissertation done and defended."

Katya gave Max a discerning glance. "Given your expertise and the lab equipment at your disposal, why don't you whip yourself up a batch, now that the free supply has ended? Is it tough to make?"

"I have no idea. They were very secretive about the formulation. The ingredients weren't written on the IV bags. Believe me, I checked. I also stole a look in their refrigerator one day when nobody was watching, but there were no spare bags. In retrospect, I wish I'd siphoned off some of my IV to analyze. But I didn't know the trial was going to be ending when it did, and I didn't want to risk jeopardizing my continued participation."

"What tests did they run on you?" I asked.

"During each session they gave us an IQ test. They also took blood and urine samples. Last week when we went in, we did the test and gave the samples, but we didn't get the infusion. They told us that was it."

"Did they ever share the results?"

"No."

"And do you feel it wearing off?"

"Definitely. Frankly, I'm nervous about it."

"Would you pay to keep taking it, if that were an option?"

"Sure."

"How much?"

Max grew a wistful smile. "I'd pay anything."

Chapter 39

BOLO

THE BUOYANCY brought about by an hour's reprieve with old friends and a bottle of wine evaporated as we exited Saba's building.

A police car was waiting.

Two militia officers sat smoking inside, their attention on the next entrance over. I put my arm around Katya's shoulder and casually guided her in the opposite direction while slouching to take a couple of inches off my height.

She leaned in and whispered. "That's the entryway to my old apartment they're watching."

"I assumed as much."

"Do you think they were looking for me?"

"Have you ever seen the police hanging around like that before?"

"No."

"Then yes, I think they were looking for you."

"But why? I haven't done anything."

Me either, I thought. *But look at me now.* "Apparently we've upset powerful people just by surviving, and I'm not inclined to placate them."

"Why are the police suddenly involved?"

"I'm guessing that when we tripped the facial recognition system at GasEx, we spooked them, whoever they are. Apparently they decided to go beyond their own goon squad."

Katya gave me a dubious look. "What would they tell the police? How could they get them looking for us?"

"If it's a powerful person making the request through someone high up in the force, they could feed us into the system as *persons of interest*. That could generate a priority BOLO, a Be-On-Look-Out dispatch, without requiring specifics as to why. The beat cops would just be ordered to bring us in for questioning. Then they'd have us."

"So what do we do?"

"We keep out of sight and hope we figure this thing out quickly, because Moscow's no longer safe." Katya's lower lip quivered, so I hastened to add, "On the good news front, we know the investigation is heading in the right direction, and we know they're not tracking our van."

We drove into the setting sun without speaking, lost in our own thoughts, trying to cope with a situation that had started badly and was spiraling downward. I noted that Katya was now mimicking my vigilance, constantly but subtly scanning the windows and mirrors for black suits, white vans, and police cars.

It took us thirty minutes to reach Dr. Tarasova's address. Her five-story apartment was an old, undesirable style of apartment building built back in the 1960's throughout the Soviet Union under Nikita Khrushchev's reign. I drove past it and parked in a shadow a couple of hundred meters further up the side road. "We have to assume they'll be watching the place. I'd have a man posted either within sight of Tarasova's door, or within the apartment itself. So we should assume both."

"Okay, what's our next move?"

"I'm going to ask you to stay here in the van and keep an eye on Tarasova's entrance while I scope out the twin neighboring building and figure out which apartment is number 32." I put in my earbuds and called Katya's iPhone. She donned her own set and answered by saying, "Don't bother. Hers is the second window from the right end on the top floor." She pointed. "The kitchen ventilation window's open and the lights in the main room are on."

"How do you know that one's hers?"

"The five-story Khrushchyovkas are all the same. I had a friend who lived in 32. I'm sure it's freezing in the winter and the roof leaks into the kitchen."

"What's the floorplan?"

"It's an efficiency. There's a kitchen, bath, entry hall, main room, closet, and balcony."

"Not a lot of places to hide."

"That's for sure."

"Won't 32 be on the third floor?"

"No, they're numbered sequentially. What's all this about? What's your plan?"

"I'm going in through the window."

Katya's face wouldn't have looked more skeptical if I'd told her I could fly. "How? It's on the fifth floor."

"Climbing to the window will be a snap. It's getting through it undetected that has me concerned. I'll have to play that part by ear. Same plan as before. You keep an eye on things from down here."

"But someone will see you."

"Not if I'm fast and time it right."

"What will you do if someone starts yelling?"

"I'll go over the roof and be down the back side before anyone can react. Don't worry about it. As long as you're keeping a watch out from below, I'll be able to focus on a quick ascent and quiet entry. Agreed?"

"Okay. You really think you can climb the building? Without falling?"

"Most residential buildings are as easy to climb as ladders. They have all kinds of pinch points, edges, and ledges. All reasonably spaced and regularly repeated. These walls are concrete panel rather than brick, which would make it a challenge if there weren't windows and balconies everywhere, but there are. And this one even has a drainpipe, which may as well be an elevator."

Katya didn't look convinced. "We're talking about five stories. That's probably sixty feet. One heck of a tree."

"See my shoes?" I crossed my left leg over my right to put my approach shoe on display. "They're designed for climbing. The tread is gummy, the support excellent, and they fit like a glove. With them, I'll stick to that wall like a spider." This wasn't quite true, of course. But to comfort her I was going for attitude rather than accuracy. "To answer your other question, the best way to avoid attention while doing something surreptitious in public is to act like you're someone in charge."

"And how do you plan to do that?"

"It will be a combination of what I do and don't do. I'll avoid cautious movements and furtive glances since they arouse suspicion — triggering alarms built into our DNA. My goal will be to avoid detection altogether, so as not to generate any reaction at all, but even if I get stuck walking past an audience that can't miss me, all I'll have to do is keep my head up and shoulders back like an authority figure. That posturing triggers the submissive sectors in most people's minds, and usually lets one slip under the radar without a second glance." I nodded, subliminally reinforcing the veracity of what I'd said. "Time to go."

Chapter 40

Monkey Business

I GOT OUT of the van, but waited to cross the road until a couple of people walking dogs had rounded the corner. With the sun down, the air had taken on a chill, but it was dry. Good climbing weather.

I made my way to Tarasova's building with my head down and hands in my pockets, like a local resident on his way home. I didn't have chalk for my palms, but they wouldn't be sweating, and with a drainpipe to climb, it really didn't matter. "Am I clear?" I asked, speaking into the mike.

Katya came right back like a pro. "There's a couple on a bench about twenty meters ahead of you, but they're looking at each other. And across the street there are numerous open curtains, but I don't see anyone actually standing at their window looking out."

"Good enough. Here goes." The concrete panels were about nine feet tall, so there wasn't much to grip. The surface itself, while ostensibly smooth, was plenty rough for smearing, the raw face-to-face friction move that would give my feet purchase. As for the ten-centimeter drainpipe, it was built fifty years ago by the Soviet war machine. Designed to withstand the never-ending strains of a brutal climate and communal living, it wasn't going anywhere. I put a hooked hand around each side at head level, and pulled back until my arms were straight and my back was engaged. Then I brought my feet up onto the wall one at a time, and began to ascend like a hungry monkey scaling a coconut palm.

It felt great.

I never feel better than when I'm climbing. There's something about the combination of mortal risk, physical exertion, and discernible progress that stimulates my brainstem like nothing else. And the greater the risk, the tougher the climb, and higher the ascent, the better I feel.

I wear approach shoes wherever I go because I'm always eager for a fix. I don't go around climbing telephone poles, but I feel better knowing the option is there. And sometimes kittens get stuck.

It took me about fifteen seconds to get my head level with the bottom of Tarasova's kitchen window, which was about two meters off to my left. As a climber I knew that my 'ape index' was 1.05, meaning that my arm-span was five percent greater than my height, or about six-foot-six. If my two-meter estimate was accurate, my reach would come up short.

"Anybody notice me?"

"Not that I can tell. You climb like a chimpanzee."

"Nicest thing you ever said to me."

I leaned as far as I could to my left, but was still a couple of inches shy of the windowsill. Rather than leaping for it, I repositioned my feet so that my right foot was pressing against the pipe from the left side, and then extended both my left arm and leg. To Katya, it would look as if I splatted against the wall in the midst of a jumping jack, but it did the trick. My left fingers found two knuckles' worth of purchase amidst the city grime and pigeon crap.

I released my right.

A shuffle and chin-up later I was looking into Tarasova's kitchen window. Fortunately, no one was looking back. "Katya, I want you to hang up on me and call Tarasova's home number. If someone answers, find some reason to keep him talking and distracted. Otherwise, let it ring for a few minutes."

"Okay. Be careful."

I positioned myself so that I was peeking through a corner of the window that was partially concealed by a potted plant. From there I could see through the kitchen and into the better-lit hallway beyond, without risk of detection by the casual glance of a resident. Of course, this only applied to people inside the apartment. From the outside, I was totally exposed.

The apartment's phone began to ring.

It kept ringing.

On the fifth ring I made my move. I pulled myself up and onto the exterior windowsill, which was only about an inch wide. From there, I reached through the small ventilation window in the top right corner, and then used the curtain to snag the latch handle and unlock the larger window.

With Scar's Glock in my hand, I pushed the window open on the eighth ring. Apparently the Tarasovs opened it on a regular basis, because the mechanism was smooth and the windowsill was clear of clutter. Either that, or karma was on my side.

Climbers learn to become a part of the rock they're climbing. It's a feeling, a mindset, a flow. They shut off all other senses and feel the rock, living from its perspective, moving in harmony with its surroundings. Serene, secure, and silent. I slipped into that mindset as I eased through the window, onto the sink, and down to the floor. Quiet as a summer breeze. Then I reengaged with the rest of the world.

The phone was still ringing.

I used a ring to cross the kitchen floor and tiny hall. On the next, I peered into the main room, the living room/bedroom combo. It contained a convertible couch, television, wardrobe, and display cabinet, but no pulse.

I exhaled. That left me the balcony, closet, and bath to clear. I could see the entire top half of the enclosed balcony from where I stood. It looked empty, but would be a good place to hide. I glided across the floor and peered through the glass. Nothing but boxes and cross-country skis.

The closet's contents also proved to be inanimate.

On my way to the bathroom, I stopped by the front door and looked out the peephole. No one appeared to be on the landing, but that didn't mean a black suit wasn't waiting behind a door or in the stairwell — locked, loaded, and listening.

Two silent steps took me to the bathroom door. Light shown through the crack at the bottom. I listened for a full minute before opening it from a crouched position, the Glock raised and ready.

Mr. Tarasov stared back at me. He was in the shower, hanging by his neck.

Chapter 41

Health Food

I WAS DETECTING A PATTERN.

I was also tiring of being one step behind.

I needed to figure out how to get one step ahead.

That was the problem with following clues: you were following. Behind by definition. Getting ahead required ideas.

I had a couple to try.

But first things first. There was no need to check Tarasov for a pulse. A swollen tongue protruded from his mouth, and stains on his jeans indicated that he'd voided his bowels. I glanced around the bathroom for a fake suicide note, something referencing his not wanting to go on without his beloved wife, but the black suits hadn't bothered with those finer details. No need. The setup itself looked good. Perfect motive. No signs of struggle.

My guess was that they'd tranquilized him before stringing him up on a belt in the shower. No other way to do it, really, since his feet were touching the bathtub floor. There would be traces of the tranquilizer in his bloodstream, but the police wouldn't find it if they weren't looking.

Getting them looking was one of my ideas.

I pulled the bathroom door shut behind me and dialed Katya. "I'm okay, but Tarasov's not. They killed him. How are you? I'm going to need about twenty minutes."

Katya took a few silent seconds to absorb that blow before coming back with, "I'm fine. The group of teenagers has grown into the double digits, but no sign of unfriendliness. Are you in danger? What are you going to be doing?"

"I'm working on getting us leads. I'll be fine." I hung up and began searching the apartment for computers, notebooks, or papers — anything that Dr. Tarasova might have brought home from work. I was sure the black suits had beat me to it, but I couldn't not look.

The size of the apartment made it a quick job, and I came up empty on all accounts. But I'd saved the best for last. That was where my second idea came into play.

Tarasova wouldn't have bothered to hide her notes or computer, because taking those home was part of her job. Not just permitted, but required. One thing, however, probably wasn't allowed. It wouldn't be left laying around in plain sight, not that there was a great deal of choice in where to lay it.

I rubbed my palms together like I was getting ready to roll dice or pick a card, and opened the refrigerator door. Milk, juice, sausage, cheese, condiments, various plastic storage containers, and a six-pack of probiotic yogurt drinks in a cardboard box.

The plastic containers were the obvious first choice, so I removed the yogurt box instead. It felt full — and it clanked. I looked inside. A dozen glass vials winked back at me. "Now we're talking."

Setting the yogurt box off to the side, I grabbed an insulated lunch box off the kitchen counter, and checked the freezer for cooling agents. No ice, corn, or peas. Although it did yield bags of frozen strawberries, blueberries, and blackberries — the constituents of a smoothie I was guessing, noting the bananas, blender, and thermos on the counter.

Seeing them gave me another idea.

I loaded the blender with fruit and milk, then secured the lid. I put the yogurt box in the lunch box, set a quart-sized ziplock bag on each side, and packed in as many frozen blueberries as would fit. Satisfied that the Brillyanc would keep cool for hours, I slung the lunch box's shoulder strap around my neck, and went out the way I'd come in.

Chapter 42

112

"WHAT'S THAT?" Katya asked, her face awash in relief and curiosity.

"That," I said, "is one step ahead."

"What?"

I was back in the driver's seat, with the lunch box on my lap. "Figuratively speaking. Literally, it's a couple of pints of frozen blueberries, and a dozen vials of Brillyanc."

"No way!"

I passed her the box. "See for yourself."

Katya unzipped the lid and pulled out the yogurt carton. She opened it up and extracted a glass vial. "Two fluid ounces. I was expecting IV bags."

"I assume the Brillyanc gets diluted with saline or some other buffering solution for the infusion. If it takes six hours to go in, there's probably some sophisticated biochemistry involved."

Katya brightened even more. "Fortunately we know a sophisticated biochemist."

"My thoughts exactly."

"What made you think to look? In a yogurt carton in the refrigerator, I mean."

"A sophisticated biochemist. Max made it clear that he'd do whatever it took to keep taking Brillyanc after the clinical trial ended. The only reason he didn't arrange it was that he didn't know the trial was ending."

"So?"

"So I figured Tarasova would feel the same. Only she did know the trial was ending. And she had access to the product. And since Brillyanc has to be kept refrigerated, I knew where to look."

Katya grew the face of a professor who'd heard the right answer. "What do we do now?"

"Call Saba, and see if he and or Max can meet us now at Leningrad train station. You can let him know we've got something for him, but don't hint as to what it is. Just in case."

"Okay. Are we going to St. Petersburg?"

"No, that's a red herring. Just in case."

"I'm picking up on a motif."

I couldn't help but smile at that. It felt good. "Leningrad station also provides tactical advantages. We do need to get out of Moscow ASAP though. Between the black suits and the police, there are too many forces working against us here. But we need more information first, and I'm not sure how best to get it. I'll give that some thought. Meanwhile, I'm going to work on getting us two steps ahead."

Katya had learned better than to ask, but her eyes flashed concern.

I put calm in my tone, and a grin on my face. "I'll be back in ten minutes."

"Be careful."

I retraced my steps from earlier that evening, and a few minutes later was back in Tarasova's kitchen. I reversed the lighting pattern in the apartment, turning on the kitchen light and turning off the main room light. After checking the blender's lid to be sure it was secure, I flipped the on switch. As the violent roar disrupted the silence, I ran back to the main room, stepped behind the curtains, raised the Glock, and waited for a black suit to come through the door.

I didn't have to wait long.

The front door opened, slowly — just a crack. The blender drowned out any noise as it screamed for attention. After a ponderous second, the door crashed all the way open, its thunk loud enough to hear over the high-pitched mechanical drone.

It was followed by nothing.

For six long seconds there was no other sign of movement from the hall. Then the chrome barrel of a large automatic emerged. Probably a Desert Eagle. Next came a leather gloved hand followed by a black sleeve. A powerful shoulder panned it back and forth nearly six feet above the floor, like a tank turret. Hallway, kitchen, main room. Light to light to dark.

The Desert Eagle stopped on dark. Then quickly, suddenly, smoothly, the rest of the body followed in from the hall. As he kicked the door shut, I squeezed my Glock's trigger.

When a bullet rips through your heart, you don't bring a hand to your chest and wobble around moaning before sagging slowly to your knees, and then toppling forward to the floor. When a bullet rips through your heart, the blood stops pumping and the oxygen stops flowing and the central nervous system effectively shorts out. It's like someone yanking your power cord. You simply drop.

Suit collapsed.

Three hundred pounds of muscle turned to three hundred pounds of beef in three-hundredths of a second. His joints all gave way at once: ankles and knees, hips and shoulders. Because he'd been a pro ready to release a magnum round, his center of gravity had been a vertical dead center. When the quarter ounce of lead I'd thrown his way came calling at 1300 feet per second it was enough to tip the balance, so when he dropped, he dropped on his back.

Well, mostly.

His legs fell akimbo in an entirely unnatural pose, and his head came to rest propped up against the edge of the wall as if he was looking at his own misplaced legs and thinking *WTF.*

The bark of my gun followed by the thud of his body and crack of his skull would normally have alerted even the most dimwitted of neighbors. But the blender was still doing its thing. I was eager to silence it, but wanted to lock the door first.

Since suit had kicked the door closed behind him, I was relatively certain that he was alone, but I wasn't willing to risk being wrong. So far I'd only seen suits in pairs.

I crept toward the front door, remaining near the wall but keeping the soft soles of my shoes on the oriental carpet rather than the hardwood floor. Stepping over the corpse and resisting the urge to look through the peephole, I slid the lock into place from the protected position of the far side.

The blender stopped wailing. A failsafe to prevent overheating, I assumed. I stood still, listened for thirty seconds, then crept to the peephole. The landing was clear.

This suit had worked alone.

I didn't bother searching the body, certain that he'd be as sterile as the last guys and wanting to leave him untouched with my next move in mind.

I was pleased with the little bit of progress I'd made — another thug down and some Brillyanc in my bag — but I felt like a climber who, having conquered a foothill, was looking up at the mountain ahead. As crazy as it sounded, even in my own head, it was time to turn up the heat.

I dialed 112, the Russian cquivalent of 911, and reported a shot fired at this address.

Chapter 43

Smoothie

I SLID INTO the driver's seat, started up the van, and hit the gas.

Katya looked up from the Brillyanc bottles, her face awash in curiosity. "What's up?"

"The police are on the way."

Katya looked around. Listened. "How do you know?"

"I called them."

"Why on Earth would you do that?"

"I left a suit upstairs. Wanted to make sure they'd find him. Put a little heat on our pursuers."

"You killed another one?" Katya's face morphed to an expression somewhere between marveled and horrified.

"They did a convincing job of making it look like Tarasov killed himself. I wanted to make sure the police didn't fall for it, so I added another body to the scene, reducing the forces against us at the same time. Kind of a two-for-one deal."

We were on the third ring road around Moscow, driving counterclockwise toward the Leningrad train station. With the fall of the Soviet Union, they'd changed the name of the city founded by Peter the Great from Leningrad back to St. Petersburg, but the train station retained its communist name.

Wanting to lighten the mood, I pulled the thermos from my pocket and handed it to Katya. "I made a smoothie."

"What!"

"Want some? It's triple berry with banana."

She didn't reply.

It was getting colder. I added a notch to the van's heater. After a couple of silent minutes, I said, "I trust you got through to Saba, and he's meeting us at the station?"

"I did. They'll both be there."

"Did he sound normal on the phone?"

"You mean, did it sound like someone had a gun to his head?"

"Yes, I suppose that's exactly what I mean."

"No, he sounded fine."

I could tell by the way she trailed off the last word that Katya had more to say, so I waited. It had been two days since we had laid on a warm rooftop in Palo Alto and watched death visit Katya's door. Since then, death had kept calling: at the hotel, at the clinic, and at the Tarasov's.

Sergeant Dix told me that at Fort Bragg they found that two to three days of constant tension was what it took to figure out if a soldier was going to break. Most who made it to the Special Forces Qualification Course could take anything the Army cared to throw at them for forty-eight hours. But by day three, with reserves depleted and nothing but misery on the horizon, a soldier's core became exposed. His baseline ability. His essence. Superficially, this was evidenced by the decision to quit or continue, a temptation the drill sergeants dangled every time they spoke.

The real game, of course, was mental. Beating the Q boiled down to a soldier's ability to disassociate his body from his mind, his being from his circumstance. This was relatively easy during the mindless procedures — the hikes, runs, and repetitive drills that form the backbone of military training. Disassociation became much tougher, however, when the physical activity was paired with judgment calls and problem solving. If a soldier could engage his higher-order thinking while simultaneously ignoring the pain and willing his body to continue beyond fatigue, then he had a chance at making it to the end. If he couldn't, then the strength of his back, heart, and lungs didn't matter.

Dix had concluded that the Q-Course was as much about self-discovery as a prestigious shoulder patch.

Katya was in that discovery phase now.

The big question was what we'd do if she decided to quit.

She broke the silence after a few miles. "Do you ever get used to it?"

"The killing?"

"Yes."

"We're all used to killing — just not people. We kill when we spray for bugs, or squash a spider, or buy a leather bag, or order a hamburger. I don't think of the individuals I've killed as people any more than you thought of the last steak you ate as Bessie."

"But they are people."

"When people are trying to kill me, I categorize them as a virus in need of eradication. I know that sounds cold, and I'm aware that the violent life I've led has skewed my perspective, but I don't want to lie to you and tell you that I cry a little every time I squeeze a trigger."

"How did you do it this time?"

"I set a trap and encouraged him to walk into it. I used the gun his colleague pressed against your temple last night in the stairwell."

I wanted to watch her process this, but we were nearing the train station so I had to keep my eyes on the road, and there was no time to stop for tea. Would she be able to rise above the individual acts and look at the big picture? Could her mathematical mind parse it into a simple kill-or-be-killed, them-or-us, details be damned? Or would the hurdle be too much for her moral framework to handle, now that her reserves were depleted, and her baseline exposed?

"You made a smoothie," she said, her voice tentative. It was a statement. A challenge. An opportunity.

"The blender was the trap. The smoothie's a reminder that we're just doing what it takes to stay alive. That we've got to play the cards we're dealt, with the big picture in mind. That despite all the crap that fate has thrown our way, life still has a lot to offer."

I looked over at Katya.

She looked back, meeting my eye. Then she unscrewed the thermos's lid and took a sip. Then another. "Pretty good."

I had my answer.

Once the smoothie was gone, Katya busied herself playing with the Brillyanc bottles. They clinked about like gold coins as I maneuvered the van through the city center's stop-and-go traffic.

When I finally hit the parking selector in an undersized spot in Leningrad station's long-term lot, I looked over to find Katya beaming her beautiful smile back at me, excitement in her eyes. "What?"

"Do you know who Rita is?"

"Rita? No, I can't say that I do."

"I don't know either. But Tarasova did. And she wrote her phone number on the inside of the yogurt carton." Katya opened the lid to reveal the note, handwritten in blue pen on the cardboard. "If I'm not mistaken, that area code is in Washington, DC."

Chapter 44

Blending

I STARED at the handwritten name paired with a 202 number and ran various scenarios through my mind.

"Who do you think Rita is?" Katya asked.

"Not a patient. Not with a DC phone number."

"Do you think she's connected to Brillyanc?"

That was my hope. "If Tarasova was just using the yogurt box as a notepad because it was handy, she'd have written it on the outside. Or torn the lid off. And this is written carefully, not a quick scribble. Given that, and the way it's hidden, I think it's clear that Rita's somehow connected to Brillyanc. What expiration date is stamped on the bottom?"

Katya closed the lid and carefully inverted the carton. "May 20."

"Still nearly a month to go. So the box is fresh, meaning the note is fresh."

"Should we call it?"

I shook my head. "Not yet. I like your attitude, but I'd like to do some research first. Meanwhile, I think your friends are probably here by now. Where are they waiting?"

"Beneath the clock in the main hallway."

I locked the van with an enthusiastic press of my thumb and hid the key under the fender. Now that we had a solid lead to follow, the smart move was to get out of Moscow before either the suits or the police got lucky. My intuition was that our investigation would eventually lead us back to Moscow, and I wanted the van ready and waiting when it did.

Katya came around to my side of the car. "What did you mean earlier when you said this meeting location gives us tactical advantages? The police are bound to be looking for us at all the major transportation hubs."

"Major train stations have thousands of people mulling about, looking this way and that, walking here and there. Having been on the other end of an operation in a place like this, I can tell you that visual fatigue sets in quickly. By now, anyone posted will have been at it for hours. Meanwhile, it gives us an anonymous place to leave the van long-term, and the ability to quickly and inconspicuously conduct countersurveillance."

I led Katya in the direction of the road rather than the station, and ducked into a kiosk I'd noted while driving in. It yielded winter jackets and watchman's caps, black for me and white for Katya. We studied our reflections in the saleswoman's smudged mirror before handing over our cash. Picking us out of the crowd dressed like this would be nearly impossible. We'd probably have to introduce ourselves to Max and Saba.

"How does it work?" Katya asked. "Counter-surveillance, I mean. What do we do?"

"Well, for starters, there are two types of people who may be looking for us: black suits, and police. The police will have seen our photos as part of a BOLO. But they'll have other duties on their plates as well. So as long as we don't do anything conspicuous, we're not likely to ping their radar. Our primary concern is the black suits. Make sense?"

"Sure."

"In essence, what we're doing is looking for people who are looking for us. Of course we need to do this in a way that allows us to see them, before they see us. Let's begin by thinking about *where* they'll be looking for us. Any guesses?"

Katya gave me a mysterious look that made my heart skip a beat. "Obviously they'll be looking at anyone approaching Saba and Max, if they know that's who we'll be meeting. If they don't, then I guess they'll be watching the entrances."

"Very good. What other focal points would be of interest? What will be the best vantage points?"

Katya tilted her head. "I suppose any perspective that also yields a view of the faces of people in line for tickets or getting onto trains would be doubly advantageous."

"Excellent. Now, *how* are they going to be doing that? Assuming they're good and they're resourceful, which they certainly appear to be."

"How are they going to be doing that?" she repeated back to herself. "Hum. In a manner that looks natural, I suppose."

"That's right. Or?"

"Or ... from someplace they either can't be seen at all, or wouldn't be noticed."

"For a theoretical mathematician, your analytical skills are pretty practical."

"Thank you."

"Given all that, *how* can we expect them to have set up surveillance?"

"How? You mean *hidden*?"

"Exactly. But hidden how? What are the two ways to hide?"

"Out of sight, or ... what's the word ... camo'd?"

"Camouflaged. How do you camouflage yourself in a train station? Keeping in mind the primary objective, which is studying faces in the locations you noted."

"You mean dressed like a ticket agent, or a janitor?"

"You're on the right track. Ticket agent would be good if it weren't for the limited perspective. Although if they were really thorough, they'd have our pictures taped in front of all the ticket agents. By contrast, janitors have freedom of movement, but they're not going to look natural studying faces, only floors."

"Okay. How about conductors or baggage handlers?"

"Now you're thinking. Limo drivers looking for their clients would be another example. Also people who would otherwise appear harmless, like a mother watching a child, or a businessman nervously checking his watch while looking around for a late colleague. And as for the hidden, that would be someone watching from above with binoculars, or studying the monitors in the security office. Whoever and wherever they are, our goal is to avoid catching their eye while we try to identify them."

"And how do we do that?"

"We begin by blending into the background. Come on, I'll show you."

Chapter 45

Reunion

I HELD OUT MY ELBOW for Katya. She looped her arm through and we began walking toward a *marshroutka*, a privately operated passenger van that served as a bus. "We'll start with the lingo," I said. "The direction we're heading is 12, as in the top of a watch face, and our rear is our 6. With our arms intertwined and our mouths conversing, you'll look natural with your head traversing 9 to 2, and I'll look natural with mine moving 10 to 3. Also, as long as your eyes follow sudden noises, or track something interesting, like a sexy skirt or a big dog or a running child, it will look natural to glance backwards. The key is to make any head movement look casual. That make sense?"

Katya swept her head to her 9. "Yes." And swept her head back to 12.

"Good," I said, performing a similar reverse move. "This applies while we're walking side by side. When we need a three-sixty search, we stop and face each other while I appear to check my phone, or you rummage through your purse."

Katya had developed a bounce in her step that I took as a good sign, although whether it meant she was enjoying the lesson or looking forward to seeing Saba, I couldn't tell. "That gives you the general idea of how to study your surroundings without appearing to do so. Offense, as it were. For defense, we modify not only our behavior, but also the context in which we'll be seen. Since they'll be looking for a couple, we want to appear as anything but. We can separate, so long as we keep a live call going, but more preferable is blending into a larger group. That could be as simple as walking beside a luggage porter with a full cart, or blending into a group of people whose outward appearance fits with our own. A warmly dressed Caucasian family would work, but not a hockey team."

I guided us so that we were next to another couple approaching the station, walking four abreast with the women in the middle. "As we enter the station, turn to the woman and compliment her on something. Get her talking to you. Try to keep it going until they stop moving."

While Katya engaged the woman to her right, I pulled out the paper I'd taken from Scar. It was folded in quarters with the photos inside. I held it in front of me like a ticket, and began glancing back and forth between it and the arc of surveillance points that afforded good views of the entrance. I saw nothing. No stationary figure in a group or alone watching the main entrance. Not near, not far. Not uniformed, not in plain clothes. There were shadows and blind spots I couldn't examine covertly, but I was confident we'd be all right if they hadn't sent their A-team.

The center of the station was bustling and clamorous. The overnight trains to St. Petersburg were the most popular, which was why I'd selected that particular station. There were tired businessmen and couples with quarreling children. There were groups of excited students and large families that appeared to be hauling everything they owned in big bags and brown boxes. All were being serviced by eager porters and weary vendors and sly hawkers and patient conductors. Controlled chaos, with a rhythm shared the world over in transportation hubs.

We stayed beside our cover couple as we walked right past an oblivious Saba and Max and onto the couple's train, but then went left as they turned right, with Katya and her new friend exchanging bon voyages.

"You did great," I said, stopping by a window that offered a good view of the way we'd come, the only way onto our train.

"Thanks. That was fun. Saba and Max didn't even notice us. What now?"

"Now call Saba and ask them to join us for a minute on the first car of this train."

Katya complied while I continued watching the pier that led to our train. We were near the front car, nearly a hundred meters down the pier. It was filling up, with departure just ten minutes away.

When the familiar Georgian forms came into view, strolling side by side along the pier, I motioned for Katya to stay there in the hallway beside the private sleeper cabins, while I moved to a position near the doorway. I called Saba when the guys were about ten feet away. Once I caught his eye, I turned so they'd follow without fanfare, leading them back to Katya's side.

"We meet again." Max held out his hand to shake mine after hugging Katya.

"Thanks for coming. Anybody ask about us or follow you or anything like that since we left?"

The Georgians looked at one another, then shrugged. "No excitement at our end, other than the curious summons," Saba said. "Katya said you had something for us?"

I pivoted to unsling the lunch box and felt my cheek burn as the window shattered to my left, and Saba's head exploded to my right.

Chapter 46

Tight Squeeze

SCREAMS ERUPTED FROM other passengers in the hallway as I dove onto Katya and Max. Three more bullets followed the first in rapid succession as we flew to the floor, suppressed sniper shots from a single gun, shattering glass and splintering wood. I shouted, "Stay down, but follow me!" and scrambled through the doorway a meter ahead to our right.

The sleeping compartment I'd invaded had upper and lower berths on each side, and a table against the back beneath a big window. Katya and Max tumbled in after me, stunned and sobbing.

The thwack of impacting bullets gave way to the silence of expectation as my friends looked up at me with wide eyes. Was the sniper adjusting his angle, preparing to begin another barrage with the first sign of life, or had he packed up and fled?

I kicked the door closed as soon as they were clear, and threw the lock. Reaching down with both hands, I helped Katya to her feet. She was trembling, but not hysterical. Max appeared to be in shock. "Max. Open the window. All the way down. Can you do that for me? Can you handle that, Max?"

He nodded.

The window split horizontally, so when opened it created a gap about four feet across, and a foot high. Enough to squeeze through.

The clock in my head said it had been about twenty seconds since the sniper's first shot signaled his presence and position. That sliver of time would feel like an eternity to an exposed professional whose modus operandi was concealment and stealth. It also created what I'd consider an unacceptable risk. By now, a hardened pro would have relocated in anticipation of our next move, and most lesser shooters would have fled. Plenty of mad men and fools also played the killing game, bringing unpredictability and adding risk, but they didn't fit in with the black suits I'd seen. I ran the odds, and made a call. "Katya, stay down. I'll be right back."

I removed Katya's backpack and the lunch box from around my neck, then crouched, opened the door, and rolled back out into the corridor. It was empty for the moment, but would soon be swarming with police.

I couldn't low-crawl to Saba through a pool of blood, given what we had to do next, so I duckwalked instead, keeping my head well below the window line.

Seeing my new friend's yellow polo drenched in crimson like a perverted New Mexico state flag made me want to forget retreat and go hunt the sniper. I was angry with myself for getting him killed, and I wanted to vent that anger by venting the shooter. But this was no time for self-indulgence. Two living souls were counting on me, and I had a mission to complete, so I did as I was trained.

I went over Saba's pockets and person, removing everything I found: watch, wallet, keys, passport, comb, a handkerchief, and a pack of gum. The longer Saba remained anonymous, the safer Max would be. I piled everything into my own pockets, and was about to return the way I'd come when I caught sight of a gold chain beneath his shirt, no doubt holding an Orthodox cross. Removing it would cost precious seconds and make a mess, but a thief would pilfer it if I didn't, so it went in my pocket as well.

Back in our commandeered cabin, Katya and Max were hugging and sobbing before the open window. "Time to go," I said. "Max, you mind going first?" Normally I'd go point, but I wanted to stay between Katya and the killer.

Max gave Katya an extra squeeze, then climbed onto the table. He worked his right arm and leg through the gap, then he pulled the rest of his body up and over the sill, dropping with a crunch to the gravel below. Katya followed with the grace of a springboarding gymnast, reminding me that she'd been one in her youth.

I passed the backpack and lunch box through to Max, then handed my new black coat and leather jacket through to Katya, concerned that my chest would be a tight squeeze. "Put my black coat on over your white one, and remove your hat. For camouflage." I was more concerned with Katya covering the bloody streaks screaming for attention than I was with altering her general profile, but avoided mention of them. I was learning.

On an exhale, I wriggled myself through the opening without drawing blood, and crunched down on the gravel beside them. We hopped the chain guardrail between the neighboring train's cars and stepped inside the proximal car with the swoosh of a pneumatic door and a short sigh of relief.

I grabbed Katya's hand and led them toward the back of the train and the front of the station, nodding politely to the other passengers we passed while hoping that the panicked looks on my colleagues' faces wouldn't cause concern. But I'd forgotten something. I felt the blood rolling down my nose just as the woman started to scream.

Chapter 47

Burner

THE SCREAMING WOMAN raised her tattooed arm and pointed. Right at me. Right at my bleeding face. Didn't she know it was rude to point?

I ignored her, but went to work wiping the blood with my left sleeve and hand as I guided Katya and Max toward the exit.

The woman didn't scream again.

We reached the last car about six minutes after the sniper's first bullet. Six minutes was long enough for the screams to have put the station authorities on alert, but too short for the city police to have sealed the station. I guessed we had another minute or two before that curtain came down.

It was going to be tight.

"We're going to run for the street where we'll grab the first taxi we can find. Forget trying to blend in, go for speed."

"What about the shooter?" Max asked with wavering voice. "Won't we be exposed?"

Only the world's best, battle-hardened professional snipers would have the nerve to stick around this long with the police closing in. Of course Russia was home to many of the best, but the odds were still in our favor. This wasn't a government operation, it was a private affair, and our choice of transportation hub had been random. "As long as we're quick, we'll be out the door before we're spotted."

And we were.

We ran right into a white Lada that had probably been working as a cab for twenty years. Once we'd disappeared onto the ring road, heading west, Katya turned my way. "I can't believe the station wasn't going crazy after the shooting."

She was seated between Max and me on the back seat, and speaking in English, lest the driver get involved. While plenty of Muscovites spoke English, the odds of an English-speaker driving a twenty-year-old cab in that economy were slim. "Judging by the lack of reaction, you'd think someone gets shot there every day."

"Maybe they do," Max replied without turning from the window.

He was right. It wouldn't be clear until ballistics were performed that a long gun had been used. Meanwhile, a Georgian with his face blown off wouldn't look that different from a Chechen, and Chechens had been terrorizing Moscow for decades. The police were probably numbed.

"Do you have someplace you can go for a few weeks?" I asked Max. "A friend or relative you can stay with until I get this sorted out?"

"You're going to sort this out?"

Max's despondent voice showed a trace of hope. I wanted to play to that, and keep him energized until he was free and clear. "Oh yeah. No doubt about that. No doubt at all. But meanwhile, it would be wise for you to keep out of sight."

He turned and leaned forward to study my face, looking for reassurance.

I saw that he was still on the dark side of despair.

"I lost a partner once. Also to a distant sniper. Also when I was standing beside him. I made that sniper wish he'd never heard my name. Made him wish he'd never been born. Took me ten days, but I did it, and I did it right. I'm going to break that record with this guy. Count on it." I lifted my chin and pointed to the spot on my cheek that burned. "If for no other reason than because the bullet was meant for me."

Max held my gaze for a few more seconds, then shifted his eyes to Katya for a few more before saying, "I've got friends with a couch."

"Good. Now, I've got something for you. Something you're going to like." I passed the lunch box to Katya.

She passed it on to Max. "Twelve vials of Brillyanc."

Max unzipped the box and looked inside. "Make that nine. Three are broken. What's with the bags of berries? An ice substitute, I assume."

"Correct. You'll need to keep it refrigerated. How long will it take you to analyze?"

"That depends on when I can get time on the mass spec. Probably a few days at least. Is there a rush?"

"Oh yeah. If I don't figure this out in the next ten days, it will be a long time before I get another chance."

"I'll see what I can do. Where are you guys headed? Or shouldn't I ask?"

"Back to the US. But we'll be in touch. Actually, you should probably keep your cell phone powered off with the battery out until things clear up. Just to be safe. Buy a burner phone to use in the meantime." I typed our cell numbers onto a note on my phone, and showed it to Max. "Memorize these and call from your burner once you learn something."

"Got it. Will do."

Chapter 48

Balancing Act

HALF AN HOUR LATER, Katya and I were on a different train departing a different station for a different country. This one was headed 720 kilometers west to Minsk. Katya curled up and fell asleep within minutes of my locking our first-class cabin's door.

I was bone-weary, but had a call to make. Assistant District Attorney Kilpatrick was expecting to hear from me, and I didn't want to disappoint. I weighed the pros against the cons and decided to remain in our cabin for the call. The train's clackety-clack provided good cover, added a bit of intrigue, and I was planning to speak softly enough that Katya would be able to sleep right through.

In the last 72, hours I'd survived multiple assassination attempts. I'd seen three people killed, and had killed five men myself. But it was dialing a phone number that put a lump in my throat. "Mister Kilpatrick. It's Kyle Achilles calling."

"Kyle Achilles. I'd say good afternoon, but that comment assumes I know what time zone you're in. Which I don't. Which I guess gets to the point of your call."

"Did you discuss my proposal with the DA?"

"I did. That was an interesting conversation, to say the least."

I waited for Kilpatrick to continue, but he was going to make me ask. Perhaps he wanted me to sweat a little. If he only knew. "What did you conclude?"

"We concluded that bail was a risky proposition. If you don't show up for trial, people will ask why you were granted bail in the first place, having been arrested for a triple homicide and all — with compelling physical evidence, the oldest motive in the book, and a colorful professional history. The discussion gets particularly awkward at that point, because of course we didn't grant bail. Not initially. That was reported in the local press. So if anyone asks, we'll be on the losing end of a news story involving a jailbreak and a cover-up. The DA asked me to tell you, 'Thanks, but no thanks.' "

Kilpatrick had some good points. Each felt like an ice pick in my ear. Or maybe a Bic.

I took a deep breath and reminded myself that assistant district attorneys spent their careers negotiating. He hadn't come close to *yes*, but he hadn't given me a flat-out *no* either.

He wanted something.

I had a pretty good idea what that was going to be. Before we went there, I wanted to balance the scorecard.

"That's not nearly as juicy or scandalous as the bumbling incompetence involved in letting me walk right out the front door."

"You had accomplices. Accomplices posing as federal agents. They'll be in nearly as much trouble as you are when we catch them."

"I don't know what you're talking about, Kilpatrick. Those were legitimate FBI agents, as far as I know. Either way, it makes the story national news if the story comes out. And it makes the FBI look bad. Of course, the master politicians in the Hoover Building aren't going to let that story spin against them. No way, no how. They'll be using your little department as a shield. Your boss will become a scapegoat, a bug deflector. Plus, you'll have the Fibbi's in your shorts for the foreseeable future. Certainly through the next election cycle."

Kilpatrick didn't respond immediately. Got me thinking he had the DA in the room with him, and they'd put me on mute. It was a good minute before he came back on the line. "I suppose you have a less controversial scenario in mind?"

"The morning of the day I was released from jail, there was an attempt made on my life. A serious, sponsored attempt involving three other inmates and a senior corrections officer. The inmates came at me in the shower while the guard stood watch. Given the nature of the attack and the imminent threat to my life, you had no alternative but to pull me out of SBCJ, at which point granting bail seemed the most sensible option."

"Is there any evidence of this alleged attempt on your life?"

"The three inmates all required medical treatment afterwards. The guard's name is Grissel. I'm sure he was paid off. I'm also confident it wasn't the first time. That's both justification for my relocation and four hashmarks in the DA's win column."

Again there was a pause. "Even in that scenario, it would be difficult for bail to make sense."

"But you'll discuss it with the DA?"

"Yes. I'll discuss it with the DA."

"I'll call you back tomorrow."

Chapter 49

Pattern Recognition

AS I CLICKED OFF the call with Kilpatrick, Katya rolled over to face me. "That didn't sound overly encouraging."

I turned so that I could study the lines of her face while I spoke. "I'm sorry I woke you. I had to get that call in today, but didn't want to risk the chance that you'd wake up here alone."

"Thank you. I got enough sleep for now. Kilpatrick's not cooperating?"

She did appear to have rebounded. Remarkable. "He is playing it out longer than I expected."

"Playing it out?"

"Negotiating."

"Negotiating for what?"

"Money."

"Doesn't he get to dictate the amount?"

"He does. But I can always walk away. I've already walked away. He has to get me to come back."

"Why do you care if you get bail? Since you're out, I mean."

"If I don't get bail, then I'm guilty of a prison escape. It was nonviolent, but they could still give me three years in jail for it. Furthermore, it makes me look guilty in the eyes of the jury. That alone would push most over the edge of reasonable doubt on the murder charges. Plus there will be a warrant out for my arrest. That could impede my investigation. Given the time pressure, I can't afford any impediments."

"And where is the investigation taking us next?"

I felt a twinge, a little warm wave scurry across my skin with her use of *us*. "Washington, if we're lucky."

I opened the iPhone's web browser and began navigating.

"You accessing one of those special CIA websites again? Tracing the yogurt box number?"

"Exactly."

"You access it through a weather website?"

I looked behind me, saw the phone's screen reflected on the window, and adjusted the angle of the screen. "You know I trust you completely, right? It's just not my call."

"I understand."

Once I reached the hidden portal, I drilled down to the page I needed, input the DC phone number, and queried the owner detail. "Unregistered. No big surprise there." I queried the call log next.

"When we get to Minsk, if there's time before our flight to Washington or wherever, can we get a room with a tub? Even if it's just for an hour?"

"Count on it."

The screen populated.

I scanned the results and then checked the header to be sure I hadn't limited the search parameters. "Rita's phone number has only been active for three weeks."

"Is that a good thing?"

"It means the trail is fresh, which is good news. But it limits the amount of data, which isn't so good."

Katya sat up and I moved next to her so she could see the screen. She scooted in closer. "All the calls are 202 area codes."

"And they're almost all outgoing. Just a few incoming calls — and those just started this week. And they're only from numbers she called during the first week." I copied the entire list and then pasted it into the phone's spreadsheet app. Then I sorted the list by number. "Most of the numbers were only dialed once, but there were a few twos, threes, and a four."

Katya pointed. "The repeated calls are all on consecutive evenings, each roughly an hour later than the one before."

Leave it to a mathematician to pick up on a pattern faster than you could spell Pythagoras. "Conclusion?"

"She was trying to catch them at home. And she doesn't leave messages. The call durations are too short."

"I agree. Now look at the last one and tell me what you see."

"It was just ten minutes ago and only lasted two seconds. And it was the second time she called that number in as many days."

"That's accurate, but not quite what I see."

Katya turned to me and raised her eyebrows.

"I see an opportunity."

Chapter 50

No Dope

WE SPENT the next couple of hours researching the recipients of Rita's calls, beginning with the latest. Chris Pine was a 35-year-old manager at Kenzie Consulting, a top-tier firm. His specialty was the public sector, which as far as I could tell meant that he helped make government operations efficient. Talk about a growth industry.

Rita's earlier calls all went to people with similarly prestigious positions. Three more management consultants, five investment bankers, a dozen big-firm lawyers, and no less than four members of Congress. All were mid-career, with most in their thirties or early forties.

I set my phone on the bed and rubbed my eyes. That tiny screen wasn't the best way to view a spreadsheet — but I wasn't complaining, I was just hurting. And feeling sleep deprived. "Congressmen aside, I don't think there's a person on the list earning less than three hundred thousand a year. I'd guess many are closer to a million."

Katya pointed to the picture on her screen. "Chris Pine looks like the actor with the same name. Took me a second to be sure it wasn't. Same square jaw, mischievous smile, and smoldering blue eyes." She cocked her head in a gesture that was growing on me. "Now that I think about it, so do you. Except you've got that Spartacus chin dimple."

"That's good news. The resemblance, I mean."

"Why's that? You planning to go into acting?"

I was glad to hear that Katya's sense of humor had remained intact. Her resilience astounded me. "No, but I suspect that I may be impersonating Mr. Pine before this is over. In person, I mean. Of course first I'll be impersonating him on the phone, about twenty-two hours and thirty-seven minutes from now."

"You're planning to be in his home when Rita calls?"

"Of course."

"But what if he's there? What if his family is there?"

"He's not married. We already know that from his file. If he's there or a girlfriend or boyfriend is there, that will complicate things, although not insurmountably. But management consultants travel all the time. Their engagements typically last for months, and the consultants only fly home on the weekends, if at all."

"How do you know that?"

"The CIA used them on occasion. Paid them more for a month than they paid me for a year." I changed the subject. "Bet you'd like some tea."

"You'd win that bet. But I don't think the overnight trains have dining cars."

"I thought I'd check with the conductor."

"You don't think he'll be sleeping?"

"He works nights. Besides, we've got the Belorussian border coming up. He'll be getting the paperwork ready for that. Lock the door behind me."

I found our conductor in a good mood, for which I decided to take credit. I'd paid him a hefty premium in cash to sell us tickets on the spot. He was in his little nook at the end of the car, sipping tea with his feet up on the edge of his mini kitchenette, and reading a Russian detective story. For twenty dollars I got us a couple of piping hot teas, a small box of chocolates, and the explanation that they only stocked enough complimentary breakfast boxes to cover the number of tickets officially sold. "Free refills on the tea," he'd said as I was leaving.

Katya cleared the chocolate box like a hustler playing pool, and I ended up taking double advantage of the free refill offer. Once the last truffle had melted in her mouth, she smiled and asked, "Why do you think you'll be impersonating Chris Pine in person after the phone call?"

"What kind of calls do you think Rita's making?"

"What kind? How should I know?"

"Deduction. A process I know you're both fond of and proficient with."

Katya humphed, but her mind started spinning. She began paging through screens on her phone, examining the downloaded records. "The calls are all placed in the evenings, to home numbers. And no messages are left. That's an unusual combination, except for sales calls. So these are likely sales calls."

"That was my conclusion."

"You think she's trying to set up a clinical trial?"

"No. Consider the recipients. What do we know about them?"

Katya plucked crumbs from the box with a moist index finger while she thought that through. "They're all successful professionals in the second quartile of their careers."

"Right. What else?"

"They're all influential and affluent. All are well-educated. All are excelling in very competitive industries."

"What does that last point tell you about them? About their personalities?"

"They're hardworking and ambitious."

"Exactly. So we've got ambitious plus affluent. I think that's the common denominator."

"Common denominator for what?"

"Selection."

"Selection for what?"

"A sales pitch."

Katya's eyes went wide and her voice kicked up a notch. "Of course. Only instead of dope, she's pushing Brillyanc."

Chapter 51

Shared Secrets

KATYA AND I stared at each other, digesting our breakthrough. I repeated it, just because it felt good. "Rita's pushing Brillyanc. In the US."

Katya's eyes flashed the same excitement I was feeling. "Max said he'd pay anything."

"To gain a significant competitive advantage, most ambitious people would."

"But she doesn't want *most* people. She wants the *most-affluent* people."

"Exactly." I grabbed a seat at the foot of Katya's bunk.

"Why? Why not cast a broad net and let the customers figure out the money part? Why not act like a typical drug dealer?"

"Secrecy."

"Drug dealers work in secret. They have to, since it's illegal."

"They work to keep their identities secret. Rita's working to keep Brillyanc's existence secret."

Katya's head rocked back skeptically. "Is that a realistic expectation? In Russia we have a saying: *Three people can keep a secret, as long as two of them are dead.*"

"We have that saying too, and it's been bugging me. But the one thing we know for sure. The one thing we know with absolute certainty, is that these people will kill to keep a secret."

"You think they're threatening their clients? 'Buy our product, and oh, by the way, if you tell anyone about it we'll kill you?' "

"No. That wouldn't be sustainable. But back to secret-keeping. The history of the world is full of it. There are state secrets, trade secrets, secret societies, and of course, clandestine organizations like the KGB and CIA. All managed to keep secrets for generations by doing one thing."

"And what's that?"

"Making their members *want* to keep the secret."

Katya began flicking her fingernails off the pad of her thumb while her big brain tackled that twist. One, two, three, four. One, two, three, four. "Seems to me that when you discover something amazing, your first impulse is to share it. But maybe that's a female thing."

"No, it applies to us hunters as well." I leaned back against the wall. Felt the train rocking rhythmically on the rails. "I remember one time in college, the ski team was on a road trip and I snuck into the home team's gymnasium to do my stretching routine. It was closed off due to construction, but I found a way in. I heard some laughter and went exploring. I found a grate in the floor that looked down over a locker room, which at that moment was packed with dozens of sorority girls posing in their bathing suits for a fundraising calendar. Every college guy's dream, right? But my first impulse wasn't to pull up a chair and enjoy the frivolity, it was to go get my fellow Buffs and share the thrill."

"Did you?"

"I did. Brought three back and we spent the next half hour enjoying a private modeling show while the girls giggled and the photographer did his thing. We began clapping as they were wrapping up with a group photo. None of us stuck around to see what happened next, but I found out later that one of our clapping shots made the cover. There was something particularly sexy about their expressions at that instant of discovery."

I stood up and began pacing. I was exhausted, but needed to keep my head in the game. "But getting back to the secret keeping, I think your point is valid. And I don't have an answer. I don't know what you do to keep a Brillyanc user from telling his closest friends."

"Maybe that's why they're targeting these professions. They want cutthroats who'll be unwilling to share any advantage that gives them a leg up."

The simplicity of her solution hit me like a splash of cold water. "Yes! That works. Although my gut tells me there's more. Something more predictable. Something the makers of Brillyanc could count on with absolute certainty."

Neither of us could crack that nut. After a long silence, Katya said, "You still haven't told me why you think you'll be impersonating Chris Pine in person before this is over."

I stopped pacing and turned to face her. "Three reasons. First of all, look at the call pattern. For starters, the calls are all under ten minutes. That's too short to close a sale on something as complicated and nuanced as Brillyanc. Second, they're all in DC. Why limit yourself geographically, unless personal contact will be involved? Finally, we know what's being sold, and it requires you to be hooked up to an IV for six hours."

"Do you think the call is just to set up a meeting?"

"I do."

"What do you tell people as smart and sophisticated as these to get them to attend that meeting?"

"That's what we're going to find out — about twenty-two hours from now."

Chapter 52

Touchdown

GRIGORI WAS NOT a big man in the physical sense. At 5'8" and weighing in at a hundred and fifty-two pounds he'd be described as *average* and *slight*. In the company of his security head, however, he looked downright diminutive. At least from afar. Up close, body language warped perceptions. Pyotr was a tiger, but Grigori had tamed him.

While Grigori adjusted his crimson tie in the big mirror that dominated his bedroom, Pyotr stood silently at attention a few steps behind. Satisfied with his appearance, Grigori turned to face his security chief. "You lost another one to Achilles. That makes it five now, if I'm not mistaken. Am I mistaken?"

"No, sir."

"I thought not." Grigori let that hang there for a second, then checked his watch. "Let's go. President Korovin is the one man I won't keep waiting."

Grigori opened the terrace door and stepped out into the inviting air of an April afternoon. He was excited. His first flight to the Kremlin's new helipad was just minutes away.

But he had one more bit of business first.

Grigori detoured from the direct route to his favorite toy, leading Pyotr right up to the rim in the corner where the south tower and the main building met at a ninety-degree angle. On clear spring days like this, a constant slipstream bellowed up from below, warm wind powered by the sunbaked southwest exposure and channeled by the cornering facades. He'd tried tossing a cigar into the gust once, to see what would happen. It had come right back up and marred his blue suit with gray ash.

Once Pyotr was beside him at the edge, Grigori pointed to the ground a hundred meters below. "Do you see that?"

Pyotr had not developed Grigori's immunity to acrophobia, but given his role he couldn't show it. Grigori punished him this way, and Pyotr had no choice but to grin and take it. Pyotr was the beast, but Grigori held the whip. "What am I looking for?" Pyotr asked.

"Not what. Who."

"All I see is tulips."

"Closer to the building. Right below where you're standing."

Pyotr scooched and leaned. "I see him now. Black suit. Who is he?"

"Your replacement."

Grigori was a hands-on guy who loved the feel of life's furry edge. That was what had driven him to the KGB all those years ago, and that was what drove him to discipline Pyotr personally today. There was a challenge inherent in Grigori's selected means, however, which boiled down to basic physics. His security chief had every physical advantage there was, working in his favor. A greater reach, younger reflexes, and a hundred pounds of muscle, to name a few. Grigori balanced the equation by adding electricity to his side. Six million volts of electricity.

Palming a mini stun gun like a magician would a card, he pointed down with his left hand, and zapped Pyotr's ass with his right.

The jolt shot Pyotr's hips forward as if they were propelled by rubber bands. As the stun gun took his central nervous system offline, Pyotr's center of gravity swung out over a hundred meters of open space, dooming him before his body had a clue what was happening. Just a tenth of a second from A-Okay to complete-systems-failure. Grigori may as well have put a bullet through his brain for all the chance Pyotr had of recovering — but this approach was much more satisfying.

Pyotr yelped, then Grigori got a couple of words in before Pyotr began wailing. "As promised."

Unlike the cigar, Pyotr wasn't blown back.

Grigori looked up before Pyotr touched down. Such a disappointment.

Back to business.

Chapter 53

Full Circle

THE HELICOPTER PILOT, a chisel-faced veteran of the Afghan war, met Grigori's eyes with a level gaze as he approached the big black bird. He showed no reaction to Pyotr's demise.

Grigori made the lasso sign.

Erik flicked a switch and the rotors started spinning with effortless grace. The twin Pratt & Whitney turbines, each capable of delivering the power of 630 horses, emitted more of a throaty growl than a thundering whine. Grigori loved the sound. Tremendous raw power. At his command.

He liked his pilot too. Ten years his senior, Erik was the only employee with whom Grigori felt a natural ease conversing man-to-man. He'd come with the helicopter, but was now Grigori's chauffeur as well.

Grigori would have preferred to sit in the front to better take in the memory of this flight, but it wouldn't do to be seen exiting from the cockpit. So he hopped in back, and donned his headset.

"We got the go-ahead from the presidential security service," Erik said by way of greeting, his voice calm and cool like a captain's should be. It was hard to faze an Afghan vet.

"Ever flown to the Kremlin before?" Grigori asked.

"Almost no one has flown to the Kremlin before. They only put the helipad in a few years ago, and it's typically reserved for the president himself and visiting heads of state. How'd you get the privilege, if you don't mind my asking?"

Truth was, there were at least a dozen Russian oligarchs who had been granted the perk by a president eager to maintain an iron-clad support base at home. But it was still the hottest ticket in aviation, and Grigori's pride swelled every time he thought of it. "A few years ago the president asked me a question. A sports question, of sorts. A year ago, I gave him an answer he liked."

"Must have been one hell of an answer."

"You should have heard the question."

As they hit the Moscow river from the south and turned northeast to follow it to the Kremlin, Erik risked a glance at Grigori. "If you were granted the privilege a year ago, why haven't you used it until today?"

"I was waiting to make a special delivery. Something worthy of the honor." He reached up to touch the vials in the left breast pocket of his suit coat. Then, remembering, he removed the mini stun gun from his right side pocket. "I'll leave your toy in the cup holder. Thanks. It was the perfect tool for the job."

~ ~ ~

This time Grigori's throat was relaxed and his palms were dry as the presidential guards escorted him to the big office. This time he knew exactly what to do upon entering. And this time he knew exactly how to answer the question: "What have you brought me, Grigori?"

As the guards clicked their heels and closed the gilded doors, Grigori walked straight to Vladimir's chess desk and took a seat. He removed two finger-sized vials from his breast pocket and positioned them upright on the squares reserved for the black king and queen. When the president looked over, he said, "Something for the hunter watching the crocodile watching the rabbit. Kind of completes the circle."

"You really did it?"

"We really did it."

"When I saw you fly in, I figured as much. What are they?"

"The king is a flea. The queen a tick."

"Okay to pick them up?"

"Sure. To you and me they're as harmless as any other flea or tick."

"And to our hunter?"

"He'll start having vision issues about a month after he's bitten. Within three months he'll be blind."

Korovin toppled the king vial and began to roll it back and forth with his index finger, watching the flea tumble while churning the scenario in his mind. "How's that possible?"

"The technology is the same that's used to create custom cancer therapies. Only instead of going after cancer cells, they're going after retinal cells. They used gene sequencers, mass spectrometers, and micro-array scanners to analyze his DNA and create a molecular profile of his cells, using the hair follicle your office supplied. Then they went to work with genetic databases and synthetic biology software to create a very specific synthetic DNA. They booted that DNA up in host cells, and then transferred those cells into pests indigenous to the Moscow region. The pests, in turn, will transmit the synthetic DNA to our hunter with their bites."

Korovin leaned forward, making no attempt to mask his enthusiasm.

Grigori was loving it.

"When I get bug bites, my doctor always inspects them. If he doesn't like what he sees, he loads me up with vitamins and antibiotics."

"The bite will look normal, as will his blood work. Even if they prophylactically treat him for everything from plague to Lyme disease it won't matter. This is a personalized bioweapon, based on his DNA. It's not anything that's ever been transmitted by a bug bite or anything else before. It won't be detected."

"Really?"

"Really. That said, I suggest we go with fleas. They're much less conspicuous, and quickly forgotten. They don't latch on and hang out the way ticks do. The docs weren't sure which host vectors would prove viable, so they tried three species. These two worked."

"How do we know they'll bite him?"

"It only takes one bite. Given the quantity of fleas that will be in the vial, and the condition they'll be in, my people tell me it's a mathematical certainty so long as you remove the cap within a meter of the target while you're both stationary. A hunting blind will be perfect."

"Will they be able to trace the condition back to the bite?"

"No. At best, it will be one of many hypotheses. But there won't be any evidence."

Korovin stood and began to pace. "But will it look natural? If they suspect foul play, they'll look for motive, and we all know where that investigation will start."

"*Cui bono.*"

"Exactly. We can't have that."

"It doesn't get any more natural than this."

"Be specific."

Grigori leaned back in his chair, tilting it up on two legs and then placing his hands behind his head. "My guys looked for a region where his DNA was already weak, something his doctors will likely be aware of. They found the predisposition we're exploiting, which is one reason we picked blindness rather than, say, cancer or a heart attack. Furthermore, since it's not an outright assassination, it doesn't fit the mold. Finally, there's the timeframe. It's quick in the big scheme of things, but there will be a full month between the flea bite and the first symptom."

Korovin sat back down. "So in summary, it's natural, untraceable, and inconspicuous?"

Grigori nodded.

After a moment of quiet appraisal, the President of Russia said the two magic words. "I'm pleased."

Chapter 54

Bubbles

THE BORDER CROSSING into Belorussia proved to be a non-event, and the flight from Minsk to DC uneventful. That was good, we were overdue for *uneventful*. The bad news was the timeline. Not only had the rush forced me to renege on my promise to get Katya a hot bath before the flight, but it also left us precious little time for reconnaissance after. By the time we got to Chris Pine's part of the city, the anticipated call was just three hours away.

Pine's apartment was a few blocks northeast of DuPont Circle on New Hampshire, which coincidentally put it within a stone's throw of the Belorussian embassy. We managed to find a hotel room directly across the street. A couple of major conventions left little selection when it came to rooms, so I sprang for a two-bedroom suite. That was fine with me — in part because it put us on the top floor with direct line of sight to Pine's apartment, and in part because I was in the mood to splurge on creature comforts. Gather ye rosebuds while ye may, and all that. Going with a suite also enabled me to keep Katya in the same room, but on the other side of a door. Something that was good for both her security and my waning willpower.

"The bath is perfect," Katya called out. "Worth the wait."

"So I'm forgiven?"

"Indeed."

It felt weird talking to Katya while she was in the tub, which itself was odd, given all that we'd been through. "Do you have your phone in there?"

"I do."

"I need you to make a call to Chris Pine's office."

"Okay. What's the goal?"

"We want to find out if he's in town, and if he is, how late he'll be in the office. If he's not in town, we want to find out when he's going to be back, and the name of his assistant."

"Okay. You know I'm the analytical type, right? Creativity isn't my thing."

I heard the Jacuzzi's jets kick in, so I spoke louder. "Would you like a little coaching?"

"Please. You can come in. I've got bubbles."

She's got bubbles. Great. Nothing sexy about that.

She did have bubbles. The Jacuzzi jets had blown them up to the rim of the tub. Besides her head, which was now plastered with wet hair, only the tops of her shoulders and her neck were visible. I moved the little vanity stool next to the tub and sat with my back to the wall so that all I saw was the bubbles covering her feet.

"If Chris answers, say, 'It's me. When are you going to be home?' If he asks you to clarify, use a silly-boy voice and say, 'It's Cathy, from across the hall. I've got a little something for you.' If he doesn't go along, tell him you must have a wrong number."

"And if he doesn't answer?"

"Ask for his assistant. Get her name — that's important — and tell her you're Chris's sister Cathy, and you want to surprise him with a visit. Say you know he travels a lot, so you wanted to know when you can expect him home."

"Wouldn't this be easier if you pretended to be his brother?"

"You think I'm being lazy?"

"I think you have a reason, and I'd like to know it. This spy stuff is new to me — and surprisingly fascinating."

Giving in to temptation, I turned to look at her. "People are generally less suspicious of women. Plus, we may be playing the distress card later on. That works best woman to woman."

"Distress card?"

"Don't muddle your mind with those details yet. Let's get this right first. Are you ready for the number?"

"What about my accent?"

"Good point." My jet lag was showing. Not a good sign.

"I could be his ex-girlfriend?"

"No. That will raise defenses. Can you fake a British accent?"

A second later, Katya replied with, "I suppose. Why would I want to talk this way, luv?"

"That's good. Say you're his sister and you've got a layover on your way back to England. If she says anything that throws you off, complain about your jet lag and ask her to repeat it." I handed her a dry washcloth to wipe her hands, and then her phone.

"What's the number?"

I gave it to her.

"It's ringing." "Yes, good afternoon. This is Catherine Pine calling for Christopher, please. Yes, Chris Pine. Is his secretary available? Yes, what's her name, please? Emma. Thank you. Yes, I'll hold." Katya looked over at me and smiled. She seemed to be enjoying herself. "Yes, good afternoon, Emma. This is Catherine calling, Christopher's sister. Yes, that's what the operator said. Are you expecting him later? Well, I guess not. That's a shame. I've got a layover I wasn't expecting and thought I'd surprise him. But I'm headed back to London in the morning, so I guess it wasn't meant to be."

I had a brainstorm and mouthed some words to Katya.

"Can you hold a second, luv?" Katya hit the mute button. A second later she unmuted. "Where was I? Oh yes. Don't tell him I called, luv. I'm going to leave a little something in his apartment and I want it to be a surprise. Thank you, you're a dear."

I clapped as Katya hung up. "You're hired."

"He won't be back until next weekend, ten days from now. He's in Hong Kong. What was that last bit about?"

I stood and stretched, my eyes averted. "Just priming the pump. I'm going to go recce Pine's place. You enjoy your soak."

"Recce?"

"Sorry. Reconnoiter. Conduct reconnaissance. I'm going to check out your brother's apartment. You be okay for half an hour or so?"

"Mmm hum."

I headed for the door, hoping I wasn't making the mistake of a lifetime by leaving her alone in the tub.

Chapter 55

To The Nines

IN THE HOTEL LOBBY, I paid eight bucks for a small roll of packing tape. It disappeared into my jacket pocket.

Chris Pine lived across the street in an Italianate eight-story. Constructed long ago from red brick and limestone, his building boasted bay windows, and looked more inviting than the smaller gray stone residences to its left and right.

I walked past the canvas-covered portico and through an alley to the back. I'd come for the view, but my nose couldn't help noticing the battle raging between the dumpster and the laundry room vent. For the moment, the fabric softener was winning.

I backed up all the way to the neighboring wall and surveyed Pine's building like I would a boulder I wanted to summit. Technically, I wouldn't be bouldering but *buildering*, although my current objective was the same. Route planning.

The easiest way to the top takes the whole ascent into account, not just the first dozen moves. There was no fire escape or drainpipe, but the middle third of the building was bumped out a couple of feet all the way to the top, to accommodate a different floor plan for the inside units, I assumed. The corner this created was a climber's dream. The ninety-degree angle gave enough opposing resistance to support a wide variety of hand and foot holds, and would speed both ascent and descent dramatically.

I moved in to inspect the bricks, and once again was delighted. Their height was a standard 76 mm, and the mortar set back a good 5 mm. That made them prime for pinching, as well as the crimping and edging I'd employ with larger masonry. Climbing Pine's place wouldn't be quite as quick as Tarasova's, but the difficulty was only about a 2 on a scale that ran all the way to 16, so I was a happy climber.

I turned around to check my exposure before heading to the lobby. Not bad. The building behind Pine's also had smaller, opaque windows on its backsides, primarily for bathrooms and stairwells, I assumed. People were more concerned about privacy than the view when it came to alleys.

Finished with the back, I headed around front. Pine's building didn't have a doorman, but it did have a concierge. This made sense to me. A traveling executive would want someone there to receive dry cleaning and packages and tend to the occasional personal request. This one was tall and lanky, with thinning hair and round, wire-rimmed glasses that made me think of colonial times. "Hi, I'm Adam," I said, holding out my hand.

"Charles. How may I help you?"

"A colleague of mine said this was a great building. Do you have any vacancies?"

"Not at the moment. We typically only see vacancies once or twice a year, and those are usually rented out in advance."

"Any coming up?"

"We've got a one bedroom becoming available in June."

"Does it have the same view as Chris's? He's in 8A."

"Mr. Pine's unit is a corner penthouse overlooking New Hampshire. The one becoming available is 8E, which isn't a corner unit, but it's also a one bedroom, and it also looks over New Hampshire."

"Could I see it?"

"I'm afraid it's occupied."

"Maybe just from the doorway?" I asked. Then I added the magic words, "I would be most grateful."

What's the difference between a bribe and a gratuity? Same two parties, same special service, same discreet transfer of cash. But the timing shifts, and timing is everything.

"I do have some dry cleaning to drop off in 8E."

Charles produced a back-in-five-minutes sign and then extracted three hangars' worth of bagged clothing from a closet behind the counter.

"I'll take the stairs," I said. "It's a thing."

No flicker of whimsy from Charles. Just a respectful, "See you up there."

I raced up eight flights of stairs and then a ninth to the roof. Cracking the door, I found the typical bare concrete architecture, with exhaust pipes and vents and a perimeter raised about eighteen inches. Someone had set up lawn chairs, the cheap folding kind you find in beachfront convenience stores. They'd also left a plastic bucket half filled with water that I presumed had once been ice. It was easy to see why. The view was fantastic. The fountain in DuPont circle was visible to the south, and beyond it, the Washington Monument, which would likely forever remind me of Barsukov's Rocket.

I tore a six-inch strip of packing tape off the roll using the built-in cutter, and plastered it over the door-latch holes. Then I tore off another to double its strength. Satisfied that it would hold, I eased the door shut, descended to eight, and joined Charles in the hallway before 8E.

Charles pulled out a Schlage master key.

I could pick most conventional locks with the paperclips I kept in my back pocket, but that could take time. With this information, breaking in would be cake. He worked the lock and said, "Kindly hold the door while I hang these. By the way, the kitchen is on the right, the bathroom's on the left, and the living room is straight ahead. The bedroom has the same southwest view."

And no alarm panel. I had everything I needed. "It's beautiful. Thank you so very much."

As he relocked 8E, Charles said, "Would you like to fill out an application?"

I pulled a hundred dollar bill from my wallet. "Let me think about it. I'm not sure about the eighth floor thing. How late will you be here?"

"Jason relieves me at eight o'clock."

I took my time going down the stairs so Charles would see me exit, which I did with a polite nod.

He reciprocated.

I took a right on New Hampshire, then a left on R. At the corner of Seventeenth, I entered what Google assured me was the nearest chain hardware store. After a quick survey of the hired help, I approached the youngest of the three employees. A skinny boy in his late teens. He was still losing the fight with acne, but no doubt winning plenty on his Xbox. "Hey Brad, I need a key," I said, reading his nameplate. "Can you hook me up?"

"You got it." Brad spun around and took me to the key machine.

Before he could ask, I said, "I need an L-style Schlage key, cut to nine on all five positions."

He took a minute to mentally process the order, which didn't follow the default input parameters. "You got the original?"

"No. I lost it. But it really doesn't matter since I know the pattern. Nine all the way across, so it will look like a little saw when it's done, with five tiny teeth. Can you do that? I can show you, if you'd like."

"I got it. Just kinda weird."

"Thanks. I got some other shopping to do. I'll be right back."

I heard the whir and metallic grind of the key-cutter going to work as I found a rubber O-ring with a quarter-inch hole. By the time I'd picked up a small screwdriver and returned to Brad, he was pulling the Schlage off his machine. He pushed it in and out of a deburring hole a couple of times, and presented it for my approval. "To the nines," he said with a touch of pride. Then chuckling to himself, he added, "Sounds like something my grandfather used to say, but I don't think he had this in mind."

It was exactly what I had in mind, however. So I thanked him, paid, and left to commit a felony.

Chapter 56

Backpacking

"I WANT TO GO WITH YOU," Katya said, her eyes twinkling and her hair aglow after the bath.

I was thrilled, but stunned. "Why? It's just a phone call. I can put Rita's call on speaker, and you can listen in on your cell phone. Same as being there, but risk free."

Katya put her hands on her hips. "Do you have any idea what this past week has been like for me?"

That wasn't the comeback I was expecting, and I had no idea where she was going with it. "I've got a pretty good idea."

"No, you don't. Not really. You're a professional, a trained spy with years in the field. You live in a world where breaking into a building or out of a jail holds as much weight as a trip to the supermarket. For you, putting a bullet through a brain or crossing a border with false papers is the equivalent of ordering brunch."

"So?"

"So I'm a twenty-eight-year-old with a PhD in mathematics from Moscow State University. My world is ethereal. I deal with probability theory and predictive computations and confused students. You and I live on the same planet, but our work lives have less in common than fish with fowl."

"I don't follow. I mean, I hear what you're saying, but I don't see what it has to do with your joining me for a felony B&E. Kinda seems you're making my point for me?"

Katya picked her mug of tea off the kitchenette counter and took a sip. Then another. "Everyone wants to visit Paris once in their lives," she said, tilting her head to the right and staring into her own mind. "Women, at least, all seem to have that common dream. But we differ on how. The vast majority opt for a tour bus trip. They want safe hotels, familiar food, and guides who speak their language. They want to hit all the must-see sights, without fail. They're willing to settle for a guaranteed B-minus experience, because it's predictable. The tourism industry has evolved to cater to them — the multitudes, the risk-averse." She met my eyes and I saw fire within.

"Then there are the backpackers. A paper map in their pocket and a few euros in their shoe. They figure things out on the fly, and enjoy an unscripted experience. They're the only people who have a shot at experiencing the real Paris, and that's only because they're willing to risk an F in order to earn an A. You follow?"

"Sure."

"I'm a backpacker, Achilles. I want to live. I want to suck up every second I can of this strange new world of yours, because I know that I'll never see it again. Soon, I'll be back in my ivory tower. And that's fine. I love it there. But while I'm here in your world, I want to live it. I'm not one to settle for a guaranteed B-minus in life."

Looking at her standing there making her case, I was overcome by the desire to walk over and crush her body to mine, kiss her like she was the last remaining source of oxygen in the universe. I wanted to run my hands up and down her slim back and through the tangles of her hair. I wanted to pick her up and take her to my bed and forget all about men in black suits and assistant district attorneys. But I was a grieving brother, and a gentleman, so I said, "As you wish."

Her mouth formed a funny smile, not unlike that famous must-see painting in Paris. "Thank you."

"But you're going to have to earn it. I'm climbing to the roof, and entering the building from there. You'll need to find another way to get past the concierge."

"What about a fire escape?"

"Building doesn't have one."

"Huh. Well, what was your Plan B? You had one, right? Back when you had me make the call to Chris's assistant?"

"That was in case there was an alarm. I was going to have you call her back from Chris's door and tell her you have a key, but forgot the alarm code, and now you'll be stuck dealing with the police if she doesn't give it to you in the next forty seconds."

Katya smiled like an eager backpacker as she pictured that scene. "But how were you going to get me to the door in the first place?"

"Charm, deceit, or subterfuge. I'd have thought of something on the fly."

Katya raised a fist. "So that's what I'll do. You ready to go?"

I took off my leather jacket, transferring my hardware store purchases to the back pocket of my jeans. "Now I'm ready. Don't you need time to plan?"

"Backpacker, remember? I'll think of something."

Chapter 57

Greasy Ladders

I EXITED Chris Pine's stairwell, winded and sweaty, ten minutes after Katya accepted my challenge. She was already there, waiting in the corridor, looking fresh as a daisy and somewhat pleased with herself.

"You have a key?" she asked.

"In a manner of speaking." I emptied my back pocket. "A *bump key* to be precise." I slipped the O-ring around Brad's handiwork and slid it back to the base. Then I inserted the key into the lock. "I'm going to put a tiny amount of torque on the key, barely enough to turn it. Now when I hit the back of the key like this..." I gave it a few straight-on whacks with the handle of the screwdriver. "The teeth bump the lower set of pins. If I get it right, the lower pins hit the upper pins like pool balls, creating a gap between the cylinder and the housing for a split-second, thereby allowing the cylinder to rotate if there's tension on it." The key turned after half a dozen bumps.

Katya grinned like a little girl on her birthday. "What's that rubber ring for?"

"It puts the teeth in the right place to bump the keys. Without it, I'd need to reposition the key every time. Still works, but it's much slower. Why don't you get your phone ready to call Emma? Just in case Chris had an alarm put in."

She did.

I opened the door.

The ringing started almost immediately.

It wasn't like any alarm countdown I'd ever heard. This was more like a digital ring tone, one of the preset options on a modern home phone. Which, of course, was exactly what it was.

Katya stepped out of my way, noting, "Rita's early."

I ran toward the source of the noise, which emanated from a wireless home phone system on the counter between the kitchen and the living room. Katya locked the door behind us as I picked up the handset and hit the speaker button. "Hello."

"Is this Chris?" The voice was a late-twenties Caucasian female with a British accent. Katya and I exchanged fancy-that glances at the ironic coincidence.

"Yes, who's this?"

"My name's Rita. A colleague of yours referred me. I've got a proposition for you."

Intriguing start. Professional and self-assured. "What kind of proposition?"

"Not the type you'd expect, I assure you. I understand that you're doing well at Kenzie. You're working hard and it's paying off, but of course the future has yet to be written. As you're well aware, ninety percent of your class will slip off the greasy ladder before reaching the partnership rung, despite their Ivy League graduate degrees, herculean work-ethics, and killer instincts."

"That's probably right. It's a high-risk, high-reward business."

"What would you say if I told you that I can eliminate the high-risk component, that I can virtually guarantee that you'll make partner? That's my proposition. Are you interested?"

"Am I interested in making partner? Of course. But your proposal doesn't strike me as credible."

"Of course it doesn't. If it did, then it wouldn't be extraordinary. And it is extraordinary, Chris, I assure you. But no doubt my assurances aren't enough — so I'd like to prove it to you."

"Prove it? How can you prove what's going to happen years from now?"

"Meet me this Friday at the Hay Adams and I'll show you."

"How do I know this isn't some kind of a scam or swindle?"

"It's the Hay Adams, Chris, not a dark alley. And I'm not asking you to show up with a bag of gold bricks. But you can't mention this to anybody, and you do need to come alone. This is a *very* exclusive offer."

I paused for a sufficient interval. "What time?"

"Eight o'clock at the bar. It's appropriately named Off the Record."

"Okay."

"And Chris?"

"Yes."

"This is a one-time offer. If you're not there for any reason, you'll never hear from me again. Then someone else gets the offer, and you'll be left alone on the greasy ladder."

Chapter 58

Naked

I LOOKED ACROSS Chris's kitchen counter at Katya. "See if you can find a spare key. I'm going to program Chris's phone to forward to my cell, in case Rita calls back."

Katya didn't even have to move to find the key. She opened the drawer before her and there it was, in an organizer that also held an assortment of business cards and office supplies. "Why do we want a key? You need it to lock the door?"

"The bump key would suffice, but this will make it easier to return if required. Tell the concierge you're a guest with a key and there's not much he can do to contradict you, not with Chris in Hong Kong."

"You're big on contingency planning."

"I run into a lot of contingencies."

"Speaking of the concierge, how are you going to explain your presence when you leave, seeing as you came in through the roof? Or are you planning to go out that way too?"

"Charles got off at eight. Jason's working now. He won't know that I didn't come in earlier. You planning to tell me how you got past Charles?"

"A woman has her secrets."

Jason barely looked up from the monitor behind his counter as we passed. Perhaps the Washington Wizards were playing. I hadn't been following the playoffs. When we were out on the street, Katya asked, "What's next?"

"I've got to call Kilpatrick right away. While I'm on the phone, would you mind checking into flights to San Francisco? There's nothing for us to do here before Friday evening."

"San Francisco? Isn't that risky?"

"There's no sense in looking around anyplace that isn't risky. Would you rather hang back here?"

"Do I have to explain the whole tour bus and backpack thing again?"

"No ma'am."

"Good. I'll look into our flight options."

Back in our suite, I scrolled through my recent calls and redialed Kilpatrick's number.

"I'd almost given up on you," Kilpatrick said by way of greeting. "Then I saw the now familiar *Blocked* message on my caller ID screen. That's quite some service you're using."

"How'd it go with your boss?" I asked.

"It was an interesting conversation. A lesson in risk management from a master politician. She's keen to avoid the hit she'll take from a prison escape, and she has no desire to become the FBI's scapegoat. But she's been at this too long not to have learned that getting caught in the cover-up is usually worse than getting caught in the crime. So even after spreading the potential blame by consulting with Senator Collins — who apparently knows your reputation from your CIA days — she's still not going to go for it without assurances."

Here it comes. "What kind of assurances."

"Well, that's just it, isn't it? There's nothing you can say. There's only what you can do."

"And what can I do?"

"It's come to our attention that your father kept his money offshore."

"You noticed that, huh?"

"We did. You've got to bring it all back, and you've got to put it all on the line. The DA is setting your bail at ten million dollars, cash. Have it wired to the account posted on our website by close of business Friday, and you've got bail. Fail to do so, and the jailbreak story goes out first thing Saturday morning, along with a warrant for your arrest and a global BOLO."

"First thing Saturday morning," I repeated. "When nobody's watching the news."

"Like I said, she's a master politician. But that's going to be working in your favor, now."

"How so?"

"She's instructed Flurry and me to support you in any way we can. She recognizes that the stronger the case for your innocence, the more likely you are to show."

"And the more interaction we have, the easier it will be for you to track me down if I don't."

"Again, master politician. But that's not all there is to it. She rounded your bail back to ten million even, from the $10.2 million I'd proposed. I wanted everything you had left from your inheritance, less your attorney's retainer, but the DA didn't want your investigation to suffer from a lack of funding."

"That was considerate of her," I said. And I meant it. "You'll get the ten million Friday."

As I pushed the button that ended the call, I felt a big gorilla climb off my back, only to become aware that I still had a whole ark on my shoulders. I'd never been into money, but ten million dollars did provide a security blanket of sorts. Now I was practically naked and feeling an unexpected breeze. A very cool breeze. I was facing a formidable opposing force, a ticking clock, and life behind bars — but I had yet to figure out why.

Chapter 59

Bad Stats

WITH TEN MILLION DOLLARS now on the line, I closed my eyes and took a deep calming breath. When Dix was putting me through the worst of my training, when I was neck-deep in the slog and sucking wind with a world of hurt ahead, he would have me focus on momentum rather than position.

I tried that now.

Just a few days ago, I'd been locked up under Grissel's thumb and slugging it out in the shower. Now I had eleven days of freedom ahead of me, several solid leads behind me, and a remarkable woman by my side. I rolled my shoulders and threw a dozen rapid jabs into the air, like a boxer headed for the ring. With the blood flowing, I used my right palm to push my chin up to the left until my neck cracked. *Bastards didn't have a chance.*

"I see it went well," Katya said, reading my face as I returned to our suite's central room.

"I had to put the ten million I inherited up as bail."

Katya did a double-take. "I had no idea your family had so much money until the police detective brought it up while questioning me. I mean, I knew your father had done well, being a doctor and having a yacht and all, but I had no idea it was seventh-power money."

"Seventh power?"

"Ten million, ten to the seventh power."

"Yeah, well, that was a recent development. While we were growing up, my dad worked for the military, so the pay was very modest by physician standards. He really only became wealthy a couple of years ago when some stock options paid off."

"So you really are putting it all on the line? There aren't millions stashed elsewhere?"

"Yep, all on the line. Crazy, right? But then, I intend to show up, so it really doesn't matter."

Katya pursed her lips. "Have you transferred the money yet?"

"No. I was going to do that now. Why do you ask?"

"I think you should reconsider. Your attorney's investigators had six months to work the case, a hundred eighty-two days. That's sixteen and a half times the amount of days we have left to solve this thing. They came up with nothing. Even if we're ten times as good as they were, we're still going to fail, statistically speaking."

"Not necessarily. What did you find out about flights to SFO?"

"There's a flight at ten tonight that gets in at one a.m. And the flights start back up at six in the morning. Personally, I say we grab a nice dinner and get a good night's sleep, and head to San Francisco in the morning. I'm guessing there's not much we can do there at one in the morning anyway. And besides, isn't there some soldier's axiom about eating and sleeping when you can?"

"You an expert on soldiers now?"

"No, but I'm pretty good with axioms."

I laughed. Just a quick, spontaneous snort, but it felt good. I realized I hadn't laughed since the party, since Colin had recalled some of the more challenging moments presented by raising two boys while toasting my father.

Katya watched me enjoy the recollection before continuing. "When I said we'd have to be ten times as good as the other investigators to catch them in the time you have left, you said 'not necessarily.' What did you mean?"

"Your equation assumes the investigators were equally competent and motivated. I can't speak to their competence, but I'm beginning to think they weren't motivated at all. So first I'm going to take you to the Old Ebbitt Grill for some lobster. Then we're going to get a few hours of sleep. Then we're going to fly to San Francisco and confront an old friend."

PART 3: ENLIGHTENMENT

Chapter 60

Finding Fear

NEW YORK CITY has a street that serves as an address and an icon and a center for its financial activity. On the opposite coast, three thousand miles and a ditched-necktie away, Silicon Valley has a road that serves the same purpose. Vondreesen Ventures boasted its Sand Hill Road address on engraved linen stationary and crisp bone business cards. According to the shapely blonde at reception, however, the firm could no longer brag of the presence of the man for which it was named.

"Mr. Vondreesen retired at the end of last year," Megan said. "We're still here to administer existing funds, but there's no new business being conducted." She was cordial and intelligent and pleasant to watch, but Megan left no doubt that her words could be taken to the bank, like a weather girl who'd made news anchor.

"I hadn't heard. I'm an old friend. Vaughn worked with my father."

Her face brightened, then clouded. Recognition then realization before her diplomatic training kicked in. "You're John's son. That dimpled chin's pretty distinctive. I should have known right away."

I bowed my head as though doffing a hat. "I need to speak with Vaughn. Some old business related to my father. Is he still living in Atherton?"

Megan gave a perfect little shake of her head. "He moved. I'm afraid I have strict instructions not to pass his contact information along to anyone. Venture capital is a stressful business, and despite his success, he was happy to leave it behind."

"Why the office, then? The rent here can't be cheap, and surely the storefront is no longer necessary, if all that's left is administration?"

She gave me an appraising stare. "I'd heard you did, shall we say, government work. It shows. To answer your question, there was a lease and a legacy to consider. I can pass along the information that you called, if you'd like to leave a number."

I knew a cue when I heard one. "No need, I'll call him directly. I trust his old cell is still in service?"

"Some things never change."

Once we were back in the parking lot, where our Tesla waited in the shade of a redwood tree, Katya said, "You gave up pretty easily back there. That tells me you already have a Plan B."

"In the modern world, people who expect privacy are bound to be disappointed. Vondreesen is no exception." I looked up his cell phone number on one program, then pasted it into another. Twenty seconds later I got a set of GPS coordinates, which I punched into the Tesla's navigation system.

A voice remarkably similar to Megan's told me the route was being calculated.

I muted her without prejudice.

"He stayed in Northern California, or at least his cell phone did. It's near the far end of Napa Valley. Should be a lovely drive."

I'd rented the Tesla because its combination of speed, style, and silence were great for covert work in Silicon Valley, but I was still surprised by the quiet operation. Just touch and go. No rumble or revving, no jolting or shifting. Just velvety power on tap. Now I had the Golden Gate Bridge and the Marin County headlands and the windy roads of the Napa hills ahead. This was going to be fun.

As we left the 101, Katya said, "You still haven't explained what you expect to learn from Vondreesen? Or how he's related to the investigation? Or why Casey's investigators would be anything but motivated?"

I adjusted my seat with a whir and a purr, dropping my right arm onto the tan leather armrest and opening myself up in Katya's direction. "The morning of the incident, a couple of beat cops picked me up in a hotel room. By then the detectives had already spent hours scouring the yacht, but I was oblivious to what had happened. I'd enjoyed a very late night, and had slept in accordingly. When Frost finally broke the news to me, Flurry was already done with you. By the time I learned they were looking at me for the murders, I already had a lawyer."

"How'd you get a lawyer before you knew you needed one?"

"I'd wondered that too, at first. But I also knew I was a few hours behind the curve, so when Vondreesen appeared with his lawyer already working the system, I didn't question it. Lawyers go with venture capitalists like salt with pepper."

"And now?"

"Now I'm wondering if that wasn't a little too convenient."

"Convenient for whom?"

"That's what I want to learn from Vondreesen."

We were driving north through Napa Valley now on the St. Helena Highway. The sun was out, the fields were green, and the air was fresh with the scent of bloom. In a sense, I'd been told I only had a few days to live, and this wasn't a bad way to spend one of them.

"Vondreesen introduced you to Casey just moments before your arrest?"

"Yup."

"If you suspect Vondreesen, then by extension you suspect Casey too. Which is why you're not convinced the investigators were fully motivated. Since Casey hired them."

"It's a working theory. But it has a big fat hole, which is why I didn't start there."

"What big fat hole?"

"If you'll recall from the party, Vondreesen is about as far from the killer profile as you can get. Rich, handsome, extremely well-connected, and a longtime friend of my father."

"When did you start to suspect him?"

"He was always a suspect. But he didn't top the list until the Brillyanc connection emerged. As it is, I still don't have the most important piece of the puzzle." I tossed the question to Katya with my eyes.

She fielded it immediately. "Motive. What could he possibly gain by killing your family and framing you for it?"

"I think I've got the motive piece, but you're close. I'm missing the linking piece."

"What's his motive? You told me he has it all: fame, fortune, influence."

"Exactly. So his motive isn't *gain*, it's *avoiding loss*. Vondreesen's motivated by fear. But fear of what? That's the missing link."

"If something scares him enough to involve him in the murder of friends, then he's not likely to open up to us about it."

"I agree. I'm going to have to put the pressure on. And since I've got my trial coming up, and he's the kind of witness who could sway a jury, I've got to do it in a way that doesn't deeply offend him."

"How do you do that?"

"I'm not sure yet, but I think it will involve your being the *bad cop* to my *good*. Are you up for that?"

Katya waited for me to look over at her before saying, "Always," with a gleam in her eye.

Chapter 61

Time Travel

AS WE MULLED OVER the upcoming confrontation with Vondreesen, our electronic guide took us off the main road and up into the wooded hills. "I've never been anyplace more beautiful," Katya said. "Not that I've been that many places."

"What about Paris?"

"Apples and oranges. Paris is man-made. This beauty is natural. But now that you mention it, with its colorful homes and rolling vineyards, Napa Valley fits the image I have of the French countryside."

"Did you grow up in Moscow?"

"I did. Spent my whole life there. Russia's not like the US. Here, you've got New York, but you've also got Washington, and Chicago, and LA, and Dallas, and Miami, and, and, and. They might not all be considered quite equal, but to each her own. In Russia, on the other hand, there's just Moscow. Everywhere else is, I don't know, Des Moines. I suppose St. Petersburg is like, say, Buffalo, but you get the point. Once you make it there you never think about going anyplace else domestic. Other than to the Black Sea for vacation. Or Paris," she added with a wink.

"What did your parents do?"

"My father was a geologist. He had a PhD from the Moscow School of Mines. My mother was a technical translator for the patent office. They were relatively prosperous, but not well-connected. When I got into MSU it was a big deal for them."

"You used the past tense."

"They passed away a couple of years ago."

"Siblings?"

"None."

None. Did I check that box now too? Or did forms have a *deceased* box for siblings? I wasn't sure. It was going to take a long time to adapt to my new status.

At a quarter to twelve, we rounded a bend on a quiet winding road and approached the last turn on our route, a few hundred yards from our destination. I stopped the Tesla beneath the arching bows of ancient oaks to study the turnoff that I presumed was Vondreesen's drive. Large blocks of chiseled gray stone flanked the entrance to an unnamed road like silent sentries. No name. No number.

"This is the place." I lowered the windows to inhale the fresh air, then checked the display on my phone. "Vondreesen's still here. Or at least his cell phone is."

Twitters of the biological variety emanated from sunny treetops all around us, but otherwise the scene was silent and serene. That changed when the Tesla's tires met the fine gravel of Vondreesen's oak-lined drive with a crunch that sounded like money.

The drive arced and rose and the woods gave way, yielding to sun-drenched fields on both left and right. They were planted with acres of new vines in long contoured rows, each wrapped in a brown tube to protect it from foraging beasts and birds.

"Oh my God," Katya said, as we crested the rise. "We *are* in the French countryside."

I eased off the gas and we crunched to a halt with wonder in our eyes. Rising above us in the midst of a clearing backed by an oak and evergreen forest was a castle the likes of which I'd only seen in storybooks and European travel brochures. "Vondreesen didn't just leave Silicon Valley when he retired. He left the twenty-first century."

Katya couldn't stop gawking. "Looks like a remnant of the Hundred Years War. Like it was lifted from the Loire Valley by a magical crane and dropped here six hundred years later."

"Moat and all."

We studied the spectacle in stunned silence for a few seconds. Square towers with crenelations and merlons rose forty feet to the left and right, while the central entryway was located on the second floor. It was reached by crossing a heavy timber drawbridge that sloped up across a moat, and was protected on both sides by a barbican. Katya asked, "What do we do now?"

"It's a bit extravagant, but at the end of the day it's just a house. We park and knock." I earned an elbow to the kidney by adding, "Just keep an eye out for archers."

The driveway wrapped around to the back of the castle, but I parked to the left of the drawbridge in a bump-out big enough to handle a dozen Teslas, or two dozen horses.

Katya wasted no time getting out of the car. "This is really cool and really creepy at the same time. And what's with the second-story entrance?"

"No weak zones on the first floor. Standard defense against barbarians."

We passed beneath the spikes of a wooden portcullis dangling above, and stopped before the massive arched oak door. True to form, there was no doorbell, although I detected electronic eyes cleverly concealed in caricatures carved into either side of the framework. A dragon and a frog. The knocker was a heavy ring of wrought iron, which I clinked three times. I half expected to hear the clank of armored footsteps, but got no response for what felt like an eternity. Then the door swung open with the grace and ease of a big bird's wing, and the king of the castle spoke — with a British accent. "Hello, Achilles."

Chapter 62

Block by Block

VONDREESEN GAVE KATYA a warm smile. "Hello Katya. Welcome. Won't you come in?" He still looked every bit a George Clooney twin, but he seemed to have lost the energetic glow that had radiated from his eyes. Perhaps retirement, while good for the spirit, took its toll on the soul.

He stepped back with a graceful move to reveal an attractive architectural amalgam of fifteenth and twenty-first-century styles. Or so I guessed, not having much experience with the former. "Still feels like you're outdoors, doesn't it?" Vondreesen said, closing the door. "It's the lighting. It's all indirect, and it uses full-spectrum bulbs that automatically adjust in brightness depending on the time of day. The chandelier is for show." He gave me a proud grin.

"The floors are original, and come from the same mix of stones as the walls, but I had them sliced thin and installed over heating elements. Now I've got the first castle in history with floors that are warm to the touch. But forgive me for prattling on. My new toys and I are still in the honeymoon phase."

I spun around, admiring the architecture. "Not at all. We're naturally curious. This is the first castle we've been to today."

"You're too kind." Vondreesen put a hand on each of our shoulders.

"The painting," I said, gesturing to the large oil that filled the wall between stairways arcing up to the left and right. "Is that Raphael's *St. George and the Dragon*?" Since this was Vondreesen's place, I wondered if it could be the original.

"Something about it doesn't feel quite right, eh?"

Man, was he good at reading people. "Yes, although I'm no expert."

"But your mind is trained to detect incongruity and remember detail. It's neither a copy nor a Raphael, but it is from his workshop. That's an original Penni. It's sixty-four times the size of Raphael's original work, and it's painted on canvas rather than wood. A great find. This way, please." He motioned to his right.

"So what's the story?" I said, spreading my arms.

"Can't a man have a castle without a story?"

"Not a chance. Not a thousand years ago. Not today."

"It was relocated and reconstructed by a French Baron and wine enthusiast named Crespin who fancied himself an entrepreneur. There's not a lot of innovative entrepreneurship going on in the French wine industry, so Crespin came to the land of opportunity. He tried to bring old-world charm to the new land, figuring that he could one-up all his competition by adding a new dimension to the wine tasting experience. He thought he could create the hottest vineyard in Northern California — a tourist attraction in addition to a tasting room."

"Kind of a Walt Disney approach."

"Indeed, although Disney chose a German castle. This was originally built in the fifteenth century in what's now a nowhere village in south-central France. He bought it for a song, and reassembled it here, block by block."

"So what happened?" Katya asked.

"He died and the project stalled. By the time his heirs quit quarreling, an Italian had beat them to the punch with *Castello di Amorosa*, which is an even grander castle not ten miles from here. The Crespin heirs missed the window of opportunity and were stuck with a pink elephant. Napa Valley doesn't need two medieval castles. I was looking for a place when it came on the market, and I liked the extra dimension it added. It's hard to beat for dinner parties, or for getting the grandkids to visit."

"It certainly has cachet."

Vondreesen gestured toward the staircase. "Please join me in the library. It's also rather special."

Chapter 63

Duped

VONDREESEN LED US up the left semicircular staircase, past St. George and the mammoth wrought-iron chandelier and through oversized double-doors into the grand library beyond, where polished hardwood floors and rich oriental rugs treated our eyes. Classic floor-to-ceiling bookshelves surrounded us, complete with rolling oak ladders, but our eyes flew to the opposite wall and grew wide.

A glass, semicircular wall bowed out into the room, running floor to ceiling and dancing with flames. The enormous ultra-modern fireplace reminded me of a commercial aquarium, but with flames rather than fish. It was a spectacular centerpiece, and made the library a memorable place to entertain Silicon Valley's most distinguished. No doubt that was Vaughn's intent. "There's a natural gas field on the property," he continued, in answer to an unstated question. "It's not large enough to justify a commercial effort, but it is sufficient to keep the home fire burning for decades."

"Why are we hardly feeling any heat?" Katya asked, as we accepted seats around the central of the three coffee tables situated before it.

"The glass wall is double-paned, with a vacuum in between, and the glass itself is coated with infrared film. I wouldn't mind a bit more heat myself, but it wouldn't be good for the books." He plucked a smoldering stogie from the oddest looking ashtray I'd ever seen, and took a puff to keep it lit. Following my eye toward the softball sized hunk of pockmarked stone, he said, "It's a moon rock."

"Never heard of them. Do they do something to the smoke?"

Vondreesen smiled at my misunderstanding. "It's literally a rock from the moon. A gift from … well, I shouldn't say."

"And you use it as an ashtray?"

"At first I just had it on the table for display purposes. Then a guest mistook it for an ashtray, and, well …"

He picked up the mini-tablet that lay beside the moon rock and asked us, "Coffee? Espresso? Something stronger?" He swiped the screen as if planning to place our order electronically.

I caught a glimpse of the display before his first stroke. It showed live images of the barbican from the dragon's and frog's points of view.

Perhaps that explained why a man who lived in a castle and could order up drinks on a tablet would answer his own door. "Black coffee would be great. And I'm guessing Katya would appreciate some chamomile tea, if it's no trouble."

She gave me a smile. "Please."

Vondreesen tapped his screen. "Melanie, two black coffees and some chamomile tea, please."

He set the tablet down with a reverent touch of pride. "Now, how can I help you?"

This was the big moment.

The moment for which I'd traveled halfway around the world and back.

The moment that could change the course of my life, sending it either into the freedom of the open seas, or crashing onto the rocks. At the very least, Vondreesen's reaction would be a barometer of my odds of avoiding jail. "As you may be aware, I've been granted bail in order to investigate my family's death. In that context, I wanted to learn more about Vitalis Pharmaceuticals. Specifically, why it folded."

Vondreesen picked up his cigar, found it lacking, and rekindled it with a torch lighter. Turning to Katya he said, "No worries," and motioned upward with his chin. "The ventilation system scrubs the air."

Turning back to me, he nodded solemnly, a grave expression on his charismatic face. Compassion and wisdom, with perhaps a hint of fear around the corners of his eyes. "You think Vitalis might somehow be connected to your tragedy?"

"It's a common denominator, shared by both my father and my brother. The police are looking at me due to economic motives, so naturally I'm looking into others."

"I see. Well, as you pointed out, Vitalis folded. It's bankrupt. Its shares are virtually worthless."

"In the US. But what about abroad? We've learned that the clinical trial only wrapped up last week."

"Is that what this is about?" He leaned back and blew smoke for a couple of beats. "Megan told me you stopped by, which means you know my office is still working, even though I retired at the end of last year. I believe she explained the logic behind that decision to you?"

"That's right."

"Well, the same goes for Vitalis. The clinical trial was prepaid, and the Russian Ministry of Health requires follow through, so we let it play out. No reason not to. Plenty of reason to let it run. It's my fiduciary responsibility to recover whatever I can for my investors, and that includes the sale of assets. Clinical trial results fall into that category."

I kept a friendly expression, but put some bite in my tone. "I can see that. But you still haven't answered my original question." I didn't repeat it. Vondreesen knew full well what it was, and of course he knew exactly why Vitalis folded.

Just then a woman walked into the room through a large oak door to the right of the fire, carrying a silver tray with a matching teapot, a French press full of coffee, three bone china cups on platinum-rimmed saucers, and a silver bowl of coco-dusted chocolate truffles. Melanie looked like she might be Megan's sister, and I wonder if Vaughn had collected the set. She unloaded the tray onto the coffee table, smiling at Katya while setting down the truffles. She poured the tea and coffee, then disappeared without a word.

Glancing up from the table, Vondreesen seemed surprised to see us looking back at him. His eyes went back and forth between us as though he was searching for something. For a good five seconds, I watched him struggle mentally while his face turned from confused to panicked. Then all at once his eyes lit up and his normal expression returned. It was as though his mind had suddenly tuned back in to its previous channel.

He leaned forward and put his elbows on his knees, cupping his right hand over his left so the cigar jutted out like a lance. Meeting my eye, he said, "Vitalis folded because I got duped."

Chapter 64

Synthetic

I LEFT MY COFFEE where it lay, and repeated Vondreesen's words. "You got duped. My family was murdered, and you tell me 'you got duped.' What the hell does that even mean?"

Two men appeared in the same doorway through which Melanie had disappeared, like guard dogs sensing a threatening change in tone. They weren't wearing suit coats or wraparound shades, but otherwise they appeared to have come from the same store as our earlier acquaintances. It could be a coincidence. Google *bodyguard* and *big, beefy, crewcut* was the image you got, more often than not with a black suit and sunglasses.

But I wasn't a believer in coincidences.

A part of me wanted them to intervene, giving me a chance to turn this discussion into an interrogation after working off some pent-up aggression. But Vondreesen held up a palm, and they backed off through the door. The scene reminded me of the way some guys will pull back their coat to reveal a concealed carry. Tactically, it was just as stupid a move.

Vondreesen seemed to sense this and dove right into the answer to my question. "Brillyanc wasn't my creation, you understand. It was brought to me. I'm a venture capitalist, not a biomedical researcher. An investor, not an inventor."

It was sad to see the great Vaughn Vondreesen making excuses. But I wasn't going to let the sympathy card distract me. It did get me wondering, however, if the castle was the late-life crisis equivalent of the mid-life crisis Ferrari, or something else entirely. "Surely you performed due diligence? In-depth analysis before pouring in millions of OPM?"

Katya recoiled at my words. "Hold on. I didn't know Colin was working with narcotics. That adds a whole new dimension to things."

"Not opium," Vondreesen said. "O.P.M. Other People's Money. And Achilles, actually VC's invest all the time without knowing if a compound is going to work. You can't definitively determine the efficacy of a new compound without performing clinical trials, and clinical trials are very expensive. That said, efficacy wasn't the problem."

"It wasn't?" Katya and I said in chorus.

"No. Brillyanc works. Beautifully, in fact. The problem was its formulation."

It was my turn to recoil. "The formulation? You mean the list of ingredients? Surely you didn't invest without knowing that?"

"No, of course not. But as I said, I was duped. The formula we were given for due diligence wasn't the same as the formulation used in the previous clinical trials — the preclinical studies, and the Phase I and II trials. It was almost the same, but a couple of amino acid side chains were different, and they make all the difference."

"You're saying they disclosed actual clinical results, but shared the wrong formulation?"

"Exactly. And furthermore, as part of the deal, we agreed to continue with their contract manufacturer — who used the original formulation without our knowledge. The result was that we didn't detect the discrepancy until we were a year into it, and then only because Colin was at the top of his game."

"What does it matter? Once you found out, couldn't you switch to the correct formulation?"

"If only! But no. Two reasons. One was the patents, all of which were filed around the wrong compound. That was critical, but not necessarily lethal. The other, however, was vital." Vondreesen, relaxing a little now that his story was flowing, took a few long puffs on his cigar before continuing. "Ask yourself why the inventors would do that? Why would they pull a switcheroo?"

I was willing to play along for now. But I wouldn't be leaving without the answers I'd come for. Barbicans and black suits didn't frighten me. Life in jail did. "You implied that it wasn't patents. So I'd guess that it was to get you to pay for the clinical trials, but not actually own anything of value in the end." I felt I'd found a thread, so I shifted my gaze to the flames and kept pulling it. "They'd keep two sets of books, so to speak, and leave you holding the bad ones while they run off to the bank with the good ones." I saw it now. I was getting excited. "My brother discovered this. He told my dad. The inventors found out and killed them to keep the se–" I cut myself off. My hopes dashed. "They killed them after Vitalis folded. There was no secret to keep at that point."

Vondreesen grew a 'nice try' smile.

Katya threw her idea into the ring. "They knew you wouldn't invest if you knew the real formulation."

"Correct."

"Because there's something that would prevent you from marketing the real formulation. Something other than efficacy or intellectual property."

"Correct again."

Katya and I each stared into the flames, racking our brains. This wasn't a twist I'd anticipated. After a minute we looked at each other. Neither of us had a clue. I started thinking aloud. "You said the product works, so we'll assume there's demand. Unless the actual formulation is too expensive?"

Vondreesen shook his head. "The pricing is inelastic. There are enough buyers to support a healthy business at virtually any price point."

"Okay. Well, we also know they can manufacture it, so we'll assume there's supply. If it's not supply or demand, what's left?"

"A regulatory issue," Katya said.

"It's all of the above," Vondreesen said. "The difference between the formulations was the difference between *organic* and *synthetic*. The formula they showed us was synthetic. The actual formula is organic, and it can't be synthesized. At least not with current technology."

"So what? You told me that price doesn't matter."

"That's right. It's not an issue of price. It's an issue of source. Unlike, say insulin, which came from pigs and cattle before it was synthesized, one of Brillyanc's key ingredients comes from an endangered species. The gallbladder of a sun bear, to be precise. Sun bears are the small ones that look like Winnie the Pooh, by the way." He spread his arms wide and rolled his eyes. "So out of the blue, we found ourselves with an insurmountable supply issue, a potential demand issue, and a killer regulatory issue."

"Three strikes and you're out," I muttered, as the implications began crashing down like the big stone blocks of castle walls.

Chapter 65

Vanishing Act

VONDREESEN SHOWED SIGNS of relaxing after dropping his bomb. His complexion improved and his facial wrinkles faded. I suspected that my appearance had gone in the opposite direction.

"Three strikes and you're out," Vondreesen repeated. "That's exactly right."

"Four, now that I think about it," I added. "In addition to a supply issue, a demand issue, and a regulatory issue, the public-opinion referees have you for ethics violations to boot."

"No choice but to fold," Katya said. "Now I understand why Colin was so confident one day, and so despondent the next. There was nothing he could do about it."

"Was this why you retired?" I asked Vondreesen.

Vondreesen blew out smoke and shook his head at the memory. "It was humiliating and it was discouraging. I let a lot of people down."

"That explains everything. Everything except the most important thing." I turned in my chair to face Vondreesen full-on. "Why would they kill my family, if there was nothing to protect?"

Vondreesen shrugged. "I asked myself that question six months ago, when it happened, and I asked myself that question six minutes ago, when you arrived. I got the same answer both times. *They* wouldn't. I can only conclude that your family's death was not related to Vitalis."

If that was true, I was screwed. I had no other leads.

But I knew it wasn't true.

The murders of Dr. Tarasova and her husband made the connection clear. "Who are *they*?" I asked.

"I'm afraid I can't tell you that."

"Can't, or won't?"

Vondreesen collapsed back into his chair, spreading his arms and exposing his chest with his hands extended well over the sides. "Anonymity was a big deal to them. Frankly, I don't think they even needed the money. What they needed was an American face. They chose mine, and I agreed because the product was so spectacular."

"You mean you let greed override your better judgment?"

Vondreesen met my verbal jab with a remorseful smile so genuine that it might have saved Nixon. What a politician. "You have to understand, that's what VC's do. We spend our lives looking for investments with the potential for phenomenal return. That's our opium. Our bliss and our addiction. Brillyanc was the biggest deal I saw in thirty years."

"Who are they?" I repeated.

"They're Russian. That's all I know. They did everything through an offshore corporation that no longer exists. The officers who signed the forms were straw men. Caribbean islanders paid for their time."

"Isn't that suspicious?"

"If you look at it as venture capital, it's atypical. But if you look at it as a large financial transaction by a wealthy party, it's commonplace. I wasn't suspicious until Colin made his discovery. Then they disappeared, and we shut it down."

"What do you mean, they disappeared?"

"Their phone number and email server went out of service. All contact was severed. Recourse became impossible."

"And all that happened before my family was murdered?"

"Months before."

I had no idea where to take the discussion. This wasn't what I was expecting — and apparently my Brillyanc had worn off. Suddenly I wasn't so sure about my decision to post bail.

I looked over at Katya. She nodded back at me. We were done here. "Thank you for your time, Vaughn. Enjoy your castle."

Chapter 66

Forgetfulness

WE SAT QUIETLY as I backed away from the moat and headed down the winding drive, the gravel crunching beneath the Tesla's tires while Vondreesen's words reverberated in our ears. The moment we touched pavement, however, Katya hit me with, "What did you think of Vondreesen's story?"

I replied in a tone that showed my frustration. "It explains everything, and it leaves us nowhere. I feel like a reporter who interviewed a presidential candidate. I know I've been fed a salad of truth and lies, but I'm struggling to separate the mix. What did you think?"

Katya twisted in her seat so that she could face me, and drew her knees up toward her chest. "The use of endangered species in medicine rings true enough. I'm not familiar with sun bears, but in Russia we hear about endangered fish often enough, due to our love of caviar. Sun bear gallbladder sounds like an Asian thing to me — lots of traditional medicine there for sure. Anyway, it would certainly explain Colin's reaction and Vitalis's sudden demise."

I concurred and watched picturesque vineyards roll by on the left and right. I was trying to remember something I knew I was forgetting. It wouldn't come. The memory-palace technique I'd drilled in prison only applied to things I deliberately worked to memorize.

The helpless frustration I was feeling made me think of Max, cut off from Brillyanc just shy of completing his dissertation. His words rang truer than ever: *I would pay anything.*

God, what a nightmare Alzheimer's must be.

I was sorely tempted to stop at one of the beautiful wineries we were passing for a glass of pinot noir and a few minutes of reflection, but we didn't have time. I'd have to hope the drive jogged my memory, and settle for whatever red they served on the plane.

I decided to attempt tricking my mind into relaxing. "Sun bears are the smallest bears, but they have the longest tongues for eating honey."

"How in the world do you know that?" Katya asked. "Did you used to work at a zoo?"

"No. I was into Winnie the Pooh as a kid. What did you think of the rest of Vondreesen's story?"

"I can't really speak to the whole investment part of the equation, but I believe Switzerland has one of the highest per capita GDP's on the planet, and their economy is based largely on secretive banking. So I suppose I buy that too." She looked back at me with her big amber eyes. "What's making you skeptical?"

"I'm always skeptical. What's bothering me is that Vondreesen's explanation is flawless. I don't like flawless. It implies engineering. Natural phenomenon are rough around the edges. They have imperfections, holes, and grit."

"He got duped. That's a pretty big hole."

"I buy that part. I'm just not sure about the details. I also don't believe that he doesn't know the identity of the Russian owner. He's too savvy to go for that."

"But?"

"But those are just feelings. Feelings are useless. We need facts. And I feel like I'm overlooking some of those. Speaking of which, did you catch that senior moment of his?"

"Right after Melanie dropped off the coffee. He seemed spooked by it. You think that may have contributed to his retirement decision?"

"It may have. It's certainly a confounding factor, and our investigation doesn't need any more of those. It also surprised me. The other times I met him he seemed, I don't know, superhuman. But for a second there I thought he was going to have a breakdown. Anyway, time to focus on the next meeting."

"Rita?"

"Exactly. By tomorrow night I have to become Chris Pine. That's not a lot of time."

"You already look like him. What else do you need?"

"I resemble him from across a room. I need to pass muster face to face. Plus, I need to brush up on his biography, and study any online videos of him I can find so that my behavior and mannerisms match. We don't know what kind of research Rita did, but whatever it was, I need to fit what she found."

"There's something else." Katya reached over and put her hand on my arm. She'd never touched me like that before. Not pointedly. Purposefully. It was something we both seemed to understand was best avoided.

"What's that?"

"I want to go with you to the pitch. I want to meet Rita."

I thought about the hand on my arm, while I contemplated my answer. "She made it clear that I was to come alone. That I couldn't mention this to anybody. But you know that, and you still want to go, which means you think your presence won't blow the deal. Why's that?"

Her hand didn't move. "Because I'm going to be just as strong a candidate for Brillyanc as Chris Pine is. I'll find someone I can play. Someone equally bright and ambitious and no less bent on climbing a greasy ladder. Perhaps Chris's coworker. Bottom line, Rita's a salesperson, right? She's not the boss. Her mandate is to sell. Sure, she might have second thoughts about working with someone who's less than perfectly obedient. But once I'm there her options become *two sales or zero*."

Katya had some good points, but I wasn't sure how far she'd thought this through. "When I ran covert meetings like Rita's doing, if I saw that my contact wasn't following instructions, I wouldn't show. If Rita's tactics are similar, she'll never know that you're a perfect second sale."

Katya tilted her head. "You're testing me, aren't you?"

I winked back. "I want to help you think things through. My mentor, Granger, was always guiding me that way."

"That's easy enough to manage. I'll keep out of sight until Rita shows. Also, she must have come to expect a little disobedience from her clients, given the egos she's working with. Furthermore, we know what she's going to pitch, so we know I'm a fit. We don't have to worry about it being a guy thing or something in very limited supply. She'll want me as a client. But still, it's your call. You're the one looking at life behind bars. I'm thinking that I can help you, if I'm there by your side." She gave my arm a squeeze, and then withdrew her hand. "No pressure."

No pressure. Right. And oh, by the way, does this dress make me look fat?

Our arrival at SFO's rental car garage saved me from an immediate answer. Pulling up next to the yellow-shirted attendant, I had a thousand things on my mind, not the least of which was the warm feel of Katya's hand.

As I looked up at the attendant's smiling face, I finally remembered what I'd forgotten: returning a rental car was predictable. Detective Frost spoke to me over the barrel of his gun. "Kyle Achilles, you're under arrest."

Chapter 67

Bad Note

"WHAT'S THE CHARGE?" I asked Frost as he locked the cuffs around my wrists with a bit too much verve.

"Prison escape."

"I'm out on bail."

"No, you're not."

Frost's smugness made me want to kick his teeth in. I held back, as I was reserving the first couple of kicks for myself.

I'd screwed up big time. Twice. I'd made a predictable move, and I'd failed to factor banking delays into my thinking. It was only Thursday. My bail payment probably still hadn't cleared. I was no expert, but this felt like a legal gray zone. I definitely didn't have time for one of those.

Frost barked across the Tesla's roof at Katya. "Stay where you are, Miss Kozara. If you interfere in any way, I'll arrest you for obstructing justice."

I looked over at Katya. Tears were streaming down her cheeks. "Stick with the plan you proposed," I said, trying to sound optimistic. I'll work this out and catch up with you as soon as possible."

"Should I call Casey?"

"Yes, but don't miss the plane. The big clock is still ticking, regardless of my current situation. Please focus on that, and let me worry about this. Now go."

Frost spun me around before Katya replied, and started marching me in what I assumed was the direction of his hidden police cruiser. I didn't resist. Once my cuffs were on, he'd swapped his automatic for a Taser, and I was sure he wouldn't hesitate to use it.

"I'll see you soon," Katya called after me, her voice squeaky, but resolute.

"So, you are sleeping with your brother's wife." Frost smirked. "The jury was still out on that, so to speak. I'll be sure to let them know."

"Why are you doing this? I have a deal with the DA. She even instructed Kilpatrick and Flurry to support my investigation. Surely, you know that."

"I know no such thing."

I wasn't inclined to believe him, but couldn't be certain. Frost was behind me in a control position, so I couldn't see his face. "We agreed on the terms for my bail yesterday. I initiated the payment as soon as we were off the phone. It's a done deal."

"Perhaps this changes things."

That was my fear, although I was screwed either way. If I went to Santa Barbara rather than DC, I'd miss the meeting with Rita.

I decided to go on the offensive. Test some hunches. Shake things up. What did I have to lose? "You're acting alone, aren't you? You've gone renegade, looking for a win."

"Caught you all by myself."

"Kilpatrick isn't going to be happy that you went behind his back. Maybe you should call him now, before this goes any further."

"Kilpatrick isn't my boss."

"That may be true, but you both work for the mayor, and I'm sure he wants harmony, not renegades."

"You seem to think you're above the law, Mister Achilles. I'm here to tell you that owning a yacht doesn't make the legal system optional."

"And apparently having the title of detective doesn't mean you have a clue," I replied. To be honest, I understood Frost's point of view. But that understanding didn't change my situation. If I wasn't at Off the Record at eight o'clock tomorrow night, I'd lose my best link to the real killers. Then the clock would run out, and I'd be living under the heel of men like Frost and Grissel for the rest of my life.

Where was Frost's car? I was scanning the rows of parked cars ahead looking for government vehicles, when it hit me. "Did you fly here?"

"Straight from Vandenberg."

That was bad news.

I had to act quickly.

As we were passing one of the garage's supporting pillars, I stopped walking and turned to face Frost. "Where's Detective Flurry? I'm sure she's in the loop. Call her if you won't call Kilpatrick."

"Keep walking."

I stuck out my chest. "Flurry's what, ten years younger than you? Fifteen? But she makes you look like the rookie."

I did my best to look smug and egg Frost on while he blasted me with his rambling retort, but my mind was elsewhere and the words didn't register.

A handcuff key has more in common with a standard screwdriver than it does with the device that unlocks your door. Like standard screwdrivers, handcuff keys are essentially identical. Like all screwdrivers, handcuff keys are merely tools designed to apply torque. Just as you can use a coin or letter opener to turn a slotted screw, you can use another improvised torquing device to release a handcuff ratchet. All you need is a tool that fits the slot, and the knowledge of how to twist it.

I pulled a paperclip from my back pocket and quickly kinked it in the proper place for Smith & Wesson cuffs. Frost had double-locked them, so working the locks was painfully slow — about four seconds for the counterclockwise move that released the locking pin, and three seconds more for the clockwise twist that retracted the ratchet. Fortunately, Frost had more than seven seconds of blathering in him.

Palming the freed left cuff in my right, I tuned Frost back in, and prepared myself for the inevitable prompt. I didn't have long to wait.

"... I'm done with you. Now get moving."

I gave Frost a defiant stare for good measure and began pivoting to my right in compliance, only to stop almost immediately. "One more thing..." Reversing my pivot to face him again, I threw my left hand at Frost's Taser arm while my right swung for the left side of his head. It was a move similar to the sap strike that had failed me in the Escalade, but Frost didn't have the black suit's lightning reflexes, so this time the blow was true to its target. The impact of the handcuff was solid enough to hurt my hand, but nothing his thick head couldn't handle. Frost wobbled for a second or two, then his eyes rolled up, his knees gave way, and he dropped into my arms.

I hoisted the unconscious detective into the bed of a nearby pickup, and laid him on his left side in what EMTs call the recovery position, with his mouth down, chin up, and arms and legs in stabilizing positions.

Pulling the reporter's notebook from the breast pocket of his blazer, I began flipping pages. The last scrawled entry was, "Silver Tesla," followed by our rental's plate number. I tucked that informational nugget away for later analysis, and penned Frost a note with my left hand on the next blank page. "Sorry about the headache. I'll make it up to you when this is over."

Chapter 68

Conflicting Interests

"YOU LEFT HIM A NOTE?" Katya said, still beaming and unable to believe my sudden reappearance on the plane.

"The guy might be a stick in the mud, but he didn't deserve a club to the head. I'll do something to make it up to him once I'm free and clear of this mess. Maybe season tickets to the Lakers."

"Not the opera, or the Polo & Racquet Club?" She replied with a wink.

I'd just made our flight to DC. When I'd plunked down next to Katya, she'd been curled up in her seat, knees to chest and phone to ear, trying to get through to Casey for the twenty-third time. Now we were cruising at 36,000 feet and giddily sipping airline wine.

"Where'd you learn to pick handcuffs? Why'd you learn to pick handcuffs?" Katya asked, giddily.

I responded in kind. "There's a lot of sit-around-and-wait time during covert operations. Usually we sparred or goofed off, but sometimes we got more inventive. That particular trick came up when we were brainstorming on all the things you could do with a paperclip. There's quite a list, actually. An impressive enough list that I've kept a couple in my back pocket ever since. You can find paperclips everywhere, and take them anywhere, and they've got dozens of practical uses. Picking handcuffs with them was the most interesting. It began as a typical male *challenge-issued, challenge-accepted* thing with a former MP, but we all ended up spending hours learning to do it blind."

"I'll never look at a paperclip the same." Katya's face clouded over as she spoke. "Wait a minute. Won't Frost have people waiting for you when we land in DC?"

"That's a distinct possibility. But I doubt it. I don't think he'll have either the time or the inclination."

"Really? It won't take him long, now that he knows the name you're using. From the rental car, I mean."

"There's still a lot of bureaucracy to press through, and it's only a five-hour flight. But I'm guessing he won't even try."

"Why ever not?"

"Couple of factors. First, he was acting alone, trying to be the hero, trying to upstage Flurry. I don't think anyone else knew what he was doing. Not Flurry or Kilpatrick anyway. So nobody is expecting an update. Why admit an embarrassing failure if you don't have to? 'Guess what? I caught him, but then he got away.' I don't think so. That goes against human nature. Second, once my wire transfer completes, I'll be out on bail. So they'd be doing my in-processing and out-processing simultaneously. That won't be good for Frost's reputation."

"In other words, you've got pride and practicality working for you."

"And spite working against me."

"So it all boils down to Frost's character."

"Exactly."

Katya finished off her Chardonnay before speaking again. "Assuming Frost's character goes your way, is it still okay with you if I come along to the meeting with Rita?"

"If you can find a solid fit, I'd love to have you by my side. But that's no small order. Remember, on top of everything else, the person you're impersonating will need to be unreachable, presumably traveling overseas. You better get started right away."

Katya did, right there on the plane using inflight Wi-Fi. By the time we arrived at Washington National, she'd found her woman.

Then we learned that Frost's pride and practicality had won out over his spitefulness. As our taxi pulled away from Washington National Airport beneath overcast skies, I thought I saw the clouds parting ahead. But maybe that was an illusion.

Chapter 69

Rules

BEFORE I KNEW IT, I was headed for the Hay Adams, free on bail, with Katya by my side. Or should I say Chris was headed there, with Alisa. I had a fresh haircut with a bit of premature gray on my temples and some makeup that altered the shape of my face and diminished my dimple. Katya was now a brunette with shoulder-length hair and black Versace glasses. We went early and entered separately, so that we'd be properly positioned when Rita arrived.

Off the Record was known as Washington's best place to be seen and not heard. It had dim lights and wood-paneled walls and plenty of plush alcoves upholstered in red. Katya went to the bar while I grabbed a corner booth. I scooted over so that it would be easy for Katya to slip in beside me once Rita took the opposite seat.

Ambient jazz music played in the background, just loud enough to keep quiet conversations private without being obtrusive. I didn't recognize the artist's sultry voice. I don't have a memory for that kind of thing, but I loved the way it melted into the piano and double bass like a dab of churned butter on a sizzling steak. I had the waitress bring me a club soda with lime, and studied the other patrons while waiting for Rita to arrive.

At the bar, lawyers and lobbyists were buzzing around Katya like yellow jackets smelling grilled meat. She was holding her own, fending them off without offending. No doubt the result of years of practice.

At precisely eight o'clock, a woman I pegged as Rita glided through the doorway like she was expecting to fuck the president. Confident. Poised. And sexy as hell.

I estimated that her outfit cost six-figures, including a low-cut couture suit of fine cream-colored wool, pumpkin-toned heels with a matching bag, and heavy gold jewelry splashed with diamonds. Rita herself had sparkling green eyes, suntanned skin, and dark hair coiffed up to reveal a long and slender neck. Marilyn Monroe and Jackie Kennedy rolled into one — here to meet me.

Here to make a sale.

She'd sold me and she had yet to say word one.

I stood as she spotted me and walked toward our booth. "I'm Rita, and I'm glad you came." It was the British voice from the phone. She held out her hand. A French manicure and a bracelet that likely cost as much as the average car. As soon as we were seated, Katya slid in beside me and extended her own hand. "I'm Alisa."

Alarm crossed Rita's face like the passing shadow of a predatory bird, but she took Katya's hand. "Pleased to meet you."

"Alisa is also an ambitious junior partner at Kenzie," I said. "She's a Princeton PhD with two great talents: predicting competitive reactions, and climbing greasy ladders."

"We're a team of sorts," Katya said, mimicking Rita's poise and confidence. "We serve as each other's sounding boards, and help each other out behind the scenes. Kind of a secret alliance."

I leaned closer to Rita. "So whatever your career-enhancing service may be, she'll be equally interested. I'm sure that with a little research you'll find that Alisa is every bit as attractive a candidate as I am. So I figured you'd be happy to include her — and double your commission check."

Rita processed this like Miss Manners finding an unexpected crunch in her food. A dab of distaste and a smidgeon of surprise, but she swallowed and smiled. "What's your last name, Alisa?"

"Abroskina. As you may have guessed from my accent, I'm originally from Russia."

"And yet you graduated Princeton, with a PhD no less. Most impressive. When were you born?"

Katya gave her Alisa's DOB.

"If you'll excuse me for a minute, I'll be right back." Rita got up and made for the door.

"Do we follow her?" Katya asked.

"We stay. She's not leaving."

"How can you be sure? I'm sorry. I shouldn't have pushed for this. That was selfish of me."

"I think you sold her. I was watching her body language. Once she got past the initial shock, she was leaning in and analyzing, not leaning out and thinking about escape. And I didn't detect deception when she said she'd be right back. There was an apologetic intonation. Slight, but detectable. She went outside to check you out. She's being cautious."

"I hope you're right."

Rita didn't return in a minute. She didn't return in two, or three, or ten. But after twelve minutes she walked back in, just like before, the belle of the ball. She slid back into her seat, proffering a stern smile. "There are rules."

Chapter 70

The Pitch

RITA MET EACH of our eyes in turn, her gaze suddenly as serious as a sphinx. "I'm making a special exception for you. A big exception. Fortunately for you and me, there is a precedent for allowing multiple members of the same organization to become clients. But as you will see, we are adamant about our rules. I need to advise you that no further exceptions will be made."

I didn't blink. "We understand."

"Very well. Rule One is Absolute Secrecy. The reasons for that will become clear shortly, but I need to get that on the table up-front. Think of it as joining the KGB. I'd say CIA, but American-style secrecy doesn't conjure up quite the same vision as the old Soviet-style. You have to accept that you will never be able to discuss what you are about to learn with anyone. Ever. And for what it's worth, you won't want to."

Rita paused to look us each in the eye. "Assuming I can deliver what I promised, are you okay with that? Please consider your answer as seriously as you would an oath of office."

"We deal with confidential client information all the time," Katya said, as we'd rehearsed. "Some of which is quite inflammatory. We're comfortable with this version of attorney-client privilege, assuming the business is legitimate."

Rita looked at me.

I nodded.

"Very good. Forgive the theatrics. You'll understand them in a moment. Now let me ask you," Rita said, leaning in. "If you had to name the one quality your firm's global managing partner possesses that got him to the position he holds today, what would it be?"

"Easy enough. He's affable and well-connected, but the driving distinction is the perception that he's always the smartest person in the room."

"Precisely. Thank you for doing my job for me. That's what I have to offer. I can make you the two smartest people in virtually any room." Rita leaned back, and gave what appeared to be a prearranged signal to our passing waitress.

"Literally, or figuratively?" I asked. "Are you selling covert information, or improved cognition?"

"You both hold advanced degrees from Ivy League universities and fast-track positions at the most prestigious consulting firm on the planet. That puts your IQ's somewhere in the range of 140, or 1 in 200. Sound about right?"

We nodded, our eyes locked on hers in rapt attention.

"I can take your IQs to 160. From 1 in 200 people, to 1 in 20,000. Add in your good looks, strong interpersonal skills, and killer work ethic, and you'll truly be one in a million."

"How's that possible?" Katya asked after a suitable period of stunned silence.

Rita was all too ready with the answer. "A new pharmaceutical. A very exclusive, very expensive new pharmaceutical. Which brings us to the next bridge you need to cross if we are to proceed."

"The cost," I said.

Rita smiled. "As junior partners at Kenzie, you're earning somewhere in the neighborhood of half a million, all in. Once you move up to partner, you'll begin earning twice that amount. And then five, ten, and even twenty times as much as you move into and through the director ranks. You know all this. It's why you're there. It's the dream. The dream, as you now see, that I can virtually guarantee." She grinned wryly.

"The cost of that dream is, of course, commensurate with the benefit. Something I'm sure you, as management consultants, can appreciate. It's ninety thousand dollars a quarter."

"That's a thousand dollars a day." I blurted my calculation a bit louder than intended. Perhaps not a bad thing. I'd fully expected a large number, but wasn't really prepared for that one. The $180,000 I'd need to cover Katya's and my first dose was virtually everything I had left after bail and this operation's other expenses.

Rita didn't miss a beat. "Roughly one-fourth the amount Kenzie charges clients for your services. Surely you wouldn't expect to pay less?"

Chapter 71

Meritocracy

THE WAITRESS ARRIVED carrying a shiny silver bucket pebbled with condensation. She set a crystal flute before each of us, and then set about unwrapping and popping the cork. Cristal Champagne, I noted. Probably costs north of $400 a bottle here. Nothing next to the $720,000 annuity Rita had just pitched, but noteworthy nonetheless.

Once the flutes were bubbling away before us and the server had moved on, I said, "You know we can afford it, but you also know that it will be a struggle at this point in our careers. You timed your pitch to ensure our complete dedication to maintaining the integrity of your system."

"I timed it to help you make the biggest leap of your careers. A single promotion at this point is worth as much as all your other advances combined." Rita picked up her flute. "Is that a financial commitment you'd be willing to take? We can either drink to your careers, or we can end the discussion here and just enjoy a nice bottle of bubbly. It's entirely up to you."

She was smooth. The perfect recruit for her job. Whoever had hired Rita knew his stuff. "You tell a good story," I said. "But how do we know there's more to it than that? Talk is cheap."

"You will, of course, have the opportunity to try before you buy. But we need to know you're committed before crossing that bridge. To put it in your parlance, we'd want a figurative LOI from you, a Letter of Intent. Your agreement to proceed at the terms discussed, assuming the product passes your scrutiny."

Katya and I looked at each other, then down at our glasses. We picked them up, and Katya said, "Here's to our careers."

The Cristal was delicious. Crisp and dry, yet smooth and buttery with a honeyed aroma that reminded me of a garden restaurant I'd visited on the Cote d'Azur. I wasn't sure if it was worth twenty bucks a swallow, but it sure beat prison fare. "How does this new pharmaceutical of yours work?"

Rita set her glass down. "An inquisitive mind. Why am I not surprised? There are two other hurdles I want to be sure you're comfortable with, before we come to that. There's a practical issue, and a philosophical one. First, the philosophical." Rita paused, meeting my gaze.

"The manufacturer has weighed the options and decided that Brillyanc — that's the name of the pharmaceutical — will be reserved for the elite. The true ruling class. They believe there's a line beyond which a democracy must yield to a meritocracy, and Brillyanc is on the other side of that line. Put another way, access to Brillyanc will be like one of Washington's exclusive clubs, where you need both an invitation to join, and the funds to do so."

Rita gave us a just-look-around-you gaze. "Now, while Brillyanc is not a club, it's also not like other pharmaceuticals. It's not medicine. It doesn't remedy a malady. There's no condition it's fixing or preventing. Everyone can live a normal, healthy life without it. Just like everyone can live without a Metropolitan Club membership." Rita paused to look at each of us. "Are you with me?"

"We understand," Katya and I replied in chorus.

"Good. Given that, the manufacturer believes there's no moral obligation to supply it to anyone. Or even to make it accessible to the majority of the population. They acknowledge, however, that the argument could be made that the greater good would be served if we were to put it in the water supply, so to speak. Like fluoride.

"With Brillyanc, we have the power to raise the IQ of the entire population, the whole human race. We could boost mankind a few rungs higher on the evolutionary ladder. But we're choosing to be selective instead. We're going surgical, rather than systemic." Again, she paused to aid our digestion.

We remained silent.

"If word of Brillyanc were to get out, the argument for widespread distribution would surely be made. Loudly and frequently. There would also be outrage regarding the pricing, since the vast majority of the population couldn't afford it even at one-tenth the price. Both of these would eventually lead to backlash against Brillyanc users. There would be witch hunts fueled by fear and jealousy."

"Like the X-Men comic books," I said.

Rita raised her sculpted eyebrows. "Exactly. So the manufacturer is not going to be marketing the product publicly, and therefore will not be seeking regulatory approval. You need to be going into this with eyes wide open. You need to be philosophically comfortable with the meritocracy approach. And you need to be one hundred percent committed to maintaining our secret, recognizing that there could be devastating personal consequences if it ever came to light."

"Why so harsh?" I asked, curious as to how much Rita would reveal.

"Not harsh. Balanced. You'd be betraying a network of the world's most powerful people, and putting billions of dollars at risk.

"So we're all in it together," Katya said. "KGB style."

"Are you okay with that?" Rita asked.

"We're used to taking risks to reap rewards," I said. "To dancing close to the line if that's what it takes to win. We know it's a dog-eat-dog world. And we're comfortable with our positions atop the food chain. What's the practical issue you referenced?"

"The practical issue," Rita repeated, her voice switching from belligerent to bemused. "That's the best part."

Chapter 72

Perks

RITA TOPPED OFF our champagne flutes, but set hers down without imbibing. "The practical issue involves the drug's administration. Once a quarter, you'll need to free up a weekend to get your Brillyanc infusion. Specifically, the second weekend of the second month of each quarter. Is that something to which you can commit?"

"We have pretty busy travel schedules," I said. "Is there any flexibility?"

Rita pursed her lips and twisted her neck to look down to the left. "Not much. The last weekend of the first month of the quarter is the only alternative, but that's on the West Coast. Over the next year we'll be adding options on other weekends, probably in Dallas and Chicago, but for now it's just DC and San Francisco on the schedule I mentioned."

She paused, and her face brightened. "Trust me, after you try it once, you'll be happy to do whatever it takes to make it thereafter. It's an unforgettable event.

"The magic begins with the pre-party. Imagine what we're talking about here." Rita flared her hands and fingers like a starburst as her voice took on the excitement of a game show host. "We're bringing together a group of the wealthiest, most powerful people in America, and we're doing it in a context where everyone wants to remain anonymous. So, we turn it into a party, the likes of which, trust me, you've never experienced. Even a Kenzie annual director's retreat wouldn't compare.

"First of all, everyone wears a costume we provide. It is a medical procedure, after all. But rather than an extra-large back-split cotton smock, you're wearing tailored black silk pajamas and Zorro-style masks to conceal your identity." Addressing Alisa, she asked, "Can you get by without your glasses? The mask will work much better without."

"No problem."

"Good. Picture yourself walking into a cocktail party the likes of which is suitable for a gathering of captains of the universe. The Cristal will be flowing freely, along with every other exquisite indulgence known to man. Some simply treat it like an exclusive costume party.

Most guests, however, take it further. Imagine how the emperors partied near the end of the Roman Empire and you'll have some idea. Combine that with the fact that everyone there is, shall we say, healthy and energetic and high on the good life, then throw in the anonymity, and most tend to lose the pesky inhibitions that constrain us in our daily lives."

Rita brought her hand down to the top button of her blouse while giving us a minute to let our imaginations run with that imagery.

Mine surely did.

"People arrive for the party between six and midnight, and then filter back to the infusion room as early as ten and as late as four in the morning to begin their overnight procedure. At that point, they're as carnally satisfied as they've ever been in their lives." She paused to take a slow sip of champagne before shifting gears.

"Now, let me tell you what's involved in the procedure itself. Brillyanc is a parenteral, so it's infused intravenously. The infusion process takes six hours, during which you'll be hooked up to an IV. Rather than a hospital bed, however, you'll enjoy a setup similar to a first-class transoceanic flight. Very chic and comfortable. After six relaxing hours, you'll be good to go for another three months. How's that sound?"

"That, uh ... sounds better than what I was expecting," I said.

"Trust me. Whatever you're imagining, it's better."

"You'll be there?"

"Best job perk in the world."

"Is it safe?" Katya asked. "Brillyanc, I mean. Not the sex."

"Totally. It naturally enhances your metabolism in a way that supplies the brain with a richer, cleaner supply of fuel. I know that sounds funny, but only until you think about it for a second, then you realize that your cognitive powers are always in flux based on how much sleep or exercise you're getting, or what you're eating or drinking." Rita raised her glass. "Right?"

"Sure. I get that," I said. "Tell me, our job requires occasional drug testing. Will anything show up there?"

"No. The only thing that will potentially test differently is your cholesterol level. If your LDL and triglycerides have increased over time, they'll drift back down as a result of your metabolic improvements. No extra charge for that."

"Is it addictive?" Katya asked.

Rita smiled — no doubt reflecting on her commission checks. "Not physically. But once you try it, you won't want to live without it."

Chapter 73

The Big Question

YOU WON'T WANT TO LIVE WITHOUT IT. I wondered if that was just an expression. I decided it was. Rita seemed genuinely excited about it, and Max and Saba had been disappointed at losing their supply, but not suicidal. "Who invented it?"

My question soured Rita's sweet expression, if only for a second. "I don't know. I'll be frank with you — this experience is like joining the Manhattan Project. The level of secrecy, I mean. We're working in a highly regulated field without an approved product, so we have to fly under the radar. On top of that, and again like the Manhattan Project, we're working with a secret weapon."

"A secret weapon?" Katya repeated.

"Brillyanc gives you the power to trounce your competition. So you'll be guarding that secret like a winning lottery ticket. That said, like using the atomic bomb, there are ethical issues. It could be considered cheating, or worse. So Brillyanc is not for the faint of heart. It's for people who are willing to do whatever it takes to succeed. True leaders, like Truman. The planet's elite."

Rita drained her glass and set it down. "That's my pitch. I know it's a lot to think about."

"Not really," I said. "When you're climbing a ladder as greasy as ours, that's all you think about. You work hard. You work smart. You make sacrifices. And you take every advantage you can get."

"Exactly," Katya said.

Rita looked back and forth between us both. "Well, all right then. The sample doesn't require a six-hour infusion. It's a shot. It will make you Brillyant for about four days, but I'll give you a week to decide if you want to go ahead. That way you'll also have a few days to begin missing your new superpower after it wears off. I'll call you exactly seven days from now, at which point you'll tell me *yes* or *no*. If *yes*, I'll give you a bank account number and you'll have 48 hours to deposit your first payment. If *no*, or if the funds don't arrive, you'll never hear from me again and the opportunity will be lost to you forever. Sound fair?"

"Sounds fair," we both said.

"Excellent. Well, I was taught to stop talking once I made a sale so I'll do that. I have a room upstairs if you'd like—" Rita had started to rise, but cut herself off and plopped back into her seat. "I only have one sample with me."

"Can we split it?" I asked. "Will that give us each a couple of days of Brillyanc?"

Rita brought forefinger to chin. "I believe the titration curve is more or less linear, so that should work. There's a bit of a ramp on either side, so you may only get the full effect for a day, but in my experience, that's really all it takes to seal the deal. Do you think a day will be enough to convince you?"

"We're pretty quick with the data processing," Katya said. "Which brings me to a question. Why not give weekly shots instead of a quarterly infusion?"

Rita was ready for that one. "The logistics don't work, given the amount of confidentiality and control required. Shall we go?" She stood, handed our waitress a stack of hundreds, and headed for the door. Not the first time she'd done this.

Walking through the lobby of the Hay Adams toward the elevators with two of the most beautiful women on the planet, I was struck by a feeling I knew I'd never forget. For those thirty seconds or so I was *that guy*. The man all others envied. Or so it appeared. As we passed a large wall mirror, I took mental photos for my album. Gathering the rosebuds while I may. If I was going to be spending the rest of my life behind bars, well, this was one record that was going to get a lot of plays.

The Hay Adams was, quite simply, the pinnacle of elegance. You can't trump a hotel that looks over the White House when it comes to glamour or prestige. Rita's room was neither glamorous nor prestigious, as its large third-floor windows looked out over a courtyard at other windows, but it was plenty elegant. Traditional decor in espresso hues, with a molded ceiling, and a queen-size bed covered in enough thick linens and puffy pillows to make you want to leap and bounce.

A sofa was positioned at the foot of the bed. Before it, the room's only light shone down on a glass coffee table. Rita led us right to it.

I took the middle seat, which wasn't optimal for talking. My relative size made me a wall of sorts between the women, as was my intent. Despite her charms, Rita was the enemy, and I wanted to shield Katya.

Rita set her small, pumpkin-toned purse on the table where it seemed to glow like a log on a fire. She flipped the gold clasp, and withdrew a couple of alcohol swabs and a Romeo & Julieta cigar tube. Noting my appraisal, she said, "Camouflage, always camouflage."

She unscrewed the little aluminum lid, tilting a filled syringe out onto her palm where it looked innocuous as baby vaccine. Then she asked the big question. "You ready to up your game? Ready to become one in a million?"

Chapter 74

Adroitly Ambitious

RITA'S INJECTION PROCEDURE was reminiscent of a phlebotomist drawing blood, except this was a deposit rather than a withdrawal. A small deposit. The syringe was just two cc's and I only got half. Katya was watching me wide-eyed the whole time, as though my transformation would be visual.

"That's all there is to it," Rita said. "You'll be a different person when you wake up in the morning."

As Katya and I switched positions on the couch, I asked, "Is there some test we should be doing to calibrate?"

Rita paused and looked up from the alcohol swab. "Good question. It's not a shades-of-gray difference. The change is dramatic enough that there's no need for a validated questionnaire like you'd be taking if this were, say, an Alzheimer's screening. You can test-drive your new neural performance any number of ways, and the neat part is that I don't need to tell you what they are. You'll know. Which, ironically, is a form of calibration in and of itself."

I was beginning to think this might be real. So far, I'd been intuitively assuming there was some trick involved. "How long have you been using it?" Katya asked, as the needle pierced her flesh.

"No personal questions. That's Rule Two: Complete Anonymity. You remember Rule One?"

"Absolute Secrecy," we said in chorus.

"Good. You'll get Rule Three when you show up for your first infusion. Or rather, on the way there."

"Speaking of which," I said. "I'd like to participate in the infusion event this weekend on the West Coast. I have a big presentation coming up in a week. Career making or breaking. So I'd love it to be Brillyant."

Rita mulled that over for a second. Looked like she hadn't received that question before. It would lock in a double commission check. I watched her struggle, but lose the fight. "I wish I could help you, but payment is required in advance. Since it's Friday night, your funds won't arrive before Monday. I learned the hard way that while many private banks work Saturdays, wire transfers don't post when the federal banks are closed."

"Suppose we were to make the transfer together, right now, using my phone?" I pulled my iPhone out of my breast pocket. I had prepared it ahead of time, as well as Katya's. Setting it on the table, I invited Rita to watch as I unlocked it with one-zero-one-zero.

"Ten-ten. Your birthdate."

"You really have done your homework."

While I logged into my numbered, offshore account, Katya extracted her own phone, pulled up a blank note, and offered it to Rita. "This will help. You can enter your account info here. That way, we'll have it for future transfers as well."

Rita's head moved back and forth between us. "You two really are on the same page." She took the phone, keying in routing and account numbers.

"You have it memorized," I said. "I'm impressed."

Rita didn't look up from her task while replying. "Wait till you see what you can do once you're Brillyant. Ten-ten will be way behind you." She finished typing and returned the phone to Katya, who set it carefully on my thigh where I could read it.

I keyed in the transfer order. "Since it's a numbered account, I put Alisa Abroskina and Chris Pine in the memo line." I presented it to Rita. "If that looks right, go ahead and hit the *send-funds* button."

She took the phone from me and studied it carefully. Not just the payee details but the website address as well. She looked up. "Looks good." She made a point of pressing send. Then she watched the transaction complete and returned the phone, which I slid gingerly back into my outer breast pocket.

"It's a good day for you," I said. "Two for one, with both signed, sealed, and delivered."

Rita returned a genuine smile. She was beautiful, and seemed sincere. "This brings us to our last point of business, a week ahead of schedule. Tomorrow evening at six o'clock a limo will meet you curbside outside Door One on the departures level of the domestic terminal at SFO. You got that?"

I repeated it back.

Katya asked, "How do we dress?"

"It doesn't matter. You'll be given a new wardrobe to change into in the car. You'll also be leaving everything with your driver. Jewelry. Cell phones. Everything. Anonymity is our first concern."

"That sounds kinda creepy," Katya said.

"Wait until you get there. You'll find it tremendously liberating. It's amazing what absolute anonymity will do for you. In fact, Alisa, for that very reason, I'd suggest that you go to the event here. Let Chris go to SF by himself. It's best if you don't know anybody, and nobody knows you."

"No worries there," I said. "We're not involved. Our relationship is strictly, shall we say, Machiavellian."

"As you wish. Just a suggestion, from experience."

"What if we have questions?" Katya asked.

"Ask them now. Once you go out the door, you'll never see or hear from me again. Rule Two."

"How did you find me?" I asked. "What made you pick me from the phonebook?"

"Rule One, Chris. But you should consider it an honor. It's not quite the Nobel Prize, but we're far more selective than either your employer or your alma mater. Anything else?"

"Yes. What do you do when people decline? Either after the initial pitch, or after the free sample?"

"It's never happened." Reading my incredulous expression, Rita added, "I'm very selective in whom I approach. I don't just look for people with sufficient income at the right point in their careers. I also look at character. I only approach people who are adroitly ambitious."

"How do you know if someone is *adroitly ambitious*?" Katya asked.

Rita looked down as the right side of her mouth drew back in a smile. Then she looked back up to meet each of our eyes in turn as hers glowed with intelligence. "It's a demonstrable quality. Picture a politician weathering a sex scandal. Or a CEO fighting corruption charges. Or a trial attorney defending a wealthy killer. In your case, Alisa, you hired a Russian hacker known as *Sciborg7* to identify and alter competing admissions applications at Princeton."

Katya was so into her role as Alisa that she blushed at Rita's revelation, while I let my eyes grow wide in wonderment. Rita had discovered that scandalous secret in just a few minutes. She had to be plugged into a resource that rivaled my CIA system. This added a new dimension to things, but I couldn't dwell on it now. "What would you do if someone declined? If they walked away?"

"And went to the authorities? To the police or FDA?" Rita clarified.

I nodded.

"Nothing."

"Nothing?"

"We'd do nothing because that's exactly what the authorities would do: nothing. What would they really have to investigate? No product. No company. No witnesses. Nothing but crazy talk." She canted her head and shrugged with open palms. "Anything else?"

She had a point. Anyone whose house had been robbed or car stolen knew that if there wasn't blood on the ground, nobody really cared.

Rita stood and we followed suit. I wasn't sure if we'd been foolish or brilliant, but we were one step closer to the truth, the truth that was trying to kill us.

Chapter 75

White Powder

WE LEFT RITA in her room and caught a cab to a Thai restaurant near Chris's apartment. Tam yum soup and a red curry dish to go. I wanted to get some non-alcoholic calories in us, and Katya was in the mood for spicy.

The wait for our order gave me time to confirm that we hadn't been followed, five minutes of which I used to visit the corner drugstore and make a few purchases. Confident that we were clean, we returned to our neighboring hotel suite with Thai in tow. "Feeling Brillyant?" I asked, while snicking the deadbolt into place.

"Feeling hungry."

"You go ahead and start. I want to check the prints."

Katya pushed the food bag. "I gotta see this. The soup will wait."

I removed a bottle of talcum powder, a big blush brush, and a can of compressed air from the drugstore bag. Then I gingerly slid the iPhone from my breast pocket, holding it only by the edges as I had when giving it to and taking it from Rita.

Katya placed hers on the table beside mine with similar care.

"I'm a bit surprised we got these," I said, delicately pouring talcum powder onto the shined surface of the dark wooden desk. "When I saw her using the cigar tube, I concluded she'd been schooled in tradecraft, but apparently it wasn't an extensive course."

I dabbed the blush brush into the talc, just enough to dust it. I'd selected the brush with the longest bristles I could find, but their grouping was still a bit dense. Using pressure as light as hummingbirds' breath, I swirled the brush around the front surface of both iPhones. The white powder revealed multiple partial prints on the bottom half of my screen, including a decent index pad in the right corner. As Katya leaned over my shoulder, I said, "That's from when she hit send."

Katya's phone had fewer prints, but we knew they were all Rita's. The jewel there was an upside-down thumbprint on the top, from when she'd handed it back. Satisfied with the dustings I'd applied, I held the compressed air can about a foot above the phone and began dispensing micro bursts through the straw, a half-second puff at a time until most of the non-adhered powder was gone.

Katya watched with fascination. "Wow! Looks good."

"White powder on black glass is about as good as it gets. I don't think fingerprinting was what Steve Jobs had in mind when designing his phones, but he got it right."

I put the camera on Katya's phone in macro mode, snapped a few pictures of the index print on my phone, then reversed the procedure and captured the thumb off hers. I used AirDrop to get both photos on my phone, and then enhanced the contrast. "We got lucky. It's better than I'd hoped. This will definitely do it if her prints are in the system."

"You think they will be?"

"She's got a British accent. If she's living here and hasn't been an American citizen since birth, she should be. We print most foreigners entering the country these days, and everyone applying for a work or immigration visa. Most professional licensures require it as well, although I'm not sure about pharmaceutical reps."

"Surely you don't think Rita's licensed?"

"Not for her current job, of course. But I'd wager she used to be legit. The pharmaceutical industry is famous for using sharp, attractive young women for reps. The way she talked about titration curves and validated questionnaires makes me think she's experienced. If I were looking for someone to sell Brillyanc, that's where I'd go to recruit."

"How long will it take to check?"

"It's usually just minutes, given computer speeds these days. The FBI processes about a hundred million fingerprint checks a year, so it's got to be quick. Their algorithms have gotten really good too. With latent prints like these, their accuracy is up over ninety percent."

I was navigating my way back through my magic CIA portal, typing while I spoke. "Why don't you get our tickets back to San Francisco while I input this. Then we'll be done for the evening and can enjoy our dinner."

I finished before Katya, and laid our food out on the table.

"How's a noon flight sound?" she asked. "Gets us there at three. I figure we'll want some buffer in case there's a delay."

When I didn't respond, she looked over at me. "What?"

"We already got a match on Rita."

Chapter 76

Dangerous Territory

KATYA'S FACE REFLECTED her marvel at the power and speed of the technology I'd employed. "Who is she? Is Rita her real name?"

I read from the fingerprint analysis report. "Margaret Rosen. Birthdate is July 30, 1988. Born in London, England. Granted an F1 student visa in 2004 to attend Columbia University. Granted permanent residency in 2014. At that time, she had a New York City address. Her employer is listed as Bricks, the pharmaceutical multinational. No criminal record."

"Anything else?"

"That's all the good stuff the FBI has, other than her social security number. I'm sure Homeland Security has extensive biographical files as a result of her immigration applications, but I'm not going to bother with that now. We've got a back door into their organization if we need it."

"If we need it?"

"If tomorrow's assault doesn't work."

Katya started in on her soup. "What did you think of her pitch?"

"I thought it was masterful. She sold me, despite the exorbitant price. I'd bet she really does bat 1000."

"But?"

"Her pitch was seamless, like Vondreesen's, but it was also fundamentally different from Vondreesen's. No mention of sun bears. Makes me wonder."

"Wonder what?"

"We've heard two entirely different reasons why Brillyanc is kept secret. Vondreesen's endangered-species explanation, and Rita's backlash-avoidance explanation. Both fit perfectly. Both feel authentic."

Katya set her spoon down and brought her hand to her chin. "There's no reason they both can't be true. They're not mutually exclusive. Perhaps they keep it simple, and just mention the one most meaningful to the recipient. Endangered-species for investors, and backlash-avoidance for users."

"Could be. I just wonder if we have the whole truth between those two parts, or if there's more. I wonder if the Russians are playing Rita, the way they did Vondreesen."

"I think you're over-analyzing."

"We'll find out tomorrow night."

"Do you think the Russians will be there?"

"You heard Rita explain the event. She made it sound like the party of a lifetime. In my experience, a person only okays that kind of expense when he plans to enjoy it himself."

Our conversation yielded to the consumption of Thai food and thoughts of what was to come. A mysterious meeting. A debaucherous party. A treacherous investigation. And the ultimate confrontation.

I still found it hard to fathom how completely my life had changed from one minute to the next, just six months ago in Santa Barbara. It was like that interrogation room had been a cocoon, only I'd gone in a butterfly and come out a caterpillar. Tomorrow I'd once again be walking into an entirely different world, masked no less, in more ways than one. That would be another cocoon. I'd either become a butterfly again, or never emerge.

"What are you thinking about?" Katya asked, with a mellowed voice and empty bowl.

"It's all coming down to tomorrow night. Exoneration, or incarceration. If they send me back to jail, it's going to be maximum security. The dullest inmates. The cruelest guards. The worst conditions. And no end in sight."

Katya's expression assumed an intensity I'd never seen her exhibit before. "It won't come to that, Achilles. You underestimate yourself. They've been sending monsters at you from every direction, and you've been swatting them away like so many flies. You seem to think it's routine, but I'm in awe. After seeing what you've done this past week, I'd bet against the sun rising before I'd bet against you winning." Her eyes were misting up. Her voice, quivering.

There was nothing I wanted to do more than cross the two steps between us and crush her body to mine. I wanted to kiss her and caress her like there was no tomorrow. But if I took those two steps now, it would all be over. Her emotions were high, her reserves depleted. She'd either recoil or reciprocate. Either way I'd be going into the most important day of my life feeling like a rat. I'd be the guy who made a pass at his brother's girl.

No doubt Katya would be similarly impacted. She'd hung in there as well as any covert operative I'd ever worked with. She seemed to have a nervous system welded from stainless steel. Bulletproof. But guilt and revulsion were entirely different forms of strain. They could bend and twist and deform. "We better get some sleep." With a wink I added, "Even superheroes need shuteye."

I drifted off, having forgotten something that would soon become unforgettable. I'd forgotten about the Brillyanc coursing through my veins.

Chapter 77

Brillyant Minds

WHEN I AWOKE, I knew what to do.

My mind was experiencing a clarity I'd only enjoyed while sitting cross-legged on sunny mountaintops after long climbs. My thoughts didn't stutter, or get hung-up, or repeat. They flowed.

Testing my Brillyanc seemed superfluous, but I needed to be sure it wasn't a hallucination. I started by trying to multiply our ten-digit phone numbers in my head. I'd taken plenty of math in college, but since graduation I'd relied on a calculator like everyone else. The Brillyanc in my blood didn't cause the result to pop up like it did on a computer screen. I had to work it out. But I could work it out. I could keep track of the digits and decimals without paper. I did know instantly that it would be one-point-something times ten to the nineteenth power, since both had 317 area codes, and 317 squared gave me 100,489. The rest took about a minute. Brillyant.

For fun, I tried calculating the square root of the product. Instantly I knew that it would begin with 317 — no great leap there. However, the next seven figures flowed as well, even though I couldn't remember ever mechanically calculating a square root before. That took about ninety seconds.

I went out to the central room, intent on retrieving the newspaper, only to find that Katya had beaten me to it. She too was dressed in a white hotel robe, but had also gone for the slippers. She lowered the paper into her lap to reveal tousled hair and a big grin. "I read the paper. The whole paper, straight through. My mind sucked up the words like a vacuum cleaner. Line after line without distraction or fuss." She folded the paper and held it out. "I remember it all. Ask me a question."

I took the paper and opened it to a random page. "What percentage of the US population–"

"One percent," Katya said, before I could finish, "is affected by schizophrenia."

"Okay. There's an article written by Bill Clinton's Drug Czar–"

"Barry McCaffrey."

Two for two. I decided to try a different kind of thinking. "Got a puzzle for you. You need to measure out exactly four liters of water, but all you've got is two jars and a water hose. One jar holds exactly three liters, the other exactly five. There are no markings on the jars. How do you do it?"

She didn't even hesitate. "Fill the five jar. Dump what you can into the three, leaving two liters. Empty the three jar, then pour the remaining two into it, leaving space for one. Refill the empty five, and pour what you can into the three. Exactly four liters will be left."

We continued to test-drive our new processors all morning, switching from trivia to the investigation as we boarded the plane and our stomachs started to tense with the knowledge of what lay ahead.

"Have you figured out how Brillyanc links to Colin's murder?" Katya asked.

I had been hoping that answer would just pop into my head. So far, no pop. "I haven't nailed down the exact motive, but there's no longer any doubt that it was some kind of cover-up related to Brillyanc. Given the way its got us thinking, this drug is clearly destined to change the world — and make many billions in the process."

"Maybe it was just money. Lots of money. Isn't that the oldest motive?" Katya looked hopeful.

I hated to dim her glow. "I don't think so. They could have just fired my father and brother. There would have been a payout involved, but nothing consequential. And it had to be something consequential against a backdrop of billions. Something that put everything at risk."

"But isn't that exactly what the sun bear sourcing does? If Colin refused to go along with the cover-up, he'd have put billions at risk."

I shook my head. "There had to be more to it than that. Sun bear sourcing doesn't explain murder. Confidentiality agreements would keep him quiet. Confidentiality agreements silence executives all the time — just look at the tobacco industry. Plus, they're marketing Brillyanc in secret, so regulatory approval and whistleblower protection doesn't apply. Meanwhile, the operation goes on. In fact, it appears to be picking up steam. Rita clearly feels like she's riding a gravy train that's got nothing but acceleration ahead. And given the way our minds are working at the moment, I can see why."

"So what then?"

I looked out the window, hoping to find the answer written in the clouds. It wasn't.

"Come on, put that Brillyant brain to work."

I tried, but just couldn't make the leap.

Speaking of leaps, the next thing I knew we were landing in San

Francisco. Put another way, we were about to leap from the frying pan into the fire.

Chapter 78

Squawk

WE LANDED at SFO with time to burn, so we swung by long-term parking to check on the Escalade. It was still parked where we'd left it. That surprised me. The smell of decomposing corpses should have drawn attention by now. I noted that the bay breeze created constant air circulation. Maybe the stench didn't have the opportunity to accumulate. For precaution's sake, we decided not to get close enough to check.

I stashed our Yates passports along with our iPhones at the baggage storage desk. That left us with just 202 area code burner phones in our pockets. Our absence of identification would raise questions if discovered, but the alternative was worse.

This whole operation was half-baked. I didn't feel good about that, but I couldn't change it either. Risk increased as prep-time decreased, and I'd had little. I was running out of time and cash and options.

Katya was drawing many an appreciative eye. Sporting the same royal blue dress she'd worn to meet Rita, she looked like she'd come off a catwalk rather than a plane. Like she'd be met by a Maserati rather than a black sedan.

"Do you think it's going to be one of those stretch limos?" she asked. "Or a typical livery car?"

"As long as it's not a black Escalade, I really don't care," I said, regretting my words immediately. "Sorry, that was indelicate of me."

"Better that I'm prepared in case it is." Katya was all made up for the big event. She looked so spectacular that when she flashed me a smile my knees almost buckled. "And I'm not worried if you're here."

We made it to Door One at five minutes to six. The area was plenty busy. Not Monday morning or Friday evening busy, but enough that cars were double-parking to disgorge departing passengers. Several of them were even black Escalades, but none paid us any heed.

The road ramped up to the departures level around a curve just before Door One, so we only caught sight of approaching cars a few seconds before they arrived. The opposite was also true. Since there was no place for a driver to wait without drawing a squawk from a surveilling cop, ours either had a spotter, or he was circling, or he was counting on our being there as the clock struck six.

A cold wind took the air temperature down to forty-five degrees. Katya crossed her arms and began rubbing her hands over her triceps. I ignored the chill. Truth was, I hated the cold as much as anyone. I'd just learned to switch off that part of my brain when in the field. I wouldn't let it register until it began to compromise finger function. Then again, I never wore dresses.

A stretch limo appeared atop the ramp at precisely six o'clock, its windows dark as onyx. It wasn't one of the obscenely long vehicles that could house an entire football team, but it was good for a rock band, and it maneuvered to a stop right before us.

The door opened by itself. An anonymous invitation.

My phone started buzzing.

I had my iPhone forwarding to my burner, just in case. And I had Chris Pine's home phone forwarding to my iPhone, just in case. I pulled it to my ear and answered. "Hello."

It wasn't the driver, or someone looking for Chris. It was Max.

I held up my left forefinger to request a minute while I pressed the receiver to my ear. Between the whistling wind and buzzing traffic, it was hard to hear.

Katya looked me a question. *Should she get in? Or should she wait?*

I swapped my left forefinger for the halt sign.

She grabbed the door, but didn't get in.

The police car squawked.

Max said something about this being the only time he could get into the lab, and wanting to let me know right away. I did the calculation. In Moscow, it was four o'clock on Sunday morning. I stuck a pinkie in my left ear and closed my eyes, straining to hear his report.

The police car squawked again.

Katya called my name.

I opened my eyes to see the limo starting to roll away. An unspoken message. Now or never. I motioned to her to get in. I walked toward the door, slowly, buying time. Having trouble hearing while unable to believe my ears. "Are you absolutely sure?" I asked.

The police car started to roll. The limo inched forward again, this time with Katya inside.

I jumped in.

The limo pulled away.

The door swung closed.

The call dropped.

Chapter 79

Rule Three

MY MIND WAS ALIGHT with the fireworks of revelation, but the limo itself was black. Black seats, black carpet, and black windows. We couldn't see the driver. We couldn't see outside. We were in a rolling blindfold, but a comfortable one.

Soft light emanated from a LED strip that ran the perimeter of the ceiling, giving life to the droplets clinging to a frosty silver bucket of champagne. On the wall, two fragrant roses in a silver bud vase shared their blossom and their scent. Directly before us was the most enticing feature of all. Perched atop the backward-facing seats at the other end of the cabin, two black Prada duffel bags displayed numbers embroidered in white silk: *204* and *205*.

A soothing but authoritative voice, presumably the driver's, interrupted the analysis churning inside my head. "Make yourselves comfortable. We'll be driving for a couple of hours, give or take. Somewhere along the route you'll need to get changed. Everything you brought with you, and everything you're wearing, goes into your bag. Everything. Your bag will stay right there until we reverse the procedure on your return. Meanwhile, your chairs recline fully, in case you want to take a nap. I understand it's going to be a long night."

Music replaced the voice. Smoky instrumental jazz fit for dark clubs rife with romantic tension.

"A couple of hours of driving could take us north to Sacramento or Santa Rosa, or south to San Jose or Monterey," Katya said. She knew it had been Max on the phone, and I could see her real question in her eyes. She wanted to know what he'd said. I was dying to tell her.

We had agreed not to say or do anything suspicious in the car, assuming we'd be under audio and video surveillance. But Max's revelations were too momentous.

"Or we could circle San Francisco, the drive an illusion in support of Rule One," I replied. "In any case, we may as well get comfortable."

I put my arm around Katya's shoulders and pulled her close, turning my head and burying my nose in her hair as though I was kissing her ear. "Max says Brillyanc is entirely synthetic," I whispered. "Which means Vondreesen's endangered species story was complete bullshit."

Katya turned her face toward mine, as though she were about to kiss me. Despite the circumstances, I felt a thrill reminiscent of my teenage years.

I could have kissed her, ostensibly for the camera. But she would have known that I meant it. I'm no expert on women, but I know they tend to be extremely sensitive about those things. So I gave her my ear.

She whispered, "I'm sure that changes things, but I'm not sure how."

My thoughts exactly. I was going to need the two-hour drive to process these twists. Katya was no doubt eager to analyze the implications as well. God her hair smelled great.

I withdrew my arm from her shoulder. "We've got two hours. Let's see what's in the bags, and then follow the driver's advice and take a nap."

I passed Katya 205 and pulled 204 onto my lap. The leather-tabbed zipper opened to reveal a red silk lining and black silk garments. Pajama bottoms rested atop mine. Katya's held a slip-nightie. "That look like your size?"

Katya ran her hand over the fabric. "It looks tailor-made."

Next, we extracted full-length robes, accented with red liners and complete with hoods. The robes were followed by slippers and masks that tied in the back. "As advertised," I said.

"Rita also said we'd be getting the rules."

"There are three," the driver said. Apparently the powers that be wanted us to be aware of the surveillance. *Not unlike the CIA.* "Rule One," the driver continued, "Absolute secrecy. You are never to reference, hint at, imply, insinuate, or otherwise indicate the existence of Brillyanc to anyone, anywhere, ever." He paused to let that sink in, before continuing.

"Rule Two: Complete Anonymity. You are neither to give nor solicit information which could lead to the identification of yourself or another. This includes where you live today or have lived in the past. It includes where you've studied, worked, or grown up. It includes references to clubs or societies or political affiliations. And of course, it includes references to family members, lineage, and nationality.

"Finally, there's Rule Three: No Exit. Up until you leave the limo, you can back out. Rule One still applies, of course, but you can walk away and make like this was all a fanciful dream. The moment you step through the door at our destination, however, Rule Two becomes compromised. There's only so much that can be done to protect anonymity, even with sanitized costumes and masks. We're only working with the most elite, and that means that there's a certain amount of fame involved. So crossing the threshold raises the stakes. You'll be under no obligation to continue paying the fees and using the product, but thereafter, a certain amount of surveillance should be expected. Enough to ensure that you're not disregarding the first two rules. Think long and hard about that before stepping out the door. You'll get the question when we arrive."

"What's the penalty?" I asked. "For breaking a rule."

The music resumed. Apparently this was meant to be a one-way conversation. And silence was the polite-society answer.

Chapter 80

Masks On

I PICKED UP my Prada bag while Katya toyed with her seat controls. "I'm going to change."

I started with the top. Jacket, tie, button-down shirt, all refolded neatly and placed in my bag. Then the bathrobe went on and the rest followed. The material wasn't really silk, but some microfiber that was both stretchy and resilient. The robe probably cost a good two hundred bucks. Everything fit like a suit from Savile Row. "How do I look?"

Katya gave me an exaggerated once over and grew a mischievous grin. "Here in the limo you look like a guy who rents for a thousand dollars an hour. I mean that in the best possible way, of course. At the party, I suppose you'll look very comfortable, and very rich. What about the mask?"

"I'll hold off on that until we arrive."

I reclined my seat until I was looking at the ceiling, giving Katya privacy. Then I closed my eyes and started processing Max's startling news and its implications for the journey ahead.

I'd gone into plenty of operational situations without detailed knowledge of the lay of the land, but this was extreme. At a minimum, I'd always had a location and a target. A person to be neutralized or liberated. A document to be retrieved or destroyed. A charge to be placed. A photo taken. A trail erased. Tonight I needed to identify the person in charge, isolate him without drawing attention, and then force him to reveal the circumstances of my family's death. All beneath the watchful eyes of men in black suits.

"I think Rita must have worked in fashion before pharmaceuticals," Katya said. "She certainly sized me up."

I opened my eyes and sat up. "Gives a new twist to the little black dress."

"I'll say. It's not just little. It's incomplete."

"Incomplete?"

"A friend of mine in college had a euphemism for it. She called it going out 'alfresco.' She found it thrilling, but it will be a first for me."

We reclined and lapsed back into contemplative silence until the driver interrupted. "We're five minutes out. Time for your masks, and your decisions. Rule Three. If either or both of you want to go back, just remain in the car. Otherwise, welcome aboard. Get ready for the time of your lives."

Katya moved back next to me, and we donned our masks. The eyeholes and nose pieces were molded but the rest was free-flowing fabric that stretched and tied easily. Mine was integrated with a skullcap, producing more of a pirate look, whereas Katya's was just the strip, pure Zorro. "Reminds me of the movie, *The Princess Bride*. Ever see it?"

Katya shook her head. "Seems an odd piece of apparel for a bride."

"Her boyfriend Westley was a pirate. He wore a mask like this. Said it was terribly comfortable. I'm not sold yet, but we'll see."

On that note, the car slowed and the music crescendoed. The driver turned and the road began to rise. A different timbre emanated from the tires, and my stomach encountered butterflies.

Katya grabbed my hand and we looked at each other in anticipation. Would it be a nightclub, or a hospital? A five-star hotel, or cabins in the woods? Would there be ten other participants? A hundred? A thousand? We'd mused on these during the flight, but even with Brillyant minds, we'd come to no conclusion.

The car crunched to a halt, along with the music. We heard similar rhythms coming from outside, as though the entrance to a trendy Parisian club lay ahead. For a few seconds we sat in relative silence, stewing in anticipation. The car rolled forward only a few feet before stopping again, like our plane had on the Dulles runway, and limos did at the Academy Awards. The ambient music became a little louder with each promotion. One more roll and the speakers were right there, not just in front but also behind. Then the door opened with a click and a whoosh, and we found ourselves looking down a candlelit tunnel.

Chapter 81

Two Blows

GRIGORI IGNORED THE FLEAS buzzing around his head. They couldn't hurt him, and he was having too much fun with the girl. He'd bid on Green, an atypically early selection from the rainbow on auction, because he felt like fucking a lawyer. Well, a law student, to be precise. This one looked like a younger version of the plaintiff's lead council in a wrongful death case GasEx was trying to settle. Grigori suspected it might actually be her daughter. Wishful thinking.

She'd proven to be quite an athlete in the sack, but not the actual daughter. Sobyanin, his new security chief, had verified her identity with a little sleight of hand. But then somehow her law school classmates had all shown up in his bed, wearing plaid skirts like private school girls. He wasn't sure how that had happened, but he didn't fight it. Quite the opposite. Did fleas buzz? He thought that was flies. With a flash of insight that made the school girls vanish, he realized this was neither fleas nor flies. It was the damn phone, vibrating on his nightstand.

He'd been dreaming.

He opened his eyes.

The law student, his forty-one-hundred-dollar auction prize, was there, but without her friends. Grigori studied her while his brain came on line. Sleeping on her back with her blonde hair tousled, he noted that her breasts were still young enough to resemble the building they were in. Looking up, he saw that the glass panes at the pyramid's pinnacle were beginning to clear with the rising sun, placing the time shortly shy of five a.m. On a Sunday. Who would dare to be calling?

He hit answer, and brought the phone to his ear. "Yes?"

"Sir, it's Sobyanin. I've got important news."

Pyotr's replacement chose to go by his last name, which along with his first matched the mayor of Moscow. While they looked nothing alike, they sounded similar, and that could come in handy on the phone. Otherwise, the jury was still out on whether Sobyanin was a good hire or not. Among other things, he didn't have Pyotr's sense of discretion. "Go ahead."

"We've got Achilles and the mathematician. They're in our limo as we speak, heading to the California party."

Grigori propped himself up on a thick white bolster. "How is that possible?"

"I don't know all the details. I just know the facial recognition program nailed them. They're disguised to resemble legitimate guests, but our software is the best in the world, and they've been within a meter of a hidden camera for the better part of an hour, feeding it data. How would you like this handled?"

Grigori was about to say something about bullets and brains when a painful memory gave him pause. A memory that still shamed him, and made his nose twitch.

He and Vladimir were in Brussels, back in 1986. Fresh KGB academy grads, number one and number two in their class, with a coveted posting and the world at their feet. Their job was classic human intelligence gathering, and toward that end they had befriended the daughter of the personal secretary to one of NATO's division commanders.

Alice was homely and rebellious and thrilled to be receiving attention from the two Austrian brothers. Especially the younger, handsome one, named Vlad. He had enough charisma to become a movie star, or a president.

They smoked grass, complained about their parents, and mused about what they wanted to do after high school. Alice wanted to go to the Sorbonne and study literature. Greg and Vlad wanted to be diplomats, like their father. A routine soon developed, where Greg would play Super Mario on Alice's coveted Nintendo, while she and Vlad snuck off to kiss.

Once Vlad had Alice locked away in her bedroom, Grigori would shift the Nintendo into autoplay mode with the assistance of some special equipment from the KGB's Operations and Technology Directorate. Then he'd go about the Motherland's business while the lovers kissed and the game prattled away.

His catch was usually modest — unclassified interoffice memos or routine correspondence. But before the director's biweekly staff meetings, they often scored valuable handwritten notes on agenda drafts.

In addition to photographing papers, Grigori and Vladimir also bugged the bedroom phone, a pushbutton model on the nightstand between the queen-size bed and the secretarial desk where Alice's mother did her off-hours work.

Grigori was in the midst of swapping out tapes when Alice caught him red-handed. She'd gone to fetch baby oil from the bathroom but Vlad had stayed behind because his pants were around his ankles. Her face made it clear she understood everything in a snap. Homely correlated with lonely, but not stupid.

Grigori had panicked and hit her upside the head with her mother's glass paperweight. It was just a single, panicked blow to the temple, but enough to render her dead.

Alice dropped to the floor with staring eyes and a nasty round dent to the left of her brow. The glass-encased rose dropped right beside her. Vladimir heard the double thunk and came running.

He too read the situation in a split second.

He too lashed out — with a fist to a nose, rather than a paperweight to a temple. "Idiot!" he'd yelled. "I could have turned her. I could have recruited her to work for us."

Grigori heard the echo of those words as he looked back and forth between the phone and the girl now in his bed. He asked Sobyanin, "Who knows about this?"

"Nobody, yet. Not even the driver. I'm the first to be notified when facial recognition gets a hit. In this case, I thought you'd want to be the second. I hope that was the right call?"

It was, but Grigori wasn't one for mollycoddling, so he left the question hanging. "I'll take it from here. You're to take no action. Tell nobody. Their cover remains intact. No one should suspect that anything is amiss."

Sobyanin agreed, and Grigori had no doubt that he would comply rigorously. The new security chief was well aware of his predecessor's fate, and appropriately acrophobic.

Chapter 82

Angels & Flames

THE CANDLELIT TUNNEL was really a tent, a canvas corridor, something the Secret Service would use to protect the president. The white candles that illuminated it were the size of paint cans. They flickered within glass fishbowls, bringing the corridor alive and beckoning guests down an enchanted path.

The limo's door closed automatically behind us as we stepped from the car onto cool flagstones, sealing our fate. Rule Three. I saw nothing but darkness behind and a big black door some thirty feet ahead. I expected the limo to pull away immediately, but it sat there blocking our retreat, waiting for us to move ahead while the music played, and the candles flickered, and our adrenaline surged.

Katya took my arm. "This feels like the modern reenactment of a fairy tale I read as a girl."

"I was thinking the same thing, except when my grandmother read it she skipped the part about Hansel and Gretel wearing skimpy black silk pajamas." Katya elbowed my kidney as we followed the path, descending below ground level toward a door set deep within a stone wall. It appeared to have neither handle nor knocker. I was about to say, "Open sesame," when it slid to the left.

We entered a dim vestibule sized about twelve feet square, with a second sliding door centered on the opposite wall. To the left and right, gold-framed dressing mirrors begged for our self-appraising gaze. Beside them, combs, sprays, and bubbling flutes of champagne rested atop Doric pedestals. As the door swished shut, a soprano voice greeted us from behind. "Welcome, two-oh-four, and two-oh-five."

We whipped around to see an angel emerging from an alcove beside the entry door. Our heavenly guide was an early-twenties model with long blonde locks and augmented breasts. She sauntered between us on strappy silver heels of dangerous height, an appraising index finger before her pouty lips.

The angel's outfit consisted of a white babydoll even shorter than Katya's slip, and nothing to mask her bright blue eyes. A long white cape of sheer material, crafted to resemble wings, trailed behind while she walked, as if blown by a breeze. "You'll use your numbers when checking in for your procedure, and when you're ready to depart. All in support of Rule Two, you understand. Just type your numbers into the pad." She gestured to a panel beside the door. "When they're ready for you, your number will appear on a screen over the door."

She began to circle us, slowly, with an appraising eye. "Meanwhile, feel free to ask an angel if there's anything at all that you need." After trailing a finger across my shoulders, she moved on to Katya. She pulled a pick comb and some spray from the nearest pedestal and began toying with Katya's hair, assuming the familiarity of a big sister, and demonstrating the skill employed in top salons. "There you go. Perfect."

She put her arms around Katya as though to embrace, but then pulled Katya's hood up into place. As I followed suit, the angel used a willowy arm to motion toward the pedestals and then the door. "Please help yourself to a flute of Cristal, and enjoy the party."

The door opened automatically to reveal a warm and fragrant space even dimmer than the vestibule, with no ceiling in sight. Smooth energetic rhythms issued from unseen speakers all around, enveloping us in a blanket of sound that gave me the urge to dance, relax, and release. Quite an accomplishment, all things considered.

Our eyes flew to a swirling tower of flame in the center of the room, and our feet followed. I knew I should be studying the room, but to do anything other than walk wide-eyed toward the flame would have appeared suspicious, so I went with it.

Surrounded by a cylinder of glass that rose majestically out of the stone floor, the centerpiece combined fans with revolving gas jets to bring personality to a duet of dancing flames. Katya took my hand and spoke into my ear. "Looks like a tango of sorts. I've never seen anything like it. It's practically alive."

It was the coolest sculpture that I had ever seen. But this wasn't the first time that I'd seen it.

Chapter 83

Unencumbered

I LOOKED UP to where the flames disappeared through the black ceiling far overhead. Given the contrast with the dark room, the glare blinded like the sun.

Katya reached out hesitantly to touch the glass. When she found it tolerable, I saw the same realization cross her face. I nodded back as her eyes went wide.

We couldn't risk discussing the revelation here. At least not until we had the lay of the land.

Turning our backs to the swirling flames, we found that the room was also alive. Our adjusting eyes picked up people all around. Most still wore their silky hooded robes, but a few were setting what was no doubt the coming trend, having shed their robes, or more. The fire gave a healthy glow to their exposed skin, and the shadows made their fit bodies appear even more toned and lithe. They were clustered in pairs and groups, some standing, some sitting, some in repose. They were talking and touching and drinking and watching — all confidently poised, but only about one in three striking me as entirely relaxed.

After thirty seconds of observation, I felt myself beginning to react. Made me suspect that they'd laced the perfume-scented air with pheromones. "Time to wander. It's only natural to explore."

Katya took my arm. "Judging by the body language, I'd say we're not the only ones here for the first time."

"I'd guess that within an hour everyone will feel loose as linguini. *Al dente* that is, warm but firm."

A labyrinth of interconnected rooms surrounded the central chamber. Some were larger, others quite small. Some relatively bare, others filled with furniture or toys. All had beds or chaise lounges or thick fur rugs on the floor, and each was lit by nothing but candles. Most were occupied by attractive people engaged verbally or otherwise in various forms of congress, some all boys and others all girls, most mixes favoring one or the other.

Meandering, we discovered that the angels really were at our service. So far, I hadn't detected their male counterparts, although the guest list appeared to be evenly split between the genders. Perhaps that was for the best.

I mapped the floor plan out in my head as we walked, avoiding eye contact and pretending to sip champagne. We were looking for one man in particular, while trying to identify anyone who might be in management. Plenty of individuals were wandering around like us, but the hooded bathrobes made it difficult to discreetly judge their age in the dim light. Those without robes all appeared to be in their thirties or forties. All were suitable for fitness magazine covers. The only point of interest so far was a second large sliding door, located directly opposite the one through which we'd initially entered. "What do you think's on the other side?" Katya asked.

"A few hundred lounge chairs paired with IV bags. I suspect it will open when the time is right."

There wasn't a staircase, back room, kitchen, or exit to be found. However, there were plenty of bars and small buffets scattered throughout the rooms, all with top-shelf drinks and exquisite finger foods. French pastries, ripe fruits, petit fours, and an endless assortment of sumptuous hors d'oeuvres. All were serviced by silent angels who seemed to appear and disappear as needed. "Let's see if we can find out where they're coming from," I whispered in Katya's ear. "Maybe they'll lead us behind the curtain."

Katya jumped on that idea. "Let's wait here for one to follow. The black caviar on those blinis is calling my assumed name."

I handed her a small porcelain plate. While Katya covered it with caviar canapés, I forked a few oysters onto my own, and discreetly emptied my drink into the mountain of ice supporting the mollusks. Between bites, she said, "I wonder if they're watching surveillance cameras, looking for glasses that need refilling and plates that need carting away?"

"Good question. Let's find out." I cleaned my plate and set it down on the marble-topped pub table beside my empty glass.

Katya followed suit.

I took her hand and guided her to the darkest corner of the room, stopping directly beneath the position I'd choose to hide a camera. I turned to face Katya and grasped her hands. From this vantage point, I could see both of the room's archways, and the buffet. I also had a view of Katya's upturned face, her scintillating eyes, and plump red lips.

Katya met my gaze, and stepped a little closer.

I only had hours if not minutes to get a look behind the curtain, find the wizard, and somehow either wring out a confession or gather the evidence I'd need to bring him to justice. This was potentially the last chance I'd ever have to avenge the death of my family. But all I wanted to do was lock Katya in a long embrace. I'd never been affected by a woman this way before. I felt drawn to her at the molecular level, and proximity made the attraction stronger.

Mother Nature was compelling me to sweep her up in my arms, carry her across the room to a velvety red couch, and make a memory that could get me through the next fifty years without regret, if it came to that. Or maybe it was just the confluence of stress and circumstance. In any case, the battle between the Archangel Gabriel and Mephistopheles was raging inside my head.

The pheromones weren't helping.

Katya released my hands and reached up with both of hers to push back my hood. Once it fell, she slipped her hands inside my robe and slid them out to the ends of my shoulders. Her touch was warm and tender and seemed to send voltage across my skin.

As our eyes locked and my throat dried, my racing mind managed to ease off the gas. Months of tension evaporated beneath her fingertips. My muscles relaxed, my blood pressure dropped, and the puzzle pieces swirling around my mind finally fell into place.

Katya must have seen it in my eyes, as her own face crinkled. "What?"

Chapter 84

Last Piece

I LOOKED DOWN into Katya's beautiful amber eyes, simultaneously relieved and distraught by the break in sexual tension. "I figured it out."

"What did you figure out?" Katya switched from one form of excitement to another just as quickly as I had, but left her hands on my shoulders.

"All of it."

"Everything?" Her voice brimmed with the unbridled excitement of a little girl with a new doll.

"All the broad strokes. Vitalis's closure. The murder of my family. The assassination attempts. The sun bears. And this party."

Katya grew a contemplative look that I was beginning to consider her trademark. Pretty fitting for a mathematics professor. "I'm sure the sun bears are the key. But I can't figure out how to turn it, so to speak."

"That's right. Ask yourself what would make you invent that kind of grand deception?"

"Invent?"

"Yes, Invent. Remember that Max discovered Brillyanc is synthetic. Why fabricate a story that's not just esoteric, but potentially damaging to your business? What purpose does it serve?"

"I don't know. Marketing isn't my thing. Maybe to drive up the price by reducing supply? Or give it cachet by making it rare or elitist?"

I shook my head. "There are simpler means of accomplishing those things. These are clever people. And completely unscrupulous."

"What purpose do the sun bears serve ... " She was getting frustrated, but she was also getting close. I could feel it.

"You're almost there. Bring it home. How did this all start?"

"With Colin's murder."

"Before that. Why was he killed?"

I saw the light go on. "He discovered something."

"Exactly. Now connect the dots."

"He was killed to conceal his discovery." She was doing the thing with her nails again. One, two, three, four. One, two, three, four.

"How does the sun bear story fit in?"

"It serves the same purpose. Concealment. It's camouflage.

Everything has been about concealing something."

"Exactly. This is all about a secret worth killing for."

"But what secret?"

Katya had hit on the billion-dollar question, but an angel had appeared over her shoulder as she spoke, quiet as a cloud. The angel gathered up our used plates and glasses.

Katya saw the white form reflected in my eyes and lowered her hands. "Should we follow?" she whispered.

I was torn. I wanted to get on with the physical investigation, but now that we were both on the same new page, I wanted to keep reading. It was helpful to talk things through with a mind as sharp, precise, and logical as Katya's. I'd never experienced a mental partnership quite so satisfying before, even with Granger.

I moved a couple empty plates from the buffet to the pub table where they'd look used. "Let's follow the next angel. I want to double-check my math with you."

Katya backed up a step. "What do you think the killer secret is?"

"It has to be product related. Brillyanc is the common denominator. My father and brother were working on it. Tarasova was working on it. All the activity surrounds it."

"But it works." Katya threw up her arms in an atypical display of emotion. "We experienced it. Max and Saba both swore by it. Colin was incredibly enthusiastic about it."

"Until he wasn't. You said he was confident one day and despondent the next."

"Right. He was."

"And shortly thereafter, Vitalis was shut down."

"Right. Vondreesen explained that with the whole sun bear, endangered species, gallbladder thing."

"But we know from Max that was a lie, because Brillyanc is entirely synthetic. So Colin must have discovered something else. Something *worse*. They made up the sun bear story to camouflage something more damning."

Katya was nodding along with me. "I like the concept, but what could that possibly be? As Vondreesen pointed out, the sun bear discovery was a triple blow. It decreased supply, and demand, and killed any chance of regulatory approval."

"It may have been a triple blow, but look around." I gestured back toward the main room. "They're still able to sell it for a thousand dollars a day."

"Oh my God, you're right. So Colin must have found something that would have prevented that."

"Exactly."

"But what?"

"It's a drug, right?" I prompted.

"Sure…" Her face lit up a second later. "Side effects."

Chapter 85

The Path

AS THE WORDS 'side effects' escaped Katya's lips, another angel walked through our room. Again Katya saw the white form reflected in my eyes. She spun around as the angel made her exit, and without a word we began to follow, our minds racing in one direction, our feet headed in another.

Within two seconds of the angel's disappearing through the archway to our right, we rounded the corner in silent pursuit — and bumped into a couple of the angels' male counterparts.

They wore black suits and black tees, and together formed the operational equivalent of a brick wall. The left suit spoke, his accent Russian. "Two-oh-four, and two-oh-five, come with us please."

I studied the faces of our adversaries, trying to get a reading on their disposition. The set of their jaws, the angle of their heads, and the tension in their necks told me they knew that I'd killed five of their friends.

Neither fight nor flight was an option. Not in that place. Not at that time. We'd have been running blind. Then and there, the smart move was to capitulate. "After you," I replied.

The left suit spun around and walked toward the back of the room, toward nothing that I could see. Katya and I followed, side by side, with the right suit trailing behind. It appeared that he was going to collide with the wall, but a panel slid silently aside just before he did. We followed him into a dark corridor lit only by blue LEDs embedded every few feet in the floor, like a luminescent highway divider.

He turned right, taking us back in the direction of what I'd speculated was the procedure room. We passed chest-high LEDs on the corridor wall every twenty feet or so, some red, some green. When I saw one slide aside just before an angel appeared, I understood that they marked the hidden doors. I couldn't tell how they were activated. They didn't slide open as we passed, so it wasn't a typical motion sensor.

Still, the door into this hidden corridor had opened before the suit as though sensing his approach. Thinking about it with my Brillyant brain, I realized that was exactly what it did.

If a person had an RFID chip, a radio frequency identifier, then the system could be programmed to react specifically to him. This would explain how the angels came and went through doors that were invisible and inaccessible to anyone else. My next thought struck like a crashing wave, sweeping me up in a moment of darkness before delivering me into the light.

Katya and I had also been tagged.

RFID chips could be as small as a grain of rice. You could easily hide one on anybody, and they had created the perfect place: our masks. With that system, they could track every guest's every move on the equivalent of an air traffic control console.

But why?

I answered my question as quickly as I'd asked it. Security, of course. Rule One.

A minute into our tour, the lead suit stopped directly before a triangle of three green LEDs. A panel slid aside after two seconds, revealing a staircase going up. Rather than entering, he stepped aside. "They're waiting for you upstairs."

Chapter 86

Burning Man

KATYA AND I both turned to face the lead suit. His angular face looked evil in the dim glow of green LED lights. She spoke first. "Who's waiting for us?"

He scoffed for an answer. Looked like Rule Two applied within the organization as well.

We turned our backs on them and started climbing. There must have been forty steps, each lit by a twin pair of green lights. After the door slid shut behind us, Katya grabbed my arm and paused. "Do you think this is routine? Something they do for all first-time partygoers?"

"No. They know who we are." I spoke low and in Russian, assuming someone was listening in, and trying not to make it easy.

"But how?" Katya replied in kind.

"I was a fool. Again. They ID'd us in the car. Our disguises are good enough to deceive people who aren't personally acquainted with Chris and Alisa, but they won't fool a sophisticated computer. Not one that's looking for us. Not one that already has our real identities to match against."

Katya clutched my hand as we neared the top. "What do we do now?" She moved around me so that she was on the stair above mine, putting our heads on the same level.

"We fight back — when the time is right. We hit them with everything we have, and don't stop until we escape."

"But we're not armed. We're in pajamas."

"That means they won't be expecting much. And not all weapons are physical."

Katya pondered that for a second, then she leaned forward and kissed me on the lips — a quick kiss, but one that spoke volumes. Before I could react she turned around, and climbed the last stair.

I stood still for a moment.

Then another shock came.

As I stepped onto the landing beside Katya, the floor began moving beneath our feet. It rotated us clockwise around a six-foot section of wall into the adjoining room. A room we'd seen before. A room with twin staircases, eighteen-foot ceilings, and a wrought-iron chandelier.

The disk we were standing on didn't stop rotating after a half-turn. We had to hop off to avoid being taken back into the hidden corridor. I watched over my shoulder with childlike fascination as the wall returned to its original position behind us — displaying a large painting from the studio of Raphael.

Two men were waiting for us when we turned back to face front. They were dressed in robes and masks, rather than black suits. "Good evening, Vaughn. Hello, Casey."

"Well done," Vondreesen said, removing his hood along with Casey. "If not a few days overdue. Let's go up to the library. I'll tell you a story."

With Casey bringing up the rear, we followed Vondreesen up the winding staircase and back into the room we'd visited a few days before. The lights were dimmer now, and the back wall flickered and glowed like one of the entryway fishbowls, bringing the whole room to life. "Looks a bit different downstairs, doesn't it? I named it *Burning Man* after the annual desert festival that inspired the design. To my knowledge, there's nothing else like it."

"It's captivating, in a Faustian sort of way," Katya said, her tone reflecting a robust emotional state.

"Tell me, Vaughn, why's it circular downstairs, but semicircular here?"

"My bedroom and private study are on the other side. You don't see through to them because the lights are out." He led us back to the central of the three coffee tables as he spoke.

We sat in the same chairs as before, with Casey in the last seat. After we'd removed our hoods and masks, Vondreesen lifted an ornate crystal bottle from the coffee table. He poured generous portions of amber liquid into four brandy snifters. "Louis XIII Cognac. They say there's a century in every bottle. I thought that appropriate, given the perspective required for what we have to discuss."

It struck me that while the elder statesman in Vondreesen was on display in high resolution, Casey seemed much less at ease. It was almost as though he had a sense of shame. Nonetheless, he kept his right hand in his bathrobe pocket, where the silhouette of a silenced pistol cast a shadow over us. I recalled that he had been a Marine — and once a Marine, always a Marine. *Semper Fi.*

Vondreesen nudged a glass in each of our directions. An invitation in lieu of a tasteless toast.

With everyone leaning in to grab a glass, I thought about snatching the moon rock off the table and braining both my nemeses. In less than three seconds I could have my revenge. Casey would probably get a bullet off, but it would be the last thing he'd do. Pyrrhic victories didn't work for me, however. And besides, I was most curious to hear Vondreesen out.

"Can I get a cigar to go with it?" I asked, not because I wanted a smoke, but because I wanted to disarm Casey — and see if Vaughn would hand me a weapon more substantial than a snifter glass. Eyeballs and nerve centers reacted poorly to contact with tobacco burning at a thousand degrees.

Chapter 87

Gorilla Marketing

VONDREESEN SMILED at my request for a cigar. I couldn't tell if he thought I was caving, or if he'd read my mind. He rose and retrieved a box, torch, and cutter from a side table. Romeo & Julieta coronas, packed in the same tubes Rita used to camouflage her syringe. Hard to believe that was a coincidence.

Katya declined.

Alas, so did Casey.

Vondreesen clipped and torched our cigars. "I was in shock when your father brought me the news about the sun bears. I got the Russian on the phone then and there. He insisted on meeting in person to discuss it. So I flew to Moscow."

I knew this was a lie. The sun bear story was a fabrication. But I decided to play along and see where Vondreesen took it. Information was power, and knowing one of Vondreesen's secrets gave me some. "Did my father go with you?"

"No. I wasn't sure where that meeting was headed, so I didn't want to expose him. By then, there had been enough indications that the man I was dealing with could be dangerous. But he made me bring Casey. Called him my consigliere, no doubt having learned about Western business by watching *The Godfather*." Vondreesen paused, as if picturing the memory.

"We met in his Moscow office. Or rather *outside* his office. He took us out onto the ledge circling his penthouse. We were thirty stories up and walking a few feet from an open edge while he explained the facts of life to us. He treated it like a walk on the beach. I nearly peed my pants. Unbelievable.

"Meanwhile two of his goons trailed us at arm's length the whole way. Those security guys you keep, uh, dispatching — they aren't mine. None of them." Vondreesen gestured toward the door. "The large gentlemen you met downstairs, Boris and Ivan, they're his. Presumably provided for operational security, but most of the time they're watching me."

I was beginning to wonder if Vondreesen really had been duped with the sun bear story. Perhaps the Russian had fed Vaughn the same grand deception he was now dishing out. Or perhaps Vaughn was just that good a bullshitter. His accent made everything sound so prim and proper. "If you're looking for pity, you're speaking to the wrong person."

Vondreesen continued as though I hadn't spoken. "The Russian told me that he'd fundamentally changed our marketing strategy. We wouldn't be taking the traditional pharmaceutical path, with its regulatory approval and physician prescription and insurance reimbursement. We weren't going to be marketing to the masses either. And we wouldn't be selling Brillyanc for a lousy two or three grand a year."

He paused for a couple of cigar puffs. "You know where he went with it. You heard Rita's pitch. But did you do the math?"

Katya was all over that. "At $360,000 per year per user, your revenues will top a billion at just 2,800 patients."

"Exactly. And ten times that amount wouldn't be a stretch. The Russian mapped it all out for me, step by step. We'd start with operational centers in DC and the Bay Area. Hand select the ripest three hundred souls in each, the top 0.01 percent of our target demographic, and make each the offer you heard. An offer they'd be fools to refuse." Vondreesen's voice brimmed with excitement as he spoke.

"The plan is to expand to another major metropolitan area every six months or so. New York, Chicago, Dallas, and LA. Then London, Paris, Frankfurt, Zurich, and Milan. Followed by Singapore, Tokyo, Beijing, Sydney, and Seoul. And let me tell you, it's happening exactly as he said it would. DC and San Francisco now have over two hundred Brillyanc users each. That's worth a hundred and fifty million dollars a year, most of it profit, and we've only been rolling Brillyanc out for half a year."

"So it's all about money?" I asked.

Vondreesen gave me a silly-boy look. "Is it ever about anything else?"

"But you have plenty of that. How much more do you need?"

Vondreesen took a long swallow from his snifter. "Let me finish. That was just the carrot. Attractive as it was to the businessman in me, of course it wasn't enough. The Russian knew it wouldn't be. So he had his goons show me the stick.

He had a big one.

You know those movies where the gangster dangles his mark over the edge of a building until he capitulates?"

"Sure."

"Well, he wasn't that kind to me. He said, 'I'll give you five seconds to think it over. That may not sound like much, but it will suffice — if you're in the right frame of mind.' Then his goons picked me up and hurled me over the edge."

Vondreesen mimicked a tossing gesture. "I was over three-hundred-feet up when they released me. That's where he got the five-second calculation, the amount of time required for a thirty-story free fall. It was dark out at the time, but the snowy ground below was illuminated by landscaping lights so I could see where I was headed. At least until I closed my eyes." Vondreesen shook his head and took another puff.

"I fell to within a few feet of an icy hedge, and then sprang back up. One of the goons had cuffed a bungee cord around my ankle while they were throwing me off. Had it hooked up to a device that looked like a fishing pole, keeping me away from the building when I bounced. The goons reeled me back up but left me hanging there by my ankle ten feet out from the edge. I was scared to death my shoe was going to come off and I'd slip loose. Haven't worn loafers since." He pointed down at his lace-ups.

"That's when he asked me if I'd decided to embrace the new marketing strategy.

"I agreed.

"Casey went along too, of course."

Chapter 88

Mission Accomplished

VONDREESEN LEANED FORWARD and poured more Louis XIII into all our glasses, although he had been the only one drinking. He took a slow sip with closed eyes before speaking. "Once I agreed to the new marketing strategy, we shut Vitalis down, just as we would have done otherwise. Your father and brother were none the wiser." He twirled the brandy around in his snifter, staring into it as he spoke.

"I had no idea the Russian was going to kill them. There was no reason for that, beyond paranoia. But as the rules have made you well aware, we're dealing with a paranoid personality. A megalomaniac with a cruel streak a mile wide." Pausing for a moment, he finally met my eyes.

I knew the big reveal was coming.

"He called me the morning after the accident, while you were still asleep. Told me what he'd done. Told me to put Casey on it. Told me that he'd impose the death penalty if you weren't convicted in court. No delays. No appeals."

I took a second to digest that twist. "You're trying to tell me that by getting me convicted for a triple homicide, Casey was really working in my best interests?"

"Yes, exactly. In that context, you can see that he did a great job. He effectively got the death penalty reduced to six years, for Chrissake. It was an incredible deal. But you turned it down." Vondreesen shrugged. "So Moscow ordered the hit."

I looked over at Casey, expecting to see him nodding along, vindicated.

He wasn't.

He just looked troubled. Preoccupied.

I turned back to Vondreesen. "You called Detective Frost after our last visit, didn't you? The minute we were out the door, you were on the phone."

"Actually, I called Frost the moment you arrived. Gave him an anonymous tip — for your benefit. Ever since your escape we've been trying to funnel you back to prison where at least your life expectancy would be measured in years rather than days. But that hasn't worked either. So here we are."

"Where, exactly, are we?"

Vondreesen set his snifter down. "I'm going to give you and Katya the same choice he gave Casey and me. But I'm going to give you a very different experience to help you make up your mind."

"What's the choice?"

"What do you do if you can't beat 'em?"

"Are you kidding me? You want us to join you? Team up with the people who killed my family? Are you out of your mind?"

"You'll be the one out of his mind, if you don't take me up on the offer. Literally. I snap my fingers and within three seconds Ivan or Boris will have put bullets in both your brains. So listen up!" Vondreesen let his words hang out there for a second. Then he patted the air in a calming gesture, sending cigar ash onto the carpet.

"First, let's get a bit of perspective. What we're talking about, in the worst-case scenario, is driving sun bears to extinction. Right? Setting spilled milk aside, that's the rub. Now, I've never seen a sun bear, and I don't expect that I ever will, but I'd still agree that their extinction is not a good thing. However, I'll ask you to ponder this: is it necessarily a bad thing? Does it really matter? Did you know that twenty-thousand species are near extinction, and that every single day dozens disappear forever? Granted, most of those are plants, and the sun bear is a mammal, but at the end of the day, doesn't it boil down to survival of the fittest?"

I wanted to end him right there. Show him who was fittest. But I held it in. The animal would emerge soon enough.

"Survivors do what it takes to survive. Are you willing to exert your positions as *prime*mates? Are you willing to do what it takes to survive? Join us and you can be a part of one of the greatest medical developments in the history of mankind, one that will help to catapult the human race forward. One that, for all we know, is just as ordained to be a part of our evolution as the printing press, light bulb, and automobile. Or you can cry over spilled milk, and join the sun bears." Vondreesen spread his hands, like a balance scale. Left, or right. The blue pill, or the red.

He seemed to genuinely believe the sun bear bullshit.

I studied the lit end of my cigar, blowing on it until the gray ash dispersed and the tip glowed red. The superficial radial nerve branches out from the base of the thumb just below the skin's surface. If I could get within striking distance of Casey's hand, I could take his trigger finger out of play in a single second. A few seconds more and I could brain them both with the moon rock. I took a puff and then met Vaughn's eye. "You killed my family. What makes you think I can ever get past that?"

"Two simple truths. First of all, Casey and I had no idea that was going to happen. It was a business decision made and executed by a paranoid mind. A changed mind. You've bested five of his men since then. Squashed them like high schoolers who walked onto an NFL field. He recognizes your talent. Appreciates it. Which is why he's sanctioned this offer."

I looked over at Katya to see how she was faring. Her expression showed that she was aghast. "What's the second simple truth?"

Vondreesen lit up before my eyes. His face regained color, and his voice resounded with verve. "Justice has already been served. The two guys you took out at Katya's apartment were the same men who set you up. They were the men who reconfigured the *Emerging Sea's* exhaust system to kill your family. Your mission is accomplished."

Chapter 89

Prime-mates

VONDREESEN'S WORDS hit me with physical force. They were a blow to my operating paradigm. The men who had killed my family were already dead. I'd killed them without knowing it.

I didn't feel any better.

A quote by Martina Navratilova popped into my mind. *The moment of victory is much too short to live for that and nothing else.*

Katya reached over and put her hand on my knee.

Apparently satisfied with my reaction to his revelation, Vondreesen plowed on. "This brings me to the cherry on top of our proposal. Casey can present the evidence required to prove that those men did it. His investigators actually did find video. You'll be free and clear, wealthy and healthy, and part of the new ruling class."

I said nothing, but sighed inside. *Free and clear!* Now I just needed a healthy resolution to the dead-or-alive issue.

Vondreesen resumed his pitch. "Speaking of the ruling class, it's time for my final slide, so to speak. Ever read Plato's *Republic*?"

"I think I read a few excerpts in a poli-sci class."

"In book VI, Plato describes his version of utopia as a place ruled by the wisest among us. Philosopher-kings, he called them. Imagine it. You'll be helping us to create Plato's Utopia. It's an idea that's been 2,400 years in the making."

I wasn't sure how much more of this crap I could take. The cigar-ashtray combo move was looking pretty good, but a more elegant play had come to mind. "Don't tell me you're doing this because of some grand vision of social justice, Vaughn. This is all about greed, pure and simple."

"Granted, self-interest may be our prime mover, but that's Adam Smith's invisible hand at work. Capitalism at its finest. Do you begrudge Sergey Brin and Larry Page their billions? Or are you just happy to have Google?"

"You've really given this a lot of thought."

"I have. Believe me."

"Good. Then I have a question for you."

"I'm all ears."

"What do you think your guests would say if you told them about the sun bears? You haven't, have you? We heard the pitch. How would they react if they knew the cost of their brilliance?"

Vondreesen chuffed. "These aren't vegetarians, Achilles. They're meat eaters. *Prime*mates. Top of the food chain."

"Are you sure?"

"Absolutely. Most of them already know. We stopped including it in the pitch because it proved unnecessary. Nobody cared. You don't think about the newborn calf when you order veal piccata."

Actually, I do pass on veal for that reason. But I was pleased with Vondreesen's pitch. It would convince some people, and probably most of the power crowd. "Okay then. Prove it. If they're still aboard after learning the truth about Brillyanc, then Katya and I are aboard too."

Katya gasped.

Vondreesen's eyes narrowed. "I'm pleased to hear that. With your training, I knew that you'd be capable of putting reason over emotion, but I didn't know if you'd be willing. How do you propose that we prove it?"

"Let's go ask them."

Vondreesen leaned back in his chair, studying me with his cigar dangling over the left arm and his Cognac over the right. The fall of his robe sleeve made it possible for me to see that he had something strapped to his right forearm. A weapon, most likely. "You know I won't allow the presence of the goons to spoil the party atmosphere, so you think that will provide an opportunity to get away. It won't. First of all, even if you could escape the castle, where would you go? We know exactly where you'll be one week from Monday. Secondly, your attorney here is armed with more than a law license."

"Yes. A subcompact with a suppressor. I saw the silhouette. What is it, Casey? You get the Smith & Wesson, or a Glock?"

Casey withdrew the silenced sidearm from the pocket of his robe. It was a clean, controlled move. Unwavering. He was comfortable with the weapon. Clearly more Texas than California.

"A Springfield XD-S," I said. "The 4.0. You must have custom retrofit the barrel to get the suppressor on. Nice weapon."

Casey didn't comment. He remained uncharacteristically quiet. Perhaps guilt had gotten his tongue. How about that, an attorney with a conscience.

I turned back to Vondreesen. "I want to make sure everyone's still onboard once they have all the facts. You can appreciate that this isn't something that's naturally easy for me to get cozy with. Putting reason over emotion will take some effort. Hearing reinforcing opinions will help."

Vondreesen took a long puff and blew the smoke out slowly before answering. "This isn't a banquet. There is no master of ceremonies.

There are no speeches. There's not even a podium. This is just a party that reinforces the elite status of the participants while reminding them of their vested interest in maintaining secrecy."

I began to speak, but Vondreesen held up his hand.

"Furthermore, I'm too familiar with your background to agree with any plan you may suggest without an appropriate measure of skepticism. Katya would have to stay here. Casey will see to her comfort while we're away."

Katya's grip tightened on my knee. I turned to meet her gaze. Tried to fill my eyes with confidence.

"That's okay with me," she said. "If that's what it takes."

Vondreesen tapped the burnt ash off the end of his cigar. "There's a group of nine here tonight. Elected officials. Members of the United States Congress, in fact."

"Your political connections," I said, half to myself.

"They've been with me from the beginning. They started using Brillyanc when your father was still running the company. Back before we knew about the sun bears. Before we got so strict about anonymity. Friends who I let into the fold."

"Why target politicians?" I asked. "Lawyers, businessmen, scientists, I get. But being a politician is all about charisma and connections. At least that's the impression I usually get when listening to some of those idiots blathering away on C-SPAN."

"Maybe that used to be the case. Maybe it still is in some districts for politicians who don't aspire to the national stage. But in an era when every word that ever comes out of your mouth can become a self-destructing missile, most politicians have to be on top of their game, all the time."

"Then there are debates and press conferences and interviews, during which the command of a tremendous array of facts can be crucial. And don't forget about all the legislation they're supposed to be reading. With Brillyanc in their bloodstream, these guys are actually reading the bills they debate."

I let my reply come out slowly, deflating tension. "Okay. I can see that. What are you thinking?"

"They get their infusions together so they can caucus. As a group, they're older than our average user by about fifteen years, and they've been to more parties than most, so they tend to be among the first to make their way back to the infusion room. They're probably already there, and at this hour we'll likely catch them before any IVs are hooked up. The solution contains a mild sedative, to make it easier to sleep with the IV in, so they won't have the angels attach them up until they're ready to sleep. We could go ask them to join us. They all know about the sun bears, and it will give you feedback direct from the representatives of over six million Americans. I'll even give you the nickel tour on the way so you can see our operation in action. Would that satisfy you?"

"Yes, Vaughn. A meeting with the congressmen would be perfect."

Chapter 90

The Tour

KATYA'S HAND was still resting on my knee. I put mine on top of hers and gave it a reassuring squeeze as Vaughn and I agreed to go fetch the nine members of congress. I could only imagine what was going through her mind.

She had said that she believed in me.

I was about to put that belief to the test.

We set our drinks and cigars aside, then donned our masks and hoods.

Vondreesen's willingness to take me without an armed escort confirmed my suspicion that he was packing something formidable up his sleeve. Turning to Casey, he said, "We'll be back in ten. Don't let her out of your sight."

Casey nodded.

Vondreesen gestured me forward. "We're going back the way we came." He wasn't going to let me get behind him. Smart move.

At the bottom of the circular stairs, the Raphael door opened before us as if by magic, revealing the hidden staircase.

"RFID, right?" I asked as we descended. "I bet you can track everyone in real time on that tablet of yours, using their numbers. That's why Boris and Ivan referred to Katya and me as 205 and 204, isn't it?"

"I take advantage of technology when I can."

Vondreesen guided me past a number of red LEDs and stopped us before one that had just turned green. The significance of the color dawned on me. Green meant the room was empty, or at least devoid of motion. The light emitting diodes made it possible to know if you could enter a room without being seen. Nice little parlor trick, quite literally in this case.

We passed through a series of sitting rooms, some in use, others not. About a third of the occupied rooms resembled cocktail hour at an exclusive members-only club. Distilled spirits, fat cigars, and lively debate on how best to master the universe. The rest were in use by groups who had shed everything but their masks. "People tend to start in twosomes, and move on to larger and larger groups as the night progresses," Vondreesen commented. "Like most of human nature, it's pretty predictable."

Eventually we entered the main room, where Burning Man was dancing. I looked up again, but even with the lights on in the library I still couldn't tell it was there. The big doorway at the back of the main room was open now, revealing a chamber lit by more than candle power. I headed toward it without prompting.

As we walked, Vondreesen began bragging. "We modeled the infusion room pods after the first-class accommodations on transoceanic jets. Each offers a broad leather chair that goes from fully flat, to seated, to any position in between. Along with a state-of-the-art entertainment system. We call it a *flight* instead of an infusion. Helps our jet-set clients put things in a familiar perspective."

"How many pods do you have?"

"Three hundred thirty-six. Enough that we could eventually handle a thousand clients by servicing one group a month, on a quarterly rotation. The way that averages out, it would make this location worth a million dollars a day."

Now there's a killer motive. "That's not bad, for a pension. Did you choose the winery for camouflage?"

"Exactly. With an estate like this, large parties with limousines coming and going are expected. That's something we think about when picking locations. I must admit, personal preference also played a role — picking Napa, I mean. Not a castle. At one time or another, every Silicon Valley executive thinks about retiring to a winery."

As we passed through the doorway, Vondreesen gestured dramatically. "Welcome to the flight zone. You can see that everyone flies first class." His voice resonated with pride. To give credit where due, it was an impressive sight. The room did resemble the first-class cabin on a Boeing 777, but was much larger, since all the passengers were 'up front.'

We made our way toward a back corner, where the pods had been rearranged into a circular configuration like tick marks on a watch face. Vondreesen reached out and grabbed my arm. "Would you recognize any member of Congress from a western state? I believe you're still registered to vote in North Carolina, not that most people would even recognize their own congressmen."

I pondered that for a sec. "I'd recognize Daniels. He was a California senator before moving on to the vice presidency. Now he presides over the senate. Not sure if that counts?"

"Well, I suppose it really doesn't matter. The point is that despite the masks, you're likely to recognize some of the people you're about to meet. I want to be sure you're completely aware of the implications of learning their identities?"

I understood Vondreesen's question for what it was. He was preemptively trying to assuage his guilt over killing me, should it come to that. He was shifting the decision onto my shoulders. I wasn't in the mood to lighten his load. "My understanding is that you'll kill me if I don't join you, regardless."

Vondreesen frowned. "Very well then. I'm glad we have that understanding."

Chapter 91

In the Balance

WE WALKED INTO the midst of the circular configuration. Nine pods were occupied, as advertised. One sat empty, like a dinner plate set in reverence for a loved one who had died. A lively discussion ground to a halt, and we found ourselves under the scrutiny of nine pairs of intelligent eyes.

"Pardon the intrusion," Vondreesen said, his British accent on full display. He was the gracious host again. He'd snapped back into that role like a turtle into a shell, and now he appeared bulletproof. "Allow me to introduce Kyle Achilles. He's brought us a bit of a special situation. One that would benefit greatly from your sage counsel. A question of ethics. Could I trouble you to join us upstairs in the library for a few minutes?"

A woman replied with a voice resembling the jazz singer I'd liked at Off the Record. She was probably in her early seventies but looked to be in her late forties. A vivacious face framed by chestnut hair so perfectly highlighted and coiffed that you'd swear she was headed for a national television appearance after paying some uber-stylist a thousand bucks. To my surprise, I recognized her. She was the one Kilpatrick said the DA consulted while covering her ass. The one who chaired a committee that oversaw CIA-related issues. Senator Colleen Collins. "We were having an ethical discussion of our own," Collins said. "It wasn't going particularly well. A side discussion might actually help to shake things loose."

To her right, a fit blonde man with a permanent tan flashed a twenty-tooth smile. "It's going to take a lot of shaking to loosen her up. But I'm game."

"Thank you," Vondreesen said.

As they rose, I got the impression that this was a group of friendly rivals — at least while the cameras weren't recording.

Vondreesen led us through one of his secret doors at the back of the room, avoiding a procession past other guests. He greeted each member individually as they entered the hidden corridor, and joked about burning off the banquet calories as we climbed the stairs, keeping the atmosphere light. The man really was a master of manipulation.

I was relieved to find Katya looking composed as we entered the library.

Casey's dour expression hadn't changed, but the room had. He'd rearranged the chairs to create a mini-amphitheater, and now sat in the corner with Katya.

Vondreesen led me to center stage while the Congressmen took their seats. With the flames behind me and the mob in front, it felt like the Salem Witch Trials.

This was it.

Time for the speech of my life.

My half-sample of Brillyanc was fading, but I hoped my jurors were still fully endowed. I needed them sharp and savvy. Modern murder trials lasted for months, but I'd only have minutes. Wild West rules, with the hangman present.

Vondreesen gestured my way, and I began. Since politicians were all professional bullshit artists, I went with the direct approach. No introduction. No small talk. "I understand you've been told that Brillyanc derives, in part, from the gallbladders of sun bears. An endangered species. Is that accurate?"

My opening hit them like an arctic breeze. Expressions turned sour, and the atmosphere morphed from convivial to grim.

I took that as a yes.

"I see you're all well aware of the implications. This makes Brillyanc a big secret. A secret my family was killed to protect." I paused in an attempt to meet each face for a second or two. Most eyes looked away, but a couple had gone wide at the mention of my family's death.

"The use of sun bear gallbladders explains why Brillyanc is not approved by the Food and Drug Administration. It also helps to justify an exorbitant price tag, while ensuring that you, its elite users, have a vested interest in keeping Brillyanc a secret." I began walking the semi-circle, addressing each audience member individually for a second or two like trial lawyers did when they were allowed to approach the jury box.

"It wouldn't do much for your reelection prospects if word of your habit got out. You'd get skewered from both sides. The tree huggers would condemn you for killing Winnie the Pooh. The bible thumpers would crucify you for using illegal drugs." All eyes were frigid now. The politicians' bonhomie replaced by steely stares.

Casey retained the serious demeanor befitting a sergeant-at-arms, but I was glad to see by the bulge in his robe that he'd shifted his aim from Katya to me.

Vaughn, suddenly looking no less nervous than Katya did beside him, extracted the tablet from the pocket of his robe and began swiping. If he was summoning the goon squad, I didn't have much time.

I returned to center stage and stood facing Senator Collins, holding her unflinching eyes. "It's all bullshit. Brillyanc is entirely synthetic. There are no animal products involved. To borrow Vaughn's phrase, you've all been duped."

I paused as a murmur broke out.

Casey tensed.

Vondreesen jumped into the gap. "Don't be silly. What would be the point of such a silly deception? There are plenty of other reasons to keep Brillyanc a secret. Everyone here benefits from our keeping it exclusive, and limiting its use to the elite alone. Am I right?"

A few congressional heads nodded. Others seemed less convinced. "Are you a chemist, Mr. Achilles? Or a physician?" The speaker had a rugged, weathered face. The Marlboro Man in his heyday, with a Texan twang.

"He's unemployed," Vondreesen said. "He used to be a spy. I thought he might be useful to us, but apparently I need to reconsider. I'm sorry to have wasted your time. Please forgive the interruption." Vondreesen turned to usher them back downstairs, but nobody moved.

I stood my ground.

Senator Collins said, "What was the point, Mr. Achilles? Why would Vaughn devise and propagate such an abstruse story?"

I needed to draw the other congressmen into the conversation, so I answered her question with a question. "When does a magician use his right hand to produce fire and smoke?"

That evoked thin smiles.

Collins said, "Were you up to something left-handed, Vaughn?"

Vondreesen said, "You've been benefitting from Brillyanc for over a year now. You know it works wonders. Your stars are all rising. As advertised. You of all people should know that talk is cheap and accusations are easy. It's actions that count, and you've all benefited from mine. Forgive me for this interruption with its spurious allegations. Let's get you back down to the flight zone."

As if on cue, Boris and Ivan entered through the doorway on the right. Seeing the crowd, they paused a few steps in.

While they looked inquisitively at Vondreesen, Casey spoke up for the first time that day. "I'd like to hear Achilles out."

"I too would like to know what he meant by *you've all been duped*," said a bald, bespectacled congressman, his voice a good fifty pounds heavier than his frail frame.

Boris and Ivan inched closer, rearing to be let off the leash.

This was the crucial moment. My life was in the balance. Would Vondreesen go with diplomacy, or war?

Chapter 92

Phone a Friend

VONDREESEN KNEW he was in a pickle. A sour one, judging by his face. His nature won the struggle. Ever the diplomat, he smiled and halted the black suits with the palm of his hand.

The room exhaled.

Boris and Ivan assumed an observation stance with their weapons still holstered.

All eyes turned to me.

With guns on both sides of me and the inferno behind, I returned my full attention to the congressmen before me. "The trick to telling a convincing lie is to stick close to the truth. I'm sure you've all heard that a time or two from political strategists."

A few nods, but only a few.

"It's true that Brillyanc will never gain regulatory approval. Vaughn was honest with you about that. But he lied when he told you it's because of the drug's provenance." I turned to look directly at Vondreesen. "The FDA would never approve Brillyanc because of its side effects."

Fear built on Vondreesen's face as I paused to let the revelation sink in and imaginations run wild.

Vaughn's reaction told me part of what I needed to know.

Up until that point, I hadn't been sure if he'd been among those duped by the sun bear story, or if he was one of the deceivers.

Now I knew.

Vondreesen was in on it.

That was bad news. If Vondreesen had been among the duped, then there was a chance I could have turned him into an ally — enemy of my enemy, and all that. Instead, I was looking at a winner-take-all battle. Normally I wouldn't mind that proposition, but Vondreesen had the benefit of knowledge, whereas I had only speculation.

I returned my attention to the jurors. Their expressions had shifted from anger to a mixture of concern and fear.

"What side effects?" the bespectacled congressman with the heavy voice asked. All eyes shifted from me to him to me again.

Casey moved a step closer to me and said, "Congressman Neblett is a neurologist."

Having an authority other than Vondreesen in the room was a bit of good luck. Neblett would be the one to sway opinions on medical matters. If I could convince him, he would convince the rest.

I was comfortable in medical discussions after growing up as the son of a physician. I'd also gone through extensive medical consultation during my Olympic-training years. Unfortunately, physicians worked from data, and I had none. I had to bet all my chips on the next hand — before I saw the last card.

I turned back to Vondreesen. I needed to see his eyes for this. They'd give me the read on that final card. I'd be gauging his reactions using the same biofeedback clues favored by psychics and fortune-tellers. With raised voice, I said, "Vaughn can tell you that, doctor. He's been experiencing those side effects."

And there it was.

The telltale flash of panic.

Vondreesen's upper eyelids rose fractionally while the lower ones tensed, the edges of his mouth pulling back ever so slightly. With those micro-expressions as confirmation, I jumped in before Vondreesen composed his retort. "He's in the early stages of Alzheimer's."

"This is complete nonsense," Vondreesen blurted. "My mental faculties have never been better. Brillyanc has no side effects. None."

Perma-tan jumped into the discussion. "Wouldn't our doctors have detected any side effects? I just had a thorough annual physical last month, and everything came out normal."

"Me too," emanated from around the semi-circle.

Neblett's head shake threw cold water on the crowd. "Neurological disorders like dementia and Alzheimer's are detected by comparative performance evaluations, rather than blood work. Those aren't routine yet."

"Could Brillyanc cause Alzheimer's?" Senator Collins asked. "Is that even possible?"

Again all eyes returned to the neurologist. "There's too much we don't know to say one way or another for certain. We do know that Brillyanc improves cognitive function. It's quite possible that it could be doing damage as well."

An idea struck me as murmuring broke out. I felt a fool for not thinking of it earlier. While the crowd digested Doctor Neblett's revelation, I walked to his side and whispered in his ear. Then I grabbed a phone off an end table, dialed, and handed it to Neblett with the speaker on.

Vondreesen dropped his diplomatic veil. "What the hell are you doing? You can't make a call. That's Rule One."

"Rules are made to be broken," I said, as the international double-ring commenced.

"Hang up! Hang up now!" Vondreesen walked our way, clearly intent on physically stopping Neblett, but Tex's hand reached out and stopped him instead.

The phone stopped ringing, and we heard, "Da, slooshayou," from the speaker.

"Max, it's Achilles. I've got you on speaker with a neurologist and some other Brillyanc users. Really quickly, tell us who you are and what you've learned about Brillyanc."

"Ah, hello. I'm a doctoral candidate in biochemistry at Moscow State University. I've also been participating in the Brillyanc clinical trial for the past eighteen months," he paused there, his voice cracking.

"Are you okay, Max?"

"No, Achilles, I'm not. I've run more tests and calculations since we spoke. I discovered that Brillyanc exposes the brain to extreme levels of oxidative stress, which is the primary exogenous cause of dementia, Alzheimer's, Parkinson's, and other neurological disorders. While it's impossible to predict individual reactions, I'd estimate that an individual's odds of developing a serious neurological disorder quadruple with every infusion. I've had six, which increases my odds four-thousand fold. So no, I'm afraid I'm not alright."

The room sat still in stunned silence. We could even hear the whooshing flames through the glass. Max's tone had been as convincing as his words.

I looked at Neblett. His face was grim. "I'm afraid that oxidative stress makes sense. It's reasonable to conclude that as our minds burn brighter, so to speak, they'll generate more 'pollution.' Furthermore, there are no routine tests for oxidative stress, so it would go undetected."

"Thank you, Max," I said. "Hang in there. I'll call you back a little later, my friend."

Neblett hung up.

Vondreesen yelled, "This is crazy! One student's tests aside, you haven't seen a shred of evidence. Real doctors get things wrong all the time. Believe me. As a venture capitalist, I know. This one's talking about conditions that can't be predicted and a pathology that can't be tested. It's poppycock. Ask yourself, whom are you going to trust? Some student six thousand miles away, or your own bodies? You feel great, right? Your minds have never been sharper, right?"

Nine chins bobbed up and down. Vondreesen had personal experience on his side, and theory rarely trumped that.

Chapter 93

Destiny

I LOOKED AROUND Vondreesen's study, meeting every gaze. Some were glowering, some closer to weeping. All verged on hysteria. The jury was still up in the air. Probably leaning against me. They all desperately wanted to believe Vondreesen. Their very lives depended on my being mistaken.

Vondreesen pressed his advantage. He spread his arms wide — a man with nothing to hide. "If what you say were true, then I'd be a victim as well. I've been taking Brillyanc longer than anyone. But it's not true."

A concurring murmur broke out.

I still had a card to play — or rather, a hunch. I took a deep breath, and did my best to speak with conviction. "Tell me, Vaughn, if it's not true, then why did you stop taking Brillyanc?"

Vondreesen's jaw slackened, but he recovered quickly and spoke confidently. "I haven't stopped taking it."

"Sure you have. It's in your eyes. They've lost their glow. At first I thought it was retirement, but looking at the gleaming eyes of all the users in this room, I know better."

"Now you're claiming to know what medicine I take? This is ridiculous."

"It's easy enough to test, Vaughn. You really want to take that path?"

Vondreesen didn't answer.

"Everybody, what's the value of Pi squared, out to ten significant figures? Raise your hand when you have it."

Neblett's hand went up after about forty seconds. Others began raising their hands ten seconds later. Within another minute all nine were up, as was Casey's.

"Time to speak up, Vaughn."

Vondreesen remained silent. He just stood there blinking.

"It's true." Collins' voice was now strained and weak. "We're all headed for the long goodbye. How could you, Vaughn?"

A room full of outraged eyes burned into the shrinking host like so many lasers.

"I ... but ... there was ... You have to understand, I–" Vondreesen turned to me. "It doesn't matter. So what if it's true? It wouldn't have changed anyone's mind. You of all people should appreciate that, Achilles." He stepped closer and poked me in the chest with his index and ring fingers, hard enough to hurt.

"Why me? Appreciate what?"

"Your namesake. Achilles. Besides his heel, what's he most famous for?"

"His choice," Collins said.

"That's right," Vondreesen said, whirling about. "Achilles chose to live a short life of glory, rather than a long life of obscurity. His personality is the archetype of everyone in this room. Nobody here would have chosen different if they'd known the truth. It's a lock. A glorious life versus an obscure chance of some disease. No contest. Hell, look at cigarettes. No glory in those, and the warning's crystal clear. Smoke these, get cancer. Yet people pay big taxes and slink off into corners to light up by the millions. I made you geniuses!"

Tex glared at his host. "You didn't give us the choice."

Vondreesen shook his head. "Don't you see? You never had a choice. Not really. It's in your nature. It's destiny." He spread his hands like a preacher.

Casey withdrew his hand from his pocket in a quick fluid move, exposing the silenced Springfield and surprising the guests. He pointed it at Vondreesen's heart.

Boris and Ivan reacted as one, leveling their sidearms on Casey.

Casey ignored them. "I want the truth. I want all of it. And I want it now."

I saw the calculation cross Vondreesen's face. Then I saw him begin to move. If he could take Casey out, Boris and Ivan would have the only other weapons in the room.

I had no great desire to save Casey. At the very least, he'd been complicit in my situation. But he was my attorney — and at the moment, one of just two people on the planet who both knew mc to be innocent and had the ability to prove it. Bottom line, I needed him alive.

There's no secret to shooting accurately indoors. Outdoors, where distances are much greater and weather factors in, you need to make all kinds of adjustments for wind, and gravity, and drag. But indoors, it's simple trigonometry.

If a true barrel is pointed directly at a target, you'll hit it. How perfect the pointing needs to be, and how steady the barrel needs to remain during the firing sequence depends on the distance to the target. The shorter the distance, the more forgiving the requirements.

There were only a few feet separating Casey from Vondreesen. It would almost be harder to miss than to hit at that distance — even if Vaughn was shooting from a tiny weapon concealed up a sleeve.

Vondreesen was already raising his hands from the palms-up position he'd assumed while pleading his case. He was just a flick of the wrist and a squeeze of the finger away from hitting Casey with the last surprise of his life.

And I couldn't stop him. I couldn't get to Vaughn in time.

I yelled, "Semper Fi!" to shock the crowd and alert Casey while spinning in a counterclockwise move. My right arm snatched up the moon rock from the table as I began a full-body side-arm pitch. I put everything I had into the throw — legs, back, shoulders, and arm — building momentum and transferring power as if I needed the rock to reach orbit. I whipped around until I was facing the inferno, and then released it as the Russians drew their guns.

Chapter 94

Royal Flush

THE HEAVY HUNK of moon rock shot from my grip as if released from a giant sling. It hurtled through a few feet of open space and transferred all its momentum into the enormous pane of curved glass at the point closest to the Russians.

An ominous cracking crunch rang from the glass wall as the rock's high-velocity crystalline structure overpowered the glass's static amorphous one, sending shock waves and breaking bonds. Then the rock breached the distal plane, releasing the vacuum and putting a whole other set of forces into play.

The vacuum's implosion sent shards of glass shooting out of the new hole like a plume of water after a cannonball strike. Shock waves rippled across the wall's remaining surface, shattering it like the world's largest light bulb, with a pop loud enough to shake books off shelves.

I continued swinging around, propelled by the momentum I'd generated. I hit the deck in the fetal position, while a barrage of glass shrapnel blew past me and into the Russians. Not all of it. My back felt as if it had been lit on fire. But Boris and Ivan took the blast like straw scarecrows in a tornado. Their clothes were shredded. Their skin was scratched and sliced and punctured and scraped. I couldn't tell immediately if anything was lethal, and I never got the chance to find out. Casey's Springfield coughed twice and both Russians dropped.

But each got a round off first.

Both missed Casey. One flew past his right shoulder, the other his left ear. They pierced the inner glass wall instead. It shattered like a windshield, sending cracks out from the 9 mm bullet holes like giant spider webs, but the wall remained standing, thanks to the infrared film.

I rolled forward as the Russians dropped, grabbing one of their bloody Glocks in each hand. Ignoring the pain in my back, I leapt to my feet with both weapons aimed and ready. For a second I was thrilled by my reversal of fortune — then my heart turned to ice.

Vondreesen had a gun to Katya's head.

He'd popped it out of his sleeve and cudgeled Casey before bringing it home under her chin. As Casey dropped and Katya screamed and nine members of Congress looked on in abject fear, Vondreesen yelled,

"Drop 'em, Achilles! Before this really gets out of hand."

Adrenaline had slowed time to a snail's pace, so half a heartbeat was all I needed to assess the situation. By aiming for the right corner of the fireplace, I'd limited the significant glass-blast damage to the part of the room where the Russians had stood. I saw a few flecks of red scattered among the congressmen, but no serious injuries.

Vondreesen had knocked Casey unconscious.

Katya was fine — other than having a gun pointed at her head.

I couldn't tell what the blast had done to my back, but I seemed to have full muscular control and wasn't feeling woozy from blood loss, yet.

Putting a bullet into Katya's head would get Vondreesen nowhere but killed.

I knew that.

He knew that.

I walked toward him without dropping my guns.

He changed tactics. He looped his left arm around Katya's neck and stooped to use her as a shield while pointing his weapon straight at my head.

I kept walking.

"I mean it. Not another step!"

I stopped with about six feet between us, judging that to be the limit beyond which fear might provoke an irrational reaction. I looked over the barrel of Vondreesen's gun to meet his eye. "What do I need to do to get you to release her?"

While Vondreesen tried to puzzle out an escape scenario, I shifted my gaze to meet Katya's wide-eyed stare, and added, "Do I have to drop and shout *rape*?"

As Katya's trigger word left my lips, I crouched to take my head below the immediate line of fire and sprang left.

Vondreesen fired once, high. Purely a reflex move, a startled response. His subcompact adding one more *crack* to the succession of explosions that had pummeled our ears since I'd released the moon rock and tipped the first domino. His next move would have been tracking my lunge to his right, where I was open and exposed and ripe for the plucking. Just a trigger squeeze away from no-more-problem. Would have been, were it not for Katya.

Before the echo of *rape* had died, Katya had bit down on Vondreesen's hand and swung her fist back between his legs with all the ferocity her fright could muster. Instead of swinging off to the right, Vondreesen's gun arm flew back toward center, coming home to cradle the jewels.

As Katya wriggled free, I brought my fist down on the top of Vondreesen's right hand, knocking the weapon from his grasp and breaking it free of the contraption that held it to his wrist.

He glared at me with fiery eyes. It wasn't Brillyanc burning there, but hatred unmasked.

Drawing strength from the emotion, he lashed out with surprising force, throwing a rapid series of left and right jabs reminiscent of engine pistons, pushing me back toward the fire. Not wanting to shoot him point-blank and risk a through-and-through that could injure someone else, I tossed the Glocks and delivered a haymaker to the underside of his chin.

He didn't drop.

He didn't scream.

He just kept coming like a possessed creature that had to let its demon out. Left-right-left-right. Punches with poor aim, but surprising force and relentless fury.

I absorbed the blows and timed my move to grab his recoiling left wrist with both hands. Planting my heels as his right fist glanced off my shoulder, I swung Vaughn around like an Olympic hammer, using his own momentum against him while throwing him off balance. Releasing my grip at the end of a forceful three-quarter turn, I sent him flying backwards into the inner glass wall at the point where the Russians' bullets had struck.

He slammed into it with his shoulders and kept right on going, the shattered glass caving in around him, the film and flame turning it into a hot crystalline hammock. For a long second Vaughn hung there like an enormous fly embedded in the windshield, startled by his situation and shocked at having survived the impact, but unable to extricate himself.

As the room looked on with rapt fascination, the added strain ripped the top of the wall free of the frame and gravity took over. Everyone gasped as the king of the castle plunged backward into the flames.

Chapter 95

Not Over

VONDREESEN'S SCREAMS CRESCENDOED, and then ceased like a phone that stopped ringing. The cessation exposed a cacophony of distressed mechanical noise. As my imagination filled in the picture, the flames changed color and smoke started billowing forth.

Everyone who had moved closer in a morbid trance now recoiled back from the smoke and the smell.

Then the Burning Man extinguished, the grotesque sounds stopped, and the heat subsided.

I looked over to see Casey beside a control panel on the wall. He'd flipped a switch.

He was standing with a dazed look on his face and the Springfield by his side. I had no idea what his next move would be, so I closed the gap with three quick strides and grabbed the weapon by its warm suppressor.

Casey didn't resist.

He let the Springfield slip into my hand.

I wasn't sure if that was a result of shock, or a tactical move. By some counts, he was next in line for a bullet.

I slapped his shoulder with my left hand as men sometimes do, and turned my attention to Katya. She was sitting in the same place she'd landed after sinking her teeth into Vaughn. I walked over and held out my free hand. She took it and I pulled her up into my arms. "You did it again, Katya. That combination move of yours is amazing."

"Promise me that will be the last time it's required."

"I can't promise until this is over. But I can hope."

"What do you mean, until it's over? It is over. Vondreesen is dead."

Before I could respond, Perma-tan shouted over the ruckus, authority in his voice. "Order! Order, everyone! Take your seats. There are decisions to make, and actions to take."

"Congressman Chip Tanner," Casey said, stepping over beside us. I turned to see lucid eyes. His moment of shock had passed. Semper Fi.

Tanner addressed his colleagues with a voice calm enough to quiet a child, but resolute enough to start a war. "What we've seen and heard tonight doesn't change the rules. We still need to maintain absolute secrecy and complete anonymity. Perhaps now more than ever. Are we agreed?"

A murmur of assent and a flourish of nods followed. Then a lone voice of dissent rose from the crowd. It came from an Asian woman who had not previously spoken. She was the group's youngest member, by my estimation. "I don't see how that's possible. We've witnessed three homicides. There's going to be an investigation. We'll have to give testimony."

"No point in any of that," Tex said. "Justice has been served. All we'd be doing is detracting from press coverage of issues that matter, and wasting taxpayer money."

"But we'll be abetting murder after the fact," she pressed. "We could be prosecuted."

Tanner wagged a finger. "With this many members of Congress involved, it's a national security issue. We're obligated to keep it quiet."

"If national security doesn't work for you, consider this," Neblett said. "If word does get out, the leadership will have no choice but to distance itself from us. We'll never see public office again, and we can forget about lobbying, consulting, and speaking engagements. We'll all become pariahs. And let's not forget the executive involvement. To quote the distinguished gentleman from Texas, what would be the point?"

Seven heads nodded back at the junior congresswoman as she looked around. She raised her chin. "I'll bow to your greater wisdom."

Senator Collins picked up the ball. "I propose that we plan to leave here in the morning, the same as always."

She turned to Casey. "Mr. McCallum, to use the appropriate euphemism, are you capable of cleaning up this mess? If we can count on you for that, it will give us a three-month window to deal with the big picture. Something I suspect Mr. Achilles will be keen to help us with."

For my benefit, Senator Collins confirmed what I already knew from Kilpatrick. "Santa Barbara is part of my constituency, and the DA is a personal friend. I'm aware of your predicament. And your history of national service."

Casey was raring to help. "First thing I'll need to do is confirm that nobody downstairs saw what happened. If anyone did, I'll remind them of the rules. Then I'll see to the cleanup."

"I'm with you, partner," Tex offered, walking over to join Casey.

Casey asked, "Any suggestions on disposal?"

I mulled that one for a few seconds, then leaned in to speak with a quiet voice. "I'm no horticulturist, but given that this is an active vineyard of considerable size, I'm guessing there's a fire pit for disposing of all the dead vines. Probably a woodchipper too."

Casey grimaced, but then swallowed it. Semper Fi.

"Look on the bright side," I said. "It's not snowing."

"What?

Tex got the movie reference, and put an arm around Casey's shoulder. "The woodchipper scene from *Fargo*."

Recognizing that my attempt to lighten the mood was probably ill-conceived, I moved to change the subject. Picking Vondreesen's tablet off the floor, I turned to Casey. "Can you unlock this?"

"Try 1999."

"A reminder of the good old days?"

Casey shook his head. "The year Vaughn's net worth went from seven figures to eight. He called it his 'no thanks' year, because with ten million in the bank, he would forever be free to do whatever he wanted."

I punched in 1999.

It worked.

As Casey and Tex set about cleaning up, I went to *settings* and switched the tablet's auto-lock feature to *never*.

I turned back to Katya. "I'm going to summon Melanie, the woman who served us coffee during our first visit. We've got to figure out if she's an asset, or a loose end."

"How could she be an asset?"

"For starters, she'll know if Boris and Ivan are the only enforcers, or if we've got more suits to dispatch. Also, we could use her help to clean up the mess. Both here and now, and then later with the bigger picture."

"But why? Why clean up at all? Isn't this perfect? Isn't this all the evidence you'll ever need to get out of jail? Especially with what you told me about Casey."

"You're right. I have what I came here for. But the picture has changed. It's grown much larger, much more devious and complex. To make things right, I've got to go back to Russia, back to where this all began."

Chapter 96

Angels

AN HOUR LATER, the congressmen were back in their pods, ostensibly playing along as though nothing had happened, but no doubt whispering up a storm.

Katya and I were on our way back to the library to regroup with Casey after a bit of first aid. I'd taken thirty-one pieces of glass shrapnel in the implosion. Fortunately, none of it had cut too deep. Katya had cleaned up my back with a pair of tweezers and a bottle of hydrogen peroxide. I'd be sleeping on my stomach for a few days, but it would heal without loss of functionality.

"We need to talk," Casey said by way of a greeting.

"You're damn right we do, but first things first. How's containment looking?"

"Six guests observed the barbecue downstairs. Tex and I have sworn them to silence. We put a little fear of the Almighty into them as well, in case they got second thoughts. You get the Russian situation figured out?"

"Melanie confirmed that Boris and Ivan were the only suits on the premises."

"That's good news. What's her personal perspective on recent developments?"

"Melanie appreciates both the legal precariousness of her position, and the danger she potentially faces at the hands of the Russians. She's eager to help in any way she can."

Casey smiled. "I bet she is."

"Now, if you don't mind, I need those details that Vaughn mentioned. The proof of my innocence."

"Don't worry about that. I mean, I've got you covered. Believe me. So long as you clean things up in Russia before the Russians start cleaning things up here, you've got nothing to worry about."

I studied Casey's face. He seemed earnest. Relaxed eyes, steady gaze, no tension around his mouth. Plus, he'd spoken pretty definitively when he pulled the trigger on Boris and Ivan.

"There's something else we need to talk about," Casey continued. "Something very important."

He motioned to the coffee table, where the five-thousand-dollar bottle of Louis XIII had miraculously remained intact, along with two of the four snifters. One still bore the lip marks of a dead man, the other remained untouched. "I'm ready for my drink now." He picked up the clean glass and took a long sip with closed eyes.

"I was so thrilled with Brillyanc," he began, his tone wistful. "I thought it was the best thing that ever happened to me. It was like my brain went from six cylinders to twelve. I reveled in the power of my own mind. I used to rev it all the time, metaphorically speaking, like it was a Lamborghini. Just like you did with the Pi multiplication bit. A brilliant move, by the way."

He took another sip and shook his head. "I should have known it was too good to be true."

He lifted his gaze and locked his eyes on mine. "And the truth is even worse than you think."

I saw Katya dry swallow at Casey's revelation.

He plowed on. "But let's get the Russian cleanup out of the way before we tackle that."

"Is Barsukov behind Brillyanc, or Antipin?" I asked, referencing GasEx's Chairman and its CEO. "I'd be inclined to say Barsukov, since he seems to have the right personality, but then Antipin is a Vondreesen clone. An elder statesman with charm to burn. Seems to me they're much more likely to be friends."

"It's Grigori Barsukov. He's been one of Russia's leading angel investors for the last ten years, which is about how long he's known Vaughn. They live on different corners of the planet, but travel in the same small, elite circles. Grigori isn't charming like Vondreesen — far from it — but he's got his own sort of charisma. Kind of an evil magnetism. And he's very slick. He's also very well-protected."

Casey put his arm on my shoulder. "I don't know how you're going to get to him. But I'm sure he'll kill us all if you don't find a way."

Chapter 97

Priorities

CASEY LOOKED GENUINELY CONCERNED. Having seen Grigori's headquarters complex, I could understand why. The GasEx chairman worked in a fortress. "You said you met him at his office. Did he happen to invite you to his home as well, given that Vaughn is an old friend and you flew halfway around the world?"

Casey raised his brows. "We did, but not because Grigori is a gracious host. He lives in his office. Literally. Like the US President lives and works at the White House. I think he enjoys the analogy. He cultivates it. He refers to his office as the East Wing and his residence as the West Wing."

"Isn't it supposed to be the other way around? Doesn't the President work in the West Wing?"

"Remember where he comes from. Grigori is KGB. East versus West. The reversal is deliberate, I'm quite sure. And as long as we're on the topic and looking at parallels, I'm sure you know what Kremlin means in English?"

"Castle," Katya said.

"Right. And that's where Grigori lives and works. His so-called Rocket is a modern castle. A fortress. He's protected against assault by a wall, a gate, guards, and a lofty perch."

"We've seen it," I said. "At least from the gate. So I've got that picture in my head. Did you get a look at the security inside?"

"Not really. He brought us in by helicopter. When you're flying in and looking down, a fortress is what comes to mind. There's the main building with the pyramid on top, like the Washington Monument would look if topped with glass, but then each corner has its own square tower attached, making the footprint look like the classic X of a castle. Also there's this." Casey gestured to the room they were sitting in. "He chose literal castles for his American outposts."

"The Washington parties are also in a castle?" Katya asked.

"I haven't been there, but I've seen a picture. It's an old limestone manor atop a hill on a large piece of secluded real estate. Definitely something that would both make William the Conqueror smile, and impress modern Washington's elite. Which brings me to the main topic of our discussion."

My mind had been working that one in the background ever since Casey divulged that the truth was worse than we thought. "This is about the *executive involvement* Senator Collins mentioned, isn't it? It's about the empty tenth pod."

Casey gave me a grim look. "That's right. Before he became the Vice President, Daniels was the junior senator from California. And before he ran for his first election, he was a friend of Vaughn's. He was also one of the very first Brillyanc users."

"And he's still using?"

"He is. Vaughn visits him once a quarter. Brings Brillyanc with him. He spends the night at the vice president's home, at the Naval Observatory.

"So you see, this story can't get out. It really is a matter of national security. If the press got word, there would be a major global scandal. Members of both the executive and legislative branches of government using a mind-altering drug that causes dementia. The Brillyanc scandal would dwarf Watergate and Benghazi."

"And Barsukov knows that Daniels is using," Katya said. "Which means so does President Korovin. Which means the Kremlin has leverage over the White House. That's what all this is about. That's what the suits were sent here to protect. It's not about billions in drug sales. It's about the global balance of power."

"Precisely," Casey said, sounding very lawyerly. "I knew about the Russians, of course. But I had no clue about the dementia. Not until your revelation. But the second you mentioned it, everything fell into place. A benefit of Brillyanc itself, ironically."

Casey drained his glass and set it down with a bit of flair. "I always thought this was about money. It is potentially worth billions, and that's the way Silicon Valley guys think. But as Katya noted, this is really about power, power at the geopolitical level. We're talking influence worth trillions. The chance to change history, move armies, and relocate borders."

"That was the plan all along," I said, speaking to myself as much as the others as the big picture gained resolution in my head. "I wondered why they'd gone with Washington, rather than New York City. I had assumed they wanted to learn from a smaller market before going for the Big Apple, but now I know better." I felt my heart skip a beat as the next shoe dropped. "Wait a minute. If there are nine members of Congress coming to Vaughn's parties, how many more have been snared by the Washington office?"

"I don't know," Casey said. "But if you don't kill Grigori, I'm afraid the whole world is going to find out."

Chapter 98

Deadly Habit

CASEY AND MELANIE agreed to maintain the impression that the great Vaughn Vondreesen was still alive. I had no doubt that they'd work tirelessly and attentively. Both their lives were on the line.

With Vondreesen's iPad and her long familiarity with his style, Melanie would be an effective impersonator in the electronic world. Casey, as Vondreesen's lawyer and consigliere, would handle his phone.

They only had to sustain the illusion for a week.

My trial was set to start next Monday, and I planned to have Grigori Barsukov buried by then. How, I hadn't a clue.

To do our part to maintain the illusion, Katya and I spent the rest of the night in our assigned pods, draining our Brillyanc into the toilet rather than our veins.

I spent much of it on Vaughn's tablet, studying his email. I found one that had been trashed but not emptied during the automatic daily purge. It was from someone named *Archangel* at a popular Russian provider. It had arrived just hours before, and said simply, "Let me know how the recruitment goes." I replied for Vaughn with, "Achilles is aboard, but we lost Boris and Ivan." Hopefully, that would buy us time. Assuming *Archangel* was Grigori. If not, Archangel would assume Vaughn was confused.

There were no calls from Russian numbers in the log on Vondreesen's phone. That was disappointing, but given Grigori's ex-KGB status, I knew he'd likely use a masking relay, so I wasn't discouraged.

In the morning, we left the party as numbers 204 and 205, returning to SFO using the same limo in which we'd come. We retrieved our documents and cell phones from storage, and took a cab into the city.

Now we were holed up in a suite at a large hotel, planning my attack on Grigori Barsukov. It wasn't going as expected.

Try to focus as I might, I was preoccupied with thoughts of Katya.

She'd kissed me just before our final meeting with Vaughn, and despite being a man, I could tell there was something in it. Then we'd spent the night in pods, and slept for the whole limo ride. Tonight, however, was going to be very different. We were looking at a big fat fork in the road. Either we'd sleep together, or we'd drift apart.

I'd punted on the decision, to the extent that it was mine to make, by getting us a two-bedroom suite. We had momentum in that regard from our stay in Washington, so the choice had not been overly awkward. I hoped. I might have detected a flinch.

"There's quite a bit about him online, both traditional press coverage and blogs." Katya was studying the man, while I was learning what I could about his GasEx office. "So far, I've only found one reference to his habits. It's in an article about a trendy club called, get this, Angels on Fire. It's a strip club on the Garden Ring. They're writing about him because apparently he flies in for it every week by helicopter. Come look at this." Katya pointed to her screen.

I walked around to her side of the table. We'd picked up a couple of MacBooks to make our round-the-clock research easier, and we had them opened back-to-back, as if we were playing Battleship.

Casey had wired a quarter-million dollars into my account to give the hunting expedition virtually unlimited resources. He'd also chartered us a jet, more for the trip out of Russia than the trip in. If I wasn't in the Santa Barbara County Courtroom at nine the following Monday morning, I'd be forfeiting my ten-million-dollar bail. With a mission as tight as this one was going to be, the hours saved by flying private might make all the difference.

The relaxed security that came with flying private would be a blessing too.

If it got to the point where I had to decide between completing the mission or making it to court, I wasn't sure which way I'd go. I was resolved not to let it come to that. Therefore Grigori had at most one week to live. His next trip to Angels on Fire was going to be his last.

Chapter 99

Gusts and Thermals

THE DRAMATIC PICTURE displayed on Katya's screen captured a wiry man in formal dress stepping from a helicopter beneath a red neon Angels on Fire sign. The caption beneath the photo read, "Pouring Gas on the Flames. GasEx Chairman Grigori Barsukov's secret indulgence."

Katya summarized the story. "Every Saturday, Angels on Fire has an auction in their Rainbow Room. Apparently it's become quite famous. A hot ticket. Seven women are selected to participate each week, and the club's owner swears none of them are professionals. Thus the excitement."

"Kind of an American Idol, but for strippers rather than singers," I said.

"There's more." Katya scrolled down. "Audience members bid while contestants dance. The winner gets a date for that evening, while the student — apparently that's what most dancers claim to be — gets the proceeds to help finance her education."

"We do that here too. At charity events. To my knowledge, the auctionees are high-society members rather than students, but what do I know?"

Katya clicked a link that brought up an arousing image. "Do high-society members perform the Dance of the Seven Veils? Because apparently that's what they're doing during the auction process. It says each contestant is assigned one of the colors of the rainbow, and is given a costume comprised of veils of that color with a matching G-string. Looks like the bidding goes on until only the G-string is left. I suppose the winner gets to remove that. If the date goes as planned."

I returned to my chair. "I'm pretty sure that here in the US, the participants don't do anything they don't want pictured on the society page."

"It says that no names are used, just colors, but the auctioneer reads a biography for each in order to flesh out the fantasy. Whoa, look at this! It costs the ruble equivalent of a thousand dollars for bidders to register. That's on top of the club's hundred-dollar entrance fee."

"Smart marketing. That's how they add cachet. They make it prestigious to hold a bidder's paddle. And you can bet the women who go to the club are all clued into that. Most won't see if you arrive in a Ferrari, but a paddle says the same thing, and it's on display all night. Tells you a lot about Grigori."

"Do you think it's a good place to get to him?"

I shrugged and drained my third cup of coffee. "First reaction? It might be. I'm not happy with the helicopter. That severely limits our options. I'm sure the club itself has security out the wazoo, on top of Grigori's personal bodyguard contingent, so taking him out inside the club would be risky for us and for bystanders. Special Operations Command would never green-light a mission with that profile. And we're not going to be equipped for an air assault. So that only leaves landing and takeoff. That might work if we could study it for a few weeks and identify a security gap. But we'll be doing this cold." The more I spoke, the less encouraged I became.

"On top of that, I've got to be in Santa Barbara Superior Court by nine Monday morning. Even with the ten-hour time change, a Saturday night operation would be cutting it close. So I'm thinking that Angels on Fire should be an option of last resort."

I was surprised to find myself feeling natural using *we* to discuss an assault operation with Katya.

She seemed to embrace it.

"Do you have an alternative? A first resort?" she asked.

"I'm thinking I'll need to treat it like a sniper mission."

"What's that mean? Are you going to shoot him from a mile away with a rifle?"

"Shoot him? Yes. With a rifle? Maybe. From a mile away? No. What I meant was that I'd lie in wait in a location that he frequents, and then take him out when he shows up."

"At Angels on Fire?"

"No. The architecture isn't suitable." I whirled my laptop around and pointed to a Google Earth image. "The distance between the helipad and door is less than ten meters, so I'd only get a few seconds, during which the helicopter's rotor wash would blow the bullet all over the place. And that's in addition to the gusts and thermals that are going to surround any building in the heart of a major city. Plus, there's no decent vantage point above the club, other than the Ministry of Foreign Affairs, and I can't hole up there with a sniper rifle."

"So where, then?"

"At his office."

Katya tilted her head and narrowed her gaze as though studying a calculus problem on a blackboard. She moved the mouse from Angels on Fire to the GasEx complex. "I'm confused. Maybe I don't get the whole sniper thing, but his building is the tallest for miles around. How do you make the trigonometry work? How can you shoot him up there? Are you just going to hope he comes out to walk around the edge, like he did with Casey and Vondreesen?"

"No, I couldn't count on that happening, and again the thermals would make it an impossible shot. I'm going to climb the building and wait for him up top."

Chapter 100

Disproportionate Response

KATYA GLANCED DOWN at me with incredulity in her eye and a question on her lips. "Even after everything I've witnessed, I still don't see how you could possibly hope to climb GasEx. I understand climbing a house with windowsills and drainpipes, but this is a skyscraper."

I was lying on a swatch of spandex like it was a bed sheet, while Katya traced my silhouette with a fabric marker. To avoid staining it with blood from my shrapnel wounds, I had thirty-one Band-Aids on my back, complete with thirty-one dabs of antiseptic. Bless her heart. The fabric resembled the blue glass of the GasEx building. We also had a swatch that matched the building's stonework, and a sewing machine.

The plan was to sew front and back sides together to create a formfitting jumpsuit. A bottom half that would fit like overalls, and a top half that would fit like a hoodie. Only my hands, feet, and face would be uncovered. The ghillie suit didn't need to be pretty. It just needed to fit without restriction through a wide range of motion. Since neither of us was an accomplished seamstress, we'd bought enough material to accommodate multiple attempts.

"Technically, the climb isn't going to be challenging," I replied. "There are corners running all the way to the top. Beyond basic skills, all that's required to conquer GasEx is physical endurance, and psychological control."

"What do you mean by psychological control?" Katya asked, as she started in with the scissors.

"Basically, that amounts to ignoring irrational emotions. In this case, the fear of falling."

"You think the fear of falling is irrational?"

"If you're not drunk or running on ice, falling is highly improbable. When's the last time you fell?"

"I don't remember."

"Exactly. But if we were walking near the edge of a cliff, you'd become very concerned about it. For millennia, only the wary lived long enough to reproduce, so now extreme caution is built into our DNA. This creates what military minds would call a disproportionate response. For example, say you were taking a bath and somehow a mouse fell in the tub. How would you react?"

Katya's face scrunched back and her lips thinned. "I'd scream and splash, then scramble from the tub and run from the room."

"Exactly. But there's no real threat posed, except to the mouse. Rodents and bugs rarely harm anyone in the civilized world, but we still react to them as if they're hand grenades."

Katya's expression told me I hadn't sold her.

"Working for the CIA, I frequently faced choices between tactics that *all* offered odds of survival much worse than rodent encounters. Over time, I conditioned myself to calibrate my psychological response to dangers based on their probability. I learned to evaluate before I react."

I'd anticipated the math bringing Katya around, but the downward tilt of her chin told me I needed to work harder. "Now I draw the line using a simple formula. If the odds of mortal harm are less than one percent, then a situation no longer triggers anxiety. And the odds that a critter will kill me, or a distant handgun can hit me, or that I'll randomly slip or trip while walking, or running, or climbing are all effectively zero."

Katya's expression told me I still wasn't there. I decided to move on.

"As for the physical endurance part, that's a combination of attitude and repetition. Can you ignore the pain? Can your muscles keep contracting? Climbing a hundred meters to the top of the GasEx building is going to be the rough equivalent of two hundred chin-ups. In prison, I was cranking out a thousand a day. So I know I won't fatigue. And I know from experience that I won't fall. Thus I can focus on the real threat, which is being seen."

Katya looked relieved, although her voice was still tentative. "Thus the camouflage suits. But they won't make you invisible."

"Right. They'll just help me blend in. So I'll still have to avoid attracting eyeballs. That means minimizing movement, sound, and length of exposure. I'm not too worried about movement or sound, since I'll be climbing at night. But speed is an issue. I'm sure there will be patrolling guards, and it could take a long time to free solo a hundred meters up a smooth corner, so I'm going to use a tool that should cut the ascent to under fifteen minutes."

Katya gestured for me to continue. Progress.

When the possibility of climbing the GasEx building first arose, I emailed an inventive climbing buddy. The latest tool he'd showcased on Facebook wouldn't arrive until morning, so I explained it to Katya along with the rest of my plan.

When I was done, Katya sat quietly for a moment, reflecting. "So your plan is to hide on the rooftop, wait for Grigori to appear, and then shoot him?"

"That's the way snipers work."

"But how will you get away?"

"That will depend on the circumstances. Probably either in the helicopter, or by climbing back down, or with a parachute."

"Will a parachute work from that height?" Katya asked with the skepticism of someone who could do terminal-velocity calculations in her head, even without Brillyanc.

"I'll pre-inflate it. There will likely be an updraft on the windward side of the building."

Katya pulled her first attempt at overalls off of the sewing machine.

I tried it on. "It's not pretty, but then, with luck nobody will ever see it."

"I hope you're not counting on luck. This hasn't been your lucky year."

Chapter 101

The Ghost

OVER THE NEXT couple of hours, we cranked out a matching pair of coveralls in the stone-colored spandex, and tops in both patterns. Then we sewed matching camouflage packs for my guns and gear. Between the two suits, I would be able to blend in anywhere on the GasEx building.

I checked the results in the hotel mirror. "I wonder if this is how Peter Parker felt after his first attempt at Spiderman?"

"More like Bruce Wayne," Katya replied. "Batman was the one with all the gear."

"How did you—" I didn't finish the question. I knew the answer. Colin was a big DC Comics fan. I'd invited a ghost into our hotel room.

Katya met my eyes.

She saw the ghost too.

"We both loved him," she said. "You, for your whole life. Me, with my whole heart. We'll never forget him. But we are forgetting something, perhaps the most important thing. Now that he's gone."

I took a step closer, catching my own reflection in the mirror. I looked like a creature from the movie Avatar, minus the big yellow eyes and prehensile tail. "What are we forgetting?"

"We're forgetting that Colin loved us too. He'd want us to be happy."

Katya's words reminded me of the first time Dix let loose on me during combat training. I never saw the blow coming. He hit me out of nowhere with a lightning combination that left me breathless and dizzy and disoriented and flat on my back. I felt like that now. Without thinking, I asked Katya, "Do you think I could make you happy?"

"You make me feel safe. And you make me feel loved. And I don't know what I'd do without you."

I found myself holding my breath. I exhaled, knowing from her tone that a *but* was coming.

"But I haven't put Colin behind me yet. And I can't move on until I have. I want to, but I can't. I need time. I've never gone through this before, so it's hard for me to estimate how long it will take."

I took a half step back.

Katya took a half step forward. "I tried looking up a ratio on grieving

— some peer-reviewed study that would orient me. It's been six months since he died, and I knew him for sixteen months. I thought there'd be an algorithm, but I didn't find anything predictive. And of course I'd been hoping to spend my whole life with him, so that would have confounded the calculation even if I had found one. And now I'm prattling on. Because I'm nervous. Because I know that someday I will be ready to move on, and I'm afraid that you won't be there when I am."

I didn't know what to say to that.

I wasn't sure what I was feeling, and I knew better than to trust my feelings even if I did, given my current circumstances. As for the long-term, my thinking didn't go beyond the trial that started next Monday. What would be the point?

So I picked her up, cradled her in my arms, and carried her to the bed. I laid her down with my chest pressed to her back and my arm around her. Then I held her hand in mine, and we fell asleep, surprisingly content.

When I awoke I felt as fresh as a sunlit field after a short summer storm. Totally relaxed even without complete release. That was when it hit me, and I literally shook.

"What is it?" Katya asked, her voice soft and innocent, still half-cloaked in slumber's shroud.

"It's not going to work."

Katya rolled over, reacting to the timbre of my voice. "What won't work?" she asked, alarmed.

"The plan."

As Katya exhaled in relief, I realized the unfortunate ambiguity of my words.

"Why not?" she asked.

"Because I figured out what Grigori is really up to. We need to take him alive."

Chapter 102

Outmaneuvered

KATYA SAT UP so fast she looked like she'd popped from a toaster. "Why do we have to take Grigori alive? What do you mean, you figured out what he's really up to? I thought that was pretty clear."

"Remember our discussion with Casey? We concluded that the Brillyanc conspiracy was more about influence than direct profit. We concluded that the ability to blackmail the vice president was potentially worth trillions."

"Sure, I remember. Giving Korovin that kind of influence is a scary thought."

"Right. Except it doesn't."

Katya's face crinkled into a confused expression that was the cutest thing I'd seen in years.

"The vice president doesn't have that kind of power. Not really. The *president* is our government's executive. The vice president decides nothing."

"So it's a money thing after all?"

"No. It's still a power play. We just overlooked one critical move."

"What's that?"

"Do you know what the vice president's job is? He only has two constitutionally mandated roles." I held up two fingers. "He's a tiebreaker in the Senate. And he takes over — if the president dies."

I watched Katya's eyes turn to ping-pong balls as she put it all together. "Grigori intends to assassinate President Silver."

"Right."

"So that Daniels will become the president."

"Right."

"And since Korovin knows that Daniels secretly used a dangerous, unapproved, mind-altering drug, he can blackmail him."

"Right."

"And given Korovin's expansionist agenda, I'm sure he'll make good use of it."

"Exactly."

"But how could he possibly kill Silver? Assassinating the President of the United States has to be the toughest assignment in the world, even if you're Korovin."

"That's what I need to ask Grigori. That's why I need to take him alive. And quickly. Silver's going to Moscow next weekend."

As Katya sat up, I had a flashback to the morning this all began in a Santa Barbara hotel room. Sophie had been beautiful, but even clothed, Katya was more spectacular. A launch-the-ships and raise-the-drawbridge miracle, with very non-biblical proportions. My train of thought went off the rails, but Katya's question put it back on. "You think he'll risk killing Silver in Moscow?"

"No. KGB guys are too crafty for that. But he might tip the first domino."

"How do you think he'll do it?"

I shook my head to reboot my thinking. "In a word? Cleverly. Your countrymen are known within intelligence circles for devising innovative and ingenious methods of assassination. They took out one famous defector with a ricin pellet fired from the tip of an umbrella. They killed another by lacing his tea with Polonium-210. They assassinated a head of state by planting a bomb beneath a chair in a sports stadium during its construction, knowing that he'd be sitting there a year later for a national celebration. Who knows what they'll devise for a man with a briefcase that launches nukes. The only thing we can be sure of is that it will be innovative, and ingenious, and nearly impossible to defend against — unless you know it's coming."

"Can't you modify your plan to kill Grigori? Use a tranquilizer dart or something to capture him instead?"

"Kills and captures are totally different beasts. Shifting from lethal to debilitating force increases the risk tenfold, and that's just the beginning. Exfiltration becomes exponentially more complicated. I could account for all of that with proper planning, but I'll have neither the time nor the conditions. I won't know Grigori's procedures or habits, and ground zero is a hundred meters up, so I won't know exactly what I'm dealing with until I get there.

"Then there's the interrogation. It's going to be noisy and it's going to take time. That will be very risky without knowing the security arrangements in advance."

I'd tied my stomach into knots while pondering this problem. Now I rolled onto my back to loosen up and avoid distraction while I tried to work it.

Katya did the same.

She got there first.

"I'll enter the auction."

"What?"

"At *Angles on Fire*. I can't guarantee that I'll get in or he'll pick me, but maybe we could figure out a way to increase the odds."

I looked at her with a combination of astonishment, appreciation, and apprehension. I had to wonder where her courage came from.

"I know you're going to object," she continued. "You'll come up with all kinds of reasons why it's a bad idea. But I want you to do me a favor instead. I want you to pretend that I'm one of your fellow CIA operatives. What would you do then?"

What was it about this woman? How had God packed so much greatness into a single petite package?

Rather than questioning the divine, I did as she asked. I swapped her image for that of Jo Monfort, a French operative I'd worked with. The scenario flowed easily from there.

"You'll get selected. There's no doubt about that. There's a better chance of Grigori dropping dead of a heart attack between now and Saturday than there is of Angels on Fire rejecting you. The same goes for Grigori's interest at the auction, particularly if you play to him. Speaking as a hot-blooded male member of the human race, I can assure you that's an iron-clad guarantee. And I'll be there, helping steer things as a fellow bidder. The big question is what we do once you win — not that I'm agreeing to this approach."

"Let's order up breakfast and think about it," Katya suggested.

"Great idea." I put a rush on our order and it arrived just as we were ready for it. Pots of strong coffee and herbal tea. A carafe of freshly squeezed grapefruit juice. A lobster omelet with brie cheese and a side of fresh fruit for her. Eggs Benedict with a side of oatmeal and a berry plate for me. Plus, a couple of big bottles of water. We'd missed a few meals as of late.

"A medical emergency," I said, as the plan materialized inside my nourished head. "That's how we do it. Once you're alone you stick him with a tranq dart. Then you call me and Max and we'll show up a few seconds later at the gate in an ambulance."

"You sure they'll let you into the compound? Even in an ambulance?"

"After you call me, you'll need to find a guard. There will probably be one waiting nearby, ready to take you away once Grigori's had his fun. Tell him Grigori had a stroke or heart attack. The guard will likely have been at the club as well, which means he'll have heard your biography. If we present you as a medical student, then you'll be credible. You can even get specific to add urgency — say he had a heart attack. Those are common enough in older guys during sex. With heart attacks, time is muscle, which gives you an excuse to push the guard faster than he can think."

"Well alright then," Katya said. "Sounds to me like we've got a plan."

As much as the idea made me cringe, I had to admit that we did.

PART 4: POLITICS

Chapter 103

Blood on Fire

GRIGORI WASN'T SURE which he enjoyed more, stepping off his helicopter on his way into Angels on Fire, or hopping back on afterwards with the catch of the week. Going in, he got to enjoy the anticipation of wielding unrivaled power. He was Klitschko entering the boxing ring. Bono with a microphone. Tarzan in the jungle. Coming out was also about anticipation, but of a very different kind. That was all about the spoils of war. The pleasures of the flesh. The appreciation of beauty in its ultimate form. He decided that it was the combination that made Saturdays in the Rainbow Room the one appointment on his calendar that was chiseled in stone.

The owner, Leo, proffered a flute of Cristal while escorting him toward his reserved seat just in time for the show. Front and center. When it came to naked women, he wasn't a back-row guy.

Vondreesen had turned him onto drinking champagne. He preferred vodka, but drank champagne at the club for the effect it had on the women. Since his wasn't the friendliest countenance around, he used the bubbly to paint himself in a softer light. The pros didn't care about such subtleties, of course. But there was no sport in bagging a pro. That was why he liked the Rainbow Room. And of course, just winning an auction was no guarantee of ultimate success. The hunt didn't end when the bill was paid.

At the back of the room, behind a velvet rope buttressed by burly guards, hundreds of horny spectators gawked and cheered. Down in front, a rainbow-shaped stage was surrounded by three rows of wide, red, armless leather chairs, spaced to allow plenty of room for the girls to mingle and maneuver. Thirty-five chairs. Seven girls. A spirited auction guaranteed, given the laws of supply and demand.

"How's this week's catch looking?" Grigori asked, accepting his drink and his chair with relish.

"Only five tens this week," Leo said with a double flash of his brow. "The other two are elevens."

Leo was a natural born salesman with a hungry wallet and a golden tongue, but Grigori knew the owner wouldn't BS him. Theirs was a long-term relationship. "Tell me about them."

"Indigo is a Mariinski ballerina whose career got cut short because her breasts grew too large. Her audition was one of a kind. I've never seen so much talent with the veils. And her energy, sheesh. Someone's up for the ride of his life."

Grigori wet his dry throat with a sip of Cristal. "And Violet? I know you save the best for last."

"I'm not sure if Violet is the best. She's definitely a contender, don't get me wrong. She's stunning, to be sure. Top to bottom, from facial symmetry to carnal chemistry, I don't think I've ever seen better. But she's different. A doctor. I know what my clients like, and I'm not sure she'll perform when it counts. I left her for last because she's a bit of a wildcard."

Grigori raised his glass to that.

The techno music shifted to a sultry rhythm reminiscent of the Strauss original, but more suitable for a modern Arabian night. Leo had a skinny DJ nicknamed Lic, which Grigori understood to be short for licorice stick. Lic was a master of mood whose massive mop of hair was forever swaying to a beat. He watched the auditions with a composer's eye, and customized mixes of the Dance of the Seven Veils for each performer based on her personality and moves.

The stage began to glow like sunrise. Leo had it backed by one of the massive screens used for the latest electronic billboards, and Lic's assistant used it to full advantage. Red made her entrance using a catwalk stride with a bit of extra wiggle, starting a chorus of wolf whistles and catcalls that Grigori knew would crescendo until all seven dancers were standing side by side in a rainbow of sexual desire.

Leo had been right, the first five all ranked as tens for someone, judging by the outbursts coming from around the room. Dark-skinned and light, slim and voluptuous, petite and modelesque. Leo had arranged to pick every patron's pocket.

When Indigo emerged, Grigori found himself on the edge of his seat. She had short, dark hair, coiffed to give her a catlike appearance that matched her moves, moves that Grigori would describe as evocatively animalistic. He made his selection then and there. He wanted a wild ride with that pretty kitty.

Finally, the doctor emerged in violet silk. Grigori inhaled sharply as she strutted his way, all luscious curves and firm jiggles. She was spectacular, but she was also different. Clearly less comfortable on stage than her fellow contenders. Not more awkward, but rather more innocent. Innocence was why these thirty-five men were here, rather than buying lap dances and massages in the club's other rooms.

The crowd seemed to sense Violet's disposition, and their moment of appraising silence erupted into an appreciative chorus that drew Grigori in. Perhaps he would have to take two home tonight. Then the good doctor winked at him as she strode past, and his blood caught fire.

Chapter 104

The FOB

MY HEART invaded my throat, as Grigori's helicopter rose toward the heavy clouds with Katya inside.

"Do you have a helicopter too?" my date cooed.

It wasn't a crazy question, given what I'd forked over for a single night of companionship. A new record according to Leo, the club owner and auctioneer. "No. When I want to fly, I use my jet." As soon as the words were out of my mouth, I knew I'd made a mistake. That was going to make my next move harder for Indigo to take.

I could see the beach at Cannes reflecting in her eyes as the ballerina digested my news. "I like jets."

My Mercedes limo pulled to the curb as we exited the club. We climbed into the back, where Indigo proceeded to lay her long, lithe legs across my lap. As I looked up, she placed a blood-red nail against her crimson lower lip.

The driver only took us a few blocks before pulling over behind an ambulance.

I gently laid my date's legs aside. "You're beautiful. But I'm going to have to take a rain check on tonight. While you were changing I got an urgent call. A close friend of President Korovin's had a heart attack. My driver will take you anywhere you want to go — anywhere but back to the club. I have my reputation to consider."

The image of Cannes faded from her eyes and her plump lower lip began to pout.

"I hope you'll leave me your number," I said, trying to avoid a scene.

Indigo pulled a lipstick from her tiny bag and scanned the limo's interior. "I don't have any paper." She gave me a grin that would jumpstart a Jeep, and wrote her number on the ceiling. "Now you can look me up whenever you want."

Indigo would land herself a jet. It was only a matter of time.

I escaped into the waiting ambulance. "Let's roll," I told an anxious Max. "Lights but no sirens."

He pulled onto the ring road, hitting the gas as the clouds let loose with a heavy spring shower.

Max was doing a lot better than when we'd spoken to him on the phone from Vondreesen's study. He was symptom free for the moment, and that news was apparently enough to let him revert back to his natural optimism. I admired him for that more than I could say.

"How'd it go?" he asked, his voice apprehensive, but tinged with excitement. We weren't in his comfort zone, but he appeared to be embracing the moment. A fellow backpacker, as Katya would put it.

"Katya's in the air, but will be touching down atop the Rocket any minute. Her call could come any time after that. Probably not less than five minutes but you never know, so use the siren if you need it."

"Any issues at the auction?"

"All the women were gorgeous. Grigori passed on the first five. They went for a low of eighteen hundred up to three and a half grand. But then he bid on the sixth. A buxom ballerina. Cost me ten thousand to win her from him."

Max whistled.

"Then only Katya was left. Grigori got into a bidding war over her with an Armenian. Neither of them wanted to go home alone. Given their egos, the auction had all kinds of hormones flying around. It threatened to get ugly."

"What did you do?"

"I covertly spritzed the Armenian with nausea-inducing spray to curb his enthusiasm, but our man still ended up paying twenty for Katya. The Armenian made a point of leaving with a whole harem on his hairy arms."

Max pulled to the side of the road precisely eighteen minutes after Katya set foot in the helicopter. We'd picked a spot roughly halfway between the presidential hospital on Michurinski Prospect, and the GasEx complex a few kilometers further south.

I had the Valdada scope from my CheyTac sniper rifle out before Max had the ambulance in park. I didn't expect to be using a long gun on this mission, but I'd come equipped for all kinds of contingencies. Better to have it and not need it, and all that.

"Keep the windshield wipers going," I said, scanning the dark sky before honing in on Grigori's rooftop lair. "The helicopter's there. Rotor's not turning."

"Any light coming from the pyramid?"

"Nothing bright enough to register."

"Is that a good sign?"

Max was subconsciously drumming his fingers on the steering wheel, relieving nervous tension. I'd seen similar tells emerge a hundred times at this stage in the mission. The team was fine as long as we were moving, but once we entered wait mode, anxiety kicked in. "It is. She'll tranq him as soon as they're alone. Lights off is a step in that direction."

That satisfied Max for about five minutes. As the windshield wipers sloshed a hypnotic rhythm, he hit me with his next nervous question. "What would be a bad sign?"

"Basically any activity other than our ringing phone."

"Should we move up to the FOB?" He asked, after another three hundred painful seconds had ticked by with his fingers drumming away. He was referencing the forward operating base we'd picked out, directly across the street from GasEx.

The FOB was a parking lot in an apartment complex. The front parking spaces gave us line of sight on both Barsukov's Rocket and the guard gate. They also left us exposed. Distant from the door was an odd and conspicuous place to park an ambulance. I hoped the heavy rain would fend off rubberneckers.

I considered asking Max to stick to the plan, and remain at our current location for another three minutes, but that would be pointlessly fastidious. Truth was, Max wasn't the only one growing nervous. "Let's do it."

Chapter 105

Alternative Scenarios

I POWERED ON the radio as we drove toward the FOB, hoping for something soothing. It came to life with a rapper venting frustrations about his mother. Odd choice for an ambulance driver. I turned it back off.

Max stopped the ambulance before the orange cones that reserved our parking spot. He looked over at me with an unstated request.

I looked out at the pouring rain, and prayed that an umbrella was the only thing I'd forgotten. "I don't want to get my makeup wet. Drive over the cones."

I'd made my face up to look like Scar's. Speaking of which … I craned my neck and spotted our stolen GasEx van. We'd parked it nearby in a less conspicuous spot. I wanted it handy, in case we needed Plan B.

Max rolled slowly forward, attempting to nudge the cones out of the way. It didn't work. Both tipped. We listened to them scraping the pavement beneath the ambulance. With a shrug, he shifted into park and glanced at his watch. "I'm sure she'll call any minute."

I indicated agreement.

She didn't call. Not within five minutes. Not within ten.

I gave the radio another try. Found some jazz.

"How long has she been in there?" Max asked, when the song ended.

"About thirty minutes. Tell me again about the tranquilizers you gave her." I knew all the details. I wouldn't have approved the mission otherwise. But it would relax Max to talk about biochemistry.

"The microinjectors in the haircombs you gave me have a very limited capacity, just a tenth of a milliliter. So we needed something that would work with a minute dose, and we needed something that would act immediately. I went with etorphine, also known as M99. It's a common veterinary tranquilizer that's lethal in humans because of our opioid sensitivity. A single drop will kill most people, a mere twentieth of a milliliter. She'll use that to knock Barsukov out. It'll drop the bastard like a bullet to the brain. Then she'll administer the antidote, naltrexone. I've got that stashed in the left cup of her bra. Before he regains his senses, she'll dose him with the chloroform stashed in the right cup, to keep him under." He nodded, reassuring himself.

"Overall the plan is more complicated than I'd like, but it's surefire, and it will leave him looking like something's definitely medically wrong. It will also wipe out his short-term memory. In that regard, M99 is like Rohypnol squared."

"Brilliant, Max. I don't know what we'd have done without you."

"Bastard killed Saba. You sure Katya's okay? What if there's more than one guy in the room. What if Barsukov wants his bodyguard to watch?"

"She's got four doses of M99. Two combs, two ends."

"Yeah, but wouldn't the presence of multiple bodies ruin the heart attack ruse?"

"Katya's very quick on her feet. She'll think of something. You should have seen her when we got attacked at the hotel. The guy who seized her was literally twice her size, and she latched onto his trigger finger like a pit bull on a bone. Saved both our lives. And then at Vondreesen's castle, she did it again."

I was speaking to myself as much as to Max. Truth was, I was kicking myself for agreeing to Katya's plan. I should have nixed it back in San Francisco, but we had the whole partner thing going. It was working for us and I didn't want to ruin it by vetoing her idea. At the time, I'd expected to come up with a better proposal once we got here.

We had four days in Moscow to prep for the Angels on Fire plan. That seemed like a lot at first, especially with my trial less than a week away, but it proved barely adequate given all the practice, equipment, and contingency planning required.

I'd searched for alternative plans at every opportunity, but had come up empty. We didn't have sufficient data on Grigori's routines to uncover weaknesses — and none were apparent. He lived and worked in a fortress. But I could have gotten more aggressive. I could have broken into the complex and poked around. I had retrieved a blue key card from the stolen GasEx van, using safe-cracking equipment brought from the US.

"How long's it been now?" Max asked. He was working hard to keep calm, but his voice was cracking like an old telephone wire.

I looked at my watch. Two-thirty. Katya had been in there nearly an hour.

The hardest part of most missions was fending off demons while waiting in the proverbial dark, but this was the worst ever. This wasn't an A-Team gone quiet. This was Katya working alone. "She can't drug him until they're alone and getting intimate. Plenty of things could cause a delay. A late dinner to set the mood. A phone call requiring immediate attention. His waiting for the Viagra to kick in."

"How do we know when our worrying becomes legitimate?"

"It's not a question of worrying. It's a question of alternative action.

The proper question is: when does it make sense to switch to Plan B? In this case, that will be when we decide Plan A is off track, because it's more likely that she's been identified or thwarted than delayed."

"And when will that be?"

I ran through alternative scenarios in my mind, weighing each against my probability meter, then racking and stacking the results. "Right about now. I'm going in."

Chapter 106

Dangerous Heights

ONE GOOD THING about Plan B was that it didn't void Plan A. If Katya called, Max could still execute the ambulance scenario.

"If a guard asks why you're alone, tell him there's another emergency, an accident with members of the Duma involved," I said, referencing Russia's parliament. "Everyone understands the hoops that have to be jumped through when politicians are involved."

Since Plan B got me into GasEx using Scar's blue key card, I didn't expect to have any human interaction at all. But just in case, I'd made my face up and styled my hair to resemble Scar's ID. Our physiques and features were in similar ballparks. In my experience, that combination would be good enough for late-night guards. They'd be second-tier, tired, and focused on the deformity.

If not, I had the Glock.

I set about changing out of my EMT uniform, into a black suit and t-shirt. My other gear was waiting for me in the GasEx van, all pre-packed and ready to go.

Max watched me with his mouth half open. "I still can't believe you're going to climb that thing, in the rain no less. But I'm sure glad that you are. What are you going to do once you reach the top?"

"Depends on what I see. I'll have you on comm the whole time, so you'll know when I do. You just remain ready to roll down here. Hopefully Katya will call, but in any case, the ambulance will likely remain our best ticket out."

"You can count on me."

"I know I can, Max. Thank you."

We bumped fists, and I left to climb a castle wall.

The employee gate responded to the stolen key card without delay, and I rolled toward the Rocket like a lion stalking a gazelle.

I had identified the southeast corner of the tower as the best place for climbing. The wind was blowing from north to south, so the southern walls were the most protected from the rain, and the southeast was the least visually exposed. I'd be hidden from neighboring apartments, the guard building, and Max. Probably better for his blood pressure that way. I parked as near as I could get without being conspicuous, and went into the back to grab my gear.

I'd decided to climb wearing the black suit rather than one of my homemade camouflaging leotards since this was a covert assault rather than a lay-in-wait sniping mission. Nonetheless, those silly suits would come along in my bag for contingencies. I was also packing a large sport parachute, heavy-duty cable ties, and a lock-picking set in addition to my shoulder-holstered Glock. My specialty items were a sonic glass-shattering pick, and a pair of sophisticated suction cups.

"How's it looking?" I said into my headset mike.

"All quiet."

"Keep an eye on the pyramid and the guardhouse with the scope. Let me know if anything changes."

"Roger that."

I ran for the southeast corner and came to a stop with my back pressed into the southern wall. It was nearing 3:00 a.m. I paused there for my final pre-engagement reconnaissance, a black figure in the shadow of a stormy night. Quiet all around, except for the wind and the rain and my pounding pulse.

I was worried about Katya.

Turning back to the building, I raised the suction cups over my head. Fashioned from the shells of a popular push-up tool, my friend had designed them specifically for use on glass. Each had a suction cup the size of a salad plate. A thumb switch alternatively blew compressed air in, and then sucked it out, enabling swift and solid attachment and detachment. His clever invention would cut my ascent time by over fifty percent. I just had to be careful not to confuse my thumbs. That was one of those mistakes you only got to make once.

I pressed my left thumb, felt the cup suck in, and pulled myself up the length of my arm. Twenty-five inches from the top of my deltoid to the center of my clenched fist. My feet now dangling, I reached my right arm up as far as I could, and depressed my thumb. Feeling it engage, I pulled myself up another couple of feet. I hit my left thumb, felt the tension release, and began to repeat. *Katya, here I come.*

I wanted to test my ability to climb without the suction cups before I reached breakneck height, so after a few pulls, I tried wedging myself into the corner. Without a rope, this cornering grip was my only safety, my only alternative to falling if the suction cups failed. I'd lined the parachute pack with an extremely tacky rubber, similar to the soles of my shoes. The opposing sticky surfaces would normally make it possible for me to cling to the corner without the use of my hands, but the rain made the pollution-coated glass too slick. I tried every angle and every technique, but nothing gave me sufficient purchase to ascend.

I was about to break a cardinal rule of climbing.

I was about to risk my life on a piece of experimental equipment.

Rain poured down on me as I looked up to the sky. Somewhere thirty stories above, the most wonderful woman I'd ever known was battling the man who had brought nightmares into my life. The man who had ended my father's and brother's dreams. Those thoughts kicked my adrenaline into overdrive, and I resumed the climb with savage intent. Left. Right. Left. Right. Twenty meters. Forty. Sixty.

I was two-thirds of the way up, about twenty stories, when the lightning started. The first bolt came with a thunderous clap that made me glad I was conditioned to working around gunfire. I said, "I'm fine," for Max's benefit, then decided this was a good time to pause and replace the air canisters. My friend said each was good for well over a hundred cycles on the suction cups, but I didn't want to push it. Failure would be catastrophic, and Katya was counting on me.

Chapter 107

Lack of Transparency

A SIMPLE STRAP ran from my belt through each suction cup's handle and back down. This loop provided a measure of safety throughout the climb, and freed up my hands for the swapping operation.

The first time I'd used one of those simple tethers was in Airborne School at Fort Benning. During the final practice exercise, before they threw us out of an actual plane, the Black Hats hoisted us up a tower about the same height as the GasEx complex. During the ascent, our parachutes were held open above our heads by a giant ring. When we reached the top, the drill was to remove the safety tether running between our belt and the ring, and then give the thumbs-up to signal that we were ready for release.

I'll never forget watching one of my fellow paratroopers get confused and give the release signal without unclipping his tether. He ended up dangling by a thread still hooked to the ring, while his inflated parachute dropped below him, caught a breeze, and started pulling him toward the ground. I'd never seen someone so scared in all my life.

But the tether did its job.

We all walked away with a deeply engrained respect for our safety equipment.

"Anything happening?" I asked Max.

"All's quiet. I don't know if that's good or bad, but I'm glad you're on your way. I've been afraid to speak. I worry about breaking your concentration."

"Good instinct. I'll talk to you in a few from the top."

I rolled onto the roof fourteen minutes after my feet left the ground. My arms and deltoids were burning, but nothing like my heart.

Grigori's rooftop terrace ran about three-meters deep, from the edge I'd just clambered over to the base of the glass pyramid. The shiny black helicopter that had delivered Katya loomed behind me, off to the right. I rolled away from the edge so I wouldn't be silhouetted against the night sky and looked for a place to stash the suction cups. I didn't plan on using them to go down, but contingency planning was like breathing. It had often kept me breathing.

The roof didn't appear to have the usual assortment of exhaust pipes and HVAC units, so I made do with stashing my tools against the wall of the nearest corner tower, which rose about a foot higher than the main building. I stashed the parachute there as well, then turned up my jacket collar in an attempt to appear like a guard stuck on perimeter patrol in the pouring rain.

"I'm on the roof," I told Max. "You see any lights on your side?"

"All's dark. I still can't believe you climbed that thing."

I palmed the Glock and crawled to the wall to Grigori's East Wing office. Cupping my eyes, I put my face up to the glass. I couldn't see anything through it. Illumination from the next lightning strike confirmed my suspicion. The glass was electronically opaqued.

The last time I'd encountered this kind of glass was in the unisex restroom of a trendy Belgian nightclub. Customers had the choice of making the door to their stall clear or leaving it opaque. I remembered doubting that many patrons would take advantage of the exhibitionist opportunity, but being certain that all would talk about it. My practical take away from that experience was the knowledge that unlike most mirrored glass, the opacity worked both ways.

I stood and checked the triangular panes one by one. They were huge. Each was roughly two meters in height, and probably weighed a hundred pounds. Twelve rows of panes rose up into the darkness, beginning with twenty-three triangles in the first row on the bottom, and of course ending with just a single triangle in the last row at the top. The entire first and second rows appeared to be opaque.

I began making my way around the pyramid. Looking for doors and signs of life. I made the full three-sixty circuit and found neither. "There aren't any traditional doors on this thing," I told Max. "Just hinges on a few of the panes. I'm guessing they swing out like doors, but they don't have traditional handles I can lever or locks I can pick. Just touch pads."

"Can you get inside?"

"I figure the odds are fifty-fifty that the touch pads will respond to my palm. Either they are biometric, or they aren't."

"Why wouldn't they be?"

"Submarines and space shuttles don't have locks on their doors, and this is no less remote. But I hesitate to try without knowing if the coast is clear on the other side. I'm going to climb the pyramid. He's got the ground-level glass electronically opaqued, but maybe there will be clear panes higher up. I'll start on the southeast wall and will work my way around, so you'll be able to see me soon."

"Roger that. I'll keep watch."

Ten minutes later, I reported back to Max. "We're out of luck. Not a single pane on the pyramid is currently transparent." I sat on the apex and looked in Max's direction for his benefit.

"What now?" he asked. "She's been in there for two hours."

I scared myself with my own reply. "I don't know."

Chapter 108

Lost Luggage

PERCHED ATOP BARSUKOV'S ROCKET like Rodin's *Thinker*, I weighed my options. I considered picking a pane to shatter and dropping in with guns blazing, Hostage Rescue Team style. The core issue with that kind of breach was that I'd only get one shot at picking the right window, and it would literally be blind. If I guessed wrong, Katya and I would both be dead, and in all likelihood, so would President Silver.

"What are you thinking?" Max asked, breaking a long silence.

"I'm thinking it's time to try the doors."

The rain had stopped and the sky had cleared, but I was still wet as a washcloth as I worked my way back down the southeast wall to the hinged pane in the corner. An electric motor the size of an orange Home Depot pail drove the axle that hinged the triangular door. It resembled the engine of the Tesla I'd rented.

Electric motors tend to be quiet, but hinges often squeak. I readied the Glock in my right and pressed my left palm against the sensory pad. A tiny red LED illuminated. "Dammit!" I swapped hands but again struck red. Grigori had gone biometric.

"Try the other doors," Max suggested. "Maybe there's a servant's entrance."

I repeated the exercise three more times. Like a champion bull, I saw nothing but red. "Good idea, but no dice."

I pulled the sonic glass-shattering pick from my waist pack just to have something to fidget with while I thought things over. I loved tools. I could happily spend hours in a hardware store looking around. This one was a beauty. Shaped to resemble an ice pick, it delivered ultrasonic vibrations like a miniature jackhammer, and shattered glass the way its big brother did concrete. Unlike a jackhammer, however, it was quiet. Alas, the shattering glass was another, much louder story.

The triangular frames probably held two panes of quarter-inch glass, separated by argon gas and electronically-opaquing film. Going through would certainly draw the attention of everyone in an adjacent room, and probably anyone in the pyramid.

Testosterone was raging inside me like that bull who'd seen red as I imagined Katya suffering within, but thanks to years of training, I managed to retain control. Shakespeare's Falstaff had been right — at times discretion was the better part of valor.

"I can't risk going in blind. I've got to wait until I can see what's going on."

"That probably won't be until morning," Max said. "I mean, why would he open a window now?"

"You're right. He wouldn't. We're in for a long wait."

I weighed the options, and decided to wait at the apex, some seventy vertical feet above Grigori's floor. I'd be in for some fancy footwork if the pane I was resting on suddenly went clear, but I was up for that. Come daylight, however, I would also be visible from the outside. "I'm going to switch into the glass-blue spandex suit."

While I was changing, Max came through on the headset. "I've been thinking about your earlier comment. The one about submarines and space shuttles not needing locks. I'm wondering if that applies to helicopters."

I felt like the slow kid in class. Inspecting the perimeter was basic operational protocol, and I'd let it slip right by. "Thanks, Max. Even without Brillyanc, you're a genius."

Grigori's Ansat helicopter wasn't the sleekest design, but then neither was Marine One. The high-gloss black paint job went a long way toward making it a stylish toy, especially when viewed by moonlight.

I didn't plan to lie in wait inside, since I didn't know if Grigori would be flying anytime soon. But contingency planning made it a wise move to get the lay of the land, and clear it of any weapons. Perhaps I'd even get lucky and find a clicker that opened the pyramid. "The helicopter's doors have locks, but they're not engaged."

I slid into the pilot's seat and found a weapon the first place I looked, holstered to the front of the pilot's chair. "I found another Glock 43. Grigori must buy them by the case. Nothing else of value up front. Time to check the back."

The rear salon was typical private-aircraft luxury. Black leather armchairs with brushed aluminum accents. No weapons back there, but welcome bottles of water and bags of pistachios. I'd failed to pack either food or drink.

I moved to the back corner of the cabin to test viewing and firing angles. Now that I had two guns, I wanted to see if I could simultaneously cover all the doors.

Something dug into my backside. I twisted to inspect it and felt my heart skip a beat. "I found Katya's cell phone. It was wedged into her chair."

"On purpose, or by accident?" Max asked.

"No way to tell. Maybe she had some reason to hide it. Maybe it slipped out. Maybe she was told to leave it. In any case, it helps explain her silence."

"What now?"

"Good question."

"You should probably leave it there. In case it wasn't an accident."

"That's what I'm thinking. I'm going to head back up the pyramid now, before first light."

"Roger that."

I put the cell phone back where I'd found it and began to leave, but stopped when an idea struck me. I pulled the pilot's Glock from my pocket, ejected the magazine, and removed all six rounds. Then I racked the slide to pop the seventh from the chamber, and slapped the empty magazine back into place. Now nothing inside the Ansat would look amiss, unless Grigori was fastidious about his pistachio count.

A thought struck me as I abandoned the helicopter in favor of the pyramid. I couldn't even be certain that Katya was inside.

Chapter 109

Plan E

DRESSED ONLY in a lacy bra and panties, Katya looked down at Grigori's convulsing body, and wondered if she'd done something wrong. She thought she'd played it just right.

As soon as they made it to his bedroom, all hot with lust and tipsy from champagne, she'd taken charge using her 'Violet' alter-ego. She issued commands in a firm but sexy voice, while moving seductively and stripping down to lingerie.

Once she had Grigori where she wanted him, with his clothes on the floor and his guard dropped, Katya mimicked the moves of Vondreesen's angel. She circled him with an index finger alternatively on her lower lip and the top of his shoulders, purring intermittently while his breathing became audible. Then *whammo!* She drove the end of her hair comb into the back of his neck.

The hidden injector obviously delivered something. He dropped like a rock. But instead of slipping into sleep-like unconsciousness, he started flopping about like a landed fish.

What had she done wrong?

The answer struck her like a slap in the face. *The antidote!* She'd been so focused on knocking him out, that she'd forgotten part-two of Max's procedure.

But first the chloroform to keep him under.

Katya dropped to her knees and removed the chloroform and M99 antidote from her bra. She found herself shaking as much as her victim, so she closed her eyes and pictured a beach with rolling waves and swaying palms until her hands were sufficiently steady.

Now she needed something to absorb the chloroform. Her eyes landed on one of Grigori's socks. Holding her breath, Katya poured half the contents of the tiny vial onto the black cotton, and placed it over Grigori's nose. She wanted him inhaling the anesthetic while she administered the antidote.

The naltrexone syringe had a long, thin needle. She pulled off the protective cap, took aim, and plunged it straight down into the thick muscle of Grigori's right thigh without second thought or ceremony.

His spasms ceased immediately.

In fact, everything seemed to stop. He looked dead.

Katya hadn't known what to expect. No doubt Max had told her, but the memory had slipped. God, she hoped she hadn't killed the pervert. The whole reason she'd gone through this humiliation was so that Achilles could learn how he planned to kill President Silver.

She put her ear to Grigori's hairy chest. His heartbeat seemed rapid for someone sleeping, more cha-cha than waltz, but it was steady.

Enough already! Time for the ambulance.

She threw her bra back on, but left the rest of her clothes on the floor, scattered amongst Grigori's. The setting would be crucial to duping his guards.

Where was her phone? It was supposed to be in the back pocket of her skinny jeans. She spent a frantic minute rummaging through discarded garments and around the bedroom, then another retracing every step they'd made since entering the door. There hadn't been much prelude to the striptease. Not at two o'clock in the morning.

Her phone simply wasn't there.

She couldn't remember seeing it while removing her clothes. Maybe it had been stolen at the club.

What did it matter? Achilles had made her memorize his number.

She plucked Grigori's cell from the front pocket of his pants — but couldn't unlock it. The query screen didn't want a fingerprint or a dot-connecting pattern. It just presented a keypad — and she didn't have the code.

Land line?

She found none.

She'd also have to use a guard's phone. That would be tricky, but since she was impersonating a doctor, she could swing it. She'd have to remain clothed only in her underwear. That would underline the sense of urgency while providing some distraction. One more indignity for the cause.

The elevator didn't respond.

She pressed and then pounded her palm against the reader, but got no response. No red light. No green light. No whirring motor. No chime. How could that be? Katya answered her own question. In the middle of the night, it was a sensible security precaution for a man waging geopolitical war.

So what then?

She could go out onto the terrace and try to catch Achilles' attention. Surely he and Max would be watching.

Neither of the doors responded either. Not the door to the terrace. Not the door to the office. Everything appeared to be locked down for the night. Grigori wasn't messing around.

Achilles had warned her that operations rarely went according to plan, but she hadn't expected so many frustrations. Time for what, Plan

C? Plan D? She'd lost count. In any case, it was time to make some noise.

She retrieved a quart pot from the kitchen, and began hammering the steel base against the elevator's brushed aluminum door. The noise was jarring to nerves already on edge, but she persisted. And persisted. At least she wouldn't need to work at appearing hysterical over Grigori's 'heart attack'.

Nobody responded.

It seemed impossible that the guards didn't hear — until she thought about it. She was thirty stories up a building made of rock and steel, and it was pouring rain outside.

So what now? What was Plan E?

She couldn't do better than 'Wait.'

Wait for Achilles.

He was probably no less frantic than she. No that wasn't right. Achilles wasn't the frantic type. No less *concerned* than she. Actually, he'd be more concerned. She knew she was safe.

Waiting wouldn't be easy. This wasn't exactly a pass-the-time-watching-tv situation. As her new circumstances sank in, Katya realized that waiting was folly. She should be contingency planning. She should be setting the stage — in case Grigori awoke before Achilles arrived. Oh goodness, she didn't want to think about that possibility.

Chapter 110

Transformations

THE SUN PEEKED over the distant horizon at 4:31 a.m. Mid-May above the fifty-fifth parallel.

Birds began chirping as I did a quick and quiet perimeter walk to confirm that all the windows were still opaque. They were. That was bad news. I was becoming visible faster than Grigori's apartment.

Since my presence at the peak would change the pyramid's silhouette against the morning sky, I lay down with my head a foot below the crest. Max, can you see me?"

"Negative."

"Let me know if that changes."

"Roger that."

The transformation began at 4:57, when the sun's first rays touched the top of the pyramid like a golden crown. "I've got action. The triangles topping the northeast and southeast walls just turned clear. Ooh, there goes the next row, three more panes. They're responding to the sun."

I looked down into Grigori's lair, which had grown to mythical proportions in my mind. His enormous east wing office was decorated in what I'd call modern minimalist chic. Rich granite floors. Black leather seating. Dark wood tables polished to a diamond shine, and a glass kidney-shaped desk. There were rooms along the inside walls. A kitchenette and a bathroom.

No lights were on.

Nobody was present.

I unclipped the tether and slid down a row, just as the windows beneath me transformed. I could see all the way through the pyramid now. That meant the top triangle on the residential walls had also cleared. *Katya should be visible.*

I scampered around and lay with my head extending over a clear section. Cupping my hands to form a bridge between my forehead and the glass, I peered inside.

The tones were lighter and warmer in the living quarters. Golden travertine floors, and honey-colored wood. "The residential half just opened. It's split down the middle into two halves. I'm over the southwest section. It's a great room, combining a living room with a kitchen. The kitchen looks fit for a Michelin-starred chef, complete with a full suite of stainless steel appliances and crowned with an island that boasts a Viking grill fit to handle an entire pig. Again no lights, no bodies."

"Katya's got to be in the bedroom then," Max said, echoing the words in my head.

I circled around the empty office, and stretched my neck to peer through the corner of the bedroom's top pane.

"Well? What do you see?"

"Not enough. The angle's not right. All I see is the top of what I assume is either the bathroom or the closet. I'm going to scooch down and wait for the next level to clear."

"You're killing me."

Max only had to suffer for a few seconds before the sun did its thing. The glass transformed, and there she was — looking right at me.

She'd been waiting.

My heart filled with joy.

"Katya's there. She looks fine. She's lying in Grigori's big white bed. She sees me. She's smiling. She's okay. She's making the telephone sign with her hand and shaking her head. Now she's pointing to Grigori, and making the sleeping sign."

I mimicked jabbing him with a hair comb.

She nodded, then repeated the sleeping sign.

"She knocked Grigori out, but apparently couldn't call."

I looked a question at her.

She smiled, pointed toward Grigori's crotch, and shook her head.

"He didn't lay a hand on her."

I blew Katya a kiss.

The next set of window panes cleared, pouring more light into the room.

Grigori stirred, and opened his eyes.

Chapter 111

Disappearing Act

AS GRIGORI SAT UP IN BED, I ducked my head back, slowly. Careful not to scrape anything that might make noise, I slid down another level and peeked back in. "They're talking now. Katya is smiling at Grigori. He's shaking his head. He looks like he's got the century's worst hangover. He's getting up. Naked. Looks like he's heading for the bathroom. Slow and wobbly."

Katya looked up and met my eye. She mimed a stabbing motion.

I shook my head. Used my thumb to give her the get-out sign.

She looked a question back at me. *Was I sure?*

I gestured with my thumb again.

Katya began pulling her clothes on.

Good move.

I brought Max up to speed.

Katya looked back up once she was dressed.

I mimicked, "Your phone's in the helicopter," and then pointed toward the bathroom.

She gave me a thumbs up. She understood. Sending Grigori to get her phone was a good way to get his pants on.

I considered dashing to the helicopter to lie in wait for Grigori to come to me, but tossed the idea. I wanted Katya safe before moving on him — and I had a better plan. One that wouldn't put Katya's safety on the line.

Grigori reappeared still walking with deliberate moves. He spent some time on his tablet while talking with Katya, who played the role of starstruck guest. Clearly he and Vondreesen had synced on the technology thing, although I wasn't sure who had led and who had followed. Another row of windows went clear, making it four of the ten.

"What's going on?" Max asked.

"I'm not sure, but Katya's dressed. Wait. She just left the room."

I made my way around the northern half of the pyramid, slow and flat so as not to capture the attention of anyone down on the street who happened to be looking up. "Katya's at a breakfast table. A woman in a maid's uniform is serving her tea. Another in a chef's outfit is busy in the kitchen."

Watching was getting dangerous. I was only about forty feet up now, and the kitchen had two hostile sets of eyes.

Then Grigori walked in, and there were three.

He was wearing black silk pajamas and fur-lined slippers. He had a coffee mug in one hand, and a phone in the other. He presented it to Katya, and they sat down to breakfast.

The next half hour was tense and painful. My cover slipped away as they ate and the sun rose, drawing me ever closer. Meanwhile Grigori was regaining his wits and getting more time to study Katya's face.

I didn't know if he'd seen the photos of her captured in the Santa Barbara courtroom, but the safe move was to assume that he had. Last night at Angels on Fire, wearing slutty makeup and silky lingerie, Katya had looked nothing like the meek mathematician who had presented herself to the Santa Barbara County Court. Even if she had, the context would have made it highly unlikely that an intoxicated, hormone-driven observer would manage to make the mental connection. But there, in the light of day, without sex on his mind and booze in his veins, the odds of Katya making it out the door were getting worse by the minute.

I studied Grigori live for the first time. He struck me as dark, energetic, and mischievous. His sunken eyes and sharp features made me think of a badger, which coincidentally was the translation of his last name. One thing I hadn't picked up on while studying pictures of him, was that his nose looked like it had been broken in a bar fight. I concluded that he hid it out of habit by turning his head for photographs.

Another layer of windows gave way to clear just as a black suit entered the room. I scrambled to slip out of sight. By the time I readjusted my position and peered back in, Katya was gone.

Chapter 112

Change of Plans

I GAVE GRIGORI'S great room a thorough visual inspection, reconfirming that Katya was gone. "Dammit!"

"What?" Max asked, alarm in his voice. I'd heard him nervously drumming away on the steering wheel, but now he was all ears.

"Katya's gone. I think she left with a man in a black suit."

"Did Grigori go with her?"

"I'm not sure. I don't think so. He was in pajamas. Hold on."

I made my way back around the pyramid, only to find that the pattern of clear panes over the office was no longer regular. Like the oculus of the Pantheon in Rome, it focused the sunshine on a single area. Peering in, I found it empty.

Only the bedroom was left. I sure hoped Grigori hadn't taken her back there. "Keep an eye on the front gate. See who's leaving. Be prepared to follow."

"Will do. But an ambulance isn't going to make for discreet surveillance."

Nothing we could do about that. "Katya's not in the bedroom either, but Grigori's there, getting dressed. Looks like he even wears a suit on Sundays."

Max's voice came back on, an octave higher. "There's a black Mercedes leaving through the front gate. The windows are tinted. I can't see inside. Should I follow?"

"Is that the only car leaving?"

"Yes."

"Go for it. Sunday morning, who else could it be?"

While Max followed the Mercedes, I had to figure out my next moves. I was running out of places to hide. With the sun rising, my silhouette would be visible to Grigori and his staff even when I was over the opaque portions of the pyramid.

I surveyed the roof in the morning light. The terrace surrounding the pyramid was featureless as a jogging track — and just as devoid of safety rails. The east and west towers were capped by skylights, smaller versions of the central pyramid. No hiding there. The north tower supported a traditional terrace, with an umbrellaed table, four chairs, and a pair of loungers. It looked like a nice place to enjoy your brandy and cigars while mastering the universe. The south tower had the helipad with the gleaming black Ansat I'd visited.

There was no decent point of concealment anywhere on the roof. If I tried hiding on a lawn chair, I'd look like a three-year-old kid who thought he was invisible while everyone chuckled. That discovery wouldn't end with tickles.

I had two options. I could either go into sniper mode by lying out of the way, still as a stone in my ghillie suit. Or I could return to the Ansat and kill anyone who came along. Not a tough choice, given the mood I was in. And I was ready for more pistachios.

I bid an Arnold Schwarzenegger farewell to Grigori as he was adjusting his tie, and slid slowly down the pyramid. From the base, I low-crawled toward the south tower and the gear I'd stashed, then made a dash for the copter.

Max broke radio silence as I shut the door, causing me to jump. "Katya just exited the limo in front of our MSU dormitory complex. She's alone. The limo is driving off. I'll pick her up, as soon as it's out of sight."

Relief flooded over me. As long as Katya was safe, everything would be okay. I could take care of myself. "That's great news! Please switch to speakerphone when you do."

I found myself nervously popping pistachios while waiting for news. This was the covert operative equivalent to giving birth. I heard the ambulance door open, and then Katya's voice. "I'm alright. I'm alright. Is Achilles on his way?"

"I'm not coming yet," I said. "I've still got to learn Grigori's plan. But tell us what happened, we're dying to know. Max, drive the ambulance someplace inconspicuous while Katya debriefs."

Katya's words came pouring out like an excited child's. "At first everything went as planned. He brought me home. I'd never flown in a helicopter before. Didn't know they were so loud on the inside. That was nice, because we didn't have to talk. I played the excited schoolgirl, and he seemed to like being the big daddy."

The tone of her voice gave me a warm feeling. I couldn't believe her level of enthusiasm. This was a math professor talking. Apparently, Max and I had been the only nervous ones.

"In his apartment, Grigori turned on classical music and poured us drinks. More Cristal. Then he led me back to the bedroom, where I took a page from that angel at Vondreesen's castle."

My phone beeped. Another call.

I interrupted Katya. "My attorney is calling. You guys keep talking. I'll be back on in a minute."

I clicked over, and Casey came on the line. "Before I go to bed, I want to be sure you're headed for the plane. The charter company says you haven't checked in yet."

"We still have time."

"Well, technically. But you're down to hours. Don't forget that in addition to flight time, which the pilot tells me will be a good twelve to thirteen hours depending on headwinds, you've got customs and clearances and bureaucracy. Then there's the traffic at both ends. You've gotta add four or five hours for that stuff, at a minimum. I don't need to remind you what's at stake, do I?"

"It's only money."

"It's ten million dollars, Achilles. Your birthright."

"Nine a.m. at the Santa Barbara Superior Court. Got it. That gives me until three a.m. Moscow time to reach the airport. How'd it go with Flurry?"

"She's happy with the evidence provided. She's been having fun with the two you left in the Escalade. Apparently they're wanted for other crimes."

"So I'm good?"

"You just get here. I'll take care of the rest. But do get here. I know this judge, and he's merciless on defendants who disobey court orders."

I clicked back over to Katya and Max. "Casey wanted to be sure I'd show up for court."

"You are tight on time," Katya said.

"It's going to get tighter. Unless Grigori flies somewhere today, I'm going to hit him tonight, when he goes to bed."

Chapter 113

Bad Reflection

IT WASN'T UNTIL AFTER MIDNIGHT that the lights went on in Grigori's bedroom —12:06 to be precise. The day of waiting had been no joyride, and I wouldn't eat another pistachio for the rest of my life, but now the departure deadline was whittling away at my nerves.

If I wasn't on my way to the airport in 174 minutes, I was going to be in contempt of court and out ten million bucks. My only ten million. Grigori's late arrival had left me precious little time for finesse during his interrogation. At the moment, that suited my mood just fine.

Judging by the extinguishing lights, Grigori finally slid between the sheets at 12:22. I gave him twenty minutes to start sawing logs, and then crept about twelve feet up until I was on the pane I knew to be directly over the center of his bed.

I'd waited so long for this moment.

Exactly 200 nights earlier, while my family and I were enjoying my father's sixtieth birthday celebration, Grigori Barsukov's men crept aboard the *Emerging Sea*. Using tools covered in my prints, they diverted the exhaust, bypassed the catalytic converter, disabled the carbon monoxide detectors, arranged the vents, and superglued shut every stateroom window but mine. Then, once everyone was sleeping soundly with full bellies and intoxicated brains, they started the motor that spewed the gas that claimed three precious lives.

Katya would be dead too, but for Colin's snoring.

I would be bearing those lost lives in mind throughout the next 138 minutes.

After readying the lock blade for action in my right hand, I buried my face in the crook of my elbow. With my eyes thus protected, I palmed the sonic pick in my left, pressed it into the glass, and hit the power.

The top pane shattered with a pop as the argon gas exploded outward. Then the second pane burst. I rode a carpet of broken glass down onto Grigori, landing on his chest with a whoosh and a crash and the melodic tinkle of crystal rain.

My nemesis screamed, but I didn't care. I already knew from Katya that nobody could hear. This scream would likely be the first of many.

I put the blade to his throat and clamped my hand over his mouth to control his movements and focus his attention before speaking. "Kyle Achilles. Pleased to meet you. Utter a word, one word, and I'll blind you."

We locked eyes.

After a second of intense staring, I moved the knife from the crease of his throat to the bridge of his crooked nose, then removed my hand, drew my Glock, and backed off the bed.

Grigori remained silent.

I grabbed hold of the puffy white duvet with my knife hand. Once my grip was solid, I backed up, pulling the duvet and about a hundred pounds of glass off my captive. "Roll over, then grab your ass with both hands."

I knew Grigori was dying to talk, longing to issue bribes and threats, but he managed to resist the urge while doing as I'd demanded. He was a man of discipline, if nothing else.

A door swooshed behind me. I spun to see two black suits entering the room, sidearms up but aimed at the moonlight coming through the missing window rather than my head.

Their eyes hadn't adjusted to the dark.

The lead suit spoke first. "You okay, Mister Barsukov? The roof alarm—"

I squeezed my Glock's trigger twice, once for each of them. The first suit dropped like a fishing sinker. The second staggered and tried to aim his gun with his right arm while his left pressed his stomach. I sent two more 9 mm parabellums on their way before he found his balance. The bedroom door slid shut as he collapsed, like the curtain on the final act.

"I might have mentioned the roof alarm. But I didn't want to end up blind." Grigori's voice rang out behind me, calm and cold. "Now drop it!"

Chapter 114

Hanging Out

WHERE HAD Grigori gotten a gun? The bastard must sleep with it under his pillow. I wondered if that was a recent development.

The gun was probably a slimline subcompact like mine. Probably from the same crate. Identical serial numbers but for the last couple of digits. Didn't really matter. What did matter was that he hadn't racked the slide. My ears pick up on that sound like a mother does her baby's cry, and I hadn't heard it.

Semiautomatics won't fire without a chambered round. Would Grigori, safe in his tower, sleep on a gun with a chambered round? Glock 43's didn't have a manual safety. I decided that a man who'd been losing bodyguards left and right just might.

I decided not to risk it.

Without turning, I slowly raised my gun arm out to my side. As it reached waist level, I said, "Did I forget to mention my friend?"

During Grigori's moment of apprehension, I flicked my left wrist with everything I had. The knife I'd pilfered from Gorilla back at the Korston Hotel was a lightweight ceramic model, so it soared a good twenty feet. As it clattered on Grigori's left, I dove to the right, spinning and bringing my Glock to bear. I had three rounds left and I used them all, aiming for Grigori's weapon. I couldn't afford a repeat of the Escalade situation, with no one left alive to interrogate.

Normally I'd have gone for the shoulder on an armed subject I needed alive, targeting the brachial plexus. Disrupting that bundle of nerves turns the arm into the functional equivalent of a bag of meat. But shooting on the move is never good for the aim, and I couldn't risk hitting his head or heart. Not with my president's life at stake.

The first two shots missed, but the third flew true. It amputated Grigori's trigger finger and sent the Glock flying from his hand. I rolled backwards and somersaulted onto my feet. Using my legs like springs to reverse my momentum, I dove and bowled Grigori back to the floor.

He howled like a dying dog.

Ignoring his screams, I rolled him over and pinned him with my knees. I trussed his wrists together behind his back, snugged them tight with cable ties, and then secured his ankles.

Still tuning out Grigori's voice so I could focus on ambient noise, I picked up his Glock and ran to the door, racking the slide as I went. Nothing ejected. There had been no chambered round. No round had loaded either. Strange.

I racked the slide again and confirmed it. The magazine was empty. That made no sense until I paired the thought with Katya spending the night in Grigori's bed. She must have emptied it just as I had the pilot's. What a woman.

Bending down over my fallen assailants, I used my left hand to confirm that neither suit's heart was pumping. Satisfied, I hit the lights and searched the corpses. No radios, just cell phones.

I dragged the nearest suit over to the corner and stopped before the panel marked as a door. Hoisting him up, I pressed his right palm against the reader.

The pane retracted.

Grigori moaned on in the background.

I released the corpse so that he flopped over the sill. There was something poetic about turning one's rival into a doorstop.

Returning to the man of the hour, I flipped him face up, grabbed the cable tie that bound his ankles, and dragged him outside onto the terrace like a caveman hauling a carcass from his cave. "Time to talk."

As we neared the building's edge, I readjusted my grip. I took him by both ankles, and swung him around until the top half of his body swept out over the building's edge. Satisfied with his precarious position, I crouched down and used my hands to anchor his ankles the way I'd do for a buddy during a sit-up test.

The little bastard had some strength in his abs. He remained rigid as a plank.

I stared into his dark, reptilian eyes and then tuned in his voice. "How's it feel to be on the other side of this equation?" I asked, remembering Vaughn's story.

Grigori said nothing. Showed nothing. His KGB roots had grown deep.

"You know me, and I know you," I continued. "So we'll dispense with the pleasantries, and get right to business. I just have one question for you. Are you ready for it?"

"I'm mildly curious," Grigori said, his voice now calm and steady. "But I won't make any promises."

What was with this guy? He had to know I'd happily kill him. I'd already gone through nine of his men. I had him dangling over a ledge. And yet we may as well have been talking about sports at the local pub. Somehow the threat had calmed him.

Normally I'd have softened him up before getting down to business, but I was very tight on time. I hit him with the trillion-dollar question. "What's the plan to kill President Silver?"

Surprise registered on his face. His scleras flared, his eyebrows rose, and his mouth opened ever so slightly. They were micro-movements, but they betrayed him. His surprise was nothing, however, compared to my own. My jaw fell when I heard his reply. "You can drop me now."

Chapter 115

Smoke Detector

I LOOKED PAST my captive toward the dark expanse beyond and the lights of Moscow far below. It was a beautiful night. Fresh air, clear skies, warm breeze. A good night for revenge.

To reach this lofty height, to mount one of the world's most powerful companies and the apex of a mighty nation, a CEO had to have superior negotiating skills. He had to be able to bluff with the best of them. But this was no ordinary negotiation. There'd be no *on-second-thought* moment. If I released Grigori's ankles, that was it. No replay. No do-over. It was all *call the priest, and make arrangements.*

You can drop me now. I let his words hang there for a moment, like a slow softball pitch. Then I did as he asked. I released my grip.

His rigid body pivoted over the rim like a seesaw.

I watched his face flash surprise once again, but the emotion that followed wasn't fear.

His words hadn't been a bluff.

I was the one who'd been bluffing.

I lunged and grabbed his ankles like an outfielder stretching for a ball. I pulled them back against the rim and slid forward on my elbows until my head was between his feet. Staring down past his crotch to his upturned head, a drop of sweat fell from my brow.

Grigori smirked as it landed on his crooked nose.

I ignored his jab and repeated my question. "What's the plan to kill President Silver?"

He didn't sniffle or stammer or spit a response. He did nothing.

Then I got it.

There were things worse than death.

For Grigori Barsukov, one of them was the repercussion that would follow from betraying his old friend, the president of Russia.

I was pretty sure I knew another.

But first I decided to shake things up, throw him off balance. "I know you've got McDonald's here in Moscow. Have you got Burger King?"

Grigori blinked. "What are you talking about?"

"I'm going to let you have it your way, Grigori." I worked my way into a crouch, then jerked up and back like I was doing an Olympic power clean. As soon as Grigori's head was clear of the edge, I took a couple of steps away from the rim and dropped him to the ground with a thud. As he groaned, I rolled him over and repeated the caveman drag. Facedown this time. Back past his fallen protectors, through the bedroom, and into the kitchen.

With another Olympic lifting move, I hoisted him up onto the island. While he watched wide-eyed, I selected a razor-sharp paring knife from the butcher's block. Setting it aside, I grabbed Grigori by the collar and hauled him atop the Viking range.

"What are you doing? I told you to drop me."

"I'm not here to do what you tell me, Grigori. I'm here to get an answer to a question."

Using cable ties, I fastened his neck to the Viking's heavy cast-iron grid. Then I secured his legs in a similar fashion. Sensing what was coming, he tried to flail, but there's not much you can do while strapped facedown by your neck and legs.

I sliced through the tie binding his wrists together behind his back. Power-handling his right arm over the edge of the island, I secured it to the handle of a drawer. His left wrist got the same treatment. The end result was no cross, but then he was no saint. The position, however, would most certainly suffice.

My watch read 1:15 a.m.

I was down to my last hundred minutes.

I walked around to the end of the island and crouched so I could meet Grigori's beady eyes. I was pleased to see him starting to sweat. "Does this place have smoke detectors?"

He closed his eyes, but didn't answer.

I hadn't really expected him to. I looked up and didn't see any, but then his was hardly the typical ceiling. I used the paring knife to slice off his black silk pajamas, just in case.

A switch on the wall caught my eye. I flipped it, and a big ventilation grid rumbled to life overhead.

Grigori began to tremble in anticipation, rattling the range's heavy grates.

I'd been tortured once, for days. That was more for sport than information. I didn't like receiving it, and I didn't like giving it. Despite what this man had done to my family, I wasn't eager to go medieval on him. But I was willing to do whatever it took to save my president. And the clock wouldn't accommodate anything but extreme measures.

Chapter 116

Nibbles

I LOOKED DOWN at the man who had killed my family, and felt my blood begin to boil. He was just a man. One man. But he'd wrought so much damage — and he was eager to inflict more.

Returning to the head of the island, I met his eye again. "I'll start with your left bicep, Grigori. I figure it'll take less than 5 minutes to cook all the way through. At that point I'll be able to snap your arm off like a chicken drumstick. Let me know if you find yourself ready to answer my question before then."

I stuffed a kitchen towel into his mouth. I figured this was the point where nine out of ten men would cave in. They'd spit out the towel and begin babbling. When Grigori didn't respond immediately, I gave him another nudge. "This Viking is my kind of art. Function meets beauty. What do you have, a dozen burners on this thing? All capable of going from a low simmer to high boil, I bet?"

Grigori's eyes remained panicked, but resolute. His jaw didn't move.

The gas burner lit right up, and I cranked it back to low. A beautiful blue flame, an inch below his flesh. He lasted longer than I'd expected. A good six seconds. Spitting out the towel, he groaned, "Okay," clearly straining to sound stoic.

"That's not an answer."

"Bugs. They're using bugs."

"What does that mean? Be clear, Grigori."

He was sucking air and rolling his eyes. "They're going to kill Silver using a custom bioweapon delivered by fleas."

1:18 a.m.

There had been talk of custom bioweapons at the CIA. Last I'd heard they were still theoretical, but just over the horizon. I'd been out of the game for over a year now, however, and with high-tech that was effectively forever.

Custom bioweapons were basically smart bombs engineered to attack a sequence of DNA. They could be designed specifically enough to only impact one person on the planet. In theory, if you could attach one to a vector that would propagate like the flu, it would go around the globe without harming anyone until it infected the intended recipient. But in practice, most biologics petered out in one or two leaps. If you wanted a real shot at success, you'd be well advised to launch it with just a single degree of separation.

"What do you mean, delivered by fleas?"

The smell was already getting to me. Much worse than what you got in the dentist chair.

"They figured out how to transfer the pathogen through flea bites. One will suffice. Now get me off this thing!"

"One more question first. Who's making the delivery?"

"Who do you think? Turn it off!"

It couldn't be, could it? "Say the name!"

"Korovin. Korovin's going to release the fleas personally."

I turned off the burner beneath his bicep, but lit the one beside his head. This one didn't expose him directly to the flame, but it was close enough to singe hair, and he'd still roast, given time. I wanted to keep him feeling the heat.

The Directorate of Operations at the CIA is essentially the military arm of the State Department. During my five years within their Special Operations Group, I'd learned to look at military matters through a diplomatic lens. I applied it now. Diplomatically, this situation was analogous to a tightrope-walking porcupine in a balloon factory. The Secret Service couldn't strip search a foreign head of state. They couldn't even pat him down. Nor could they confront him verbally. Even if they could find a pretext, that was no solution.

You can't catch the head of a nuclear state red-handed in the ultimate act of war, and expect to avoid a major geopolitical crisis. You couldn't even hint at your suspicion. The more I thought about it, the sicker I felt. If the press caught wind of this, the talking heads of 24-hour news would have the citizens of the planet's two most heavily armed nations clamoring for military action.

I couldn't allow that to happen under any circumstances.

Preventing it would be a challenge. With gossip this juicy, there would be no keeping it from the press. Saint Peter himself would be tempted to talk. I was going to have to work to contain the story with the same fervor I'd employ to stop the act itself.

Assuming everything Grigori had told me was true.

Time for verification.

I put my hand on the burner control inches from Grigori's nose. "How'd you get Silver's DNA?"

I knew a DNA sample was necessary to create a personalized bioweapon, and I knew the Secret Service actively guarded Silver's, sweeping up behind him wherever he went like the hypervigilant mother of a newborn

"They got it early. Before he even announced his candidacy."

That made sense. I suspected my former colleagues did the same with most global VIPs, as a precautionary measure. "Who created the weapon?" I asked.

"Bioresearchers in Kazan. Led by Dr. Mikhail Galkin."

"Where do I find Galkin?"

"He was at the medical school, but I think he's gone now. His contact info is on my tablet."

I ran back to the bedroom and retrieved the iPad from Grigori's nightstand. I held it up to his right index finger until it unlocked. The first thing I did was disable the password protection. The next thing I did was find Galkin under the contacts. Kazan State Medical University. One of the best in Eastern Europe. He appeared legit.

"When's Korovin planning to expose Silver to the fleas?"

"On a hunting trip."

"Be more specific."

Grigori managed to smile through his tears. "Sunrise this morning."

Chapter 117

Russian Brillyanc

SUNRISE THIS MORNING! If that really was Korovin's plan, it might already be too late to save the president. I didn't have Silver on speed dial. I couldn't warn him.

What were my options?

Calling the Secret Service tip line wouldn't be fast enough. They were fielding over three thousand threats a day. 'Weaponized fleas' probably wouldn't sound like the most credible among them. By the time I got anyone to believe me, the president would be infected. Even if speed weren't a concern, I couldn't risk dumping information as sensitive and juicy as this into such a big bureaucracy. It would inevitably leak.

My own thoughts echoed in my head. *If that was true.* How did I know? "What will the flea bite do to Silver?"

I saw indecision cross Grigori's face, so I twisted the burner control.

"It's going to make him blind. He's genetically susceptible. It won't appear suspicious."

I believed him.

I had what I needed. I had what I'd come to Russia and risked my freedom and Katya's life for. Now I just had to deliver the news, quickly, and without instigating a nuclear war.

"Would you like me to leave?"

Grigori turned his head to study my face.

I supposed it was a loaded question.

"Yes."

"Call your pilot."

"My hands are tied."

"Walk me through it."

I turned off the burner, and he did. We called right there from his tablet. ETA twenty minutes. It would be 1:40 in the morning. Adding five minutes for the Ansat to be flight ready took the clock to 1:45.

Grigori told the pilot to go straight to the helicopter. Said he'd come out once the rotor was spinning.

I dialed Katya and Max, although there was no way I could reveal what I'd learned over the phone. Every major intelligence service in the world was dialed into Moscow's cellular networks. And with President

Silver in town, they'd all be tuned in. My update could snowball into Armageddon. "The good news is that the mission is accomplished. The bad news is that we have another emergency. I need you to red-light and siren the ambulance over to the American Embassy. Let the Marine guard know that former CIA operative Kyle Achilles is about to arrive by helicopter with 'information critical and urgent to US national defense.' Use that exact language. Make it clear that the helicopter is a civilian Ansat, with no explosives or armaments aboard."

"What's going on? Are you okay?" Katya asked.

"What if they don't believe us?" Max asked.

"I'm fine. If there's an issue, have them contact CIA Director Wiley in Langley. He doesn't like me, but he'll definitely remember me." I gave them my agency identification number, then I hung up. My brevity was cruel, but there would be time for kindness later.

Running to the bedroom, I killed the lights and pulled the corpse out of the doorway and out of sight. I used the butcher block to prop open the door so I'd hear the helicopter turbine come to life.

Grigori's moans and groans were gaining volume. His self-control had been depleted.

I hit the bathroom next and inspected myself in the mirror. I was a mess. I'd worn the black suit over the blue spandex for extra protection from the breaking glass, but had suffered dozens of tiny glass cuts nonetheless. They covered my front side, including the parts of my face not shielded by my elbow. A Marine security guard wouldn't get much flack if he shot me first and asked questions later.

Grigori's suits weren't a viable alternative. Much too small. I'd have to go with something less fresh.

I swapped clothes with the first guard I'd shot. His only had a single bullet hole, and the black fabric hid the blood. In the back of my mind I wondered if that was the reason for the color selection.

I used the kitchen's main sink to quickly scrub my face, hair, and hands. Not perfect, but hopefully sufficient to avoid a bullet between the eyes.

The sound of a rotor revving-up reached my ears.

Time to bid farewell to Grigori.

I returned to the crouch that allowed me to meet his eyes. I studied the man who had ruined hundreds of lives, and was attempting to impact millions more. "One last question. Why did you keep the clinical trial going after Vitalis folded?"

Grigori's eyes lit up, and he managed a twisted smile. "Americans." He spit the word out. "You may have power, but you certainly lack cunning. The trial was for the next phase of the plan, of course."

"The next phase?" I couldn't help but ask, as worry seized my heart.

His smile grew. "The Russian phase. Brillyanc without side effects."

I thought about that for a moment. What he said made sense. Perfect sense. Yet he'd ultimately cancelled the trial. "But you failed. Seems to me, you're lacking American ingenuity."

His smile faded.

"You killed Martha Achilles, and John Achilles, and Colin Achilles. You killed Saba Mamaladze, and Tanya Tarasova, and her husband. No doubt you've killed many others. I'm going to light a candle now, one in each of their memories."

While I ignited the first of the Viking's six burners, Grigori began bellowing like no man ever had before. He roared and he moaned, he wailed and he screamed. By the time I'd set the sixth burner aflame, I was wondering if his cries would shatter the pyramid.

I made it halfway to the door.

As much as I hated this man, as much as Grigori deserved to roast in the flames of hell, I wasn't that guy. I spun around and shot a bullet through the flaming tip of his crooked nose.

Chapter 118

Tough Old Bird

DRESSED AS I WAS in a GasEx guard's uniform, I didn't raise the pilot's defenses until I was in the copilot's chair with my weapon trained on his heart.

My conscript was probably around sixty in calendar years, but a hundred experientially. He was what most would call a tough old bird, with thick gray hair kept close-cropped, a weather-beaten face, and eyes that told you they'd seen it all. The no-nonsense type.

I got right to it. "The US Embassy. Land inside the fence."

He looked from my gun to my face. "I can't do that. The American Embassy is just a block from the prime minister's office. It's restricted air space. We'll be shot down."

"What's your name?"

"Erik."

"You fly Hinds in Afghanistan, Erik?" I asked, referring to the iconic beefy Soviet attack helicopter.

"I did."

"Then figure it out. Fast and low."

"That may get us to the compound, but we'll be shredded by ground fire if we try to land inside. Marines don't mess around."

"I've arranged for clearance."

Erik didn't appear convinced. I couldn't blame him. Unlike Hinds, I was pretty sure the undersides of Ansats weren't armor-plated. "And if I say no?"

"I'll shoot you, and steal a car."

His eyes drifted toward the base of his chair.

"I emptied the magazine. Nonetheless, I'd appreciate your keeping your hands on the controls."

Something flashed across Erik's eyes. Might have been admiration. Might have been hope. "What about Grigori?"

"He's tied up in the kitchen. Won't be joining us."

Erik turned to the windshield. "Flight time is about four minutes." He lifted the collective and pushed the cyclic toward the moonlit silver snake that was the Moscow River.

"I've got no beef with you, Erik. Take care of me, and you'll be fine.

Cross me, and I'll add you to the list."

He didn't ask what list. Afghan vets had instincts.

I pointed my Glock at his crotch, and called Katya. "Are you there yet?"

I had to struggle to hear her reply over the rotor noise, even with my earbuds placed under the helicopter's headphones. "We're at the front gate."

"They still haven't let you in?"

"We're still talking over the intercom."

"Dammit! Do you know who's on the other side?"

"I think it's still the duty sergeant. It is two o'clock in the morning."

"Tell him the helicopter is three minutes out. Tell him to get the ambassador out of bed. Repeat the words, 'information critical and urgent to US national defense.' "

"I told him all that, Achilles. I don't think he believes me. I may have authority in the classroom, but I'm just a Russian girl to this Marine."

"He'll believe you when he hears the rotors. Tell him to open the window."

"Okay. Also, Casey called to remind you that we need to get to the airport."

"I'll see you soon."

Erik flew us north over the Sparrow Hills, then down to the middle of the Moscow river, low and fast. Low enough that I could have yanked fish from the water with a hand net. Fast enough that the net would have snapped like a twig in a hurricane.

We flew under the third-ring road, wetting the skids. Then we splashed them again beneath the Borodinskiy Bridge. Just before the metro bridge, we cut inland and skimmed over side streets like an experienced cab driver.

This vet knew his stuff.

The US Embassy compound occupies an entire city block at the nine o'clock position on Moscow's Garden Ring Road. The public face is a famous white and yellow building of the same grand old architectural style used on most of Moscow's classic buildings. This was where the ambassador had his formal office, and where Russian visa applicants and Americans requiring consular assistance were serviced. But this building wasn't where matters of critical import were discussed. To see sexy foreign-policy action, you had to go deeper into the compound, to a cube-shaped edifice of sandstone and reflective glass.

Approaching at a height lower than many of the surrounding buildings, I was pleased to see floodlights covering the parking lot before the cube. As we swooped in, I also saw a familiar ambulance parked outside the gate.

Lights began to swarm around us from every direction, like TIE fighters defending the Death Star. Even more directed were the red dots of laser sights shining from dozens of M4 carbines.

Erik set us down center circle, killed the rotor, and raised his hands.

Chapter 119

All the Fuss

I LOOKED OVER at the pilot as the Marine embassy guards surrounded our helicopter. "Thank you, Erik. You're dismissed."

He didn't reply.

I exited the Ansat with my hands behind my head, and walked slowly toward the building's entrance. Marines in full battle gear materialized on my left and right. They grabbed my wrists and shoulders and marched me clear of the decelerating rotors.

We stopped before a third Marine who searched me while two more stood ready with M9 Berettas directed rock-steady at my head. Within seconds, my Glock and lock blade were gone, as was my cell phone and Grigori's tablet. A metal detector followed, and an explosive-sniffing German Shepherd did its thing. Finally, the Berettas backed off and a familiar freckled face appeared. "Hello, Achilles."

Michael McArthur and I had gone through the advanced field-operative course in the same six-man cohort. The experience hadn't been entirely pleasant. Granger had put me through an individual training program in lieu of the CIA's basic course — on account of my atypical background. Therefore, at the advanced-course, I was the new guy.

Initially, they all resented my special status, considering the Olympics a cake walk compared to what the five of them had been through. But between my marksmanship and stamina, I eventually earned their respect, and there was no bad blood at graduation.

Five years had passed since then.

I hadn't seen or heard of Mac since.

If inclined, he could slash through all the red tape surrounding my unusual arrival and brazen request. The identity verification. The credibility assessment. The escalation to a primary decision maker. If inclined.

Knowing he'd have an appreciation for human intelligence hot from the field, I opened with, "I've got ears-only intel for Ambassador Jamison. Information of a hyper-critical nature."

Mac studied me in silence for a good three seconds. "What about my boss, the Moscow Station Chief?"

I'd thought about that while Erik was dodging telephone wires on our flight in. "My information is diplomatically inflammatory and extremely sensitive. I think that should be Jamison's call."

Mac waved off the Marines. "Come with me."

I followed him through an anonymous federal corridor to a room with a thick door, no windows, and a round table suitable for six. He motioned for me to take a seat, but remained standing by the door. This wasn't the occasion to catch up or relive old times, so he remained silent.

I spun a chair around so I could sit while facing him. "The other two, the Russian man and woman who arrived by ambulance. They're on our side."

Mac acknowledged with a single nod. "They're comfortable in another room. What about the pilot?"

"I can't say. He flew me here at the point of my gun. His boss was evil incarnate, but as far as I know Erik was just hired help."

"Good to know."

Ambassador Jamison entered, dressed in jeans and a Naval Academy sweatshirt. The job of US Ambassador to the Russian Federation was the pinnacle post in the diplomatic corps. It didn't go to top contributors or friends of the president, like some island nations and minor European states. It was assigned based solely on merit. Jamison was nearing seventy, but word was that his mind was sharp as ever, and he looked amazingly fit.

As Mac closed the door behind him, Jamison took a seat. He studied my frazzled face for a silent second before speaking. "Tell me, Mr. Achilles. What's all the fuss about?"

Chapter 120

Two Vials

JAMISON AND I rocketed across the Russian countryside in his ambassadorial limo, blue lights flashing on the roof, American flag flapping on the hood, sirens silent. They would have been superfluous. The ambassador had requested a police escort, and the mayor of Moscow had accommodated. With the US President in town, this was no time for petty power plays.

We were sixty-five kilometers from the Kremlin when the limo roared through gates that armed guards closed behind us in haste. Sixty-six kilometers by the time we pulled up to the main entrance of President Korovin's hunting dacha.

I looked over at the ambassador. He appeared nervous. We'd spent one hour at the embassy debating tactics, and another perfecting the plan during the drive. Two hours wasn't a lot, given the diplomatic minefield we'd be navigating. Maximizing the odds of President Silver surviving while minimizing the odds of instigating a war required a tightrope balancing act.

I voiced a final word of encouragement. "Ninety-nine-point-eight percent is pretty good. Nothing's ever a hundred."

He nodded, but his expression didn't change. "Beyond that door, two rivals are having breakfast. Both have nuclear briefcases. I pray we're right."

Stepping from the limo to the snap of an enormous presidential security service officer's salute, I experienced a first. I cringed at the sight of an American flag.

"Ambassador Jamison, Mister Achilles, if you'll follow me please." Without another word, the officer did an about-face and led us through double doors held open by silent soldiers. Our guides' shoulders were so broad, I wondered if he'd have to twist to pass cleanly through a normal door. I wasn't sure how nimble that made him, but his physique certainly was intimidating. To Korovin's further credit, I'd never seen a better body shield.

We paused in the vestibule, ostensibly for our guide to receive instructions through his earpiece, but almost certainly for us to be scanned. You couldn't pat down diplomats without raising eyebrows, but you could secretly subject them to millimeter wave scans that produced detailed 3D images.

The pause gave us a moment to look around.

I'd never been to Naval Support Facility Thurmont, better known as Camp David, but I understood that the US President's weekend retreat was essentially a compound of high-end log cabins and lodges. By contrast, the Russian President's was more like the home of a German king. Marble floors, arched plaster ceilings ornamented with gold filigree, and large oil paintings of men with muskets and dead animals.

Satisfied, for one reason or another, Shoulders resumed walking. We wound our way to a dining room large enough to house an orchestra, and ornate enough to host a black-tie dinner. A left turn through an archway in the corner took us to a private dining room with a bay window that hinted at first light. Seated before it, dressed not in tuxedos but rather in hunting garb, were two of the world's most famous faces.

We stopped and waited to be acknowledged.

President Silver put down his coffee cup and turned our way. "Good morning, Ambassador."

"Good morning, Mister President. President Korovin. Pardon the intrusion at this early hour. We understood that your plan was to be in the hunting blind at dawn, and we needed to catch you first."

"Well then, you're just in time," Silver said.

"Mister Achilles needs a word in private, if you don't mind, Mister President. This will only take a minute."

Silver turned back to Korovin. "If you'll pardon me, Vladimir, apparently I need a minute."

Korovin inclined his head with no change of expression. "But of course."

Silver stood and Shoulders led us toward the back of the room while Ambassador Jamison remained with President Korovin. The guard paused beside a doorway and motioned for us to enter the sitting room beyond.

We did.

Shoulders shut the door behind us.

Two hundred days had passed since my family had been murdered. Fifteen days since a dedicated master sergeant had broken me out of jail. Nine days since Katya and I had gone undercover at a dead man's party. And four hours since I'd killed the man who was ultimately behind it all. Now I was twenty meters from the most powerful man in the world, and alone with his intended victim, the President of the United States.

President Silver looked older than on TV, but somehow more charismatic and intelligent. His thick head of hair befit his surname, and his deep blue eyes had a magnetism I knew I'd never forget. "Please allow me to see if that's a bathroom," I said, heading for a door a few steps from the one we'd entered.

It was.

I flipped on the light.

"If you'd come this way, Mister President."

While Silver complied, I turned on both faucets and motioned for him to close the door. To his credit, Silver went along without question. I supposed that handlers and security practices were among the many things to which presidents are forced to become accustomed.

"I'm sure you've got one hell of a story for me, Mister Achilles?"

I removed two vials of insect repellant from my breast pocket. "I do. While I relay it, would you kindly remove your clothes."

Chapter 121

Epic Choices

I STEPPED OFF the chartered jet into the balmy Santa Barbara air at eight o'clock, Tuesday morning.

I was a full day late.

My bail was forfeit.

I couldn't explain my tardiness. Not to Casey. Not to ADA Kilpatrick. Not to Judge Hallows. Long ago I'd sworn to keep my nation's secrets — regardless of how inconvenient. I suppose I could have asked President Silver for a favor. But that would have felt like putting a price on what I'd done. Besides, I didn't need the money — not now that I was done with legal fees.

As I walked out of the courtroom later that morning, a free man on the broad marble steps with a beautiful woman by his side, I heard a familiar voice. "I owe you an apology."

Katya and I turned to see a petite, ship-shape form approaching from a few paces behind. "Detective Flurry. How nice to see you where the sun is shining."

"I swallowed their bait," she said. "Hook, line, and sinker. I'd hoped I was better than that."

"Neither of us had a clue what we were up against."

"But *you* figured it out."

"Not for six months. And even then, I had to go to extremes."

Flurry half smiled, then got down to business. "I know how they did it. But I don't know why. Care to clue me in?"

"Professional curiosity?"

"You could call it that."

"They had a big secret to keep." I turned back around, put my arm around Katya's waist, and resumed walking down those broad marble steps.

"What about Rita?" Katya asked. "Will she be going to jail?"

"No. That would require a trial, and we can't have that. She's a victim of Brillyanc herself. She'll live in fear for the rest of her life. That's punishment enough for someone who didn't know what she was really doing."

"You're just being nice because she's pretty."

Perhaps I was. Perhaps I was just sick of negativity.

"Where to?" Katya asked, as we closed the doors of her Ford. Just two words, but a gigantic question. She knew it. I knew it. It had been hanging out there since that day she walked into the visitation room at the Santa Barbara County Jail. Now that those bars were forever behind me, a decision was finally due.

"When I left government service a year and a month ago, it was because I was disillusioned with the bureaucratic process that's baked in. I wanted to have right and wrong guide my life, not politicians. The question I couldn't answer was what to do next. Politics is the way of the world, after all. Whether it's the government or the private sector, if you have a boss, he's going to be looking for personal gain." I shook my head at the memory of my last boss and our final confrontation in his corner office at Langley.

"I spent a year throwing myself against rock faces and wandering about the corners of Europe, trying to find an answer. Then I spent six months in jail, learning to count my blessings."

I turned to face Katya, whose attention was locked on me so intently that I felt I should remind her to breathe. "The last two weeks were the toughest of my life. They were also the most productive. We altered history, Katya. Together we saved hundreds if not thousands of lives. We rid the world of a scourge. Wielded justice where it was overdue. No bosses. No rules. Just you and me and boundless determination. That's what I want to do. For the rest of my life."

Katya crossed her arms. "Like your namesake, the original Achilles. You've made the epic choice."

I said nothing.

"But how? How do you — I don't even know how to phrase it — identify the dirty work that needs doing? The Barsukovs and Vondreesens are hidden beneath cloaks and shadows. They're few … and far between."

I took her hands. "I'm not so sure about *few*. But I fear you're right regarding *far-between*."

Katya's eyes darted back and forth between my face and our hands. "But I work at a University. I'm not free to wander about in search of adventure."

"I know. And it's eating me up."

Chapter 122

From Time to Time

THE SAN FRANCISCO OFFICE of Senator Colleen Collins was elegant, but not grand. It befit a woman who was both distinguished and of-the-people. The sky-blue carpet she'd selected was appropriately uplifting, and it had the added benefit of bringing out her eyes, eyes that were smiling at me.

She motioned me to a cream-colored armchair that looked great but was probably a bear to maintain. With that voice that should be singing jazz, she said, "Thank you for coming."

"It's a pleasure, if an unexpected one. I didn't think I'd see you again."

"Really? It was inevitable."

"How's that?"

"Allow me to enlighten you, Mister Achilles. Secrets are like walls. They have people on both sides. They try to keep you out, but once you're in, you're in. You've scaled a couple of tall walls of late. That puts you in rarefied air, with some pretty lofty company."

"A couple of walls?"

"I chair the Senate Subcommittee on Emerging Threats and Technologies, and in that role, I have regular contact with the National Security Committee. President Silver told me what you did."

I hadn't told the president the full story there in the bathroom. Ambassador Jamison and I had agreed that it could be diplomatically dangerous to give Silver news of such a vile, personal attack right before he spent the morning with the man who had plotted his genetically engineered demise. Not while they were both just an arm's reach from nuclear triggers. So I'd told him part of the truth. Enough to make him sufficiently worried about the dangers of insect bites to be extremely thorough in his bug spray application. "How is the president?"

"He's still pretty shaken. Theory is one thing, but having someone actually create a personalized smart bomb with your name on it is quite another."

"I can only imagine."

"It goes without saying that he's deeply grateful for what you did. He told me he's comforted to know that you're out there." She paused, her face fraught with emotion. "That wasn't just a political bromide. He really meant it. He went on to explain that despite having a dozen forces out there working to protect him and our nation, from the Secret Service to the FBI to the United States Marines, there are still gaps. Gaps that no federal force could ever fill, because they're too small, and we're too big and bureaucratic."

She shrugged. "Of course he could never admit any of this publicly. Never even hint at it. But I could, I can, with you. Because you're already on our side of the wall."

Climbing has its privileges.

"Silver suggested that on occasion he might need a force of one. And that on such occasion, he might want to call on you, through me, to help out. He wanted to know if you'd be willing? As would I."

At that moment, I wished I had a shot of Brillyanc to help process the load Senator Collins had thrown at me. Not really, but that got me thinking. "How's the cleanup going? The elimination of Brillyanc?"

"Grigori Barsukov's penchant for secrecy made that a relatively simple task. Very few people knew the formula, and we were able to identify and neutralize all of them — one way or another. Federal forces are excellent for that. We've also put flags in place that will alert the FDA if someone is purchasing the raw materials in suspicious proportions."

"What about the users?"

"They've all been discreetly informed of their situation." Collins paused, and I noted that she was playing nervously with the hem of her jacket. "I see by your eyes that you're thinking about my situation. In short, I got lucky. Good genes and a California diet overflowing with antioxidants. Looks like I dodged a bullet. But of course I'll be monitoring my mental health as regularly as my blood pressure. That will be a monthly reminder of how close we came to a dangerous fork in history's path, not that I'll need one. Every time I forget something for the rest of my life I'll probably be holding my breath."

"And Daniels?"

"The jury is still out on the VP. And by jury, I mean his medical advisers. He'll be taking monthly tests as well. Meanwhile, he's started playing one of those computer games specially designed to keep an aging brain sharp, and he's dining on fruit and vegetable smoothies three times a day."

I wondered if there had been a heated debate in the White House Situation Room involving everyone from political strategists to constitutional scholars to medical and security advisers, or if the discussion had been limited to a quiet three-way between Silver, Daniels, and Collins in the president's study.

I was enjoying this backstage pass to history in the making, and longed to know more, but didn't press. That feeling gave me the only answer that really mattered.

I wanted to spend more time behind the curtain.

"So what do you think, Achilles? Can I call on you, from time to time, at the behest of a grateful president?"

NOTES ON PUSHING BRILLIANCE

In the last words of this novel, Achilles faces the toughest decision of his life. Does he follow his passion, or follow his heart? It's eating him up. I didn't answer it here because to do so would not have been genuine. Neither Achilles nor I can answer it until the dust settles and he sees what comes next.

That happens in Book 2, *The Lies Of Spies*, which you're about to read.

If you're skeptical about Achilles' climbing feats, watch the fascinating trailer of the 2018 National Geographic film *Free Solo*, or search "free solo climbing" on YouTube. What you'll see is mind-blowing.

For more information on the threat faced by bioengineered weapons, read "Hacking the President's DNA," published in the November 2012 issue of The Atlantic.

Brillyanc is a fictitious product, but the link between oxidative stress and cognitive function is well established. Google Scholar is the place to search if you're in the mood for heavy reading.

All of the above and more can also be found on the Pinterest Board: Author Tim Tigner, Research for *Pushing Brilliance*.

AUTHOR'S NOTE

Dear Reader,

THANK YOU for reading PUSHING BRILLIANCE. I hope you enjoyed it. On the other hand, if my writing wasn't your style, I thank you for giving me a try. I appreciate the fact that tastes vary. (Personally, I love cilantro but hate brussels sprouts.)

For those who had fun, I'm pleased to note that Kyle and Katya's story continues in THE LIES OF SPIES. I also have a special offer. If you email me at PushingBrilliance @timtigner.com, I will immediately forward you the story of **Creating Kyle Achilles**. I think you'll find it fascinating. I'll also keep you informed of future releases.

Thanks for your kind reviews and attention,

The Lies of Spies

Tim Tigner

This novel is dedicated to Dick Hill, the golden voice who brings my audiobooks to life. Thank you, my friend.

THE LIES OF SPIES

PART 1: ASSIGNMENTS

Chapter 1
Damned Spot

Washington D.C.

"CAN YOU GET THE BLOOD OUT?" Reggie asked, unbuttoning the pinpoint oxford and handing it to his landlady.

Mrs. Pettygrove accepted the soiled shirt with a liver-spotted hand and an inquisitive glance. "Solid white is easy, dear. Lots of options. Don't you worry, I'll get it out. Leave your shoes too. They'll be waiting for you in the morning."

Reggie looked down to study his black wingtips in the dim glow of the Georgetown brownstone's entryway light. "My shoes are fine. You shined them just two days ago."

"*Fine* isn't good enough." Her singsong voice was tinged with excitement. "Not for you, and certainly not for the White House. I want them to be beautiful."

Reggie slipped off his shoes — more to see the twinkle in those wizened blue eyes than for the service itself. "You're too good to me."

"Better than some people, apparently. Would you care to tell me whose blood you're wearing?"

Reggie showed her some teeth. "Let's just say it's a lawyer's."

"Everyone in Washington's a lawyer, dear."

He winked and turned toward the stairs that led up to his room, knowing that no offense would be taken. She understood that discretion was his first duty. "Good night, Mrs. Pettygrove. Thanks again."

Reggie served as President William Silver's personal aide, or *body man* as most referred to him. It was a unique role. On the one hand, he was a servant, a valet. On the other, Reggie enjoyed virtually unparalleled intimacy with both the great man and the highest office. Only Brock Sparkman, the president's new chief of staff, was as tapped into the psyche of the commander-in-chief.

Reggie went everywhere the president went, mentally two steps ahead while physically three steps behind. His job was to anticipate Silver's personal needs and attend to them. With Reggie relieving him of petty problems and everyday worries, America's chief executive was free to dedicate his big brain to the nation's business.

Officially, Reggie knew little of import. Although he held a Top-Secret clearance, as everyone close to the president did, he didn't have

SCI clearance. He didn't have access to the Sensitive Compartmented Information, the sexy stuff. Nevertheless, very little happened in the Oval Office or on Air Force One of which Reggie wasn't aware.

He pieced together a few words here, and a few words there, when a door was left open or he was leaving a room. The subsequent amalgamation was unavoidable when one had a keen intellect and a curious mind. Sometimes it didn't even take that much. Today in Cadillac One, for example, in between the president's routine update with his chief of staff and a call with the governor of Wisconsin, the secretary of defense had phoned regarding an administrative matter but had ended up briefing the president on a space-based defense platform that was right out of the movies — except that apparently it wasn't.

Of course, Reggie would never even hint at the knowledge he'd acquired, much less speak of it. His loyalty to his president was absolute. His patriotism emphatic and sincere. Still, late at night, when the president was finally tucked in and Reggie got to enjoy a few quiet moments before passing out on his pillow, he found pride in knowing as much about Silver's social relationships as the first lady, as much about Silver's congressional relationships as the minority whip, and as much about Silver's foreign relationships as the director of the CIA. Not bad for a young man whose upbringing had been anything but privileged.

Pulling back the covers, Reggie found himself shaking his head as he reflected on his conversation with Mrs. Pettygrove. *Can you get the blood out?* In this town, that was a loaded question. Reggie's conscience was clean, but he knew that many on Capitol Hill had souls resembling Lady Macbeth's. How fortunate he was, to be working for the good guys.

As he drifted off, Reggie had no inkling of the remarkable revelation he'd overhear the next morning while in the presence of those good guys — or the colossal confrontation that would result.

Chapter 2
Big Decision

Air Force One

PRESIDENT WILLIAM SILVER looked out the window to the left of his desk as Air Force One broke through the morning clouds. Funny how it was always sunny if you just climbed high enough. He tried to use that analogy as a guiding principle for his presidency — but Washington didn't make it easy.

Today, however, he wouldn't be rising above. Today, he would be diving down. He'd be sinking to the bottom of the barrel, taking the fight to the enemy.

Silver wasn't entirely comfortable with that.

Without turning from the window, he said, "Reggie, I'm ready for Collins and Sparkman now."

"Right away, Mr. President."

Used to be you had to press an intercom button, Silver mused. Nowadays, all he had to do was begin speaking with a name and the walls somehow knew who to connect. It was convenient, and the Secret Service loved it, but Silver found it a bit creepy — if he thought about it. So he tried not to.

Collins and Sparkman arrived simultaneously, but not together. Senator Colleen Collins was still getting to know his new chief of staff. She was a Californian with 36 years of Capitol Hill experience — and the new chair of the Senate Select Committee on Intelligence. A *grande dame* as it were, with power, class, and a scintillating intellect. At seventy-something, she appeared early-fifties, with perfectly coiffed chestnut hair, glowing skin, and a perky disposition.

Brock Sparkman, on the other hand, was a behind-the-scenes bulldog of a guy. The Washington Beltway equivalent of a 4-star general. Lots of bark, lots of bite, and a reputation for sacrificing political correctness in favor of expediency. Having Sparkman prep the battlefields allowed Silver to drive hard bargains without sacrificing affability.

Both Collins and Sparkman were extremely effective, albeit in very different ways.

Standing before his desk, both were giving him a funny look, as though a big bug was nesting on his nose.

"What?"

"Are you feeling well, Mr. President?" Collins asked.

She knew him too well. "I've been struggling with a special circumstance for some time now, and the accompanying decision. I finally made it, and it's *execution* time, which is why you're here."

"Execution time?" Sparkman repeated, while he and Collins took seats in response to Silver's gesture. "I haven't heard you use that phrase before."

Silver concurred with a nod, pleased with his chief of staff's astute grasp of nuance. "How long do we go back, Brock?"

"All the way to freshman orientation, Mr. President."

"Right. And in the forty years that have flown by since, have you ever known me to be vengeful?"

"No sir."

"Impulsive?"

"No sir."

"Irrational?"

"No sir. You battled your way to the pinnacle of political power by never allowing rogue emotions to get the better of your fine mind." Sparkman's tone was analytical rather than obsequious.

Silver nodded in acknowledgment, and turned his attention to Senator Collins. "And you, Colleen. Have you ever known me to put the personal above the professional?"

"No, Mr. President, I have not."

"Have you ever known me to be reckless with affairs of state?"

"No, sir."

"And as the ranking elected official focused on intelligence affairs, have you ever known me to be daft, rash, or unreasonable?"

"No, sir. I've always been proud to have you as my president."

Satisfied with the results of his verbal priming, Silver found the courage to proceed as planned. "I've asked you here to discuss a personal issue involving the Russian president. One which, as far as I know, has no precedent."

Collins and Sparkman leaned closer, but kept quiet. Their eyes were locked on his, their expressions anxious.

President Silver mimicked their pose and lowered his voice. "The bottom line is this: I've decided to order President Korovin's assassination."

Chapter 3
Preemptive Measures

Air Force One

PRESIDENT SILVER studied the staring faces across the desk. Collins appeared relieved. Sparkman, by contrast, looked like his priest had just told him his mother was a Martian. He seemed to be waiting for a modifier that wasn't going to come. Sparkman's expression ran a gamut of emotions until at last he turned to Collins. When he saw the look on her face, he began shaking his head. Turning back to Silver he asked, "What am I missing? Is this some inside joke? Because with all due respect, Mr. President, you can't seriously be considering an unprovoked attack on another nuclear power."

"He's dead serious, Brock." Collins' tone bore no ambiguity.

Sparkman's shoulders slumped. "We have an agenda. An agenda reflecting the promises made to the people that put you in The Oval. If you — I can't believe I'm even uttering these words — if you send in the Special Forces to assassinate the president of Russia, word will leak and that will all be gone. Your entire second term will be tied up with just two things." Sparkman held up a couple of fingers. "The desperate struggle to avoid nuclear war, and a fruitless endeavor to keep you out of jail."

Silver sat silently, waiting for Sparkman's analytical center to regain control.

Not there yet, Sparkman turned back to Collins. "I can't believe you're swallowing this without gagging, Colleen. What do you know that I don't?"

Silver nodded at Collins, giving her approval.

Collins reached out to put a hand on Sparkman's shoulder. Perhaps they were better acquainted than he'd realized, Silver thought. More likely it was just the reflexive move of a savvy politician. While Sparkman looked on with widening eyes, Collins began. "About three months ago, President Korovin launched an attack against President Silver using a customized bioweapon. But for the actions of a former CIA operative who stumbled across the plot, your boss would now be blind."

Sparkman wouldn't have looked more stunned if Collins had ripped off a mask to reveal a robotic face. "Blind! Customized bioweapon! What's going on here? I feel like I just woke up in Bizarro World. Why am I only hearing about this now?"

"Containment."

"Containment? I'm the bloody White House Chief of Staff! I'm the one who does the containing!"

Collins kept her hand firmly in place. "You weren't chief of staff at the time. You're only hearing about it now for exactly the reasons you elucidated earlier. If word were to get out, geopolitical stability would be jeopardized. Stock markets would crash. The global economy would suffer. And everything else on the agenda would go out the window as we scrambled to avoid World War III."

Sparkman flopped back in his chair. "You're serious." After a moment of silent reflection, he asked Silver, "What on earth was Korovin trying to accomplish?"

"He wanted to further his expansionist agenda by weakening the opposition," the president replied.

"Surely Korovin couldn't have expected to get away with it?"

"Actually, he almost did. His plan was ingenious. The blindness would have appeared entirely natural. He was exploiting a genetic predisposition."

Sparkman's face softened as his frustration gave way to empathy. "Why didn't you tell me when I took the job?"

Silver met his eye. "The day I learned of the plot, I decided not to tell anyone. Not until I'd thought it through. And I haven't told anyone. Not even the first lady. This news is simply too volatile to feed with any oxygen at all."

"But—"

"Senator Collins knows because she also got sucked up in the Korovin conspiracy. The only other people who know are our former ambassador to Russia, and the operative who uncovered and thwarted Korovin's plot."

"So what's changed? Why the sudden decision to act?"

"The decision's not sudden. Acutely aware of the potential consequences of rash action, I spent a few months reflecting, adding the objectivity that only time provides. I gave it a hundred days, and decided that I'll never feel safe so long as Korovin is out there. I've also concluded that my G20 counterparts aren't safe either. Not with Korovin still eager to implement his expansionist agenda."

Sparkman took a deep breath. "Can I safely infer that during those hundred days you figured out how to eliminate Korovin without sparking World War III? Because in that regard, I don't have a clue, Mr. President."

"That's precisely why we're meeting today." Silver redirected his gaze to Collins, who was waiting with a knowing twinkle in her blue eyes.

She spoke a single word. "Achilles?"

Silver's lips spread in a shallow smile. "Achilles."

Sparkman leaned forward. "Is that a code name?"

"It's a last name," Silver said. "Kyle Achilles was the operative who saved me from Korovin's custom bioweapon."

"Is he CIA?"

"Used to be. He's been out for almost two years now."

"Doing what?"

"Colleen, why don't you field that question," the president said.

Collins cleared her throat, buying a second to think. "Achilles has been doing some contemplating of his own. His life's held a few disappointments. He was an Olympic biathlete until an injury ended his career. He then swapped sports, getting into competitive rock climbing until Garrison Granger recruited him for the CIA's Special Operations Group. Achilles ended up as Granger's go-to guy for top ops, but once Rider took the helm and forced Granger out, Achilles became frustrated and left. Since then, he's been in a transitional period."

"Transitional period?

A single knock interrupted their discussion, and Reggie Pepper slipped into the room.

President Silver held up an index finger, putting Reggie on pause while nodding to Collins to continue. He didn't want to lose momentum with Sparkman. While his subordinate, and absolutely loyal, Sparkman was anything but a yes-man. It was important to Silver that his chief of staff buy in wholeheartedly, as this was a momentous decision.

Collins resumed. "After the CIA, Achilles returned to climbing until he got caught up in the Korovin conspiracy. It sucked up about seven months of his life, and now he's climbing again."

"You think he'll want another crack at Korovin?"

"I know he does. President Silver left Achilles with the expectation that he might call on him from time to time if circumstances warranted an off-the-books, one-man op. I'm the designated intermediary, the firewall as you'd say, due to our mutual history with the Korovin conspiracy."

Sparkman refocused on Silver. "So you did see this coming?"

"You know I like to be prepared." Silver was glad to see Sparkman warming to the idea. Now that the fire was lit, he knew his chief of staff would shepherd it. He turned to face the door. "What is it?"

"Theresa May requested a call," Reggie said, referencing the United Kingdom's prime minister. "She says it's urgent."

"Thank you." Silver nodded in dismissal.

"Was that wise?" Sparkman asked, once the door had closed.

"Reggie? His loyalty is absolute. He'd never breathe a word. I'd bet my life on that."

"Speaking of placing bets," Collins said. "What exactly is your plan for Achilles?"

Chapter 4
Sunrise

The Kremlin

THE PRESIDENTIAL GUARDS didn't query Ignaty Filippov as he barreled toward the gilded doors.

They didn't dare.

Sixteen years earlier, one of their colleagues had delayed Ignaty to ask if he was expected. That guard had later written that northern Siberia was only cold three months out of the year: June, July, and August. The other nine were *very* cold.

President Korovin raised his left index finger as his chief strategist burst in, but didn't look up. He was on a call. "Thank you, Nicolas. I'll look forward to seeing you at the summit."

The moment Korovin cradled the corded phone, Ignaty waved a flash drive. "Miss Muffet came through!"

Miss Muffet was the code name of Russia's most valuable spy. While not officially under his direct command, Ignaty's rank in Korovin's power structure gave him the ability to assume virtual command of pretty much anything he wanted. As chief strategist, this extended to a few key espionage operations.

"Your White House mole?"

Ignaty grinned in response, then waited for Korovin to connect the dots. It only took the president a second. His mind should be listed beside the other natural wonders of the world.

"Sunrise?"

"Sunrise!"

Sunrise was the code name assigned to the largest defense project in U.S. history. Also the most tightly guarded one since the Manhattan Project. Ignaty had been digging for the details ever since the $70 billion project appeared in the DOD budget, and Korovin bugged him about it daily.

"Tell me."

"*Sunrise* will give the Americans complete control of space: spacecraft, space stations, and space satellites." He emphasized the latter because that was the game changer. The death blow. Without satellites, both civilian and military communications would cease to function. Ignaty knew Korovin's quick mind would grasp that implication immediately.

The president's terse response confirmed as much. "How?"

Ignaty grabbed a chair, and laid it all out: the mechanical operations, the military implications, and the political fallout.

Korovin maintained a poker face throughout, but Ignaty wasn't fooled. He knew his boss felt each revelation like a lash from a cane. It was a side of the great man to which only his closest aides were privy.

Behind all the posturing and poise, the collapse of the Soviet Union still weighed heavily on Korovin's broad shoulders. He woke with the pain of disgrace each morning, and he went to bed limping from fatigue each night. In between, he smiled publicly for the cameras while privately vowing to set things right.

An average politician would accept Russia's decline as the inevitable outcome of a failed ideology, but Korovin was determined to restore Russia's parity with the U.S. before leaving office. And it was working. As the international press frequently lamented, he was making measurable progress — one sly step at a time. Russia's voters were also taking notice. As the local broadcasts proudly proclaimed, the bold commander had put hope back on the horizon.

Sunrise would squash the dream like a beetle beneath a boot.

Again Korovin cut to the crux with a one-word question. "When?"

"It's scheduled to go live in three."

"That soon? Three years?"

"It leverages existing systems." Ignaty saw evidence of the damage he was inflicting reflected in Korovin's cornflower eyes. He may as well be slipping a stiletto between the president's ribs.

Korovin blew air and leaned back, shifting his gaze to the shimmering crystals of his chandelier. After a full minute of somber silence, he said, "Give it to me."

"What?" Ignaty asked, knowing full well. Long history or not, only a fool would interrupt the most powerful man on Earth with bad news alone.

"Our solution."

Ignaty lived for moments like these — and he remained alive because of them. Still, he made the president wait a few seconds for it. "I call it *Operation Sunset. Sunset* will do far more than neutralize *Sunrise. Sunset* will bring America to its knees."

By the time Ignaty finished presenting his masterpiece, Korovin was pacing like a caged tiger smelling prey. He kept moving for a few minutes after Ignaty concluded. When he finally broke the silence, his question caught Ignaty by surprise. As usual, Korovin's mind had raced miles ahead. "What's on the flash drive you held up when you first walked in?"

Ignaty extracted the silver sliver from his pocket. "A recording. It's for our next discussion."

"Next discussion? You've got something else? Something on par with *Sunrise*?"

Just wait till you hear this one. Ignaty was about to make himself utterly indispensable. "What can I tell you? Miss Muffet's a goldmine."

Korovin chuffed. "You can tell me how she does it."

Ignaty simply proffered the drive. "We've discussed that, and we've agreed that it's really better for your own peace of mind if you don't know the operational details."

Korovin accepted the device. "You want me to listen to it?"

"You'll want to hear the original."

Korovin accepted the recording without breaking eye contact. "What's on it?"

"A conversation President Silver had yesterday aboard Air Force One."

"Muffet's got ears in the presidential plane? And you don't want me to know how she does it?"

Ignaty said nothing.

"What are they discussing?"

Ignaty knew better than to prevaricate or sugarcoat. "Silver's sending someone to kill you."

Chapter 5
Sixth Sense

Palo Alto, California

ACHILLES LOOKED DOWN from the chin-up bar at the display on his vibrating phone: *Caller ID Blocked*. He could only smile, remembering some calls he'd made using that feature. It might just be a telemarketer, but he was feeling lucky.

He dropped to the ground, wiped the sweat from his brow, and hit *accept*. "Hello."

"Achilles, do you know who this is?"

You betcha he did. He'd been waiting three months for Senator Collins to call. "I do."

"If you're still interested, I'd like to meet. Late tomorrow night."

"I'm interested."

"Can you be at my DC home by midnight? Best if you're already there when I arrive."

Achilles didn't have her DC address. She was testing him. "I can."

"Excellent. Please ensure that you're not seen by anyone, or caught on any camera. I'll leave the back door unlocked. Deactivate the alarm with my zip code, twice in succession. Got it?"

"Got it."

"Good. I'm looking forward to seeing you. I'd say *give my best to Katya*, but of course she can't know we spoke." Collins clicked off before Achilles could acknowledge. Katya was his significant other, but not in the usual context. Theirs was a platonic relationship — for the moment. The remnant of a complicated history. Achilles thought of their relationship as a work-in-progress, when he thought of it, which was often.

* * *

Twenty-eight hours later, Achilles slid open the back door to Senator Collins' DC home. The security alarm was silenced by the double zip code as promised, but his mental alarm blared as he crept from the kitchen to the base of the stairs.

He wasn't alone in the house.

Most people can sense another presence in a room — if they're paying attention. They don't know how they sense it, they just do. In fact, their lizard brain is registering a sympathetic energy field. Another biological grouping of bellowing lungs, pulsing arteries, and firing neurons. Another soul.

It's an ability spies are wise to hone.

Unfortunately, determining intent is another matter altogether. There is no friend-or-foe identifier couched in biologic emissions. Perhaps the senator had arrived early, and was power-napping on the couch, but Achilles feared something far more sinister.

He stood silently in the dark, trying to get another ping on his mental radar.

Nothing came.

He'd planned to find a plush chair and wait in the dark, stakeout style, setting the mood for what he hoped would be the start of something big. Instead, he began to explore.

The ground floor consisted entirely of common areas, with the exception of Collins' study. Achilles cleared each room in quick order, finding no one.

He was halfway up the stairs when the next ping punched him in the nose. Or rather, the first hydrocarbon molecules. The unmistakable scent of gun oil. He didn't know if the California senator kept a firearm in her home, but he doubted that she spent a lot of time with Hoppe's oil and cotton rags. *Sinister it was.*

He'd come here to begin a mission, but apparently the mission had already begun. He just didn't know what it was.

Freezing in place, ears perked, nose practically twitching, Achilles considered his options. He could retreat. He could call 9-1-1. Or he could attempt to intercept Collins on her way home. None of those felt right. There were a hundred million able-bodied patriots in the fifty United States, and from all of them the President had selected him. It wasn't for his ability to retreat or pick up a phone.

Achilles just wished he'd brought a gun.

He didn't routinely carry anymore. He liked to travel light, and as a civilian he didn't feel the need to augment his capabilities with gunpowder and lead.

Determined to have that be the mission's last stupid mistake, he palmed the slim tactical knife that lived beside the paperclips in the back pocket of his jeans. He engaged the blade slowly, so that it locked open without an audible click, and resumed his quiet climb.

Once he reached the upstairs hallway, he only needed seconds to pinpoint the source of both scent and vibe. They emanated from behind a single door, not the double. A guest bedroom, not the master. A bedroom that overlooked the front drive.

The shooter was in there, lying in wait. Achilles could sense him.

He pictured the intruder, clad in slim-fitting black fatigues, with leather driving gloves and a balaclava — a shadow peering through the blinds.

How long would it take that shadow to react to the opening door? How many seconds would he require to assess the threat Achilles presented, bring his weapon around, acquire a kill zone, and squeeze? About two seconds, Achilles figured. Closer to three if he was using a long gun — but a long gun seemed unlikely.

Why enter the house if you planned to take the senator out on the street? Better to wait for her to fall asleep, then creep down the hall and strike in the dead of night. A spray to an inhaling nose. A needle beneath a polished fingernail. A drop between open lips. So many swift and stealthy ways to stop a heart.

But why? Why would anyone want Collins dead? He wished she'd given him a clue. Whatever was happening, it was happening faster than she'd anticipated.

Achilles began rehearsing assault scenarios based on likely layouts of the hot bedroom.

He didn't get very far.

Red and blue lights began dancing across the hardwood floor, simultaneously signaling he was out of time and complicating the situation. Senator Collins was home, and she wasn't alone. She had arrived with a motorcade — the presidential motorcade.

Chapter 6
The Beast

Washington D.C.

ACHILLES BROUGHT THE LOCK BLADE up to eye level as he braced for the breach, and glanced at the gleaming tip. If he didn't have steel poised atop the killing place within two seconds of turning the knob, he'd be on his way to dead. He pushed that thought aside with the same discipline he practiced on every rock climb, and turned his focus to execution.

Ready ... set ...

"Come in, Achilles."

Achilles had probably heard that exact phrase a thousand times during his thirty-two years, but not once had it couched so much meaning. And never before had it been uttered by that voice.

The door between Achilles and the shooter was constructed from solid pine boards arranged in a boxy ornamental pattern. Dense enough to take the oomph out of all but a magnum round. But if the speaker intended to shoot him, surely he would have waited another half second for the door to open.

Achilles palmed the lock blade, poising it for an underhand throw. He focused in the direction of the voice, and twisted the knob.

The man standing before the bay window radiated a soldierly vibe. Thin lips sported a satisfied smirk beneath eyes that had undoubtedly witnessed war. They spent a second sizing each other up in the glow of red and blue revolving lights, then the man spoke. "Silver asked me to join your meeting with Collins. Name's Foxley."

Foxley's fit body was average in height and looked to have about forty years' worth of wear. Close-cropped brown hair, sharp features, and a confident disposition completed the picture. He was not visibly holding a weapon — but then neither was Achilles.

"Silver invited you?" Achilles asked, closing the gap between them as he spoke.

"Well, Chief of Staff Sparkman actually. I work for him from time to time. Off the books."

The presidential limo, *aka* Cadillac One, *aka* The Beast, had stopped directly below them in Collins' semicircular drive. The Secret Service agent was shutting the door behind Collins as Achilles looked down. "Silver isn't joining us?" he asked Foxley.

"I don't know. At this point it really doesn't matter, does it? By sending the limo, his endorsement of whatever Collins says is clear."

"Why would Collins need a presidential endorsement?"

Foxley's smirk broadened. "Obviously the ask is going to be both big and outrageous."

"So you don't know what this is about?"

"I only know two things: This op is classified tighter than the hit on Bin Laden, and I'm here to support you." He spoke the last bit like it was an accusation.

They listened to Collins enter while the motorcade drove away and Achilles evaluated what he'd just heard. Experience with men in uniform taught him that it was wise to tackle trouble up front and head on. "You don't sound happy to be serving as support."

Foxley squared off. He had broad, angular shoulders that poked up like the poles on a tent. "I'm sure there's a good reason for leaving the senior guy in the rear. That is where they keep the generals, after all."

"What makes you think you're senior — other than your birthdate?"

Foxley snorted. "Serbia, Iraq, Afghanistan, Pakistan, and Libya." He stepped close enough that their feet nearly touched. "You've never set foot on a battlefield. Don't get me wrong, I know you're an accomplished athlete. Olympian and all. But it's a whole different world when second place gets you a bronze casket rather than a silver medal."

Obviously Foxley had only seen Achilles' unclassified file.

"You boys can come down now," Collins called.

Foxley broke eye contact and headed for the door. Five minutes later the three of them were seated in the senator's breakfast alcove holding mugs of black coffee and speaking softly. All very normal — except that it was midnight rather than morning, and the topic of conversation was a presidential assassination.

Chapter 7
The Abduction

Sochi, Russia

MAX ARISTOV LEANED OVER to kiss the love of his life as the wheels of Aeroflot flight 1122 screeched down onto Sochi's sun-drenched runway. Even though they'd been dating for years, he still felt a thrill every time Zoya Zolotova kissed him back. She was *the* Zoya Zolotova — actress, movie star, sex symbol.

While closing his eyes to savor the perfect start to their momentous vacation, a flight attendant triggered his sixth sense.

"What is it?" Zoya asked. "You were there with me, but I felt you slip away."

Zoya was as attuned to people's feelings as he was to potential threats. Max had literally identified, assessed, and dismissed the intruder in the blink of an eye, but she'd still detected the blip. "Nothing. A photographer."

Zoya's eyes smiled at the news. With a Golden Eagle nomination for Best Supporting Actress, she was finally, officially, a film star. In Russia at least. Outside the former Soviet Bloc nobody had ever heard of her.

She was dying to break through to the international stage, of course. Max secretly feared that would never happen. While she remained breathtaking, one in one-thousand, her beauty had peaked while the Russian film industry was in a dip. MosFilm was on the rise again, thanks to President Korovin, but not in time to capture Zoya in full bloom.

She flashed a disarming smile at the flight attendant. "May I see the picture?"

The flight attendant blushed, but obliged.

Max knew why Zoya was asking. As a schoolgirl, Zoya had received a poster of Robert Doisneau's *The Kiss* as a gift, and had since spent countless hours living in that Parisian scene. Now her bedroom was full of pictures of kissing couples. Stolen shots, never posed. Some famous, some taken by Zoya herself. Nine included Max. Today, Zoya was hoping for the tenth.

"I like it," Zoya said, her voice sincere. She could fake sincerity better than most politicians, but Max knew her well enough to recognize the genuine emotion.

Performing his part in their practiced routine, Max whipped out his own phone and accepted an AirDrop of the photo before Zoya surreptitiously deleted the original and returned the phone with a kind, "Thank you."

As they entered the main terminal of Sochi International, a large, dark-suited man wearing thin black gloves stepped into their path and spoke without preamble. "Come with me please." His face was expressionless, and his attitude neither commanding nor deferential, but Max knew an order when he heard one. The gloved man beckoned toward an emergency exit which a second, equally large suit then opened.

"You didn't tell me we were being met," Zoya said, her tone inquisitive. *Should I be worried?*

Rather than replying, Max turned and kissed her. It was one for the wall, one of those Victory Day, just-off-the-ship kisses, with one arm on the small of her back and the other behind her neck. He bent her backwards and poured his heart into her as though worried their lips might never touch again.

They'd been dating for four years exactly, yet their love still grew day-by-day. Max remained amazed that Zoya had fallen for him. One wouldn't expect an actress to find much in common with a spy. He sought shadows while she required bright lights. He eyed promotion, while she pursued fame. But at the end of the day, they were both actors. He just didn't get retakes.

Confident that their flamboyant display of affection would generate plenty of witnesses with supporting photographs should this exit become a disappearance, Max took Zoya's arm and followed the lead of their escorts.

The emergency exit took them down to an empty ground level hallway. Walking four abreast, with the big black suits on either end like mobile castle battlements, they marched toward distant double doors. Once they reached them, the suits opened both doors in unison, bombarding the corridor with hot air and bright light. While Max's eyes adjusted and his pulse raced, the suits each raised an arm, gesturing toward the tarmac — and a waiting helicopter.

Chapter 8
The Silence

Black Sea Coast, Russia

MAX WALKED into the August sunshine with his woman on his arm and his head held high, uncertain if he'd just flipped heads or tails. His thoughts jumped to the latter. Russia was famous for making people disappear, and assassinations via helicopter were not uncommon with high-profile targets. Mechanical failures didn't raise eyebrows in the former Soviet Union. Then again, using a 200 million ruble machine when a two-ruble bullet would suffice was hardly the Russian government's way.

What could be the SVR's motive? Max wondered. The top brass back at Foreign Intelligence Service headquarters in Moscow were singing his praises. He'd just pulled off a major espionage coup in Switzerland. In fact, he was expecting to return from this long overdue vacation to a promotion — one that would bring him in from the field. One that would allow him to start a family with Zoya, knowing that he'd be home most nights rather than away and incommunicado for months at a time.

Had he done so well that his boss now considered him a threat? That was a distinct possibility. Zoya occasionally chided him for what she called an *independent streak*, her polite way of saying he wasn't kiss-ass enough.

Max didn't see their suitcases waiting in the big black bird. Perhaps they were in a luggage compartment. Did helicopters have luggage compartments? he wondered.

"What about our bags?" Zoya shouted over the powerful growl of the engine.

"They've already stashed them in back," Max said, hoping for the best. He slipped on his headset and asked the pilot, "How long is the flight?"

The pilot didn't answer.

Max couldn't tell if that was because the channel wasn't open, or because the pilot was instructed not to talk. He'd ask again later.

The Ansat rose above the new airport with effortless grace and pointed its nose northwest toward Sochi, rather than south toward their exclusive beachfront resort. The relative position of the Black Sea made this obvious, so Zoya immediately picked up on the navigational discrepancy. Max could see it in her eyes. But she didn't say anything. She just held his hand and wore her *public mask*, the pleasantly neutral expression designed to thwart predatory paparazzi.

As they thundered over the Black Sea coast, leaving Sochi far behind, Max racked his brains for what lay ahead. Not much. Krasnodar region with its surrounding seaside resorts were a few hundred kilometers ahead, but those weren't as nice as the one now behind them. Still further northwest was the Crimean Peninsula, famous for the 1945 Yalta Conference and the 2014 Crimean Crisis. But the distance would likely warrant a plane rather than a helicopter.

Max was flummoxed, but like the actress beside him, he didn't show it. Instead he gave the pilot another try. "I flew Black Sharks and Alligators back in my service days," he said, referencing the military helicopters by their nicknames. "They were fast, but as long as nobody's shooting, I'll take the comfort you've got here over speed. How long you been flying?"

Again, no answer.

With nothing to lose, Max kept at it. "I still get behind a stick once a year or so, just so I don't lose the feel. Know what I mean?"

Nothing.

Resigned to accepting his temporary state of ignorance, Max worked to keep Zoya occupied by pointing out scenery below, most of which was craggy rocks and uninhabited coniferous coastline. Beautiful, but foreboding.

Eighty minutes into the flight, the hum of the rotor shifted and the Ansat veered inland over thick forest. This turned into an approach arc that brought them around until they were flying back toward the sea and their apparent destination. Near the water's edge, a magnificent estate with manicured grounds and picturesque gardens appeared in a hilltop clearing.

"What is it?" Zoya asked, speaking through her headset microphone for the first time.

"It looks like the palace at Versailles," Max said, feeding Zoya the recollection of a favorite trip with a cheerful lilt.

"That's just what I was thinking. But this isn't the center of France. This is the middle of nowhere."

Indeed it was. The plot thickened.

In Russian fairy tales, magnificent homes in the woods were always owned by witches. Max had lost his childish naiveté long ago, but his career had made him all too familiar with the true face of evil.

The pilot landed on the middle one of three helipads, just a few meters from a Mercedes S65 whose gleaming black paint job matched their helicopter's. Three helipads, Max thought. Much more impressive than a three-car garage.

No words were spoken as the Ansat powered down, its roar turning to a purr, but the open Mercedes passenger door made the next move clear even as the pilot's continued silence brought a smile to Max's lips. He recognized a pattern.

Max helped Zoya down from the Ansat and wrapped an arm around her waist as they walked toward the car.

She turned her head and whispered, "Why aren't they speaking to us?"

"They've been ordered to forget us, and they're taking their orders seriously."

"Forget us," Zoya repeated. "Are we going to disappear?"

Max pulled her tight, but didn't stop walking. "Yes."

Chapter 9
The Twin

Black Sea Coast, Russia

"WHY ARE YOU SO CALM?" Zoya whispered, her lips to Max's ear and her fingers on his pulse. She was speaking English as the Mercedes whisked them toward the palace, something she often did in public to hinder eavesdropping.

Max didn't answer. He was deep in thought.

Zoya persisted. "Isn't this the perfect time for you to use one of your secret agent tricks to take over the car so we can make a break for it?"

Max concluded his analysis and cut Zoya off with a single shake of his head. "This may look like a palace, but it's a fortress. During the helicopter approach, did you notice that there's only one passage carved through the forest, and that road's got more curves than a scared snake? It's designed to prevent an assault, but it works the same for an escape. No doubt they can also raise barricades and dragon's teeth with the touch of a button. We wouldn't even make it to the main road."

"So you're not going to do anything? You're just going to sit back and let us disappear?"

He squeezed her hand. "It's not the Siberian kind of disappearing they have in mind, or the Sicilian kind. It's the covert assignment kind."

Zoya's voice trembled as she squeezed his hand back. "What do you mean?"

"Everyone thinks we're on vacation. Nobody will miss us for three weeks. At this very moment, two people resembling us are probably checking into our room, toting our luggage and using our names. Meanwhile, we're going to be asked to do something very secretive, something that can't be traced to us, or by extension, to Russia." As if to accentuate his point, the Mercedes continued past the palace's front entrance without slowing.

"Why didn't you say so in the first place, Max? I was scared. Really scared." Her hand relaxed, and her tears started flowing.

Max wiped his love's red cheeks with his sleeve, before meeting her eye. "I wanted you to be braced for what's to come."

She recoiled as the panic returned.

Max used his index finger to draw a circle in the air as he continued the explanation. "Helicopter transport isn't the usual protocol for a mission briefing. Whatever they're going to ask of us, it's not going to be . . . small."

Zoya swallowed hard as the Mercedes slowed and descended through a side drive into an underground portico reminiscent of the entrance to a grand hotel. The instant their forward velocity hit zero, a giant of a man in a soldier's uniform opened their door like a valet and said, "Welcome to Seaside."

He motioned them toward another door which was held open by a similarly impressive soldier and which in turn revealed a third man waiting inside. The third man wore the insignia of a colonel in the presidential security service, and a face Max recognized. Igor Pushkin.

Colonel Pushkin had been Cadet Pushkin when they'd gone through the KGB Academy together. With their heads shaved and uniforms on, the two could have been twins. They certainly fought like brothers.

The instigator of their discord was Arkady Usatov, the son of the Academy's commandant, and Pushkin's best friend. For four years, Arkady and Pushkin made a sport of getting Max into trouble with drill instructors, professors, and women through cases of mistaken identity. Given Arkady's protected status, Max just had to take it with a tight lip and a burning heart.

Max's heart still burned, even though graduation was twenty years behind them, and he hadn't spoken to Pushkin since.

Apparently they weren't going to speak today either. As Max and Zoya entered an enormous circular entry hall reminiscent of a Roman temple, Pushkin simply used a sweeping arm to point them up a broad marble staircase.

Chapter 10
The Proposal

Black Sea Coast, Russia

ARM-IN-ARM, Max and Zoya climbed toward a domed ceiling decorated with a fresco of the Greek gods in their heavenly abode. Max loved museums. He found poetry in the idea that you could achieve immortality by pouring years of your life into a spread of canvas or a chunk of stone. But today his appreciation of the beauty surrounding him was lost to other emotions. Relief primarily. Relief that they were going up stairs rather than down.

As they reached the landing where the stairway split left and right before doubling back, Zoya whispered, "That officer looks just like you. Could that be why we're here? They need a body double?"

Wishful thinking, Max thought. He leaned over and kissed her cheek. "I love you so."

Pushkin hadn't told them where to go once they reached the main floor, implying that there would either be another guide or their destination would be obvious. Obvious was an overstatement, but an open double doorway beckoned them from the distant end of a long promenade. Still arm-in-arm and with footsteps now echoing on marble, they walked past life-sized sculptures and oil paintings bigger than barn doors toward the unknown.

"Who owns this place?" Zoya asked, still whispering. "I know we don't have one, but you'd think a palace like this could only belong to a tsar."

Technically, Russia hadn't been ruled by a tsar since Nicholas II, who was deposed at the start of the Russian Revolution. Effectively, it had fallen back under a monarch's rule some seventeen years ago. Heredity aside, the main difference between a president and a king was a parliamentary system of checks and balances. Although his title was president, Korovin hadn't been checked or balanced for years. Anyone who tried, ended up in jail or dead. "You're right," Max said. "I'm sure it does."

Zoya stopped walking when they neared the double doorway. She just halted and turned and wrapped her arms around his waist. She looked up at him with her big brown eyes and waited for him to return the stare.

He did.

"You were going to propose to me, weren't you? At the resort? Tonight, for the fourth anniversary of our first date?"

Actually, Max was undecided. He'd planned to, wanted to, desperately, but he was hesitant because his big promotion hadn't yet been granted.

Women were usually a mystery to Max, but this was not one of those times. He held her gaze without waver, as tears came to his eyes. "I want to marry you more than I want anything else in the world."

"Well then ask me."

Now? Here? Were they on camera? The thoughts and implications pummeled him, even as he pulled the ring from his pocket and dropped to one knee.

Chapter 11
The Assignment

Washington D.C.

THE COBALT BLUE MUGS were etched with the seal of the United States Senate. The coffee was fresh-ground and thick. The conversation, however, was more tense than cordial. Collins had left her flowery words and embellishing phrases on the Senate floor.

Foxley ate it up.

He loved the no-nonsense approach top politicians tended to take when behind closed doors. What he didn't like was that Collins kept her big blue eyes locked on Achilles like a teacher on her pet. When she finally did turn her gaze his way, Foxley couldn't believe the words that followed. "President Silver has reason to be concerned that President Korovin will make an attempt on his life."

"What!" Foxley blurted, unable to help himself. The idea was too provocative. And yet, he noted with more than a little consternation, Achilles didn't seem surprised.

Collins turned back to Achilles and continued as though Foxley hadn't spoken. "Therefore, after long and careful debate, President Silver has decided to eliminate the threat. Given your native language skills, your relevant clandestine experience, and perhaps most importantly, your personal history with Korovin, you are uniquely and ideally qualified for the job. Given your civilian status and independent stature, you're also a good diplomatic fit." Collins emphasized *diplomatic*, and then paused for a sip while her words reverberated between their ears.

Again, Foxley was flabbergasted. What *personal history* did Achilles have with Korovin? What *relevant clandestine experience*? Neither was even hinted at in Achilles' FBI file.

Collins set down her mug and continued talking directly to Achilles. "Your primary concern, job number one, is to ensure that nothing you do can ever be traced back to your government. If the U.S. were to be implicated in the assassination of the Russian head of state, the world would begin to worry about nuclear war. And even though we'd likely avoid the red button, the strain would rattle the planet. Who knows what nuts would shake out? Best if his death looks to be natural. If not natural, then an accident. If not an accident, then anonymous. If not anonymous, then for the assassin's personal reasons. Are we clear?"

Foxley remained silent as Achilles said, "Crystal."

"Outside the three of us, only Silver and Sparkman know of this assignment," Collins said, looking Foxley's way again. "Not the Chairman of the Joint Chiefs, not the National Security Advisor, not the Directors of the CIA or the FBI. That's just five people, gentleman. The circle must never, ever, reach six. Are we clear?"

"Yes ma'am," they replied in chorus.

"Good. It goes without saying that there will be no paperwork. No get-out-of-jail-free card. And of course no parade once the deed is done. If bad meets worse, I trust you'll take matters into your own hands — one way or another. Any questions, or can I move on to operations?"

Foxley shook his head along with Achilles. Crazy though it might sound, they knew the drill.

"Geopolitics and nuclear arsenals aside, operations really is the rub," Collins said, her tone more congenial now that they were over the hump. "Korovin is the most highly-protected man in the world. I say *most* rather than *best* out of deference to the home team. That said, Russia's Federal Protective Service, FSO, is five times the size of the Secret Service. They have 3,000 employees whose sole responsibility is Korovin's personal security."

"That makes for a pretty tight net," Foxley said, trying to be the wise voice of experience.

Nobody reacted.

"The CIA has spent months looking for holes in that net," Collins continued. "Michael McArthur, the CIA Station Chief in Moscow, finally found one. Just one. It's up to you to figure out how to exploit it."

Collins produced two crimson red flash drives. They looked bulkier than most Foxley had seen. She set them down on the white tiled tabletop and used a French manicured index finger to slide one over to each of them. "There's a few thousand pages of research notes, and a ten-page summary report. None of it can be copied, printed, or transferred. The files will erase if you try. Read it all, and memorize what you need. The drives will auto-erase in seventy-two hours, but destroy them anyway once you're done. They're flammable. Any questions?"

"I have one," Foxley said. "I've listened to everything you've said, but have yet to decipher the exact nature of my role."

"It's crucial," Collins said, giving him an encouraging smile. "I understand you've handled a number of sensitive assignments for Sparkman. *Quick, quiet, and without complications* was how he summarized your service. He said that if you had a business card, those words would be engraved on it. Sparkman also said you were well connected within the world of shadow operations. That you are a master of procurement. Everything from cutting-edge weapons to surveillance systems, passports, and visas."

The one and perhaps only good thing about politicians, Foxley thought, was their talent for making you feel important while speaking face-to-face. "That about sums it up. But it doesn't really clarify my role."

"Your role, Mr. Foxley, consists of two parts. Number one, you act as a cutout, so that Achilles has no direct relevant communication with anyone employed by the government during the course of this assignment. And number two, you supply him with anything he needs, be it information, documentation, or equipment — all sourced from non-governmental channels. Your fee and funding will come through the same cloaked channel Sparkman has used in the past. Clear and copacetic?"

"Clear and copacetic."

"And Achilles," Collins continued, redirecting her charm. "Whatever you need, Foxley's your man. I trust the two of you will come up with some clever means of communication that avoids leaving any trail of association."

After both men nodded, she said, "Well then, I suppose that's it. We've just changed the course of human history over a single pot of coffee."

"I have a question," Achilles said, arresting the other two as they began to rise. "Silver's not an impulsive man. He's a planner. He must have given thought to what happens next. In Russia, I mean. When Korovin's gone."

"Indeed he has," Collins said. "Vasily Lukin talks tough in public, but privately he's a great admirer of the West. Silver is convinced we can get him into the Kremlin. Then the West will enjoy its first substantive ally since Gorbachev, and we'll be a big step closer to world peace."

"I like the sound of it, but there is one problem with that," Achilles said. "Covert operations rarely go according to plan."

Chapter 12
The Gap

Washington D.C.

ACHILLES WATCHED the video from Collins' flash drive for a second time, while processing the summary report he'd just read. He was intrigued, disturbed, and certain the ghost of George Orwell was laughing at that very moment.

Foxley was still working his phone regarding some private affair.

They'd holed up in a hotel suite with a bag of Honeycrisp apples and a pot of strong coffee to knock out a plan. Foxley had some prior business to wrap up, but Achilles had dived right into the CIA station chief's report.

"I'm done with the summary," he said, grabbing an apple.

Foxley set his phone on the table, face down. "What's your conclusion?"

The wiry veteran had warmed up a bit since their first encounter in Collins' guest bedroom, which was to say he was only mildly hostile. He was still finding the second fiddle role a hard pill to swallow, even after Collins' references to Achilles' undocumented accomplishments had sucked the puff out of his chest.

Achilles closed the laptop and wiped his lips with the back of his hand. "McArthur did his job. His analysis was thorough, his tactical instincts are spot-on, and his logic is tight."

"So he did find a gap in Korovin's security?"

Achilles waggled his hand. "More like an opportunity."

"Why don't you give me a summary," Foxley suggested, leaning back with his hands behind his head. "Then we'll sleep on it."

Checking his watch, Achilles saw that it was 3:00 a.m. *Not a bad plan.* Referencing the English translation of *Kremlin*, he said, "Korovin literally lives and works in a castle. When he spends the night in his Moscow home rather than the official Kremlin residence, he flies to and from work in a helicopter equipped with countermeasures capable of defeating guided missiles. When he drives, his motorcade includes a shell game of six armed and armored specialty vehicles — in addition to a police escort. The only other place he visits regularly is his weekend home on the Black Sea. McArthur says it was designed with defense in mind, and suggests that given its remote location, it's even more secure than the Kremlin."

"What about past attempts?" Foxley asked.

"There have been a dozen serious assassination attempts over the years. All targeted him at pre-announced events or en route thereto. None came close to succeeding. The problem is, you can't get within a kilometer of him. As you noted earlier, a 3,000-person FSO security detail makes for a pretty tight net."

Foxley leaned forward. "But McArthur found a gap."

Achilles nodded. "Korovin stole a move from Shakespeare's *King Henry*. On occasion, he slips his own security, dons a disguise, and goes out into the Moscow night."

"How's he getting out?"

"He exits the Kremlin through the employee entrance."

"Then what?"

"Then he wanders around like thousands of tourists and tens of thousands of Muscovites do every day, exploring the beehive of activity surrounding Red Square. It's like he's on a two-hour pass from his gilded cage."

"How often?"

Achilles took a big bite of apple, then gestured with it while he chewed. "There's the rub. They only have two data points, and they're nine weeks apart."

"So it might not be a habit. And it's not predictable."

"Exactly."

"How'd they discover it?"

Achilles opened his laptop and hit play while turning the screen so Foxley could see it too. "That's the cool part. They found him using a sophisticated identification system that essentially works like fingerprint analysis, identifying the existence and relative position of mappable features. But instead of inspecting a static image, it analyzes a video. And rather than loops and whorls, it measures bone lengths and motion corridors."

The video, obviously a zoom from a distant fixed location, showed the Kremlin employee entrance. As figures came and went, the computer drew stick figure skeletons atop them, then it populated the figures with bone lengths, motion arcs, and relative angles. When it found Korovin, his photo popped up, as did a grid comparing measurement points and a conclusion: 99.99 percent probability.

Foxley looked pleased for the first time. "Gait analysis. I'm familiar with it. It's a new program, but we've already got cameras trained on hundreds of points of interest."

"How do you know that, given your lack of official status?" Achilles asked, stroking Foxley's ego.

"When your job's procurement, you need to know what's available to procure. And I'm well connected."

Achilles nodded. "Why do you think Korovin risks it?"

Foxley pulled a blade from his sleeve and began spinning it on the table top. "You tell me. You're the boss."

Achilles didn't demur. "As the whole world knows, Korovin's got no shortage of testosterone. He does it for the thrill of defying authority — the only authority he ever has to listen to. And for the rush of risk. You and I know that primal pull all too well."

Foxley began dipping his finger in and out of the spinning blade's path. "But he's got so much to lose. Give me ultimate power and I'm not going to risk losing it over something stupid."

Foxley's naïveté surprised Achilles. "He's not thinking about what he has to lose, any more than you do picking up a gun, or I do climbing a cliff, or a politician does unzipping his fly. He's not thinking at all, he's feeling. The rush is immediate, and guaranteed, whereas the risk is theoretical, and remote."

Foxley nodded without looking up.

"You have any ideas, beyond spending the next couple of months waiting to get lucky?" Achilles asked.

Foxley brought a finger down atop his knife's grip, halting the rotation with the tip pointed in Achilles' direction. "Nope. You?"

Achilles tossed his apple core into the air, then snatched Foxley's blade and flicked it up hard enough to pin the core to the ceiling. "I've got one, but it's risky."

Chapter 13
The Question

Black Sea Coast, Russia

ARM-IN-ARM and all of ten-seconds betrothed, Max and Zoya walked through the double doors and into the largest sitting room either had ever seen. A presidential parlor. Whatever awaited them there, they would face it as a couple.

A billboard-sized window dead ahead in the southern wall pulled their gaze. The picturesque gardens it framed were backed by the white-capped waters of the Black Sea, creating a living masterpiece. Walking toward the window as if drawn by a string, they passed plush furnishings and enormous vases flush with fragrant flowers. "When money is no object," Max whispered.

A familiar voice boomed behind them, ending their momentary reprieve. "Ever see an eagle kill a bear?"

They whirled around to see one of the most recognizable faces on the planet. Russian President Vladimir Korovin was walking toward them from a back corner of the room.

For a split second Max wondered why Korovin hadn't begun with introductions, but then realized how silly that would be. They obviously knew him, and he obviously knew them. The fact that they'd never met was irrelevant.

"I'll take your silence as a *no*," Korovin continued. "It's hard to imagine, right? Big eagles weigh five kilos, whereas small bears weigh fifty. Eagles have beaks and talons, but bears have teeth and claws. Any ideas?" Korovin gestured toward a welcoming set of armchairs encircling a radiant coffee table. Looking closer, Max saw that it appeared to be made entirely of amber.

Korovin struck Max as being even more charismatic in person than on a flat screen. His cornflower-blue eyes telegraphed an intelligence that was captivating, if not cooling. By contrast, the inner energy he radiated like bottled sunshine gave him a politician's trademark warmth.

"Tools," Max said, answering Korovin's question instinctively. Whenever he faced long odds in the field, he looked for leverage, he looked for a tool.

Korovin locked his eyes on Max's. "Good answer. Can you

elaborate?"

"The eagle finds a means of leveraging an advantage."

"And what advantage is that?"

Even with the eyes of the world's most powerful man boring into his, Max could ponder, process, and analyze with the best of them. Perhaps that was why he was so good as a spy.

He tackled the question without a discernible pause. Eagles had better eyesight. A broader perspective. And they were faster. None of those felt sufficient, however, so Max went with his first instinct. "They can fly."

"Very good. Morozov was right about you," Korovin said, referring to the head of the SVR. "But you've only supplied half the answer…"

Zoya fidgeted in her chair. This wasn't her venue, but she knew people and was a master of distilling situations. Like Max, she sensed that he was thinking for their lives.

In Max's experience, solving puzzles often involved a change of viewpoint. A sideways glance, a zoom in, or a zoom out. In his mind, he stepped back from the problem, broadening his perspective. From a distance, the puzzle proposed by Korovin didn't look like an eagle against a bear, but rather small against big. *When could small beat big?*

He didn't know enough about the habits of eagles and bears to get specific, but then perhaps he didn't have to. "Eagles pick an advantageous time and place. They look for circumstances that will magnify their ability to inflict damage while flying."

"Yes," Korovin said, his gleaming eyes reflecting light from the window. "To kill a bear, an eagle will wait for it to wander near the edge of a cliff. Then the eagle will swoop in, grab the bear by a hind leg, and drag it over."

"And you need us to drag a bear off a cliff," Max said.

"Because our English gives us the ability to fly undetected," Zoya said, surprising all with her first words. "And you need a couple."

Korovin studied Zoya for a long moment, perceptibly pleased by her conclusion. "You're half right."

Chapter 14
The Cliff

Black Sea Coast, Russia

PRESIDENT KOROVIN gave Zoya an appraising glance that didn't sit well with Max. Then again, despite the five-star treatment, nothing about their unplanned diversion had been comfortable. Funny that. They'd been met by a private helicopter, then given a chauffeured limo ride — to a palace. Yet they hadn't enjoyed a minute of it. Apparently, perspective could control one's enjoyment of just about anything. Max would remember that, the next time he was looking into the abyss.

"By the way," Korovin said, his eyes still locked on Zoya. "I'm a great admirer of your work. I thought your performance in *Wayward Days* was magnificent. Speaking of eagles, you should have won the golden one."

While Zoya accepted the compliment with characteristic grace, Max's thoughts returned to Korovin's prior comment. He wondered which half of Zoya's guess was right; the need for English, or the need for a couple?

Korovin returned to business without clarifying that point. Speaking with a touch of pride and a dramatic flair, he said, "Nobody knows you're here. The men who met you at the airport didn't know where the helicopter was going. The pilot and driver were instructed to avoid learning your identities. The security personnel here at Seaside don't exist outside these walls. Meanwhile another couple has taken your place in Sochi, and will spend most of the next three weeks in your suite, eating room service and making love behind closed doors."

Korovin spread his hands with a flourish. "There's a reason for all that skullduggery, of course. Russia has a delicate problem you can help me solve." He brought his hands back together in a forceful clap.

"You're too young to remember what it was like when Russia and the U.S. were both superpowers, with the world split between us. But I do. I've vowed to return Russia to its former glory before I leave this world, and I'm hoping you can help me make it so."

As Korovin paused to let that sink in, Max couldn't help but note that Korovin had implicitly confirmed the widely held suspicion that he intended to cling to power for the rest of his life.

"As everyone is well aware, and my popularity ratings signify, I have

TIM TIGNER

been very busy restoring Russia's former glory. Our wealth, prestige, and territory are all growing. We're back at the big table again. But, since we're still far from the head, I've decided to broaden my tactics." He looked from Max to Zoya and back to Max again.

"In addition to raising Russia, I've decided to bring our rivals down." He pounded fist to palm forcefully enough to make Zoya jump.

"Since our defense budget is one-tenth the size of America's, we have to attack like an eagle with a bear. And of course the attack must be both invisible, and untraceable. I could never speak or even hint at our involvement, either before or after such an event — either publicly or privately. To do so would be the equivalent of locking an eagle in a low ceilinged room with an angry bear." Again his arms went wide, as if he considered himself a maestro conducting their emotions. "Thus the unconventional nature of your summons."

Max and Zoya nodded their understanding. It was perfectly logical. No trouble at all. They were happy to be there.

"If you want great rewards, you have to take great risks. I'm considering risking everything . . . on you." Korovin paused there, inviting comment.

Max wanted to ask why Zoya was there, rather than a female SVR agent. But that would be crossing the line between asking a question, and questioning Korovin's plan. He had no illusions about his status. He was interviewing for a job. Either he would get it — or he'd be killed. Korovin had told them little, but he'd said too much to let them walk away.

Max looked over Korovin's shoulder and out the window for a second. He pictured the helicopter flying them home, and wondered whether there were sharks in those windswept waters. Then he refocused on his host, and asked an appropriate question. "Surely the Americans will be able to figure out who masterminded their misfortune?"

Korovin was ready for it. "These days, the list of suspects will be long. It will include both nation states and terrorist networks." He cracked a thin smile. "But I'm not relying on obfuscation. Instead, I've made provisions to put the Chinese at the top of that list."

Zoya jumped back into the conversation. "How?"

"The Government of China will fund *Operation Sunset*. Chinese operatives working undercover in America will assemble the tool using components sourced from China, and then those same Chinese operatives will install it. We'll talk more about the specifics later."

"Why China?" Max asked.

Korovin nodded his approval of the question. "America is heavily dependent on the Chinese for everything from currency loans to cheap goods to 1.4 billion consumers. Driving a wedge between Beijing and Washington will cause tremendous collateral damage. A priceless bonus, so to speak."

Whatever you thought of Korovin, Max reflected, you couldn't deny that he was a master strategist. "What's our tool?"

"I'm glad you asked. Actually, if you break it down, *Operation Sunset* has two. The *talons* and the *cliff*, so to speak. The talons come in the form of electronic devices the size of smart phones."

"And the cliff?" Max asked on cue.

"We're going to use the same cliff that made Bin Laden so effective. We are going to drag America over a cliff of fear."

Chapter 15
SDI

Black Sea Coast, Russia

AFTER DROPPING his big revelation on them, President Korovin directed his gaze toward the back of the room. Looking over his shoulder, Max saw a short bald man with big ears and a bushy mustache moving toward them like he'd been launched from a battleship.

"Zoya Zolotova, and Max Aristov, allow me to introduce Ignaty Filippov."

"Good afternoon," the new arrival said, his tone clipped and efficient. He shook their hands brusquely, then canted his head back toward the door and added, "You're with me, Max."

Max's first thought wasn't to question what this no-nonsense guy wanted. He assumed Ignaty would be briefing him on the details of *Operation Sunset*. His first thought was that he'd be leaving Zoya alone with a man known for his wandering eyes and boundless virility.

Max wasn't the jealous type. If he had been, he would never have gotten involved with Zoya. Anyone dating a woman so beautiful and famous would have to anticipate tremendous competitive attention. Married or single, young or old, Max knew that every man whose plumbing still worked would dream of testing her pipes. But he trusted Zoya to faithfully dismiss their solicitations, and he managed to leave it at that. President Korovin, however, was a different species of beast.

Feeling powerless as he met Zoya's eye, Max squeezed her shoulder as he rose to dutifully follow Ignaty. They passed half a dozen statues of Greco-Roman athletes in combative, contemplative, or victorious poses, before Ignaty led him into another sitting room. Much smaller than the grand parlor they'd vacated, this one resembled a gentleman's club, with dark wood paneled walls, a pub-style bar in the corner, and heavy ashtrays on the coffee tables. The room smelled of cigar smoke, but only mildly. Clearly the palace's ventilation system was first rate.

"Feel like a Punch?" Ignaty asked deadpan before lifting a box of the famous cigars. No doubt this wasn't his first time using the double entendre.

"You have a Champion?" Max said, thinking fast after reading the band on a discarded butt.

"I do indeed. Funny, I'd pictured you as more of a Magnum guy."

Their big-dog dance completed to mutual satisfaction, the two alpha males dropped into plush burgundy lounge chairs, whereupon Ignaty clipped and torched their Punch Champions. They enjoyed a few initial puffs in shared silence before Ignaty fired his opening salvo. "There's been a race going on for years behind the scenes. A very important, very intense technological race — and the Americans are about to beat us across the finish line."

"Do tell."

"You familiar with Vulcan Fisher?"

"The aerospace company that recently landed the biggest defense contract in U.S. history?"

"You heard about that," Ignaty said, picking something invisible off his lip. "If you tell me you know the details, I'm going home right now. You can have my job."

"Morozov had planned to send me on recon, but another assignment came up."

"Yes, Switzerland. I heard. Congratulations."

"Thank you."

Ignaty blew a long jet of smoke. "Back to Vulcan Fisher. Their project is codenamed *Sunrise*, and like the best codenames, it holds meaning without giving anything away. Ever since the Gorbachev/ Reagan Years, we've been dreaming of so-called *Star Wars* defense systems. Are you familiar with the concept?"

"Lasers in space," Max said, his heartbeat now rising from more than just the nicotine. "Officially called SDI, the Strategic Defense Initiative."

"Exactly. But after years of sexy headlines and tens of billions of dollars worth of failed attempts, technical and budget issues finally tabled SDI in favor of more conventional systems."

Max saw where this was going. "Are you telling me Vulcan Fisher cracked SDI?"

"Yes. Just three years from now, the U.S. will gain *absolute* and *permanent* military control of *everything* in the earth's atmosphere — and everything below it." Ignaty paused for a long, tension-raising puff before blowing smoke in Max's direction. "They'll essentially have their fist wrapped around the planet — unless you stop it."

Chapter 16
The News

Black Sea Coast, Russia

MAX PRIDED HIMSELF on staying a step ahead of his bosses and peers. While they were out drinking, he was home reading. While they were chasing women or watching sports, he was looking for trends and calculating odds. But he had not seen this coming. Last he'd heard, SDI was dead. Now Ignaty was vesting it with complete military control of the planet.

Max decided to adopt Korovin's trademark style when querying the president's chief strategist. "How? What?"

Ignaty leaned forward, resting an elbow on each knee. "Laser, satellite, and computing technologies have grown exponentially since the 1980s. We're light-years ahead now, and apparently Vulcan Fisher is further ahead still. What do you know about them from your earlier, almost-assignment?"

"Vulcan Fisher is a pioneer in satellite and drone technologies. Their roots are in aeronautics — aircraft control systems — where they remain the global leader."

Ignaty concurred with a long drag on his cigar. "The biggest hurdle to overcome in a laser defense system is power generation. You basically need a nuclear power plant, and we're not talking the nuclear submarine type. We're talking Fukushima. We're talking putting something the size of a football stadium on a spaceship." Ignaty scooched forward to the edge of his chair, tapped the ash off his cigar, and gave Max the real punch. "Well, apparently Vulcan Fisher has gotten so precise with their satellite capabilities, that they've eliminated the need to put the laser into orbit."

"I don't follow."

"Nor did our physicists, at first. It literally takes a leap of perspective." Ignaty paused there, enjoying the tease.

Max remained silent, unwilling to ask.

"Vulcan Fisher will be building a huge, land-based laser that will shoot a beam straight up to a master satellite, which can then redirect the energy like a sophisticated disco-ball. By bouncing beams off additional satellites orbiting around the globe, they'll literally have the power to fry any and all other electronic equipment in orbit or on the ground, all at the speed of light." Ignaty snapped the fingers of his free left hand, then settled back into his chair.

"So many questions," Max began, thinking out loud. "Where are they building the laser?"

Ignaty answered without enthusiasm. Apparently he wasn't impressed. "We don't know. They'll probably use an island in the South Pacific, where the air is clean, the clouds are few and far between, and there are no people for thousands of miles around."

"How long will it take?"

Ignaty gave a look that said, strike two. "The system goes live in three years."

Max cursed himself. Ignaty had already supplied that answer. Max didn't let his nerves show as he took his third swing. "How do I stop it?"

Ignaty pecked the air with his cigar. "Now there's a trillion-dollar question. Let me begin to answer it with a question of my own. What's modern America's greatest weakness? I'll give you a hint to get you started. Why is Korovin more powerful than Silver, despite the relative size of both his army and his economy?"

Max was pleased to be back on familiar ground. Geopolitics was his thing. "Korovin can do whatever he wants. Silver is hamstrung by legislative and judicial branches. He needs Congressional approval for most things. In other words, he can't act without the permission of his political rivals."

"So?"

"So America's greatest weakness is bureaucracy. Its legal system."

Ignaty again tapped his cigar against the air in approval. "The day after Bin Laden knocked down the World Trade Center, President Bush was on the airwaves, promising to rebuild it, *Better and stronger than ever! A symbol of American resilience.* And the whole world cheered him on.

"It took them fourteen years. Fourteen years to reopen a single building. And that was with American pride on the line, and the world cheering them on. Why?"

"Legal battles."

"Legal battles," Ignaty confirmed. "While scores of American lawyers waged their war at a thousand dollars an hour, Korovin rebuilt all of Moscow. In the time it took America to construct a single new landmark, Russia reconstructed its entire capital city. If Korovin wants something, he gets it. If Silver wants something…"

"He has to ask for it," Max supplied.

"Exactly. So the way to stop Vulcan Fisher …"

"Is to wrap it up in red tape."

"You got it! Do that, and by the time their sun is ready to rise, we'll already have our star in place."

When Max didn't respond immediately, Ignaty said, "You look disappointed."

"No. No. I'm honored."

"Not sexy, is that it? You were thinking James Bond, super spy, only to find that you'd been handed an accounting assignment?"

Max said nothing.

"Well, wait till you hear how you're going to generate that red tape."

Max felt his heartbeat quicken.

"You're going to make Bin Laden look like the cave-dwelling amateur he really was. I'll pour some poison, and tell you all about it."

The brandy came out, fresh cigars were lit, and Ignaty regaled Max with the details of *Operation Sunset*.

Two hours later, when the alpha males joined Zoya and President Korovin for a surf and turf dinner, Max was feeling even better than he had been when they first landed in Sochi on vacation. He had been selected by none other than the president of Russia to lead a mission that would shift the global balance of power.

Zoya too was wearing a smile that broadcast delight as she reveled in the company of her powerful new friend. But even before Max kissed his fiancée's cheek, he knew that she was acting. Something was tearing her up inside.

First it struck him that his news was not likely to improve her mood. Then he realized that he had yet to hear hers.

Chapter 17
Soul Food

Black Sea Coast, Russia

AS THEY WATCHED their new recruits depart, Korovin turned to his chief strategist. "When you gave me the broad strokes of *Sunset*, I thought you were about to propose that we find some way to use the American's own weapon against them. I was expecting you to suggest reprogramming the laser to blow up the Capital during Silver's next State of the Union address, or something like that."

"A frontal assault," Ignaty replied.

"Yes, exactly. Bold and glorious, but straight at their defenses."

"That would be an amateur mistake. The IFF safeguards on *Sunrise* will be triple or quadruple redundant. Attempting to trick it into misidentifying a friend as a foe would be a fool's errand."

"Agreed. Your solution is far more practical, simpler even. It's genius. How'd you come up with it?"

Ignaty felt warm honey running through his veins. Korovin wasn't one to waste words on praise. The president saved the sweet sounds for affairs of state, while adopting a more practical attitude toward domestic affairs. Ignaty knew his boss figured that keeping one's job was all the endorsement anyone should need. In that sense, he praised everyone on his staff, every day. While this pragmatic system satisfied the minds of the Kremlin staff, it left holes in their souls. But not today. Today Ignaty felt complete. "I was working on strategies for keeping America's economic progress in check when we cracked the *Sunrise* code. So I started playing chess on two boards, so to speak."

"And you figured out how to combine them," Korovin said, completing Ignaty's sentence. "The plan is beautiful, but of course planning is the easy part. Max has a hell of a task ahead of him."

Ignaty was enjoying this rare glimpse beneath the armor of the president's psyche — at the hole in his soul. "I trust you were impressed?"

"He's got a quick mind, and good strategic reflexes. Morozov says his operational instincts are first rate, and Morozov isn't easily impressed. But it's one man against an entire American defense corporation. We're asking a lot."

"It's always one man. Doesn't matter how big the team. You of all people surely know that."

Korovin nodded, but remained silent.

"Max will find a way."

"You don't think he'll be too distracted?"

Ignaty knew this was sensitive ground, so he trod lightly. "By the Zoya thing?"

"Exactly."

"I'll just ride him hard; he won't have time to think about it."

Chapter 18
Dangerous Heights

South Lake Tahoe, California

THE THWAP-THWAP-THWAP of a helicopter rotor grew increasingly closer, breaking Achilles' concentration. Not a good development when you were 400 feet up the side of a cliff without a rope. Achilles reaffirmed the grip of all four points of contact and risked a glimpse over his shoulder. The helicopter was medevac red. Some climber was having a bad morning — which was a bit surprising in that he hadn't seen anyone out yet. The inky darkness had only yielded to dawn's first light about twenty minutes earlier.

After a week of getting nowhere on the Korovin assassination plan, Achilles had driven to a favorite climbing spot to work the problem with an unencumbered mind. He did his best thinking while climbing, and Lover's Leap was perfect for that purpose.

Popular with San Francisco, Sacramento, and Silicon Valley residents looking to tackle tough climbs without battling Yosemite's crowds, Lover's Leap was a jewel just south of Lake Tahoe. Achilles loved it both for the spectacular views, and because it was well maintained. When you climbed without ropes, you needed solid surfaces free of grit and growth. The steady flow up the vertical visage of Lover's Leap meant he didn't have to devote time to tedious prep work.

Speaking of prep work, Achilles was on his own when it came to developing the Korovin plan. By Foxley's own admission, he was a doer, not a planner. Achilles suspected that the abdication was driven more by Foxley's political instincts than his self-awareness. The task had appeared impossible when Collins presented it, and seven days later it still did. Failure, nonetheless, would rest entirely on Achilles' shoulders.

The medevac helicopter kept closing in, its roar vibrating everything that clung to the granite, including Achilles himself. Achilles stayed put until its red tail rotor disappeared from view, eclipsed by the cliff top some 200 feet above his head. Soon the silence of a mountain dawn enveloped him once again, and Achilles resumed his ascent in peace.

Given the data they had, the Korovin assassination resembled a deer hunt. Instead of watching a stream at dawn, Achilles would be watching the Kremlin's employee exit after dusk. Unfortunately, that was where the similarities ended. He couldn't erect a hunting blind on Red Square. He couldn't even loiter in the area. The FSO kept eyes on the Kremlin's surroundings like a fat man on his doughnuts.

As bad as the observation challenge was, the timing aspect was worse. Korovin didn't come out daily like a deer to a stream. His appearances were rare and unpredictable. Achilles had to be there, watching, every evening Korovin was in the Kremlin. If he missed one opportunity, it might be months before he got another.

Despite the seemingly insurmountable challenge this mission presented, Achilles was thrilled to be back in the espionage game. Thrilled to be putting his talents to use to serve his president and his country. And thrilled to be ridding the world of the scourge that was President Korovin.

If he found a way to accomplish his mission, Achilles had no doubt that President Silver would call on him again. Then he'd be sitting pretty, doing patriotic work for a well-meaning man, without bureaucracy or a boss. If he failed, Achilles didn't know what he'd do. Anything else would feel like settling for second place. The conclusion was obvious: he couldn't fail.

Easier said than done.

The valley was coming to life below as the sun began peeking above the mountains, stirring up the breeze and waking the birds. Achilles was looking forward to greeting the morning from atop the cliff. He'd sit cross-legged with the sun warming his back while the shadow of the granite monolith slowly receded from the valley. If all went according to plan, the Korovin solution would blossom in his brain like one of the blooms below.

The sun seemed to be right there before him as he poked his head over the crest, like a bare bulb hanging in an attic, or a flashlight in the eyes. Achilles checked his watch once his pupils had adjusted. The 600-foot ascent had taken him twenty-eight minutes. Far from a record, but mighty respectable for a meditative climb on a cliff rated a 5.11 — which put it near the difficult end of the technical-climbing spectrum.

As he rose to full height in salute of the sun, Achilles made a discovery that put a shadow on his meditation plan and set off warning bells. He wasn't alone.

PART 2: REVELATIONS

Chapter 19
The Partner

Seattle, Washington

"ARE WE HAPPY?" Ignaty asked Max, his voice sounding more like a child's than his own. They were using Voice Over Internet Protocol delivered via The Onion Router using 256-bit encryption and voice-scrambling technology. The setup caused a four-second communication delay, but with those stacked systems, even the NSA was powerless to eavesdrop.

Max cleared his throat. "I don't know yet. Wang's not due for another twenty minutes. How on earth did you hook up with this guy?"

Ignaty's reply came through four seconds later. "One of our Seattle operatives bumped into him. They were both chasing the same technology. Wang was coming out as our guy was going in, so to speak, and offered to sell him the information. For cash. Our guy didn't take him up on it, but he did let Morozov know that Wang was for sale. Morozov proposed him to me — at the same time he proposed you."

Max suspected there was more to it than that. So far Wang was proving to be the most unusual agent Max had ever worked with. "I'm sure you ran a full background check. What did you learn?"

"Wang runs China's industrial espionage network in the Pacific Northwest. He's been in Seattle for nearly a decade, and has established an entire cell of spies. His clandestine operatives are all in the U.S. on legitimate work visas, all hired as programmers and engineers by unsuspecting technology corporations looking to save a buck. The Americans think they're getting high-quality talent on the cheap. What they've really bought themselves is a big fat security gap."

"The human version of spyware," Max said.

Ignaty emitted an annoying chuckle. "Sometimes old school rules. Why are you asking about Wang?"

"He's not what I was expecting."

"How so?"

"Have you met him?"

"No. Everything has been done remotely — to disguise our nationality. You're the only Russian to have a face-to-face meeting with him since that initial agent — and he thinks you're British."

Max knew he was getting on Ignaty's nerves, but pressed anyway. "That's kind of my point. You've got me playing the dapper Englishman to an audience of one, but that one is a stumpy, soft-spoken peasant, with thinning hair, a hygiene problem, and an addiction to American soap operas. As the Brits would say, we're chalk and cheese."

"What you have in common is money. You have it, he wants it. There's no penalty for running too sophisticated an operation. On the other hand, getting sloppy could be catastrophic. Make sure he doesn't figure out that you're Russian and we'll be fine."

A knock at the door preempted Max's next comment. "Speak of the devil."

"Let me know as soon as you've verified the product. Don't wait for me to call you tomorrow."

Ignaty didn't show it, but Max knew he was nervous. When you sent your money to China, you were never quite sure what would come back. If Wang's delivery of the first *Sunset* devices failed to meet specifications, it was going to get ugly. There would be a shit storm, a cyclone of fury and frustration spinning out of the Kremlin. Max would be stuck in the center of it.

He hated the rules of engagement on this assignment. Only half a dozen people on the planet knew of Korovin's plan, and Ignaty had made it abundantly clear that Max was to keep it that way. *No Russian involvement! Everything local must go through Wang.* This extreme secrecy requirement crippled his ability to operate. He felt like a surgeon forced to wear mittens.

Besides Max, Zoya, Korovin, and Ignaty, two electrical engineers were the only people with advance knowledge of *Sunset.* One engineer had done the design work, and the other had written the code. Max had met neither, but they'd spoken on the phone and Ignaty had shown him their prototype before he flew to Seattle. He was not impressed. The circuit board was the size of a shoe box, replete with a rat's nest of wires and a bedazzling array of soldered components. To Max, it looked more like a high school science project than the pinnacle of global warfare.

Ignaty had assured him that benchtop designs always looked that way.

They'd sent the *Sunset* prototype off to Shenzhen, where Chinese engineers had optimized the design for small-batch production and miniaturized it to the size of a smart phone. They'd sent back a full set of schematics along with detailed assembly instructions.

All in Mandarin.

All accomplished without their knowledge of where or how the circuit board they'd replicated would be used.

Max had asked how that was possible. One of the Russian engineers explained it. "Imagine a hundred translators working on one chapter of a book. Each may know a line or two, but none will know the scene. And since they don't know what this circuit board plugs into, they'll have no clue about the bigger story."

Now the man who was using those schematics and instructions to build fifty *Sunset* units was knocking at Max's Seattle hotel room door. He, too, would never know the whole story. He might piece it together after the fifty planes crashed — but he'd be running for his life by then.

Wang shook off his umbrella in the hallway before bringing the stench of cigarette smoke into Max's room. "It must be sunny somewhere."

Max took Wang's habitual greeting as his mechanism for coping with Seattle's gloomy climate. He stepped aside and the Chinese spy entered, water still dripping off his big black umbrella. In his left hand he carried a plastic bag holding two white cartons of Chinese food.

Wang set the bag on the kitchenette counter, hung his umbrella on the doorknob, and said, "Dig in."

Max extracted both containers. One was hot and heavy, the other cold and light. He opened the hot one. Singapore noodles.

"That's mine," Wang said, breaking open a pair of chopsticks.

Max took a second to study his partner in light of what Ignaty had just told him. He wondered if Wang's chopped English, and in fact his whole rumpled appearance, might be camouflage used to slip under the radar, like TV's Detective Colombo. Impossible to tell.

Wang stuffed a pile of yellow noodles and shrimp in his mouth, then gestured toward the cold carton with his empty chopsticks.

Max unclasped the lid to find something far more savory than Singapore Noodles: a *Sunset* device.

Chapter 20
Green Lights

Seattle, Washington

MAX STRUGGLED to control his amazement as he pulled the circuit board from the carton. The sight bore no resemblance to the bulky tangle of colorful wires and crude components he'd seen in Moscow. Rather it reminded him of what he saw whenever he opened up a computer — a completely undecipherable green board replete with metallic lines and tiny black and silver bug-like attachments.

"The pilot unit," Wang said, his mouth half full of curry noodles. "You know what that means."

Max did know. Wang was all about the money. "You'll get the second installment once I've verified it."

If only Wang knew. Ignaty had arranged for the money trail to lead straight to China — not just the country, but the government. Through a string of intermediaries, Ignaty had paid a compromised Chinese official ten million dollars to transfer three million from a government account to the account of a shell corporation in Shenzhen. The official immediately refunded the government's money from his ill-gotten proceeds, and then resigned. He was probably living it up in Thailand under a false name. Meanwhile, the government-funded Shenzhen shell corporation was paying all the *Sunset* expenses.

"One hundred thousand," Wang said, clearly happy with the number's sound. He was getting $2 million for about $20 thousand worth of work. The premium was paying for speed, installation, and absolute secrecy. Wang had received $100,000 up front, would get another $100,000 for today's delivery of a pilot unit, and then he'd receive $300,000 more once all fifty were delivered. The $1.5 million balloon payment was due once his team had successfully installed them. "Soon okay? The team is anxious."

Max had no idea how much of the two million Wang was sharing with his team, but if it was more than ten percent he'd be surprised. "I'll verify functionality tonight, and will wire the money tomorrow, if I'm happy."

"You will be happy," Wang said, before spontaneously breaking into song. "Don't worry, do do do do do do, be happy."

"Bobby McFerrin big in Beijing?"

"Bobby McFerrin big everywhere thirty years ago. No so much anymore. Want some noodle?"

"No thanks. It's lasagna night downstairs. My favorite." Max was living in an extended-stay hotel, the kind that served a buffet breakfast and dinner and cleaned your room once a week. Eighty bucks a night, all-inclusive, for stays of a month or more. As a security precaution, he slept in a neighboring room Wang didn't know about. Both were discretely located in a little dog-leg alcove at the end of the second-floor hall.

"Come on," Wang prompted, shoveling a hefty pile of noodles into the now-empty second container with the back half of his chopsticks. "It's good." He proffered a second set of chopsticks to Max. "You try the show yet?"

Max accepted the food. Was this really his life? Takeout and soap opera talk with a lonely Chinese spy. *"General Hospital?"*

"Yes. It's very addictive. Is that a teapot?"

"You never told me how you got hooked?" Max tried to sound as though he cared while rising to brew tea.

"Usually I only busy before and after normal working hours. During the day, I watch TV. Improve my English. Shall I tell you about it? Or would you rather tell me what that little contraption actually do?" He gestured toward the pilot unit.

While they ate their noodles, Wang summarized the spaghetti bowl of relationships connecting the Quartermaines and the Spencers in the longest-running soap opera in American history. Max smiled and nodded, chewed and swallowed, and tried not to think about the impossible task ahead.

Once the noodles were eaten and the tea was drunk and the fortunes were told, Wang disappeared back into the rainy night. Max waited three minutes before crossing the hall to the room where he actually slept and worked.

He chained and bolted the door, drew the curtains, and turned on the news to create cover noise. Satisfied that he would not be detected or disturbed, he set to work installing Wang's delivery into a Boeing autopilot system Ignaty had borrowed from an imprisoned oligarch's aircraft.

Three hours and two cups of coffee later, relief washed over Max. Four green lights winked back at him from the diagnostic display.

His project had literally been greenlighted. The road ahead remained long and treacherous, but he'd passed the first major milestone. He had verified that when a Chinese-made *Sunset* unit was installed in an American aircraft, Russia would gain remote control of its autopilot system.

Chapter 21
Wrong Song

Seattle, Washington

THEY MET AT A KARAOKE BAR. Wang's suggestion, of course. Max had learned by then to spare himself the argument and just to go along with his little friend.

As a newcomer to the karaoke scene, he'd expected to find the kind of place where the brave or the drunk sang on a barroom stage. He'd expected to huddle over a tiny table in the back, sipping sake and whispering with Wang while watching participants mimic moves from music videos. What he found instead was a place that rented out rooms by the hour, mini-studios with wraparound couches and private karaoke systems.

"Reservation for Li," he told an attendant dressed like a Catholic schoolgirl. Wang, who benefited from the natural cover of the second most popular Chinese surname, used Li on these occasions. Li — Max had checked — was *the* most popular Chinese surname.

"All the way back on the left," the girl said, still chewing gum. "Hello Kitty."

Max was puzzled by the odd closing remark until he opened the door and saw Wang sitting beneath the yellow nose and pink bow of a cartoon cat. The room was wallpapered in pink and white stripes, and the white Naugahyde couch sported pink, bow-shaped accent pillows. "Quite the place you picked."

"It must be sunny somewhere," Wang replied, gesturing toward the coat rack where his big black umbrella hung. He started up the music with the instrumental version of Katy Perry's *Firework* while Max removed his raincoat.

Max took a seat before a shot glass as Wang poured the baijiu. Embracing the inevitable, he raised his glass. "Gan Bei!"

Wang responded in kind.

Max downed the warm 'Chinese vodka' in one swallow, clanked his glass back onto the table, and asked, "What's the forecast?"

"Five days, my friend. All fifty will be ready in just five days."

Max could see Ignaty smiling all the way from Moscow. "That's fantastic."

"I aim to please. But you don't look so happy."

Max refilled their glasses from the ceramic bottle. He was about to cross a bridge, break a protocol, and expose himself. But his only alternative was turning to Ignaty for help, and that tactic wasn't likely to end well. "How long have you been assigned to Seattle?"

"Nine years last month."

"So you've had extensive dealings with all the big players."

"By this point I know them better than my wife."

"You're married?" Max couldn't keep the surprise from his voice. Not once had his partner-in-crime hinted at the existence of a Mrs. Wang. Not in anything he said. Not in the way he behaved. He didn't act anything like a man who had a woman caring for his needs or correcting his rudimentary ways.

"With children. Two girls."

"They here?"

"No. They are back in Beijing."

That explained a lot. Max was curious to know more, but knew he'd be wise to pick Wang's brain before there was too much alcohol sloshing around it. He raised his glass. "To your family."

They drank.

After a polite pause, during which the play list moved on to the unfortunate choice of U2's *With or Without You*, Max asked. "Do you have anyone at Vulcan Fisher?"

Wang's lips morphed into a knowing smile. "Forget about them."

"Why do you say that?"

"The software companies, the electronics companies, the medical device companies, those are one thing. The defense contractors, those are fish from a different river.

"So you don't have a man there?"

"Not for lack of trying. Their operations security is through the roof. Well beyond Department Of Defense requirements. Everyone needs a security clearance. That means U.S. citizenship and a thorough background investigation. Even the best legends rarely survive those."

Max had read everything he could find on Vulcan Fisher's operations security via job boards and chat rooms and SEC filings and contract award disclosures. None of it had been encouraging, but he had yet to set foot inside. Talk was cheap, and everyone boasted. On the ground, attentive eyes could discover the discrepancies between theory and practice. The loopholes humans created because they were impatient, or lazy, or wanted to screw or smoke or drink. But spotting those took luck and time, and he was hoping for a shortcut — courtesy of Wang's nine years of experience.

"What do you know about their security systems and procedures?"

"It's all tip-top. That's what you Brits say, right? Tip-top."

"We do indeed."

Wang chortled for a reason unapparent to Max. "It starts at the front gate. Employee parking stickers and picture ID cards are checked by a gate guard using a setup similar to a military installation. No coincidence there. Once inside, you'll find electronic locks on all the doors. Their key cards are coded by department, so nobody can wander into areas that don't concern them."

Max had expected as much. "What about biometrics?"

"They have palm scanners on the doors in R&D."

That was okay. He didn't need R&D. "Anything else?"

"Yessiree. GPS chips in the key cards automatically track everyone throughout the compound. Plus they now have gait monitors strategically placed to help combat impersonations."

Max decided it would be senseless to allow pride to hold him back now. He was already in the Hello Kitty room. "How do the gait monitors work?"

Wang pushed away his glass and leaned back on the couch. "They funnel inbound traffic single file through a ten-foot corridor that uses backscatter scans to measure the position and movement of anatomic landmarks, like femur length and hip sway. Computers then compare those data points against the employee database to verify a match."

Suddenly Wang didn't sound so much like a Chinese peasant. More like Detective Colombo making a bust. "So what happens if Bob sprains his ankle and starts walking with a limp?"

Wang shrugged. "I don't know. It's a new system. Their own system. But I think it learns, adding to its database with each new measurement. Apparently it's smart enough to account for deviations. It has to be, given the range of female footwear."

"Great."

"You want my advice?"

"Sure."

"Pass. Whatever the project, save yourself a whole lot of heartache and pass. It's impossible."

"I can't pass. *We* can't pass."

Wang blinked as his mouth cracked. "Wait a minute. You're talking about your *current* project? *Our* project? Are you telling me that I'm not getting my $1.5 million until we do the install at Vulcan Fisher?"

Technically speaking, there was another option. They could do the install at Boeing. But it was a defense contractor as well, and to disclose that information would be to give Wang the other half of the puzzle.

At the moment, Wang had no idea what the devices he was building actually did. They were circuit boards. Remote control overrides. Theoretically they could go in any electronic system. VF made a wide variety of those, much of it sexier than autopilot systems. Drones and satellites would come to mind first. But Max couldn't afford to give Wang a clue. Despite appearances, Wang was an accomplished intelligence agent — and Max was framing his employer.

With a bright red face and a pointing index finger, Wang lashed out. "You told me you had a plan for the install. I asked you if you had access, and you said *No problem*. No problem. Those were your exact words."

Max met his eye, trying to assert a calming presence. "I was sure I would — by the time you were ready."

"*Ma la ge bi!*" Wang screamed, slamming his fists on the table.

Max took a sip of baijiu.

Without further word, Wang rose and stomped out the door.

Chapter 22
The Awakening

ACHILLES OPENED his eyes to the sight of an unfamiliar face. His head hurt, his ears rung, and he had that groggy feeling you get when woken in the middle of a dream.

"Can you hear me?"

The woman's loaded question helped to part the fog. People didn't utter those words without a reason, and the ache in the back of his head supplied one. "Where am I?"

Tears dropped onto his cheeks. The woman leaned down and kissed his forehead, bumping his chin with something. When she sat back up, Achilles saw a round medallion hanging from her slender neck, an intricate pattern wrought from silver surrounding a dime-sized opal that gleamed like it was on fire. His eyes didn't linger on it, however. The woman who had just kissed him was beautiful. And obviously relieved. Had she hit him with her car? Was he waking from a coma?

He repeated his question, but the ringing in his ears muted her hesitant reply.

Achilles turned his eyes to his surroundings. He wasn't in a hospital room. There were no tubes connected to his veins, and there was no monitoring equipment to be seen. Oddly enough, he wasn't in a room at all, or even a bed. He was lying beneath dawn's blue sky on a plump orange cushion. The type of cushion you find poolside on loungers at upscale resorts. Surely there was a story behind the location, perhaps one involving a large quantity of liquor, although drinking wasn't his thing.

In a flash he understood.

The inevitable had happened.

He'd finally fallen.

Falling for free solo climbers was like prostate cancer for the rest of the male race. If you hung in there long enough, it was bound to happen. "I fell, right?"

He studied the woman as she composed her reply. She looked simultaneously stunning and stressed, like a Ferrari that had been taken off-road. She showed all the signs of attentive upkeep, with everything polished, plucked, and trimmed, and yet her hair had been left to air dry and her face was devoid of makeup. Apparently he wasn't the only one who'd had a rough night. "No, *mon chou*, you didn't fall. But you hit your head doing something equally reckless. How do you feel?" As the ringing faded away, he noted that her voice was soft and sweet and slightly accented. French if he wasn't mistaken.

He answered her honestly. "I'm confused."

"No doubt." She stroked his cheek. "But I'll take confused over the alternatives. I've been worried sick about you for the past thirty-two hours."

Achilles' brain began catching up with his ears. She'd called him *mon chou*, a French term of endearment. The puzzles were multiplying, along with his list of questions. "How did I hit my head?"

He tried to prop himself up on his elbows, but she gently pressed him back down, the words *take it easy* written large in her big, beautiful eyes.

"I'm not sure. Maybe you slipped, but my guess is that something flew into it."

"Flew into it? Like a bird or a baseball?"

"God only knows. Everything was flying about in the hurricane."

"Hurricane?"

A dark cloud crossed her features. "You don't remember?"

Achilles started to shake his head, but stopped short when his injury screamed.

She reached out and lightly stroked his hair. It was a very intimate gesture. "Hurricane Noreen. It grew to Category 4 in less than twenty-four hours, with 150 mile per hour winds. Caught everyone by surprise. We hunkered down to ride it out. We were curled up on the couch, watching the terrifying NOAA images while reporters shouted and the storm pounded. A couple of hours into it we heard a horrible crash overhead and the TV went blank. You tried switching to internet coverage, but when you discovered that it was also out, you resolved to go up on the roof and fix the satellite dish. I tried to stop you, but … well you know how you are."

Her face was so fraught with conflicting emotions that Achilles felt worse for her than for himself. She took a deep, composing breath, and continued. "That was around eleven PM. I was worried out of my mind by eleven-thirty when you still weren't back. At midnight, I went up after you."

"Into the hurricane? Onto the roof?" Achilles propped himself up onto his elbows, this time without pushback. He was indeed on the flat roof of a single-story home.

She focused on his face while he studied his surroundings. The lush vegetation around the oceanfront home looked like it had been blasted by a water cannon, but otherwise the scene before him was paradise.

Finding it difficult to digest the onslaught of implications with a head that rang like a gong, Achilles lay back down. "What happened next?"

Chapter 23
Recognition

ACHILLES' SAVIOR repeated his question with anguish in her eyes, reliving the moment. "What happened next…"

She took his hands. "I'd never stepped into a hurricane before. Everyone has felt strong wind, but this was ridiculous. I could barely stand up against it. The rain blasted sideways, as if from a fire hose. When I didn't see you, my first thought was that you'd blown away. But it's a big roof and the night was dark as a cave, so I began searching for you on my hands and knees." She gripped his hands tighter.

"Searching for you was bad, but actually finding you was the worst moment of my life. You were laying face-down, positioned like a chalk outline at a murder scene, with water sluicing all around you and the wind ripping at your clothes. I thought you were dead."

She paused to steady her nerves with a deep breath. "The only light I had was the flashlight on my phone, but when I set it down to check your pulse the water shorted it out. So I was stuck feeling you out in the dark. My heart leapt when I found your pulse. Then I felt your breathing, but with all the water I couldn't tell if you were bleeding. You wouldn't wake up, and I was afraid to shake you. So I just lay down next to you, to help keep you warm."

Achilles felt dumbfounded by the whole situation — and his lack of memory surrounding not just the accident, but everything leading up to it. And yet there he was, on a rooftop. Looking around, her story made perfect sense. Much more sense than anything else he could come up with. He returned his gaze to her.

"You back with me now?"

Despite the crazy conditions, he couldn't help but find her French accent adorable. "I'm back. Please continue."

"The storm faded rapidly about an hour after I found you. Some time later you started to toss about. That comforted me, because then I knew you weren't paralyzed. I decided it was safe to move you. But I didn't want to drag you, and of course you're too heavy for me to carry.

So I decided to bring a bed to you." She let go of his hands, and began gesturing.

"I went down and got a couple of dry cushions out of the shed. I rolled you onto one and lay down on the other. When the sun rose, I examined you as thoroughly as I could. The only wound I found was that nasty one on your head."

Achilles stared up at his courageous savior, with her big brown eyes and her mane of dark locks, and he felt a mighty wave of gratitude wash over his heart. Uplifting though that was, it still left him drifting in a sea of confusion. This wonderful woman had just risked her own life to save his. She'd also shown great presence of mind — and yet hadn't thought to call an ambulance.

Stress did funny things.

He probed the back of his head with a couple of fingers. It was tender, and there was a large lump with some scabbing, but he'd suffered worse. Of course it wasn't the damage to the outside that posed the danger. The real risk from head injuries like his was a subdural hematoma. "I feel fine, but we should probably call an ambulance. Just to be sure."

She recoiled with a scowl. "Don't you think I'd have done that already, if it was possible?"

"It's not?"

She grabbed two iPhones off the rooftop and spread them into a V like playing cards to display their blank screens. "It was your idea to use them like flashlights during the hurricane."

"Of course. Sorry. I'm not at my best. Let's drive to the hospital. Maybe stop for breakfast on the way. I'm starving."

Her jaw dropped a little, and her lower lip began to quiver. When she spoke, her words came out low and slow. "Where do you think we are?"

That was a good question.

He'd gone to Lover's Leap to do some climbing while puzzling out the Korovin assassination. Nothing helped to focus his mind like a good climb. He didn't remember coming back. He also didn't remember a hurricane ever striking Northern California. His hunger gave way to an uneasy feeling in his stomach.

Rather than risking saying something stupid, he rose to his feet for some direct reconnaissance. Beyond the rooftop was lush green vegetation, and beyond the vegetation was glistening white sand, and beyond the sand was sparkling blue water. Beautiful turquoise-blue ocean water — not the dark, Northern California kind.

He spun around, slowly, taking in the beautiful scene. For half the circle, he enjoyed a beachfront view. For the other hundred-eighty degrees or so, greenery extended toward a large boulder or volcanic cone that jutted out of the sea and rose hundreds of feet into the air. Aside from the windswept appearance rendered by 150 mile per hour winds, it was pure tropical paradise. A climber's paradise. His kind of place — but unfamiliar.

He turned back to the woman.

She wore a mask of panic and was studying his face as though the secret to eternal youth was written on his forehead. No sense tiptoeing at this point. "I have no idea where we are. I don't recognize this place. And, I'm sorry, but I also don't recognize you."

Chapter 24
Miss Muffet

The Kremlin

IGNATY LOOKED DOWN at the ringing phone. It wasn't his cell phone. It was his encrypted VOIP phone, the one he used to communicate with agents in the field. At the moment he only had two active agents, Max and Muffet, and he wasn't expecting a call from either.

He hit accept. "I'm listening."

"I think they're on to me."

It was Miss Muffet, his White House mole. His gold mine. His miracle worker. If he lost her now, it would be disastrous. Korovin was all over Ignaty for daily updates, and without Muffet he'd be blind in Washington. He would do whatever it took to keep her in place until *Sunset* was complete and the FBI investigation was derailed chasing wild Chinese geese. But he doubted they were on to her. "What makes you say that?"

"Just a feeling," she said, clearly trying to sound certain.

Muffet wasn't a typical agent. In fact, she was the opposite of typical, which was what made her so effective. You never saw her coming. But that cloak came with a price. She needed coddling.

To the extent that Ignaty understood empathy, he could empathize. She didn't have anyone else. That was by design. He'd gotten her as the result of a long con that involved taking out her husband while leaving her penniless and thus ripe for the plucking. He'd positioned himself as her white knight, and now he had to play the part. That wasn't always easy. She was needy and vulnerable, but far from stupid. "Did you see anything that makes you suspicious?"

"Not exactly."

"Hear anything?"

"No. It's not like that. As I said, it's more of a feeling." Her voice trembled with an odd combination of fear and resolve. "I've been giving you a lot lately. Very sensitive, very valuable information. I know you must be acting on it, and I know those actions are sure to lead to investigations — investigations which put me at risk."

She was right about that. The mother of all investigations would be launched just a few short weeks from now. He didn't expect Miss Muffet to survive *Sunset*, but he planned to ride her hard, right off that cliff.

Now that he thought about it, Ignaty realized that she wasn't just being paranoid. Her intuition was spot-on. Of course, he wasn't about to tell her that. "They're always investigating, but they never get anywhere. It took them an entire decade to find Bin Laden. You've got nothing to worry about."

"Maybe yes, maybe no," she replied, her voice showing increasing signs of strain. "But if you want me to take that chance, you're going to have to improve our arrangement."

Ignaty couldn't believe it. Little Miss Muffet was shaking him down. He had to smile at that. He was paying her $1,000 per transmission, giving her an income of about $3,000 a week. It was enough for her to live comfortably, even in Washington, but not enough for her to get ahead. Apparently she'd figured that out. "What did you have in mind?"

"Something more commensurate with the risk."

Commensurate, Ignaty repeated to himself. Was she a lawyer now? "Have you thought about the risk of my finding another source? What would you do then?"

"Good question. What would I do then? I don't know. So I need to be prepared. Financially prepared."

Who'd put steel in her spine all of a sudden? Had she been watching reruns of some 1980's detective series? Ignaty decided to shake her tree and shake it hard, make her grateful for what she had. But later. For now, he would mollify her. Keep her producing. "What would make you happy?"

"I want to be paid what my work is worth. I want $100,000 per transmission."

Ignaty inhaled deeply, audibly. Apparently that shaking couldn't wait.

The money wasn't an issue. He had unlimited funds, and Muffet's transmissions would be a bargain even at $1 million apiece. But the independence that she'd gain if she had financial freedom posed a threat. Ignaty couldn't abide threats.

Time for a bit of brinksmanship.

"How about this. How about you let me know when $1,000 is sounding good again, and we'll see if I still need you." He disconnected the call.

Chapter 25
All that Jas

ACHILLES STUDIED the face of his savior. She didn't scream or slap or freak out at the revelation that he didn't recall her. She just stared at him while a single tear rolled from each of her big dark eyes.

Without a word, she took his hand and led him across the roof. They climbed down through a trap door into a utility room, then passed through a pantry into a million dollar kitchen.

She repositioned two chairs so they could sit knee to knee, while holding hands. After inhaling deeply, she looked him in the eye, and began. "My name is Sophia. Sophia ... Dufour ... Achilles. But you call me Jas. We've been married for seven months."

Achilles was too shocked to reply.

"We're on Nuikaohao Island, which is an islet really, in the Hawaiian chain. It belongs to my parents, but they won't be here until the first week of January. They're in Cannes through New Year. I'm just rambling now. I'm sorry. I'm a bit scared and don't know what to say. I've been scared sick ever since I found you. I'm an artist, not a doctor."

"So we're the only ones on . . ."

"Nui-kao-hao," Jas repeated. "It means big goat horn, which is the shape of the rock formation that constitutes most of the island. Your favorite feature, of course."

"There are no natives, or neighbors, or servants on Nuikaohao?"

"Just us. We're only sixty kilometers from Kauai, which we can cover in thirty minutes on the speedboat in calm seas. But the hurricane took the speedboat."

"The hurricane took the speedboat," he repeated, allowing the situation to sink in. "So we're stuck? On an island? Without a boat or phone or internet?"

"The whole island chain is a mess, I'm sure. Hurricane Noreen caught everyone unaware. It was calm before the storm, of course, so we didn't have warning."

"Surely there would have been alerts?"

"Undoubtedly there were. But you were out climbing all day, and I was busy painting, listening to my playlist, not a broadcast. We didn't check the news until the storm hit our island. Then we saw the huge spinning white cloud on the radar map and nearly had heart attacks."

Achilles could picture that scene. He'd sat out many a tense situation waiting for news. "If we're living on a private island, surely we have a two-way radio?"

"It was on the boat."

"That was shortsighted."

"Not everyone thinks like you do, Achilles. My parents aren't always expecting armageddon. And to be fair, this is Hawaii, not Karachi. They obviously built the house right, it's hardly got a scratch."

Yeah, just the satellite dish. Achilles was used to planning for double and triple redundancy of critical systems, but he knew Jas was right. That wasn't the norm. He regretted his outburst. Still, the contractor should have protected the dish. Although, come to think of it, he wasn't sure how you'd do that. He'd never seen a dish in a cage. "Sorry. What's the plan?"

Her features relaxed in response to his words, making Achilles feel bad about adding to her tension. "I'm sure the Coast Guard will be by to check on us any time now. I'm a bit surprised they haven't shown up yet. They know we're here, as we registered with them back on Kauai. But I'm sure they have their hands full dealing with the damage Noreen inflicted on the main islands."

"Why are we here?"

"Vacationing in Hawaii? For free? In a luxury home on a private island with an art studio and a 312-foot sea cliff you said would rate at least a 5.12?"

Hard to argue with that, not that he was trying to be argumentative. Achilles was just trying to gain his bearings. Find solid ground. She'd just given him some by speaking the language of climbing. Jas's 5.12 remark told him a lot about both her and their relationship. The "5" on Nuikaohao's cliff meant that climbing it required technical skill, that it was significantly more vertical than horizontal. The 12 indicated the difficulty on a scale running from 1 up to 15. To tackle a 5.12, a person had to be comfortable climbing rock faces that would appear impossible to anyone but a pro.

His failure to take Jas's emotional strain into consideration concerned him. It told him that he was off his game. That was understandable, but disconcerting. He paused to confirm that he wasn't imagining everything. Odd experiences with strangers were common enough while dreaming. But he quickly dismissed the thought. The edges of his perception weren't cloudy. Time wasn't amorphous. And, come to think of it, he had to pee. "Where's the bathroom?"

She pointed over his left shoulder. "I'll get breakfast started."

The master bathroom was the size of some inner-city apartments. It included opposing his-and-hers sinks with generous granite countertops, and a walk-in glass-brick shower. A bathtub easily large enough for two rested beneath a picture window that framed the Big Goat Horn.

Achilles made quick use of the facilities and then checked his pupils in the mirror while turning the lights on and off. They responded. A good sign that the knock to his noggin hadn't been too severe.

He moved on to the makeup station he'd passed while walking through the master bedroom. It was a white wooden desk topped with a trifold mirror and ornamented with carved roses. Resting atop the right wing, behind a ceramic curling iron and an overstuffed makeup bag, a silver framed photo gleamed in the morning sunlight. A wedding couple on a beach.

He picked it up.

The groom was standing in the surf with his shoes off and his black tuxedo pants rolled up. He was holding the bride in his arms and they were both beaming. The bride was the woman cooking his breakfast. Achilles was the groom.

Chapter 26
Beyond Marriage

Hawaii

ACHILLES STARED at the picture in disbelief. He was married.

To a woman he didn't know.

Or was he? Achilles scrutinized the picture of his face. The cheekbones, the chin, the hairline. No doubt it was him. The image itself gave him a familiar feeling. He had seen it before. But he still couldn't remember the day, or more importantly, the bride.

Only once in his remembered-life had Achilles contemplated marriage. But that was during an odd relationship, one that had never been consummated. Apparently Katya had moved on, or he had. The thought pained him. He wondered if Katya was also married now, but decided he'd hold off on asking Jas that question. He'd only been bumped on the head, not beheaded.

Before returning to the kitchen and his wife, Achilles struggled to dredge his most recent memories from the depths of his throbbing brain. Those memories weren't in Hawaii, that was for sure. After a good minute of beating the bushes, he couldn't dig up anything more recent than his trip to South Lake Tahoe, where he'd climbed Lover's Leap.

"These are the last of the eggs," Jas said, setting two-thirds of a steaming mushroom and Parmesan omelette down before him. "Let's enjoy them."

Achilles set his hand atop hers as she let go of the plate, in the tender way lovers do. He drew his hand along hers, stopping to study her diamond engagement ring, and matching platinum wedding band, hoping this would spark a memory. "You wear your rings on your left hand, the American way."

"Right," she said, drawing out the *i* to make it clear that she always had. "And you're not wearing one at all, in the climbing tradition. How's your head feeling?"

Achilles took a bite of his breakfast before responding. Delicious. Eggs browned but moist, the mushrooms flavorful, the cheese punchy. He followed the first bite with another big one before answering. He was ravenous. "It's sore, but not screaming."

He had dozens of big questions to answer, but his mind wasn't ready for another major dump at the moment. Memory loss and a surprise wife were enough before breakfast. He didn't want to talk about his health either, so he went with something lighter. "Why do I call you Jas?"

Achilles' heart skipped a beat as she flashed a breathtaking smile. *Wow! His marriage was making more sense by the minute.*

"The first time we met, you said I reminded you of Princess Jasmine from Disney's movie *Aladdin*. You've been calling me Jas ever since. I like it, even though I know it's wishful thinking on both our parts."

The nickname didn't strike him as much of a stretch at all. But then he was stretching into the realm of the surreal by asking a stranger basic questions about himself, and getting revelations as answers. The next question slipped out. "And how long ago was that?"

She looked up for a sec to do the calculation. "About twenty months. We met New Year's Day, 2018, in a Honolulu convenience store. It was about the only place open on the island. You needed trail mix, and I needed dramamine, and both were sold out. That spoiled each of our plans, and we ended up grabbing brunch at the Hilton on Waikiki Beach. You started talking about climbing, and I mentioned that I had a private cliff that nobody could possibly climb, and you ended up accepting my challenge."

He could easily picture the scene she'd painted. A beautiful woman, a tropical hideaway, and a challenging cliff. He'd have jumped on that like Jack from a box.

But he didn't remember it.

He was missing at least two years.

Chapter 27
The Revelation

Hawaii

"WHAT'S THE LAST THING YOU REMEMBER?" Jas asked, in what seemed to be her favorite refrain. She appeared to be taking it personally that he didn't remember her.

Hard to fault your wife for that.

They'd spent the day taking it easy while waiting for the Coast Guard to show. It was almost like a normal vacation. They ate fruit salad for lunch, and Caesar salad with grilled fish for dinner, leading Achilles to understand how his wife maintained her enviable figure. They walked hand-in-hand on the beach and napped arm-in-arm on the hammock while Achilles enjoyed the experience of rediscovering why he'd fallen in love.

Jas was curious and clever and full of *joie de vivre*. She brought that love of life to her paintings, which captured couples at tender times in city settings. She kept the faces in her paintings out of sight and out of focus, to help the viewer step into the scene. Achilles also delighted in the way she rendered lights, giving the canvas great depth while bringing the background to life.

Over dinner, he discovered that she knew lines from all his favorite movies. His French girl even shared his love of the outdoors. Their bellies full, they were now snuggled up on a beach blanket beneath a bright canopy of stars, studying their fire pit's flickering flames, in what Achilles hoped was a prelude to getting to know her as a woman.

He'd had to dig down through the woodpile to find dry kindling, but it was worth it to smell the sweet Koa smoke and hear the logs snapping away over the ocean's rhythmic roar. While he'd been preparing the fire, she'd disappeared only to surprise him with a bottle of white Burgundy from her father's wine store. Alcohol was probably contraindicated for head injury victims, but just what the doctor ordered following extreme emotional stress, so they generously called it a wash and promised to limit their alcohol consumption to a single bottle.

"It's all there, you know," she said. "Given that you're not displaying other signs of cognitive malfunction, the blow to your head almost certainly didn't destroy the neurons holding your memories. It just disrupted the synapse trail leading to them."

"Were you a doctor before you became a painter?" Achilles asked, careful to get his intonation right.

Jas scrunched her face. "I keep forgetting all the things you've forgotten. My grandmother died of Alzheimer's. It was horrible. My father worries that he's next, so he does his research and shares it with me."

"How does that help me? The neural pathway thing I mean." He took a sip of wine, then snugged his glass into the sand and pulled a long glowing stick from the fire.

Jas flipped her hair out of the way. "If you think of your brain as a neighborhood, and your memories as houses, then the sidewalks are your synapses. The bump to your head likely crushed one or two paving stones, but the others are still there. All you need to do to access your lost memories is bridge the connection anew. Make sense?"

"Sure. But how do I build that bridge?"

"We follow the sidewalk as far as we can and then try to jump to the other side."

"I get the metaphor, but what do we *actually* do?"

"We retrace the path of your last memories again and again. We should find that we can push them a bit further each time. Before we know it, we'll be on the other side."

That sounded sensible enough to Achilles. "Thanks."

"Don't thank me, silly. Tell me the last thing you remember."

"Climbing Lover's Leap."

"When? Do you remember the date?"

"August of 2017."

"Good. Now give me the details. Why were you there?"

"I had just received a big assignment. A tough mission with what seemed to be an insurmountable problem. I'd gone home to Palo Alto to ponder it, but wasn't getting anywhere. So I drove up to South Lake Tahoe to meditate on it — which as you know I do best while climbing."

"What problem were you trying to solve?"

Achilles couldn't go into specifics. Most of his adult life was classified for national security reasons. The bulk of what he knew was factoids that civilians couldn't care less about, but the details of that particular assignment would make front page news around the world.

When he didn't answer right away, Jas prompted him with, "Did you figure it out?"

Good question, he thought, grabbing his wine glass. "I don't know. Not that I recall."

"Focus on the fire, and try to remember."

Her instincts were solid. The sound of the ocean and flicker of flames were classic hypnotic prompts.

He thought back to the meeting in Senator Collins' DC home, his follow-up research with Foxley, and his subsequent solo attempt to puzzle it out at home. He tried to point his mind down the right path and set it free while the fire crackled and the ocean swished, but he couldn't make the leap.

He was about to confess failure, when Jas said, "Wait a minute! Did you say August of 2017?"

"That's right.

Her face lit up with excitement. "That's when you were working on the Korovin assassination."

Chapter 28
The Relief

Hawaii

ACHILLES FOUND Jas's words no less startling than a sudden slap to the face, but he managed to keep hold of his wine. He took a sip to buy a second of thought. "I told you about the Korovin assassination?"

"Of course you did. I'm your wife. We agreed early on never to keep things from each other. Not the big things, anyway." She raised her own wine glass. "Assassinating one head of state at the request of another is as big as things come."

"Apparently. But, wow, I still can't believe I told you something that inflammatory."

Jas shook her head. "You're forgetting what a marriage is. When they're good — and ours is good — two people become one. We share everything, in good times and bad and all that."

Achilles just nodded, unable to believe that he'd broken security protocol. Perhaps his experience with Katya had loosened him up? She had played a major role in his initial battle with Korovin. Had history repeated itself with Jas?

Jas continued while Achilles was still processing. "In fact, we wouldn't have met if it weren't for Korovin."

"Really? How's that?"

"You'd just completed that assignment when we first met. That was why you were in Hawaii. You were decompressing. Of course, I didn't know that at the time. You didn't tell me until after we were married."

Achilles felt a wave of relief wash over him from head-to-toe, releasing tensions he didn't know he'd had. For him to have told Jas about that, an assignment that was not only his deepest, darkest secret, but one of his nation's, he must really trust her. Really love her.

Looking over at her sparkling eyes and the little shadows cast by her jaw and cheekbones in the firelight, he was overcome with a tremendous urge to make love to her. It burst forth from deep inside his core, like lava erupting from a volcano. Hot and steamy and irrepressible.

He had a lot of lava built up.

For the last three months of his active memory — the memory still synaptically accessible — he'd been cohabiting his Palo Alto home with another woman. A very special woman.

Katya Kozara was, without a doubt, the most amazing woman he'd met. At least before Jas. But of course there had been a twist in their relationship. A big twist. One of those gut-churning, conscience-grating, sleep-stealing twists that life tends to present — just to keep you from getting too comfortable.

Katya had been his brother's fiancée.

Colin Achilles died the same night he proposed to Katya. Then Achilles and Katya grew close investigating the incident that killed Colin. That same incident left them both in need of housing, and Achilles in possession of a home not far from Katya's job at Stanford. At the time, it would have felt odd for them not to cohabitate. But reflecting on it now, with the objectivity that only time can lend, Achilles' home life struck him like the setup to a reality TV show.

Despite the confounding complications that tore his heart this way and that, he felt drawn to Katya at the molecular level. Genetically programmed to love her. And though they'd never openly discussed it, he'd sensed that she felt the same. But the ghost of Colin was ever present, complicating their feelings and confounding their emotions. So they had decided to give it time, and live platonically. Her postdoc at Stanford would only last a year. They'd make a decision when it was time for her to move on.

Now he knew where they'd landed on that question — and the decision both shocked and saddened him.

Mentally, a seemly period of grieving and reflection had suited Achilles. Physically, that decision had sentenced him to a state of sexual frustration. Looking over at Jas now, all that pent-up energy came crashing back against his sense of restraint like a horde of barbarians on a castle gate. Then enlightenment struck, and for the second time that day, Achilles enjoyed the sensation of relief washing over him. Although new to married life, he was pretty sure that matrimony meant he didn't have to fight his natural urges.

Achilles stood and helped Jas to her feet with an extended hand.

"What?" she asked, a knowing twinkle in her eye, but a bit of strain in her voice.

"Let's go see if we can jog some memories loose."

Chapter 29
The Struggle

Hawaii

ACHILLES LED HIS WIFE by the hand back to their bedroom. When they reached the foot of their bed, he pulled her toward him, wrapped his arms around the small of her back, and pulled her lips up to meet his. What a lucky man he was, to be able to kiss his beautiful wife — again — for the first time.

Jas was about six inches shorter than he, and although more model than centerfold, he expected to find her slim figure soft in all the right places. As their mouths met, and her flesh melted into his, the universe seemed to condense down to the place where their lips touched, like the birth of a star. Time stopped ticking and space stopped moving and Achilles felt himself utterly lost in the moment.

Then Jas pulled back.

"How about a hot bath?" She proposed. "Let me clean you up. Make sure everything looks alright before we raise your blood pressure."

He wanted to say, *How about after*, but feared getting his marriage off on the wrong foot. He could hold out. They weren't going anywhere. They were literally stranded on an island.

Yes, he thought, *his situation was improving by the second*. It was all a matter of perspective.

Jas squirted some soap and twisted the taps and warm water sluiced into the tiled tub from a silver spigot. Judging by the two-seater's size, it would take a few minutes. "I'll refresh our drinks and grab a couple candles," Jas said. "Why don't you go ahead and climb in."

Achilles complied, but not before pausing to inspect his naked body in the mirror to see what it looked like at thirty-four years. No noticeable wear and tear, was his immediate conclusion. His hair was thick and dark, and there were no new scars on display. His body still looked pumped from the stint he'd spent in jail at the beginning of his thirty-second year, cranking out various calisthenics by the thousand each day. It was indeed a day to appreciate silver linings.

The lights went out as Achilles slid into the tub and he turned his head to see Jas in the doorway. She was holding a tray with their refreshed wine glasses and a pair of fat white candles, already aglow.

"How's the water?"

"It's missing something," Achilles said with a wink.

Jas closed the gap and emptied her tray on the tub surround before leaning over him to hit a button. The spa's jets whooshed to life, blowing bubbles and spreading the scent of honeysuckle.

"I meant some*one*. The water's missing you."

"Well here I am."

And there she was — for all of a second or two. Jas stepped out of her clothes quicker than an ape could peel a banana. With a lithe move that afforded Achilles only a brief glimpse of her darker regions, and a murmured "Aaah," she disappeared beneath a blanket of suds.

"I think we've got enough bubbles," Achilles said, extinguishing the jets. "The hot water won't damage your opal?"

"My great-grandmother's good-luck charm? Nah. I never take it off." Jas handed him his wine. "Now where were we? You were telling me about the Korovin job."

"Actually, you may know more about it than I do. I don't remember much. Was I successful?"

Jas raised her wine glass. "You were. Lukin is now Russia's president."

"Wow!" Achilles found himself plunged back into the thick of big-revelation day. "How did I do it?"

"Try to remember. Bridge the gap. What was the plan?"

He didn't remember.

Frustrated by his inability to break through, Achilles reached under the water and found a leg. He pulled. Jas slid closer, but stopped his progress when her feet hit the back wall. Rather than folding her legs to come closer, she put her wine glass between them. "*Ah ah ah.* Work first, play later."

Achilles took a long sip of wine, and attempted to refocus. He tried to put his frontal lobe before his libido. It was a struggle. With the warm water and wonderful wine working their magic on his nervous system, and the profound relief he felt knowing that he'd justified his president's faith, Achilles found himself fading. To say that it had been a big day would be like calling King Kong a big gorilla.

But he was still looking forward to the honeymoon.

Jas was watching him with a mischievous expression on her lovely lips. "I know what you need." Before he could query her further, she was out of the tub.

She dried off with a plush white towel that contrasted nicely with her taut, tanned skin, then slipped into a matching white robe she conjured from thin air. For her next trick, Jas made his towel appear along with one of those small bottles of scented oil that cost as much as liquid gold. "Finish up your wine. It's time for your massage."

Chapter 30
Close Call

Seattle, Washington

MAX LOOKED at his watch for the fourth time in as many minutes. Two minutes to go. He wasn't looking forward to Ignaty's call.

Meanwhile, Wang was on Max's mind. The Chinese spy had been unresponsive since learning that Vulcan Fisher was their target. Max was confident that Wang would eventually come around — $1.5 million buys a whole lot of forgiveness and understanding — but until he did, Max seemed stuck.

His own attempts to locate a crack in VF's security had borne no fruit. In addition to researching everything from emergency response procedures to factory tours, he'd tried stoking his creative fires by running along the waterfront and meditating in a park. Nothing had helped. Normally, he'd experiment. But this was hardly a trial-and-error situation. The Americans took espionage seriously. A slip-up could be worse than death.

His computer chimed on time and as planned. "Tell me," Ignaty said.

Ignaty had insisted on a daily call rather than the usual message board. Theoretically this was to avoid any chance of confusion, given the exceptionally high stakes, but Max felt certain that Ignaty had gone that route in order to maximize the pressure he could inflict. Ignaty was that kind of guy. Even with the Mickey-Mouse voice distortion, Max could still sense the glee as he twisted the knife.

Max put as much enthusiasm into his voice as he could muster. "Delivery in five days."

"Five days? All fifty of them?"

"All fifty."

Ignaty didn't say, "Excellent!" or even "That's early." He said, "Are you ready for them?"

"I will be."

"So that's a *no.*"

It was uncanny just how intuitive that bristle-faced ferret could be. Max wanted to point out that he was one man, working alone, in a foreign country, against the most secure corporation on the planet. But those were excuses. He wanted to ask for permission to reach out to

SVR assets in the area, fellow foreign intelligence agents who had undoubtedly already analyzed Vulcan Fisher for weaknesses. But Ignaty had already denied that request with a reprimand that made him feel like a schoolboy. *What didn't he understand about the consequences to Russia if the inevitable extensive American investigation turned up anything implying Russian involvement?* Ignaty was right. In the aftermath of the operation, the FBI would offer millions for information. If Max made queries, someone would remember. The consequences would not be pretty. "That's a *no*."

"That's disappointing."

Max had planned to ask about Zoya, but this clearly wasn't the time. Operations security protocol prevented him from contacting her directly, but Ignaty had promised to pass along news and relay messages. What an ill-conceived plan that was, passing verbal I-love-you's via Ignaty. Get real. During their first call, he realized that he'd never get anything more than a *she's-fine* even if he asked. But today, anything would sound good. He needed the boost he'd get from even that brief third-party interaction with her. God, how he missed her. His fiancée. He decided to risk it. "What's the latest from Zoya?"

"She loves you. She misses you. She's pregnant."

"What!" If ever there was a time when you didn't want a four-second communication delay, this was it.

"Just kidding. But what if she were? What world would you be bringing that child into? One where daddy is a hero, or a national disgrace?"

Max's shoulders slumped even as his neck recovered from the emotional whiplash. "I better get back to it then."

"See that you do."

Chapter 31
The Request

Hawaii

ACHILLES OPENED HIS EYES, and once again found a beautiful woman looking down at him. This time he recognized her face and knew her name. This time he was lying on a proper mattress, beneath a puffy white duvet and a circulating ceiling fan. Oh what a difference a day makes.

And a night.

He turned toward his bride, studying her face in the morning light as if for the first time. She was already dressed in a tawny t-shirt that accented the highlights in her hair and the amber flecks in her big brown eyes.

"Ready to get to work?" Jas asked. "I'm not letting you out of this bed until you remember me."

He reached back and ran his index finger over the lump on his head. It was still angry, but it wasn't screaming.

Jas studied him. "What is it? Your head bothering you?"

"A little."

"All the more reason to stay in bed."

"I need my morning coffee."

Jas gestured with her chin.

Achilles looked behind him to see a covered bowl, a silver thermos flask, and an empty mug. He sat up, poured the coffee, and lifted the lid off the bowl.

"Steel-cut organic oats, with raspberries," Jas said. "That sound about right?"

"That sounds perfect." Sipping the coffee, Achilles found the taste divine. Fresh and bold. Chock full of caffeine, minerals, and antioxidants. What a woman.

Reading his expression, Jas flashed him a million-dollar smile. "Better?"

"Much better."

"Good. Can we get back to healing your mind?"

"Bring it on."

She sat beside him on the edge of the bed and brought her anxious eyes to his. "Two years ago, you were climbing Lover's Leap, and trying to devise a plan. Tell me about it."

Achilles balked. He was eager to oblige Jas for oh so many reasons, but this first step was a hurdle. Obviously they'd already discussed the important stuff. She already knew the damning details. The sensational headlines. The secrets worth killing for. Silver had asked him to assassinate Korovin, and he had complied. The things she didn't know were just footnotes. Still, it wasn't in his nature to discuss operations with outsiders. Perhaps that was the rub. The fundamental mistake of a bachelor's mind. She wasn't an outsider. They were a team. A marital team. A successful team. A team made strong by sharing everything.

"What is it?" Jas asked, setting her hand atop his.

"Nothing. I'm just a slow learner." He shook his head and took another sip of coffee. "We identified a gap in Korovin's security. A gap he created himself."

"Really? That doesn't sound like Korovin. He was so security conscious that he never even used a cell phone."

"Yeah, well, apparently the rare exception gave him the strength to stick with the rule."

Jas nodded understanding. "Like the fashion model who allows herself the occasional chocolate truffle. What did he do?"

"He occasionally slipped his security and exposed himself."

"When? How?"

"The details don't matter. The problem was figuring out how to exploit his behavior, because it was so unpredictable."

Jas withdrew her hand. "The details are all that matter! That's how we're going to extend the path back to your lost memories. Detail by detail. Brick by brick. I need you to remember, Achilles. I need a husband who knows me and loves me despite everything he knows."

Achilles set his mug down a bit too roughly, sloshing coffee. He ignored it. "I don't know the next move. I don't know what I did. I'm just as stuck now as I was back then."

Jas looked like she was about to cry. "I thought we had it. You got my hopes up. I need you to remember me. Surely you understand that."

"I'll try. I promise. It's absolutely my top priority. It's important for me to remember everything. Especially the day I met you — the luckiest day of my life."

His words evoked a smile, giving Achilles hope that he'd eventually get the hang of the husband thing.

"Your oatmeal's getting cold," she said.

Achilles broke eye contact to look over at the bowl on his nightstand. He scooped up a spoonful with a raspberry on top. "How's Silver's second term going?"

Jas tensed up.

Looking back over he saw that the fire in her big beautiful eyes had faded. She lifted a hand to his shoulder. "I'm sorry, Achilles. President Silver had a stroke shortly after Korovin died. It killed him. Matthews is now president."

Achilles was no psychologist, but he was certain their textbooks included phrases like *tipping point, inciting incident,* and *precipitating event.* The news that fate had prematurely snatched away yet another pillar of his self-identity felt like one of those.

"I'm going to get some air," he said, rising from the bed and heading for his closet.

Most would consider his wardrobe an amusing if not an odd sight. During the extended backpacking trip that Achilles had taken immediately after leaving the CIA, he had learned to appreciate the efficiency of limiting his base wardrobe to under ten pounds. A pair of loose blue jeans, a set of khaki cargo shorts, a couple of soft white Tees, and some cotton undergarments were all he really needed. His feet only had one home: approach shoes — the special soft-soled sneakers that were an efficient hybrid of a hiking boot and a climbing shoe. Buy them in black, and they were one-size-fits-all as far as most occasions were concerned. Rounding off his wardrobe was a single luxury item, a quality black leather jacket. That should have been all he saw when he slid aside the mirrored door, but apparently he'd made a concession to married life or island life or both. His lonely shelves also supported a set of swim trunks, blue with a white stripe, and some flip flops, brown rubber and natural leather. Gifts he guessed.

"Please, Achilles. Come back to bed. Back to me. Let's talk."

The climbing clothes went on with practiced familiarity. Twelve seconds flat. He looked up from the second shoelace to see Jas standing there in the closet doorway with her ankles crossed and her arms outstretched. Naked.

His throat turned dry, and his breath came up short. If memory served, he'd passed out during the massage.

Her legs were long and lean and looked like they could go for miles and miles. She only got better heading north from there. "Stay with me," she said. "Talk to me. We don't know what's going on with your head. You need to take it easy until we get you checked out. Don't be rash."

Chapter 32
The Accomplice

Seattle, Washington

"THIS COULD BE THE ONE," Wang said, his eyes still glued to the binoculars.

Max sure hoped so. There was only so much more *General Hospital* talk he could take. Still, he was happy to suck it up as penance if it made Wang happy.

They were peering through the window of a hot sheets motel across the road from Callie's Club. The enormous bar was frequented by airmen and soldiers from the neighboring joint base, and by Vulcan Fisher employees, many of whom were retired airmen and soldiers. A neon sign in the window promised live music and dollar longnecks, while Callie's winking logo hinted at something more.

Wang had finally come around. As upset and intimidated as he was by the prospect of slipping into Vulcan Fisher for a midnight soldering session, the siren song of a seven-figure payday had proved irresistible. And as it turned out, Wang had been holding back. He'd been to Vulcan Fisher just six weeks earlier.

"He looks nothing like me," Max replied.

"Right age, right height. You not so fat, but people lose weight. The hair you can fix."

"His nose is twice the size of mine and his eyes are set much deeper. You think we all look alike, don't you?"

"You really want to have that conversation? A Caucasian talking to an Asian? I look nothing like the guy whose ID I copied, but Vulcan Fisher's lily-white guards never blinked."

The two spies watched another car with a VF parking permit pull into Callie's lot. Four guys dressed in jeans and sneakers piled out. Rats from the local lab. One was black. Another was both vertically challenged and pumping lots of iron to compensate. But the remaining two had potential. They sported both the right general appearance and regular facial features, although the blonde one wore a wedding ring. Max was encouraged. "Two show potential."

"Well all right then!" Wang said, punching his shoulder. "You see. All kinds of good things happen when the sun is shining."

The sun was indeed their friend today. No rain meant no raincoats, leaving ID cards exposed. They'd likely have come off in the bar anyway — Callie kept it warm and thus welcoming for thirsty servicemen sick of the cold — but Max was happy to take a sure thing. The lack of outerwear also helped speed up target assessment.

Wang's plan for covert entry into Vulcan Fisher had two steps. The first was ID replication. They had to borrow a suitable ID long enough to copy it, and then return it before it was missed. The second step was ensuring that the target would not go into work the next morning. Couldn't have two Lester Winkelmans showing up, not with a security system as sophisticated as Vulcan Fisher's.

Entering the bar half a minute after his prey, Max saw that the foursome had snagged a table up by the stage. A good sign. They were more interested in entertainment than conversation. Their waitress, a healthy college student dressed in short black shorts and a tight Callie's T-shirt, was already filling frosty mugs from their first pitcher.

Max grabbed a seat that put them between him and the stage. Both his potential marks were taking notice of the charms their waitress had on display. A promising sign. He knew that married men cheated all the time, but now that he was engaged himself he found it freshly repugnant. He couldn't imagine cheating on Zoya. Then again, by landing the most beautiful woman he'd ever met, he had stacked the deck.

Wang elbowed him. "Which one do you like most?"

"Blondie's facial features are a better match, but he's about four inches too short. Will that be a problem with the gait analysis?"

"Almost certainly. But remember the gait monitors aren't installed everywhere. You might be able to avoid them. That would be a good idea in any case. I don't know how accurate they've gotten. They're supposed to be adaptive, learning as they add data points. Getting harder to fool every day."

"Your advice?"

Wang studied them for a second. "Go with the tall guy. His build is more like yours."

"But his face is longer and thinner." Max began thinking aloud. "I suppose I could let my jaw hang loose, and wear glasses. His center hair part is unusual enough that the guard's gaze will gravitate to it. If I get that right, I should be okay."

"Assuming he wore it that way when he took his security picture."

"Men don't change their hairstyle. Only women."

"Okay then," Wang said, raising his phone in a victory gesture. "We've got our first choice, and a backup. I'll let Lucy know."

Callie's was a target-rich environment for practitioners of the oldest profession, and as long as those practitioners were discreet, Callie didn't protest. Word was, that was how she earned her seed capital. In any case, she was giving this Seattle neighborhood exactly what it wanted.

Max thought Lucy looked even better live than in the picture Wang had shown him. Reputedly a law student at U-Dub, Lucy was in her early-twenties and vivacious. She had a blonde ponytail, long athletic legs, and a mischievous kitty vibe. She'd reportedly cost Max $5,000, although he'd assumed Wang was skimming at least half off the top. Now he wasn't so sure.

In response to Wang's text, Lucy grabbed a seat at the empty table next to the boys. Positioning herself just inches from target number one, she laid her long, bare legs up on the neighboring chair like a fresh cake in the window. While necks began straining, Lucy turned her eyes to the stage and began nodding her head with the beat of the Nickelback tribute band.

Target number two rose as the song drew to a close. He grabbed a seat at Lucy's table. Skillfully leveraging both the tiny musical gap and the title of the last song, Max heard him ask, "What would you do if today was your last day?" Max didn't hear her answer, but based on her response it was obviously friendly. A few seconds later the mark was flagging their waitress.

"Do we want man number two?" Wang asked, his phone out and ready to text Lucy.

"Number one would be better, but that could get complicated. We might not get either." As Max weighed the potential downsides of trying to upgrade, Wang's phone vibrated. Max looked over at the screen. It read: "+$1k for 2."

Chapter 33
The Horn

Hawaii

ACHILLES WAS NOTHING IF NOT DISCIPLINED. He'd worked his way to Olympic bronze in the biathlon before a back injury had dashed his dreams of gold. Then he'd served with distinction in the CIA's Special Operations Group until the joy was gone. Both careers had demanded the constant sacrifice of short-term desires for long-term goals. He wasn't certain that clearing his head would be considered a long-term goal, but he was certainly sacrificing his short-term desire to achieve it.

A very strong short-term desire.

Jas looked more astonished than upset as he headed for the door.

Free solo climbing isn't as reckless as it sounds. You don't just walk — or in this case swim — up to a class 5 cliff face and start climbing without a rope. Not if you hope to survive. First you plan your route and prep the rock. Before working your way up from the bottom with nothing but a sure grip between you and the Almighty, you work your way down from the top — on a rope. You prepare for the insanity by brushing away grit and growth and removing any rock that's not firmly fixed. That way every hold you lunge or leap or strain for will be solid and sure and clean. Only when the prep is done, do free solo climbers tackle the tough climbs aided only by bravado and a bag of chalk.

Even without his memory, Achilles instantly knew the best route to take up Nuikaohao. Experienced climbers see routes on rocks' faces the way cosmetic surgeons see wrinkles on humans. It's automatic. From the water, it appeared that the cliff face angled outward, more like the prow of a mighty ship than the horn of a big goat. Perhaps the Polynesians had named it before a mighty ship ever reached their shores.

Pulling himself up out of the warm waves at the start of the obvious route, he had expected to slip into a familiar groove, both literally and figuratively. Let the meditation begin!

But he didn't slip into a familiar groove.

The meditation didn't begin.

The peace of mind did not come.

Time and again his chosen grip was slick and his foothold was slippery. At first he attributed the discrepancy to Hurricane Noreen, assuming that her wild winds and torrential rains had washed away the chalk and deposited the grit. But that hypothesis faded fast. No amount of blowing and blasting could account for the abundance of moss and loose stone he found on the favored routes.

Achilles didn't need another mystery at the moment. He was supposed to be clearing his mind, not adding to the clutter. Surely there was a simple explanation? One that temporarily escaped his frazzled neurons. One that would be revealed once he reached the top.

After more than an hour of false starts and double backs on half a dozen routes, he gave up on the seaside approach, and attacked Nuikaohao from the island side. The Big Goat Horn didn't present a technical challenge when attacked from behind, but a deep, vegetation-covered crevasse almost ruined his day. Even without further mishap, Achilles had a mild sweat going by the time he reached the glorious summit.

The view atop his vacation island did not disappoint, but the experience was a flop. He was hoping the awe-inspiring scene, previously rendered in moments of free solo triumph, would spark his synapses and bridge his memory gap in the fashion Jas had described. But the scene before him didn't feel familiar.

From atop its bald head, Nuikaohao looked like a green teardrop on a turquoise sea. A private paradise.

Centered on what looked like about half an acre of flat land, the house was a sprawling single-story structure with a flat roof, a wraparound deck, and an elaborate swimming pool. The walkway to the water was paved with intermittent flagstones, reminding Achilles of his damaged neural pathways. The dock itself was mangled in the middle and clearly missing the docking section where their speedboat had been ripped away.

Other islands were discernible as shadows at or near the horizon. The only visible boat was miles away, and not headed in their direction. He and Jas were all alone.

With those preliminaries out of the way, Achilles set about trying to explain the mystery that had led to his landside climb. Once he found the anchor used to tether the rope in his preparatory climbs, he'd know what route he'd taken and the explanation would unfold from there.

Climbing anchors looked like big sewing needles, steel eyelets screwed into holes drilled deep into solid rock. Their coloring blended with the gray rock, but their preferred placement on smooth protruding surfaces tended to make them easy to spot.

He quickly found an obvious potential installation point, a flat-faced monolith jutting above the top plane. Plenty of birds had left their mark upon the protuberance, but not a single drill or hammer. He concluded that it was too far from his chosen route, and began looking elsewhere.

None of the other obvious installation points yielded fruit either. All the rock atop Nuikaohao was virgin. He dropped to his hands and knees and studied the edge for signs of prior climbs. Again, nothing.

Achilles switched to a crosslegged position and angled himself to sit with his face toward the rising sun. With open palms atop naked knees, he began to ponder this latest chilling discovery. One-by-one, the implications crashed against his consciousness like the waves upon the cliff face below.

He'd never climbed Nuikaohao before today.

Therefore he had not vacationed on this island.

Therefore either Jas had lied to him, or he was missing something big. What could that be? Like an astrophysicist, he needed a grand unifying theory.

As the sun baked his face, and the wind blew his hair, Achilles recollected the relevant conversations with his wife. Everything she'd said made sense at the time. All had fit together and felt right. But clearly all wasn't accurate. Were her words confusion or deception?

If deception, then why? By whom? And which side of the script was Jas on? Were they both victims of some psychological experiment? Or was she part of the deception? Jas bore no resemblance to any agent he'd ever known.

Spies develop the espionage equivalent of gaydar. They can detect their own. A few minutes with Jas was enough to know that she hadn't joined the club. She was neither acutely aware of her physical environment nor constantly contingency planning. She wasn't thinking about escape routes or counterattacks or defensive positions — habits that quickly became second nature to undercover agents. At least the ones who managed to keep a step ahead of the reaper's scythe.

So who was she? Had she knowingly lied? Toward what end?

Achilles knew at least one way to find out.

Chapter 34
The Incursion

Seattle, Washington

MAX FIGURED President Korovin had to be leaning hard on Ignaty, given the barrage of questions coming over the phone. "How are you going to breach security? What size of team are you taking in? How long will the system modifications take?"

Max hated supplying management with detail. Espionage assignments weren't like military maneuvers. Covert operations were best left fluid, leaving operatives free to adapt to opportunities, rather than feeling funneled into preconceived plans based on outdated intel.

Ignaty wasn't having it.

Max tried to keep it broad. "For tomorrow's reconnaissance, we're using stolen IDs. How we'll get in for the final installation operation is still TBD. Wang estimates that he needs five hours for that — assuming we can infiltrate with a ten-man team."

Max only got the four-second encryption reprieve before Ignaty redirected his assault. "What's the sweet spot in the manufacturing process? I assume it's got to be pretty late to avoid detection of the additional circuit board?"

Sounded like Ignaty had been consulting the engineers. Fortunately, Max had a knack for technical detail. "Ideally, we'll install *Sunset* after both manufacturing and quality control are completed. We're targeting the gap between QC and packaging for our midnight screw-and-solder party. We'll aim to grab the autopilot systems off either quality control's outgoing rack or packaging's *incoming* one."

"What if they're not left at either location overnight?"

"Then we'll be stuck working in either packaging or shipping."

"It has to happen this month."

Max was well aware of that. Boeing's entire next delivery was going to Southwest Airlines, which only flew domestic. Keeping the terror confined to U.S. territory was paramount to the plan. Korovin insisted on it being a wholly American tragedy. This was both to limit the investigation, and to ensure that it would create a new day, like Pearl Harbor and 9/11.

Max had no doubt that it would.

Sunset would replace 9/11 at the forefront of the American mind, just as World War II had World War I. It would shut down virtually all air travel for months if not years to come. By the time the investigations were completed, the congressional committees had debated, the preventative measures had been devised, the funding approved, the implementation contracts awarded, and the work actually ordered, it would be years. By the time the airports were rebuilt and the public trust was regained, decades were likely to pass. Meanwhile, the loss of air travel would devastate the American economy.

"It will happen this month," Max said, putting a certainty he didn't feel into his voice. "I've learned that product routinely sits for days between departments, due to bottlenecks here and there. We'll have time."

"How are you going to know when the autopilot systems reach the target racks?"

"That's part of tomorrow's reconnaissance mission."

"Details. I need details."

Of course you do, Max thought, rolling his eyes. "I'll be installing fake emergency lighting systems outside QC and packaging. They'll have cameras and wireless transmitters hidden inside."

"Clever," Ignaty said, surprising and delighting Max. "Last question: How are you going to get the free rein to walk around Vulcan Fisher while you do all that work?"

It was Ignaty's best question.

Twelve hours after he'd asked it, Max was about to verify his answer.

He'd brought Wang with him to Vulcan Fisher, both to double the reconnaissance coverage and for camouflage. Two men walking around together would be virtually invisible and appear far less suspicious than one man alone, particularly if the two didn't look like a team. The sight of a tall, elegant Brit with a toolbox and a short, disheveled Asian with a white lab coat and clipboard hardly screamed of collusion.

But first they had to get inside.

"It must be sunny somewhere," Wang said, extending two copied Vulcan Fisher ID cards out the car window.

The guard grunted but didn't reply as he scanned each of them.

His scanner resembled those used by checkout clerks, but with an LCD screen stuck on top. The guard spent about as much time examining the headshots that popped up with each click as clerks did when processing tomatoes. Hardly a surprise, given the rush hour lineup and pouring rain. Max figured he probably could have skipped the itchy blonde wig.

The requisite Vulcan Fisher parking sticker also proved to be no obstacle at all. Max wondered why they even bothered. All he'd had to do to get one was photograph someone else's and run to a copy shop. But he wasn't complaining. Anything that gave VF a false sense of security sounded good to him.

"This way," Wang said, the moment they hit the lobby.

"I thought we'd agreed to start at QC, and it's straight ahead."

"The direct path goes through one of the gait monitors. We can get around it by cutting through the break room."

They'd only just entered, but Max was already tiring of lugging his toolbox around. With two battery-stuffed surveillance systems stashed beneath its tool tray, the toolbox weighed forty pounds. But avoiding detection was job one, so he followed Wang without protest. If they blew it today, he was totally screwed.

Max found the break room detour reassuring, in that nobody gave them a second glance. Granted, everyone was busy stashing lunch boxes in cubbies and exchanging morning pleasantries, but then that only highlighted the beauty of slipping in with the morning rush. He hoped to be back out the front gate before boredom struck and eyes began to wander.

Wang stopped short as they exited the break room. "They moved it."

"Moved what?"

"The gait monitor. They moved it further down the hall. We can't circumvent it."

"So what do we do?"

Wang drummed his fingers on his clipboard. "Nothing. We're screwed."

Chapter 35
Rogue

Bangkok, Thailand

PRESIDENT SILVER exited Bangkok's Leboa State Tower straight into The Beast, which roared out of the underground parking structure, amidst a circus of red and blue lights. He'd enjoyed his second spectacular rooftop dinner in as many nights as part of a whirlwind Asian tour. The trip had been productive, but he was looking forward to waking up in Washington.

Reggie was waiting on the limo's backward facing seat with an encouraging smile, a growing to-do list, and a dreamy look in his eyes. Silver himself had been inspired by the open-air dinner venue, some 820 feet above the expansive beehive that was the Thai capital. He could only imagine what his young valet was feeling. "You look impressed."

"Very, Mr. President. I didn't think anything could beat last night's dinner atop Singapore's Supertree, but Sirocco just did."

"I find such visits to be a healthy reminder that Washington isn't the center of everyone's world. Helps me to ignore the silliness that so often pervades The Beltway." Silver nodded toward Reggie's notebook. "What have you got for me?"

"Sparkman's top of the list, Mr. President. He indicated that it was urgent, and asked that Senator Collins be patched in from California for the call."

"How long do we have?"

"The airport is twenty minutes away."

Silver pulled off his necktie and hit the speaker button as Bangkok's vibrant amalgam of ancient-and-modern, rich-and-poor, rushed by beyond the 5-inch thick bulletproof glass. "Give me Sparkman and Collins."

The secure call connected some seconds later, without audible ring or fanfare. Sparkman spoke first. "Good evening, Mr. President. We have news."

"Go ahead."

"Vasily Lukin has been assassinated. He was taken out by an RPG in the doorway to his Moscow residence."

Silver felt gut punched. "Oh goodness." He began thinking out loud. "That leaves two hardliners as Korovin's likely successors."

"That's right, Mr. President. Grachev and Sobko. If Korovin leaves office, they'll be tripping over each other as they scramble to the right, vying for the nationalist vote. Russia could become even more expansionist."

"The timing is quite a coincidence," Silver said, his frown digging deeper.

"Yes, sir. And that's not the only development. Ibex has gone dark."

Ibex was the code name that Sparkman had assigned Achilles. Silver had asked and learned that it referenced the alpine goats with no fear of heights. "What do you mean, gone dark?"

"He's unresponsive. Incommunicado. We've heard nothing from him, and we can't reach him. It's been 72 hours."

"You think there's a connection with Lukin's death, that Ibex has been captured and interrogated?"

Sparkman shocked Silver with his answer. "No, Mr. President. I think he sold out."

"I don't agree with that assessment," Collins interjected, speaking for the first time. "I'm sure there's another explanation."

"What, exactly, are we explaining?" Silver said, looking over at Reggie. At moments like these he'd gladly switch jobs with his body man, if only for an hour. Just long enough to work the cramps out of his shoulders before the weight of the world came crashing back down.

Sparkman rushed to clarify. "As a precautionary measure, Sylvester put a tracking pellet on Ibex." Sylvester was the codename for Foxley, Sparkman's sly go-to man for black ops.

"And?"

"And it shows Ibex on a private Hawaiian island."

"That's hardly incriminating," Collins pushed back. "Alcatraz is also an island."

Silver closed his eyes and took a calming breath as Sparkman continued. "The satellite imagery we have shows the island's only other occupant to be a woman. The only activity we've been able to observe indicates a relationship far more amicable than hostile, but it's inconclusive. Without re-tasking the satellite, we only get coverage one hour in twenty-four. Given the sensitivity, and the paperwork trail, I didn't order the re-tasking."

"Good. Don't. We can't draw any attention to this. What's the move?"

"I sent Sylvester in. We should have answers shortly."

"I'm sure those answers will be exonerating, Mr. President," Collins said.

"I would like to agree with you, Colleen, and if it weren't for Lukin I'd be certain that you're right. But Lukin is too big a coincidence when you remember who we're dealing with. Korovin can be incredibly compelling, and he has unlimited resources. If he somehow wrangled word of our op, or even if he just anticipated it, he could apply virtually limitless leverage. Remember what Archimedes said about that?"

Sparkman supplied the answer without delay. "Give me a lever long enough and a fulcrum on which to place it, and I shall move the world."

Silver decided to leave it there. No sense speculating further. "I'll expect Sylvester's report by the time I awake in Washington."

Chapter 36
Honey, I'm Home

Hawaii

INSIGHT HIT ACHILLES when he was midway down the Big Goat Horn. He was leaping between rocks when the conclusion illuminated his brain like a beam of blinding light piercing a bat cave, a sudden revelation that gave definition to the landscape and set his thoughts aflutter.

It had to be Korovin.

With that one leap, that single assumption of *Who*, everything else made sense. The *What*, the *When*, the *Where*, and most importantly, the *Why*.

The *What* was a grand scheme. So grand, so all-encompassing, that there were no visible edges to pull back. The fact that anyone would go to so much trouble just to trick him, a relative nobody, was incomprehensible. Some tactical genius must have constructed an elaborate script. That mastermind then acquired — rented, leased, borrowed, purchased, or stole — an entire island. He simulated the damage wrought by a hurricane, presumably using tractors and water cannons. He populated his "stage" with a French woman selected to be just Achilles' type and he trained her to act just right. Then he taught her enough that she could play her role, for days, without detection.

The arrogance required by Achilles to even consider such an elaborate and expensive scenario was astounding.

Until you considered the source.

Until you factored in Korovin and his fortune.

Forbes estimated Korovin's net worth at $200 billion. Other financial institutions pegged his ill-gotten gains at twice that amount. Achilles had once calculated that with just one billion dollars, you could spend $10,000 an hour for a decade and not run out of money. In that context, the Korovin context, the grand scheme was literally no trouble at all.

The *When* was key to understanding it all. Why make Achilles believe that two years have passed? His spy brain leapt to a couple of sound strategic reasons. One was to fabricate historical events. His marriage and two presidential deaths, for starters. Another strategic reason was to make current events less sensitive for discussion by framing them as historical events. Prior to an attack, it's crucial to keep an enemy unaware of what's coming, but after the fact, the enemy already knows.

The *Where* made perfect sense in this context. It had to be someplace isolated from all communication. Not an easy feat in the satellite age. A cabin in the woods might work. Or perhaps a mental asylum. But a fancy private island offered additional advantages. More control for one. The kicker, though, was acceptability. Who wouldn't want to believe that their future didn't hold a beautiful wife and vacations on a private Hawaiian island?

Then there was *Why*. In retrospect, Jas's tactical focus made this crystal clear. She wanted to know how Achilles planned to kill Korovin. Her synapse-reconstruction scheme was a brilliant way of slipping beneath the radar and onto topic. And why not discuss it with a wife who already knew the big picture, especially with both the target and the man who ordered it already dead?

Achilles was about to continue his descent through the tropical forest when another, more disturbing question hit him. *How?* How had Korovin learned of Silver's plan? How did he know that Achilles was to be his executioner? And how was it that someone with that knowledge wouldn't know of the security gap revealed by the Moscow station chief's research?

Those were crucial questions — but he'd come back to them later. For the moment, he needed to focus on staying alive.

While he jogged down Nuikaohao, Achilles used a tried-and-true tactic for strategizing. He mentally consulted his mentor Granger.

The man who'd recruited him into the CIA had an unparalleled talent for cutting to the crux of a matter, and Achilles found that when he imitated him, his critical thinking improved. Funny how the human mind worked.

"What's your top priority? Right now, at this moment?"

"Getting back to Jas."

"Why?"

"The longer I'm away, the more suspicious she'll get. The more suspicious she gets, the more likely she'll be to say enough's enough. I didn't give her the specifics of Korovin's security gap, but I probably supplied enough for Korovin to figure it out. Assuming, of course, that she is Korovin's spy."

"Is there another explanation? Any other scenario that accounts for her lies?"

"No."

"So you fell for a honey trap. The oldest trick in the espionage book."

"This one came with a pretty big twist."

"Yeah, but you fell for it. You fell for it because she's so beautiful. So desirable. You wanted it to be true. With the honey trap, the guys always do."

"I fell for it because she's so convincing. I still can't believe she's a spy. Is she even French? Or is she really Russian?"

"It doesn't matter. You're losing focus. Get back on track. Is she working alone? Physically? Is there anyone else on the island?"

"Too risky. It's such a small island, and they had to allow for the possibility that the operation would drag on for days."

"I agree. So what's their backup plan if the shit hits the fan?"

"The cavalry must be close by. Watching. Listening. She mentioned the Coast Guard."

"So you'll need to get her someplace they don't have eyes and ears. You'll need to get her alone, and then apply pressure. More than you'll want to. Once you get past her prepared line of BS to the actual operational situation, you can set a trap of your own."

"I agree."

"Thing is, that's the obvious play. They'll have accounted for that in their contingency planning."

"Right. But how? She can't carry a gun."

"Maybe she's a kung-fu master. Maybe she's got poisoned fingernails. Maybe she—"

"She's got a panic button. Her opal amulet. It's always around her neck. One good squeeze and the cavalry appears."

"Well then you better make sure it's out of reach when you make your move."

"Agreed."

"So what's the play?"

"By ear."

"A hostage situation is the most likely outcome — and that won't work."

"Why not?"

"You know why."

Achilles did. Even if Jas was Korovin's spy. Even if she'd planned to play him and turn him over to the brute squad, he couldn't bring himself to hurt her. "She won't know that I'm bluffing."

"She's much more empathetic than you. And she's obviously got your number."

"What else can I do?"

Even Granger didn't have that answer.

When Achilles emerged from the jungle and into the clearing, he expected to find Jas waiting on the back deck with two glasses, a bottle of wine, and a relieved look. But nobody was there.

He kept jogging.

Jogging looked natural enough for an athlete returning home from a workout, and it minimized both his exposure and her preparation time. Funny how he was looking at everything anew now that he was an operative again.

He studied the deck boards to avoid those most likely to creak, and used his eyeballs more than his neck to direct his gaze. Nothing untoward registered. His ears caught only the roar of the ocean and wind-rustled leaves, his nose only the smell of blooming flowers and the salty sea.

Aware that he was likely on camera, he couldn't do anything but head straight for the back door. He slid it aside without a surfeit of sound, and stepped silently into the family room. This wasn't going to be a "Honey, I'm home!" moment.

The smell hit him as he was closing the door. Smokeless propellant. The unmistakable scent of a fired gun.

Chapter 37
Try This

Seattle, Washington

MAX SHIFTED HIS GAZE from Wang to the problematic piece of equipment. Gait monitors were similar to the body scanners used at airports except that they were ten times as long and didn't require you to stop moving. The one down the hall only rose to waist height, leaving any adult walking through it open to observation. The attendant doing the observing was positioned about twenty feet further down the corridor in a setup similar to a TSA passport checking station, but with the addition of a large screen.

Max knew he should abort.

But he also knew he wasn't going to.

Time was tight, Ignaty was breathing down his neck, and the gait monitor would still be there when he came back. Best to think fast and act faster. Perhaps an alternative approach? He looked back at Wang. "We could try packaging or shipping first, and then circle back."

Wang shook his head, dashing Max's hopes. "The branch off to those departments is also on the other side." As he finished speaking, Wang began tapping his clipboard. A thought had arrived. "You went with Bradly's ID, right?"

Back at the bar, and with the promise of an extra grand, Lucy had sold the idea of a threesome to both of her marks, men Max now knew to be Bradly Richards and Michael Grumley. Once she got them back to her room, she'd led them to the shower to kick things off. While they'd sudsed up, Wang's techie cloned their IDs and spritzed their clothes with poison oak extract. Today, Bradley and Michael would be far too consumed with scratching their privates and researching STDs to think about coming to work.

Lucy's entrepreneurial move gave Max the choice between a better facial match with Bradley and a better body match with Michael. He'd gone with the face, partly because challenges would climax in a face-to-face confrontation, and partly because Bradley worked in maintenance. "That's right. Best facial match."

"Did you also bring a mylar envelope?"

"I stitched one into my back pocket."

"Good. Use it to shield your ID from the gait monitor, and try to blend in with a crowd."

Max nodded. "Makes sense."

"Best we split up," Wang added. "I'll go first. See you on the other side — or at the rendezvous."

Max turned around and went back to the break room. He stopped just inside the door, presumably to check a vibrating phone but actually to transfer his ID to the pocket lined with mylar film. His blip would suddenly disappear off the radar, but as one of thousands now on the system, he didn't expect that to raise a loud alarm. Technical glitches happened all the time.

He studied his phone's screen until the last group of morning stragglers began exiting the break room, at which point he blended into their midst.

While walking through the gait monitor with others both before and behind him, Max tried to pay the guard no more attention than a piece of furniture. The attitude was not reciprocated.

"Excuse me, sir. Do you have your ID?"

Max ignored him.

"Sir!"

Max looked up. "Me? Of course."

"May I see it." Not a question.

Max set the toolbox down and dutifully produced Bradley's ID.

The guard ran it beneath a scanner and received the requisite chime.

Max waited patiently. Bored even. To accomplish this, he used an old trick Zoya had taught him: picturing an elevator button.

"Have you got electronic equipment in your toolbox, Mr. Richards?"

Max raised his eyebrows. "That's it. Magnetic interference. Happened once before."

"If you could just walk back through without the toolbox."

Max accepted the ID and retreated down the opposite side of the corridor, thinking fast. He had three options, all messy. He could keep walking. He could slip the ID back into the mylar pocket. Or he could roll the dice with the gait monitor.

He decided to go with option three, hoping fortune would favor the bold.

Entering the scanner, he kept his friendly gaze on the guard, but caught a glimpse of Wang standing before a bulletin board further down the corridor. Max was almost at the end when the podium began beeping, and the guard began frowning.

The guard silenced the alarm.

Max put on a perplexed look without altering his pace. He needed to close the gap between them. "Did my equipment screw things up?"

"I don't see how it could."

"Here, let's see if that's it." Max reached the toolbox and unclasped its lid.

"That's not necessary. In any case I've got to call this in."

"I bet this is it," Max said, removing a black box sized and shaped like a cigarette pack but sprouting a pair of short metal antennae. He offered it to the guard, but at the last moment lunged and plunged the taser into his chest.

Chapter 38
The Assassin

Hawaii

AS THE SCENT of smokeless propellant triggered all sorts of physiological reactions, prepping his body for combat, Achilles cursed his carelessness. Once again he was headed into a firefight without a firearm. This time, he didn't even have a knife. When this episode was behind him, he was going to have a serious sit down with his pacifist side. Meanwhile, he was certain that the real owners of the island home would have a gun safe stocked with serious hardware for defense against pirates. Alas, he had neither the location nor the combination or the time.

Jas would surely have a gun too — stashed somewhere, just in case. But the same problems applied.

The questions kept coming as he crept down the hall. Had Jas been the shooter or the target? In either case, the shot indicated that they were not alone on their little island. Had the third party been there all along? Or had they arrived while Achilles was climbing?

His ears detected nothing but ocean waves as the telltale scent grew stronger. A few stealthy strides took him to the arched entryway beyond which lay the kitchen and family room. The heart of the house.

He spotted Jas immediately. She was seated before a writing desk in the far corner. She'd whirled her chair around to face back in his direction, but her eyes were staring at the ceiling, and her arms were dangling straight down. With the kitchen counter blocking his view, he couldn't see below her breast, but that was enough to know that she was either unconscious, or dead.

He ran to her.

Achilles knew that was a mistake, but his impulse center overrode the warning. Apparently his heart hadn't heard that she probably wasn't his wife.

As he reached her side, a familiar voice called out from behind the kitchen bar. "I caught her sending a coded message. The old-fashioned kind, with a one-time pad. You believe that?"

Achilles whirled about to see Foxley crouched in a classic shooter's stance. Shielded to his shoulders by the kitchen island between them, he was holding not one, but two handguns. Achilles recognized the rectangular snout of a Glock in Foxley's right hand, whereas his left held an odd, round-barreled weapon that looked even more sinister but was probably less.

The guns didn't waver while he spoke. "I couldn't read the Russian, but obviously you're the victim of a double-cross. Food for thought while you spend the rest of your life in a traitor's jail."

Achilles brushed the words aside. Obviously, Foxley had mixed good information with bad assumptions. Achilles would address the false conclusions in a minute. For the moment, Jas had his attention.

He spotted the red tail of a tranquilizer dart beneath her left breast. Although difficult to discern against the fabric of her shirt, he now saw that it was rising and falling with her breath.

Achilles used his right hand to verify that Jas's carotid pulse was strong and stable while his left covertly plucked and palmed the dart. "How'd you find me?"

Foxley grinned. Keeping the Glock rock steady, he set the tranquilizer gun down on the counter and pulled a cell phone from his back pocket. Working left-handed, he unlocked it, exposing an open app which he flashed. It showed a map with a pulsating red dot.

"You tracked me? How? An isotope injection?"

"Nothing so sophisticated. Your predictability made it easy. I put a pellet in your shoe."

Achilles frowned. That was a downside to a spartan wardrobe that he hadn't previously considered.

Foxley returned the cell to his back pocket and again palmed the tranq gun in his left hand. "President Silver didn't think you'd sell out. But I told him everyone had his price. Speaking of which, nice island. Might have been tempted myself. But I'm surprised you fell for a honey trap. An amateur mistake. I thought you were better than that."

"You got it all wrong, Foxley."

Foxley's tone turned harsh. "Tell that to Lukin."

"Korovin's successor? What's he got to do with this?" Achilles' processor was whirring away while he spoke. Offensive tactics. Defensive tactics. Situational analysis. Too much here was not what it seemed — to either of them.

"Lukin got gunned down shortly after you went off the grid. I suppose you're going to pretend that was a coincidence?"

Achilles was only half-listening to Foxley. His mind had snagged on something important. "Did she see you coming? Did she grab her amulet?"

"What? Look—"

Foxley's head exploded into a red cloud before Achilles' eyes as a staccato symphony assaulted his ears. The back of Achilles' mind automatically deciphered and mapped every sound. The two guns that shot Foxley. The sickening splats of lead on flesh. The two guns that Foxley fired in shock. The crack of the Glock's bullet impacting the writing desk. The thwack of a dart impaling Jas's chest. The crunch of Foxley's skull against the marble floor.

Achilles dropped as quickly as Foxley did, although driven by reflex rather than gravity. He caught a brief glimpse of the assailants before the kitchen island obscured his view. It wasn't encouraging. Two large crew-cut men wearing Coast Guard uniforms and pointing automatic pistols. They were turning from Foxley's position toward his like the turrets on twin tanks.

Given his distance from the goons, Achilles guessed that he had about three seconds to live — two seconds for them to reacquire line-of-sight, plus a bonus second for them to aim and fire. Two armed men on the move, one unarmed man on the floor. He might buy another second by turning over the writing desk to use as a shield, but then what? If he had a blanket he could throw it over both himself and Jas to make a desperate run for the jungle, assuming they wouldn't fire on their partner. But there was no blanket and he refused to use a woman as a shield. Some things weren't for sale at any price.

Rolling onto his back, Achilles drove the dart he'd pulled from Jas's chest into his own. Then with legs splayed and mouth agape, he forced himself to go limp and close his eyes.

Chapter 39
Leaps of Faith

Seattle, Washington

WITH THE GUARD momentarily stunned by the taser, knocking him out with a quick uppercut was child's play for Max. He even felt a flash of guilt for cheating. But no doubt the victim would welcome a concussion to avoid the alternatives.

As the guard collapsed into his arms, Max looked around the corridor like a kid who'd tripped and fallen. Nobody had seen him! Slipping in with the last of the stragglers had paid off in an unexpected way.

Of course, the next passer-by would sound the alarm — unless he could dispose of the unconscious guard. There was no obvious place to stash him, and Max couldn't prop the limp body back up on the bar stool. The physics of flesh didn't work that way.

The toolbox was also an issue. Lugging it out would slow him down. Stashing it wouldn't work either, no matter how good a job he did. The surveillance tapes would show it there one minute and gone the next. A frantic hunt would ensue. They'd be worried about a bomb.

They'd be worried about a bomb, Max repeated to himself. There was an idea. He re-clasped the toolbox lid and left it beside the body. An unconscious guard. A big black box. Imaginations would run wild. Fear would change the focus — from finding the intruder to saving themselves.

Or so he hoped.

Max ran. Not back to the lobby, but rather toward shipping — with its receiving bays and cargo trucks. He picked up his knees and pumped his arms and made like the building was about to explode.

He'd just turned off the main corridor when his chest began to buzz. *Taser! No, not a taser.* His right hand quickly confirmed something worse.

His amulet was vibrating.

Zoya had hit her panic button.

While the original pair to Zoya's panic button was with the team circling Nuikaohao on a Coast Guard boat, Max had insisted on receiving a duplicate copy for his own peace of mind. As long as it didn't buzz, he knew Zoya was fine. The rest was details — details he was better off not knowing or thinking about. But her physical safety was where he'd drawn the line.

Now she was in danger.

At the worst possible moment.

Max tried to push his fiancée from his mind as he barged through a large set of double doors and into Vulcan Fisher's cavernous shipping bay. Twelve sets of plastic curtains danced along the opposite wall, attempting to keep the cold Seattle climate from blowing through the truck-loading doors. They looked like the pearly gates to him. They signified freedom.

Between him and them, scores of heavy-duty racks rose to the ceiling, partitioned two-pallets wide. They sat atop a shiny concrete floor gridded out with blue lines and numbers and forklift corridors. Someday soon, one of those racks would be packed with fifty autopilot systems destined for Boeing. And if Max did his job, each would weigh about three ounces more than usual.

He went straight for the nearest plastic curtain, attempting to walk casually but purposefully, while studying the shipping activity. Three trucks were loading, and two were unloading, including a UPS truck. Max set Big Brown in his sights, knowing it wouldn't loiter. UPS drivers were paid for speed. With a bit of skullduggery, he could quickly subdue this one and ride out wearing the borrowed brown cap and jacket. Quick and clean.

The alarm ruined that plan.

It sounded just as Max was slipping beneath a curtain into the pouring rain. Not the constant deafening ring of a fire alarm. Rather, three squawks followed by a pause, and then three more squawks.

They'd found the unconscious guard and suspicious black box.

Safety and security protocols would be snapping into place. No doubt the UPS driver would be matched with his license, and his truck would be searched. Soon they'd be reviewing security tape. It would lead them straight to him.

Now Max had no time, and no plan.

He wondered if Wang was already clear.

The sound of a slamming door pulled Max from his momentary stupor. Which truck? Not the one right next to him.

He dropped to the puddled cement and began sliding under the truck, but then thought better of it and rolled back out. He ran forward to the gap between the cab and the trailer and leapt up into the tight confines, sloshing as he went. From there he jumped and got hold of the trailer's roof.

A little voice asked, *What are you doing, Max?*

The sound of a starting engine interrupted his discouraging answer.

Max pulled himself up onto the roof and looked around. The rig next to him was blowing smoke. It wasn't a semi, but rather a forty-foot container truck. No doubt headed for the port.

He'd have to jump for it.

Over a six-foot gap.

Under the pouring rain.

He took a running leap as the target truck started to roll. He didn't try to remain on his feet. He landed and went straight into a forward flop. Two hundred pounds of flesh smacking down onto cold, wet corrugated metal. He skidded to a stop with both arms over the far edge. He'd be bruised in the morning, but still breathing.

Max wriggled back to center and spread himself like a starfish. To avoid sliding off as the truck gathered speed, he clamped down with all ten fingers and sucked himself down to minimize his profile and maximize friction. After a few seconds of stability, Max decided he'd be okay clinging to the corrugated ripples while they were within the compound. Once the driver hit the highway, however, they'd be scraping him off the next vehicle's windshield.

First things first. He still had to make it out the gate.

Max popped up his head for a quick reconnoiter. Positioned centrally atop the container, he was about thirteen feet off the ground and three feet in from each side. Assuming Max stuck up about one foot, and the guard's eyes were about six feet off the ground, how far back would that guard have to stand to see him? Max couldn't work the trigonometry at the moment. Not with Zoya's peril and his second-to-second survival on his mind.

And it really didn't matter.

The truck was rolling and the guard gate approaching. Whatever the calculation, he was committed.

Chapter 40
Boris

Hawaii

PLAYING POSSUM was a first for Achilles. It went against his nature — although it was tougher than it looked. As anyone who has suffered from insomnia will tell you, it's not easy to force yourself to relax. Attempting to do so after witnessing a violent homicide is particularly difficult. Add in the clomping boots of approaching assassins, the smell of gunfire, and a self-inflicted chest wound, and it's a near impossibility.

But Achilles had been training his whole life to control the beat of his heart and bend the focus of his mind. In biathlons, he trained to shoot straight in the midst of extreme cardiovascular challenges — with the world watching and national pride on the line. On climbs, he had no choice but to maintain a relentless focus on his action rather than his position — for hours on end, with his life on the line. To have allowed his heart or mind to wander whether braced behind a gun or a thousand feet up a cliff would have meant losing — and losing was the one thing Achilles refused to do.

That was what gave him an advantage now. Achilles refused to lose.

Lying exposed atop the polished travertine tile, eyes closed and legs akimbo, he didn't think about the bullets that might rupture his flesh. He didn't worry about the pain that might explode his brain. He didn't contemplate the loss that might occur. He pushed all the 'mights' from his mind and disconnected his ears and collapsed all thought down to a single point of focus: his breath. In … … … Out … … … In … … … Out … … …

Immediately following the split-second assessment of his situation and the available alternatives, Achilles mentally played out the possum ploy. He concluded that the critical seconds would be the first few. That's when the assassins would assess the situation, searching for threats.

As they came around the counter with their weapons raised and their adrenaline pumping and their senses peaked, their eyes would fly to the red plumage jutting out of his chest. If the feathered tranquilizer dart wasn't rising and falling at a slow and steady sleeping speed, instinct would act on their trigger fingers.

If that initial sweep raised no alarms, their next point of focus would be the plume protruding from Jas's chest. Her unconscious condition would reinforce the conclusion that he'd been drugged. Then it would all come down to orders. To that extent, Achilles' fate was a coin flip. Dead or alive. What had they been told to do? Capture him alive? Take him out? Bring him in? Improvise?

The kick came at the start of Achilles' third breath cycle, a swift combat boot to his left thigh. Had he thought about it, Achilles would have been pleased. As far as nerve centers went, the legs were bottom of the list, whereas for bone depth and density they were on top. Tactically, the Russian had made a poor choice. He'd gone for convenience, the easy target.

But Achilles didn't think about it. The kick was the equivalent of a thousand-foot drop he chose to ignore. Despite the pressure, despite the pain, despite the horrific circumstance, he focused exclusively on his breath. In … … … Out … … …

Three breath cycles later, Achilles brought his attention back to the world beyond his lungs. Someone was right there, inches away, standing silent as a sentry in the night. Footsteps also registered, distant but approaching. Coming from the end of the hall. Then a single word, spoken in Russian. "Clear."

Inches from his shoulder, Achilles heard the other goon exhale and shift his feet.

"Who do you think he is?" the returning scout asked.

"Doesn't matter. He isn't anymore, and he didn't bring friends."

"Good point. What now?"

"We bring them both in. Use whatever Zoya learned to extract the rest from Achilles."

"Lead pipes and blowtorches…" The scout mused. "So be it. What about Boris?"

So Jas's real name was Zoya, but who was Boris? Achilles wondered. *Could Foxley have been Russian?*

"We lose him on the way to Kauai."

"Chains?"

"Yep. But first we clean up here. Ignaty wants it left spotless."

Achilles answered his own question by placing it in the context of a hit squad. *Boris* was an inside joke. A reference to a shared history with a dead man. A corpse was a *Boris* to these guys.

"I thought Ignaty had a crew coming?"

"They're just repairing the dock and the dish. No wetwork."

"Whatever. How long will these two be out?"

"Depends on the tranq. A few hours, give or take. You want to carry the departed back to the boat, or mop up his brains?"

"I'll man the mop."

"Be my guest. But tend to the target first. I don't want any surprises.

You got the zip ties, right?"

"Yeah. You might want to sack Boris before you drag him to the boat. We got enough mess."

"Roger that."

As the men clunked about, Achilles readied himself for the battles ahead, internal and external. Lying limp while they tied him up would be the mental equivalent of climbing a cliff while looking down.

Various interpretations of "tie this guy up" began spinning around his head. Hands in front, or behind? What about legs? Ankles bound? Hog-tied? He could fight with bound arms, especially in front. If they stopped there, he could wait for the moment to be right.

Bound legs were another story.

If the Russian grabbed his ankles, Achilles would need to attack immediately. Regardless of other circumstances.

It would only be seconds now.

Chapter 41
The Trucker & The Frog

Seattle, Washington

MAX WAS LISTENING to the reverberations of his own heartbeat through cold steel when the truck's engine re-engaged. It lurched back into motion only to rumble to another stop seconds later.

With his ear pressed to the wet metal three feet from the roof's edge, his vision was limited to what he could see on the horizon off the left side of the truck — when raindrops weren't blinding his eyes. As disconcerting as he found it, Max didn't dare risk raising his head. He consoled himself with the thought that it might be tactically advantageous to defer to his other senses, that his performance might be enhanced, like a racehorse with blinders on.

The roof of the guard hut came into view during the next advance. It was just a few arm-lengths away. Max plowed his concentration into his left ear. He heard voices over the engine noise and pouring rain, but couldn't make out what they were saying. Then the engine stopped, and their words became decipherable.

"Nobody's with you?"

"Nope."

A car horn beeped behind them. Two short beeps. A courteous nudge.

"You sure?"

"What ya see is what ya get. You see anybody up there in my bed, let me know. It's been a while, know what I mean?"

"What about in back?"

"No way."

"How can you be sure?"

"This 'ere container's going ta Hamburg. It's packed solid. If he's not Tom Thumb, he ain't in there."

"Why don't we take a look."

"Man, this little fiasco of yours has cost me enough time already. I got a schedule to keep."

Another beep. A longer, single blast.

The rumble started up again, along with Max's breathing. Apparently the guard had conceded with a nod.

Geckos cling to walls and ceilings using the electromagnetic attraction of van der Waals force. Max prayed that force would be with him as he tried to hold tight. His prayers got louder as the truck picked up speed. Of course, if he did get a grip, then he'd probably freeze. Sixty-mile an hour wind and pouring rain would have him hypothermic within minutes.

For the first time in his life, Max began begging for a red light. He spewed out offers related to churchgoing and unborn children, but the only intersection between his truck and the highway still came up green.

As they turned onto the cloverleaf that began a ninety-minute drive up I-5 to the Port of Seattle, Max decided to give up what little purchase he had and make a dash for the sheltered space between the cab and the container. What choice did he have?

With arms and legs spread wide for maximum stability, he began wriggling forward like a lizard with its tail on fire. He only had a few seconds to cover some fifteen feet.

The wind and rain began driving him backwards the moment he released his grip. For every foot he gained, he lost six inches to backward slide.

He didn't make it to the forward edge in time.

The truck hit the straightaway when he was still a couple of yards short, and began accelerating to highway speed. Now desperate, Max risked a glance back over his shoulder, hoping to see a flatbed truck hauling sand. He saw a big fat windshield instead, wipers humming.

As his blonde wig was ripped from his head, the sick side of his brain mused that people went through windshields all the time, albeit from the inside out. Then the acceleration paused while the driver shifted gears, and Max took the biggest risk of his life. He went airborne. He leapt like a frog.

Whether it was the force of fear or a shifting wind or divine intervention, Max would never know, but he covered the gap in that single bound. He crashed into the back of the truck's cab and then dropped into the filthy fissure that separated it from the container.

The driver hit the brakes before Max had squirmed into a sustainable position.

Max scrambled to standing while the truck began kicking up rocks off the side of the road. He remained motionless once it stopped, knowing the driver would be listening. After a lengthy pause, the door opened. Max slipped out the right side, and timed his drop to the ground to coincide with the driver's. The instant his feet hit pavement he began jogging back toward the cloverleaf, a shadow in the pouring rain.

He didn't hesitate or look back as the driver yelled. Better not to give the trucker any more information than he already had, in case he was inclined to make a call. But Max doubted that he would. His benefactor seemed like a mind-his-own-business kind of guy.

As Max jogged along that rain-soaked highway, having pulled his feet from the fire by hook and crook and miracle, his thoughts shifted to a single point of focus. They skipped right over his own miserable condition and the smoldering remains of his operation to the only thing that really mattered. What had happened to Zoya?

Chapter 42
Tetherball

Hawaii

ACHILLES LISTENED intently as the Russians moved around, opening and closing cabinet doors. They were looking for cleaning supplies, he supposed. One set of heavy boots thunked back his way, and a package of zip ties thwacked onto the floor beside his head.

He didn't flinch.

Rough hands grabbed him by the hip and shoulder and rolled him onto his stomach with enough force to snap the tranq needle off in his chest.

He remained limp.

The Russian pinned Achilles' left hand against the small of his back and wrapped a zip-tie around it. Bad sign. He was going to use a tie on each wrist, like links on a chain, and join them with a third wrapped multiple times. An interrogation industry best-practice.

Achilles felt his last chance of a conventional fight slipping away. He was crossing a bridge, in the wrong direction. But he'd be a fool to attack with the other Russian still in the room. If they weren't armed, then maybe. But they were.

The first plastic strap cried victory with its trademark *ziiiip*.

The right hand followed, as did another mocking *ziiiip*.

Achilles started thinking about scissors and knives. Where to get them. How to hold them. Timelines and percentages. While he mapped out a plan of attack, the other Russian finally left, hauling Foxley's bagged corpse back to the boat.

Achilles reckoned he had about sixty seconds before the odds returned to two-against-one. For the moment, however, the odds were even — except that he'd be fighting with his hands tied behind his back. And the Russian had a gun.

The instant his captor walked away around the counter, Achilles opened his eyes.

Fifty seconds left.

Face-down on the travertine didn't make for a great viewing angle, but if he focused properly, the sliding glass door twenty feet ahead sufficed as a makeshift mirror. It was probably coated with UV-reflective hurricane film.

When his captor ducked down behind the counter to clean up Foxley's gray matter, Achilles rolled into action.

Forty seconds.

While his captor kindly obliged him with the cover of a sickly sweeping sound, Achilles wriggled onto his knees and then his feet. Crouching to remain below counter height, he crept to the corner of the bar and peeked around.

He found eyes peering back at him from just a few feet away.

Twenty seconds.

The Russkie proved to be quick of wit. He had a white plastic dustpan in his left hand, and a matching whisk broom in his right. Within a second of his unexpected discovery he'd brought both to bear. The Russian flicked the dustpan's crimson contents straight at Achilles' eyes, and flung the broom right after. Had Achilles not moved, he'd have been blinded in a most unpleasant manner.

But he did move.

He rose and lunged forward onto his left leg, fast enough that the Russian couldn't adjust his aim. While the gray matter and crimson blood-encrusted broom flew toward his waist, Achilles' right knee exploded upward from beneath his assailant's chin, channeling every ounce of energy his body could bring to bear. Had the Russian not been rising himself, had he not already put his mandibular bone in motion, there would have been a mighty crack, as his jaw shattered, and his teeth broke loose, and any soft tissue stuck in their midst was severed forever more.

But the Russian was rising.

Rather than colliding with an object at rest, Achilles' knee served to accelerate the chin's ascent, exponentially and with a twist. By raising the Russkie's skull much faster than the spine to which it was connected, it behaved like a tethered ball. This abrupt change of trajectory transferred most of the kinetic energy directly onto the fulcrum, which in this case was the poor bastard's third cervical disk.

Achilles heard a horrific crunch and watched the shocked eyes grow wide. Then his tormentor toppled backward onto the marble floor, where the crack of his skull resonated like a delayed echo of Foxley's.

As Achilles reached for the kitchen knife he'd use to free his hands, the body began to tremble and quiver beneath its bugged-out eyes.

Ten seconds.

But not really.

While Achilles was still working the knife and absorbed in the assessment of what his knee strike had done, an approaching voice called from the hall.

"You know, I never did a movie star. What do you say we have some fun? Take some pictures? We could even—"

As the speaker came into view, Achilles hopped up onto the counter, and the race was on. Foxley's Glock was right there where he'd dropped it, beside the sink that had caught the tranquilizer gun.

The Russian rapist's Gyurza was in a holster on his hip.

In a pure physics equation, the Russian would win. No contest at all. A practiced move. A quick draw. Grab, point, pull. The Gyurza doesn't even have a safety.

But it wasn't a pure physics equation.

This scenario packed a powerful surprise for the Russian. Fifty seconds earlier, he'd been joking with a dead man about Boris. Then he'd rounded a corner with sex on his mind and found his friend writhing and gasping and glaring away like a big landed fish.

The stunning surprise bought Achilles a couple of crucial seconds. Only two, but enough for him to grab the Glock's grip and begin pulling. Like a short kid shooting pool with the cue behind his back, Achilles was guesstimating. But only with the first round. As it drilled the dishwasher door, he recalibrated and put the second into his opponent's hip, spinning him down and around like a crashing helicopter. The third hit center mass. Not necessarily the heart itself, but close enough as makes no difference.

Chapter 43
What-ifs

Seattle, Washington

THE RENDEZVOUS location Wang had selected in case the shit hit the fan was the food court at the Tacoma Mall. Lots of traffic, plenty of exits, and the apathetic attitudes of minimum-wage workers in temporary jobs. A person could sit there from open until close and be seen by ten thousand eyes but never be noticed — if he kept to himself and didn't light anything on fire.

Wang wasn't there.

He should have been on his third cup of tea by the time Max dragged his wet ass up to the table. Surely Wang had arrived hours before. He had a car. Max had the whole container truck adventure followed by the wait for an Uber — once he'd made it off the highway and gotten presentable with the aid of a comb and a cap and the gas station restroom's entire stock of paper towels.

What now?

He couldn't do anything but wait. He didn't have a phone number for Wang, and he didn't know where he lived. All he had was a bank account number and an email address. Both, no doubt, untraceable.

With the immediate danger behind him and his adrenaline spent, Max went for a Venti coffee. He sipped it for ninety minutes with no sign of his partner, then bought a pretzel to calm his stomach.

He imagined Wang getting thumb-screwed at that very moment, locked away in a dark corner of Vulcan Fisher with their head of security. No doubt their security chief was former military. Max pictured a sergeant major with more service stripes on his sleeve than hairs on his head. A man who knew the price of winning a war, and the value of avoiding bad publicity. A man who wouldn't hesitate to go medieval on a foreign national caught spying, before dumping his corpse in Puget Sound.

Max's own predicament didn't feel much better. He might have evaded capture, but he hadn't avoided torture. He was tortured by worry for Zoya. Why had she pressed the panic button? Had that been an accidental slip of the wrist, or had the worst happened? Not knowing was killing him.

Max couldn't call Ignaty without his computer's encrypted VOIP programs. Even if he could, he'd be a fool to do so before learning what happened to Wang. Ignaty would just give him the runaround until he got the results of today's mission. The last time they'd talked, Ignaty had stressed that President Korovin was eagerly awaiting today's update on his pet project. Bottom line: Max couldn't call Ignaty to learn about Zoya before he had a plan to complete his mission.

So he did the only thing he could do. He watched the mindless mall rats wander their maze, and waited for Wang to show.

For the first time since that fateful day that he and Zoya had been diverted from their Sochi vacation, Max had the opportunity to ruminate on the big picture. *Operation Sunset* still blew his mind. The sheer impact of it. The more he thought about it, the less comfortable he became with the historical role Korovin had thrust on him. As a spy, his job was to bring tactical advantages to his motherland. Despite the stigma, espionage was meaningful, time-honored work. Dangerous, but universal.

Operation Sunset, by contrast, wasn't directly benefitting Russia. It was waging war. An underhanded, unprovoked, undeclared war. A war that would claim many thousands of civilian lives. *Sunset* crossed a line.

Max wasn't sure what he was going to do about that.

Today, it seemed he wasn't sure about anything.

With nothing else to do, he kept waiting.

He waited while the terrifying *What-ifs?* grew bigger, and the tempting *What-nexts?* grew bolder. He waited while acid ate away his stomach lining and his bowels turned to water. Finally, when he could wait no more, he went to the restroom, and found Wang.

Chapter 44
The Getaway

Hawaii

ACHILLES USED the kitchen knife to free his hands, then took a moment to assess his situation while rubbing his wrists. Yes, he was better off than the guys at his feet, but not by a lot. Korovin literally had an army available. The bodies before him were just the tip of a mighty spear.

And Korovin wasn't even Achilles' chief concern.

According to the late Agent Foxley, President Silver believed that Achilles had sold out, taken a payoff from the Russian president in exchange for vital information. Unfortunately, that was understandable, given what Achilles now knew.

Achilles had disappeared shortly after learning Silver's plan. He'd vanished. Gone black. Then Lukin had been assassinated. The next data point Silver had was of Achilles living it up on a private island with a beautiful Russian movie star.

Now Foxley would fail to report in. He'd be presumed dead, and Achilles would take the blame.

Minutes from now, the presidents of two powerful nations would each realize they had a personal problem. A problem best quashed by killing Achilles. God only knew the covert resources they'd call on to hunt him down.

He had to get moving.

Granger had once told him, "When you're on the run, confound and confuse." That sounded like a good game plan.

Achilles began by tossing the dead men's weapons, papers, and electronics into a backpack. He'd inspect them at a later time in another place. Meanwhile he noted that each corpse had the expected phone, and one also wore an amulet similar to Zoya's. The sight of it confirmed Achilles' assumption and gave him an idea.

He unclasped the amulet from around Zoya's neck, and removed its back using an eyeglass screwdriver found in a kitchen drawer. Inside was a tiny circuit board and a relatively large battery. Setting that assembly aside, he removed his shoes and searched the soles. Foxley's GPS pellet wasn't in the heel, as expected, but rather under the edge of the left arch, where less pressure would be applied. About the size of a BB, it had been so expertly installed that it was tough to find even when he knew what he was looking for.

Achilles seated the pellet in Zoya's amulet where the battery had been, and returned it to her neck. He wasn't sure what this insurance policy would ultimately accomplish, but if nothing else, it fit the *confound-and-confuse* pattern.

He used surplus zip ties to bind Zoya's arms and ankles. She'd be going with him.

Since they'd be using the Coast Guard boat, Achilles stripped the unbloodied Russian, and changed into his stolen uniform.

Time for more confounding.

He hoisted the disrobed Russian onto his shoulder and headed for the jungle. Knowing that half the world's covert intelligence assets were about to come after him was nothing if not motivating.

Even with the extra two hundred pounds, Achilles reached the concealed crevasse in just three minutes. Ten minutes after that he had both Russkies stashed where they'd never be found.

Zoya felt weightless after the brutes. He laid her down on the aft deck next to Foxley and a pile of anchor chain. The vessel was the one he'd seen from atop Nuikaohao. Its bulbous orange hull ringed a modest cabin, but boasted big engines, lots of lights, and a powerful radio. The Russians had undoubtedly stripped the boat of tracking devices after stealing it, but Achilles was going to treat it like a hot potato nonetheless.

A quick cleanup of the house was all that remained. Just enough to add confusion. The bullet holes were inconclusive, but the blood told a definitive story. He'd pondered the problem of expunging it while hauling the corpses to their final resting place. He didn't have time for anything fancy, and burning the house seemed too extreme. Deciding that delaying any forensic findings would be good enough, he doused the dirty zones with the kitchen faucet sprayer, and sopped everything up with bath towels. Then he emptied a gallon of bleach on top of what remained and left it to dry. Three minutes total.

Besides his clothes, Achilles had only stuffed two items into the backpack he was bringing to the boat along with the big bag of blood-soaked towels. The first was a bottle of ammonia. The second was his wedding picture, still in its silver frame.

He paused near the edge of the dock and pulled out the captured cell phones. Although he'd like to mine them for data, he didn't have the pass codes and he couldn't risk taking them with him. Not with GPS. Besides, anything interesting in them should also be in Zoya's head.

After calculating the right distance from the waves, he dragged a shallow ditch with his heel and dropped the phones into the sand. When the tide came in, a few hours from now, it would simultaneously short out the phones and bury them, confusing the timeline and adding to the mystery. This simple little move might even postpone Korovin's pursuit.

Achilles checked his watch. Twenty-four minutes from extinguishing the Russians to igniting the outboard motors. Thirty more minutes to Kauai. Could Korovin react in under an hour? Would he have men waiting at the marinas? Achilles had no idea. Regardless, once he hit Kauai, another race would begin.

Meanwhile, he'd leverage the Coast Guard boat's autopilot function. It was time he had a talk with his wife.

Chapter 45
Daggers & Buttons

The Kremlin

IGNATY PLOWED past the guards and into Korovin's office without a sideways glance. One had to flaunt their power on occasion to keep it fresh in people's minds. Plus Kremlin staffers tended to get a bit full of themselves. Ignaty liked to remind them that working close to the sun doesn't make you a star.

Korovin looked up from a paper report. His paranoia regarding electronic communications of all sorts translated into lots of reading — and a personal micro shredder the size of a refrigerator. The president made use of it before meeting Ignaty's eye.

Once the shredding sound abated, Ignaty said, "There's good news and bad from Hawaii. Bad news is we've had a glitch. Zoya hit her panic button. The crew responded as planned, but never reported back. Once they went black, I scrambled a second crew from California. They just reported that the island is deserted. Everybody has disappeared: Achilles, Zoya, and both of my men."

"Didn't you have a tracker on Zoya?"

"It went black."

"Satellites?"

"We didn't use them. In retrospect, that was shortsighted. I didn't think we'd need it for an op on an island that's smaller than Gorky Park, and I didn't want to draw attention. The Americans monitor our satellite movements."

"What's the assumption?"

"Achilles figured it out and escaped."

"Does the White House know?"

Ignaty was pleased to be able to answer that question, if only partially. Miss Muffet had called him back just three hours after he'd hung up on her, asking for forgiveness — and a bonus. She had spine, that one, and he admired her for it. He'd agreed to include an extra $10,000 in the next payment.

"That's not clear, Mr. President. Our mole only transmits once a day at best, so we won't know today's thinking until tomorrow at the earliest. The last we heard, our plan had worked. The combination of

Achilles having gone black and Lukin being killed convinced the Oval Office that he had sold out."

Korovin rose and began to pace. "Last I heard, Achilles fell for the ruse. How'd he figure it out? How'd he escape? You think he had help?"

Ignaty took a chair, hoping to calm his boss down. "He couldn't have summoned help. Besides Zoya's panic button and the two-way pager she used to send and receive coded messages, there was no communication equipment on the island. That was a big point of contention with Max, who wanted to be able to call or at least write, but I convinced him that Achilles was bound to conduct a thorough search in a moment of doubt. We eventually agreed that any communication or surveillance equipment would compromise the mission and Zoya's safety."

Korovin stopped pacing and stared out his window for a good twenty seconds. "So he set a trap. He set off Zoya's panic button, and ambushed the response team. You obviously underestimated this guy. How are you going to fix it?"

Ignaty put on a confident grin. "Like wolves hunting wildebeest. We're going to isolate him, and then spook him into an ambush of our own."

"I want details."

Ignaty told him.

Korovin accepted the plan with a stone face. "Have the island returned to its original state. I don't want any physical evidence to support Achilles' story, if he gets a chance to tell it."

"Already done."

Apparently satisfied, Korovin changed gears. "What about *Sunset?*"

Ignaty didn't sugarcoat it. "Max seems to be struggling with Vulcan Fisher's security."

"We always knew that would be the tough nut. You assured me he'd find a way to crack it."

"He will."

"Zoya's disappearance can't be helping his focus. How's he reacting?"

"He doesn't know."

"I thought he had a replica of the panic button?"

"We haven't spoken since it went off."

Korovin's face contracted. "That's surprising. I'd have thought he'd call immediately. What are you going to tell him when he does?"

"I'll tell him it was a false alarm. A slip of the wrist. I'll tell him how my guys went running and nearly blew the mission to protect her, but found her unharmed and apologetic."

"Will he buy it?"

"I'm sure he'll have his doubts, but there's nothing he can do with them."

Korovin grabbed a Japanese kaiken from his display cabinet and began toying with the blade. "Will he remain focused on the job?"

Ignaty took the president's fidgeting as a good sign. It signaled the shift to tactical thinking that accompanied his acceptance of the facts at hand. "I'll keep the pressure on. Dangle some carrot, wave some stick."

"What if she turns up dead? Or doesn't turn up at all?"

"We just need to make sure he completes *Sunset* before that happens."

"He'll be … very angry."

"She may well be alive. No sense upsetting him unnecessarily. He's a pro, he'll understand that. May I move on to the good news?"

Korovin smiled with the right half of his mouth, then gestured with the dagger. *Proceed.*

"Zoya got a transmission off before she hit the panic button."

"Mission accomplished? She got the assassination plan?"

"Not entirely, but I think she learned enough. Tell me, Mr. President, have you been sneaking out at night?"

Chapter 46
Trial & Error

Seattle, Washington

WANG HAD CONSIDERED walking away from his "extracurricular activity" a dozen times in the past few hours. The Brit — or Israeli, or East European, or whoever Max really was — had just upped the risk exponentially. Vulcan Fisher had already been a fortress. Now the drawbridge was raised and the archers were on the walls.

But Wang didn't walk away.

He needed the money.

As Max turned from the urinal, Wang studied his face. Expressions were best read up close during unguarded moments. Max was far from unguarded, but as moments went, this was the least guarded he was likely to get. A certain amount of relaxation was required to get things flowing.

"Where have you been?" Max asked, using the mixed tone of a parent speaking to a found child.

"That's my question," Wang replied. "Last I saw, you'd been flagged by the guard. Then the alarm went off. Then you showed up three hours late looking like someone who'd put up a fight, and lost."

"You think I cut a deal?"

"Fear the wolf in front, and the tiger behind."

"Is that some ancient way of saying you think they caught me and put the screws on?"

"That was one of several working hypotheses. After watching you drink coffee for an hour, I became convinced that you were alone — as far as you knew. After two hours, I determined that you weren't being watched."

"So why are we talking in here?"

"Since this doesn't seem to be my lucky day, I decided to proceed with extra caution."

Max zipped up. "Satisfied? Can we flush and move on? Debrief somewhere more private? Somewhere I can get a drink and a steak?" Max gestured with his arm, inviting Wang to go first.

Wang didn't move.

Max kept his arm extended in gesture. "Please."

Wang shook his head in reluctant consent. "Buy yourself some fresh clothes, then meet me at BJ's Brewhouse." With that, Wang turned and walked away.

By moonlighting for Max, Wang had climbed way out on a limb. He couldn't afford to inject impatience or incompetence or hubris into the delicate balancing act. One rash move might break the branch. There was no sense trying to explain his precarious position to Max either. Foreigners couldn't relate to his predicament.

The Government of China had 1.4 billion people at its disposal. Against those odds, it was virtually impossible for anyone to become indispensable. Wang's boss would replace him without a second thought at the first whiff of scandal. Westerners weren't nearly so vulnerable.

As his wife Qi constantly and relentlessly reminded him, the only security Wang could ever hope to achieve was the kind that came with a big bank balance. With that dream in mind, he decided to stick with it. For now.

When Max slid into the booth across from him wearing a new black Abercrombie hoodie, Wang had a pitcher of pale ale and a plate of loaded nachos waiting.

Max ignored the food and drink. He skipped the history discussion as well, and went straight to future actions. "How are we going to get around the gait monitors?"

Wang snorted. He'd enjoyed a beer while waiting, and now couldn't help it. "You have an invisibility cloak?"

Max remained rigid. "What I have is a call to make. My boss expects a detailed progress report tonight. If that report looks anything like the current draft, you can kiss your million-dollar payday goodbye."

"Million-five."

"The gait monitors. Can we fool them? Dodge them? Hack them?"

Wang fought back his building frustration. "If I knew how to do that, don't you think I would have suggested it earlier? I've given you everything but the east wind."

"You're always spouting proverbs."

"I'm eternally hopeful."

"Well I have one for you: *when men work with one mind, mountains can be moved.* Let's think about the monitors."

"The monitors aren't commercial yet, so we haven't been able to study them. As for dodging, you saw the arrangement. The only way around is to enter through the exit lane. That might be possible in conjunction with a distraction, but it would be risky, and it would only work once."

"What about the roof? Instead of going around could we go over?"

Wang grabbed a nacho for himself before responding. "The roof hatches are monitored and alarmed."

"How about hacking?"

"They're a top-shelf U.S. defense contractor. I've got a guy who can penetrate just about any organization on the planet, but these guys are using custom systems on top of the best federal standards. With billions on the line, they're smart enough to hire top talent and buy or invent cutting-edge equipment."

"There must be a weak link."

"*It takes more than one cold night for a river to freeze deep.*"

"What?"

"I'm sure there is a weak link, but finding it will take time. Lots of trial and error. You've already used up our allocation of error."

Wang could see that his last jab wounded Max. He could see him reliving the ordeal in his mind. Then Max's pained expression brightened as if a wind had parted clouds. His chin lifted and his misty eyes began to twinkle with hope.

"Were you shooting straight about your guy? Can he really hack any organization on the planet?"

Chapter 47
Ties that Bind

Hawaii

ACHILLES DOUSED a rag with ammonia and cupped it under Zoya's nose. Her eyes flew open as she gasped and whipped her head to the side. She coughed twice in rapid succession, and then a third time. "What happened?"

Before Achilles could answer, she discovered that her ankles and wrists were bound. "What's going on?" Her question sounded sweet and sincere, but she hadn't yet gotten her game face on. Her eyes indicated that she knew.

"A colleague of mine shot you with a tranquilizer dart. Then your friends showed up and killed him. Then I showed up and killed them." He nodded, but kept his gaze on her eyes. "That about sums it up."

She didn't say anything. Twice she started to speak, but both times she stopped. Achilles could empathize. What could she say? Obviously, her jig was up, and her life was in the hands of a man who'd just confessed to killing two of her colleagues. Lies might provoke him, but so might the truth.

Finally she twisted and rocked her way onto her knees so that she could see over the side of the speedboat. "Where are we?"

"Off the western coast of Kauai. You're looking at a wilderness preserve."

"What are we doing here?"

"That's my question, *Zoya*. I suggest you think carefully about how you answer it."

His captive cringed at the use of her real name.

Achilles had been busy since commandeering the stolen Coast Guard vessel. He began the rest of his life by circling Nuikaohao in search of Foxley's boat. All part of his confound and confuse strategy. He discovered a battleship-gray speedboat tied up on the western edge of the island in a spot where the jungle extended to the water's edge. Achilles considered switching to the more anonymous craft, but decided to stick with the Coast Guard vessel so that he could search it thoroughly during the ride. There was no time for a search at that moment. Remaining on the island was like sitting in an acid bath. Every second was doing damage.

He transferred Foxley back to his own boat, sans anchor chain. Then he found Oahu on the navigation system some seventy miles to the southeast, engaged the autopilot, and dove off the back while Foxley sped away. Confuse and confound.

Back aboard the Coast Guard vessel, Achilles programmed its autopilot and then went to work. While the twin Mercury outboards rocketed him and the spy named Zoya toward Kauai, he searched the boat. There wasn't much to it, so he found the Russian team's Murphy bag even before Nuikaohao had dropped out of sight.

The stash of emergency essentials included about a hundred-thousand dollars in cash, a comprehensive disguise kit, and four Florida drivers' licenses. Two with pictures of the dead Russian goons. One with Zoya's image. And the fourth with his own photograph. All ironically issued with the last name Murphy, and hailing from the same address on Poinsettia Road.

Zoya spoke at last. "You seem to know who I am, but do you really know who I am?"

Actually, he did. He'd used Foxley's phone — unlocked with his thumbprint — to take Zoya's picture. Then he'd run a search using her image and first name typed in Cyrillic. Rather than a few low-probability potential matches, he'd gotten thousands of hits from Russian websites. Zoya, the woman who'd slipped beneath his radar and his sheets, actually was an actress. A celebrated movie star no less. She'd been nominated by the Russian Motion Picture Academy for a Best Supporting Actress award. The find made Achilles feel slightly less incompetent about falling for her act.

"I do know. And I agree with your fans. You should have won the Golden Eagle."

Zoya's face reddened. Some actors could force a fake blush, but none could prevent a real one. "When did you figure it out?"

"What are we doing here?"

"I'm an actress."

"What are we doing here?"

Her features hardened. "My president asked me to help prevent his assassination."

"By pretending to be my wife?"

"Would you have preferred thumb screws? I was doing you a favor."

She had him there. "Why didn't Korovin go with thumb screws?"

Achilles saw Zoya flinch at the mention of Korovin's name. He wondered whether that was because it made the situation real, or because of the way Korovin made her feel.

"They said plans for future covert actions weren't verifiable information — and that you'd know as much. Therefore you'd never reveal the true plan to kill him. He said a con was the only surefire way to know."

As the cold logic of Korovin's plan sunk in, Achilles found himself acutely aware of his surroundings. The rocking of the boat on the waves, and the warm, fragrant maritime breeze. This was an odd place for an interrogation. He decided to use it to his advantage.

He plunked down onto the deck across from Zoya, mirroring her pose minus the zip ties. Locking his eyes on hers, he let his mind race ahead. He was about to get crushed between two battling giants. Korovin from the east, and Silver from the west. The Russian president was correct in coming after him. The American president was mistaken. But how could Achilles convince Silver of his innocence?

Secrecy was the rub.

Given Achilles' mission, it was imperative that nobody ever learn that he and Silver had a relationship. Nobody. Ever. Achilles couldn't call or visit or write. He couldn't pass a note or wait in a favored bar. To reach Silver, one had to circumvent gatekeepers and security protocols and official records. Plus the Secret Service.

He was screwed.

It hit him out of the blue. There was one thing he could do without either violating Silver's trust or jeopardizing national security. He could reach out through the one living intermediary who already knew the plan.

And there was the second rub.

It was his only move. Korovin would come to the same conclusion.

The race was on.

His strategy set, Achilles turned to tactics, and his captive's role. "I appreciate the situation Korovin put you in. Do you understand your new situation?"

Zoya held up her bound wrists and feet in a modified yoga pose. An accurate and eloquent summary of her predicament.

"If you come with me to California to visit an old friend, and if you tell her everything you told me as convincingly as you just did, there's a chance you'll return to the movies. But if you do anything other than help me make that happen, I'll—"

"You don't need to say it," Zoya interjected. "I understand. Let's go."

Chapter 48
Technicalities

Seattle, Washington

MAX FELT LIKE a man who had just been told his cancer was in remission. He was at once thrilled and afraid. Thrilled to be breathing deep breaths of hope again, and afraid that with Wang's next words his euphoria would slip away.

He wanted to enjoy the feeling for a few minutes, but there was no time for that. He had to press on. He couldn't relax until he knew Zoya was safe. Setting down his beer, he asked Wang the big question. "Can your guy hack into shipping companies?"

"Shipping companies . . . Shipping companies. Huh." Wang spun his umbrella on the restaurant's floor. "You're thinking of doing the install en route. Clever. How'd you come up with that?"

Max reached out and stopped the umbrella. "I rode out of Vulcan Fisher on top of a truck. Can you do it? Can your guy hack a shipper?"

Wang ignored the aggression and grabbed a nacho. "Shipping companies are easy."

"Really?"

"Small ones are unsophisticated, low-budget operations. Big ones have nodes in every strip mall, literally thousands of access points. And the information, while occasionally sensitive, is hardly secret."

Max felt a surge of hot blood bringing warmth to weary muscles. He'd finally caught a break.

Wang inched closer, catching Max's enthusiasm. "Which shipper will they be using?"

Max pictured the assortment of trucks he'd seen a few hours before. "I don't know. They don't appear to be exclusive to anyone."

"Who's the shipment going to?"

Max didn't want to tell Wang that, lest he guess the goal of the operation. "It's a ground shipment."

"Long-haul, or short?"

"What's it matter?"

"Companies specialize. Helps narrow down the list."

"Short-haul."

"How short?"

"What's it matter?"

"Just thinking ahead. If it's same-day pickup and delivery, that doesn't leave us a lot of time to work with."

Max saw the point. He was coming to appreciate Wang and his area of expertise more and more.

As a special operative, Max had subconsciously looked down on Wang the way surgeons did on general practitioners. Industrial spies were good guys, nothing wrong with them, but they didn't control life and death with a scalpel. "Let's cross that bridge when we come to it. First thing we have to do is figure out which company they'll be using."

"And how do you plan to do that? We can't hack them until we know who they are, and we can't hack Vulcan Fisher to find out. Feels like a chicken-and-egg scenario."

Good question. "The shipment we need isn't a one-off. It's part of a regular order. If I get you a list of the shippers VF uses, can your guy get me a list of all the shipments each made for Vulcan Fisher during the past year?"

Wang popped the last of the nachos into his mouth while he pondered that one. Max could see that he was growing ever more excited. "That would take a lot of work, not to mention a lot of skill. Where will you get the list of shippers?"

Max had no idea, but figured it had to be easier than getting around the gait monitor. "Let me worry about that. Just answer the question. Can you do it?"

"Can I get you boys some more nachos? Or maybe some sliders?" Their waitress spoke with a Southern accent that Max would have found charming under other conditions. He brushed her away without looking up.

Wang spent another second savoring Max's suffering while he pretended to ponder. The obvious ploy made Max want to slap him. "Technically, it's well within our capabilities."

"Why do you say *technically*?"

"Well, because *financially* this is beyond the scope of our agreement. Well beyond."

So that was the source of his partner's jubilation. Wang had him by the short hairs. Ignaty wasn't going to like that. "How much?"

"Another $1.5 million."

PART 3: SURPRISES

Chapter 49
Bad News

San Francisco, California

DESPITE CHAIRING the committee that oversaw CIA operations, Senator Colleen Collins was not a technophile. She had aides to manage the requisite social media postings, and she navigated her calendar with a gold Cross pencil rather than her index finger and thumbs. But there was one modern feature of her custom Blackberry phone that Collins leveraged with relish — the ability to assign custom ringtones.

This evening it wasn't Norah Jones' soothing voice that beckoned from the tub's ledge, indicating a family call. Rather, the *William Tell Overture* disturbed her habitual soak, and sent her heart galloping. She pulled herself out of the steamy water, grabbed her bathrobe, and hit the speaker button. "Good evening, Mr. President."

"Good evening, Senator. Your message said it was urgent?"

"My message?" Collins' mind raced even as she spoke. At seventy-two, fears of mental deterioration were never far from her mind, but a staff error seemed far more likely. "I'm sorry, Mr. President, I fear there's been a miscommunication."

"No worries. As it happens, I wanted to speak with you anyway. Sylvester is now missing."

Collins paused with just one slipper on and her bathrobe unbelted. Foxley had gone after Achilles, and now he was missing too. "Oh, no."

"Yes. I'm afraid this reinforces the obvious initial conclusion. First Ibex goes quiet, his assignment incomplete. Then Lukin is assassinated, indicating a related information leak. Then Sylvester tracks Ibex to a private paradise only to disappear without a trace. As sad as it makes me to say it, we have to go with the evidence and conclude that Ibex sold out."

Collins cinched her bathrobe belt with a bit too much verve. "Sir, while I respect the logic, I don't believe that for a moment. Ibex's patriotism is beyond question. You know that from personal experience."

"I do, Colleen. And your assessment of his past actions mirrors my own. But people change. They reappraise. Reconsider." Silver was speaking with his stumping voice, a sonorous blend of sympathy and certainty that played to both the heart and mind. "Stress changes people, and Lord knows he's had plenty of that. Plus we screwed him financially after that last incident. And let's not forget that he walked away from the CIA."

Collins would have walked away too, if staying meant working for Wylie Rider. But of course she couldn't say as much to the man who'd put him there. Instead she said, "His reasons for leaving were understandable."

"Perhaps. But it was a radical move, an abandonment of government service. I fear we've just seen the pattern repeat. He wouldn't be the first man coaxed off course by a beautiful woman."

Collins couldn't believe she was having this conversation — for so many reasons. Even after thirty-six years of life behind the big curtain as a member of the United States Congress, she found it hard to fathom that she was discussing international espionage and assassination with the president of the United States — much less in a fuzzy white robe and slippers. As she walked into her bedroom, aiming for her writing desk, Colleen found herself in a scene even more surreal.

"Are you still there?" Silver asked.

She was there. She was also staring into the business end of a large semi-automatic handgun. Ironically, not one of the weapons she'd introduced legislation to ban. Three feet beyond it, a leather-gloved hand held a fat index finger to a thin pair of lips. After allowing a second for the scene to register, the hand dipped down to a pocket. It pulled out a sign which it held like a limo driver at the airport. The top line of text stated the gunman's demand. It said: READ THIS ALOUD.

Collins looked at the black muzzle before her, then back at the text. "Let me call you back, Mr. President. Ibex just walked in the door."

Chapter 50
The Call

San Francisco, California

ACHILLES FELT Zoya begin to tremble beside him as their cab neared Senator Collins' San Francisco home. Zoya had kept it together for the first 2,400 miles, but like most marathons, the last stretch was proving to be the toughest.

Achilles found it ironic that the Russians' escape pack had made it possible for him to whisk Zoya back to the continental U.S. undetected. The airline had readily accepted their cash in exchange for first-class tickets once presented with driver's licenses for Frank and Barbara Murphy. And of course once he had Zoya on the plane, things got easier. There wasn't anywhere she could go, or anyone she could talk to.

Once the other passengers became absorbed in their books and movies, and the flight attendants were busy prepping in the galley, he hit her with the question he'd been dying to ask. "How did I end up on Hawaii?"

Zoya looked over with miserable eyes, and spoke without inflection. "They ambushed you at the top of a climb. Drugged you and flew you out on a medical helicopter."

Achilles nodded. "Lover's Leap."

"What?"

"That was where they did it."

"That doesn't sound right. It was a place with a funny name. A different funny name. Some fruit."

"Strawberry?" Achilles suggested, naming the two-horse town south of Lake Tahoe that housed Lover's Leap.

"Yes, Strawberry. The drugs kept your memory of the capture from forming and caused your headache."

He bought that.

While they were on a roll, Achilles pulled the wedding photo out of his bag. "What about this?"

"Staged on the beach near Sochi. That's me with a model standing in for you. They added your face using Photoshop."

Achilles shook his head. "But the picture feels familiar."

"They used the face from a press photo taken when you made the

Olympic team. That's why you look so happy — and why it has a familiar feel."

Zoya returned her gaze to the window.

Her introspective mood suited Achilles just fine. He too had options to weigh and scenarios to game out in his mind.

He tossed her a grenade during dinner. It slipped out when he was reflecting on his relationship with Katya. "What does Max think of your latest role?"

She looked surprised at the mention of her boyfriend's name. Then resigned. Then sad. "The tabloid press. We love them and we hate them."

"You keep telling the reporters it's not serious, but they keep taking pictures of you with him. Makes me wonder if you're staying single just to keep the headlines coming."

"It's a rough business."

"You still haven't answered my question."

She turned to meet his eyes full-on for the first time since the boat.

Achilles saw a world of misery looking back at him. Was it real or part of an act? That was the problem. He had no way to know. He wouldn't be played again. Fool-me-once and all that.

"He's not happy with it," she said, sounding sincere.

"But he didn't stop it."

"How could he have?"

"He probably couldn't have. But did he try?"

Zoya didn't answer, which was answer enough.

Achilles didn't press. He had his own relationship issues to sort out.

But that sorting would come later. First he had to make it through San Francisco arrivals. If the Russians were quick and resourceful enough, they would have men waiting at the airport. Big, hard men who took no chances and showed no mercy.

Without letting go of Zoya's hand, Achilles hit a gift shop across from their gate. He paid cash for black 49ers hooded sweat suits, and then pulled Zoya into a family restroom. After a quick change of clothes, Achilles used the Russian's disguise kits against them. Satisfied with what he didn't see while looking at Zoya and in the mirror, he led his captive out through another terminal's baggage claim and straight into a waiting cab.

As the cab left SFO behind, heading north for the city, he turned toward Zoya and spoke in Russian. "Time to remove your stage makeup. For this next scene, you'll be playing yourself."

"Who are we visiting, exactly?"

Achilles peeled the slim mustache from his face before answering. "She's a senator — the tough, wise kind. Not a pretty-boy blowhard. Under normal circumstances you'd like her. During her last election she set a record for the most popular votes in senate history."

"What will she do with me?"

Achilles told it to her straight. "That will depend on the larger context as she sees it. And how much she likes you. And my recommendation."

"Is there any chance she'll let me go?" Zoya's voice cracked as she spoke, and Achilles caught the cabbie checking on them in the mirror.

"There is. Your celebrity will help to diminish her fears that if released you'll become a threat. But her first inclination as a guardian of national security will be to make you vanish without a trace and then let the professionals take their time pumping you for information in a dark basement."

"I don't have any information."

"You have plenty. If you actually tell her everything, she may decide there's nothing more to gain. But if she senses you withholding, then she'll go with that first inclination."

Zoya hugged her own chest a little tighter. "You say her, but it's really you. The two of you. Isn't it?"

She was right. Achilles had a tough call to make.

Chapter 51
Pacific Heights

San Francisco, California

ACHILLES DIDN'T ANSWER Zoya's question about his inclinations. The truth was, he was conflicted about her. On the one hand, she'd only been doing the job her president had asked of her. On the other, she'd been cruelly manipulating him as a prelude to execution. He decided to see how she played it with Collins.

The cab pulled to the curb in Pacific Heights. "Fifty-two dollars."

The driver didn't seem to notice the transformation his passengers had undergone. Like the people beside you on a crowded bus or plane, they'd been accommodated, but ignored. If questioned, he might recall that he'd been asked to drive by a hardware store en route, but that too would quickly fade. Achilles handed over three twenties from the Russian's stash, and pulled Zoya behind him into the misty night. "Keep the change."

Achilles had given the driver an address a block from the senator's, on the assumption that her home was under enemy surveillance. For appearance sake, he began walking up the drive of the house before them with his left arm locked through Zoya's right. Only once the cab had turned the corner did he reverse their course.

Using the maps app on Foxley's phone — which now had a new SIM card, making it untraceable — Achilles found the Tudor style home that was directly below Collins' on the steep hillside. All the houses in the prestigious neighborhood faced north, out toward Angel Island and the Golden Gate Bridge. The higher homes on each block, like Collins', had their main entrance on the back of the house, whereas the ones down below had entrances at the front.

He paused once the angle was right to study Collins' house. The hill was so steep that her ground floor was on the same plane as the roof of the home below. From what Achilles could see, only the third floor had lights on.

He glanced over at Zoya. Once they'd started moving, she'd stopped trembling and reengaged. Just like a soldier.

Zoya caught him looking at her. "Which one is hers?"

"The white one up above with the Beaux Arts façade."

She studied it with a faraway look in her eye. "What's the plan?"

Achilles waited for a woman being towed by a Dalmatian to pass before answering. "You have no money, no identification, and no cell phone. I'm stronger, faster, and more familiar with the neighborhood."

"I get it. I'd be a fool to run."

"It would be a big mistake. If you think we don't have informants within your consulate, or that we don't monitor their incoming calls, think again."

Rather than come back at him, Zoya nodded toward the bag in his hand. A purchase he'd picked up on the way from the airport. "Why did you buy enough rope to moor a yacht? Surely you could incapacitate me with a few zip ties or three feet of clothesline."

Achilles ignored the query as he compared the homes before him to Google's satellite image. The fronts appeared the same live as in the picture, so hopefully the backs were as well. According to Zillow, ownership hadn't changed for over a decade either. While far from conclusive, that was a sign that their security systems would be dated.

Despite their seven and eight-figure prices, Pacific Heights homes had negligible side yards. Enough for the trash cans and a source of natural light, if you were lucky. Achilles led Zoya up to a metal gate on the left side of his target address.

A security light protested their approach.

He ignored it.

The gate rose eight feet in height, and occupied the entire width of space between the house and the wall that separated it from the neighbor's lot. An earlier misting of rain left it glistening beneath the floodlight. Achilles interlocked his fingers to create a stirrup, and said, "You're going over first."

Zoya shrugged, gave him her foot, and used his boost to spring over the gate like a rabbit hopping a hedge.

Achilles followed on her heels by swinging his legs up and around until he was practically inverted, and then dropping to her side. They'd landed in a cobblestoned alley devoid of ornamentation or vegetation. The path before them was lined with bicycles, both adult and child sizes. "Follow me."

Sticking as close as possible to the house wall, Achilles led his prisoner through the side yard toward the backyard. He stopped just shy of the corner. Pointing to a position about fifteen feet off the ground, he said, "See the security light?"

"Sure."

"I'm hoping you can unscrew the lightbulbs if I give you a lift."

"It's awfully high."

He knelt down like Atlas. "Climb up onto my shoulders, and brace your hands on the wall so they can walk up it while I stand."

She complied without question, catching the attention of the motion detector in the process. The security lights blazed to life, illuminating the entire backyard, which boasted a covered Jacuzzi and built-in barbecue.

"Ignore the lights," he said, clamping his hands over her feet and rising to full height.

"I still can't reach it."

Achilles scooched his open palms under her sneakers and shoulder-pressed her three feet higher.

Zoya extinguished one bulb, then the other, plunging them back into the quasi darkness of a cloudy city night.

Achilles reversed the lifting procedure and lowered her back to the ground. "Good job. Warm-up's over." She followed his gaze to the senator's terrace, three stories above.

Chapter 52
The View

San Francisco, California

ZOYA WINCED as Achilles secured the knot that tethered her like a vicious dog. It wasn't that long ago that she'd been on top of the world, with a best-supporting-actress nomination on her résumé and a wonderful man by her side. Then her vacation had been commandeered by none other than the president of Russia, and now she was being led to trial on a leash.

She kept hoping she'd wake up to find Max by her side. She'd regale him with tales of her amazing nightmare over a breakfast of fresh berries and hot peppermint tea. But no matter how hard she pinched, she was still stuck in the surreal world of spies.

Now Achilles expected her to climb a three-story building. At night.

"When I give the signal, you hold the rope out in front of you with both hands while you lean back into the harness as though it was a chair. Then just walk up the wall."

Zoya looked down at her bindings in a new light. The rope construction looping around her waist and thighs did remind her of the seat on a toddler's swing. Fancy that. "Okay."

Achilles had tied the other end of the rope to his backpack, while dropping the coil itself to the ground between them. They were standing at the back left corner of Senator Collins' house, preparing to ascend fifty feet into the dark. Apparently with American spies, hopping a gate, disabling security lights, and scaling the fences between yards was considered a warm-up.

Zoya thought she knew a better way to reach Senator Collins' terrace. She grabbed Achilles' elbow to get his attention. "Wouldn't it be easier to break in here at ground level and climb the stairs?"

He looked down at her hand. "The senator has a zoned security system, allowing her to arm the ground floors while walking about freely upstairs. Besides, this will be plenty easy."

Plenty easy for whom? "You've been here before?"

Achilles nodded. "Once."

With that he turned around and began climbing the senator's back wall faster than she could scale a ladder. He used windowsills and ornamental fixtures and other handholds as well as footholds she couldn't discern. She found him staring back over the ledge of the third-floor terrace before she'd exhaled.

He gestured for her to grab the rope with both hands.

She did.

The rope went tight, and then Achilles disappeared from sight. A moment later, Zoya felt herself being drawn skyward.

She lost her balance and banged into the wall, bruising her shoulder. Achilles seemed to sense this and paused. *What had he said to do? Use the rope like a chair and walk up the wall?* She maneuvered her legs out in front of her until both were perpendicular to the wall.

The rope cut into the crease between her buttocks and thighs like a misplaced thong two sizes too small. It was uncomfortable, but bearable.

The lifting resumed.

She found herself picturing Achilles pulling hand-over-hand in concert with the rhythm of the rope's movements. She grabbed hold like she was choking a chicken, while doing her best to lean back into the rope harness. Step-by-step, she walked up the wall. The sensation reminded her of the ascent at the beginning of a rollercoaster ride, except there was no ominous clicking sound, just her ragged breath and the city soundscape. No doubt the view behind her was beautiful, but she wasn't about to turn and look.

As she neared the top, Zoya saw the soles of Achilles' feet braced against the railing on either side of the rope, but no other part of him. He must be leaning backward in a pose similar to her own, heaving ho.

"Just like a pro," Achilles said, as she scrambled over the rail.

Zoya took in Senator Collins' million-dollar vista as Achilles went to work releasing her harness. About a dozen blocks of houses stretched out below them, with the dark waters of San Francisco Bay beyond and a few concentrations of light visible far in the distance on the other side. Off to their left, the Golden Gate Bridge framed the scene.

Achilles must have used some special tying technique, because he got the harness off her quicker than she could untangle knotted shoe laces. He let the rope drop to the terrace floor.

She rubbed the chafed areas, "What now?"

Achilles pointed toward a sliding glass door set in a wall of floor-to-ceiling windows. "I believe that's her bedroom, although I've never been."

The drapes were drawn, but Zoya saw a warm glow emanating around the edges. "So we just knock?"

"That would be the polite thing to do, but the consequences would be unpredictable. It's not the front door. Let's see if it's unlocked."

Chapter 53
Red, White & Blue

San Francisco, California

ZOYA IMAGINED how she'd react in Senator Collins' shoes, if a couple of spies appeared in her bedroom after dark. First she'd scream, then she'd run. If Collins was more like Max, she'd grab the Beretta she kept between the mattress and the headboard and shoot them both in the legs. Nothing fatal, but enough to assess their intentions from a position of power. That scenario raised a question. "Is Collins married?"

"Only to her job."

"Boyfriend?"

"I'm not sure, but she's in her seventies, so I doubt we'll be interrupting anything too wild."

"I was thinking more Wild West."

"Quickdraw Collins? I don't think we have to worry about that." Achilles gave the terrace door a gentle tug.

It yielded.

He slid the glass aside just enough to part the curtains and peep through. After a few silent seconds of observation, he slid the door open another foot and ushered her inside with one hand to his lips and the other on her hand.

Zoya smelled the sweet combination of magnolia and mandarin she knew to be *J'adore* perfume, as well as something more metallic. She heard nothing. Perhaps the lights were on a timer, and the senator wasn't home. What would Achilles do then? Would they have to hide out until her return — a day, a week, or a month from now? Didn't senators have two homes? One in their district, the other in Washington?

Achilles closed the door behind them before pulling aside the curtains.

She felt him go tense.

He ushered her two steps forward across the carpeting, then halted, stone still.

She studied the bedroom of one of the most powerful women on Earth. Beyond the plush seating arrangement near the window, a big bed with a European-style white duvet dominated the room. It was flanked by end tables supporting electronic necessities and piled high with reports and romance novels — the only clutter in an otherwise immaculate environment. The bed faced the wall to their left, which was adorned with a white marble fireplace and a modern television, both dormant. A long hip-high dresser topped with family photos completed the scene.

Achilles pointed to his ear, his face now fraught with concern.

She didn't hear anything.

He released her hand and walked silently toward the archway before them. It appeared to lead between his-and-hers closets to the master bath. Staring in the direction of Achilles' movement, Zoya detected the flickering of candlelight.

She stayed rooted, while he forged ahead. She expected to hear the sound of splashing water accompanied by the startled senator's scream. She got the splash, but the scream was from Achilles. *"No! No! No!"*

Zoya ran toward him rather than away, surprising herself. She stopped just as suddenly upon entering the bathroom. The decor was all done in various shades of white — the tile, the marble countertops, the walls — all accented by brushed nickel fixtures. Right out of a catalogue. The exception was the bathtub, which was filled with red.

Zoya had made a few movies involving murders. A hanging, a stabbing, some gunshot wounds. They'd looked similar enough, but had felt nothing like this. They'd been staged. This was tragic.

Despondency and despair washed over Zoya like a bloody wave, making her stomach sick. She realized now that Collins had been a beacon of hope. A potential source of salvation in an otherwise pitch-black night. She'd been fixated on that guiding light all the way from Hawaii. Now her last ray of hope was extinguished and she felt herself plunging into darkness.

Achilles was also in agony. Zoya could sense it. He'd lost more than hope; he'd lost a friend.

Zoya didn't speak. She didn't scream. She just turned and ran.

Chapter 54
Flight Plans

Russian Airspace

THE FLIGHT ATTENDANT summoned Ignaty shortly after takeoff. Her name was Oxana, and in Ignaty's opinion, she was the highlight of Korovin's plane. She was also his mistress. One of several.

It was almost worth the verbal thrashing from the president that usually ensued, just to follow her heart-shaped ass up the aisle. But Ignaty wouldn't be getting a thrashing today, so the summons was pure pleasure.

Korovin flew to Seaside most weekends. This delighted Ignaty. With a private plane and helicopter at their disposal, the trip only took a couple of hours — not much more than the average Muscovite's daily commute. The remote setting provided infinitely fewer distractions than Moscow, improving Korovin's mood, and increasing Ignaty's face time.

"Have you caught Achilles yet?" Korovin said, as soon as Oxana closed the burl-wood door. He was seated before a silver bowl of nuts and a bone china tea service. With the glow of sunset pouring through the single open window bathing the president in golden light, the scene resembled those rendered by Rembrandt.

Ignaty slid into the deep cream leather seat opposite his boss. "I expect to have Achilles within the next twenty-four hours. My guys are waiting in ambush at the one place he's guaranteed to show. Meanwhile, the frame worked, so he's neutralized. Any moment now, Senator Collins' body will be discovered and an APB will go out on Achilles. A massive manhunt will ensue."

Korovin grunted. "Still no sign of Zoya?"

"Nothing. I'm not optimistic."

"That's a shame," Korovin said, shelling a pistachio. "We can't let Max know until it's over."

"Agreed."

"What's the latest on *Sunset?*"

Ignaty scooted forward, relieved to have made it to the good news unscathed. "Max came through."

"He cracked Vulcan Fisher?" Korovin tossed the nut into his mouth and the shells over his shoulder.

"Not exactly. He thought outside the box. He's hacking the shipping company instead. He's going to adjust the pickup time in their records, and change the pickup address to a location he's rented down the street."

"Okay…"

"Then he'll pick up the units as originally scheduled, install the *Sunset* devices—"

"And have the original shipper collect the modified units from the new address, for delivery to Boeing as scheduled," Korovin said, completing the thought as was his habit. "I like it. What can go wrong?"

"The plan creates discrepancies. Obviously minor discrepancies of time and location, but also product discrepancies, as a result of repackaging."

"What makes you think they'll go unnoticed?"

"They don't need to go unnoticed, although I believe they will. They just need to go unreported."

"So you're betting on lazy."

"And an abhorrence of bureaucracy, a lack of accountability, and the managed chaos that defines life in large organizations. In the lean-manufacturing climate, people are way too busy and scorecard oriented to care about anything that's not formally identified as a problem."

Korovin nodded his approval, and grabbed a few more nuts. "I can see the news reports already. Have you done any modeling?"

"Of the damage?"

"Yeah."

Ignaty was thrilled to share that data. The obvious comparison to Bin Laden made him out to be a strategic genius. "Southwest configures their 737s to fit 143 passengers. Adding in crew and allowing for a few empty seats, I estimate 140 people per plane. Multiply that by fifty aircraft and that's seven thousand souls. More than double the 9/11 casualty count — and that's just the base."

"Just the base?"

"Once you add in the ground casualties, the airport employees and passengers waiting to board when the planes come through the terminals at 140 knots, shattering glass, twisting steel, and spewing jet fuel, the numbers will skyrocket."

"How much?"

"That's much less predictable, but by targeting the middle of the busiest terminal we'll add hundreds more casualties per plane. It's safe to say the total will top ten thousand, but I think we'll see closer to thirty or forty thousand if we go with a major travel day, as planned."

Korovin pushed the nuts Ignaty's way. "It will be good shock value if we can add a zero to the 9/11 casualty count. I can see the newscasters going wild with a 10X comparison."

"Agreed."

"Of course the lasting damage will come with the subsequent paralysis and loss of infrastructure. That's the real prize. With that in mind, I want you to target the planes to cause maximal structural damage to the airport, rather than immediate loss of life."

"Will do."

The president blessed Ignaty with a rare smile. "What else have you got for me?"

Ignaty recognized the perfect opportunity to slip in his bad news. A flea on the camel's back. "Wang extorted an extra $1.5 million for his hacking services."

Korovin chuffed. He'd predicted as much. "Has he figured out who we are or what we're up to?"

"Max thinks the British illusion is still holding. More importantly, he's certain Wang has no inkling of the end game. But he warns that Wang is very smart, so our risk increases with our exposure."

"He has to figure it out eventually, right?"

"Once we hand him the autopilot systems to modify, it won't be much of a leap."

Korovin began flicking pistachio shells off the table with his finger, aiming for the trashcan by his desk, but missing. "By then the millions will be within his grasp. He won't have the willpower to back away. He'll find some justification to go through with it, to earn his payday — people always do. We just have to keep him hungry. Tell Max not to pay any of it, including this latest $1.5 million, until Wang's work is done and Boeing has the modified units."

"Will do."

"What's the plan for Wang when it's over?"

"I expect that he plans to disappear, which is perfect. It reinforces our ruse. But if he decides to stick around with his newfound wealth, that wouldn't necessarily be bad either. Assuming he knows nothing that links *Sunset* to us."

"Agreed," Korovin said, flicking his last shell, and scoring. "What about Max?"

Ignaty turned to the window to study the stars before answering.

Chapter 55
Shifting Priorities

San Francisco, California

"NO! NO! NO!" Achilles fought back the gag reflex as he leapt to Senator Collins' side. She was laying with her head flopped against the rim of her tub and her arms dangling in the water. If it weren't for the crimson, she'd have appeared to be sleeping.

He thrust his fingers against her exposed left carotid while his eyes tried to penetrate the water. If she had a pulse, it was too weak for him to feel. With trembling fingers, it was hard to tell. Trembling fingers, he couldn't remember that ever happening before.

Snatching the phone off the tubside cradle, he hit 9-1-1 and the speaker button. While the call connected, he pulled Collins' arms out of the water. Her left wrist had several long slits. He spoke the moment he heard the click. "I need an ambulance immediatcly at this address. Senator Colleen Collins' wrist has been slit. She's unconscious and has lost a lot of blood."

The responding voice was crisp and cool. "Please confirm the address."

Achilles gave the house number and hung up immediately. He needed his hands working the medical emergency and his brain crunching this big twist to his predicament.

Grabbing the senator beneath her armpits, he dragged her out of the tub and onto thc floor, so that her ankles hooked on the rim. His assumption was that maximizing blood flow to the brain was priority number one, and that elevating her feet would help. "Zoya, grab me a belt and a towel."

He used his left hand to compress the senator's left wrist while elevating it straight up. Zoya didn't reply and he didn't hear her moving. He turned his head to find himself alone. "Zoya, I need your help!"

He pulled the belt off Collins' bathrobe and wrapped one end around her wounds, tying it off as tightly as he could, with the knot over the cuts. *Zoya had run, goddamnit!* He lashed the free end of the belt around the faucet in order to keep her arm raised, then started CPR.

A whirlwind of rage and sorrow and fear swirled within him as he rhythmically pressed his big palm down against Collins' fragile breast.

He hadn't realized how much she meant to him until that moment, when he held her life in his hands.

They hadn't enjoyed much time together, but the hours they'd shared had been intense. His feelings weren't so much love, as respect and admiration. "Don't die on me, Colleen. Just hold on a little longer. The world still needs you."

He continued the chest compressions for a few minutes before stopping to check for a pulse. Fearful of what he'd find, he put his ear to her heart and fingertips to her neck. He heard it and he felt it! She had a pulse, weak but steady.

His first sigh of relief went into her mouth, the start of rescue breathing. During the second breath he heard noise downstairs. Was it Zoya, or the paramedics? If it was the paramedics, he should leave — get away and go after Zoya. But he couldn't be certain that it was the paramedics, and he couldn't leave without passing Colleen into competent hands. He gave her one more breath, then shouted "Top floor master bath!"

He heard the clumping of burdened feet running up stairs, and a moment later two medics joined him. The first was toting a large medical bag, the second carried a stretcher. "I found her in the tub seconds before I made the call. I don't know how long she'd been bleeding. I couldn't tell if she had a pulse but she's got one now. I gave her CPR."

Achilles stepped aside and let the professionals take over.

While they set about stabilizing her on the stretcher, he went out the sliding glass door, and over the rail.

He ran down the hill toward the bay, keeping his eyes open for Zoya but knowing it was hopeless. He flagged the first cab he saw by running out in front of it and holding up both hands. The Ford Fusion screeched to a stop three feet before him, its bearded driver too shocked to curse.

Achilles practically dove into the back seat. "How long to Palo Alto?"

"Man that was dangerous."

"This is life or death. Please start driving. How long?"

"This time of night, about forty-five minutes. Depends on the address."

Achilles rattled off the block he wanted, then added, "If you get me there in thirty minutes, I'll tip you a thousand bucks."

The driver met his eye in the mirror. Achilles studied him right back. He saw hope and ambition and a clenched jaw. "If I get a ticket, I could lose my job."

"So let me drive. You still get the thousand."

"Then I definitely get fired."

"You're burning clock. Life or death, man. Decide!"

The driver studied Achilles for another second and then floored the gas. "It's 8:26 p.m."

Achilles knew exactly what time it was. Katya's favorite yoga class ended at 8:30. It was down in Santa Clara, fifteen miles south of their home, but Katya made the drive because she loved the instructor, a Latvian woman who'd won an international competition for best human pretzel or something like that.

They hit Highway 101 after five minutes of scooting through residential streets with no regard for speed limits or stop signs. Now that they were on a straightaway, the driver met his eye in the mirror. "Show me the money."

Achilles pulled ten of the Russians hundred-dollar bills from his backpack and held them up.

The driver nodded once and returned his focus to the road. He'd been scanning it like a Humvee driver in Baghdad. Achilles wondered if he actually had been, but didn't ask. They both needed to focus elsewhere.

Achilles wished he'd had time to search the streets around Collins' house for Zoya. A cab would have been perfect for that kind of tactical reconnaissance. She might even have inadvertently approached him.

But Zoya was no longer his primary concern.

Whoever went after Collins, would go after Katya next.

Chapter 56
Three Strikes

Palo Alto, California

ACHILLES GAVE the driver an intersection a block south of his house as their destination. This afforded him the opportunity to scan for goons as they drove by. He didn't spot any. Hope surged in his chest when he noted that the garage light wasn't on. Katya hadn't arrived in the last couple of minutes. He just might have beaten her.

The driver announced "8:58" as they screeched to a halt.

Achilles pushed the thousand dollars through the slot. "Please don't double back along these side streets. I don't want anyone to see your car twice."

"Whatever you say. Thanks, man!"

Achilles made it to his neighbor's backyard thirty seconds after exiting the cab. The Khan's black lab came running as he vaulted the fence. Achilles landed in a crouch and extended his hand. "How's my Puck? How's Pucky?" His playful tone and a ruffle behind the ear calmed the dog right down.

The fence dividing the Khan's yard from his own was a six-foot redwood construction, but it was a row of Cypress trees that provided the real cover. Achilles rolled over the fence and melted down between the branches, where he squatted to surveil the scene.

The home he shared with Katya appeared tranquil, but then so could shark-infested waters. He would proceed as though Jaws was inside until investigation proved otherwise.

Like all homes in the city of Stanford and the heart of Silicon Valley, the residence he'd inherited was priced at about ten times what people from the American heartland would expect. It was nice, but nothing spectacular. A two-story tawny stucco with a red-tiled roof and a semicircular drive around a Spanish fountain.

He approached the back patio like a fox on the prowl, low and silent and alert. Having been a covert operative for five years, Achilles knew exactly what he'd do if Russian intelligence had sent him to kidnap Katya. He'd slip into her house and wait for her to come home. Why grab someone on the street, where confounding factors abound — bystanders and video cameras and traffic? Much better to set up shop at home and do the dirty work in the predictable isolation of the victim's own garage.

Achilles planned his incursion accordingly.

His thoughts moved to the alarm. He had a top-notch system, but there was only so much electronics could do. Home alarms all shared a weakness, a keypad that gave hackers access to the motherboard. Achilles had added a layer to his security by installing his control panel within a wall safe that opened with a palm scan. Sixty seconds wasn't a lot of grace period when you had two systems to overcome, even if you were SVR. But Achilles knew there were two constants that killed even the best of operatives: bad luck and the unexpected.

For the second time in as many hours, Achilles found himself looking through a glass door at curtains. Beyond these were a kitchen to the right and a dining room to the left. No light was coming through, so he pressed his ear to the glass and listened. Silence.

Achilles didn't have his keys. They hadn't made it to the island. His patio door closed with a standard latch, as there wasn't much to be gained by upgrading the lock on a piece of glass, not with patio bricks at hand. But Achilles had no need for picks or bricks since he knew where the Hide-A-Key was. He grabbed it from the magnetic box he'd secreted beneath one of the outside lights, and eased it into the lock.

The opening of the door should have resulted in the low annoying hum of an alarm counting down. But he heard nothing.

Had Katya failed to arm it? Or was this a Jaws scenario?

Achilles sensed them the moment he closed the door. He knew the scent and rhythm of his house, and both were now atypical. A deep inhale detected sweaty clothing tainted by cigarette smoke. It wasn't until that realization slipped its cold hand around his heart that he realized he was, again, unarmed.

That's three strikes.

Best practice for home defense was to have a handgun in every living space, preferably secreted with the grip properly positioned for a hasty grab. Achilles knew that, but hadn't bothered. This was California, not Texas, and he'd been worried about spooking Katya. That was ironic, since the stated reason for her living with him rather than alone was for her security. But relationships were complicated beasts, hoofed with nuance and bridled with compromise. And he'd figured that between the Ruger he made her pack in her purse, and the small arsenal he kept locked in his bedroom, they were covered.

He began mapping out the weapons that were at his immediate disposal, the blades and missiles and blunt objects that populated most rooms disguised as knick-knacks and furnishings. The walnut butcher's block to his right, full of Swiss knives. The polished-rock bookends just beyond, embracing Katya's cookbooks. The cast iron skillet sitting atop the stove. The—

A familiar rumble interrupted his mental rehearsal. The garage door was opening.

Chapter 57
Big & Bigger

Palo Alto, California

THEY CAME from the living room as the garage door groaned. Big men in heavy boots. Men who had to duck and twist to fit through standard doors. Achilles was no lightweight. At six-foot-two he sent the arrow to 220 pounds. But these guys would have to weigh in on livestock scales. Worse still, the fact that they'd been sitting so calmly and quietly spoke to exceptional discipline.

They stopped on the hinged side of the door to the garage. No doubt they planned to grab Katya the instant she stepped inside. That's when they saw him.

Achilles was already moving. He had a bookend in each hand and their skulls in his sights. From a physics perspective this was as foolish as a quarterback assailing two linebackers. Any football, rugby, or billiard fan watching would expect him to bounce off onto his back, and be crushed in the ensuing scrum.

But combat didn't work like contact sports.

Games are rigged to oppose equivalent forces, and designed to accommodate repeat performances. Sportsmen seek playoffs and tournaments and season-ticket sales, while rallying fans and courting huge contracts.

Battle, by comparison, is a single-serving proposition dished out to mismatched forces. Combatants seek quick and decisive resolutions through disproportionate advantages.

Funnel some muscle into a section of sharpened steel, and one gladiator could remove another's head. Add enough speed to an eight-gram piece of copper-jacketed lead, and a girl could drop a 1,000-pound gorilla. Initiate a chain reaction in fissile material, and one maniac could kill a million men. In warfare, you looked for leverage.

Achilles didn't have a sword or a gun or a bomb, but he knew how to apply superior force. And he knew his opponents' minds.

When you're twice the size of an average Joe, you don't back off or step down. You lean in. You flex your chest and ground your feet and become a wall. It's part of the big-dog identity, and it happens every time.

These two didn't reach for their guns. No time. They twisted and braced, their left shoulders coming forward and their right feet going back in a synchronous display of instinctive reaction.

Achilles did the unexpected. He jumped. He sprang like an assailant in a martial arts movie, his legs leading like lances.

Normally that would have been a suicide move.

Normally giving two hostile giants one leg each would be begging for a breaking, turkey wishbone style. *Snap, crackle, pop!*

But this wasn't a blunder. It was a gambit.

Achilles wasn't making a hail-Mary move, he was serving up a distraction. As the giants seized his legs, they exposed their heads. With their arms engaged, and their attention distracted, their noggins were teed up like shiny steel nails on a soft pine board, just begging for a pounding.

Achilles used the same muscles that had once propelled the poles that had pushed the skis that had earned his country Olympic bronze. Muscles that he'd kept conditioned by pulling his body up thousand-foot cliffs. He charged those muscles with the anger and frustration bred by Russian deception and born of recent lies, and he brought the bookends down with unstoppable force, smack in the center of those two big heads.

The crack was sickening, the splash grotesque, and the smell alone enough to make a vulture vomit. But all Achilles felt was relief as his assailants tumbled to the floor.

Achilles knew they were dead before his arms stopped moving, so he relaxed and rolled with it. By the time he'd regained his feet, there was a puddle of blood the length of a pool table on the hardwood floor, and Katya had slammed her car door.

Chapter 58
Two for the Road

Palo Alto, California

"KATYA, DON'T COME IN!" Achilles shouted. "Just hold on a second. I'll come out to the garage."

"Okay. Welcome home. Good timing. I've got great news! Are you all right?"

"I'm fine. Just a sec."

He wanted to shroud the bodies, and he wanted to do it with something devoid of sentimental value. Almost everything in the house had belonged to his father or stepmother, and now that they were gone everything was a bit sacred. Even the silly stuff.

He found a gray king-size blanket in the hallway linen closet that looked to be fresh from Macy's shelf, and carried it back to the mess. "Just one more minute."

There was no way to work without tracking blood around, so he decided to ignore it and mop up later. He relieved the assassins of their weapons, then made them easier to cover.

Grabbing first one and then the other, he pulled the assassins out straight like springboard divers and then lined them up side-by-side atop the coagulating puddle. Satisfied, he flopped their arms back down by their sides.

"What's that slapping sound?"

If ever a question deserved an oblique answer, that was it. "Housekeeping. Almost done."

He swooshed the blanket up and let it settle over them. It immediately started turning a telltale red, but the amorphous mass was far less disturbing than what preceded. How could he explain it in a way that wouldn't frighten Katya? His friends back at Langley would nod their approval and ask for a beer if he told it to them straight, but he expected a stronger reaction from a mathematics professor.

Glancing down, Achilles found his own appearance to be amazingly unremarkable from the ankles up. All the blood spatter had been directed away.

Slipping off his shoes, he tried to lighten his own mood and facial expression with a silent homage to Chevy Chase. *Yes, dear. I hit a water buffalo on the way home, and I just couldn't bring myself to leave it there.*

He opened the garage door to find Katya braced and poised on the other side of her Ford, with her Ruger pointing straight at him.

His heart filled with love and pride. She was so composed. So resilient. And she'd come so far.

Katya had completed her Ph.D. in mathematics at Moscow State University, and was now doing post-doc work at Stanford. After spending her whole life in academia, she'd been swept up in a very violent conspiracy that eventually made her the target of assassins. Rather than running away and cowering in a corner, Katya had actively embraced the investigation for the experience of it. That beautiful, brilliant woman had a core of iron.

In the aftermath of their adventure, Achilles had bought her a handgun and taught her to use it. They'd looked at the Glock 19 and 42, the Kahr CW9, and the Sig Sauer P238, but she found the Ruger LC9 to be the most comfortable — once he finally got one into her hand. That took a few trips to a dealer who specialized in arming women, and the purchase of a designer concealed-carry purse.

As she lowered her Ruger, he said, "Sorry about that."

Katya's shoulders slumped and her face softened and she began walking toward him. "Are you okay? Welcome home! I wasn't expecting you, but I'm so glad you're here. I've got good news."

Achilles wanted to run to her and pick her up in his arms and smother her with passionate kisses as a prelude to things to come. Things too long in coming. He thought he'd lost her forever after waking up on that island. As painful as that had been, he now realized it had been a gift. Now he knew for certain how much he truly loved her. And reflection in that context had given him a new perspective. He wouldn't try to replace Colin. He'd pick up where Colin had left off.

But not now.

Before focusing on the future, he had to ensure that they'd both have one. So he didn't rush forth and embrace her. He didn't press his lips to hers or pull her body close. He remained in the doorway, blocking her path. "Before we get to that, there's something I need to tell you."

Her face darkened as she approached. "Okay."

"You remember that time we left a black Escalade in long-term parking at SFO?" It was a rhetorical question. Of course she did. The Cadillac had contained a couple of corpses.

A wave of dread crossed Katya's face as she stopped before him and nodded with wide eyes.

"I've got a similar situation." He used his head to motion toward the bodies now blocked from her view by the door.

Her eyes went even wider, and silent tears started flowing.

Achilles reached out and pulled her into his arms. As he buried his nose in her honey-blonde hair, he was reminded of the last woman he'd hugged and the problems still ahead.

The team lying at his feet was a speed bump, not a finish line. He still had a long way to go. Correction, *they* had a long way to go. Whatever he did, he couldn't leave Katya alone.

He picked her up and carried her to the living room couch, far from the disturbing view.

"Is this related to the assignment Senator Collins gave you on behalf of President Silver?"

Katya had helped him uncover Korovin's earlier plot to kill Silver, so she was familiar with Achilles' very special, very sensitive relationship with the American president. But Achilles hadn't told her the details of his mission. All she knew was that Collins had given him a highly classified assignment, a mission that would take him off the grid for a month or so.

Katya hadn't pressed for details, and she hadn't even seemed surprised by the news. She understood him and seemed to appreciate his value. "Yes. It's related to my assignment. And I'm going to tell you all about it. Everything. But not here. Not now. We need to leave right away."

Chapter 59
Connecting the Dots

Palo Alto, California

ACHILLES' SHOULDER WAS WET, but Katya's tears had stopped flowing by the time she looked up. "Where are we going? For how long?" Her voice was returning to normal. The analytical math professor was re-emerging.

Achilles kept his hands on her shoulders. "It could be a while. Probably a month, maybe more. Throw your essentials in your purse. I've got a backpack for any must-haves that won't fit. I'll grab our passports and deal with the, um, mess I made."

"Are we going far?"

"I'm not sure."

"Achilles, you're not making sense."

He supposed he wasn't. You couldn't play fast-and-loose with logic around a Stanford mathematics professor.

He pulled Foxley's phone from his back pocket and powered it on. Explaining who Zoya was and how he happened to be tracking her using a dead American assassin's equipment wasn't just a long story, it was a minefield. They didn't have time to navigate it now. Achilles didn't know what protocols the Russians now rotting on his floor had put in place, or what back-up might be nearby and waiting.

As the screen came to life, a map formed around a blinking red dot. It was moving at highway speed. Zoya had crossed the Bay Bridge out of the city and was headed north on I-80 through Berkley. Had she stolen a car? Hitchhiked? Or had someone picked her up? Either of the first two were fine with him. The third would complicate things, and might spell the end.

He pointed to the red dot. "We need to catch up with that."

Katya frowned. "What is it?"

"Did you happen to see the Russian film *Wayward Days*?"

"Afraid I missed that one."

"The red dot represents one of its stars, Zoya Zolotova. She's the only link I have to information of great geopolitical importance. Information that might also save my life."

Katya blinked a couple of times. "I didn't see that answer coming.

But knowing you I'm only shocked, not completely bewildered. I do know Zoya Zolotova from other performances. She was also a sex symbol, if memory serves."

Achilles nodded noncommittally. He wasn't about to go there. Not now, anyway. "I'll tell you everything — once we're moving. It's not safe for us to stay here any longer. Grab your essentials while I clean up. I'm going to have to go outside to find their car, so keep your gun handy until I return." He tapped his pockets to make sure he had the guns of both assassins. He was learning.

Achilles gave Katya a hug and ran back to the mess. He pulled the blanket back and emptied the pockets of both Russians into his backpack, keeping only their rental car keys at hand. A Chevy Tahoe, color black — according to the keychain.

Satisfied with his salvage, he headed for the front door.

A big black bag in the entryway stopped him short and spiked his adrenaline.

It was the kind of briefcase that loaded from the top so you could carry larger, heavier loads. Textbooks or legal binders or reams of advertising materials. He shouted back to Katya. "Did you arm the alarm when you left for yoga?"

"Of course. I always do. Just like you asked me — many times."

The palm scanner on the wall above the briefcase was completely black. Normally there was a green LED in the bottom corner. He pressed his palm against it. That should have brought the display to life, but nothing happened. Not a thing. The scanner was as dormant as the picture frame it resembled. They'd cut the power to it, but not to the house. The lights were working and the refrigerator was humming away. The microwave clock hadn't been blinking.

He tried opening the briefcase, but found it locked. He grabbed the handle, tested the briefcase's weight, and found it unexpectedly heavy. A good fifty pounds. He pulled a paperclip from his back pocket, straightened part and then kinked the end by pressing it against the lock housing. The basic briefcase locks only took a few seconds each before their clasps thwacked back in quick succession.

He flipped the lids open and peered inside. A top shelf held some basic tools, screwdrivers, tape, and knives. He lifted it slowly, checking for resistance and wires. The main compartment was brimming with rolls of thick copper wire. Three across, the rolls ran end-to-end. A bit puzzling to put it mildly until he saw the switch built into the side of the briefcase. A simple on-off toggle. "Holy guacamole!"

Chapter 60
Critical Condition

Palo Alto, California

BY THE TIME Achilles had loaded the dead bodies, bloody blanket, and black briefcase into the back of the rental car, Zoya's red dot had cleared the Bay Area. By the time he'd scrubbed the floor, set out the trash, and emptied his safe of the things they'd need, Zoya's red dot was on the I-5 heading north.

Interstate 5 was the main West Coast highway, stretching all the way from Mexico to Canada. It passed through every major city in California, Oregon, and Washington — except for San Francisco, which it only passed near.

Katya slid into the Tahoe's passenger seat and looked at the screen. She'd been ready long before he had, but for obvious reasons had chosen not to wait in their commandeered car. "Do you know where Zoya's headed?"

"I'm surprised she's in a car at all. I would have thought she'd go straight to the consulate in San Francisco. That's where we were, San Francisco."

"Well maybe that's exactly why she didn't go there."

Achilles turned north on Highway 101. "Maybe, but that doesn't help."

"Are you sure? Wouldn't the same logic send her to the next closest consulate?"

"That's in L.A. She's headed north."

"You're wrong."

"Look at the dot."

"No, I mean about the consulate. There isn't one in L.A. But we do have one in Seattle."

One point for Katya. "Huh. That's gotta be at least a ten-hour drive."

Katya had her phone out. "Google says twelve. She could drive through the night, and be there when they open in the morning. Meanwhile, if it weren't for the tracker you'd be tearing apart San Francisco."

"God, you're smart."

"We could fly and leapfrog her."

Achilles pondered that approach for a second. "That's risky. If we're wrong, we'll lose a lot of time overshooting her. See if you can find a flight out of Sacramento. Either to Seattle or better yet Portland. If she's still racing north by the time we reach Sacramento, we'll fly."

Katya used her thumbs while Achilles burned rubber. "The best I can find gets us into Portland at 8:30 a.m."

"That's too late. Did you try Alaskan and Southwest?"

"Yep."

"Give the Sacramento Executive Airport a call. Tell them you've got two people desperate to be in Portland by 4:00 a.m. Maybe they can arrange to charter a plane. If they can, use your Kate Yates alias for the reservation."

Katya got right on it. By the time they reached the I-5, she'd completed her third call. "We're good to go."

Good to go, Achilles repeated to himself with a shake of the head. Some math professor.

As they raced toward Sacramento, closing in on the red dot inch-by-inch, Achilles explained how it had come to pass that he was running for his life from both American and Russian covert operatives. In a stolen car. With two dead hit men in the trunk. In pursuit of a Russian film star.

"It all started with Silver asking you to assassinate Korovin?"

"Near as I can figure."

"Why you? Why not the CIA?"

"Because Silver couldn't risk having the U.S. government implicated if details leaked or the operation went sideways, as covert-ops all too often do. One loose lip and we'd all be sunk. Can you imagine anything more dangerous than two feuding men clenching nuclear control panels while millions of proud and patriotic supporters cheer them on?"

"But you used to be CIA," Katya prodded, going after his logic. "Doesn't that make using you the same thing — as far as political perception is concerned?"

"Not with all that's happened since I left. As you know, I had problems with the government, and Korovin killed my family. Lone wolf would be an easy sell. The media would eat it up."

With the stage set, Achilles continued his story, starting with his island awakening. He walked Katya through everything, step-by-step.

She stayed quiet throughout. It wasn't until he choked up during the bloody bathtub scene that she chose to interrupt him. "So you don't know if Colleen's alive?"

"I hated to leave, but I'd done all I could. As soon as the shock of finding her wore off, I realized I had to get to you. If I hadn't . . ." Achilles wanted to tell Katya how losing her had caused him to realize just how much she meant to him. How it had felt like the tragedy of his life. How he wanted to pick up where his brother had left off.

But he found himself holding back.

This wasn't the time to unfurl those emotions. Too many other winds were blowing.

Katya changed the subject. "What if Collins dies, and we don't catch Zoya? What do we do then?"

"I don't know."

"With your going AWOL right before Lukin's death, I can see why Silver would suspect you of selling out — especially given your recent financial escapades. Then Foxley finds you in Hawaii, but disappears. Then Collins is nearly assassinated."

"Yeah. Korovin's a mastermind."

"You really think he's running this personally?"

Achilles thought about that for a second. "I doubt he's more than one step removed. He's probably got a razor-sharp strategist on point, acting as both brains and buffer. Can't wait to get my hands on him."

"Or her."

"Or her," Achilles repeated, remembering how effective Zoya had been.

They lapsed into silence for a few miles until Achilles blurted, "You said you had news! Back when you were still in the garage, you said my timing was good because you had great news."

"Now's not the time. The airport exit is just one mile ahead."

Achilles smiled to himself as he checked the red dot. They both had hot items on hold for cooler times. He had a lot to look forward to — if he got out of this alive. "Zoya's still on course. Still about ninety minutes ahead." She was driving a steady 72 mph. Fast, but not fast enough for a highway ticket. Smart if you were in a stolen car without a driver's license. She was probably tailing a truck just to be sure.

Achilles ran some calculations. If he drove 90 mph, he'd catch up before she hit Seattle. But he too was in a stolen car, and while he had a driver's license, he also had a couple of corpses in the back. "Let's risk the plane. If we get caught with this car, it's all over."

As he exited I-5, he said, "We might not have to wait to learn about Colleen. She's a senator. She might be in the news."

Katya picked up her phone. "I'll Google it. Hey you just missed our turn."

"That was the Executive Airport."

"Which is where we're going."

"Yeah, but we can't leave this car there. We have to hit long-term parking at the commercial airport and then take a cab."

"Of course."

A moment later, Katya said, "Channel 4 just posted a video on Senator Collins two minutes ago."

Achilles had to keep his eyes scanning for airport signs, but his ears honed in on the chipper reporter's voice. "Senator Colleen Collins was rushed to the emergency room at the California Pacific Medical Center earlier this evening after an anonymous 9-1-1 call. Details are unconfirmed, but her condition is listed as critical. In conjunction with this, police are now searching for Kyle Achilles, the Bay Area resident who won a bronze medal in the biathlon at the 2010 Winter Olympics. Anyone with information ..."

Chapter 61
Boys & Toys

Sacramento, California

KATYA DIDN'T EXHALE until the news video summarizing the attack on Collins had ended. After a moment of stunned silence, she looked over at Achilles. His knuckles had turned white on the steering wheel. "Why are they looking for you?"

Achilles slowly shook his head with clenched jaw and furrowed brow before responding. "Clearly there are multiple forces at work. I made the 9-1-1 call, and the EMTs caught a glimpse of me at the scene, but that should have taken time to process. I'm guessing that the real killer planted evidence against me. I didn't have time to search the scene. But that's not what bothers me."

"No?"

"No. The speed of the publicity was too quick. Something like this, where rushed judgments lead to lawsuits and lost careers, the CYA process takes time."

"What are you saying?"

"There's pressure from the top. The very top."

Katya felt her stomach drop. "President Silver?"

"He sent Foxley after me, and Foxley disappeared. Now the only other person knowledgeable of the operation is at death's door." Achilles pounded the wheel as he spoke.

"Can we still risk the airport?" Katya asked, disturbed by the panicky tenor of her own voice.

"We have to. It would be a bigger risk to let Zoya get away."

Katya wasn't so sure. "But your picture is on the news, and they probably have the news running all the time at the airport."

Achilles turned to give her a reassuring smile. "The pilot's not going to be waiting around in the terminal. They'll call him in and he'll go straight to pre-flight inspection. Plus I've got a mustache and some glasses in my backpack. We'll be fine if you do the talking."

Katya lacked Achilles' confidence, but experience had taught her to trust his instincts on operational matters.

Achilles left the motor running after they parked in the back section of Sacramento International's economy lot. He got out, causing the door to begin a steady reminder chime.

"What are you doing?"

"I want to see something."

Katya watched him reach around and pull a big black briefcase from behind her seat. Given the way he struggled with it, she figured it was full of gold bricks. "What is that?"

"I think this is what Korovin's thugs used to defeat my alarm. I'm pretty sure it's an EMP."

Katya wasn't sure she'd heard correctly. "An electromagnetic pulse device? Those are real?" She thought the electronics-frying energy bombs were still science fiction.

"Sure, they're actually pretty easy to make. But they don't discriminate, so I want you to take our phones out of range."

"You're going to test it on the Tahoe?"

Achilles nodded. "As a favor to the detectives discovering the bodies. It will add excitement to their investigation." He gave her a wink and handed her his cell phone. "Please turn on the radio."

There were some parts of the Y chromosome that Katya would simply never understand. She complied with a half-smile and shake of her head, then realized that her half-smile had been Achilles' objective. Despite all the strain he was under, he was still trying to lighten her mood — in his own weird way.

A commercial for the radio station interrupted her momentary reprieve. She wondered why all stations advertised themselves on themselves, even the ones claiming to be commercial free. Seemed counterproductive to her.

Achilles gestured. "If you'll back up about a hundred feet that should be plenty."

"You're really going to set that thing off? Isn't it dangerous?"

"Only to cyborgs and people with pacemakers."

She backed away until Achilles gave her the thumbs up. Then all of a sudden the chiming stopped, the radio went silent, the motor stopped, and the dome light extinguished. Achilles said, "Cool!"

Katya returned to his side, feeling a mixture of wonderment and worry. "How did you know it wasn't a bomb?"

"Only religious fundamentalists put the detonation trigger on the actual bomb. Everyone else uses a remote. Besides, it was stuffed with wire, not explosives."

"They could have been at the bottom."

"The weight told me it was all battery and wire."

Katya wouldn't have risked it, but then she wasn't the pro.

She took a second to ponder that, to learn from it. Achilles won, constantly and consistently, by putting everything on the line and then giving it everything he had. He took things further than most people would dare to go, and did so not just without hesitation, but apparently without worry. She knew by now that it wasn't an act. You couldn't fake courage on the side of a cliff. Her conclusion: Either he was a whole lot better at running probability calculations than she was, or his instincts were of a different breed.

As they wiped the Tahoe's shiny surfaces free of prints, she asked, "Why did the motor shut off? This isn't a Prius or Tesla, it runs on gas."

"All cars are computer-controlled."

"Huh." She thought of the Lada she'd driven back in Moscow and wasn't so sure, but didn't comment.

"Let's go."

Katya was surprised to see Achilles hauling the heavy briefcase. "Why are you bringing that?" She knew the answer even before he replied: boys and their toys.

"It's a pretty cool weapon. Why leave it behind if we don't have to?"

Chapter 62
Grim Reflections

Portland, Oregon

THE RED DOT was still heading north along I-5 when Kyle and Katya Yates boarded their chartered Piper. It was fast-approaching Portland when Captain Roberts landed them in The City of Roses. By the time they had rented two surveillance cars and loaded up with Egg McMuffins and drive-through coffee, it was at the city limits. As they pulled onto the I-5 with their car radios Bluetooth-synced to their cell phones, Zoya was only eight minutes behind.

Katya had not liked the idea of separating from Achilles in different cars, but she found herself appreciating the time alone to think and reflect. Achilles had confessed to feeling deep sadness about *drifting apart from her* upon learning that he'd married Zoya. That gave Katya a lot to think about.

She knew that Achilles loved her, and of course she loved him too, although they hadn't spoken of it or acted on it. They had almost yielded to their urges once — during an exceptionally stressful moment back before she'd moved in. But Colin had only been gone for six months at that point, and she'd told Achilles that she needed more time.

He'd respected her wishes.

His recent expression of remorse was the closest he'd come to bringing the subject up since she'd moved in.

Katya realized that the prospect of Achilles marrying Zoya had the same effect on her. She didn't like the feeling.

She diagnosed her predominant emotions as grief and jealousy. Then she couldn't resist Googling Zoya's image. There were hundreds of them online. Some very sexy. She'd been hoping to find pictures worse than the one in her head, but had found the opposite instead. Now she couldn't help but imagine Achilles making love to the beautiful movie star. The scene made her sad.

Katya had just decided that this was a good thing, the two of them having the same reaction, when she remembered her big news. How would that affect things? Under normal circumstances, they'd have spent the evening discussing it. She'd have made a nice dinner of chicken picatta or stuffed grouper, and grabbed a bottle of good wine.

They'd have sat outside, and ate and talked it through while the sun set over the Cypress trees. But with everything else going on, her news hadn't even come up.

That concerned her. The fact her big life event didn't make the agenda was distressing. It highlighted the downside of life with Achilles. Nothing she did could compare to the coups he pulled off.

Her heart felt like it was in a blender. On the one hand, she was now more certain than ever that Achilles was the man for her. On the other hand, she didn't know if she could adopt the lifestyle required to live with him. In fact, given her feelings regarding today's big revelation, she was certain that she couldn't. For the moment, anyway.

Katya decided she'd endured enough self-reflection for one sitting. With the cruise control set on 65 miles per hour and the road straight ahead, she picked up her phone to check for news on Collins.

She'd just finished reading the story a few words at a time, when Achilles' voice came over the speaker. "Zoya's just a mile back now, with her cruise control still set on 72 mph. When she closes to a quarter mile, I'll let you know so you can set yours for 72 miles per hour as well. That will keep you a quarter-mile ahead. I'll follow her from a quarter-mile behind."

"Okay. I just saw a report that Collins is in a coma."

"I suppose that's better than dead. Did they mention me?"

"Yep. Same story."

Achilles didn't reply.

She had no idea how Achilles was going to get out of this one. She decided to change the topic, confident that somehow he'd find a way. He always did. "What's the plan for catching Zoya?"

"The Russian consulate in Seattle is just an office in a downtown high rise, so she won't be able to drive into it like she could a diplomatic compound. We'll grab her when she parks."

"Then what?"

He didn't answer.

"Achilles?"

"I haven't figured that part out yet."

Chapter 63
Old Tricks, New Tricks

Seattle, Washington

ZOYA WAS HAVING TROUBLE reading the street signs as she exited I-5 in Seattle, not because of the dim morning lighting or the heavy rain, but rather due to her tears. She thought she'd cried them all out in the first six hours of her marathon drive, but obviously she had more. And these were different tears. Those had been tears of frustration. These were tears of relief.

For eight hundred miles she'd expected to see flashing lights or flood lights. She'd strained to hear helicopter rotors and police sirens. But in the end, her trip had been entirely uneventful.

That was a small miracle.

She wasn't just an escaped Russian spy operating on American soil — a designation so far from anything related to her own self-identity that it still completely blew her mind — she was also a car thief.

In the heat and shock of a startling confrontation, she'd summoned not only the courage to run, but also the presence of mind to think and act tactically. She hadn't just run out into the night. She'd snatched the senator's keys from the seashell bowl by the front door and stolen her Cadillac. Then she'd found the Chevron card in the armrest and the parking money. And even now, twelve hours later, she still couldn't think of a better plan than the one she'd devised in the heat of a murder scene.

Zoya was shocked by her own performance.

She'd been conscripted into a devious con by none other than the president of Russia, compelled to act as another man's wife, and forced to reconcile the fact that her fiancé had allowed her to be prostituted, yet she was still in control of her emotions. And despite being captured and bound and threatened and hauled halfway around the world and back again, she was still performing, still thinking fast on her feet. Now that she'd found a quiet moment to exhale, she felt entitled to a few tears.

But only briefly.

Just enough for a quick release.

This was no time to let her guard down. Sooner or later someone would notice that Collins' car was missing. Probably sooner given the high profile of the case. And when they did, the police could probably just punch some registration code into their big computer and see exactly where she was.

She had to distance herself from Collins' Cadillac. To do so, she followed signs to the train station.

Located just south of the center of downtown Seattle, near the intersection of I-5 and I-90, and within the shadow of CenturyLink Stadium, King Street was an epicenter of mindless commuter movement and anonymous transient activity.

She'd come there on instinct, drawing on her limited espionage experience. Four years earlier, she had made use of her French by playing a Russian spy in a French miniseries. Although the role didn't fulfill her dream of breaking her into the French film industry, it did lead her to Max. As she learned later, he'd been in Paris on an actual espionage mission.

Max had approached her one night after filming as she was leaving the hotel restaurant. In a characteristically bold move, he had pretended to be the author of the novel on which the show was based. He'd flashed his brilliant smile and asked in Russian if she'd like some tips. Who could say no to that?

He'd led her to the hotel bar, and they'd discussed her character over Irish coffee. In the miniseries, Zoya seduced a nuclear scientist in order to lure him to the bad section of Paris where his murder could look accidental. Max had proposed that she might score points with the director if she suggested leaving the scientist's keys in the ignition of his unlocked car, so that its theft would add to the illusion. She did, and the director revised the scene.

Max confessed his white lie after receiving his reward the following evening. Then he asked her for another date.

Four years later, she actually was a spy leaving a car to be stolen.

As she closed the trunk, with the senator's raincoat and umbrella now in hand, Zoya saw a couple of boys wearing low-riding pants and big baseball caps approaching. The trunk noise caused them to look up and meet her eye. They didn't strike her as formal gang members, more like bored high school dropouts, but she was no expert on American inner-city youth.

She scurried back to the driver's seat and immediately locked the door. Rubbing her amulet for luck, she studied the two in the side mirror. They didn't give her a second glance. When they passed without slowing, she made a snap decision.

She lowered the passenger window. "Either of you guys have a driver's license?"

They stopped and then backed up, reversing themselves like a rewound video rather than turning around. "Say what?" The shorter, thicker boy asked.

"If either of you has a driver's license, you could make some money."

"How much?" the leader asked.

"Doin' what?" asked the taller one.

Both sets of hands remained plunged in pockets.

Zoya resisted the urge to look down and see what they might be holding. "Driving this car back to San Francisco for me earns you a thousand bucks each."

"This sweet ride?"

"San Francisco?"

"Interested?" Zoya asked.

"Hell yeah."

"What's the catch?"

Zoya gave them her conspiratorial shrug and put a bit of mischief in her eye. "It's my ex's car. I needed to borrow it, and now I can't take it back."

The two looked at each other, then backed away to converse in private. But only for a moment. Their next words were as predicted. "Show us the money."

"He pays. When you deliver to the address on the registration. Otherwise, how do I know you won't just sell the car? It cost over sixty thousand dollars just nine months ago. You could easily get twenty, twenty-five, maybe even thirty thousand for it, even without the title. So you need incentive."

Again the two backed up and put their capped heads together. Their words weren't decipherable, but their excitement was as evident as the conspiratorial looks on their faces.

Sixty seconds later Zoya was alone on the wet pavement beneath a pink paisley umbrella, wearing a golden raincoat over black 49ers sweats, and holding pitifully little in her pockets. She had a stolen Chevron card, four dollars in change, a box of TicTac mints, a bottle of water, and a company name.

Vulcan Fisher.

She had come to Seattle to find Max. Now all she had to do — as a hunted spy, on enemy territory, without a car or computer or contacts or cash — was figure out how.

Chapter 64
Sleeveless

Seattle, Washington

IN *WAYWARD DAYS*, Zoya played a woman who runs away from her abusive husband, a major in the Moscow City Police. At the start of her signature scene, she awakes from a concussive blow, and experiences clarity of thought despite her throbbing headache. She rounds up all the valuables in their apartment, and storms out with a vow never to return.

Her first stop is a pawn shop. Arriving with a bruised face, disheveled hair, and a wild gaze, she dumps her plunder on the counter. It's quite a haul, as it includes a large stash of watches and jewelry that her husband had either accepted as bribes or pilfered from drunks. In a hallmark moment, the unctuous thug behind the counter asks, "Anything else?" once they agreed on the price for each piece. "Just one more thing," she replies, slipping off her wedding ring and flicking it onto the pile. That's when the police arrive, and her wayward days begin.

Despite it being the scene that won her the Golden Eagle nomination, Zoya wasn't hoping for a repeat performance as she dropped Jas's wedding and engagement rings onto the counter at Seattle Pawn. Nonetheless, she expected that her expression was just as contemptuous as it had been in the movie. The engagement ring wasn't the one Max had given her, of course. Ignaty Filippov had swapped Max's out for one he called "more Western." She held the gaudy bauble in the same esteem that a slave would her collar — but of course she didn't show it.

"How much you looking for?" the pawn broker asked after a quick, initial appraisal.

"I know what they're worth, so you can drop the act. My ex paid $15,000 for the set just six months ago. I'll settle for $10,000."

"Where'd he buy them?" the broker asked, suspicion in his eyes.

Zoya thought fast. Could experts tell where jewelry was from? Did it matter? Or was he just trying to rattle her. "Moscow."

The man emitted a satisfied chuff and brought the jeweler's loupe back to his eye. Fifteen minutes later, Zoya left the little shop with $7,500 cash in her hand, and hope in her heart.

She took a cab to Pacific Place mall and found her way to the dress section of Barneys New York, where she began looking for a very specific item. She didn't find anything close to what she needed. BCBG Max Azria was similarly disappointing, although it yielded suitable shoes and undergarments. She was almost ready to search for a fabric store when a dress at Club Monaco caught her eye. The style was entirely wrong with a scoop neck and long sleeves, but the color was a perfect rendition of the striking violet purple she needed. "Do you have this in a size two?"

They did, and the dress looked custom fit.

At the checkout counter, Zoya asked another question. "May I borrow your scissors?"

"Of course."

While the sales associate looked on with wide eyes, Zoya carefully cut off both sleeves and turned the scoop neck into a V. "Much too hot out, don't you think?"

As Zoya held the defiled dress up to admire her work, the sales associate said, "You're not going to be able to return it now."

Zoya had to laugh at that one.

Her outburst brought a smile to the clerk's face as well. "No one's ever done that before."

Zoya gave her a wink. "I prefer setting trends, to following them. Where's the ladies room?"

The girl inclined her head. "Just outside to the right."

Appraising her handiwork in the bathroom mirror, Zoya had a mixed reaction. On the upside, she'd achieved the look she was going for. On the downside, she appeared a lot older than the reference image imprinted on her mind's eye. This gave her pause.

No woman enjoyed aging, but the process was particularly distressing for actresses. Although actors benefited from increasing opportunities until age 46, the numbers were depressingly different for their female counterparts. Actresses' careers peaked at 30, and it was almost always downhill from there.

Standing there studying herself in the mirror of a mall bathroom with 30 nearly a decade behind her, Zoya asked herself if she wanted to continue fighting what was ultimately a losing battle. Wouldn't she be better off getting out on top and moving on to something else, like Gwyneth Paltrow had? But what? *My how the last few weeks were affecting her in unexpected ways.*

Zoya wasn't sure if her fresh perspective was a good or bad thing. What she did know was that the prospect of embracing any old role, just so long as it allowed her to keep acting, had become a lot less appealing.

Still, what alternative did she have?

That, of course, was a question for another day. For now she had her hands full just ensuring that she'd have a future beyond bars. The next few hours would be crucial in that regard.

Chapter 65
Purple Flowers

Seattle, Washington

ESPIONAGE was hardly routine work, but it routinely involved repetitive work. Mind-numbing jobs as far from the glamor of James Bond as suburban Seattle was from MI6. Jobs the campus recruiters never mentioned when they came calling.

Max was in the midst of one of those grinds now. To get to the excitement of intercepting Vulcan Fisher's shipment to Boeing, he first had to find out *who* was doing the shipping, and then *when*. Thus the mind-numbing task of watching trucks come and go.

He had installed a video camera on the light pole directly across the street from Vulcan Fisher's main entrance drive. It was a bit distant, but the only electrified alternative, atop the Vulcan Fisher bus stop, was too risky. The guard hut was just a hundred feet away, and bored public transit riders were constantly milling about. Someone would surely spot his camera, and either steal or confiscate it.

After a few minutes of watching the live feed, Max decided to watch the recording instead — at a much faster speed. 10X proved to be too fast. He might miss a truck if his mind wandered or his eyes averted for more than a single second. But 5X was tolerable. His schedule evolved from that. Every five hours, he'd set aside his other work, grab a large coffee, and sit for sixty minutes with his eyes glued to the screen. Still a shit-sandwich of a job, but cut into bite-size pieces.

In between surveillance sessions, he divided his time between investigating the companies whose trucks he'd seen coming and going, and working out the plan's other details. He found sources for trucks and uniforms. He identified warehouse spaces available to lease and made appointments to see them. He ordered Vulcan Fisher signage. Pulling off an illusion required a lot of attention to detail.

As his second day of reconnaissance drew to a close, Max figured he was in decent shape. He'd identified twelve potential shippers, and had winnowed the dozen down to just three by excluding those that weren't a match due to cargo type or weight or destination. Wang's guy was already at work hacking into those three while Max continued the grind. He'd force himself to keep at it until they identified the one shipper delivering autopilot systems to Boeing.

Max had just finished the last sip of his latest coffee when he slapped the pause button and stared at the screen. He was looking at a contradiction. Something he couldn't mistake, and yet something that couldn't be true.

He zoomed in on the bottom right side of his screen. The Vulcan Fisher bus stop was a typical city structure, with a roof, back, and single sidewall. This one had a not-so-subtle billboard advertising Callie's Club.

Max had learned to ignore that quadrant of the screen during his surveillance sessions. He was afraid of getting so mesmerized by people-watching that he'd fail to notice the arriving and departing trucks. But his eye had been drawn by a purple dress. It was an instinctive reaction to a flash of color, like a honeybee to a flower.

Pictures of beautiful women held special spots in the memories of most men. Some were iconic, most were sexy. For their breakthrough photos, Marilyn had posed in white, Farrah in red, and Zoya in purple. Each had managed to provoke the same primal reaction. All had been plastered across countless bedrooms and dorms.

With every click of the zoom, Max's heart grew and his head became more certain. It wasn't a look-alike or a hallucination or wishful thinking. The woman in the sleeveless purple dress actually was Zoya.

Impossible — and yet he'd bet his life on it.

He looked at the video's timestamp. Ninety minutes ago.

Swapping over to the live feed, he held his breath while it connected. *Please! Please! Please!*

She was there! Zoya was still at the bus stop. She was alone with three younger guys, all sporting well-worn flannel shirts and lustful stares.

Chapter 66
First Things First

Seattle, Washington

MAX'S RENTAL CAR was a mid-size blue Ford, a perfect combination of unremarkable and peppy. He took full advantage of peppy as he raced toward Vulcan Fisher with foxhole prayers spewing from his lips. Being unremarkable would come in handy when he arrived, if his prayers were answered and Zoya was still there.

Among the thousands of questions he had for his fiancée, the most pressing was if she was under surveillance. Was she bait? Or was there another, far more complicated story?

He covered the four miles in as many minutes and caught a glorious glimpse of purple from a hundred yards away. Zoya was still out in front of the covered bench, dangling like a lure, but clutching a silver Club Monaco bag. She'd walked all the way to the curb as though she were trying to hail a cab, but the intent seemed to be to get away from the flannel shirts. They'd risen and were standing behind her like hyenas who'd cornered a gazelle.

Max's plan was to conduct careful countersurveillance. He'd confirm her presence from the far lane at cruising speed, then double back, park at a distance, and search for watchers on foot. That plan went out the window when one of the men reached out for Zoya's shoulder.

Max floored the gas, swerved into the curb lane, and slammed the brakes just before the bus stop. His Ford screeched to a stop with the back tire thunking against the curb inches from Zoya's feet. He leaned over, pushed the passenger door open, and yelled in Russian, "Zoya get in!"

As soon as her right ankle cleared the door, Max hit the gas, rocketing the car ahead and slamming the door closed. "Is anyone watching you?" he asked, his foot to the floor, his eyes darting furiously between the traffic ahead and the traffic behind, scanning for openings and searching for pursuit.

"No."

"Are you sure?" he asked. With a stroke of good luck, he caught a green arrow and took the left turn at 50 mph.

"I escaped in San Francisco. Drove here through the night. Nobody followed." Her voice was fraught with deep emotions. Fear, relief, and surprise.

Max was consoled but confused. He didn't slow down. Better safe than sorry. "I've been so worried about you! I've been going out of my mind ever since you hit the panic button. Ignaty told me it was an accident. I wanted to believe him, but I didn't."

"I hit it when someone showed up at the island. He shot me with a tranquilizer just after I sent off my report."

"Who was it?" Max interrupted.

"I don't know. By the time I woke up he was dead, as was my support team."

"What!" Max looked over into Zoya's eyes, and his heart melted.

"When I awoke, Achilles had me tied up on a boat."

Max reached over and stroked her thigh. "But you escaped? For real? Achilles didn't let you get away so you'd lead him to me?"

"No way. I got away when his friend was killed. And he doesn't know about Seattle. We never discussed your mission. Never even broached the topic. He was completely focused on his own mission and predicament." Zoya was speaking fast, as if she couldn't wait to get the words out.

Max interrupted her. "Throw everything out the window just in case. Everything you had with you on the island. Everything he gave you." He lowered her window.

She looked down at her shopping bag, then tossed it.

"What about the clothes you're wearing?"

"I just bought these."

"No phone?"

"No phone."

"Great." He reached out and stroked her thigh. "Please continue with the story."

She did, and what a story it was.

Max was in a hurry to get Zoya back to his room, but her tale was so enthralling that he feared accidentally hitting a pedestrian or rear-ending another car. Making a flash decision, he took a dangerous turn from the far lane into a Walmart where he proceeded to perform a series of evasive maneuvers in the huge parking lot that would either shake or expose any tail. Satisfied that they were indeed alone, he hid the Ford between two vans in the employee back lot, and turned to the love of his life.

As Zoya described her journey from Hawaii to San Francisco to Seattle, he couldn't believe that she'd managed to keep her wits and composure about her throughout it all. He felt love and pride welling up inside, overwhelming the fear and doubt that had inhabited his heart for the last few days.

He gave her thigh a big squeeze. "That was a brilliant move on your part, waiting at a place you knew I'd be passing, wearing an outfit you knew would catch my eye."

Zoya blushed, her smile dislodging a few tears of joy. "I didn't know what else to do. I'd thought about going to the consulate in San Francisco. The moment Achilles gave the Hawaiian airline ticket agent our destination, it crossed my mind. But later he actually warned me that the CIA had eyes and ears there."

Max used the back of his finger to wipe away her tears. "That would have been a bad idea anyway. We're supposed to be vacationing in Sochi. Korovin and Ignaty would both have had fits if anyone learned otherwise. Maybe if you'd completed your mission, but it wouldn't have gone well if you'd added a security breach to a failure."

Zoya's face scrunched.

"I'm sorry," Max said. "That was insensitive."

"That's not it. Well, not entirely. I didn't fail! I got most of the plan from Achilles."

"And they know that?"

"Of course."

"Then why didn't they pull you out?"

"I'd literally just sent the message when the guy with the tranquilizer gun showed up. Ignaty had me using some old-fashioned code."

"A manual transliteration cypher."

"That's it. Took forever."

Max was all too familiar with one-time pads. The SVR liked them because they were unbreakable even in the face of American and Chinese supercomputers. If you didn't have the pad, you couldn't break the code. Period. "What do you mean by *most* of the plan?"

"The CIA discovered that Korovin occasionally slips his bodyguard on purpose."

"When? Where? How?"

"Achilles didn't say."

Max thought about that for a sec. "It doesn't matter, not if you can ask Korovin himself for the details. You could have sent the *mission-accomplished* signal."

"I wasn't certain at the time."

Max exhaled a long sigh of relief. "Well that changes everything."

"What do we do now?"

He flashed his eyebrows. "First things first."

Chapter 67
Changing Plans

Seattle, Washington

WITHIN SECONDS of Zoya completing her story, she and Max were making out in the Walmart parking lot like teenagers shipping off to war. Max eventually came up for air. "Let's buy you a quick change of clothes, then get back to my room."

Zoya reached for her door handle. "Sounds good. Can we stop for dinner on the way? I'm starving."

"I'd rather avoid public places for a while. We're probably safe if the boys took the Caddy to a chop shop. They'd kill the GPS first thing. But if the boys actually are driving it back to San Francisco, Achilles will shift the hunt to Seattle the moment they're caught. He'll have every cop in this place carrying our photos in no time."

Zoya shook her head. "I'm not sure Achilles will involve anybody else. Remember, he needed me to prove his innocence. Without me, he'll be forced to avoid the authorities."

Max hadn't considered that. "You're probably right. But we need to factor in that your escape changes his situation. He may be desperate, and desperate people can be unpredictable. Illogical. Anyway, just to be safe, we'll eat at my hotel. The food is nothing special, but it's not bad."

Zoya looked happy with the idea. Giddy even. "Okay. Then what?"

"Then we make love until morning. In the morning we'll watch the news and go from there. We may need to change rooms. We might be better off staying put. Kinda depends."

They were in and out of Walmart in under ten minutes, toting a bag of generic clothes. Max then drove his fiancée back to his hotel as planned, but their love making didn't wait until after dinner. Since the purple dress was so eye-catching, he wanted her to change before going down to dinner. But the moment she slipped the dress off her slender shoulders, the dinner plan was postponed.

As he pushed her back onto the bed, the images that had haunted his dreams and hijacked his idle mind came calling like marauders at a tea party. Zoya and Achilles sharing a bed, sharing a bath, sharing whatever the American saw fit. It was the last thing he wanted on his mind at that moment, so of course it appeared.

Zoya sensed the intrusion. "What is it?"

Max didn't know what to say. But he also couldn't keep silent. "Did he . . . Was he . . ."

"Max, don't!" Zoya put a finger to his lips. "Just don't. I love you."

"I know, but you . . ." He grimaced as his unfortunate choice of pronoun wounded her like a twisting knife.

"Don't you tell me what *I* did! I did what I had to do. If you didn't like it, the time to speak up was at Seaside."

"But—"

"No! No buts. I don't want to talk about it ever again. You understand? You've never been the jealous type. Don't start now. If you need to talk about it, you talk about it with someone else. I'm not going to relive it. Not now. Not ever."

Max held up his hands. "Okay. You're right. I'm sorry."

Zoya rolled over and sat up on the edge of the bed. "Now feed me. I'm hungry. Then after dinner I want a hot shower." Her voice transitioned from commanding to playful as she spoke, and Max knew they'd be okay. "A long, hot, soapy shower."

They grabbed a corner table and sat facing the TV mounted over their heads in order to minimize the exposure of their faces to the other guests, most of whom appeared Asian. That night's menu was pork chops with sauerkraut. Not bad.

While the television looped repetitive news, and Max pictured the headlines soon to come, Zoya ate two chops with a mixed salad and buttered rolls. More calories than Max had ever seen her consume in one meal — with the possible exception of a box of Godiva chocolates.

He was on his second free beer when a photo of Senator Collins appeared on the screen, followed by one of Achilles in a Team USA jersey. "They're blaming Achilles." He spoke low and in Russian, once the story yielded to a car commercial. "He must have run. That's perfect."

"Why is that perfect?"

"It means he's isolated. So he's not talking. The APB will also hamper his movements. Hard for him to come after *you* when *he's* on the run."

"So you think we're safe?"

"I think we've got good news to report."

"Can the report wait?"

The look in Zoya's eyes sent a wave of relief flooding over Max. "It can wait."

He was feeling like a new man as they returned to the room. The night before, he'd drudged back to the second floor with a world of worry weighing heavily on his shoulders. Tonight he was practically skipping.

"Race you to the shower," Zoya said, as his card key chimed a greeting.

He chased after her, right into the muzzle of a gun.

Chapter 68
Poof!

Seattle, Washington

THERE WERE TIMES and places and means for defeating firearms pointed in your face, but Max knew this wasn't one of them. The Glock's muzzle was four feet from his nose — too close to dodge, too far to grab. The man wielding it held a second gun pointed at Max's right thigh. That was the hot trigger, Max knew. There'd be no hesitation. Not from this man. Not from Achilles.

"Well played," Max said. "I'm impressed. Zoya was certain the Collins' murder wasn't an act, and she's obviously a pro when it comes to acting." He was talking to buy thinking time. His world had just turned upside down. He needed to adapt and analyze.

His immediate read was that his was a lose-lose situation. Either the American government would kill him, or Korovin would. At the moment, he was in custody on a capital offense. A captured spy. If he escaped, he'd be an operative who had failed his president on a pet mission of grave strategic importance. There was no way to win — without rewriting the rules.

But he had to win, because Zoya was in the same boat. HE HAD TO WIN! "I'm sure you have a lot of questions. Shall we take a seat?"

Achilles cocked his head, sending that dimpled chin of his toward the left, away from the door. "You know the drill. Put your hands behind your head. Turn around. Get on your knees."

Max didn't resist. His body went along while his mind worked the problem. A problem that also included a beautiful Russian woman holding a Ruger on Zoya. Acting on impulse, he addressed her, his charm on full display. "You must be Katya. It's a pleasure to meet you. We have so much in common."

Katya didn't bite.

Max pressed on. "We both made sacrifices that included giving our loves to another for the sake of a mission."

Achilles kicked him hard in the back, propelling him face down onto the floor where a foot pressed him down while rock-hard hands zip-tied his wrists behind his waist.

Max didn't struggle. With Zoya in the picture, he knew that the smart move was to focus on the mental fight while yielding to the physical. He had to find a way to turn his lose-lose scenario into a win-win. A win for him *and* a win for Achilles.

Max locked on Zoya's big browns with a sideways glance. The fear that met his eyes put a pick through his heart. He blew a kiss, but then closed his eyes. He had to concentrate.

"Coast is clear," he heard Katya say. The first words she had uttered.

Max felt himself being lifted to his feet. Picked up by his waistband and collar like a bag of garden bark. Achilles was extraordinarily strong, and he seemed to want Max to know it.

"Not a peep. Not a trip. Not a fumble," Achilles growled before pushing Max out the door.

They didn't head for the emergency exit, the back stairwell that would dump them in the parking lot and presumably a waiting car. Instead Achilles guided them toward the lobby.

But they didn't go far.

Achilles pushed him into a room across the hall and three doors down.

The extended stay suites all had separate bedrooms and living areas, but this room was a double. Two bedrooms divided by a combination living/cooking/eating area. Achilles pushed Max toward the dining table and said, "Take the seat facing the window. Zoya, you're to his left, facing the TV."

Max's neurons were practically steaming from overuse by the time additional zip ties cinched his shins to the chair legs with their trademark hum. And then it appeared. Poof! Like one of those drone videos, where a quiet Pakistani shack instantaneously transforms into a big gray cloud. An utter and instantaneous change of circumstance. Only this one was constructive. Max had his win-win plan.

Chapter 69
Revelations

Seattle, Washington

ACHILLES WANTED to sigh as he cinched the last zip tie into place, but of course he couldn't show relief. Relief implied prior weakness, and the circumstances called for nothing but strength.

He had a fine line to walk in the coming hours, and perhaps days. Negotiating successfully with a mind of Max's caliber would require both bluster and bluffing.

Achilles recognized Max when he got his first good look at him in the Walmart parking lot. That was when he did the research that pinged positive on a CIA database. Zoya's boyfriend was known to be a senior operative of the SVR, Russia's foreign intelligence service. His appearance did resemble that of a British aristocrat, and reportedly he could speak both English and German without a Russian accent.

Suddenly Zoya's Seattle run made perfect sense.

But it also raised the question of what Max was up to. He was too far from Hawaii to be working with her in any kind of supportive role. He may as well have stayed in Russia. If he wasn't there to support her, then why?

Apparently his assignment included a deep cover role, as even Zoya didn't have the means to contact him directly. The bus stop move proved that. So what was Max doing in Seattle?

Zoya interrupted his thoughts. "How did you find me? I was certain I wasn't being followed. Was it satellites?"

"Technically, yes. GPS. I put a tracker in your necklace."

Zoya gasped, as her hand flew to her neck.

"We'd planned to intercept you at the consulate. But you ditched the car in a rather creative way, so on a hunch we decided to watch you. Then you hit the pawn shop and went clothes shopping, and we really got intrigued. It was Katya who figured out what you were doing at the bus stop. She recognized your outfit from a famous photograph."

Achilles turned to Max. "As for you, Agent Aristov, we've got a lot to discuss. I'm sure you're aware that I'm not with the judicial branch of the government. I don't get points for frying spies. Of course, the moment I pick up that phone and call Seattle PD, or the FBI, or some other agency, the scorecard becomes exactly that. Your skin. I'm hoping we can avoid that."

"You're not going to pick up the phone, regardless," Max said. "That would be MAD. Mutually assured destruction. The first person arrested would be you."

"You think?"

"I think I don't even need a phone. I think I could get you arrested just by screaming, right here, right now. 'It's the guy from the TV! The one who killed the senator! That Olympian! Help! He's tied me up!' Some dumb hick might even burst in, recognize you, and free me. Or get shot trying."

Achilles maintained a neutral face, although he suspected that Max might be right. Putting some scorn into his voice, he opened their poker match with a bluff. "The TV report was just a ploy to get you to drop your guard. The APB has already been cancelled."

Max's retort was just as quick and forceful. "No, it hasn't. I know that because I know why it was issued in the first place." Max paused there for a moment before adding, "I'm guessing that you don't."

"Don't try to bluff me," Achilles pushed back. "Your best play here is to win my confidence. *I* called 9-1-1. Zoya knows that to be a fact. Then the medics saw me."

Max smiled and shook his head. "You and I both know that forensics aren't that quick. We also know it takes time to give the green light to get the media involved with something so sensitive. Lawsuits launch and careers crash when reporting jumps the gun. We're talking about a ranking senator and an Olympic hero."

Achilles hated to ask. From a negotiating standpoint it was a weak move. But intuition inclined him to play along nonetheless. Max was looking more like a man with a plan than a cornered cat. Achilles wanted to know that plan. "You have another explanation for the rapid response?"

Max didn't smile or gloat. He simply laid it out as one would to a friend. "The alert went out because President Silver personally gave the order."

Chapter 70
The Proposal

Seattle, Washington

ACHILLES SUSPECTED Silver's direct involvement in issuing the APB for his arrest, but it still pained him to hear a stranger say it aloud.

Rather than let it rattle him, he studied his opponent. Max obviously wanted to be asked how he could possibly have that information, so Achilles asked himself instead.

The answer came quickly.

The Russians had a source in the White House. That fit the bigger puzzle. The same source had tipped Korovin off about Achilles' mission.

Katya rose. "I'm going to make some tea."

Achilles kept his eyes on Max. "You're offering a trade? Your freedom for the identity of the White House leak?"

Max flashed his eyebrows in a surprisingly disarming manner. "I'm glad to see that your mind moves quickly. That will serve us well, given what's ahead."

This time Achilles did bite. "And what exactly is ahead?"

"The national media is broadcasting the warrant for your arrest, because the president of the United States thinks you've betrayed him and your country. The SVR is sending assassins after you, because President Korovin personally wants you dead. At this point, your odds of surviving until the end of the week are a long shot to say the least."

Achilles wasn't going to let Max derail him. "Well then it's a good thing I've got you to corroborate my story."

"Corroborate what? Your secret assignment to assassinate the Russian president? There are only two people besides Silver you're cleared to talk with about that. One's dead and the other's in a coma. You can't get to Silver without exposing your relationship, which would be treasonous. And of course Silver will shoot you himself if you disclose his plan to anybody else. As the final strap on your straitjacket, it's well known in intelligence circles that the Director of the CIA would love to see you discredited, so your old friends aren't going to help."

Achilles was astounded by the breadth of Max's knowledge. Whoever was tipping the Russians off had to be as close to Silver as the First Lady. "I've still got contacts."

"I'm sure you do. But reaching out would put them in a pickle, be risky for you, and messy all around."

With Katya's expression becoming ever more panic-stricken, and Zoya looking as perplexed and intrigued as he felt, Achilles decided it was time to ask. "What are you proposing?"

Max flashed a smile. "What's my position?"

Katya put four white mugs of tea on the table. Of course, only she and Achilles could drink it. The others had their hands tied behind their backs. As she looked at him over her mug, Achilles realized that was Katya's point. Nice.

He decided to table the White House leak for the moment. Things were complicated enough without it. "Your position is that you and your girl have been caught spying in America. Regardless of what happens to me, you'll both be looking at dying in a dark cell if I pick up that phone."

Again, Max surprised him. "Actually, our position is worse than that. We're dead whether we cut a deal with you or not. Korovin either kills us for failing, or he kills us for talking. Your president sent an assassin after you when he thought you'd betrayed him. Surely you don't think Korovin is any softer?"

Max was right. Politicians of presidential caliber didn't tolerate loose ends — and the Russian version of disavowal was even more extreme than the American. "What kind of a deal are you looking for then?"

"Actually, there's no deal you can offer us."

"We have witness protection."

"And you think that program is more secure than the White House?"

Again Max had a point.

Now Zoya was looking panicked, while Katya had become perplexed. Achilles, on the other hand, was totally intrigued. "I'm listening."

Max met each of the women's eyes in turn, then stopped with his gaze locked on Achilles'. "My proposal is straightforward and simple. I'm proposing that we work together to complete your initial mission."

"My initial mission," Achilles repeated.

"That's right. In exchange for our freedom, I'll help you assassinate President Korovin."

Chapter 71
Double Down

Seattle, Washington

ACHILLES TURNED to Katya while digesting the startling offer, not bothering to hide his surprise. *Max wanted to help him kill Korovin.* He considered taking her off to the corner to talk in private, but he didn't want to give Max and Zoya an opportunity to sync. Besides, what would be the point? This wasn't a typical negotiation. Despite the picture Max had tried to paint, the power of position was all Achilles.

Katya spoke first. "I can't fault his logic."

"I can't either. But I'm sure there's a catch or three." Achilles turned back to Max. "Who's the White House leak?"

"You're testing me."

"Of course. But I'm also giving you a chance to start earning my trust."

Max looked down at the steaming mug before him. "Discussions are always easier over tea."

"First the name. Then the tea. We'll have plenty more to discuss."

"Agreed. The truth is, I don't know the name. I'm not even entirely sure there is a name."

"You mean the leak is electronic?"

"Could be. The information is extremely high level, and often detailed, but very hit or miss."

"Like you can only hear discussions taking place in a certain room?"

"Exactly. Furthermore, it can't be tasked. We can't request specific information. If we could, Korovin would have learned the details of his security gap that way and the whole Hawaiian fiasco could have been avoided. As it is, all he learned was that you had been tasked with his assassination."

Again Katya said, "I can't fault his logic."

Achilles couldn't help but be moved by Max's revelation. If nothing else, his rival had just given away a huge bargaining chip. Achilles could not dismiss the possibility that this was a gambit, a sacrifice designed to put him in check a few moves down the line. But he also couldn't make the mistake of failing to act for lack of perfect information. "That's worth a left hand."

Achilles zip-tied Max's and Zoya's right hands to the backs of their chairs. Then he freed their left arms with his pocket knife.

Once the four of them had enjoyed a few sips of Lipton, he hit Max with the big question. "Even working together, how could we possibly get to Korovin? He just completed a very sophisticated mission to uncover the one weakness the CIA identified. No doubt it's already plugged."

"If I tell you how, do we have a deal?"

"Specifically?"

"Once Korovin is dead, we go free. Directly. No side trips to Langley or elsewhere."

Achilles looked around the table. He wondered if there'd been as unlikely a meeting since Potsdam. Top spies from two rival nations. Paired with two of the world's most beautiful women. Working out the assassination of the world's most powerful man. Over tea. Geopolitics in its most basic and perhaps most efficient form.

This was what Achilles lived for. "My mission's not that simple anymore. With Lukin gone, either Sobko or Grachev would become Russia's next president. Neither would be acceptable to Silver or the State Department or the American people."

"Surely you don't want to leave Korovin in place?"

"Surely I don't want to trade bad for worse — which either Grachev or Sobko might well be. I also don't want to disregard the spirit of my assignment. Silver's play wasn't just removing Korovin. His ultimate goal was improving U.S.-Russian relations. I'd think you'd share that goal, as it will improve the plight of the Russian people. At the moment, your compatriots are slowly suffocating under a cloud of sanctions."

Max finished off his tea, then met Achilles' eye with a rock-steady gaze. "So what are *you* proposing?"

Achilles was glad to be back in the driver's seat. "I'm telling you that we have a deal, but only if we take your proposal one step further. If you want to earn your freedom, you'll have to help me eliminate Sobko and Grachev as well as Korovin."

Chapter 72
The Bad Part

Seattle, Washington

ACHILLES WATCHED Max spin his mug on the table as he contemplated the counterproposal. Max wasn't taking the triple elimination demand lightly. Achilles saw that as a good sign. Sobko and Grachev didn't have Korovin's level of protection, but as leading members of parliament, they still surrounded themselves with machine-gun toting muscle.

Max brought his hand down on the spinning mug. "We'll have to deal with them first. Once Korovin's gone, they'll become paranoid. And rightly so, as each will be trying to eliminate the other, one way or another in order to snare the presidency."

"Agreed," Achilles said, noting that Max had become uneasy.

Max looked up as if reading Achilles' mind. "I don't have a plan for them."

"Nor do I. But they'll be much easier than Korovin."

"Easier, but far from easy. They're both well protected." Max canted his head and stared into his own mind. "Still, between us, I'm sure we can figure something out."

Achilles stood, presumably to stretch but really to study Zoya's reaction to what Max was saying. Although he was all too familiar with her exceptional acting skills, Achilles believed he read genuine surprise in Zoya's eyes.

Katya must have picked up on that as well, as she shook things up a bit. "What will the two of you do, once Korovin's dead? Will you try to somehow slip back into your former lives?"

"That's something we have yet to work out," Max said, looking at Zoya. "Obviously, this scenario wasn't planned. Whatever we decide, it will be better than the current alternatives."

"Okay then," Achilles said. "How do we get to Korovin?"

Max flexed his right shoulder forward. A gentleman's request.

Achilles had searched Max thoroughly, from his scalp to his shoes. He'd confiscated his cell phone, and with some satisfaction had removed his amulet. Max wouldn't pose a threat even without his ankles incapacitated. Achilles had ten years and forty pounds on him. So while

Katya refreshed everyone's tea, Achilles went ahead and freed both his captives' right arms.

Zoya immediately began rubbing her newly-freed wrist.

Max just brought his right hand up to join his left around his mug. "I'm sure you know of Korovin's great distrust of electronic communications. It's been widely publicized in the popular media. It comes from the years he spent as an intelligence operative. They convinced him that electronic transmissions were *never* safe."

Nods all around the table.

Achilles noted that Zoya seemed just as interested in hearing this as he and Katya were.

Max continued with all eyes locked on his. "I'm sure you're also familiar with the speculation surrounding Korovin's wealth. While the amounts reported in the press are always guesstimates, they're usually twelve figures. Hundreds of billions." He paused, allowing them to orient. "I did the math once. If you've got a billion dollars, you could spend ten thousand dollars an hour, every hour, for ten years and still have over a hundred million dollars left. So one billion is already more than anyone should be able to spend in a lifetime. And Korovin's probably got at least a hundred billion. None of it legally obtained, of course."

Achilles could only smile at the thought that he and Max had both made the same calculation.

"This combination — his distrust of electronic communication, combined with his need to conceal and manage extreme wealth — leaves Korovin with a unique problem."

Achilles liked where this was going, and chimed in. "A problem further complicated by an extremely high profile, and the knowledge that hundreds of thousands of people want him removed from office."

"Exactly. Who can you trust with a hundred billion stolen dollars? That's perhaps Korovin's most tightly guarded secret. I doubt anyone but Korovin himself knows."

"Other than you," Achilles said.

"Other than me," Max echoed.

"And how do *you* happen to know?"

Max spread his hands. "A mixture of serendipity, coincidence, and professional curiosity."

Achilles could buy that. He'd press for the details later. "Do you have a plan for using that information to kill him?"

"I have some ideas, but we'll need to refine them on the ground. In Switzerland. Which brings me to the part no one's going to like. Nobody at this table will be happy with my proposition. Not you, not Katya, not Zoya, and not me."

Chapter 73
Difficult Choices

Seattle, Washington

KATYA GREW UP in Moscow during the collapse of the Soviet Union and Russia's tortuous transition from communism to capitalism. Crazy times, but she did her best to ignore the chaos by focusing intently on her education.

The strategy worked out well. She earned her degree from the same doctoral program that produced some of the world's greatest mathematicians, including five Fields Medal winners. Even after meeting Colin Achilles and realizing that she might one day move from Moscow, Katya remained faithful to her nose-to-the-books plan. Again her diligence produced the desired result. She secured a highly-coveted postdoctoral position at Stanford University.

Then Colin was killed, and in the aftermath his brother entered her life. To save her from the same assassins, Achilles dragged Katya halfway around the world and back. With both their lives on the line and no classroom in sight, they solved Colin's murder and much more. Rather than becoming flustered or frightened by the novelty and danger, Katya found the experience fascinating. Perhaps more so in retrospect than at the time, but the realization that she enjoyed it was a shocking bit of self-discovery nonetheless.

Today she was getting a replay of that deep dive into the lies of spies.

Sitting in a hotel room across from Max and Achilles, Katya found herself regarding the experience as a gift. She'd been invited to history's table. She was participating in a spy summit — and she was loving it.

It was an experience she wouldn't trade for anything.

Well, almost.

Maybe.

Just a day earlier, Stanford had offered her a tenure-track faculty position. Tenure. At Stanford. In her line of work, it didn't get any better than that. The offer was the grand culmination of a great dream. The prize at the end of her lifelong race.

But it was an anchoring position.

Professors bought houses.

Achilles' lifestyle was about as diametrically opposed to a professor's as it was possible to get. He trotted the globe, assignment to assignment, for weeks and months at a time. Forget the white picket fence; he didn't even carry a suitcase.

Would he ever give that up?

Could he turn his back on Silver?

She doubted it. And she couldn't blame him. Not after experiencing this. The logical conclusion was as inescapable as it was unavoidable. She was going to have to choose.

But this wasn't the time for that discussion. For once, she was happy to have a good reason for procrastination.

She returned her focus to Max. He was about to reveal his grand plan.

"The part of the plan that you're not going to like," Max said, "relates to my current assignment. It's very high-profile. Korovin personally recruited me for it, and his chief strategist, a bald little mustached prick named Ignaty Filippov is keeping close personal track of my progress. There's no way I can leave it unattended."

Surely, Katya thought, he wasn't maneuvering to stay in Seattle while Achilles flew off to Europe alone? That would be an obvious trap. Was Max proposing to send Zoya with Achilles, as a hostage of sorts? Katya didn't like that idea either, but for an altogether different reason.

Achilles' face remained stoic. "What are you proposing?"

"My job here is largely coordinating the work of a third party. A non-Russian. I'm going to propose that while you and I run off to Moscow and Switzerland, Zoya and Katya stay here to manage my guy."

Katya felt her heart skip a beat. Was Max seriously attempting to draft her into an espionage operation against America?

Achilles' cool reaction shocked her further still. "Doesn't Ignaty have you under surveillance?"

"No. He's too big on operations security for that. We speak on a daily basis, but that's VOIP over TOR so my location is masked."

Achilles nodded. Clearly, that acronym jumble made sense to him. "Tell me about the U.S. operation."

Achilles' tone and Max's demeanor both tightened with that question. They both knew that Max would be crossing the Rubicon by answering.

Max took a deep breath. "It's industrial espionage. The target is Vulcan Fisher. I'm sure you heard about the defense contract they just won, the largest in history. Well, Korovin is determined to learn all about it."

Katya found her thoughts drifting to Zoya while Max went on about space lasers and satellite communications. Zoya wasn't just strikingly beautiful, she was interesting. Her large features broadcast both energy and emotion. At the moment, she was maintaining a statuesque facade, but on the screen Katya had seen her shift from shy to sultry in a heartbeat.

What charms had she used on Achilles? How had she chosen to ply secrets from him? Had she drawn him into the illusion by playing the frisky vixen? The attentive nurse? The worried wife in need of consoling? How had she faked familiarity their first time? Was she a method actor? Had she convinced herself that she loved him to make it real? Had she enjoyed it? Had he? Did he picture her naked when he looked at her now?

"I don't believe you," Achilles said, his tone yanking Katya back to the present. "You're lying. Korovin's not going to have his chief strategist personally running an industrial espionage assignment. There's got to be more to it than that. Much more."

By the time she'd refocused, Achilles was on his feet with two guns out and pointing.

Zoya's mask broke, revealing fear. Max raised his arms, open palms facing forward. "The local mission is not relevant to our killing Korovin."

"So why lie about it?"

"We can't afford the distraction."

"If you think I'm leaving Katya here without a thorough understanding of what's going on, you're sadly mistaken. If you think I'm running off to Europe with you, without a vice-grip around your balls, you're delusional. You want a partner? You make me one. Otherwise, I'm picking up the phone and taking my chances."

Chapter 74
Casualty Counts

Seattle, Washington

ACHILLES HAD GUNS pointed at the chests of both Russians, but his eyes were locked on Max's.

"Tell him, kotyonok," Zoya said. "He's not bluffing."

Max shook his head back and forth, struggling visibly. When he stopped, his gaze was on Zoya. "The Vulcan Fisher project is Korovin's baby. If it stops moving, so do we."

Katya waded in, surprising everyone. "Nobody's telling you it has to stop. Zoya and I will keep it going."

"We haven't heard what it is yet," Achilles said.

Max nodded, acknowledging the validity of Achilles' conclusion. They hadn't heard.

Achilles didn't let up. "But you've got no chance of keeping it going if you don't tell me all about it, and quick."

Max's expression morphed from defeated to resigned. His shoulders slumped, and his voice lost its bluster. "Korovin calls it *Operation Sunset*. He's building a device that will allow him to crash airplanes into U.S. airports during the Thanksgiving travel rush."

"How many planes?" Katya blurted.

Max swallowed audibly. "Fifty."

"Fifty planes," Achilles repeated reflexively. He pictured the tailfin of a jumbo jet protruding from a flaming terminal, then multiplied the image by fifty. "That will start a war. But unlike Bin Laden, Korovin can't hide."

Max arched his eyebrows. "Korovin won't need to. It will look like a Chinese operation. Chinese money is funding it. Chinese workers are following Chinese blueprints to build it. And soon, Chinese operatives will covertly install it on fifty airplanes."

"Why make it look like a Chinese operation?" Katya asked.

"What kind of device?" Achilles asked.

Max turned to Katya first. "China is America's biggest creditor and trading partner. By straining U.S.-China relations, Korovin will weaken them both — and, of course, deflect blame from Russia. It's a brilliant strategy, and it's being expertly executed. He's going to wage and win this war for less than the cost of a single MiG jet."

While Katya chewed on that, Max turned back to Achilles. "As for the device, it's fundamentally very simple. He developed an override for the Vulcan Fisher autopilot system used on Boeing 737s. When powered off, the additional circuit board is completely undetectable, unless you happen to crack open the casing and compare what you see to the manufacturer's blueprint. When powered on, however, the circuit boards turn 737s into remote-controlled drones. They lock out manual control."

Achilles pondered that for a second, with chin resting on fist. "What if the autopilot system isn't engaged? What if the pilot is flying manually?"

"Doesn't matter. Like a phone that isn't being used, it can still be made to 'ring' at any time by dialing the right number."

"Surely the attack will be stopped after the first one or two planes go down. They'll never crash all fifty," Katya said, her voice barely above a whisper. "Not that one or two wouldn't be bad enough."

Max shook his head. "Do you have any idea how many commercial aircraft are in U.S. airspace during peak hours?"

Nobody replied.

Max met Katya's eye. "Over five thousand. Airplanes aren't making money if they're not in the air, so the airlines keep them in constant motion."

"God help us," Katya said, bringing hand to mouth.

"So Korovin's fifty planes will be less than one-percent of those flying," Achilles said. "Spreading resources way too thin. There will be pandemonium."

"Right. And nobody — not the pilots or their air traffic controllers — is going to be paying attention to anything but their own disaster during the first few minutes of each attack," Max added, meeting each of their eyes. "Think about that scene as it unravels in real time on the ground. During landing, 737s are still moving at about 150 miles per hour. To crash them into a terminal, Korovin will only need to alter their course by about half a mile. That's just ten seconds of flight time. By the time the pilots yell *Oh God!* and figure out they can't switch to manual, they'll be part of a flaming graveyard."

Max paused to allow the horrific scene to sink in before he continued painting the picture of *Operation Sunset*. "Ignaty will know the airline schedules ahead of time, and will aim for a zero hour that has all fifty in the air, and a bunch landing. His fifty drone pilots — working out of a warehouse in Shenzhen — will engage all the *Sunset* systems at once. Those that aren't landing will start a dive toward a close, previously-selected major airport terminal. Hysteria and confusion will reign for twenty minutes or so. Then the operation will be over, and the paralysis will begin."

"The paralysis?" Katya asked.

Max nodded, no joy in his eyes. "For starters, you'll still have about five thousand aircraft in the air. Many with no place to land. All afraid to be next. That's over a million hysterical people — people who, along with their families, are unlikely to ever fly again." Max began counting off points with chops of his hand.

"Pictures of smoldering airports will be on every smart phone and television screen within minutes of the first crash." *Chop.*

"People will be fleeing the remaining airports like they're radioactive." *Chop.*

"Air traffic control will order all aircraft out of urban airspace." *Chop.*

"The authorities will start evacuating rural highways to use as landing strips. Within a few hours those million-plus passengers will be on the ground someplace other than their intended destinations." *Chop.*

Max spread his hands. "How long do you think it will be before the government allows *any* commercial aircraft into U.S. airspace? How long before they even figure out precisely what happened?"

"Months, at a minimum," Achilles said. "Then they'll need to develop preventative measures. That will take years, as will repairing the airport terminals. The American psyche will take even longer."

"Why?" Katya asked. "Why would Korovin want to do that, even if he could get away with it? How does Russia benefit from terrorist activity?"

"It will cripple the U.S. economy," Achilles said. "The U.S. isn't just a military powerhouse, it's an economic one. This will bring America's economy down closer to Russia's size. The military will follow."

Achilles felt the puzzle pieces snapping into place as he spoke. The plan was multidimensional, and absolutely brilliant. The picture in his mind grew larger, large enough for him to bring it full circle. "It will bankrupt Vulcan Fisher. Once the investigation reveals that it was the VF autopilot systems that enabled the terrorism, they'll be crushed beneath lawsuits. All work will stop on *Operation Sunrise.*"

Max nodded his head with a grim smile.

"Someone else will just pick that up, won't they?" Katya asked.

"Not possible," Achilles said. "You can be sure Vulcan Fisher has filed dozens of patents on enabling technologies. Those will be tied up in legal battles for years as VF shareholders try to maximize their value. Plus the budget will be gone, used to rebuild airports."

Max folded his hands across his chest. "Very good. In the course of a single hour, Korovin will cripple his chief rival's economic engine and derail the most significant military operation since the Manhattan Project. On top of all that, America's biggest creditor and trading partner will take the blame. All without a single Russian casualty."

That cinched it for Achilles. He was all-in on Max's plan. He was going to crush Korovin, and Sobko, and Grachev. "Switzerland, here we come."

PART 4: ASSASSINATIONS

Chapter 75
Shots Fired

The Kremlin

PRESIDENT KOROVIN began each morning with his personal trainer. Workouts were the closest thing in his life to a religion. Still, on this special occasion, Ignaty felt comfortable disrupting his boss's sacred time.

Korovin was on the elliptical machine when Ignaty slipped into his private gym. The boxing champ who trained him was voicing encouragement, and Korovin's legs were pumping at an impressive speed, but the president's focus was on the TV screen. He wasn't watching a motivational movie or the latest news. It was a famous American talk show host, interviewing Julian Assange.

Ignaty jumped in, speaking loud enough to be heard over the whirring mechanism and blaring television. "What is it with you and Charlie Rose? I thought we were done with him."

"He's coming back for another helping," Korovin replied, referencing his earlier interview with Rose.

"He's not your friend."

"He's not my enemy either. I want the Americans to get used to having me in their living room." Korovin paused the recording, but didn't slow his stride. "What have you got for me?"

Ignaty laid his smart phone on the elliptical's control panel. It displayed a gruesome photograph.

The president studied the picture without any discernible change of expression. "Looks like the last guy who pissed off Shark," he said, referencing his trainer. "Who is it?"

"That's Achilles. Zoya hit him in the face with a pair of marine binoculars swung by the strap."

"He's dead?"

"He's dead, and she's back with Max in Seattle."

The elliptical beeped three times as Korovin completed the circuit, reinforcing the victorious mood.

Shark backed away as the president slowed to a stop with a contemplative expression on his sweaty brow. "Did Achilles talk to anyone?"

"She says no. The APB did the trick. Kept him isolated."

Korovin grabbed his hand towel and wiped his face. "How close are we on *Sunset*?"

Ignaty knew better than to expect an attaboy for eliminating Achilles. Still, some kind of acknowledgement would have been nice. "That's not clear yet. The Chinese hackers are still working the shippers, but there's no magic involved so I'm not anticipating a problem. We should know soon."

"Are we certain the Chinese don't know they're working for us?

"We're certain. Everything flows through Wang, and Max is the only person in contact with him. And you know Max. You'd peg him as British or German or even Israeli before considering Russian."

Korovin tossed his sweaty towel back at Shark, but kept his eyes on Ignaty. "Okay. Keep on him. We dodged a bullet with Achilles. Let's make sure that's the last one Silver fires before his planes start dropping from the sky."

Chapter 76
Feeding the Beasts

Seattle, Washington

ZOYA WAS ANGRY. She was angry with Korovin for involving her in his devious plans. She was angry with Max for not standing up to him. She was angry with Achilles, for outsmarting her with the amulet. And she was angry with Katya for being so nice. But most of all, Zoya was angry with herself.

Still, she had a job to do, and this one had its challenges. It was testing her acting skills to be flirting like a schoolgirl while boiling on the inside. Of course, on this job her acting skills were secondary to her appearance. In fact, if she looked half as good in her yoga outfit as Katya did in hers, then the quality of her acting might make no difference at all.

She and Katya actually did have similar appearances and could easily pass as cousins if not sisters. They were both slim and on the tall side of average height. They both had the pronounced jaw and cheek lines common among Russian women, complemented by otherwise regular facial features. Katya just had a lighter color palette — hair, skin, and eyes — and was athletic looking, whereas Zoya gave a more sultry vibe. The big difference was that at twenty-eight, Katya was younger by ten years.

Zoya redirected her coquettish gaze from the man working out across the gym toward her partner in crime. "I can't believe we're actually doing this of our own accord."

Katya looked up from her hamstring stretch. "Can you think of an alternative?"

They were at Summit Fitness, taking advantage of a free trial membership to seduce Billy Richards. A muscle-bound former supply officer who'd given the Army twenty years, Billy was now the regional manager for *Solid Green*, a shipping company that specialized in high-security short haul transportation.

The shipping records obtained by Wang's hackers showed that Vulcan Fisher used Solid Green for shipments to Boeing. But contrary to earlier promises, the hackers had been unable to learn the specifics of future shipments. They whined that Solid Green's defense-grade servers were sealed up tighter than scared oysters. The best the hackers could do was supply the women with a flash drive and a fresh plan. If Zoya could open their file on one of Solid Green's networked computers, the drive would auto-install a back door. Then Wang's hacker would have free rein to view and modify whatever they wanted.

Two days of observation and research had led the women to believe that Billy was their best bet. He had an obvious weakness. Given all the time he spent before the mirror at Summit Fitness, he was clearly too fond of himself. Tonight they hoped to exploit his narcissism.

Zoya put her flexibility on display with eagle pose, and replied to Katya with a hushed voice. "My failure to invent an alternative is what's eating me. I'd been upset with my president and my fiancé for colluding to use my sexuality to get their job done, but now that I've got the opportunity to orchestrate my own operation, I've cast myself in the sex kitten role again."

Katya gave her an understanding smile. Of course, Katya would understand. She was every bit as beautiful as Zoya had ever been, and she was still in her prime. "The male sex drive is one of the most powerful forces in nature. It's universal, its— Wait a minute, your fiancé? I didn't know you and Max were engaged. But then of course you wouldn't have worn your ring to …" Katya's words trailed off. She'd inadvertently opened a sensitive subject.

"It was a foxhole proposal," Zoya replied, already feeling better after her moment of venting.

"What?"

"Max literally asked me to marry him on the way into the meeting with Korovin. He took a knee right there in the marble hallway. Speaking of which, I've got to tell you about Korovin's vacation house. Un-be-lievable! But later. The show's about to start."

Billy was working his way around the free-weight circuit. They'd positioned themselves on mats between the benches and the mirrors. Right next to the big dumbbells. Zoya was playing a hunch.

She'd been stealing glances at Billy for the past twenty minutes. Always just long enough to get caught and blush. Finally it was time for his dumbbell routine.

Billy went for the largest pair, of course. The pair not three feet from her head.

"What on earth are you going to do with those monsters?" she asked him.

"Just feeding the beasts," he said with a wink.

She stood as he took a seat on a bench. "I gotta see this. I thought those big ones were only there for show."

Billy swung the dumbbells up as he dropped to his back. He was trying to make it look easy, but popping veins betrayed the strain. Zoya counted out loud as he started pumping. She increased her pitch with each count, so that by the time he reached eight, she was ecstatic.

After he'd reversed the positioning move, swinging the dumbbells down while sitting up, she said, "Isn't that dangerous?"

"Not if you do it right."

"Is there a trick you can show me?"

"Sure. We might want to start with something lighter though."

After half an hour of private coaching, Zoya made her move. "Well, thank you, Billy. I hope to see you again sometime."

He reacted like she'd poked his eye, but recovered quickly. "Well, how about dinner? I know a great place just up the road. Best surf and turf around."

"I'd love to, but I have to get my roommate back to her computer so she can work. Maybe some other time."

"Your friend can join us."

Zoya put her hands on her hips in a way that puffed out her chest. "Nice try. But as I told you, she has to *work*. She teaches math online. Her class starts in forty-five minutes, and it will take us forty just to get home."

Billy was not going to be so easily deterred. "Let her take your car. I'll bring you home after dinner."

Zoya put a pout on her face. It was a childish expression that Max always said he found sexy for some inexplicable reason. "She can't drive. She's just visiting from the Ukraine. That's why her class is starting at this hour."

"What if, ah, what if … Can she use any computer? My office is just across the street. Nice and safe and quiet. High-speed internet. We've even got tea. Ukrainians drink tea, right? I could set her up real nice." Zoya struggled not to flinch as he draped one of his sweaty beasts around her shoulder and turned his hungry gaze to Katya. "Maybe we could even bring dessert back to the office."

Chapter 77
Emergency

Zurich, Switzerland

"THAT'S OUR MAN," Max said. "Severin Glick."

Achilles studied the Swiss banker through powerful binoculars. Thick white hair, elfin ears, red marks from reading glasses on a long, thin nose. In a bathing suit, he didn't resemble a banking titan, but put him in a couture three-piece and throw some silk around his neck and he'd look quite at home on the cover of Forbes. He certainly looked fit for a man of sixty years.

They were perched on the limb of a mighty oak tree, up the hillside overlooking Glick's estate. As the sun peeked over the hill to their backs, Achilles watched Korovin's money man do a graceful dive into his backyard pool and begin swimming laps while the water bled heat into the crisp mountain air.

Max continued the briefing. "He's one of seven senior partners at The Saussure Group. Because Saussure is a privately-owned bank, I don't know much more. Obviously, I wasn't able to use SVR assets to investigate."

Achilles set down his binoculars. "How did you manage to connect him to Korovin in the first place?"

As Max looked over, Achilles knew they were thinking the same thing. Neither could believe they were having this discussion.

Theirs was a very unusual relationship, to put it mildly. There were lots of forces at play. Deep down it was clear to both that they had a lot in common. They just happened to be born onto rival teams. But then they'd spent their careers not just fighting hard, but killing and conniving and risking life and limb, to beat the other's team.

The personal lives of the two spies further confounded their relationship. On the one hand, they were both paired with exceptional Russian women. On the other, Zoya had been married off to Achilles, by none other than Max's boss, the very man whom Achilles had been assigned to kill.

Max acknowledged all this with a single nod of his head. It was a simple gesture, but it was enough, spy-to-spy and man-to-man. "I was in Zurich on another case. My academy roommate is stationed here at the embassy, so of course we caught up for a night out. We hopped clubs while he regaled me with tales of wild parties in Swiss chalets filled with flavored schnapps and hot tubs and willing women. He even invited me to one that coming Friday, but I had to pass.

"Then he called me early Saturday morning. He was stuck in Brunnen, but he had a standing appointment in Zurich he couldn't miss. An envelope exchange."

"Let me guess, with Glick?"

"Right, although he knew neither Glick's name nor position. He'd been told the contact was Code 6 — a covert asset not to be engaged in any way."

Achilles could see where this was going. "But as a secret stand-in, you weren't threatened with Code 6 sanctions. So you indulged your curiosity, followed him, and learned his identity."

Max smiled. "Nice guys who play by the rules don't get ahead in the SVR."

"Did you risk looking inside the envelopes?"

Max gave him a "What do you think?" grin. "The letter from Korovin had no *to*, no *from*, and of course no signature. Just two columns of code—notations like 1PPVLO and 5MSPTR."

"Did you crack the code?"

"Yes. But only because I'd learned Glick's identity."

"As a banker?"

"Exactly. In that context, it's relatively easy to decipher 1PPVLO into *One percentage point of Valero Energy Corporation*, and 5MMSPTR into *five million shares of PetroChina Company*."

"How do you know if it's a buy or sell order?"

"Simple bookkeeping convention. Debits on the left, credits on the right."

"What about the return letter from Glick?"

"That one I couldn't risk opening. The envelope wasn't the same type we had at the embassy, so I couldn't replace it with a fresh one, the way I had Korovin's. I assume it was Glick's weekly portfolio report."

"You assume? We're risking everything on your assumption?"

Max shrugged. "Remember the question I posed back in Seattle? How does a man who refuses to risk electronic communication manage his stolen billions?"

While Achilles mulled over the uncertainty that had just cast a big shadow over their operation, Glick hopped out of the pool and into a thick, royal-blue robe. By the time Glick disappeared into his home, Achilles came to the same conclusion as Max. The fact that he did, hinted at another potential problem. "Do you think your friend also figured it out?"

Max's face scrunched. "In addition to Glick's identity, he'd need Korovin's personal eyes-only mail code, which he'd be very unlikely to have. That's highly classified information."

Achilles knew that mail delivered through diplomatic pouches often used codes rather than addresses to conceal the identities of both the sending and receiving parties. "How do *you* know Korovin's personal code?"

"I didn't know it at the time I followed Glick. But when I saw it on an envelope the day Korovin gave me the *Sunset* assignment, I put it all together."

With Glick back inside, it was time to come out of the tree. Achilles went first. "So how do we turn Glick's identity into a kill shot?"

"I have an idea. But I think it would be helpful if you reached the same conclusion independently. Now that you know what I do."

Achilles saw the wisdom in that, and began thinking out loud. "Beginning with the end in mind, we have two approaches. We could either go to Russia posing as Glick, or we could lure Korovin to Switzerland. Of the two, luring Korovin here for the kill is preferable, because that gets him out of his castle."

"Agreed."

"To lure Korovin here, we've got weekly letters, back and forth, eyes-only between Korovin and the Swiss banker managing his stolen billions."

"Right."

"And of course we've got Glick's location and identity. What else do we know?" Achilles chewed on that for a few seconds. "We know that Korovin goes to great lengths to keep Glick's identity secret. He does this to hide his stolen treasure, thus protecting it and his position."

"Exactly."

"So Korovin and Glick never speak. And they never meet. Because Korovin doesn't trust telephones, and his movements are tracked."

"Except when he slips away," Max corrected. "As your boys discovered."

"Right. Except when he slips away. And what would make him want to slip away to visit Glick? Some kind of banking emergency? A huge and unexpected loss of portfolio value, I assume."

"That was my conclusion."

Achilles pondered the plan for a few seconds. "I'm not sure that will be provocative enough. If it's too big, he'll assume it's a typo. Five billion instead of fifty. If it's too small, we can't be certain that he'll immediately hop on a plane."

Max canted his head. "You have something else in mind? Something more provocative?"

Achilles looked back toward the Swiss mansion. "I'm thinking Korovin is about to acquire a major stake in Vulcan Fisher."

Chapter 78
Winsome Whisper

Seattle, Washington

WANG PAUSED before climbing aboard the first of three yachts. This was a big step in his career and his life. A turning point. A beginning and an end.

The yacht broker watched him, sensing Wang's excitement and apprehension, but assuming an altogether different causation. "Take your time exploring. I'll wait here in case you have any questions."

"Any chance I could borrow your phone to call my wife. She needs to be in on the decision."

"By all means. By all means." The salesman couldn't wait to hand over his phone.

"She's in China," Wang added. "But I'll pay for the call."

Bobby waved his hand. "Forget about it. It's important to me that she be happy with your selection."

Wang had to give the guy credit for not flinching. He accepted the Samsung and leapt from the dock. The craft he landed on was a schooner built in 2008. *Yacht* was a generous term for the sailboats he was inspecting. Although the three under Wang's consideration were fifty feet long on average, all were well-used and far from flashy. Still, they had everything one needed to live. Any of them would make a fine hideout, and each could be sailed on the open ocean by just one man.

He'd been expecting the schooner to rock when he hopped aboard, but it didn't. Perhaps that was the result of the 3,000-pound keel the broker raved about. Wang ducked into the cabin and dialed China.

"Wei." Qi's voice was groggy.

"How are the girls?"

"They're sleeping. As was I."

"School going okay?" Wang asked, dismissing the first yacht at first glance. Just not his style. Too cramped and gloomy. It felt more like a prison than a getaway.

"Same as always," Qi mumbled. "Why are you calling?"

"I've got news."

He decided to leave her hanging for a few seconds, hoping that would recalibrate her attitude.

The second boat was a fifty footer made in France, a Beneteau Oceanis named the *Winsome Whisper*. Although older, it was more modern inside, and looked easier to handle. Three suitable staterooms, and a big common area. He even liked the name. That was important. Changing a boat's name was bad luck.

"Tell me," Qi said, her tone much more attentive.

"I found out who's funding my side project. It's the Russians."

"The Russians," she repeated. "That's good, right? They've got money. Are you sure it's them?"

"I'm sure. They reassigned the slick Brit and now I'm working with a couple of obvious Natashas."

"How much do you think we can get?" Qi asked, most definitely awake now.

It was only *we* when it came to money, Wang noted. All other topics were either *I* or *you*. But he didn't let the observation get him down. He was about to beat the Russians at their own game, and make a mint in the process.

His people told him that the circuit boards they'd been ordered to produce were most likely a manual override. They speculated that engineers had taken some Vulcan Fisher system and figured out how to hijack it. Well, now Wang was going to do the same. He was having his engineers add an override to the Russian system. Nothing nearly as sophisticated as theirs. Nothing either of the Natashas would notice. Just a simple circuit breaker with a 256-bit encryption code. A code that would lock the Russians out of their own devices.

Wang's favorite pastime of late was speculating how much the Russians would pay him for that code, once the units were installed and they were at his mercy. That was his wife's favorite question of late as well. Besides their two daughters, a shared dream of that payday was the only thing he and Qi still had in common.

He took a deep breath, and answered his wife's question, knowing that the conversation would quickly turn unpleasant. "How much they'll pay depends on what the system does. If the Russians are plotting to gain control of fifty military satellites, the value might be billions. If it's drones, that might be worth a few hundred million."

"Really?"

"Yes, but it might be something far less exciting. In fact it probably is. If it were big, they wouldn't be leaving it in the hands of girls."

"Can you find out?"

"I'm thinking it doesn't matter."

"You're talking in circles," Qi said, using an exasperated tone he heard far too often.

Wang wasn't surprised by the criticism. His mind had been spinning for days.

He'd been toying with the idea of pulling a double-cross and disappearing ever since securing the extra $1.5 million for the hacking job. The windfall had stoked his imagination and whet his appetite. Then the Russians had replaced Max with amateurs and made his decision a no-brainer. He'd even made preliminary arrangements to get Qi and the girls out of China, although they didn't know that yet.

The tricky part of this stage of his plan was figuring out how much he could extort. The wise part would be tamping that number down to what he could get away with.

Bracing himself for the backlash he knew would come, Wang said, "I plan to ask for twenty million, regardless. No more, no less."

"What! If you can get a billion, you ask for a billion. Even your dumb uncle knows that much. Just imagine how we could live as billionaires!"

"The trick isn't just *getting* the money. It's *living* to spend it."

Qi took her time responding, and when she did, her voice was clipped. "Why only twenty?"

"It's not *only twenty*. It's twenty million dollars. Say that, Qi. Twenty million American dollars."

"I'd rather say one billion."

Wang looked out over the dark water of Puget Sound and took another deep breath. "Twenty million is my Goldilocks number."

"Your Goldilocks number? Are you telling me you've met someone?"

Oh, that it were so, Wang thought. "It's a reference to the fairytale. Twenty million is just the right size. It's big enough for us to live like royalty for the rest of our lives, yet hopefully small enough in context that the Russians won't think twice before paying it. Twenty million feels just right."

"What if it's not a big project?"

That was Wang's worry. "Then we forget about the extortion. If the project is not worth twenty million dollars, then crossing the Russians won't be worth the risk. They don't mess around."

He knew Qi wouldn't give up that easily. He could picture her standing with hands on hips and a steely stare on her scowling face. She said, "Do you want to hear *my* Goldilocks number?"

Wang wasn't about to start that negotiation, so he changed the subject. "Did I tell you where I am?"

By the time Wang hung up with his wife, he was sold on the *Winsome Whisper*. He really liked the French style. He'd look at the third boat, the 52-foot ketch, but only to keep from tipping his hand in the subsequent negotiation. The Beneteau was the boat for him. All that remained was a bit of haggling.

And of course, the operation that let him afford it.

The way he figured it, as long as his demand was financially inconsequential, *and* he could remain hidden from the moment he made it until the Russians paid, he was golden for the rest of his life.

Thus the boat.

He'd anchor it somewhere off the beaten track in Puget Sound, and he wouldn't come up on deck until he saw his bank balance rise. Then he'd send them the activation code and turn the bow toward Mexico.

If the project was big enough.

But he couldn't wait to buy the boat until he was certain of the project's size. He had too much to prepare. The time had come to roll the dice and take a leap of faith that the project's size meant the Russians wouldn't think twice about an extra twenty million.

He rejoined Bobby on the dock. "Thanks for the phone. Pending a satisfactory technical inspection, I'll pay one-eighty for the *Winsome Whisper*. Today. In cash."

Chapter 79
The Lion's Roar

Zurich, Switzerland

THE SWISS, like the Germans, are a people in love with rules. Not legalities — the technicalities that American tort and defense attorneys are so fond of — but rather codes of conduct. Civility permeates the Swiss psyche, and so order pervades Switzerland. Swiss streets are immaculate not because they have more people cleaning them, but because nobody litters. That wouldn't be proper.

Today Achilles and Max were going to take advantage of their orderly nature. And they were doing it in a flatbed delivery truck. As the German speaker, Max was driving.

"Can I help you?" Glick's gate guard asked, setting aside his morning coffee.

"We're here to deliver the replacement lions."

"What? Lions? You have the wrong address."

"Marble lions," Max clarified. "We're with Evergreen Gardens. During the last service, we had a mishap with a shovel. Knocked the paw off one of the sculptures you have guarding the front door."

In fact, Achilles had shot the paw off two days prior while the gardeners were working on the other side of the estate. He'd been up in the same oak they'd used for their initial reconnaissance, some two hundred yards away, using a Remington 700 with a Kestrel 308 Suppressor.

"Oh yes," The guard said, frowning. "I saw the result. You brought a new one?"

"We brought two. So they'd match."

The guard came out of his booth to inspect the back of their vehicle, which looked like a tow truck but with a crane. Roped in beside the crane, the guard saw twin Carrara marble lions looking back at him, their paws raised in a gesture similar to the regal emblem on his gate. The Saussure Group's emblem. "Your truck doesn't have the Evergreen Gardens logo."

The guard was no slouch, Achilles realized. What else would he notice?

Max didn't blink "It's a rental. We don't usually need a crane, but those statues weigh two hundred forty kilos each."

The guard stepped back for a second, admiring look. "They're beautiful. How long will this take?"

"Less than two hours."

The guard nodded. Long enough to do a proper job, but not enough to dawdle. "Be sure it does. I expect Mr. Glick back at 10:00 a.m. As you know, he prefers his help to remain as invisible as garden elves." The guard made a note in his log, pressed a button, and the big wrought-iron double-gate swung wide.

Glick's neoclassical estate had a circular drive surrounding a water feature that had more in common with Trevi Fountain than with Achilles' modest lawn fixture. Achilles voiced his admiration. "This has to be the nicest private residence I've ever visited."

Max backed the truck up toward the front door. "You should see Korovin's Black Sea estate. It looks like the Palace of Versailles, although it probably has one more of everything, just for the record."

The lions on the flat bed behind them were the real deal, and the guard's appraisal had been spot on. They were stunning. Drilling holes in them had taken six hours. The Italian craftsman had grimaced throughout the delicate process. But in the end, each lion had a bore hole ten centimeters wide and a meter deep rising up within its base. Enough to pack over 7,500 cubic centimeters of ANFO explosive, and Tovex boosters.

They had used ammonium nitrate fuel oil rather than military explosive because mining explosive was far less regulated and much more widely available. This made it infinitely easier to obtain, something they did from a hungry quarryman.

ANFO had the added advantage of being made of the same core ingredients as fertilizer, so the dogs wouldn't go wild when sniffing it in the garden. Although Achilles didn't expect them to detect it sealed under all that marble.

The plan was to detonate the two lions as Korovin passed between them on his way to the front door. There was no type of armor or contingent of bodyguards that could save him from a blast of that magnitude. The quantity of ANFO packed into the lions would level the entire front half of Glick's estate. Crushed between competing shockwaves like a bug between colliding bowling balls, the president of Russia would simply vanish.

Chapter 80
Best Laid Plans

Zurich, Switzerland

ACHILLES AND MAX had been working around the clock since the first draft of their plan came together during Glick's morning swim. Max had focused on luring Korovin to Zurich, while Achilles prepared to kill him once he got there. Now that they were back together for the explosive-lion installation, they finally had the opportunity to catch up.

Or so they'd thought. Manhandling the heavy beasts ended up demanding much more focus than either spy had anticipated.

"How'd the letter swap go?" Achilles asked, once they'd finally lowered the second lion into place.

Max wiped the sweat from his regal brow with a crisp white handkerchief. "It was easier than it should have been. I knew which mail slot it would be in, from the last time I picked it up. And of course my face was familiar to both personnel and guards. But borrowing the envelope for the switcheroo was so easy it was anticlimactic. Wait till you see the video."

Back in the Seattle hotel room, Achilles had insisted on a couple of safeguards before agreeing to go with Max's proposal. The first was that Max and Zoya would not be allowed to communicate during the mission. He reasoned that if they couldn't talk, they couldn't plot subterfuge. The second safeguard was that whenever he and Max were separated, Max would wear a button camera that Achilles could either watch live or from a cloud recording. Neither precaution was foolproof, but they weren't flimsy either.

"How'd you make the new letter look like the old?"

Max went to work with a whisk broom, cleaning up around the base of his lion. "The letter itself was nothing special. Laser printing on plain white paper. Completely anonymous. Adding 4.9 percent of Vulcan Fisher stock to Korovin's portfolio was as simple as replicating his letter with 4.9PPVCFR added to the buy column. Then all I had to do was seal it up in a fresh diplomatic envelope labeled with Glick's delivery code, and return it to the proper mail slot for my friend to deliver."

Achilles detected no signs of deception, nor could he think of a reason for Max to lie, but he would still scrutinize the video. Trust but verify.

"You get the passports?" Achilles wanted fresh false identities for their upcoming trip to Moscow. Max said he knew a guy in that department, and he had taken their passport photos with him to the embassy.

"We're all set."

Achilles checked his watch. Quarter to ten. The installation had taken longer than he'd planned. "We need to get moving. I don't want the guard coming around. Make sure the wires are well hidden."

They'd identified two weaknesses to the exploding lions plan. The first involved the mechanics of the detonation. Remote detonation required them to leave a signal receiver outside the lions. It was small enough to hide in a nearby bush, but it had to be hard-wired.

The wire was tiny, but scrutiny on the Glick estate was high. Rather than leaving the connecting wire exposed during the week it would take for Korovin to learn of his Vulcan Fisher ownership, they decided to come back later with the signal receiver and hard wire the connections. Meanwhile they'd tuck the wires out of sight in the tiny gaps between the statues' edges and the stone walkway.

The second weakness was the need to identify Korovin quickly. They'd likely only have a couple of seconds. Just the brief period of time during which he'd be walking from his car to the front door. Given the secrecy with which Korovin would treat this trip, they expected him to show up in an unmarked car, perhaps even wearing a disguise. He might well be surrounded by bodyguards, or using an umbrella. In any case, they didn't want to get it wrong. So when they returned to connect the signal receiver, they'd plant video cameras as well.

"I'm thinking the spiraled hedges look good for the cameras," Achilles said, as they tidied up. "They'll give us both left and right angles. I'll take pictures to help us prep."

"Sounds like a plan."

Once they'd packed up and started the truck, Achilles asked, "You really think Korovin will come?"

Max drove toward the gate, giving the guard a wave and a smile before answering. "I'm absolutely certain that he will."

"How can you possibly know that?"

Max looked over and met Achilles' eye, revealing a rare glimpse of raw emotion. "Because if he doesn't show, I'm dead."

Achilles thought about Max's position as the gates parted, allowing them to exit the first stage of their mission and enter the second. He and Max were both all-in on this one. Evidence of their collusion would eventually show up — if anyone was looking. If Korovin was still alive when that happened, there'd be no way for either of them to talk themselves out of a traitor's jail. Achilles held Max's eye, while nodding back. "You and me both."

Chapter 81
Brainstorming

Zurich, Switzerland

MAX STUDIED the steely gray clouds sweeping in over the Swiss Alps for a few seconds before turning his gaze back to Achilles. Their collaboration on the Korovin affair had been going unexpectedly smoothly — even for a couple of pros accustomed to unconventional assignments — but their differing viewpoints on the Sobko and Grachev assassinations portended a thunderous clash. "It's a perfect fit, Achilles. Two shooters, two targets, two simultaneous shots. There's no guesswork, no grunt work, and most importantly, no risk of capture. All we have to do is uncover or orchestrate their joint appearance someplace they'll be susceptible to sniper fire."

Achilles set his coffee down and shook his head. His demeanor reminded Max of what he'd seen back in Seattle — *before* Achilles had cut his bonds.

After installing the explosive lions, they'd driven straight from Glick's estate to a coffee house a few villages over to plot their next moves. Time was tight, very tight, so they were still dressed for garden work. They only had a few days to take out two high-profile targets. Neither would be nearly as tough as Korovin, which was why all prior focus had been on the president. But now that the Korovin job was set, the task of eliminating his hard-line successors loomed large and daunting.

Achilles looked up from his coffee. "A sniper shot is too high-profile. Lukin was killed just a few days ago. If we add Grachev and Sobko to the list, who knows how Korovin will react."

"It doesn't matter," Max persisted. "Korovin's not going to ignore Glick's stock purchase. It presses three of his hot buttons — his pet project, his penchant for privacy, and his personal fortune."

"We don't know that. And it's not just Korovin I'm worried about. The more Russians we eliminate, the more the world will look beyond Russia's borders to find the assassin."

"Not our problem," Max replied, studying his sparring partner. Achilles' eye color varied with the environment like no other irises Max had seen. Blue, brown, green, or black. Give the American spy a vivid shirt and his eyes appeared to match. Today Achilles was wearing the olive outfit of an upscale gardener, but at the moment his eyes looked more like the thunderheads now rolling in. Emotion was overpowering optics.

Achilles clenched his jaw before replying. "I won't ignore the spirit of my mission just to make it easier to complete. President Silver is counting on me. He's relying on my judgment as much as my skills."

Max fought the urge to lean away. "So what do you suggest?"

After a few seconds of silent tension, Achilles thunked the white marble table three times with index and middle finger. "We get them to resign."

"Sounds good," Max said, working hard to sound sincere. "Any idea how?"

The eyes twinkled, like a lightning flash in the clouds, and Achilles' whole demeanor shifted along with his tone. "Why *should* they resign?"

Max was thrilled by the attitude shift, but befuddled by the question. "I don't follow."

"Why don't they deserve to be in office?"

"I'm sorry Achilles, you've lost me."

Achilles' upbeat expression didn't change. He'd latched onto something, and Max's opacity wasn't fazing him. "What do they have to hide?"

"You mean corruption?"

"Exactly."

"All our politicians are corrupt."

"Sure, but they all hide it. If exposed, they'd go to jail for it. Right?"

"You want to blackmail them into resigning?"

"I do."

Max felt his stomach drop. He'd been excited for a second. "We don't have time for a long play. Blackmail ops require multiple stages. Before you can catch your targets, you have to identify their weaknesses, create an exploitation plan — then lure them, hook them, and reel them in."

"Not necessarily."

"Anybody ever tell you you're cryptic?"

Achilles chuckled, leading Max to believe he'd stumbled onto an inside joke. "You just hit on Katya's favorite refrain."

The mention of Katya made Max think of Zoya. He'd been trying not to. He knew she was fine and that she was facing no imminent physical danger. But he still felt guilty about pulling her out of her world and plunging her into his — the cold water at the deep end — and then abandoning her.

"I was watching the news last night," Achilles continued. "Charlie

Rose is going to be interviewing Korovin again in a few days."

"So?"

Achilles waved the air. "Forget about that for the moment. What do Grachev and Sobko want more than anything?"

Finally an easy question, Max thought. "Korovin's job."

"Right."

Now Max saw where Achilles was going. "They'd both kill for the opportunity to be interviewed by Charlie Rose. Especially if each thought he were the only one given the honor."

Achilles nodded.

Max's moment of clarity vanished like the sun behind the clouds. "But how do we turn their desire for Charlie Rose interviews into their resignations?"

Achilles' eyes flashed again, and Max knew he had it. "Guile."

Chapter 82
Five Days

Seattle, Washington

THE APPLE STORE in Seattle's University Village had more in common with a beehive than with the neighboring shops. Katya found it perfect for their meeting with Wang. Two Caucasian women in bright red polo shirts huddled in intense discussion with a rumpled Asian man clutching a big black umbrella would blend right in.

Wang arrived wearing a pleasant expression rather than his usual befuddled frown. "You did good work. We own Solid Green now. Electronically at least."

Katya leaned closer. "So when's the shipment?"

"Fifty Command-R Autopilot Systems, going to Boeing?"

Katya found Wang's attitude a bit too enthusiastic. "That's right."

"Pickup is Friday at 8:00 am."

"Five days from now?"

Wang nodded.

Suddenly the danger seemed more real. Katya could also sense tension seeping from Zoya, although she got the impression that her partner's angst was caused by more than the impending date.

Katya reached over and grabbed Wang's umbrella. To her surprise, he let her take it. She gave it a spin on the floor and asked, "Is your team ready for the install?"

"Of course. It will take about an hour to rework each system. That includes cracking open the casing, soldering on the additional circuit boards, and resealing the system. Ten men working means five hours. Add in two more hours for packaging at both ends and a third for buffer and you're looking at an eight-hour turnaround."

"You're satisfied with the workshop Max arranged? Everything is in order?" Max had subleased a warehouse just down the street from Vulcan Fisher for Wang's team to work in.

"Already set up."

"Good."

Wang reclaimed his umbrella. "Do I have the go-ahead to update Solid Green's pickup instructions? Five p.m. Friday at the new address?"

Katya looked at Zoya. She still looked bothered, but she nodded.

Turning back to Wang, she said, "You do."

"Very well then. I'll see you Friday morning. Good luck."

Zoya reached out to stop Wang. "Hold on. We should meet Tuesday for a dry run."

Wang's face spoke before he did. "I don't think that's necessary. My team has been to the facility. It checked out."

"Not your call. We've got a tight turnaround, and only one shot."

Wang turned to Katya.

Katya didn't know what Zoya was thinking, but she'd come to respect her intuition. "I agree. Shall we say 8:30 Tuesday morning? We'll be there with the truck."

Wang didn't fold. "You forget, my guys have regular jobs. This is moonlighting for them. One sick day is not a big deal, but I don't want to push it."

Zoya didn't back down. "Just you then. It's important that we think it through live."

Wang wriggled his teeth for a moment before deciding for himself that *yes, that would be a good idea.* "All right. See you Tuesday morning."

Katya waited for Wang to leave before asking, "What's bothering you?"

"We screwed up."

"What are you talking about?"

"Max didn't want Wang to know what system he'd be working on — until the last minute."

Katya put hands to hips. "There was no way around it. Not with Wang's team looking for monthly shipments of fifty units to the same address."

"We should have thought of something."

Katya agreed. Now that Wang knew what system the units were going on, he could guess their game plan. There wasn't much ambiguity to how you would use hijacked autopilot systems. "I see your point. But it's done. I'm more concerned about how we're going to stop this thing. We can't actually give Korovin control of those planes. What if Achilles and Max aren't able to kill him?"

"If they fail, we alert Boeing. But I know Max won't fail. He never does."

Katya thought back to what she'd heard about Achilles' last assignment with the CIA. "To us they look superhuman, but there's a first time for everything."

Zoya didn't reply.

"Why did you press for the dry run on Tuesday?"

"I've never trusted Wang. As one professional evaluating another, I can tell you he's acting when he plays the peasant brought in from the rice fields. There's a lot going on beneath the tranquil surface. When he mentioned the Command-R system, he got unduly excited. Something's going on."

"I picked up on that too. But what can we do about it?"

"I think we should watch where he goes."

"He warned us not to try. Plus he's a pro. He's been operating under the radar in Seattle for years."

"I know. But I've got a plan. Actually, you gave it to me."

Katya's phone vibrated before she could ask. "It's Achilles. Let's go somewhere more quiet."

She accepted the call but didn't speak until they were out on the street. "Hi."

"Hi. Is Zoya with you?"

"Yes. Why, is something wrong?"

Katya hated that they had to keep their calls so businesslike. She wanted the details. She wanted to know how he was feeling, what he was thinking, and if he too was staring at the wall for half the night. Probably not. His nervous system was tougher than a manhole cover.

"Nothing's wrong. Is it safe to put me on speaker?"

"You're on."

"Zoya, what's the name of your friend at MosFilm? The magician with makeup and masks? The one you worked with on *The Hunchback of Notre Dame?*"

"Mila."

In the background, Max said, "Mila, that's right."

Katya saw Zoya brighten at the sound of Max's voice. As tough as Katya had it, Zoya had it worse.

Achilles continued, "Zoya, can you call Mila and tell her you've got a big, urgent project for her. Tell her it pays *ten times* her normal rate, but it has to be confidential, and it has to be tomorrow."

"I can call. She'll want details. She likes to be prepared."

"Tell her you've got a six-foot-two 31-year-old who needs to pass for Charlie Rose. In person."

"The talk show host?" Katya asked.

"That's the one. He's six-foot-three and 75 years old. You think she'll be up for it?"

Zoya said, "Mila loves challenges, but there's only so much she can do. Aging you won't be a problem, but how much you end up looking like Charlie Rose will depend on the similarities of your build and bone structure."

"That's all we can ask. Thanks, Zoya. Katya, I need you to get a Google Voice number for New York City. Then I need you to use it to make some calls. I'm going to give you a list. Are you ready?"

Chapter 83
Masks & Promises

Moscow, Russia

"YOU'RE NOT GOING TO LIKE IT," Mila said, holding up the straight razor. "And this is only phase one."

Achilles took a second to study the master makeup artist. When he'd pictured her prior to their meeting, he'd imagined someone in her late-fifties with big hair and a bulky apron. Mila looked more like Taylor Swift in glasses. And she didn't appear to be joking. "Go ahead."

Mila set her straight razor down and picked up the electric. As she went to work, Achilles found himself remembering the words to a cadence sung on long runs during his CIA training. In Sergeant Dix's southern drawl, he heard, "Sat me in that barber's chair. Spun me around, I had no hair."

Zoya had really come through, not only by getting Mila to agree to a meeting, but also by getting her excited about the project. By the time he and Max had arrived, she'd already loaded enough Charlie Rose video into her Autodesk software system to create a life-size 360-degree model of the celebrity's head. It would generate the outside of the rubber mask. The next step was creating a similar model of Achilles' head for the inside. To get perfect pictures and a perfect fit, he needed to be bald.

Achilles studied his new look in the mirror. He was well-tanned from thousands of hours climbing cliffs, but the density of his dark hair had kept his scalp white. The contrast, now visible, looked ridiculous.

While he thought about that, Max held up a photograph and asked Mila, "Can you make me look like this guy? Enough to fool people who haven't seen him for years?"

She appraised the photo with pursed lips. "You just have this single passport photo?"

"That's right."

Mila held the photo up beside Max's head and compared them. "Your eyes are similar, and that's the key. If the eyes match a person's memory, their mind tends to fill in the rest. I can make this work."

"Can you do it without shaving my head?"

"If you plan to keep the same hairline you have now, I can just grease your hair back for the mold."

"Excellent." Max gave Achilles a taunting wink.

Achilles ran a hand over his smooth scalp in a mock salute. "Who is it?"

"A guy I went through the academy with. A real asshole named Arkady Usatov. Wouldn't mind causing him a few problems. His best friend from back then now heads security at Korovin's summer home. That's what made me think of him."

"That opens up options. I like it."

Achilles turned back to Mila. "Mind if I play devil's advocate?"

"By all means." She flashed him a confident smile.

"I know these rubber masks look real on film, but will they work in real life?"

Mila was ready for that one. "The short answer is *yes — for a while.* Let's break it down. The hair will be perfect. Millions of people are walking around all the time with hairpieces that go unnoticed. The skin is where it gets tricky."

While she spoke, Mila was using a camera to scan Achilles' head into her computer. "We'll start with your hands. There's a famous example of a young Asian man flying from Hong Kong to Vancouver wearing a rubber mask that disguised him as an old Caucasian. He got caught not because of his face, but rather his hands. They were too young. We'll be painting liver spots, wrinkles, and veins onto yours with dyes."

On the screen, Mila dragged the 3D image of Charlie Rose's head on top of his. "This is very good. Your bone structures are similar. Cheek bones, eye sockets, ear placement, all blend acceptably. You must have similar ancestry, in the evolutionary sense." She stopped nodding, and her tone changed. "His face is longer, so you'll have to relax your jaw. Show me your teeth."

Achilles did.

"Close enough. Neither of you have any unusual dental features." She resumed ticking boxes on the computer screen. "Our ears and noses never stop growing. Did you know that?"

"Sounds familiar."

"This makes it hard for older people to appear young. But of course those adjustments are easy going the other way." She completed the last of the query fields and hit return. "Okay. In about four hours, we'll have the base of your mask. Meanwhile, we'll get started with your hands."

"What will the mask be made of?"

"Clear silicone. To which we'll apply makeup."

"And that will look natural?"

"Of course. Women wear it all the time without anyone noticing. But you're particularly fortunate in that respect."

"How so?"

"Charlie Rose's face is constantly covered in pancake makeup for the cameras. People will expect it. The makeup will make your mask look more real, not less."

Achilles hadn't thought of that. "Any behavioral tips — things I can do to sell the disguise?"

Mila slid her jaw to the left. "Distance will be your friend. You'll be able to fool everyone who doesn't know Charlie personally at two meters or more. Once people close to within handshake range, it becomes hit or miss. Try to minimize interaction at that distance. And don't face people head-on. Give them your profile, and then give them something else to look at. If they're close and you can't control where they're looking, try to show them your back."

"Anything else?"

"Wear something distracting. A tie with a print that requires deciphering, or a flower on your lapel that appears about to fall. Something to draw the eye from your face."

As Achilles made mental notes, his phone began vibrating. It had to be Katya calling. "Can we take two minutes before you start on my hands?"

"But of course. I'm ready for another one of those delicious chocolates you brought."

Achilles put the phone to his ear. "How'd it go?"

"I got them both!" Katya's bright voice conjured up a picture of her beautiful smile.

Their plan had been a simple one. Call Grachev and tell him: *Charlie was interested in interviewing one of Korovin's potential successors, while he was in town to interview the president. Would the parliamentary leader be interested, or should she call Sobko instead? Charlie only had a two-hour window.* Of course, Sobko got the call as well.

"So we're set?" Achilles asked. "The day after tomorrow?"

"They couldn't sign up fast enough. Grachev is at 4 p.m. Sobko's at 8 p.m."

The only thing Achilles liked about politicians was their predictability. Unfortunately, that quality didn't extend to their bodyguards. Regardless of the quality of their makeup, the danger of detection by pros like those would be significant. Achilles found himself reminded of the proverb, *Be careful what you wish for.*

Chapter 84
The Metropole

Moscow, Russia

MAX COULDN'T BELIEVE the transformation Mila had created. Achilles was Charlie Rose.

At least from across the room.

If he didn't speak.

Or move.

"You're not walking like a 75-year-old. Rose is fit, but he's not spry."

Achilles tried to modify his gait. "Thanks. Zoya, any suggestions on how I could do that? We're about out of time."

Zoya was watching him via Skype. "What's the furthest you ever ran without stopping?"

"26.2 miles."

"Remember how sore you felt the next morning?"

"More or less."

"Walk like that. And put some pebbles in your shoes."

Max checked his watch. "I gotta go. I'll see you at the Metropole." He still wasn't allowed to speak openly with Zoya. He understood why, but it still pissed him off.

Playing the role of Charlie Rose's secretary, Katya had booked top-floor corner suites at two landmark hotels within a stone's throw of the Kremlin. The Kempinski and the Metropole. She'd also arranged for two chauffeured stretch limousines and three first-class bodyguards.

Max went straight from Mila's office at MosFilm into the first limo.

"The Metropole," he told the driver. Max was dressed in a working-class suit. The kind worn five days a week with wrinkle-free shirts. The kind appropriate to blue-collar work in white-collar surroundings.

Turning to the bodyguard beside him in the back, he said, "What's your name?"

"Ivanov."

"You know who we're protecting, Ivanov?"

"That American reporter. Rose."

"That's right. We're the advance team. Your job is to stick with me until I say otherwise, and to stay silent until you're off the clock. Not a word, not to anyone. It's *quiet day*, you got that?"

The bodyguard nodded.

"Good man. When I say the word, your job will be to clear everyone from the room. Everyone but Grachev, Rose, and me. No exceptions. Got it?"

Ivanov nodded again.

"Good man."

The Metropol was only about ten kilometers from MosFilm, but it took Max forty minutes with Moscow traffic. This was his second trip of the day. He'd been setting up the hotel rooms during the hours it took Mila to get Achilles resembling Charlie Rose.

Federation Council Chairman Sergey Grachev arrived just as Max and Ivanov were exiting their limo. It was easy to tell the cars of Russian officials. They had special license plates with flags and three numbers, and the lower the number, the higher the rank. Grachev, a bull of a man who resembled a Siberian wrestler more than a politician, was technically the second most powerful man in parliament after the unpopular prime minister. But as a relative newcomer to the stage, his license plate was only 008.

Three people and a German Shepherd climbed out of the black SUV with Grachev. Their functions couldn't have been more clear if they'd been printed on signs. Eight of the legs obviously belonged to Grachev's bodyguards, the other two belonged to a lovely assistant.

Max approached her only to have two hundred pounds of beef step into his path. The blocker had congenial features, making him suitable for background photographs, but the Krinkov short assault rifle slung across his chest more than compensated for any perception of weakness.

Ivanov moved in to face off with him, one bulldog to another. Max ignored them and, putting some flair into his gesticulations, greeted the woman in English with his British accent on full display. "I'm Tony Swan. I'll be running the shoot. If you'll come with me, we'll get Chairman Grachev set up. Mr. Rose will be here shortly."

Without waiting for an answer, Max turned and entered the Metropole. Ivanov followed a step behind to the right. Grachev, his assistant, and the two assault rifles trailed a few meters back with the dog.

Max hadn't counted on a dog.

Chapter 85
Final Sweeps

Moscow, Russia

IT HAD BEEN FOUR DAYS since Max had handled the ANFO that went into Glick's new marble lions. Now he was getting into an elevator with an explosive-sniffing dog. He tried to recall what he knew about canine capabilities, but was still drawing a blank when the doors swooshed closed and sealed him in.

He inhaled deeply, but detected only sweat and gun oil. Then the dog began to fidget — but no menacing growl followed. As the express elevator rocketed them toward the penthouse floor, Max let out a silent sigh and set about using the mirrored wall to study his opponents.

Grachev looked older in person than on TV, but nonetheless radiated a commanding general's energy. His assistant, a thirty-something looker in a stylish gray suit, made a phrase come to mind. *The best that money could buy*.

Max couldn't help but give his own disguise one final inspection. His silicone mask had been delayed by a technical glitch, so he'd taken advantage of the expectation for finding eccentrics among the show biz crowd, and had gone with the look of a British film star from the 1950's. He'd combed his hair straight back and dusted it gray with some of Mila's powder. Then he'd complemented the hairstyle with a mustache, sideburns, and glasses. The result was a persona so out of character that even Zoya wouldn't recognize him. Most satisfactory.

Max turned to address Grachev after they'd cleared the elevator. They were standing in an area reserved for penthouse suite guests only. The lounge was a five-star room itself, complete with beverage and concierge service. "Mr. Chairman, I'm sure you can appreciate that like most artists, Mr. Rose is very particular about the way he works."

Grachev nodded tentatively.

"He's adamant about not permitting any distraction. As the camera operator, I'll be the *only* third party permitted in the room during your interview. I'm sure your staff will be comfortable out here for ninety minutes." He gestured to the soft furniture surrounding them.

Grachev didn't look convinced. "I'm sure you can appreciate, Mr.

Swan, that men in my position require certain security precautions."

Max held up his arms as if surrendering. "Of course. Of course. If your security detail wants to do their thing while we're waiting for Charlie, they're most welcome. Most welcome, indeed. Meanwhile, let's get you seated by the camera so we can perfect your lighting. Time's tight, so we'll want to roll the minute Charlie arrives."

While the dog went to work methodically sniffing the suite, and the bodyguards did their best impression of storm troopers, Max led Grachev to his seat.

The two chairs were set up facing each other in the middle of the room, with the makeup artist Max had hired standing between them. As Tiffany went to work fitting Grachev with an apron, Max signaled Achilles using a clicker concealed in his pocket. Taking Charlie's chair, he said, "I'll have three cameras rolling the whole time. One on you. One on Charlie. One that captures both of you. For any particular moment, the editors back in New York will use the one that best captures the dramatic tension."

"I'm familiar with the procedure." Grachev's deep baritone resounded off the walls, making Max glad there would be two doors between him and his guards. "But I'm surprised you'll be managing the equipment all by yourself. Usually there's a team of four or five."

"Charlie likes to keep it simple, the producers like to keep it cheap, and modern technology makes both possible. Personally, I like being indispensable," he added with a wink that bounced off Grachev, but fit Swan's colorful character.

A bit of bustle erupted from the direction of the suite's entrance.

They turned to see Charlie enter. He headed straight for Grachev, his right hand extended.

Tiffany, busy putting makeup on Grachev's face, prevented him from rising. Grachev just smiled and poked his own right hand out from beneath the apron.

Achilles started coughing into his left. "Excuse me." He shook Grachev's hand while trying to clear his throat. "Give me a minute," he added, and turned toward the master bedroom and its private bath.

Max spoke up for all to hear. "Okay, we need to clear out! Everybody, please! This will take about an hour and a half. I'm sure you'll be comfortable in the lounge."

Tiffany made two final strokes with her brush, then ran for the door, leaving her kit behind.

Ivanov dutifully herded everyone toward the lounge before becoming the last to leave.

Max bolted the door behind him.

Chapter 86
The Bear

Seattle, Washington

"WHAT IS IT with you and that umbrella?" Katya asked, as Wang twirled it round his hand. "You have a dagger in the tip? Cyanide pellets perhaps?"

Wang looked back and forth between the women and his umbrella. "Sometimes an umbrella is just for the rain."

He looked at his watch, then exhaled loudly and returned his attention to the walls.

There wasn't much to see in the warehouse they'd rented. Ten unmanned assembly stations equipped with soldering irons, screwdrivers, magnifying glasses, and grounding pads. Ten large tables for the unpacking / repacking operation. The rest was bare concrete and old workers' rights posters.

When Katya's gaze wandered back to his, Wang said, "Actually there is a story. When I was young, we had a terrible monsoon season. The whole village flooded. We moved to higher ground, but I was still wet for an entire month. Once the water finally receded, there was nothing left of our home. We moved to the city after that. Now I hate the rain."

"And they sent you to Seattle." Katya almost felt for the spy.

Wang nodded.

They'd rendezvoused to inspect the truck that would be used in Friday's operation. It had yet to show up.

Katya had offered an independent trucker twenty thousand dollars to paint his truck to match the ones used by Solid Green, and make the pickup Friday morning. Not bad pay for a paint-job and a morning's work.

But apparently not good enough.

"Let me show you something." Zoya's upbeat voice buoyed their moods. She pulled out her phone, opened the music app, and selected *Singing in the Rain* from her song list. As Gene Kelly began belting out the classic, she took Wang's umbrella and started dancing about the warehouse floor.

She was masterful. Clearly she'd performed the routine professionally at some point in her career. By the time the song ended, Zoya was sleek with sweat and Wang appeared to be smiling for the first time in years.

The truck still hadn't arrived.

Zoya bowed, returned the umbrella, and rained on the parade. "I think our driver took the money and ran."

"How much did you pay him in advance?" Wang asked, fiddling on his phone.

Katya said, "Half."

Wang's expression said *bad move.* "Half the pay, none of the work, and zero risk." He shook his head. "Never trust a fox with your chicken. Do you have a backup candidate?"

Katya held her ground against the two of them. "We'll find one."

Wang checked his watch. "I've got to go. You might want to stick around in case it was a flat tire, or a speeding ticket. If he doesn't show, you best get right on finding a replacement. Tick tock." He started to turn, but paused. "Thanks for the show. I'll never look at my umbrella quite the same again." He lifted it in a wave, then turned and walked out to the curb.

Ninety seconds later a car showed up.

Nothing traceable.

Wang went everywhere using Uber.

Zoya looked at her watch as he pulled away. "How long until the truck is actually due?"

"Twenty minutes," Katya replied after checking her phone. She opened an app and added, "Same goes for the first ping."

Zoya had used the dance to tag Wang's umbrella with a *Bear*, a tracking device that *hibernated.* Pulled from Max's bag of tricks, Bears powered on just once every seven hours, and only for long enough to emit a single ping. A 500-millisecond cycle time meant the detection window was only one second in 50,000. Odds they were willing to take. Bears were almost useless for tailing active targets, but good for creating maps over time. With luck, the Bear would pinpoint Wang's lair. Just in case.

Zoya glanced over Katya's shoulder at the map of greater Seattle now displayed on the screen. "I'm starting to enjoy this."

Chapter 87
Two Minutes

Moscow, Russia

ACHILLES EMERGED from the bathroom and headed straight for his interview chair, his hand resting on his stomach the whole way. Speaking to Grachev, he said, "Excuse me, Sergey. I think I got some bad shrimp on the plane." He let out another cough as he finished.

A colleague of Mila's had coached Achilles on imitating Charlie's voice, but he knew it remained the weakest link. Both Grachev and Sobko spoke excellent English, and would likely have listened to Rose speak without interpretation.

Achilles met Grachev's eye, then cocked his head. "Tiffany missed the left side of your nose. Tony, will you ..." He made a brushing motion with his hand.

"Of course," Max said. "Good eye."

Achilles knew that the big makeup brush Max extracted from his sleeve concealed a hypodermic needle amidst its bristles, but he couldn't discern it. Grachev also never saw it coming. As the needle pierced his neck, he went from relaxed to rigid to relaxed in the course of three seconds.

Achilles breathed easier with Act One of his impersonation routine successfully completed. The rest, while less pleasant, would be more predictable.

When Grachev awoke some five minutes later to the pungent kick of smelling salts, he found himself in an entirely different position from when he'd gone under. His neck was tethered to his left ankle, by a taut cable running behind his chair. Another bound his chest and biceps, while a third looped around his right thigh. The combination immobilized him and discouraged struggling — even with free hands.

He was going to need his hands.

But he wouldn't be needing his mouth, so Max had duct taped it.

As Grachev's eyes sprang wide and his nose tried to figure out how to react, Achilles said, "Calm down. With a bit of cooperation, this will all be over in a few minutes and you'll be back on your feet. No worse for the wear."

Grachev began yelling as best he could. The result was neither intelligible, nor loud.

"There's no need to talk, Sergey. Only to type. All you need to do is show us something, and we'll be on our way."

More unintelligible blather. He was really working it. The chairman's pride was at odds with his position, and his glaring eyes reflected his outrage. *This couldn't be!*

Achilles peeled off another six inch strip of duct tape with that unmistakable sound, and pressed it down atop the first. This didn't substantially change the physics, but it reinforced Achilles' point. "As soon as you calm down, we'll get started."

With venom practically squirting from his eyes, Grachev began waving his fists to the degree his bound upper arms would allow. This tightened the cable around his neck, causing him to choke.

Achilles waited.

Grachev's panic grew but his struggles subsided. Then the big old cuss noticed his right leg and his face paled. Achilles had wondered how long that would take.

They'd removed his shoe, rolled his pant leg up to his knee, and locked his ankle into a custom stockade. With his leg extended straight out in front, it looked like a pig set to roast over a fire — or more accurately, a big fat candle.

When Achilles smelled hot urine, he knew the moment was right. "We're going to ask you to show us something on the computer. Once you do, we're all done. We're leaving. You with me so far?"

Grachev nodded.

"Good. Now, as you may have noticed, you're unable to speak. That's intentional. We won't be listening to anything you have to say until this is over. Are we clear? We're literally not going to listen to your bullshit, so the smart move is not to bother. Get it?"

Another nod.

"Excellent. Now, there's been a lot of speculation on exactly how much of the people's money you've stolen while in office. The estimates I've seen range as high as two billion." Achilles pulled out a laptop computer. "What you're going to do is show us the money. Once you've identified at least $500 million in active accounts, we're done. Are we clear?"

Grachev's eyes began spewing venom again.

"I'll take that as a *yes*. You're going to pull up your bank accounts, and show the cameras the money you've stolen. Now, are you ready for the good news?"

Grachev appeared to be attempting to pulverize his own molars, but he nodded.

"The good news is that you get a two-minute grace period. Plenty of time to let your fingers do the talking — if you don't waste precious seconds on the aforementioned bullshit. And we highly recommend that you don't, because after two minutes, we light the candle."

Chapter 88
The Candle

Moscow, Russia

ACHILLES LOCKED HIS EYES on Grachev's once the politician finally looked up from the fat candle poised beneath his exposed flesh. Achilles waited for the motors to stop whirring and resignation to kick in, then he threw the next blow. "The candle doesn't get extinguished until either you're done typing or both legs are done cooking. Personally, I'd strongly suggest you strive to show us the money before the candle ever gets lit, but then maybe I'm just too fond of my legs. Are we clear?"

The remaining bravado drained from Grachev's eyes like a flushing toilet.

"Are we clear?" Achilles repeated. "Or shall we skip the grace period and move straight to the candle?"

Grachev nodded.

"Good. Now aren't you glad we plugged your pie hole? Think of all the flesh we're saving."

Grachev looked away.

Achilles regained the politician's attention by setting an open laptop before him. "Here's the computer. The internet connection is high-speed, you'll be glad to know."

Grachev reflexively positioned his hands on the keyboard. Max gave the go-ahead, and Achilles spoke to the camera. "Chairman Grachev, you've stolen hundreds of millions of dollars from the people of Russia. The time has come for you to show us where it is." He opened the stopwatch app on his phone and hit the green button. "You have two minutes."

Achilles didn't know what to expect. Neither he nor Max had used the classic foot-to-the-fire tactic before. Modern interrogation techniques generally leveraged an unlimited supply of the one thing

Max and Achilles didn't have: time. They had an hour to accomplish what Guantanamo Bay hadn't managed in a decade. But then, Grachev was no fundamentalist, and freedom was a big fat carrot.

Grachev pulled up the notepad application and typed. "I don't have the login information in my head."

Achilles pointed to the timer. "One minute fifty seconds."

Grachev typed. "$1Billion at Credit Suisse. I don't know the number."

"One minute forty seconds."

Achilles pulled out the lighter they'd selected. It was the long type used on fireplaces and barbecues. He clicked it once and got a flame.

Grachev clawed the air for answers with panic stricken eyes.

Achilles looked over at Max. He was remaining behind the cameras since his disguise wasn't quite as impenetrable. Max had one lens focused on Grachev's face, a second on the computer screen, and a third capturing the whole scene.

Max gave a thumbs up.

Achilles said, "Ninety seconds. You're not fooling anybody, Mr. Chairman. Guys like you check your bank balances more often than your in-boxes."

Grachev sat staring and sweating and seething as he ran the permutations.

Achilles stopped counting time. He held up the stopwatch so his prisoner could see it, but turned away to lessen Grachev's shame.

Grachev caved with fifty-eight seconds left.

His fingers began flying across the keys. Then he groaned. Achilles turned to see the website spinning a circle in thought. Spinning. Spinning. Achilles began to wonder if this was a trick he hadn't foreseen.

The website relented with twenty seconds left on the clock. Then a security question took it down to nine.

Grachev typed like he was already on fire.

A second security question popped up with just two seconds remaining.

Another groan.

Achilles clicked the lighter to life. He put it to the candle. As the flame caught, the account summary exploded onto the screen. Three-comma's worth of Swiss francs. Roughly two billion dollars.

Max whistled.

Grachev began shouting incomprehensibly but emphatically.

Achilles licked his fingers as he met Grachev's eye. Then, with a satisfying pinch and an appropriate hiss, he extinguished both the flame and the chairman's career. "The videos sync live with the cloud, so rest assured they've already left the building. The two of us are about to do the same — while you take another nap.

"On our way out, we'll tell your guys that you got an important call and asked for privacy. We'll stress that you asked not to be disturbed for a few minutes. We suggest that you play along to avoid embarrassment."

Grachev didn't attempt to reply. He'd learned to respect the duct tape.

"The money will be gone by then, but resign from parliament within forty-eight hours, and we'll put ten percent back. Stay retired, and we'll return another ten percent on every anniversary of today's date. Nobody need ever know of your humiliation. Be content with what you have. Let enough be enough."

As Max again brought the needle to Grachev's neck, Achilles added, "They say that misery loves company. Well, Mr. Chairman, you'll be glad to know that you're not alone."

Chapter 89
Two Possibilities

The Kremlin

THE SHATTERING GLASS brought the presidential bodyguards running, two crashing through the double doors and a third bursting in the private entrance.

Korovin held up his hand. "It's all right, guys. Just had a disagreement with my teacup."

He'd tried to hurtle it through the window, but of course china couldn't penetrate bulletproof glass, so the cup swallowed the surplus energy and shattered like a fragmentation grenade.

As the guards backed out, weapons holstered, Korovin addressed the senior officer. "Get me Ignaty."

The president's day had started off badly and gotten worse. Grachev and Sobko had both resigned for personal reasons — and he'd learned about it from the paper. He didn't know what upset him more, losing his two biggest allies in parliament or learning of it after the fact. It was a slap in the face. If the Middle-Eastern summit didn't have him so pressed for time, he'd have tracked them down immediately to voice his disappointment.

The double doors opened, and Ignaty walked in. "This about Grachev and Sobko?"

"No. But we will get to that."

"How else can I help?"

"Sit." Korovin indicated the chessboard abutting the front of his desk. He wanted Ignaty positioned with their faces aligned.

The president took the opposing chair and locked his eyes like lasers on Ignaty. "I just acquired 4.9 percent of Vulcan Fisher's common stock. Four billion dollars worth."

"What! Why on earth would you do that? It's about to tank. Worse yet, it puts you in the picture."

Korovin stared in silence.

"But of course you know that," Ignaty added.

"I didn't order it."

"Glick acted independently?"

Ignaty struck Korovin as genuinely surprised, and deeply concerned.

Then again, deception was his job description. "I just got my weekly report, and there it was."

"That can't be a coincidence."

"No, it can't." Korovin kept his eyes riveted on Ignaty's. It wasn't pleasant. His chief strategist's head looked like a volleyball with a bristly brown brush stuck on — below the nose, not above.

Ignaty didn't blink.

Korovin pressed on. "You're the only person besides me who knows about Glick. The only one. And you're the only person of consequence to know about *Operation Sunset*. Unless you've told anybody about either? If so, if anything slipped your mind, this would definitely be the time to enlighten me."

"I've told nobody, absolutely nobody, about either." Ignaty looked and sounded sincere.

Korovin remained fixed on his strategist's facial features. "So how do you explain it? Put your strategic hat on. Speculate for me."

Ignaty leaned back and looked up, his hands cradling the back of his head. After six seconds of staring at the chandelier he said, "My best guess: the CIA."

Korovin had run that permutation. "That's the worst-case scenario. If it's true, *Sunset* is dead, and they have me by the short hairs. But I don't think it's true."

"Why not?"

"4.9 percent is a strategic number. It's just below the disclosure requirement. Why would the CIA stop there?"

"It's meant to be a warning shot, not a fatal wound."

Korovin pulled the black queen from the desk drawer and rolled it around the chessboard as he thought. "Let's assume you're right. If the CIA knows, then the information had to come through human intelligence. There's no electronic communication to intercept. Never has been."

"You think they got to Glick?"

"I think they either got to him — or you."

Ignaty's eyes bugged as words leapt from his lips. "Well then, I think it's Glick. Do you want me to go to Switzerland? Take a couple of guys with a nail gun and cheese grater?"

"No," Korovin replied, his voice a hammer hitting a nail. "I want you to stay at the Kremlin. I'm going to handle this myself."

"But you're hosting the summit tomorrow. You need to be here — and surely you won't risk calling?"

"Zurich is a three-hour flight. I'll leave now and come back tonight." Korovin locked his gaze on Ignaty's bugged eyes. "Wait for me."

Chapter 90
Bombs Away

Zurich, Switzerland

THE BLACK MERCEDES G65 SUV blew past the gate, kicking up gravel as it shot around the circular drive.

Achilles had gotten a good feeling when he saw the gates opening with no car in sight. A first since he and Max had started their around-the-clock surveillance. "You ready on the detonator?"

"Oh yeah," Max replied over their scrambled comm.

They each had a detonator — for redundancy and so neither would ever know for certain who had killed Korovin. Ambiguity might be useful, if the lie detectors ever came out.

This time they weren't positioned shoulder-to-shoulder. Max was perched in the tree they'd used for reconnaissance. Achilles was three stories up on a neighboring mansion's roof, also about two-hundred yards from target. He wanted them to have a 360-degree perspective on the house, in addition to line-of-sight views of the lions.

Just in case.

Large quantities of explosives called for extreme caution.

Achilles was dressed in coveralls that matched the slate tiles, and had three pieces of equipment: a suppressed Remington with a Bushnell scope, a monitor showing the video of Glick's front door, and a remote detonator for the explosives. Max was similarly equipped.

"I can't believe I'm actually about to do this," Max said. "Assassinate my president. I'm supposed to be on the beach right now."

"Exactly. You're supposed to be on the beach. Korovin brought this on himself."

The Mercedes looked as though it was going to ram Glick's front door, but it slid to a stop instead — nearly crashing into the marble lions.

"That's one mad president!" Max added. "Good call on the Vulcan Fisher stock."

Achilles' focus was elsewhere, and his mood far less celebratory. "I lost the camera feed!"

"Bollocks! Me too. Korovin's car must have knocked something loose. I'm glad we brought the scopes."

That explanation didn't sit right with Achilles as he put the scope's reticle head-height between the lions. Something felt wrong. He just couldn't nail it. "Good thing we went with explosives rather than a long gun. That parking job cut Korovin's exposure time down to a single second."

"And we've got wind," Max added.

The mansion's front door opened wide, revealing — no one.

In response to the silent invitation, both of the SUV's front doors opened. Men whose height and width resembled commercial refrigerators exited on either side. After a quick 360-degree appraisal, they opened the rear passenger door.

The man who stepped into view was almost certainly Korovin. The thin hair and predatory posture made him unmistakable even in wraparound shades.

"Confirmed," Max and Achilles both said at once.

Achilles pressed his detonator button.

Nothing happened.

He hit it again. Still nothing. "I've got a malfunction."

"Me too. What the—"

With no time left for a proper rifle shot, they watched in helpless frustration as Korovin disappeared into the mansion.

The bodyguards took up posts at the ends of their car. Battlements protecting a mobile castle.

Max came back on. "The Mercedes must have hit the detonator's receiver."

Achilles head caught up with his gut. "No. He's got a signal jammer in the SUV. That explains the camera malfunction too."

"You're right," Max said. "I see the array on the Mercedes roof."

Achilles pounded a fist against a slate tile. "Damn! I should have anticipated it."

"No wait. Our comm units are working."

Achilles puzzled on that for a second. "We must both be outside the blackout radius. Portable jammers have limited power, but still have to cover the full signal spectrum, so they go broad but not deep."

"What do we do now?" Max asked.

"I don't know. The jammer's overpowering our detonation transmission. The only ways to beat a jammer are to outpower it or turn it off."

While Achilles was studying the scene and weighing the options, Max asked, "What if we shot out the array?"

"We'd alert the guards. Who knows what they'd do then." Achilles thought about the EMP he'd recovered from the goons at his house. He still had it. An EMP would take out the jammer — but it would fry the detonator as well.

"Stealth?" Max suggested.

"Let's game it out. One of us infiltrates while the other sits behind a sniper scope. The ground guy has to get into the Mercedes, power down the jammer, and exfiltrate. All undetected. Virtually impossible with two pros watching."

"What if we take out both guards with sniper shots? Synchronized fire."

"We still need to infiltrate and exfiltrate without tripping an alarm or alerting Glick's gate guard."

"We have to risk it," Max pressed, the weight of the world in his voice.

Achilles thought out loud. "We know how to get onto the grounds. It's a mansion, not a fort. The security's good, but passive. Fences, not dogs. A gate guard, but no patrol. The odds aren't good, but they're probably the best we'll ever get."

He had his conclusion.

Achilles reached for his rifle. "You get a bead on the north guy. I'll take south. We drop them, then I go in while you cover."

Chapter 91
The Replay

Zurich, Switzerland

WIND WAS WORRISOME when you needed a head shot, so Max was worried. Both of Korovin's bodyguards were wearing body armor, therefore head shots it had to be. He and Achilles. Two cold bores. One bullet each.

They were both about two hundred yards out, Max to the north, Achilles to the south. On a competition range, two hundred yards was the equivalent of a three-foot putt. But they weren't on a range. He was in a tree, and Achilles was on a roof. Max's oak was pretty stable. He was on the big branches. But the slightest sway could be enough when your target was only six inches wide. Achilles' rooftop wasn't moving, but he had an updraft to contend with.

Achilles' voice came through on his earpiece. "Got mine. Got yours?"

The guards were standing at either end of the SUV like bookends. Both faced away from the house, studying their surroundings through aviator shades. Scanning for threats. Looking for them.

"Roger that. Initiating."

Max had a voice-activated timer app open and ready. He spoke to it. "Timer start!"

The lovely British lady began counting down loud enough for Achilles to hear her as well and synchronize their trigger squeezes. "Twenty. Nineteen. Eighteen…"

Max made himself relax.

He had the barrel braced on a branch as sturdy as a bipod. His chest and forearms rested on another. At two hundred yards, he didn't need to worry about vibration from his heart rate. That came into play with distances of a thousand yards or more. But breathing moved the needle. He'd hold his breath for the last few seconds of the count. Meanwhile he focused on relieving muscle tension and making the Remington part of his body.

With six seconds left on the count, the red dot in his reticle was rock steady. Then Plan B fell apart.

Korovin burst through the front door after just a few minutes inside.

The guards reacted instantly, the north one moving to the driver's door, the south one to the passenger side. Korovin was out of sight in two seconds.

"Abort," Achilles said. "No point shooting. Move to fallback."

Max abandoned the reticle and cursed his luck as the Mercedes roared away, spraying gravel.

Five minutes later, he was back in the Audi, letting the ramifications of his failure sink in.

The moment Achilles slid in beside him, Max voiced his conclusion. "We're screwed."

Achilles didn't reply.

Max pulled onto the winding residential road and headed up into the mountains. He had no destination other than release — and the A8 provided 450 turbocharged horses to achieve it.

Achilles sat contemplatively while Max tested the Audi's ability to stick to curves and dodge sheep.

After ten kilometers of going nowhere fast, his phone rang. A call forwarded from his computer. "It's Ignaty."

"Take it on the speaker."

Max used a steering wheel button to accept the call, and Ignaty's voice came over the Audi's speakers. "Report."

"No issues of note. Just preparatory grunt work. We're on target and on schedule."

"Everything happens Friday?"

"That's right."

"How's Wang behaving?"

"Like a man who knows we're putting the caviar on his blini."

"No concerns?"

"None."

"Alert me immediately if anything changes." Ignaty hung up without waiting for a response.

Achilles gave him a wry smile. "My last handler was a charmer too."

Max barely heard him over the voices in his head. "I've got to get back to Seattle where I can be seen."

Achilles' expression soured and his voice became stern. "Not an option. Either Korovin's going to his grave, or you're going to jail."

Max hit the brakes, skidding the Audi to a stop on the cliff side of the road, dangerously close to the edge. "We can't kill him now! We blew it. Korovin knows."

"What does he know?" Achilles asked.

"He knows that someone's onto him."

"How does that change anything? Korovin was paranoid in the first place. He doesn't know who's behind the stock purchase. Or why."

Max wasn't mollified. "There's a limited number of candidates. I'm on the list, because I know about Vulcan Fisher."

"All the more reason to take him out."

"Easier said than done. I don't have another backdoor pass."

Achilles turned to face him full on, exposing unwarranted excitement. "I was thinking about that while you were scaring the wool off sheep. We don't need another pass. We can still use the one we have."

Max wondered if Achilles had hit his head climbing down off the neighboring mansion. "Are you crazy? Now Korovin and Glick both know their communications are compromised."

Achilles' demeanor didn't change. He looked the same way he had when dreaming up the Charlie Rose con. "What did they say?"

"I don't know," Max replied. "I was in a tree at the time."

"You didn't have to be in the room to know how that conversation went."

Max found Achilles' self-assuredness maddening. "What are you talking about?"

"You saw Korovin leave. He was only in there for two minutes. Given that, I guarantee you their meeting went like this. Korovin stormed in and asked, 'Why did you buy four billion worth of Vulcan Fisher?' Glick replied, 'I was just following your orders.' Korovin looked him in the eye, saw fear but not deception, and decided he needed to reevaluate. They both agreed to look into it, and Korovin raced home to his summit."

Max had to concede the point. Anger and frustration had clouded his thinking. "I buy that. But I don't see how that gives us another backdoor pass."

Beaming eyes told Max that Achilles did. "We play to it."

Chapter 92
Ten X

Zurich, Switzerland

THE BLACK MERCEDES G65 SUV blew past the gate, spraying gravel as it shot around the circular drive.

Again it came to a stop abutting the marble lions.

This time the pair of Russians who exited weren't quite refrigerator-sized, although their dark suits matched those of their predecessors. The passenger was six-foot-two and 220 pounds, the driver an even six-foot and closer to 180 pounds. While Max walked around the car, Achilles bent down as if to tie his shoe.

A quick scan confirmed that the detonator was still in place.

If all went as planned, he'd snatch it up on the way out. They'd leave the explosive in place. Without the detonator, the ANFO would be no more threatening than the marble surrounding it.

Achilles stood and met Max's eye before pivoting toward the door. They'd phoned ahead to give a few minutes warning, as Korovin had the day before. Just as the gate had opened during their approach, so the front door did now.

The two marched in.

Glick had a home to die for. A decorator's dream. Marble and mahogany. Mosaics of brightly colored glass and the Dutch Masters rendered in oil. Vaulted ceilings, curved walls, and a sweeping staircase.

The king of the castle stood before them trying to appear regal with his tail between his legs. He was dressed in a charcoal gray suit with a dove gray shirt, both custom of course, and flawlessly pressed. His silver tie matched the reading glasses in his breast pocket and gave luster to his thick white hair. "Good morning, gentlemen."

"Let's move to your home office, shall we," Achilles said. No introduction. Not a question.

"But of course. Can I offer you a coffee? Some schnapps?"

"Is it upstairs?" Max asked, ignoring the drink offer.

"Yes. Right this way."

The study door slid aside automatically before the master of the house, and closed just the same behind. More like the starship *Enterprise* than *Walmart*.

Glick's home office was everything you'd expect from the banker who managed the money of the man many considered to be the world's wealthiest criminal. Since Glick was Swiss, it was more austere than flashy, but wealth suffused the space nonetheless. The Persian rugs, the investment-grade artwork, the antique furnishings. *Nice*, Achilles thought, *but not worth ten thousand times the IKEA alternative.*

Glick gestured them to plush seating overlooking distant snow-capped mountains.

Achilles and Max remained standing. "We'll be working on your computer."

"I'll get my laptop," Glick replied. "Please, have a seat."

They sat at the edge of their chairs, rather than sinking into them.

Glick returned with a slim silver computer, his face an obsequious mask. "Now, how can I help the president?"

Achilles let the tension build before responding. "He's not a happy man. You're fortunate he has the summit to distract him."

Glick said nothing, but his expression didn't reflect fortunate feelings.

"Despite the security breach, he's decided to give you a second chance."

Glick exhaled. He'd been expecting worse — but then he hadn't heard the details.

"Assuming that's what you'd like?" Achilles queried.

"But of course. Of course. He won't regret it."

"Good attitude. Time to get specific. What is the total combined value of Mr. Korovin's holdings as of this morning?"

Glick donned his reading glasses and began typing. "In U.S. dollars?"

"Yes."

"9,989,641,717."

"That sounds right," Achilles said, although in fact he'd been hoping for a much larger number. If Glick only had $10 billion, then Korovin must be using dozens of bankers. That diversification wouldn't affect today's plan, but it would create complications down the line. "Here's the plan. It comes in two parts."

"I'm listening," Glick said, scooching forward.

"Today we're going to transfer nine billion to other accounts." Achilles held Glick's eye, making it clear there was no wriggle room. "Then, next Sunday, you're going to present Korovin with your strategy to turn the billion that remains in your control, back into ten billion." Achilles paused to allow Glick to absorb the one-two blow.

Glick managed to retain his composure. Achilles figured that was the first lesson in Swiss banking school. Never pucker.

Achilles waited.

Glick finally found his tongue. "I'm to take one billion and increase it ten-fold?"

"As quickly as possible."

"Meanwhile we'll be transferring 90 percent of his current holdings out of my bank?"

The banker's speech remained serene as a swan on a pond, but Achilles knew his mind was thrashing beneath the surface.

That was perfect.

Achilles wanted Glick's mental faculties devoted to self-control. "It could be 100 percent. Your call. But the president thought you would appreciate the chance to make things right."

"Yes, of course. Of course." Still no strain or stutter. The banker was very good. "And he's returning Sunday? This Sunday? For the growth strategy presentation. Back to ten billion. As quickly as possible."

"No."

"No?"

Achilles shook his head. "We will be picking you up and taking you to him."

Max spoke for the first time. "His weekend home on the Black Sea. Lovely place."

Chapter 93
The Good Life

Zurich, Switzerland

MAX AND ACHILLES were back in divide-and-conquer mode. The tight timeline demanded it.

Max knew that Achilles hadn't planned to ever let him off a leash, but a combination of earned trust and forced practicality had scuttled that operating paradigm on the second day of their joint mission. Now, with successes behind them in Zurich and Moscow, they were functioning as efficiently as any team Max had ever been a part of, and far better than most.

But this bonhomie hadn't convinced Achilles to tell Max more than he needed to know — or allow Max to speak with Zoya. Max respected Achilles' operational discipline, but he didn't like it.

Today's divide-and-conquer approach had Achilles off hiding their stolen money while Max was arranging the transportation they'd need during their second attempt on Korovin's life. Later today, they would reunite in Austria to acquire a special weapon system for that assault. Achilles hadn't provided any detail on that special weapon — he tended to be cryptic when it came to operational details — but he had piqued Max's curiosity by promising something extraordinary.

Max was finding his current assignment pretty cool as well. He'd been tasked with chartering a private helicopter and jet — and thanks to the Glick operation, he had unlimited funds with which to do it.

The jet would take them from Switzerland to Russia, and then from Russia to the United States. The helicopter would be for transport within Russia, specifically from Sochi International Airport to Korovin's Seaside home and back — the same route he and Zoya had flown some four weeks earlier, the day this whole crazy caper began.

Switzerland was exceptionally well-suited for making private travel arrangements. As one of the world's most established and grand headquarters for clandestine banking, the neutral nation in the heart of Europe was geared to cater to the world's wealthiest citizens and their many privacy peccadilloes.

Max had operated undercover in Switzerland before, but this was the first time he'd posed as one of the uber-wealthy individuals they loved so much. He was rather looking forward to the experience.

Walking through the sliding glass door of Zurich's Private Aviation Center dressed in an exquisite, freshly-fitted suit and polished Bally loafers more comfortable than bathroom slippers, Max wasn't entirely sure what to expect. Would it resemble any other airline terminal or look more like the lobby of one of Switzerland's private banks, effusing symbols of wealth and security? What he found reminded him of a 4-star hotel lobby: polished marble floors and solid custom furnishings. The engineer in him recognized a design intended to retain a fresh appearance despite high traffic levels while requiring only minimal maintenance. Lacking were the live flower arrangements and original artwork you found in 5-star establishments — although the women behind the counter appeared top-shelf.

"Hello, I'm Kendra. May I help you?" one of them said. With her platinum blonde hair and million-franc smile, she was as welcoming as a warm blanket on a cold night.

Max noted that Kendra somehow knew to address him in English. He wondered if that was a default setting or a judgment call. In either case, he was glad she hadn't spoken Russian. Max prided himself on being mistaken for a Brit and used that accent in his reply. "I'm most hopeful that you can. Herr Leibniz over at Baumann Brothers recommends you most highly, most highly indeed," he said, referencing a banker he'd seen mentioned in *Le News* while extending his hand. "Name's Archibald Vanklompenberg. I need to charter a long-range jet and an executive helicopter."

"That was very kind of Herr Leibniz," Kendra said with a flash of her bright blue eyes. "You have indeed come to the right place, Mr. Vanklompenberg. Let's start with the helicopter. When do you need it?"

"Please, call me Archibald. Everyone does — Vanklompenberg is a bit of a mouthful." Max paused there.

"Very well, Archibald. When would you like to travel?"

"I shall require the helicopter this Sunday."

Kendra's nod indicated this would not be a problem. "From where to where?"

Max looked left then right before returning his focus to the agent's plump red lips. He lowered his tone. "That's where it gets a bit complicated."

Her lips spread into a knowing smile. Kendra was accustomed to *complicated*. She pandered to clientele who'd inherited half the world and yet somehow seemed perpetually dissatisfied. "Why don't we have a seat and you can walk me through it."

She picked up the tablet on which she'd been typing and gestured toward the fat burgundy armchairs off to her right. "Would you care for a coffee or perhaps something from the bar?"

Over espresso, Archibald was delighted to learn that the Sochi helicopter rental was no trouble at all. Nor was the long-haul jet. The price for the combo was well into six figures, but like most of Kendra's clients, Archibald Vanklompenberg did not dwell on that. Impeccable, invisible, imperturbable service was what mattered. That and one final point.

Setting down his second espresso, he said, "Now that I know you're able to accommodate us from a logistical perspective, I need to run our other requirement by you."

"Other requirement," Kendra replied, a smile on her face but *here-it-comes* in her eyes.

"We need these charters to appear routine."

She chewed on that one for a second, like a perky weather girl encountering an unexpected cloud formation. "What you've described is perfectly routine, I assure you. We regularly fly all over the Russian Federation and often to places far more remote than Sochi."

Archibald shook his head at his own shortcoming. "Forgive me, I wasn't clear. I literally need the flights to be booked in the name of one of your routine clients. We don't want to raise any eyebrows or generate any paperwork in our names."

Kendra's smile faded as the processor began whirring behind her beautiful blue eyes.

Max set the hook before her lips got too far. "Anonymity is our objective, and we're willing to pay for it."

Kendra reacted as expected to the magic words. This time she was the one who looked left and right and lowered her voice. "There's an engineering company we work with that does a lot of business in and around Sochi. They are one of our more price-sensitive clients. I suspect that if money's no object, they'd be willing to accommodate you."

Man, was it great to be rich, Max thought, suddenly reconsidering his government service career. "Excellent. And you, Kendra, would you mind brokering the deal for, say, a ten-percent commission? I'd rather not be involved."

Chapter 94
Forged Bonds

Switzerland

NICCOLO BOLZANO stubbed out his cigarette and shook his head at Achilles while a smile spread ear to ear. "When you asked for forty numbered accounts spread across Europe, Asia, and the Caribbean, I was prepared for a hundred million or so — but nine billion. Mamma mia."

Achilles had the same reaction when he started thinking about Korovin's money, the money now in his possession. *Million* and *billion* sounded similar, and the words were used interchangeably in colloquial conversations, but the enormous difference became blindingly obvious in context. A million seconds was about twelve days, whereas a billion seconds was nearly thirty-two years. "Is that going to be a problem?"

"No no no. It's only zeros," Niccolo replied, his arms as active as his lips. "Given your security concerns, I'd suggest no fewer than seven anonymous interjurisdictional leaps before parking it across your forty accounts. We'll split and shuffle each deposit before transferring it, making every leap the electronic equivalent of three-card Monte."

Niccolo had once helped Achilles track down an arms trafficker. A Swiss-Italian, he was the polar opposite of Severin Glick in everything but ability. Jet black hair slicked back, a portly physique, and compulsive addictions to both nicotine and caffeine. Despite soulful gray eyes, he always struck Achilles as a man clutching to life by both breasts and daring her to defy him.

"How long will it take?" Achilles asked.

"With most bankers, you'd be looking at three weeks and astronomical fees. But I know which countries and banks are geared to take direct international wires without undue bureaucracy, so there won't be any inquiries or hold-ups. Working full-time, I can do it all in three days. The cost will be peanuts."

Achilles was sure that Niccolo's definition of peanuts varied from his own, but then it was Korovin's money, so he didn't really care.

The last time Achilles had worked with Niccolo, the banker had refused payment with a wave of his cigarette. Granted, giving up a modest government fee in lieu of having the CIA owe you one was a shrewd move, but Achilles had appreciated the gesture.

Today, Niccolo would reap his reward.

Achilles reached out and put a hand on Niccolo's shoulder. "What do you say we agree on three million total in fees? You keep whatever the banks don't take."

Niccolo kept a straight face. "Three million for three days. I can live with that."

"Glad to hear it."

"Let me buy you lunch, the best ragù Napoletano you ever tasted. Then I'll fire up the espresso machine, and we'll get to work."

Achilles double-squeezed Niccolo's shoulder, then removed his hand. "Once all this is done, I'll gladly take you up on your kind offer, my friend. Today, however, I have to hit the road. My plate is as full as your ashtray. Speaking of which, remember to leave ten million in the Bank of Austria account. I need operating funds."

Niccolo bowed agreement. "Sounds like a fun operation."

Achilles paused at the door as Niccolo's final comment sank in. "Actually, I've been looking forward to this operation for a long time."

Niccolo grew a knowing look. As a man who moved billions, he saw a lot of dreams realized. "Ciao, my friend. Godspeed."

Achilles hopped back into the A8 and rocketed off toward Austria. He was looking forward to an even more exciting appointment.

While he'd been in with Niccolo, Max had been chartering a Gulfstream jet and an Ansat helicopter. In an hour, the two spies were due to rendezvous in the west Austrian city of Bregenz, where alumni from Glock and Steyr had combined brainpans to form the specialty weapons company, SPOX.

As he sped through the beautiful mountains overlooking Lake Constance, Achilles reflected on his evolving relationship with his Russian partner. Common goals had pressed them into an alliance defined by rivalry and fraught with suspicion. Then circumstances had forced them through a few flaming hoops, side-by-side. Now, as they approached the ultimate undercover operation, Achilles realized the tie that bound them felt more like a bond than a chain.

Max was already waiting when Achilles pulled into the wooded parking lot. "Doesn't look like much," Max said by way of greeting. Indeed, there was nothing notable about the exterior of the single-story structure, aside from its picturesque location between Lake Constance and Mount Pfänder. "What's SPOX stand for?"

"Technically, it stands for Special Operations Experts, but really it's a nod to their flagship product."

"And what's that?"

Achilles opened the lobby door. "Something that will remind you of Star Trek."

Chapter 95
The FP1

Bregenz, Austria

THIRTY MINUTES and 20,000 euros after opening SPOX's door, Achilles and Max were both standing bare-chested before bathroom sinks, shaving their armpits. It was a necessary part of the weapon customization process, according to Hans and Gunter, the technicians assigned to them.

Achilles looked over at his exposed partner, and thought about how far they'd come. Then he thought about how far they still had to go. As their axillary hair dropped into the sink in what looked more like prep for the ballet than battle, he decided to take a load off Max's mind. "Zoya never slept with me. She prevaricated with everything she had."

Max met his eye in the mirror, but didn't speak.

"Just thought you should know."

The door opened and Hans' big blonde head appeared. "We're ready when you are."

Max gave Achilles an after-you gesture, and they followed the Austrian technician into a room that looked like a cross between a surgical suite and a barber shop.

Hans swept a big hairy arm toward a couple of inversion tables. "Please."

Once they were strapped in and dangling with their heads below their feet, Hans and Gunter went to work securing plastic baggies to their smooth armpits. Hans talked them through it as he worked. "These are the power packs for the FP1." He held up four objects the size of squashed ping-pong balls, then dropped one into each of their bags while Gunter mixed something with a spatula. "They are specifically engineered to deliver a nanosecond electrical pulse."

Gunter moved in and began pouring a thick flesh-toned liquid around the power packs, while Hans set an egg timer and continued his explanation. "The molding material is the same stuff dentists use to make impressions. It will help the power packs stay snugly in place while secreted beneath your arms."

Achilles found it a very peculiar feeling, having his armpits and only his armpits filled with warm liquid.

Once Gunter finished, Hans said, "Now clench down around the power packs, so your elbows are by your sides and your hands cross your chest, like this." He demonstrated.

"What's a nanosecond electrical pulse?" Max asked.

Gunter opened his mouth for the first time since his introduction. He was as tall as Hans, but only about half his weight. He wore a trimmed mustache and beard that gave his gaunt face an elfin appearance. "I'm sure you're familiar with stun guns. Nanosecond electrical pulse devices are a similar, but next-generation technology. And they're military grade. Less than a second of contact will knock out an average soldier for three minutes."

Max looked over at Achilles, his expression a mixture of surprise and skepticism. "Why haven't I heard of them?"

Gunter ran his fingers over his hairy chin. "The technology is still theoretical, according to the experts. Research has been going on for years all over the world, but without success — so far as anybody knows. We happened to find the right pulse parameters, but we're keeping that information confidential until we're ready to commercialize."

"Is the technology lethal?" Achilles asked.

Gunter nodded. "Potentially. Although even traditional stun guns kill people under the right circumstances."

"Under what circumstances is the FP1 lethal?" Achilles asked.

"We don't know. Our data is limited, but we expect casualty rates as high as 0.2 percent from these early models. That's something you'll want to keep in mind. They're definitely military grade and by military, we're not talking UN peace keepers."

After two minutes of set time, the timer rang. Gunter extracted the baggies while Hans returned Achilles and Max to seated positions. The molds looked like childhood Play-Doh creations.

Hans and Gunter peeled off the plastic and trimmed the excess material from the edges, careful to avoid clipping the long wires protruding from the apex. Once satisfied with their craftsmanship, each handed one over, wearing proud expressions. "The little knob beside the micro-USB charging port is the on-off switch. Of course, the long wires deliver the charge. We'll customize their length next."

The technicians went to work gluing the power packs into place and cementing the flesh-toned wires along the undersides of their arms. "You're sure these won't set off a metal detector or register on a wand?" Achilles asked.

Gunter smiled reassuringly. "Absolutely. The FP1 was designed with that in mind. The wires are low mass, well-insulated, and nonferrous. The power pack is also nonmetallic as far as metal detectors are concerned."

"Really? What is it?"

Hans raised a fat finger. "That's proprietary. But I assure you, it won't be detected."

Achilles pictured Korovin's bodyguards. "Does it have enough juice to work against a big guy?"

Hans got a twinkle in his eye, and his basso voice became unexpectedly jovial. "We tested it on cattle. Went to a slaughter house and stood by the conveyor belt. We used our fingers to subdue the cows, rather than the stunning device the workers usually employ. It dropped the poor beasts like a bullet to the brain. Kept them down for over a minute. Coolest thing you ever saw." Hans crossed his big arms on his chest while nodding to himself. "Makes you feel a bit godlike, to be honest."

Achilles was satisfied. Korovin's guards were big, but they didn't weigh a thousand pounds. "What's FP1 stand for?"

"Finger Phaser One. Hey, speaking of batteries," Hans added, changing the subject. "Did you know that traditional stun guns are powered by a single 9-volt battery?"

Max jumped on the question. "Yeah, those are good for two to five minutes of discharge, in my experience. What will we get from these?"

"About one minute. But that's a hundred knockouts, if you don't dawdle."

"No dawdling," Achilles repeated. "Got it. What if we want to knock someone out for longer than three minutes? Will multiple zaps add up?"

"More or less. But don't forget the lethality factor. Best to think of nanosecond electrical pulses like a drug, with overdose potential."

After giving them a second to digest the implications, Hans continued. "You have a decision to make regarding the placement of the electrodes. The most convenient for application purposes is at the tips of your index and middle fingers. But then you have wires running across the palms of your hands. That's both more visible and easier to accidentally knock loose. It's also very dangerous. Easy to accidentally self-inflict by making a fist or grabbing a conductive surface. The alternative site is here." He pointed to the pinky side of his hand, just above his wrist. The karate-chop surface. "Lower risk of detection. Less likely to dislodge. But a bit less convenient for zapping."

"What do you recommend?" Max asked.

"Do you expect to use it in a combat situation or by stealth?"

"Could be either."

"You really don't want them uncovered on your fingertips during a fight."

Achilles frowned. "We really need stealth."

"Are you right-handed?"

"Yes," both spies replied.

"Then I'd go with the finger electrodes on your left hand, and the palm configuration on your right. I'll show you best-practice knockout moves for both applications."

He paused to get their nods of approval. "But I need to warn you, in the strongest possible terms. If you aren't vigilant with the insulating covers or precise with your assault technique, you'll find yourselves unconscious at the worst possible moment."

"That's a hell of a backfire," Max said.

Achilles concurred. A lethal backfire. The FP1 would never make it to market. Bad for Hans and Gunter. Good for him and Max. Korovin would never see it coming.

Chapter 96
Complete Control

Seattle, Washington

WANG'S BIG DAY had finally arrived and by some miracle so had the diverted shipment of fifty autopilot units. Having carefully unpacked the systems to facilitate a seamless resealing, his ten technicians were now busy soldering the auxiliary circuit boards into place.

Both sets.

While his Russian minders looked on — oblivious to the double cross taking place under their cute little noses.

Max might have noticed that Wang's men were adding two boards to each system rather than one, but not these two. Whoever pulled Max out in favor of a couple of women had made a $20 million mistake.

Twenty million, he repeated to himself. Nothing wrong with that.

Despite his wife's daily pleas to go for the gold, Wang had resisted the urge to get greedy. Qi had a point. He might get a billion dollars if he asked for it. But his experience indicated that a torture session followed by a bullet between the eyes was far more likely. Why risk it? Twenty million would give them everything he needed — without the headache.

Later tonight, once the systems were safely inside Boeing's gates, he'd place a phone call and demand payment for the activation code that would switch off the second circuit board. Then he'd disappear onto the *Winsome Whisper* and wait for his bank to provide confirmation that he'd never suffer through another rainy day.

Looking over his shoulder, he saw the fair-haired Russian looking back. Near as he could figure, this was the only time a woman that beautiful had ever stared at him.

She met his gaze with surprising confidence and reflected that sentiment in her tone. "We're running out of time."

This one was proving to be far more analytical than her appearance suggested. Still, analytical wasn't the same as technical. Wang remained confident that he could manage her. He echoed her confident demeanor. "We've still got two hours."

"That's my point. With twenty-five percent of the time remaining, we've still got forty percent of the workload."

It was true, his ten technicians had only modified thirty units. The addition of the override circuit was not factored into the timeline. "They're picking up speed. It may come down to the wire, but we'll make it. Meanwhile, may I suggest you back away from the tables? That may help them focus."

Rather than backing up, she looked over to her colleague. The dark-haired one with soulful eyes was seated on the floor, focused on her laptop rather than his ten men. As he watched, she too stood up and came his way.

"We were expecting a single soldering operation. But they're adding two components."

"Is that a question?"

"Why the variance?" the fair-haired one asked, ganging up on him.

Wang pushed back. "I didn't set your expectations. So I can't speak to variances."

"Only the larger of the circuit boards is in the drawing package." Dark hair pointed to her computer screen.

Wang didn't give an inch. "Don't blame me if you don't have the complete package. The big one is the override unit. The smaller attachment enables communications. Together, they form a single system."

Wang actually had no idea how the system worked, but that seemed logical to him. The way he figured it, autopilot systems normally handed off control to a computer, which then interfaced with all the other systems on the aircraft to safely and efficiently follow the flight plan. With *Sunset* in place, the autopilot system would irrevocably pass that control to a remote operator instead, essentially turning the aircraft into a drone.

The women stared at him.

He stared back with confidence. As his father liked to say, the rice was already cooked. They only had two choices: proceed with the operation or cancel it. No way they would call it quits based solely on suspicion.

Wang had them in a corner. He knew it, and their eyes told him they knew it too.

Chapter 97
Bit of Coin

Seattle, Washington

ZOYA HAD ANTICIPATED feeling a sense of relief once her mission was complete, but her shoulders remained tied in knots, and her appetite hadn't returned. Sure, Max and Achilles were still in the thick of it, but that didn't account for her nervous tension. The guys were pros, and Max always came through. She and Katya had been the wildcards. But they'd done their part and done it well.

The problem, she realized, was what they'd done — and what it could lead to. "I don't know how the guys do it."

Katya was clearly having similar thoughts, but held up her chopsticks in apology until she swallowed her sushi. "Men are better at compartmentalizing their emotions. And at breaking things down into binary constituencies. Us or them. Live or die." She gestured back and forth with her chopsticks like a metronome. "Women tend to feel situations from all angles, along with the connections in between."

Zoya agreed. "I can't ignore the angle that we just gave Korovin the power to kill tens of thousands of civilians."

"He already has a nuclear arsenal. This doesn't change anything." Katya's expression indicated she realized her mistake even as she spoke the words.

Zoya called her on it. "Of course it does. *Sunset* won't be traceable to him. We gave him the power to get away with mass murder."

Katya nodded. "You're right. But he won't. Achilles and Max will see to that. Even if they aren't successful on their current mission, all they have to do is alert Boeing."

"Unless they're too late."

Katya started to reply but coughed instead. "Excuse me, the wasabi has quite a kick." She fanned her mouth. "They won't be too late. I know next to nothing about aircraft manufacturing, but even if installing autopilot systems is the last step in the process, it will still take time for the airline to put them into service. I'm sure there's paperwork involved."

"I was reading up on that. Boeing is delivering fifty 737s a month. And they use just-in-time manufacturing, so they're not holding

Katya's phone started vibrating. "It's a Seattle prefix, but I don't recognize the number." She looked around. They were in a corner booth, with nobody else close by. "I'll put it on speaker."

Zoya appreciated the gesture.

Katya accepted the call, but didn't speak.

"Hello?" It was Wang's sing-song voice.

"Yes," Katya said.

"It's me. I have some information. It's very confidential. Can we talk?"

"Hold on," Katya said. She plugged in her earbuds, and gave Zoya one. "Go ahead."

"Our shipment has been delivered. Boeing just logged it in."

"You followed the truck?"

"Obviously."

"Why? We paid you the moment the truck was loaded."

"Yes, well, that was just a down payment. I'm going to require twenty more. Million that is. Paid in Bitcoin."

After the women paused to look at each other, Katya said, "Or?"

"Or the units will be useless. You were right earlier to suspect me. That second component wasn't part of the original package. It was my own add-on."

Zoya reached over and disconnected the call.

"What did you do that for?"

"He's screwing us. I don't want him to enjoy it too much."

Katya's wide eyes turned jolly as Wang called right back. "What does it do?" she asked without preamble.

Wang took a second to compose himself. "Think of it as a drawbridge. Without the activation code that lowers the bridge, your circuit board won't link up with the autopilot system."

"And the cost for lowering the bridge is twenty million."

"Precisely."

"You little weasel. We don't have twenty million."

"I'm sure you can get it. I'm sure you could get a billion if required to. But I want to keep things simple. Twenty million is a very modest price, a pin-prick, not decapitation."

"It will take some time."

"Of course. But I expect you'll get a rapid response. Twenty-four hours should give you plenty of time. And just so you know, Bitcoin works 'round the clock."

Katya left him hanging for a few ticks. "Where and when do we meet?"

Wang chuckled before replying in a derisive tone. "Oh, there will be no meeting. No communication either. I'm about to paste my account number on our message board. You'll need to switch the 6s and 9s.

Repeat that back."

"We'll need to switch the 6s and 9s."

"Good. When the money shows up in my account, I'll post the activation code. Same rule applies to it. Switch the 6s and 9s. Are we clear?"

"How do we know you'll deliver the code once we deliver the money?"

Wang was ready with a one word answer. "Logic."

"Logic?"

"If I weren't satisfied with that sum, I'd be asking for more. Good enough?"

No arguing with that, Zoya thought. He could have asked for twenty billion.

"Good enough," Katya said.

"Are we clear?"

"Yes, we're clear."

"Good. Because we won't be speaking again."

Chapter 98
The Plan

Seattle, Washington

ZOYA WAS GLAD that Wang was blackmailing them, because it meant she'd get to speak with Max. Familiarity with Ignaty's mindset would be important to their discussion of Wang's treachery, and Achilles didn't have it.

Once Katya explained the situation to Achilles, he agreed. Max came on speakerphone a few seconds later. "I'm sure Ignaty will wire the money. No doubt the Bitcoin requirement will have him cursing the walls, but Wang was smart to stick to a modest figure. Paying is a no-brainer."

Just hearing Max's voice imbued Zoya with a calm she hadn't felt in days. As that warm blanket settled over her shoulders, hope began winning the battle raging in her heart.

"That's good to hear," Katya said, nodding along with Zoya.

The women were in a roadside motel room whose highlights included a grimy window overlooking a parking lot, and a heating unit louder than a lawnmower. Once their part of *Sunset* was completed, they'd decided to distance themselves from the scene. Both had longed for a five-star resort with room service and fine linen and spa treatments that would wash away the stresses and strains of Korovin and Wang. But both had opted for a place that took cash without questions and resolved not to think about all the mileage on their mattresses.

Achilles was the next to speak. "Is the Bear working? Do you have a map of Wang's location?"

"We're not sure," Katya said. "His beeps are coming from the middle of Puget Sound. Either there's a malfunction, or he's on a boat, or he tossed the umbrella on a garbage scow. We didn't want to risk investigating without your guidance."

"I think he'll ditch his wife before that umbrella," Max said. "But the Bear's not going to be much use tracking a moving target. We need to keep tabs on him until this is over. He may become crucial to our operation at some point. With so many variables in play, it's impossible to predict. I also worry about him selling *Sunset* to someone else, a terrorist group with lots of money, for example."

"What does it matter?" Zoya asked. "You can alert Boeing. They'll remove the autopilot systems."

"We don't want the story to get out," Achilles said. "Korovin had a brilliant idea. Best it dies with him."

"Agreed," Max added. "I'd hate to risk spooking the public. That would give Korovin part of what he wants. What's all that noise I'm hearing?"

"That's the heater in our motel room. It's not the Ritz."

"We'll get you to the Ritz when this is done. Meanwhile pack up and go after Wang. Don't engage, just observe."

"Do you still have the tracking pellet I put in Zoya's necklace?" Achilles asked.

"Sure. We kept it."

"If Wang is on a boat, and you can find it, getting that pellet aboard would solve our tracking problem. Assuming the battery still has juice."

The ladies looked at each other, pleased. "Okay. We'll call you for instructions when we know more."

Achilles popped their balloon. "I'm afraid we might not be available. We're going to be flying and then pretty intensely engaged. You'll need to play it by ear. Just don't take risks. And don't let Wang spot you."

"Use binoculars, and move at night," Max added. "If conditions look right to place the tracker, don't step onto the boat, he'll feel that. Work from the dock, out of sight of any window."

"Where should we put the pellet?"

"Doesn't matter," Achilles said. "The signal will work from anywhere. Just squeeze some epoxy into an inconspicuous corner and push the pellet inside."

"What if he's not docked?"

"That's when things get tricky. If he's on open water, you might need to get creative."

Zoya watched Katya processing all this. She had a habit of running her fingernails over the palm of her left thumb: *one two three four, one two three four.* And her fingers were really flying now. "What if he's not on a boat? What if he found the Bear and tossed it?"

"You'll think of some other way to find him," Achilles said. "You're two of the smartest people on the planet. But cross that bridge when you come to it. Don't borrow trouble for now."

"So this is it?" Zoya asked, her voice cracking. "You're actually going to Russia to do that thing?"

"We don't have a choice," Max said.

"We could just run away. With all that money, surely we could work something out."

"We didn't earn that money, and we haven't earned our freedom. You know the deal we made."

Zoya looked over at Katya. "Surely Achilles won't hold you to that. Not after Wang and Zurich and everything else we've done."

Katya looked like she wasn't sure how Achilles would respond, giving Zoya a sinking feeling. Before she could protest, Max made the issue irrelevant. "This is important, Zoya. You've seen first-hand how Korovin thinks, and how ruthless and committed he is. He has to go. I've got the opportunity, and I'm going to take it."

"But—"

Max cut her off. "They say you don't get to choose your fate, but at least now I know mine."

Chapter 99
Two Sentences

Black Sea Coast, Russia

THE WINDY CLIFF out in front of his seaside home was Korovin's favorite place in the world. With the Black Sea slapping rough rocks far below, the expansive green garden blooming fragrantly behind, and an endless blue horizon marred only by the occasional cloud, it was an analogy of his life.

At the moment, however, he wasn't reflecting on the prosperity he'd created or pondering the challenges ahead. He was focused on the danger all around, contemplating the penalty for a single misstep. But not with dread.

Oddly enough, he loved precarious positions like this.

Only those who took the greatest risks could reap the grandest rewards.

Korovin looked down at the letter in his hand for the third time. Just two simple sentences, but a lot to digest.

He wasn't aware of Ignaty's presence until his strategist spoke from just a few steps behind. "We've done it!"

Korovin turned his back to the wind and faced the man he'd summoned. "What have we done?"

"I just received confirmation from my man at Boeing. The *Sunset* units have arrived!"

Korovin couldn't help but smile inside. What a coup! With one bold stroke he would cripple his greatest rival and make another take the fall. You had to go back 3,300 years to the Trojan Horse to find a tactic as ingenious and grand. "No hitches? No glitches? No unexpected developments?"

"Just one." Ignaty paused for dramatic effect as he tended to do. "Wang discovered what we were up to and figured out how to exploit it. The sly fox added a component during the assembly operation. Now *Sunset* won't engage without his encryption code. He wants twenty million for it. Paid in Bitcoin."

Korovin wasn't sure he'd heard correctly with the wind. "Twenty million? With an *m*, not a *b*?"

Ignaty nodded. "Paid in Bitcoin. Obviously he doesn't know it's us.

Max says Wang's convinced he's dealing with a terrorist operation."

Korovin gamed it out in his mind.

Ignaty waited.

When the president looked up, his analysis complete, Ignaty said, "So we'll pay Wang, get the code, then kill him."

"No."

"No? *No* to the payment, or *no* to the killing? Surely we won't let him get away with blackmailing us."

Korovin threw a derisive look at his chief strategist. "*Who* won't let him get away with it? Pride doesn't factor in when you're anonymous. Besides, we're better off having Wang out there. No doubt he's skilled at evasion. Best to keep the FBI busy tracking him."

Ignaty took a moment to ponder Korovin's insight. "And if they catch him?"

"It doesn't matter."

Ignaty nodded deferentially, quickly catching on once pointed in the right direction. "You're right."

"Bitcoin works nonstop, right?" asked Korovin.

"24/7/365."

"All the same, tell Max to make no contact for 48 hours. I want Wang to sweat. Make the transfer Monday evening, just before the banks close."

"Consider it done."

Ignaty turned to leave, but Korovin grabbed his bicep. "That wasn't why I summoned you." Korovin raised the letter. "This was."

"What is it?"

"Glick's weekly report." This time it was Korovin who paused for dramatic effect.

The solution to the stock scandal had eluded the president. His mind tended to untangle perplexing puzzles in the middle of the night. When the international press called him a tactical genius, they had no clue it was usually his unconscious mind they were complimenting. But this time there was nothing to compliment. The summit had come and gone, and he was still bamboozled.

With Glick appearing ever more innocent, Korovin kept coming back to the only other person who knew the whole story. He kept coming back to Ignaty.

He looked Ignaty in the eye. "Glick says he thought of something important, something he forgot to mention in Zurich. He's coming here tomorrow to tell me about it in person."

Ignaty's eyes grew wide. "He can't be seen with you."

"He won't be. For the record, he'll be at a resort in Sochi, just like Max and Zoya."

Ignaty shifted his gaze to the sea. "What do you think he remembered?"

"I don't know." Korovin waited for Ignaty to look back over before adding, "But I'd kill to find out."

Chapter 100
The Return

Black Sea Coast, Russia

MAX LOOKED DOWN at the rocky coastline whizzing by below at 260 kilometers per hour. As surprising as his first helicopter flight to Seaside had been, Max found his return trip even more remarkable.

This time the Ansat's cargo included a Swiss banker, an ex-CIA agent, and an EMP device.

This time he was in disguise and at the stick.

This time he knew the game plan, but Korovin didn't.

As his president's summer home came into view on the horizon, Max was certain that no fewer than two anti-aircraft systems had their missiles locked on his exhaust. But he couldn't spot the stations. And he knew he'd never see the missile coming. Not at 2,000 meters per second. If Korovin had somehow seen through the ruse, Max's world would go from light to black without a blink in between.

He reached up to scratch his face, but stopped himself in time. His silicone mask was driving him crazy. It itched inside. Mila hadn't warned him about that, and Achilles hadn't said a thing after his Charlie Rose impersonation. If it was an allergy, he hoped it wouldn't cause his face to swell. It was mission-critical that his face look normal when the mask came off.

No time to worry about that now. Max alerted his passengers to their position. "We're on approach."

"It's remarkable," Glick said. "I was expecting extravagance, but this is also enormous."

"It's a fortress," Achilles replied.

In the role of Alex Azarov, a Zurich-based member of Korovin's staff, Achilles had been pouring on the charm ever since they picked up Glick at his home earlier that morning. Collegial chit-chat, kind gestures, and supportive expressions, all designed to put the banker at ease. "Korovin runs it like a fortress, too," Achilles said. "Do yourself a favor, and keep quiet until we're alone with him. I understand the guards speak English poorly, so you'd be wise not to risk an unfortunate misinterpretation. Beautiful though it may be, for the men working security it's a high-stress environment."

Glick's white eyebrows shot up. "You *understand*? You don't *know*?"

"Like you, I work for Korovin internationally. I've never been to Seaside, but I've heard rumors."

"I didn't realize," Glick said. "And I see your point. Thank you."

"One other piece of advice," Achilles said. "Don't let them separate us."

Glick blinked non-comprehension.

Achilles clarified. "People disappear when there are no witnesses."

Glick paled, then turned back to the window.

Achilles did the same.

Max returned his gaze to the windshield. He and Achilles would be walking multiple tightropes over the next few minutes, jumping from one to another like circus performers on steroids.

Achilles' first act was getting Glick to Korovin before Glick figured out that he hadn't actually been invited. Meanwhile, Max had to finagle his way into the guardroom without arousing suspicion. Once they were both positioned, the serious acrobatic acts would begin.

Max watched with growing trepidation while a black Mercedes sedan and a matching SUV pulled up on either side of the central helipad. He announced the sighting to his passengers. "The welcoming committee has arrived." Ten seconds later he put the skids center-circle on the concrete.

Achilles ushered Glick out the door and toward the limo as Max powered down. He looked back to meet Max's eye before stepping into the Mercedes. They'd be completely reliant on each other for the remainder of the operation. If either slipped up, neither would leave Seaside alive.

The SUV driver walked over as Max stepped out of the powered-down bird. Just one guy, but sized like a Siberian mountain. "You're with me," he said, his deep voice rumbling like thunder.

Max extended a hand. "Arkady Usatov."

"Anton Guryev."

"Mind if I sit up front?"

"Suit yourself. It's a short drive."

Max slid in and Guryev hit the gas.

"Where will I be waiting?" Max asked, trying to get his thoughts off his itching face. Surely there weren't really ants crawling all over it.

"There's a lounge you'll find comfortable. We call it the Waiting Room."

"Could you take me to the security office instead? Colonel Pushkin is an old friend."

Guryev raised a brow. Just one. "You know Igor Gregorivich?"

"We were close at the academy."

"Does he know you're coming?"

"No. I'd forgotten he was here. Just remembered on the way in. I'd love to see him. It's been a while."

Guryev turned his head in an open appraisal. Max looked back. The man had a jaw like a granite cliff. "I'll look into that."

One way or another, Max had to get to the guardroom right away. If finesse wouldn't work, he'd have to use force. "I'm just not sure how long we'll be here. I got the impression my guy's meeting with Korovin would be very quick."

"I don't know what Pushkin was like back at the Academy, but nowadays he doesn't like surprises."

"It will be a pleasant surprise. I promise."

Guryev again raised one brow. "Suit yourself."

"Say, you don't happen to have an allergy pill or three, do you?"

"Ask Vanya when we get to the security office. He's always sneezing. Maybe you'll get lucky."

Rather than following Achilles' sedan toward the underground entrance portico Max had used the last time, Guryev kept going around the side of the palace to a parking lot abutting a service entrance. It reminded Max of the back door to a large hotel, except that all the cars were black Mercedes. No private vehicles. Apparently everyone who worked there, lived there as well — boosting both security and secrecy.

"How many people work here?" Max asked as they got out.

"There's a base of about twenty, but that doubles when the president's in residence, which is most weekends. It quadruples if he's got official guests."

"Not a bad gig."

"Best posting I ever had."

Watching Guryev cast a hulking shadow on the door, Max hoped Hans hadn't been bullshitting about the FP1 dropping cattle.

The service wing resembled the rest of the building. It boasted high ceilings and walls trimmed with ornate wainscoting, although no artwork was wasted on the space above.

Guryev led him toward a vault-like steel door. "We're in here." He held his palm up to the scanner, but before the little red light turned green, the door swung open from the inside.

Colonel Igor Pushkin stepped out.

Max cringed internally at the stroke of bad luck. He needed to end up on the other side of the door, and he'd particularly wanted to be there when Pushkin first saw him, in case his disguise came up short.

Pushkin's eyes moved quickly from Guryev to Max, where they stopped and scanned with partial recognition.

Max was banking on the flip of a coin, the hope that Pushkin had not seen his old roommate for years. "Good to see you, Igor."

"Arkady Usatov," Pushkin said, appraising him with a look that definitely wasn't *pleased to see you.*

Max struggled to retain his best poker face, which of course wasn't his face at all. His real face was practically a mirror image of the one staring back at him.

Pushkin poked two fingers into Max's chest. "I thought I told you I never wanted to see you again!"

Chapter 101
One Ping

Black Sea Coast, Russia

AS THE MERCEDES pulled away from the helipad, Achilles flirted with the idea that the head wound he'd received back on Nuikaohao was more serious than he realized. Why else would he be making a move against one of the best-protected men on the planet, on his home turf, armed only with audacity and a few electrical tricks?

Fortunately, an acceptable answer came quickly. He'd promised his president. That and a lack of alternatives. And revenge for Senator Collins. And to settle an old score. And finally, because he could. This was his calling.

Achilles wondered how Katya was doing at that very moment. He wished he'd been able to size Wang up before sending Katya after him. Max had assured him that the Chinese spy wasn't the violent type, and since Zoya was equally involved in the chase, Achilles took him at his word. Still, as the extortion twist had shown, operations were unpredictable.

The Mercedes zipped past Seaside's grand entrance, just as Max had predicted. Shortly thereafter, they descended into a semicircular underground portico reminiscent of a fancy city-center hotel.

Large men waited there with solemn faces and security wands.

Achilles and Glick each got their own greeter. "Welcome to Seaside. Please raise your arms."

Achilles clutched his phone and complied. "We're here on Korovin's invitation."

"Obviously."

The guard got friendly when Achilles' belt buckle hummed. Achilles held back an impulsive quip, and a second later the search was over. The FP1 hadn't registered. Hans was a man of his word.

Glick's guard pointed them up a bifurcating marble staircase. They ascended into a domed atrium whose frescoes could have been painted by Michelangelo. Under normal circumstances, Achilles would have been in awe, but today all he saw was a battlefield.

Up top, the guard again took the lead, guiding them down a hallway the length of a football stadium and the style of an art museum. The further they walked down its white marble floor, the more blood drained from Glick's face. The sight reminded Achilles of an observation he'd made many times in the field: courage wasn't linked to rank.

Back in Switzerland, Glick's wealth and position made him as much a demigod as the Greek statues they were passing. And no doubt, given his financial acumen, some of that was deserved. But here at Seaside, the successful Swiss banker clearly realized he was but a flea on the big dog's back. Easily rubbed out, if Korovin wanted to scratch.

The guard opened an arched door on the side of the hall. He gestured Achilles into a wood-paneled room resembling a gentlemen's club. "You can wait here. There's satellite TV, espresso, and cigars. Or feel free to help yourself to something stronger if you'd like."

Achilles' feet didn't respond to the gesture. "I'll be sticking with Severin."

"No, you'll be doing as you're told and waiting here. Korovin's only scheduled to meet with Glick."

"We're a team." Achilles turned to the banker, placing the ball in his court. While Glick blinked like a computer stuck processing, Achilles brought his hands behind his back and peeled the rubber pads from his palm and fingertips, exposing the FP1 electrodes.

Glick finally snapped to. "Yes, we're a team. I'm sure the schedule means *the Glick party*, which includes Mr. Azarov."

"If the president wants him, I'll come back."

Fear straightened Glick's spine, and he snapped into haughty banker mode. He spoke nothing further, but his expression said plenty.

The guard stared back for a few silent seconds, then broke. "Follow me."

As their footsteps echoed off the polished marble, Achilles felt his phone vibrate. Once. Only once. Bad news.

He fell a half pace back and snuck a peek at the screen to confirm that he hadn't missed the second ping. He hadn't. Max was having issues with security.

Life was about to get complicated.

Chapter 102
Two Fingers

Black Sea Coast, Russia

MAX LOOKED DOWN at the colonel's fingers as they poked into his chest, and felt Guryev tense beside him. *It will be a pleasant surprise*, he'd promised. A fight between the old best friends was not a scenario Max had considered.

Exposing the electrodes on the side of his right hand and tips of his left index and middle fingers would take a good three seconds. He couldn't do it haphazardly or he'd risk knocking himself out. And he couldn't do it while under direct observation. Too conspicuous. He'd have to charm his way through this situation.

Max met Pushkin's eye. "That was a long time ago, old friend. Let's not allow one bad event to overshadow all the good. I apologize, most sincerely."

If it weren't for the chance of his electrodes being noticed during this moment of intense scrutiny, Max would hold out his hand at this point. Instead he remained still. Very awkward.

Pushkin stared back at him.

Max thought Pushkin's eyes were much crueler than his own, but the color sure looked the same.

Pushkin tilted his head down the hall. "I was about to get some coffee."

"Coffee's good," Max said, feeling his diaphragm relax. "But I have a better idea."

Both men turned to him.

Max rapped his knuckles on his chest. A resonant metallic thunk-thunk came back. "Viru Valge vodka. A gold medal winner from Estonia. A gift from their ambassador to Mr. Glick, who was kind enough to share. What could be better than old friends and fine spirits on a quiet Sunday afternoon?"

Pushkin cocked his head. "Estonian, you say? I do like their women. I guess I could give their best vodka a try. What do you say, Gura? You up for a little trip to Tallinn?"

Guryev placed his palm back on the scanner, opening the guardroom door.

The audacious plan Max and Achilles had devised was full of risks, gambles, and suppositions. As professional spies, that was business as usual for both of them. But Max was still holding his breath as the door swung open. He was going to have to neutralize everyone in the suite, so he was praying it wouldn't be a crowd.

Like everything at the palace, the security office was grand. Sixteen laptop-size screens surrounded a large central display. All were angled to be easily observable by a single guard. That guard ignored them, keeping his eyes on his work, strictly following protocol with his boss in the room.

Also on the wall before the guard, a dedicated box hosted a big red button and a smaller yellow one. Both begged to be slapped. A siren and a silent alarm, no doubt. Next to them, Max saw a keyhole rather than a green button. If the op went to hell, he'd be powerless to silence the alarm.

Max took a second to study the big screen over the guard's shoulder. It showed the president with his feet up on an ottoman and his face glued to the tablet in his hand.

Glick and Achilles had yet to arrive.

Pushkin followed his gaze. "The large screen always shows the president. The smaller ones either jump to new motion or shuffle at six-second intervals according to some fancy algorithm designed to maintain vigilance."

"I'm impressed," Max said, while his mind worked the problem. He had three men to contend with. Three was one too many for his hands, but better than it could have been. In the best of worlds, he'd orchestrate a simultaneous two-handed zap. Drop Guryev and Pushkin before either knew anything was happening. Now he had to wage a three-on-one assault against men wearing ear-mikes and guns while Achilles waited anxiously for the *all-clear* signal, a double vibration on his phone.

Max walked over to the seated guard. "Vanya, I heard you might have an allergy pill to spare?"

Vanya reached over to the drawer on his left and extracted a bottle without looking away from his charge. Surely he wasn't this disciplined when Pushkin was out of the room? "Help yourself."

Max dumped two tiny white pills into his hand and dry swallowed them. "Thanks."

With one potential disaster averted, Max decided it was time to get clever. He pulled the copper flask from his breast pocket, and turned back to Pushkin. "I don't suppose you have any ice handy?"

"Vanya will get us some."

The guard spun around and jumped to his feet. "Right away, Colonel."

As Vanya left the room, Pushkin gestured toward the monitors he'd just vacated. "This is just the passive civilian stuff." He pointed to the opposite wall, which boasted six computer stations. "We've got active military defenses like you wouldn't believe. Radar. Sonar. Air, land, and sea defensive systems. The Kremlin has nothing on Seaside."

Max was impressed, but not overly so. After all, he was there. "Where is everybody?"

"Korovin likes it quiet. This is his place to get away from the Moscow beehive. And frankly, nothing ever happens here. We're too isolated."

"An old drunk guy showed up once," Guryev said. "Some kids from the nearest town let him off at the foot of the drive as a prank. I choppered him to Novorossiysk and left him there. Figured if he didn't come back, it would stoke a legend."

Pushkin half-smiled at the memory.

Max found that an encouraging sign. He unscrewed the flask's lid and took a sip. He'd gotten used to room-temperature liquor while drinking baijiu with Wang. "It's pretty good at any temperature." He handed the vodka to Pushkin.

Pushkin ventured a sip. "Smooth. I'm sure those Estonian distillers are of Russian heritage." He took a longer swallow.

While Pushkin handed the flask to Guryev, Max put his hands behind his back and carefully peeled the rubber pads off the electrodes on his palm and fingers. As the electricians would say, he was now *hot*.

"What's the symbol on the flask?" Guryev asked after nodding his approval of the taste. "Is that also Estonian?"

That was Max's cue. "This is the coolest flask you've ever seen. Got it from a Swiss metallurgist." He leaned in and spoke conspiratorially. "Screw the lid on and lay it on the table. I'll show you something cool."

As Guryev began screwing, Achilles and Glick appeared on a side monitor. They were outside the lounge where Max had met with Ignaty. They were less than a minute from Korovin's parlor.

Max was out of time.

The big steel door clicked open and Vanya walked in with four plain white coffee mugs full of ice.

Max ran his hand over a pocket and gave his clicker a single tap, signaling Achilles *not-yet*.

They'd both be improvising now.

The tightrope was getting higher.

Every second would count.

"There we go," Guryev said, emptying the flask between the mugs.

As the four men each grabbed one, Max waited for the right moment to strike. He'd only get one chance.

Pushkin gave his chilled vodka a sip, and nodded approval. Normally Russians would slam shots of chilled vodka, straight from the freezer. But military men also learned quickly to adapt to circumstance. "So you're living in Switzerland now?"

"Yeah, Zurich. Flying birds for the bankers. It's not as nice as your gig, but I can't complain."

The men each took another sip.

Guryev held up the empty container. "What were you going to show us?"

"Wait till you see this. Lay the flask on the table," Max said, willing Achilles to keep things under control for just a few seconds more.

Guryev laid down the flask.

Max pressed the index and middle fingers from his right hand down on one corner. "Now do this. Everyone at once." He pulled his hand back.

The men looked skeptical, but complied.

This time Max reached out with his left hand. Positioning his hot fingers an inch above the fourth corner, he said. "Press down firmly, like you're trying to bend it." When he saw their fingernails turn white, he pressed down as well.

Nothing happened.

Chapter 103
Perseus

Black Sea Coast, Russia

ACHILLES HAD NEVER SEEN a room as grand as the parlor at President Korovin's seaside home. Certainly not in a private residence. With the nervous Swiss banker by his side, he tried to take it all in as his feet propelled him toward the enormous picture window dominating the far wall. Between the ornate garden in the foreground and the white-capped waters of the Black Sea beyond, Korovin enjoyed an ever-changing view reminiscent of great gallery canvasses.

"Ever own a pet python?"

The curious query hit them from behind. The voice was familiar and anticipated but jolting nonetheless. They whirled about to see Korovin gliding toward them with the grace of a jungle cat.

Korovin continued his train of thought without introduction or pause. "I owned one once. A gift from the president of Vietnam. Named him Perseus. Kept him here at Seaside, where the staff grew rather fond of him. They kept Perseus fat and friendly on a diet of rats and rabbits and *stray dogs.*"

Achilles had no idea where this was going, but he found the tactic fascinating. The good news was that Korovin was burning clock, giving Max time to work. The bad news was that poor Glick might faint.

"For years, the python was a conversation piece at meetings like this, and I grew as fond of him as a man can of a snake. Then Perseus changed. For a month he ate nothing, while at the same time his length grew by nearly a meter." Korovin held out one open palm, then the other, demonstrating the apparent contradiction. "Concerned, I called a vet. A specialist. Flew him in from Hanoi. Care to guess what the vet asked me?"

Both visitors shook their heads.

"He asked me if Perseus was free to roam the house. My parlor, my study, my bedroom. I told him yes, that was part of the fun. *Where's Perseus?* became a welcome distraction.*" Korovin looked left and right, his arms still spread. "Care to guess what the vet told me?"

Achilles felt Glick trembling as again he shook his head.

"He told me, 'Mr. President, I'm afraid your pet is preparing to eat you.' " Korovin brought his hands together in a clap as his eyes locked on Glick.

Glick said nothing.

Achilles said nothing.

Korovin said, "What have you come to tell me, Severin?"

Glick cleared his throat. "I've brought your capital growth strategy, Mr. President."

"My capital growth strategy?"

"Yes. Ten-fold growth in ten years. An annual growth rate of twenty-five percent." Glick's demeanor eased a little as the topic turned to his comfort zone.

The easing didn't last.

Korovin didn't smile. He didn't tilt his head. He didn't move his hands. He just stared at Glick with unblinking eyes, while Achilles waited for his phone to vibrate twice.

"Do you think that's my primary concern? Do you think I lack for money?"

The question hit the Swiss banker like a poke in the eye, but he quickly came around. "I'm sure you have other more pressing concerns, but money is the one I'm best suited to help you with."

Korovin shook his head. "I want to hear about the Vulcan Fisher purchase."

"I sold off all your shares. Immediately. As we agreed last weekend in Zurich. I called in some favors and got it all done with no net loss. The error cost you nothing."

"Cost me nothing. Cost me nothing." Korovin turned to Achilles, frustration writ large on his face. "Who are you?"

Anytime now, Max. Replying in Russian so Glick wouldn't understand, Achilles said, "Alex Azarov. Mr. Glick thought it might be wise to bring a translator. Another set of ears, really, given your excellent English, just to avoid any misunderstandings."

The president did not look impressed. "If Severin thinks I'd hesitate to swing the axe just because two heads are on the block, well, I'm afraid you'll find he's mistaken."

Korovin turned back to Glick. "Did you, or did you not, think of anything new regarding the origins of the Vulcan Fisher purchase?"

Glick looked at Achilles.

Come on, Max. "Mr. Glick doesn't want to get anyone in trouble, but there was an incident that appears suspicious, in retrospect. One that slipped his mind. On the way from the exchange with the embassy courier, he stopped at his usual coffee shop. One of the other patrons tripped and bumped into him."

Korovin turned to Glick. "You got pick-pocketed?"

Glick had no foreknowledge of the ruse Achilles had just employed. For a second he froze, then his professional instincts kicked in. "I can't think of any other explanation."

As Korovin leaned in and Glick cowered back, Achilles inched into striking range. *Hurry up, Max.*

"Did you bring me a name?" Korovin pressed.

Glick couldn't look to Achilles for guidance. Korovin would see right through that. "No."

"A videotape?"

"No."

Korovin spread his arms. "Well, in the past this would have been the point where I'd introduce you to Perseus. But since he's no longer with us, my security chief will have to do."

Chapter 104
Hostile Intent

Black Sea Coast, Russia

GURYEV LOOKED UP from the flask. "Feels a bit tingly. You said you got this from a Swiss metallurgist?"

Max didn't understand why the guards hadn't collapsed from electrical shock. The flask was pure copper. Highly conductive. He'd pressed both FP1 electrodes firmly against it, delivering the nanosecond electrical pulse.

The answer hit him like a hammer to the forehead while he smiled sheepishly at his drinking companions. People only get shocked if they have flesh *between* the electrodes.

As the guards withdrew their hands, Max knew it would all be over if he didn't come up with another idea fast. It might already be over but he couldn't risk a glance at the big screen to find out — not with all eyes on him.

Thinking fast, he said, "I guess the flask has to be full to work. The tingling should have been much stronger. Something about conducting the electrical force between people. Try it this way." He flipped the flask over and pressed both his thumbs on it in a gesture reminiscent of a few drinking games.

Pushkin shook his head and sipped his vodka while Vanya and Guryev played along.

As soon as their thumbs were down, Max said, "No, like this."

He brought his hands down on theirs, pressing electrodes directly into their flesh.

Vanya and Guryev dropped without a sound. It was as if Max had hit an off switch. One second they were upright and animated, the next they were slumped over each other like pigs on the slaughterhouse floor.

Max lost a second to surprise.

Pushkin didn't. Years as a bodyguard had honed his reflexes. He jumped back and reached for his gun.

Max lunged after him. All he had to do was touch Pushkin's skin with his left forefingers or the edge of his right hand — and time was on his side. Before Pushkin could aim, Max would be on him.

Pushkin somehow sensed this and shifted into a defensive crouch rather than going for his weapon. Korovin had picked a man with a quick tactical mind.

Max had no choice but to follow through with the lunge. He aimed his hands at the colonel's throat and put all his weight into it.

Pushkin thrust his arms up and grabbed Max by the wrists. His hands clamped down like steel bands. Then Pushkin went with Max's momentum rather than fighting it, using a classic Aikido move. The two flew back and collided with Vanya's chair, sending it to the ground as they landed with a thud.

Immediately both combatants started to roll. Max tried to roll free. Pushkin tried to roll on top. They ended up writhing around on their sides, neither able to get atop the other. Each refusing to relinquish his grip.

Pushkin tried to pull Max's hands ever further from his throat.

Max strained to make skin contact.

Although the two were of the same size and general build, the security chief had thousands more hours in the gym. Max realized that without a tactical triumph, he was going to lose. Eventually Pushkin's greater strength would wrangle Max's arms into joint locks. Then his elbows would snap and it would all be over.

Max had to find an advantage. He had to outwit his opponent.

Pushkin moved first. He bucked and wrapped his legs around Max's in a scissor hold. Then he began to squeeze.

Max fought it by writhing like a live fish on a hot skillet.

Pushkin conserved his energy by going with the motion. He was waiting for Max to fatigue.

Eventually Max built up enough momentum to roll atop the colonel. As he reached the apex of the roll, he put everything he had into pressing his hands back together, towards Pushkin's throat. The instant his opponent pushed back, Max reversed directions.

Their arms flew wide.

Max brought his forehead down on Pushkin's nose like a boot-heel on a roach.

The colonel momentarily relaxed his grip as the crunch resounded and the blood spurted and the expletives escaped his lips.

Max yanked his hands back through Pushkin's slacked fingers, bringing the electrodes into contact with exposed flesh.

The colonel collapsed as quickly as a man who'd taken a bullet to the brain.

Max reached for the clicker without even pausing to check the big screen. He pressed the button — two times.

Chapter 105
Concurrence

Black Sea Coast, Russia

AS KOROVIN REACHED for the device that would summon security, Achilles held out his phone in a blocking move. "Here you go, Mr. President. Pictures of the pickpocket."

Korovin paused, giving Achilles a killer look.

Achilles remained calm and composed. "As I said, Mr. Glick is hesitant to get anyone in trouble. But he's also eager to cooperate."

"Show me."

Achilles pulled up a surveillance photo and passed Korovin the phone.

As Korovin accepted it, the phone vibrated. Twice. "What's that?"

Achilles checked the screen, then locked his eyes on those famous cornflower blues. "Good news, Mr. President. Justice will finally be served."

Korovin stared back.

Achilles waited for the flash of fear, then he zapped the president's hand.

Korovin collapsed.

Glick yelped. "My God! What have you done! Is he alive? We'll be killed."

"Yes, we will. Unless you play along."

"Play along?"

"The president just had a stroke — you hear me Severin? Korovin just collapsed." Achilles held Glick's eye until the banker nodded. Then he scooped Korovin onto his shoulder in a fireman's carry. "Let's go. We've got to fly him to a hospital. Immediately. Otherwise he may never recover."

Achilles didn't lead them out the way they'd come in. He headed straight for the palace's main entrance. They made it to within fifty feet when two guards stepped into the path ahead.

Achilles shouted without slowing down. "The president's had a stroke. If we don't get him to a hospital right away, he could die! Open the doors."

The guards didn't move. No doubt they were shocked by the sight of their virile president slung over some stranger's shoulder like a sack of flour.

Achilles kept pressing. "Colonel Pushkin's on his way with a car. There's no time to spare if we're going to avoid brain damage."

"Who are you?"

Achilles didn't want to zap these two. That would be asking for trouble. *Where was Max?* "Alex Azarov. I'm on the Swiss detail. I'm also a medic. Korovin will suffer brain damage if we don't get him a shot of alteplase within the next few minutes. I've got one in my medical bag. It's in my helicopter. Step aside!"

He watched the guards run the calculation. Brain damage was above their pay grade. "You said Pushkin's on his way?"

"He's probably here already. Open the doors!"

The guards opened the doors.

Achilles ran through with Glick and the guards behind.

Max wasn't there.

"Call Pushkin!" Achilles commanded.

"Where's Dr. Dedov?" One guard pressed.

"Here comes Pushkin," the second guard said, pointing to an approaching SUV. As the black Mercedes turned toward them, a sedan also came into view heading toward the helipad.

"Dedov's meeting us at the helicopter," Achilles said, knowing that summoning the doctor had been part of Max's plan and hoping that was him.

Max brought the SUV to a screeching halt.

The guards leapt to open the passenger doors.

Achilles saw that Max had removed his silicone mask and changed into Pushkin's uniform. He hoped the visual similarity was sufficient for a few rushed seconds of exposure in the heat of a crisis, but he didn't dwell on the thought. Instead he dove into the back seat with Korovin while Glick grabbed the front.

Max didn't wait for the guards to shut the doors before gunning the gas. "Sorry for the delay. I had three thugs to disable."

"Is Korovin's pilot up ahead with the doctor?"

"I assume so. I just barked the order into the mike."

A groan from Korovin drew all eyes.

Achilles turned and slapped the president's face.

Korovin's eyes sprung open. "What happened? Where am I?"

"Your past caught up with you, Mr. President."

Korovin's face registered fear.

Achilles wanted to identify himself. He wanted Korovin to know it was he who had beaten him. But duty defeated pride. "President Silver asked me to send you a message."

Korovin tried to sit up but Achilles held him down. "What message?"

"He wanted me to tell you, 'I win.'" Achilles gave the words a second to sink in, then zapped Korovin on the neck.

"What was that about?" Glick asked, his adrenal glands finally working.

Max reached over and clamped Glick's thigh. "This isn't the time for questions. Trust me, you want everything to be a blur. One second Korovin started slurring his speech, the next he collapsed from a stroke. We rushed him to a hospital. End of detail. End of story."

Glick didn't reply.

Up ahead the Mercedes sedan screeched to a stop beside Korovin's big white helicopter. The driver got out and ran to the cockpit. The passenger got out and looked back their way. He was holding a medical bag.

Max parked beside the black Ansat they'd flown in on and said, "Follow me, Glick."

As Max and Glick ran toward their helicopter, Dr. Dedov hastened over to open Achilles' door.

"Let's get him in the presidential helicopter," Achilles said, without introduction.

"What happened?" the doctor asked as they lifted Korovin.

"We were having a discussion when the president began experiencing facial palsy and dysarthria, then syncope."

Dedov's face paled. "Sounds like a severe stroke."

"Exactly. The moment he collapsed I threw him over my shoulder and ran for the door. There's no time to lose." Achilles maneuvered Korovin onto the presidential helicopter's rear bench, zapping him repeatedly in the process, as insurance.

Max burst in while the engine roared to life, shouting "I brought your bag, doctor."

Achilles grabbed the bag and set it down by Korovin's head. As Max ran back to power up their Ansat, Achilles flipped open the top of his bag.

"What are you doing?" Dr. Dedov asked.

Achilles plucked a syringe and a glass vial off the bag's top shelf. "Alteplase. Do you concur?"

"I do and I've got my own, already titrated. Get out of my way."

"Bird's ready to fly," Korovin's pilot shouted over the intercom.

"What's going on?" a fourth voice demanded.

Both men whirled about to see Ignaty Filippov in the doorway, with two guards at his shoulders.

Chapter 106
Great Expectations

Seattle, Washington

WANG POKED HIS HEAD ABOVE DECK, just to feel a few seconds of sunlight on his face. He was finding maritime life a bit more challenging than expected. Given the strategic imperative of keeping out of sight, he was essentially sentenced to solitary confinement below deck during the day. Granted, his prison cell was made of polished teak and cream leather rather than bare concrete and cold steel, but the glamor wore off quickly all the same.

He was already browsing the online brokers, looking at bigger boats. Los Angeles, San Diego, Cabo San Lucas, Puerto Vallarta. Any of those venues would do. The trick was getting there — with a big bank balance.

He'd anchored the *Winsome Whisper* fifty feet from shore and a half-mile from a small marina north of Seattle. Even if the Russians somehow learned he was on a boat, they'd still never find him, if he remained careful. Puget Sound covered over a thousand square miles of serpentine waterways. He'd become a ghost in the fog and would remain that way until making his break for Mexico.

Wang would weigh anchor the moment the money arrived.

If it ever arrived.

It was overdue.

He'd been certain they'd transfer the $20 million within twenty-four hours. But it had been thirty-six. Perhaps they didn't know Bitcoin worked around the clock. Perhaps there had been a delay. Surely they weren't searching for him? Not for a mere twenty million.

A ping from his computer set Wang's pulse racing. He'd set up an automatic alert with his Bitcoin account so he'd know the minute his deposit arrived. Turning around, he ducked back below deck and hustled over to his laptop. The ping hadn't been Bitcoin. It was a message from his wife.

"Did the money arrive?"

When they wanted to communicate beyond the reach of the Chinese Ministry of State Security, Wang and Qi used a private chatroom on a deep web message board. You had to know the address to find it, and even if the Chinese Ministry of State Security stumbled upon it, they'd still have no way of knowing who was chatting.

Qi knew he was on the boat and glued to his computer. Ignoring her even for a minute wasn't an option. He typed, "You'll know as soon as I do. How are the kids?"

"Same as always. Messy and noisy and demanding endless attention. It's hardly a vacation without help."

His family was in Hong Kong. It was purportedly a vacation, but really a staging area for their disappearance. He had sent them false passports and airplane tickets, Hong Kong to Tokyo, then Tokyo to Mexico City. If the $20 million came through, they'd disappear and meet up with him somewhere along the Mexican Riviera to begin their new life.

Hopefully, a much more amicable one.

Qi had been born into a life of privilege, but six months after Wang had married her, Qi's father had been convicted of corruption and executed, plunging her family into poverty and disgrace. She had become bitter and resentful and somehow seemed to blame him for it all. Wang had hoped that having children would bring her around, realign her hormones and selfish priorities, but the twin girls only seemed to remind her of all the advantages she no longer enjoyed. After listening to his wife whine nonstop for two years, Wang had requested a foreign assignment, ostensibly for the increased pay, but actually for the relief.

"Are the girls enjoying Hong Kong?"

"I suppose. I'm going to let you get back to sunning on the yacht while I care for our children. I still can't believe you only asked for twenty million." Qi closed the conversation, thereby erasing their dialogue.

Wang wished he could forget it so easily.

He went online to check his bank balance, just in case the automatic alert hadn't worked. No such luck.

He clicked over to the tab displaying a lightly used 98-foot yacht for sale in Cabo San Lucas. Plenty of room to spread out there. The price wasn't listed but he figured he could get it for two million if he showed up with cash and bargained hard.

Chapter 107
Change Of Status

Black Sea Coast, Russia

IT COULD ALL FALL APART right here, Achilles thought. The burly guards behind Ignaty looked serious as cyanide and primed to react.

Ignaty leapt aboard the helicopter with surprising grace and repeated his question, yelling over the whooping turbine. "What the hell is going on!"

Achilles turned toward Dr. Dedov, who was busy inspecting Korovin. Speaking loud enough for all to hear, he said, "You get the president to a stroke center. I'll bring Ignaty up to speed."

Dedov nodded with enthusiasm. "Agreed."

Achilles grabbed Ignaty by the arm, causing the two guards to tense like chained Rottweilers. He guided Ignaty back onto the helipad, but waited for the mighty bird to lift into the sky before shouting over the roar. "The president had a stroke while talking to his banker. He has to get to a hospital immediately. If you want to follow with Colonel Pushkin and me in the banker's bird, you're welcome. Otherwise I'm sure one of the guards will drive you."

Without waiting for a reply, Achilles turned and ran toward the Ansat.

Ignaty and the two guards followed.

Achilles whirled around as he cleared the door. "We've only got room for one."

Ignaty didn't even pause, he just barreled on in.

Doing his part to salvage their escape, Max pulled the collective lever the instant Ignaty was inside, raising the helicopter off the ground before the guards could ask questions and throwing Ignaty to the floor.

Achilles pulled Korovin's strategist toward a seat as Max banked south in pursuit of Korovin's bird, slamming the door.

Ignaty looked around, his eyes coming to rest on Max in his Pushkin disguise. His brow was just starting to furrow when Achilles beckoned.

Ignaty leaned in to hear.

Achilles said, "You lose," and zapped him. *What a wonderful weapon.*

As Ignaty went limp, Achilles called to Max. "How's it looking?"

"What the hell is going on?" Glick yelled.

Achilles silenced the banker with a look.

Max said, "We're in good shape for the moment, but that could change any minute. You should get up here."

First things first. Achilles carefully worked his hands up to his armpits and turned off the FP1's, giving Hans and Gunter a mental salute in the process.

Free to operate normally, Achilles pulled a package of thick black zip ties and an extra-large black canvas duffel from a storage pocket. He pressed both into Glick's hands, then grabbed Glick by the shoulders and looked him in the eye. "Bend Ignaty's legs and bind his wrists beneath his knees, like he's doing a cannonball into that beautiful pool of yours. Then stuff him into the bag and fix his ankles together. Pretend your life depends on him not being able to escape — because it might."

Glick nodded slowly. He was dazed but adapting as competing chemicals rebounded across his central nervous system like pool balls after a professional break.

Achilles moved to the front passenger seat and scanned the horizon through the windshield. Korovin's helicopter was less than a kilometer ahead, racing south toward Sochi at 260 kilometers per hour. He looked down at the windswept Black Sea waters below, then over at the coniferous coastline a few hundred meters to their left. "Looks perfect to me."

Max said, "I agree."

Achilles pulled up a special app on his phone and dialed in a ten-digit code. The result was the picture of a big button. It glowed red, indicating a connection. Achilles had learned his lesson with the lions in Switzerland and gone with a detonation frequency at the high end of the military spectrum, well beyond what would normally be jammed.

When he pressed the button, the EMP secreted in the medical bag would come to life. Once powered up, it would emit a powerful electromagnetic pulse encompassing the entire DC-to-daylight frequency range. Quick as a lightning strike, it would fry every bit of electronic circuitry within a four meter radius.

Destroying any modern vehicle's computer system is like cutting off its head. When the vehicle is a helicopter, the beheading is catastrophic. With nothing sending signals to the turbine, the rotors stop turning. And with nothing relaying commands, the levers and sticks and switches stop responding. The absence of flight controls and vertical lift transforms the $10 million instrument into the aeronautical equivalent of a catapulted rock.

That was exactly what Korovin's copter would look like as its rotor stopped and its trajectory shifted and the downward plunge began. At their altitude, it would take about thirty seconds to reach the waves. It wasn't hard for Achilles to imagine what those thirty seconds would be like for the two conscious souls aboard. Achilles felt for the doctor and the pilot, but better them than the lives of the tens of thousands of American civilians their boss had planned on murdering.

He knew that the presidential helicopter wouldn't plunge *into* the sea, but rather *onto* it. With a forward velocity of 260 kilometers per hour and a downward velocity in the same ballpark, Korovin's ride wouldn't slip beneath the surface like a coin tossed into a fountain. It would burst apart on impact like a toy hit by a train.

Max said, "Do it. Do it now."

Achilles said, "Here's to a better tomorrow," and he pressed the button.

Chapter 108
The End

Black Sea Coast, Russia

PRESIDENT KOROVIN'S EYELIDS RETRACTED as if released by springs. He'd been roused by a jolt of panic that welled up from deep within. His subconscious mind had sensed something terribly wrong.

As he gained focus, he saw that he wasn't in his study, but rather was aboard his helicopter. It wasn't his pounding headache creating the background noise, but rather the rumbling rotor.

He sat up, gritting his teeth against the explosive pain throbbing between his ears, while his doctor looked on with grave concern in his eyes. "What happened? Why are we in the helicopter? What's going on?"

Dr. Dedov reached out and put a hand on his shoulder. "You had a stroke, Mr. President. We're rushing you to the hospital in Sochi."

"A stroke? No, no. I was attacked, in my office, by the bankers. Bankers sent by President Silver."

Dedov studied him with concern writ large across his face. "Strokes play tricks on the mind, Mr. President. Please, lay back down. It's important that you remain calm."

Korovin's mind was racing. It didn't feel impeded. He had a whale of a headache, but maintained clarity of thought. "Where's Pushkin? I want to talk to him. Now!"

"He's right behind us in another helicopter. I believe Ignaty is with him as well."

Now Korovin was confused. Panic swept back over him, putting ice in his veins. "They know about this?"

"Yes, of course, they—" Dedov stopped speaking as the mighty turbine powering the helicopter suddenly turned silent, like a roaring lion shot in the head.

For a moment, Korovin enjoyed an almost magical feeling, soaring silently high above the waves. Then his stomach leapt up as the downward plunge began. "Erik, what's going on?" Korovin yelled to his pilot, an unflappable veteran of the Afghan war.

The pilot didn't reply, his focus obviously elsewhere.

"What's going on!" Korovin demanded.

After a few seconds that felt more like centuries, Erik said, "We lost all systems, Mr. President. The bird may as well be a rock." His voice was matter-of-fact in tone.

"How's that possible? Surely there's something you can do. Don't rotors grab the wind even without power?"

"I have no control, Mr. President. Everything is dead. Goodbye, sir."

Nyet nyet nyet. This couldn't be. Not him. Not yet. He was Vladimir Korovin. President of Russia. The richest, most powerful man in the world. He was only sixty-four. He still had a third of his life to live. The best third. The third that would see Russian preeminence restored. He couldn't possibly die now. Fate wouldn't allow it.

And yet it was happening.

He only had seconds to live.

The physics were undeniable.

How had this happened? Who had beaten him? Silver wasn't smart enough to mastermind this plan.

Was it Ignaty? No. He'd go down with the ship. People feared him, but they didn't like him. Without presidential backup, Ignaty wouldn't be feared any more. Old enemies would eat him alive.

As Korovin hurtled ever closer to the frigid white-capped waves, clarity struck him like the flash of blinding light that was about to follow. He knew who had done this to him. He could feel it in the depths of his soul. It was the man who had foiled his plan once before. The American spy. Korovin spit the name with his last breath, like Troy's greatest warrior had 3,300 years before. "Achilles."

Chapter 109
Underestimations

Seattle, Washington

KATYA HEARD ZOYA WINCE from two steps ahead. "Catch another thorn?"

"These things are unbelievable. A trek like this merits the Holy Grail, not a Chinese weasel. How long until the next ping?"

Katya looked at her watch. "Just two minutes. We're cutting it close."

Working almost as much by feel as by vision, they were trudging through the dark, wild woods that separated the location of the Bear's last ping from the nearest road. The muddy forest floor sucked at their shoes while the undergrowth grabbed their bare ankles. Urban camouflage didn't work so well in the jungle.

Judging by the satellite map, they expected to spot Wang's boat from the road. Then they arrived to find a thick forest blocking their view of the water. A forest full of brambles.

"What are we going to do if he's sailed on?" Zoya asked.

Good question, Katya thought, scrunching her toes to retain her shoe. "All we can do is race to the site of the next ping."

"What if it's not close to shore?"

Katya didn't want to think about that. If it weren't after midnight, they could charter a boat with a knowledgeable captain. Perhaps even find one with diving gear so he could put the tracker on the hull. But at best it would be eight hours before that became a viable option. "We'll think of something."

Katya looked down toward the tops of her feet. She couldn't see them clearly in the dark but was certain they were scratched up if not bloody, beginning from the point where her flats left off. She was starting to appreciate Achilles' stubbornness when it came to footwear.

The woods went right up to the water's edge, but faint moonlight reflecting off the water alerted them to its proximity. "Do you see a boat?" Katya whispered.

"No. Pass me the binoculars."

As Katya was handing them over, the console in her pocket beeped. She pulled it out and turned her back to the water before pressing the button that brought the display to life. It showed a map with different color dots. A red one pinpointed the latest ping. The three prior pings were displayed in shades of orange and yellow. A green dot marked their location. To her great relief, all five dots were tightly grouped.

"According to this, he's off to our left."

They both strained against the darkness.

Zoya spoke first. "I see him. No running lights. Just a darker hole in the water."

Katya's lips parted into a broad smile as she also spotted the yacht some 150 feet from shore. *We've got you now.*

Wang's tactic for extorting twenty million had been a brilliant one. With no means of contacting him, there was no way to negotiate or trick or trap. He'd created the ultimate take-it-or-leave-it situation. And he'd been right about the figures. No doubt Korovin would have paid a thousand times his asking price.

But Wang had underestimated them.

He'd been so focused on his own con with the circuitry, that he had missed theirs with the umbrella. She drew great satisfaction from that little coup. Alas, it wasn't yet a victory. Wang could still slip away, still outwit them.

"Oh, no," Zoya whispered. "The phone's dead. No way to call for help in the morning."

And the guys can't call us, Katya thought.

"What should we do?" Zoya pressed.

Katya unzipped her fanny pack and removed everything but the tracking pellet and tube of waterproof epoxy. She handed the contents to Zoya as an unspoken answer.

"You can't be serious?"

Katya looked out at the yacht, then down at the dark water. As she pulled her shirt up over her head, she wondered just how cold it was.

Chapter 110
Alternative Scenarios

Sochi, Russia

BOARDING THE JET with Max and Glick, Achilles reconfirmed Palm Beach, Florida as their destination. Palm Beach was where the former U.S. Ambassador to Russia had retired. Achilles knew Ambassador Jamison from the last time he'd run awry of a Korovin scheme — and more importantly, Ambassador Jamison already knew that Korovin had tried to kill Silver. Achilles could talk to him without betraying the president's confidence.

Of course, he might not get the chance. Jamison might — and in fact was obligated to — arrest Achilles on sight.

Achilles had called the ambassador at his Palm Beach home while shuttling between the helicopter and the jet at Sochi International Airport. On the phone, he'd found Jamison's tone to be cordial but clipped. In other words, ambiguous. Not that Achilles had expected much better. He was a wanted man, after all — wanted by none other than POTUS himself.

But Jamison had agreed to meet.

Assuming Achilles actually got the meeting, rather than an express train to jail, his plan was to tell the ambassador everything, then trust in Jamison's ability to manage this exceptionally sensitive intelligence windfall with diplomatic aplomb. Between the Korovin assassination, the Filippov capture, the hidden billions, and *Operation Sunset*, Achilles would be dumping quite a load on the elder statesman's shoulders. Still, he expected Jamison to welcome it. Retired or not, Jamison would always be like him — a man of action.

But their meeting wouldn't be for many hours.

Sochi to Palm Beach was a 6,400-mile flight and had to include a refueling stop. He and Max would use the travel time to catch up with Katya and Zoya and to decide the fates of Severin Glick and Ignaty Filippov.

Assuming they ever got off the ground.

Although they didn't speak of it, Max, Glick, and Achilles expected to find themselves surrounded by flashing lights and laser sights at any moment. Achilles pictured speeding police cars and special agents in battle gear. He envisioned handcuffs and jail cells and a long extradition battle.

But outside his mind's eye, nothing unusual happened.

Once the pilot announced that they'd cleared Russian airspace, Glick took on the look of a kid who'd just survived his first ride on Disney's Space Mountain: thrilled but discombobulated, shaken but giddy. Achilles used the moment to inform the banker of his options. "We've got an offer for you. One we think you're going to like."

Glick's expression lost some of its luster, but remained ebullient. "You have my full attention."

So Glick listened. And as he listened, the lost luster returned — even as his eyes grew wider. Once Achilles finished, he said, "Tell me again."

Achilles was happy to indulge the banker. He'd played his part, albeit unknowingly, and for that Achilles was grateful. So he summarized: "You know better than anyone that Korovin was paranoid about his money. Beyond his secret bankers, the other people like you, nobody knows where Korovin kept his billions. Even if one of his heirs does, they can't go after it. It's all stolen. You lead us to it, all of it, and you get to retire."

"Retire as in — I run off with nobody knowing I've got a billion of Korovin's dollars in the bank?"

"Not quite nobody," Max said. "*We* know."

"And not a billion in the bank," Achilles added. "That's a bit extreme. So let's agree that in exchange for identifying the other bankers holding Korovin's money, you'll keep a hundred million. The rest, you'll donate to legitimate charities. Anonymously, of course."

Glick pursed his lips, but Achilles could read the excitement in his eyes. Apparently the prospect of a $100 million payday was enough to crack even a polished Swiss banker's veneer. "I don't actually *know* the identities of the other bankers holding Korovin's money. I only *suspect.*"

"And your suspicions are based on?"

Glick gave up the fight and smiled. "There aren't that many people managing tens of billions of anonymous dollars. Among those that are, most are easy to rule out as Korovin's bankers. Korovin's not interested in vanity purchases like sports teams or movie studios or Picassos, so I know the people looking at those aren't working for him. He's also got different investment directives from Saudi princes and Chinese tycoons. So when I vet the few remaining opportunities suitable for Korovin's portfolio, I find myself repeatedly bumping into the same small group. It's basic deduction from there."

"Your instinct and logic are good enough for me," said Achilles. "Max?"

"I agree."

Achilles turned back to Glick. "Do you think you can live with our proposal? Forever? No second thoughts?" He put some stick into his tone, rather than getting explicit about the other option.

Glick's slow nod grew faster as he processed the angles and implications. He understood that the alternative would be far less pleasant. "Yes. That's most agreeable. Anonymously donating $900 million in a responsible manner will take some time, but I shall apply myself whole heartedly, with diligence and deference."

"Good."

"Might I ask a question?"

Achilles locked his eyes on Glick's. "As long as you never ask another."

Glick blinked once, then said, "I was going to ask what you did with the nine billion you transferred last week. But on second thought, I'm quite certain I don't care."

"That's the attitude! On that note, we've got two options regarding your next steps. Option A is taking you with us to meet with the U.S. authorities, so you can explain what happened. Of course, then the retirement plan we just discussed will become contingent upon their figuring out how to permit it, while respecting national security requirements."

Glick closed his eyes for a calming moment. "And Option B?"

Achilles put a hand on Glick's shoulder so that a thumb rested in the hollow of his neck. "You swear on your life to never breathe a word, not one word, of the last week's events to anyone. Ever. You do that, and we let you off in the Azores when we stop to refuel."

Glick didn't hesitate. "If there's one thing Swiss bankers are known for, it's our ability to keep a secret. Not as well known but no less true is our love of tropical islands. Option B will suit me just fine."

"I thought it might," Achilles replied, already planning a few future reminders to keep Glick from getting too comfortable and forgetting his vow.

Glick held out his hand, and shook with both spies.

Achilles turned to Max. "What do you say, shall we go deal with our friend in the back?"

"Let's try the ladies again, first."

They'd tried calling Katya and Zoya as soon as the jet was wheels up, but the call had gone to voicemail. It was a maddening situation because the dead phone could signify everything, or nothing at all. Achilles had been fighting panic by remaining busy. Now that they had a natural break, he felt the walls closing in.

He ran his hand over his smooth scalp, while Max grabbed the phone off the Gulfstream's bulkhead and hit redial. Achilles had worn his hair short for most of his life, but Mila had given him his first skinhead. He couldn't stop touching it as the bristly hair began growing back in.

"They're still not answering," Max reported, maintaining a brave face.

"Probably forgot to recharge it last night."

Achilles felt his heart drop, yet again. What a yo-yo of a day this had been. But he'd vowed to remain optimistic. "Yeah, Katya's like that. Leave a message. Have them fly to Palm Beach, check in at The Breakers, and wait for us."

Max left the message and cradled the phone.

Achilles gestured toward the cargo hold. "Let's go talk to Ignaty. I think he's had sufficient time to soak up his situation."

Max nodded, stone-faced. "Will you let me be the one to deliver the big news?"

Achilles didn't hesitate. "Of course. I know the two of you have a history."

Chapter 111
Oversight

Seattle, Washington

KATYA BEGAN TO SHIVER as she swam up behind the *Winsome Whisper*. The water was deadly calm and dangerously cold. She had hoped for better from September.

Back on the bank with Zoya, she had almost jumped right back out when the frigid river first bit her toes. But once in the water she thought of Achilles and Max and all they were going through. She didn't dare let them down over a bit of discomfort. What circumstances were they suffering at that very moment?

With worry on her mind, Katya reached the back of the boat. She grasped the swimming platform with a light touch, so as not to rock it. The overhang wasn't just a good handhold, it provided the perfect place for concealing the tracking pellet.

She pulled the epoxy from her fanny pack with trembling fingers, ripped the caps off the twin tubes with her teeth, and spit them into the black water. Eager to complete her mission and get out of the drink, Katya wedged the tips into the corner where the platform met the hull and applied force to the plunger.

Nothing happened.

She pressed harder.

Still nothing.

Looking closer, Katya spotted the problem. The tips had to be cut off — and she didn't have a knife. With a roll of her eyes, she started in with her teeth. *Was this stuff poisonous?* She wondered. After a few seconds of fruitless chewing, she realized that it didn't matter. She'd freeze to death before she severed the thick plastic. She had to get out of the water, and if she was getting out anyway, the epoxy was superfluous.

That alternative course of action posed another predicament. Could she climb aboard without rocking the boat? She didn't have enough experience with yachts to know how sensitive the *Winsome Whisper* would be to her 120 pounds, but she had to assume that any sudden move in these calm conditions would be enough to alert Wang. Achilles had suggested gradually increasing the natural rise and fall of the boat, but in this calm, there wasn't any natural movement. With no time to waste mulling options, the math professor in her made the snap decision to go with the slow-and-steady approach. She couldn't change her mass, but she could diminish the force she imparted by minimizing her acceleration.

Positioning herself just left of the swimming platform, she pulled herself up inch by inch, handhold by handhold, until she could grasp the top railing with both hands extended overhead. She slowly stopped kicking, allowing the boat to absorb her weight gradually. Once she and the boat had settled into this new arrangement, she walked both her hands out to the sides, until they were as wide as she could get them, and her breasts were just above the waterline.

For three deep breaths, she built strength and focus, then she began to pull. She didn't heave or jerk. She kept the pressure steady, trying to picture shipyard cranes in place of her skinny little shoulders. Slow and steady. She nearly lost it at the midpoint where her arms had the least leverage, but the thought of Achilles' encouraging smile helped her to break through, and a second later she exhaled a sigh of relief as her elbows locked into place.

Katya maintained muscular discipline until she'd lifted her right leg up atop the swimming platform, then she slowly dumped her weight into it.

The boat remained steady.

The breeze froze her wet flesh even as the danger ignited Katya's core. She buoyed her mood by recalling the old statistical joke that on average her temperature was just right.

Not wanting to remain in this exposed position any longer than she had to, Katya immediately began searching for a proper place to hide the tracking pellet. As she scanned the bare deck beneath the dim glow of clouded crescent moonlight, she wondered what Wang would do if he came out and found her, clinging naked to the back of his boat. Would he shoot her? Hold her hostage? Attempt something even worse? Oddly enough, her first thought after that unpleasant image was that she couldn't die before giving Achilles her big news. Funny how the very day she received the culminating offer of her career, something even more momentous had come along. God laughs while man plans.

After resolving not to waste her next opportunity to talk with Achilles, she found the answer to her current problem right before her eyes. A seat cushion. Probably nautical blue in daylight, at night it looked black in contrast with the white yacht.

She leaned over with a slow, deliberate move and found the end of the slipcover's zipper. The sea air hadn't been kind to the mechanism. When it didn't respond to a few gentle tugs, she put some oomph into it. This gave her the inch she needed, but it also sent the epoxy tube clattering to the deck with a reverberation that may as well have been a bowling ball striking ten pins.

Struggling to remain calm, she stuffed the tracking pellet into the cushion and reversed the zip. Her mission was accomplished but not complete. The telltale epoxy tube was a few feet away, laying where Wang couldn't miss it. She made the split-second decision to retrieve it rather than immediately abandoning ship. Working as quickly as she could without generating sound or sway, Katya stepped over the rail and onto the aft deck. Snatching up the offending object, she hurled it back the way she'd come with all the force her frightened frame could muster. It soared like a frisbee further than she'd have thought possible and disappeared with a distant bloop.

"What was that?"

Katya spun about at the sound of the familiar voice to find herself looking down the barrel of the largest handgun she'd ever seen.

Chapter 112
The Rat

Airborne, over Europe

ACHILLES AND MAX went aft through the bathroom to the jet's luggage compartment, leaving Glick alone in the main cabin to contemplate his new life. Throwing open the small door, there was no mistaking the strange sight that met their eyes. When they'd loaded Ignaty through the luggage hatch, packed in the big black duffel, he'd resembled a fat golf bag. Now that he was awake and squirming, that illusion was shattered.

Ignaty had information critical to America's national security, and Achilles and Max only had a few hours to get it. They had worked out a ruse to frighten their captive into talking. Some might consider their tactic cruel, and to be honest Achilles wasn't entirely comfortable with the plan, but it was far better than the fingernail-pulling, bone-breaking alternative, and if their acting skills were up to par, it would be much more effective.

"No cries for help," Achilles noted, slipping into character and kicking off the psychological game by speaking loud enough for Ignaty to hear through the bag. "I was certain he'd be a whiner. Desk-jockeys usually are."

Max leaned in toward Achilles' ear and spoke low. "I couldn't find anything else to use as a gag, so I stuffed a wig in his mouth. I'm guessing he thinks it's a rat."

Achilles cringed at the image, but didn't comment.

Ignaty didn't speak even after Max ripped off the tape and pulled the soggy hairball from his mouth, but his eyes were talking — impolitely.

"So the strategy guy has nothing to say," Max said. "Too proud to snivel. Too blind to bargain."

Ignaty remained quiet.

"You did miss a lot of excitement while you were snoozing. Allow me to fill you in. Achilles, please show our prisoner the video."

Achilles pulled up the helicopter crash on his cell phone and put the screen a foot from Ignaty's face. "Care to guess? I'll give you a hint. It's not porn."

When Ignaty didn't respond, Achilles hit *play*.

To his credit, Ignaty didn't begin blathering as Korovin's helicopter disintegrated. Instead he asked, "Where are we going?"

"Not a bad start," Max said, playing his role beautifully. "What do you think, Achilles? Pretty efficient question if you ask me. An inclusive pronoun, and a structure that will provide a whole lot of context from a one-word answer."

Following the script, Achilles grabbed two thick luggage straps off a rack and handed one to Max. With Ignaty watching wide-eyed, Achilles secured one end around his own waist while Max did the same. Then each clipped the other end to a D-ring on the wall. "Sorry, we only have two of these."

Ignaty began to tremble as Achilles walked over to the luggage loading hatch and put his hand on the big red handle. There were safeties that needed to be manipulated both there and in the cockpit before the handle would actually release the door, but those technical details weren't front of mind, judging by Ignaty's face. Hardly surprising, since he'd just seen them kill Korovin. "I jumped from a Gulfstream GV once, over a Middle-Eastern city that will go unnamed. It was like getting sucked up by a vacuum cleaner and spit out into space."

"How'd that turn out?" Max asked.

"Just fine. I actually enjoyed it. Of course, I had oxygen, insulated clothing, and a parachute." Achilles drummed the handle. "I think you should explain to Ignaty that you and I are going to the U.S. Whether he'll be landing with us or in the Atlantic is entirely dependent on his answer to a single question."

Both spies turned their heads to look at *Sunset's* architect. Achilles had to give Ignaty credit for keeping it together. Many a rough-and-ready man would be babbling by now.

"What question?" Ignaty asked.

Max held up a finger, halting Achilles. "Let's reposition his hands behind his back before you ask. If I don't like the answer, I want to be able to kick him in the balls. Send him out into space with a split scrotum. Can't do that with the current configuration."

Achilles whispered in Ignaty's ear while he cut and reapplied the zip ties. "It would be a favor, really. Kinda keep your mind off things to come. Takes a long time to fall from 30,000 feet."

With Ignaty now hog-tied, wrists to ankles, Achilles propped him up on his knees and leaned his back against the exterior hatch. He put one hand on the red handle and the other on Ignaty's shoulder. "Just one question. I suggest a prompt and accurate answer. He's been dying to do this for quite some time now. Are you ready?"

Ignaty looked back and forth between the solemn faces of his captors, then nodded.

"Good. Here it comes. How did you learn about my mission?"

"What happens if I tell you?"

Max drew his leg back for the punt while Achilles shook his head.

"Reggie Pepper," Ignaty blurted. "Do you know Reggie Pepper?"

"Never heard of him," Max said.

"I met him once," Achilles said. "He's the president's body man — a young, fit guy who shadows Silver and serves as his extra set of arms."

Ignaty nodded. "That's Reggie. Good kid. I put a voice recorder in his shoe."

Chapter 113
Complications

Seattle, Washington

WANG HAD SPENT PLENTY OF TIME sighting in targets, and he particularly liked doing so over the serrated barrel of his SIG MPX submachine gun, but this was the first time that he'd seen a nearly naked woman in the crosshairs. Even wet as a drowned rat, stunned into silence, and trembling, the Russian was stunning.

"What was that?" Wang repeated. "What did you throw?"

She blinked a few times before answering. "My phone. The water ruined it."

"You expected otherwise?"

"It was in a bag, but the bag leaked."

Wang had a long list of questions far more serious than phone mechanics but securing the site had to come first. "Unbuckle your fanny pack and let it drop to the deck."

She complied. There was no thunk when it fell.

Wang stepped aside and gestured with the MPX for her to step down into the cabin. He paid particular attention to her eyes throughout, looking for a tell that she wasn't alone.

Her gaze didn't drift.

He snatched up her bag and followed her in. "Have a seat at the table. Lay your palms flat atop it."

She complied. "Can I borrow a bathrobe?"

He unzipped the fanny pack and looked inside. It was empty. "Who are you with?"

"I'm alone. Obviously."

She was still trembling. He was no master interrogator but that was probably a good thing. "Where's Max?"

"He's out of the country."

"Moscow?"

She nodded.

"And the brunette?"

"Back at the hotel, waiting for my call to confirm that you're still with your umbrella."

"With my umbrella?"

"That's how I found you. The other day, while dancing, my colleague put a tracking device on your umbrella. Just a precaution but obviously a good one."

Wang wanted to kick himself. If it was true, he'd been played. By women.

If it wasn't true, if there was more to the story, then his goose was cooked. He had three, thirty-round magazines for his MDX. Ninety bullets. Plenty for a power play or small skirmish, but laughably insufficient if the Russians were coming.

Keeping the MPX trained between her naked breasts, Wang grabbed the umbrella from the hook by the door. "Where'd she hide it?"

"On the inside, near the tip I think."

Rather than opening the umbrella, Wang felt for it. There was too much other stuff at the hub to tell. His eyes locked on those of his hostage, he said, "I spent some time in Dallas last year. Texans have a saying that fits this situation nicely." He paused to let her tension build. "You mess with the bull, you get the horns."

"It's there," she said, clearly trying to sound certain. "Can you at least turn the heat on?"

Wang grabbed a purple U-Dub sweatshirt from the same rack that held the umbrella and tossed it to her. While she pulled it over her head, he opened the umbrella and felt inside. Sure enough, his fingers found a kidney-bean sized something glued to the apex. Without further fuss, he opened the outside door, closed the umbrella, and hurled it over the rail like a spear.

While his old friend sank to the bottom of Puget Sound, Wang's mind began racing for his life, working the permutations of his predicament. If the Russian was alone, now she was cut off. If she wasn't alone, then there was nothing he could do about it. Whoever was out there would have called for the cavalry by now. Wang would run the hostage ploy when they showed up, of course, but he wasn't going to delude himself about how that would end. Escape was his only option. For that, he'd have to employ both quick and nimble movements, and Sun Tzu style cunning.

He took two brisk steps toward the girl and pressed the tip of the MDX between her breasts. "What was your plan?"

She stared down at the gun. "My plan?"

"Why did you come here?"

"To confirm that you were on the boat with the umbrella, that you hadn't discovered the tracker and sent it off on another boat as a decoy. I watched the boat for a long time, but nobody ever came out, so I had to swim."

That made sense to Wang. Had he found the tracker, he might have done exactly as she'd suggested. "And what were you going to do, once you found me."

"Spook you into turning over the activation code without payment."

"Spook me?" Wang blurted with incredulity before giving her the once over with his eyes. "How were *you* going to do that?"

"That's what the phone was for. I was going to leave it on the boat — and then call you."

The simplicity of her plan hit him like an ice bath. Apparently he wasn't the only one familiar with *The Art Of War*. Wang pictured himself reacting to a ringing phone that wasn't supposed to be there. In his circumstances, it would be the audible equivalent of spotting the red dot of a laser sight on his chest. "How do I know you're not making that up?"

She spread her arms. "Can you think of another explanation why *I'd* be here rather than a SWAT team?"

He couldn't. But he could think of a telling question. "Why bother? Why not just pay? It's only $20 million. You Russians shouldn't have to think twice about a paltry sum like that."

"Would you want to tell your boss that he has to cough up $20 million because you screwed up? It's more than our lives are worth. We don't work for terribly understanding men. Surely you can appreciate that."

Wang could. He chided himself for failing to anticipate that angle.

Cracks were forming in his well-laid plan, and he was becoming nervous that his bright future might shatter, leaving nothing but dark days ahead — at best.

He took a deep breath and shooed away the worry birds. He had to get moving. Fast and unpredictably.

They'd expect him to head west for the open waters of the Pacific or north toward Canada and the Salish Sea, so he decided to turn the *Winsome Whisper* south and get lost among the lesser waterways leading to Puget Sound. There were many hundreds of miles of coastline down there, much of it winding through locales with minimal habitation. He knew. He had studied the maps. Just in case.

Wang resolved that he wouldn't be bested. He'd blown a battle, but whatever it took, he'd still win the war. "Get up!"

Her eyes grew wide. "Where are we going?"

"You're going into lockup — where you'll stay, until the $20 million is paid. If it's not paid promptly or if you give me problems, well…" Wang gestured toward the dark waters with his gun. "You'll be following the phone and the umbrella."

Chapter 114
Panic

Seattle, Washington

WHEN MUTE MEN in black suits diverted her and Max into a helicopter, Zoya had become nervous. When she'd been conscripted into conning an American spy out of his deepest secret, she became anxious. When Achilles had uncovered her ruse, her tension turned into panic. But it wasn't until Zoya saw Wang capturing Katya at gunpoint that she worried she might lose control.

Zoya scanned her surroundings, literally looking for an answer while struggling to remain calm. She was on a riverbank at midnight in the middle of nowhere, with a dead phone and no backup plan. On top of that, she was mentally exhausted, physically depleted, and Max was halfway around the world.

But she couldn't let Katya down. As bad as Zoya had it, Katya had it worse.

What could she do?

Zoya grappled for answers as she clung to sanity. Had Katya successfully planted the tracking pellet? Zoya would have to recharge her phone to find out. Was that what she should do? Should she run back to the hotel and charge the phone, then try to contact Max and Achilles? Or should she stay there, watching the boat and waiting for the opportunity to assist Katya?

Wang made the decision for her. The *Winsome Whisper* began moving. It came about and turned south. She watched it for a few minutes to be sure it wouldn't come about again. Sure enough, it continued heading inland up the river rather than out toward the open water of the ocean. Strange.

Why would Wang do that?

The only explanation Zoya could think of was that he wasn't planning to make his getaway by boat. Having been discovered, Wang had decided to return to his car. But she had no idea where he'd parked. With seven hours between Bear pings, he'd gone from the city to the open water in a single jump.

He must have a car parked somewhere. On second thought, maybe not. Every time they'd met with him, Wang had used Uber.

Zoya shook her head. It didn't really matter. She couldn't follow Wang's boat by foot or by car. Her only hope was electronic tracking, and for that she needed a charged phone.

She spun about and began running through the woods, ignoring the assaulting brambles and branches. By the time she reached the car, Zoya was certain she was bleeding from dozens of nicks and scratches, but she didn't bother checking. No time for that.

She hit the gas and shot roadside gravel from beneath the tires of their modest rental car. Come what may, she wasn't going to let Katya down.

Chapter 115
Diverted

Airborne, over the Atlantic Ocean

THEY WERE ON APPROACH to Palm Beach International Airport when the phone finally rang. Both Achilles and Max jumped at it, desperate for news from the women. They'd placed six calls since boarding the jet; all had gone to voicemail. Achilles hit *Speaker* so Max would also hear. "Katya?"

"Oh, thank goodness," Zoya's voice replied, her tone expressing immense relief. She got straight to the point. "Wang captured Katya."

"What?" both men replied in chorus.

"She was planting the tracking pellet on the boat when he caught her."

"Is she alright? Where is she now?" Achilles asked.

"Are you safe?" asked Max.

"I'm fine. I don't know how Katya is. Wang sailed off with her aboard."

"Where are you now?" Max asked.

"I'm back at the hotel. I had to recharge the phone."

"How did you get away?" Achilles asked.

"Wang didn't know I was there. He wasn't docked when he caught Katya, he was anchored in the middle of nowhere. Katya swam out to plant the tracker and got caught." Zoya spoke rapidly, her voice pitched high with strain, her breathing audible.

Achilles felt a baseball-size lump form in his throat.

Max saw him struggling and hopped in with the big question. "Is the tracker working? Do you know where they are?"

"I'm not sure. The phone died. The tracker uses a phone app — but of course you know that." Zoya took a calming breath. "I called you the moment the battery came to life."

"Can you check it now?"

"Yes, I'm doing that."

Achilles began praying like he never had before. If the app showed a blank screen, if Katya was out in the wind at the whim of a foreign agent. "Well?"

"It's loading."

"How long ago was she captured?" Max asked.

"About an hour. I watched until the boat started moving. Then I ran to the car and sped back to the hotel."

Achilles' mind was racing. Whether the tracker was working or not, he had to go after Katya. Max was going to have to deal with Ignaty and brief Jamison alone. The ambassador wasn't going to like that.

Chapter 116
Mrs. Pettygrove

Palm Beach, Florida

AMBASSADOR JAMISON was momentarily of two minds when he received Achilles' call. On the one hand, Achilles was the subject of a manhunt initiated by none other than President Silver himself. On the other, he was a special operative Jamison personally knew to be extraordinarily patriotic and exceptionally capable.

Ultimately, the choice was easy. After forty years of service in the diplomatic corps, Jamison would choose to follow his own instincts every time over anything any politician said. And now that he was retired, he finally had the freedom to do so.

But he wasn't prone to make rash moves or come up short on contingency planning. So he called the head of the Secret Service, an old, personal friend, and had a couple of top agents flown in to accompany him to "a highly sensitive, off-the-books rendezvous." Then he booked an Imperial Suite at The Breakers, and waited for the appointed hour, pleased to have more on his agenda than chasing a little white ball.

Or so he thought.

Jamison's initial reservations came crashing back to the forefront of his mind when his guests arrived, and Achilles wasn't among them. "Where's Achilles?"

"I'm right here, Ambassador." The lead member of the duo held up a phone displaying Achilles' image against the backdrop of an airplane fuselage. "The mission took a twist since we last spoke. Katya has been abducted. I'm on my way to Seattle to rescue her."

Jamison found himself caught momentarily flat-footed. He was stuck between two thorny affairs, neither of which he'd anticipated.

"Allow me to introduce Max Aristov," Achilles continued. "He's holding the phone."

Max held out a hand, and spoke using a British accent. "Pleasure to meet you, Ambassador Jamison."

After they'd shaken hands, Achilles continued. "I believe you'll recognize the other gentleman, the one in plasticuffs?"

Jamison looked down to see a sweater draped over wrists, then up to see big ears and a brushy mustache beneath a bald dome. He felt his stomach drop. "Are you kidding me! You kidnapped Ignaty Filippov, Korovin's chief strategist?"

"Nobody knows he's missing, per se. Everybody thinks he's dead. It's a long story, and Max is going to tell you all of it."

Jamison didn't know what he'd been expecting, but *everybody thinks he's dead* wasn't it. He rubbed the bridge of his nose. In situations like these — and he'd seen quite a few as a career diplomat regularly assigned to the toughest of postings — the smart move was to listen.

He turned his attention from the phone to Max. "Why don't you start from the beginning."

"Perhaps it would be best to isolate Ignaty in another room before I begin."

Jamison made a motion, and one of the agents escorted the Russian strategist from the room.

With the sound of the sea seeping through the screen door, and the remaining Secret Service agent standing still as a statue in the corner, they took seats around the suite's glass-topped dining table, and Max began. "My fiancée and I were on our way to a vacation in Sochi when we were diverted to a helicopter."

From Zoya's impersonation assignment to Achilles' amnesiac awakening on a private island, Max kept the ambassador transfixed. Jamison hadn't been this caught up in a story since debriefing with Seal Team Six after one of their Ukrainian ops. Midway through, Achilles had to sign off to focus on his current mission, but it hardly mattered. Max had an impressive grasp of the facts and their context, along with quite the oratorical flare.

Max was explaining how Achilles had determined Jas was a Russian spy when the ambassador couldn't bite his tongue any more. "How did the Russians learn about an assignment of which only Silver, Sparkman, Collins, and Foxley knew? Surely none of them broke operations security?"

Max nodded. "That's something we just extracted from Ignaty. He put a voice recorder in Reggie Pepper's shoe."

"The president's body man?"

"That's right."

"Nonsense. You can't bring a transmitter into the White House without the Secret Service's knowledge."

"That's the genius," Max said, nodding along. "It isn't a transmitter. It has no electronic signal to detect. It's just a tiny digital recorder. Not enough metal to ping a magnetometer but enough memory to record for a week."

Jamison chewed on that for a second. "If it doesn't transmit, then the Russians have to retrieve and replace it on a regular basis. Old-school style. That's easier said than done. I've met Reggie, and he's sharp as a Samurai sword. He'd be hard to play more than once."

Max gestured toward the door through which Ignaty had disappeared. "Ignaty may be a first-class wanker, but he's also a world-class mastermind. More on his activities later — much more. On the Pepper operation, Ignaty's brainstorm was using an FSB agent who avoided detection because she's nowhere near the mold of a typical spy."

Jamison raised his eyebrows on cue.

"It's his landlady. A sweet old thing, according to Ignaty. A real wolf in sheep's clothing. Mrs. Pettygrove is so proud of her young tenant that she irons his shirts and polishes his shoes as part of her patriotic duty."

"Brilliant. Bloody brilliant," Jamison mumbled while lowering his head in defeat. "It bothers me, the extent to which we're supplanting clever minds with high technology. It's costing us our old-school edge and leaving us vulnerable to low-tech tactics."

Max gave him a look that said he didn't know the half of it.

Jamison pressed him. "How long has this been going on? What other secrets have the Russians learned?"

"Ignaty has all that information. He used it to advise Korovin on just how far he could press his expansionist agenda without serious pushback. We haven't gotten all the details because we've only had him in custody for a few hours, but I'm sure President Silver's people will find the means to access it all. Rest assured that every notable fact is locked up in his big brain. The man's a walking computer."

"What about the landlady?" Jamison asked. "Is she in custody? Or did you leave her in play as a source of disinformation?"

"She's still in play. But I doubt she'll be valuable as a source of disinformation."

"Why's that?" Jamison asked, standing to stretch his legs.

"There have been some other changes we need to tell you about. You're going to want to remain seated for those."

Chapter 117
Wangled

Seattle, Washington

KATYA HAD NEVER BEEN THE WORRYING TYPE. She had her parents to thank for that. They'd raised her in Moscow during *perestroika*, when the Soviet Union was dissolving and modern Russia was forming, and socio-economic upheaval was a way of life. If they'd wasted energy worrying, they wouldn't have survived.

To this day, Katya found worry to be a useless emotion. *Nose to the grindstone* remained her style. *Make your own luck* and all that. But there was no grindstone in the *Winsome Whisper* stateroom that now jailed her. She was alone with her thoughts. Theoretically it was peaceful, although she had to keep the bathroom fan running to drown out the incessant sound of soap operas drifting in from whatever you called the main room — she wasn't up on her maritime terminology.

Wang ignored her. Like a jailer, he brought her food a few times a day. Bits of whatever he was eating. Mostly spiced rice or noodles with vegetables mixed in.

He used those instances to visually check on her, but didn't speak, and he ignored her questions. She reasoned that he was distancing himself from her, in case the $20 million didn't come through.

Katya knew that should have worried her, but amazingly it didn't. By now, Achilles knew Wang had her, and that meant Wang was the one who needed to be worried. She couldn't tell if he was or not. To her, Wang seemed more anxious than nervous. He was a planner, and he had faith in his plan. To Wang's credit, it was a good one. It would have worked had Zoya's operation not brought Achilles into Max's picture. But it had, and now a tracking pellet was acting like a bull's-eye on Wang's forehead.

Hopefully.

If the battery hadn't died.

Or it hadn't stopped working for some other reason.

If it had, then Achilles would use Korovin's money to pay the $20 million. Hopefully Wang would live up to his word to set her free. Of course, he might choose not to. He might be giving her the cold shoulder because he planned to kill her anyway, but Katya chose not to worry about that. Not now, anyway. She'd cross the bridge to panic-town if and when the money appeared and not a second before.

She set her fork and bowl down by the door. She always set them there when she was done eating to discourage Wang from entering. He was a man, after all, and men had needs. The eye-full he'd gotten during her capture surely hadn't helped him to stifle those impulses. Another thing for her not to think about.

As she sat back on the bed, Katya found herself smiling. She was smiling because she had used her time alone in the stateroom to make a decision and that decision felt good.

When you're faced with the possibility of an early death, it's only natural to spend time thinking about life. The prospect of losing everything gave Katya the ability to strip away all the meaningless fluff that cluttered her mind on a typical day — the objects and events and awards ostensibly related to self-worth but genuinely meaningless — and instead focus on what truly mattered. She realized that *what* she did was not nearly as important as *who* she did it with, so long as she felt safe and free to grow. The fact that Achilles would always keep her safe, no matter what, meant more than any job ever could.

Did she love him — the way she had loved his brother Colin?

Yes, of course she did. Deeply. Passionately even. She'd been suppressing her feelings beneath a blanket of grief for Colin, but locked up facing the great abyss, her emotions were bare. Achilles had a passion for life and exploration and contribution like no one she'd ever met. He was an Olympian through-and-through, and she'd been blind not to embrace the opportunity to live her life by his side.

Her hand drifted to her sensitive place with that thought on her mind, and then the door crashed open. Upon glimpsing her contented expression, Wang's face registered surprise. But only briefly. The anger that had propelled him through the door quickly returned to center stage. "The money is late."

"I'm sure it's coming," Katya said a little too quickly while scrambling to her feet.

Wang continued to scrutinize her with his eyes, as if trying to read her thoughts. "I've decided to send them a bit of encouragement." He raised his big gun. "Come with me."

"Where are we going?"

"You'll see."

Images began racing through her mind, unpleasant images, the kind of images she'd previously kept at bay.

Her feet didn't move.

Her eyes locked on Wang's, trying to read intent. His eyes locked right back on hers, as if drilling into her soul.

A ping broke the silence, like the ringing of a countertop bell. Wang's expression changed. He blinked and smiled and whirled around, then ran from the room.

Katya stood still for a shocked second, afraid to move.

A boisterous shout broke the calm of their yacht as it slid through the black waters in the dark of night. *"Ta ma de! Wo zhong le!"*

She crept to the doorway and spotted Wang before a laptop computer on the opposite side of the main room. His arms were raised in victory and he was hopping about like his pants were on fire.

The money had come through.

Achilles didn't know where she was.

The tracking signal must have died.

Chapter 118
National Security

Palm Beach, Florida

MAX CONTINUED with his story, while Jamison rubbed his temples. He left nothing out, from Zoya's escape to Collins' attempted murder. From his own capture and interrogation to their teaming up against Korovin.

Jamison maintained his diplomatic facade throughout the storytelling. No doubt he had endured outrageous United Nations conferences, hosted hopeless international summits, and presided over contentious trade talks — all with the tranquility of a Tibetan monk. But once Max revealed the details of *Operation Sunset*, his dam burst. He bolted to his feet and began speaking with a raised voice. "Fifty planes! Crashing into fifty airport terminals! All at the same time! Tell me you've stopped it! Tell me it can't possibly happen!"

"You're safe for the moment," Max said.

"For the moment? That's not good enough. What does that even mean?"

"It's likely that the planes aren't even in service. And if they are, only Wang has the override code. He's on a boat in the middle of Puget Sound, waiting for his $20 million retirement fund to arrive."

"What if he gets depressed? Goes berserk? Joins ISIS?"

Max kept his own voice calm. He had to recruit Jamison — and the biggest news was yet to come. "Taking over the autopilot systems requires a lot more than a computer and a code. *Sunset* essentially re-couples the aircraft's controls with remote controls. The operator still needs a setup similar to the ones used by drone pilots. Actually, Wang needs fifty drone stations if he wants to use them all at once."

Jamison took a deep breath and sat back down. "Does Korovin have such a setup?"

"My understanding is that fifty drone stations are ready and waiting — in a warehouse in Beijing."

"Beijing?"

"That's right. All part of the plan to blame *Sunset* on the Chinese. But Korovin doesn't have them. Actually Korovin doesn't have anything. He's dead."

Again Jamison looked like he'd blown a gasket. Again he leapt to his feet. "What?"

Max pulled up a video on his phone. "This shows Korovin's helicopter en route from his home on the Black Sea to a hospital in Sochi."

Jamison watched as the big white bird with the presidential seal suddenly changed trajectory and plummeted toward the sea, where it disintegrated upon impact. He hit the replay button and watched it again. When it finished the second time, he looked pale. "What happened?"

"An electromagnetic pulse detonated within Korovin's helicopter and obliterated all the electronics in the blink of an eye — propulsion, navigation, and communication."

Jamison shook his head in disbelief. "I haven't heard a word about it."

"I suspect the Russians are trying to piece together what happened. As far as his staff at Seaside knew, he was being rushed to the hospital. Kremlin staff knew nothing about it. I'm sure it took time before either group figured out that he was missing."

Jamison nodded along. "They'd keep that information very close to the vest until the details were cleared up and a succession plan was put in place. Knowing that's their predilection, the media speculates that Korovin's dead and a coverup is underway every time he drops out of view for more than a few days."

"This time they'll be right."

"So what's your prediction?"

"I'm sure they've started a very quiet search. But as you saw, his helicopter's not going to be an easy find." Max began counting out points on his fingers. "His destination leaving Seaside was unknown, the black box is fried, the location is remote, and the actual flight path is nearly 200 miles long. Eventually some debris will wash up and they'll backtrack it to the presidential helicopter, but I doubt it will be anytime soon."

Jamison looked toward the phone. "It's time I called the president."

Max raised a finger. "If I may make a suggestion?"

"Go ahead."

"Tell him about Korovin, but leave out *Sunset*. Achilles is busy wrapping that up."

"I thought he was rescuing Katya?"

"The two are linked. Show a bit of faith, and you'll be able to present President Silver a *fait accompli* tomorrow. Complete with spin and everything."

Jamison shook his head. "I can't withhold information vital to national security from the president."

"You can if giving him that information would create additional national security issues."

Jamison gave Max a sideways glance. "I don't follow."

"Maintaining the president's health is an issue of national security. You'll already be red-lining his blood pressure when you tell him that control over half the world's foreign nuclear arsenal is about to change hands. If you pile on concern about an imminent domestic terror attack, an attack that would dwarf 9/11, he's likely to stroke out. And there's another, even more serious national security concern."

"What's that?"

"The main objective at this point has to be keeping *Sunset* quiet, thereby avoiding the crippling mass panic that would undoubtedly ensue if word got out. Can we agree on that?"

Jamison rocked his head back and forth a few times. "I guess. Assuming you're 100% certain regarding its operational status. What's your point?"

"My point is this: If the president learns about *Sunset* while it's still an active operation, a lot more people are going to end up in the know. Most likely across multiple agencies. The odds of a leak will grow beyond any reasonable hope of containment. You'll end up with a nation gripped by mass hysteria. The subsequent accusations and investigations instigated by rival politicians will consume the remainder of Silver's administration. Telling him is against his best interests — and those of national security. Better to avoid all that and allow the president to enjoy plausible deniability in case the plan does eventually leak."

Jamison paused a few beats before replying. "What did you mean earlier, when you said the package you'd present would be 'complete with spin'?"

Max felt hope ignite in his chest. He'd gotten Jamison onto the fence. "When a story is contained, you can control the timing and context in which it's released. As a diplomat, you certainly appreciate the tremendous tactical value that control provides. Achilles has developed a plan that will make *Operation Sunset* work in America's favor, but he has to cue it up first. Give him twenty-four hours to do so, Ambassador. He'll come through. It's what he does."

Chapter 119
Yippee!

Seattle, Washington

ACHILLES' PRAYER had been answered. The tracking pellet was still transmitting. He knew where to find Katya! With that one bit of information in his possession, Achilles knew there wasn't a force on earth that could keep him from rescuing her. It was only a matter of time — and a little planning.

When the jet door opened on the Seattle-Tacoma tarmac, Achilles caught sight of Zoya waiting for him beside a rental car far more modest than anything else at the private jet terminal. As he ran across the pavement and into her embrace, an onslaught of mixed emotions flooded his cortex. Regardless of where they'd started, the fire of combat had formed strong bonds between them, bonds that wouldn't wash away with time.

A second-and-a-half of sentiment was all the delay Achilles could abide. He pulled back from the hug and launched into business. "Were you able to buy the supplies I asked for?"

Zoya nodded, her expression as muddled as his feelings. "It's all in the trunk. I wasn't sure about the wetsuit sizing, so I bought three."

"Attagirl!"

Achilles transferred everything to the back seat, and followed it in. "Try and get to within a mile of their location. Someplace you can park near the water."

"Way ahead of you," Zoya replied. "There's a roadside picnic area on the bank about half a mile from where Wang dropped anchor for the night."

Sixty-seven minutes later, having dressed and packed for the assault, and set up Wang's $20 million payment, Achilles waded into the waveless water. A Sea Scooter diver propulsion system hung from his left hand, eighteen pounds of battery and propeller, while a waterproof pack clung to the small of his back, holding the good stuff.

He checked his watch: 22:18. With half a mile to cover and a three mile per hour propulsion speed, it would take him ten minutes to reach the *Winsome Whisper*. He added a couple minutes for contingency, and said. "Initiate the Bitcoin transfer at 22:30."

Zoya checked her own watch. "Twelve minutes. Will do." She wore a brave face but looked a lot more nervous than he felt. "Good luck, Achilles."

"No worries. She'll be fine."

Achilles slid the rest of the way into the water, brought his right hand to the Sea Scooter's handle, and squeezed the trigger. With a quiet hum, he began torpedoing through the dark water that separated him from the woman he loved. The experience brought back one of his worst memories and feelings he'd worked hard to forget. How long had it been since he'd clung to the back of that submerging sub? Better not to think about it.

Achilles hadn't wanted to be burdened with scuba equipment, so he was swimming like a dolphin, coming up for air as necessary. It was dark, so he figured the odds of being spotted were slim-to-none. The water was chilling even in a wetsuit. He shivered at the thought of what Katya had gone through.

He took one last big breath and submersed for the final stretch of the journey.

All was still quiet when he cut the Sea Scooter's motor and drifted up to the surface just behind Wang's boat. Checking his watch, he found himself with three minutes to spare. He grabbed hold of the swimming platform and released the Sea Scooter. While it sank, he studied the *Winsome Whisper's* architecture, and began a mental rehearsal of his next moves.

Achilles hadn't met Wang, but from what Max and Zoya had told him, the Chinese spy was a normal guy. Given that, Achilles expected the arrival of $20 million to initiate a chain reaction, a cascade of emotional outbursts and physical reactions known in espionage circles as a distraction.

Satisfied with the choreography he'd composed to move from the water to the interior cabins with minimal disturbance, he took another glance at his watch. No sooner had he raised the luminescent dial than "*Ta ma de! Wo zhong le!*" met his ears. The Mandarin version of *Yippee!* if he wasn't mistaken.

Chapter 120
Payback

Seattle, Washington

WANG WAS ECSTATIC. He'd done it! He'd recognized an opportunity, and he'd played it just right. He'd danced the fine line between boldness and foolishness while navigating a labyrinth of nuance and misdirection, and he'd come out on the far side with a yacht and $20 million in the bank.

He'd earned his freedom.

The way things were going, Qi might even come around and blossom back into the flower she'd been before her father's downfall. And if she didn't, well...

Still pounding the air in victory, he turned around to face his captive. Her calm expression had morphed to something far more fearful, and he felt his heart drop. "It's all right," he said. "The money came through. You get to go home."

Her expression softened. "You're really going to let me go?"

"Of course. I'm no killer. I've never shot anyone." As Wang gestured toward the SIG MPX submachine gun lying on the dining table, an explosion of pain erupted from his left thigh and he fell to the deck. His hands flew to the source of the searing pain, where they too turned red even as the gunshot registered on his ears.

"You'll be alright," a deep voice boomed from behind, reverting his attention to the external environment. "That is, if I don't shoot you again."

Wang pressed down on both ends of the gunshot wound, but craned his head around to see a big man in a black wetsuit pointing a Glock at the center of his face.

"Are you okay, Katya?" the man asked, his eyes still locked on Wang's.

"I'm fine," she replied. "I was only worried for a second, right after the payment came through."

"He didn't hurt you? In any way?" The man's eyes narrowed as he spoke.

"No. He's been a gentleman, Achilles. And I've been fine. I knew you'd come."

Wang hoped the man was as much a believer in karma as he was. The

nickname by which Katya had called him wasn't particularly
encouraging.

"Toss Wang a pillowcase so he can bandage his wound," Achilles said
to Katya. "Then come over here behind me."

Wang wasn't sure what to make of this twist of fate, but he was glad
to have the opportunity to tend to his leg. He'd always wondered what it
felt like to be shot. Now he knew. It stung like the sting from a six-foot
scorpion. His fingers, now slick and red, quickly found both entry and
exit wounds. Each was bleeding, but not profusely, and there was no
bone in between. A clean through-and-through. A disabling shot.
Tactically, a smart move — with a bit of payback mixed in.

While Wang cinched the pillowcase around his wounds, Achilles
asked, "Where are your weapons?"

Wang didn't look up. "It's on the table."

"And your backup piece?"

"None."

"Don't play games. You play, you lose." The booming voice left no
room for doubt. *Just give me an excuse* was written large between the lines.

Wang weighed his predicament. Achilles' actions made it clear that he
was a clever man who would err on the side of caution. Wang decided
to play it straight. "There's a subcompact between the cushions of the
dining table bench."

Achilles didn't divert his gaze. "When I search the boat, am I going to
find any other weapons?"

"No."

"Swear on your life?"

Wang finished with the bandage and met his captor's eye. "Come to
think of it, there's a flash-bang taped under the dining table. And a
spear gun in the bow gear box. Obviously knives here and there. Oh,
and a second subcompact under the pillow in the master stateroom."

Achilles grabbed one of the dining chairs and set it beside Wang.
Then he pulled him up onto it with his left hand. Wang winced, but
managed not to scream. The adrenaline was going to work.

"Hands behind your back," Achilles commanded.

Wang complied. He then sat still as Achilles zip-tied his hands to the
latticework with quick precision.

Apparently satisfied, Achilles retrieved the Ruger from between the
cushions and the flash-bang from beneath the table. He chambered a
round in the Ruger and handed it to Katya who accepted it with a
familiarity Wang wouldn't have anticipated. Next, Achilles made the
flash-bang disappear into a fanny pack, from which he proceeded to
extract a bagged cell phone.

Powering it on with a satisfied smile, he passed it to Katya and spoke
without taking his eyes off Wang. "Speed dial 1 for Zoya. Let her know
we're fine."

While Katya made the call, Wang studied his captor. He looked like a Super Bowl quarterback. Big, strong, and serious, with determined, intelligent eyes and hands that looked capable of cracking walnuts. Wang had no idea what those hands had in store for him, and he wasn't particularly eager to find out.

Chapter 121
Just One Thing

Seattle, Washington

ACHILLES SLID onto the bench directly across from where Wang was bound. Aside from Wang's incapacitated hands and Achilles' Glock, they looked quite civilized seated there over a mug of tea and a half-eaten sleeve of Fig Newtons. Achilles sat silent until Katya was off the phone, at which point he accepted it back and she slid in beside him. Turning to her he said, "I'm going to ask you again because I need to be certain. It's very important. He really didn't hurt you? Not in any way?"

"No. He just locked me in a stateroom and left me alone. I'm fine."

Achilles turned back to Wang. His expression suddenly much softer, he delivered the first of three big reveals. "I'm here to make a video. A documentary — in which you're going to be the star. In that video, you're going to tell me how you and your colleagues manufactured and installed the autopilot system overrides. You're going to tell it to me again and again, until we get it right. A complete confession. Once you've got it perfect, you're going to repeat it in Chinese. As you speak, a colleague of mine will be verifying the accuracy of your translation."

Wang found himself nodding tentative agreement. After a few seconds of rapid processing, he verbalized it. "Okay."

"Once we're satisfied," Achilles continued, "you sail off."

Wang wasn't sure he believed his ears. "I sail off?"

"To someplace sunny," Achilles added with a wink.

Wang wanted to believe him. His read of the body language told him he could believe him. But Wang had been at this game too long to take anything at face value, especially anything that seemed too good to be true. But he didn't want to risk insulting the man who held his fate in his hands, so instead he decided to probe. "And my money?"

Achilles' features lightened even further. "Yours to keep."

"I don't understand."

"You'll figure it out." He paused, apparently expecting Wang to do just that — right then, right there.

Wang put his mind to it. The modified autopilot units would be removed immediately, so the hijacking could never happen. The government would cloak the entire affair under the deepest, darkest, tightest national security classification. So why did they want his confession? It came to him like a thunderclap, and Achilles' expression said he saw it in Wang's eyes. "You've got a big bargaining chip with Beijing."

Achilles nodded.

"But, in fact, Beijing knows nothing about this operation."

Achilles shrugged.

Wang understood. It didn't matter. Politics revolved around perception, not reality. Of course, if and when the American government played that card in some big back room negotiation, Wang would become the most hunted man on the planet.

But he was already planning on disappearing.

He was already expecting them to look for him. One didn't just walk away from the Chinese Ministry of State Security. When he failed to return from vacation, the BOLO would go out. That had always been inevitable. Faking your death wasn't an option when you also needed your family to disappear. "Very clever. But it's the Russians you should be going after."

Achilles returned a stare so steely it turned Wang's throat dry.

Wang got the message and moved to change the subject. "There's nothing else I have to do?"

"Just one thing."

"What's that?"

"Don't ever get caught."

Chapter 122
Arrest

Washington D.C.

REGGIE SAT in stunned silence while the White House Chief of Staff personally delivered the news that sweet Mrs. Pettygrove, his landlady and surrogate mother, was actually a Russian spy. It was the worst news of his life — until seconds later when Sparkman revealed that she'd been able to eavesdrop on everything Reggie had heard while wearing his wingtips. Every foray into the Oval Office, every ride in The Beast, every trip on Air Force One. It was a staggering blow to a man who would sooner walk out the window of the Washington Monument than betray the person he loved and respected more than any other.

During Sparkman's verbal horse whipping, Reggie came to understand that the only reason he wasn't in hot water legally was that the scenario made everyone from the president to the Secret Service to the FBI to the CIA look bad. There wasn't going to be any legal hot water. The whole Pettygrove affair would never be entered into any record. With President Korovin gone and Ignaty Filippov "vanished" to some secret CIA cell that would never see the light of day, there wasn't much to clean up, other than Pettygrove herself.

Of course, the Pentagon, CIA, and State Department would be busy for months, if not years, updating their plans and processes to account for Russia having inside information, but much of that was assumed anyway and accounted for through routine procedural rotation. Or at least, that's what the few politicians in the know chose to tell themselves.

To Reggie's great surprise and delight, he was conscripted as point-man on the arrest of Mrs. Pettygrove. The CIA convinced the FBI that the old lady would be in possession of a suicide pill. So the decision was made to send Reggie home with a tranquilizer gun. To knock her out before she knew the jig was up. Of course, no ordinary tranquilizer gun would do, not for the apprehension of their chief historic rival's greatest asset. So Reggie found himself walking up the steps of Mrs. Pettygrove's Georgetown brownstone clutching a Langley-issue umbrella.

The entryway light was on as always, although it appeared different to Reggie tonight. It had always been a mark of affection, an indulgence even, extended by a considerate widow who ordinarily watched her electric bill. Now it looked more like a spotlight at Checkpoint Charlie.

The landlady didn't materialize as he entered, eager to wish him a good evening in hopes of extending the greeting into a bit of companionship. That wasn't unprecedented. Sometimes he arrived while she was "indisposed," so he gave her a moment.

Normally she'd trot out from her suite at the back of the main room, wearing a fuzzy pink bathrobe. But tonight she didn't come.

His eyes drifted down to the umbrella. A nervous tick. He called out. "Mrs. Pettygrove."

Nothing.

Normally he'd head up to his room, eager to hit his pillow without delay, but this was no normal night. He headed toward her suite instead. "Mrs. Pettygrove? Are you okay?"

Her room was what Reggie thought of as B&B classic. A four-poster bed draped in a white spread adorned with pink roses, and a few pieces of antique wooden furniture. "Mrs. Pettygrove?"

The bathroom light was on, so he moved toward it. "Are you okay?" Reggie gave the old wooden door a quiet triple-rap using the knuckles of his left hand.

No answer.

Holding the umbrella poised and ready in his right hand, he twisted the knob with his left.

The bathroom was empty.

Mrs. Pettygrove wasn't home, and Reggie knew she never would be.

Chapter 123
Redistribution

Bel Air, California

THE PARTY FUNDRAISER didn't make national news, because it wasn't an election year, but the rich still turned out to mingle with the famous. The Bel Air home belonged to the showrunner of several of television's most-celebrated series, and the guest list included scores of red-carpet regulars paying homage and laying down $50,000 a plate to dine with royalty from Hollywood and D.C.

Achilles, Katya, Zoya, and Max had come in with the caterers, but rather than heading for the kitchen, they made their way up to the owner's study where they could wait without being seen. They found ball gowns and tuxedos waiting, all perfectly sized and accessorized.

No sooner had the four exchanged their server uniforms for formal wear than someone rapped on the door. Achilles opened it to find President Silver, along with Chief of Staff Sparkman, Ambassador Jamison and, to Achilles' great relief, a lovely grande dame. Senator Colleen Collins looked as vibrant as ever despite her recent brush with death.

As their eyes met, Silver said, "Once again, we're meeting under unusual circumstances. And once again, I find myself and our nation in your debt."

As on their first encounter, Silver struck Achilles as exceptionally charming and charismatic. A real head-turner of a man. "It was a team effort, and I'm sure you'll agree that I had an extraordinary one."

"Indeed," Silver said with a flash of his blue eyes, before moving on and extending his hand. "Katya, I'm sorry it's taken us this long to meet. I trust you can appreciate the rationale for my prior lack of attention."

"It's my pleasure, Mr. President."

"Zoya, I must say you're even more lovely in person than on the screen."

"Thank you, Mr. President. It's an honor to meet you."

"I'm sure this won't be the last time. And Max. Welcome to the other side. I'm confident you'll enjoy our hemisphere. People breathe freer here."

"Thank you, Mr. President."

"Now, if we could all grab a seat. I know we have serious business before us and a limited amount of time."

They settled into opposing couches. The four politicians sat on one side and the four operatives on the other, with a lacquered coffee table carved entirely from a redwood stump in between. All eyes turned to the president.

"I'll start with the update. As you know, the government of Russia has not yet announced Korovin's demise. Our sources say the search for him is frantic, but highly confined. They're not even certain that he's dead. Some speculate that he's shaking the trees to find out who his friends really are. Others think he ran off or was kidnapped. The whole situation's a bit reminiscent of Malaysian Airlines Flight 370, except for the lack of publicity."

Everybody nodded along politely.

"The only people with direct knowledge of Korovin's last known whereabouts all speak of a stroke, but none of them have first-hand knowledge of his collapse. And none of the last people to see him are ranking members of government. We're using the window of uncertainty to prepare the ground for Gorsky to assume the presidency. Both Grachev and Sobko have been anonymously reminded of their predicaments, and we're confident they'll remain retired. So overall the geopolitical balance is poised to take a big step toward stability."

"As you planned," Achilles said. "More or less."

"More or less," Silver repeated with a smile. "Now, I've considered your proposal for dealing with information containment. Given Katya's relationship with you and Stanford, I'm not concerned. We'll get her citizenship processed and have her sign a SF-312 Nondisclosure Agreement within a week."

"Thank you, Mr. President."

Silver nodded graciously before turning to Max and Zoya. "I'm afraid your personal history makes things a bit more complicated."

"We understand."

Silver redirected his gaze to Achilles. "I read your proposal with interest. It was unconventional, to say the least. Would you care to add anything in person?"

"Just a bit of perspective, Mr. President."

Silver nodded the go ahead.

"Think of it as a modified version of the witness protection program. Like informants who turn against the mob, we're giving them new jobs."

Silver nodded. "It's an intriguing proposal, to say the least. Clandestinely dispensing Korovin's stolen billions back into Russia under the charitable guise of the Bill and Melinda Gates Foundation. Do I understand correctly that they'll be keeping their identities?"

"That's right. Since Korovin kept their assignment completely confidential, and Ignaty is in custody, nobody in Russia knows what they've done. They don't need to hide."

Silver chewed on that for a second before responding. "Do you actually have Korovin's billions?"

"We know where to get it. My suggestion is that we allow Max and Zoya to coordinate the recovery, which should take anywhere from three to six months. Once it's all in the bank, they go to work for the Gates Foundation, distributing it. It will take a lifetime to properly steward that much money."

"A life sentence to golden handcuffs," Silver said with a knowing smile.

Turning toward Max but focusing on Zoya, the president asked, "Are you really ready to give up your acting career?"

"My age means I will likely have to give it up before too long in any case. Better to do so while I'm on top, before I do anything I might later be ashamed of."

"And this new line of work suits you? You'll need to keep a much lower profile than other celebrities who've turned to charitable causes. You can't become a George Clooney, Angelina Jolie, or Bono. You'll have to ensure that Bill and Melinda get all the headlines."

"I can think of nothing I'd rather do with my life," Zoya said. "Korovin was good for his cronies and the capital, but the rest of Russia suffered mightily under his reign. There's a lot of good work to be done. As for my future husband, I can assure you he is, and will always be, of a like mind."

Max nodded.

"Well then, I believe we're all in agreement." Silver rose, and everyone jumped to follow. "I should get back to the party. People keep pretty tight tabs on me, and we're reaching the reasonable limit of a bathroom break."

After shaking hands all around, Silver paused beside Jamison and Sparkman to address them from the door. "I know Senator Collins would like a few words with Achilles. Meanwhile, I believe Bill and Melinda are eager to meet their new recruits."

Chapter 124
The Kiss

Bel Air, California

SENATOR COLLINS held up her wrist. "We both got scars on this assignment."

"I'm not sure what you mean," Achilles replied.

The two of them were talking at one end of the enormous upstairs study, while the three Russians were engaged with their own lively discussion in an opposite corner. Achilles couldn't help but admire the scene, which reflected the ladies excellent use of their long-promised spa day. Katya's honey-blonde hair was done up to display her long neck and accent her broad Slavic jaw. As if that wasn't enough to draw every eye in the room, she also wore an off-the-shoulder red dress, one guaranteed to add ten beats to every pulse. Zoya was decked out in an emerald green gown fit for a big-budget movie premier. She had styled her thick mane of dark hair such that it cascaded around her slender shoulders, adding an animalistic energy to her exceptionally glamorous appearance. Then there was Max, who appeared every bit the British aristocrat in a tuxedo with the same classic cut as Achilles'. He'd look right at home beside Zoya as they wined and dined and danced their way around the world, coordinating big-budget charity campaigns.

Collins put her hand on Achilles' shoulder. "I read your report — both the typed words and those between the lines. For a while, you believed they'd stolen two years of your life. You began living in a different paradigm, a world without either the work or the woman you hold most dear. That has to shake a person — and leave a few scars."

Achilles took tender hold of Collins' free hand, but didn't speak.

"In the wake of all that, and with two nations working to stop you, you and your unlikely crew fixed the Russian succession planning problem, completed your initial mission, and even returned Korovin's stolen billions to the Russian people. I'm shocked, awed, and thrilled to know that someone like you is out there keeping me safe." Her eyes began to tear. "But I'm also concerned for the toll these last weeks must have taken."

Achilles wasn't sure what to say to that. Honestly, he was no worse for the wear. In fact, he was better off than he'd been before. He'd done some good, settled a score, made some friends, and gained clarity on what mattered most.

His eyes drifted over Collins' shoulder toward Katya. She was so beautiful. An appropriate answer to Collins' comment appeared while he stared at Katya with ensorcelled eyes.

Returning his gaze to the woman before him, Achilles spoke softly. "At rock climbing competitions, people always ask me how I can free solo. Some understand the thrill of the climb, but most say they'd be paralyzed by fear if they didn't have ropes. They want to know what my secret is."

Collins' eyes sparkled with wisdom. "What do you tell them?"

Achilles shrugged. "I tell them my secret."

She held his hand and waited.

"I'm not afraid to die. I'm afraid not to live."

"Just like the original," Collins said with a knowing smile. "But you have to admit, your definition of living is atypical, to say the least."

"Perhaps I take things a bit further than the norm, but I think most people prefer to live life unencumbered — many just don't know it."

She nodded knowingly and released his hand. "I think it's safe for us to join the party, but a word of advice if I may?"

"By all means."

"I wouldn't let Katya off my arm if I were you — half the hunks in Hollywood are down there!"

* * *

John Mayer was belting out an acoustic version of *Half of My Heart* when Achilles led Katya onto the dance floor.

She put her arms around his neck. "You look kinda silly with a shaved head. It's so white."

He gazed into her upturned eyes, and pulled her warm body to his. Nothing had ever felt better. "You look spectacular."

They began to move with the music.

Mayer sang about the struggles of giving one's heart away. The loss of freedom. The fear of falling short. The lifestyle change. All the worries felt familiar. None of them mattered anymore.

As Achilles pulled Katya closer, he felt his heart mend, right there amid the swaying crowd. He hadn't realized that it had ripped, but he felt it coming together.

Katya saw the healing happen, and he knew that she felt it too.

Tears welled up in her eyes, and he kissed her.

AUTHOR'S NOTE

Dear Reader,

By this point, you and I have a thing going. You've let me into your head for hours at a time and found it a comfortable experience. So there's a fit. A cognitive connection. Because of that, I thought you might be interested in learning more about the guy behind the keyboard —and how I ended up there.

If you've read the biography on my website or Amazon page, you're already aware that my background is, shall we say, adventurous. What you probably don't know is that becoming an author was my greatest adventure of all. To get that story and stay informed of my new releases, send an email to TheLiesOfSpies@timtigner.com.

Thanks for your kind attention,

NOTES ON THE LIES OF SPIES

I draw heavily on my background when constructing plots, but I also do extensive research. If you're curious or skeptical about something, you might want to check out the Pinterest Board [https://www.pinterest.com/authortimtigner/research-for-the-lies-of-spies-achilles-2/] I used to store my research. Unfortunately, Pinterest doesn't let you organize the pins on a board, but if you look around you'll find links to the Russian president's palace on the Black Sea and articles on his banking and communication habits, the military stun gun that was the basis for the FP1, the militarization of space including a system like Sunrise, actual gait analysis systems, the American president's limo and body man, the Russian president's helicopter, rock climbing, silicon masks, and many of the locations in the novel.

I'd like to give a special call-out here to Tim Ellwood, a dedicated fan who self-tested a taser's ability to shock multiple people at once by touching it to a conductive surface. Like Max with his vodka flask, Tim concluded that you need flesh between the two electrodes for the taser to work.

WANT MORE ACHILLES

Turn the page for a preview of *Falling Stars*, book #3 in the Kyle Achilles series. **Please note**: Before consuming that story in its entirety, I'd recommend reading the prequel novella *Chasing Ivan*.

FALLING STARS

1

Raven

Versailles, France

THE DRONE PERCHED atop the slate roof like the big black bird for which it was named, saving battery, waiting to strike. Its minders waited nearby in a black Tesla Model X: a pilot, an engineer and the team leader.

Under normal operational security protocols, the three Russians would have hidden away, out of sight, as drone commanders usually did. But this wasn't a normal operation.

This was a test run.

A learning exercise.

All three team members needed to experience the first human capture directly.

The pilot needed confirmation that Raven's cameras were sufficient for combat operations. The engineer needed confirmation that Raven's weapons would work as designed. The team leader needed feedback, immediate and first-hand. If they unearthed any flaws, he'd have to figure out how to fix them, fast.

The house beneath the slate roof was typical old-European city-center. A centuries-old stone-block facade abutting both neighbors on a cobblestone street. The street lights were also classic. Old gas lamps turned electric, now yielding to dawn. The neighborhood was still asleep, other than the baker—and the three Russians in their silent Tesla.

"Why this particular house?" Boris asked.

Michael glanced over at the design engineer. Initially surprised to hear him speak, Michael quickly understood that the query wasn't chitchat or idle curiosity. It was a technical question from a technical man. Boris could build anything. Fix anything. Create anything. He was Leonardo DaVinci reincarnate. But like many savants, his talents ceased at humanity's edge. He was often oblivious to things beyond the mechanical realm. "It's not the house that's special. It's the occupant," Michael replied.

Boris grunted dismissively without turning from the window, his interest extinguished.

"And what's special about her?" Pavel called out from the Tesla's third row. The pilot was former military. He knew better than to ask indulgent questions. But Boris had cracked the door and curiosity had emerged.

Michael kept his eyes on the house while replying. "What makes you think it's a woman?"

"You told Boris the target weighed fifty kilos."

So he had. One point for Pavel. Michael decided to toss him a warning disguised as a bone. "Ivan has a score to settle. She interfered with one of our operations a few years back. Today, she gets what's coming."

Their employer was literally a living legend. *Ivan the Ghost* was the man to whom the wealthy turned when they needed dirty deeds done without a trace.

Or at least he used to be.

Ivan didn't take jobs anymore.

He'd given up his work-for-hire business in order to develop Raven, and the plan that went with it. If that plan worked, and Ivan's plans always worked, he would rake in billions. With a *b*. If it didn't, well, Michael chose not to think about that. Like most geniuses, Ivan had a temper. And like most pioneers, he could be ruthless with those around him when things didn't go his way.

But they would go his way.

Ivan wasn't just a genius. He was meticulous.

Before driving half the night to Versailles' city center, he had them run Raven through tests. Dozens of tests. Dogs at first. Then calves. The trial attacks were nothing short of mesmerizing.

The drone itself was impressive, if not a technological breakthrough. A scaled-up version of the quadcopter you could buy at any hobby store. They powered it using breakthrough battery technology from the lab of John Goodenough—stolen of course—and framed it with the same carbon-fiber construction used on racing bikes and tennis rackets. Boris built it to carry 250 pounds of active cargo, and hinged it to fold up for transport by SUV.

Raven's main offensive mechanism was the true marvel—both for its apparent simplicity and for its amazing action. They named it *The Claw* because it was Raven's grasping mechanism, although to Michael it looked more like a snake than a talon.

Roughly the width of a broomstick and thirty feet in length, The Claw was constructed from segments of aluminum tube, anodized black and ingeniously cut to articulate. If properly positioned, The Claw would wrap around the victim's waist with the push of a single button, automatically applying enough pressure to squeeze flesh without crushing bone. Boris insisted that the mechanics were rudimentary, but The Claw's speed and grace still stole Michael's breath every time he saw it in operation.

Of course, the trick to a clean capture was getting The Claw close enough to strike. Pets and livestock were one thing, humans were literally a different breed.

Given Raven's speed and nimble nature, Pavel was confident that he could catch anyone outdoors. The way he figured it, about a third of the victims would behave like a deer in the headlights, too frightened to react. Another third would allow curiosity to override judgment, rubbernecking until it was too late. For the final third, the warrior class, there was the taser.

Under normal circumstances, Michael was certain this particular target would require the taser. She was a fighter. But today she wouldn't get the chance. Not with Raven silently perched and The Claw ready to strike.

"How long have you worked for Ivan?" Pavel asked, breaking the silence from behind the Drone Mobile Command Unit. He was trying to make the question sound casual, but came up short.

Michael weighed his response. In fact, he'd been with Ivan since Ivan was in middle school. Michael had just won Russia's welterweight youth boxing championship when Ivan's hard-charging father had recruited him to be a companion and mentor to his son. It was Michael's first paid position, and it would be his last. After twenty years, Michael knew he was destined to be with Ivan to the end—be it abominably bitter or unbelievably sweet. "Long enough to know that he treats those who please him extremely well—and those who don't, accordingly."

A mood of grim reflection wrapped around the Tesla like a black burial shroud.

But only for a moment.

Before another word was spoken, the front door of the house opened, and Jo Monfort emerged.

2

Not a Dream

Versailles, France

JOSEPHINE MONFORT stepped onto the stoop of her house and began to stretch. She'd always loved her early morning runs, but ever since moving to the posh Paris suburb of Versailles, they'd been positively blissful. This was her meditative time, her opportunity to put her body to work and her mind at ease. What better place for that than the grounds of the legendary palace built by Louis XIII? What better time than dawn—when the birds were chirping, the bread was baking, and the tourists were sleeping?

Jo braced her hands against the cool stone and leaned back into her calves. She'd dreamed of swarms of locusts, and was eager to push that pestilent thought from her mind. A good run would be perfect.

Two seconds into her stretch, she sensed an ozone disturbance off to her left, like a television coming to life in a cool, dry room. A flash of movement followed, then something brushed against her waist. Something hard. Something cold. Faster than she could flinch it wrapped itself around her, like a cattle lasso or a boa constrictor.

She seized the end of the object with both hands while sizing it up. A steel cable gripped her waist. No not a cable, a mechanical construction. And not steel, more like black aluminum. She had to be dreaming. This couldn't possibly be real.

Time slowed, just like in a dream. She became capable of calculating actions between heartbeats and planning battles between breaths, but she could not escape the feeling that this couldn't possibly be happening.

Willing herself to wake up, Jo wrapped her right hand around the loose end of the coil and her left around the lower loop. She tried pulling them apart.

The object pressed back. It felt alive.

She clawed at the mechanical creature this way and that, trying to pry it from her flesh.

It wouldn't budge. Not a millimeter. Not with everything she had.

She didn't stop.

It got worse.

A billowing hum erupted from the rooftop some twenty feet above her head. It sounded like a swarm of locusts and signaled the second stage of the assault. That explained her earlier dream but shed no light on her present inexplicable condition.

She traced the tail of the mechanical snake up to the source of the sound, a shadow of an object now emerging from atop her home. A big black UFO. No, not a UFO. A drone.

The object that ensnared her was much smaller than a military craft, but much larger than a civilian one. Roughly the size of a mattress, it was shaped like an X with propellers extending from each corner. The snaking cable descended from a spool in the center. It resembled the line dropped from a Coast Guard helicopter, although this was clearly no rescue.

Jo's hands continued to battle her bindings while her brain grappled for answers. If this was an assassination, why not use a gun? If an abduction, why not a couple of thugs and a panel van? There had to be something bigger, deeper, or broader behind the attack. Something strategic. Something sinister. Something …

The answer struck her as swiftly and unexpectedly as the snake. Ivan! Ivan the Ghost. The grandest strategist of them all.

Jo had been part of the team that put a big black mark on Ivan's otherwise flawless record. She had long suspected that he would not forget, that he'd have his revenge, that this day would come. But Ivan had disappeared, and most believed that he was either dead or retired. Apparently he had fooled everyone, yet again.

Without relaxing her grip on the snake, Jo studied the drone hovering overhead. No doubt it had cameras. Was Ivan observing her now? Was he going to watch as the metallic snake crushed her to death?

Convinced that she couldn't overpower the metallic snake, Jo began searching for another weakness. Her focus shifted skyward and settled on the propellers humming overhead. Could she stop them with sticks or stones?

As if in answer, their pitch increased, and her situation went from bad to worse.

The drone lifted skyward and her feet left the ground. Before she could reorient, Jo found herself dangling like a hooked fish.

Desperate to stop her ascent, she lunged for the lamppost. It was the old fashioned kind, a fluted black steel cylinder that crooked to suspend its lamp from above. A functional ornament retained by a city that clung to its grandiose past.

The fingers of her right hand caught the fluting. Pulling carefully on that precious purchase, she swung closer to the pole, but the drone's ascent denied her left hand a grip. Without a second to spare, Jo brought her legs into play. Quick as a falling cat she twisted and arced and swung them around the pole, crossing her ankles as the drone drove her higher.

Her legs latched around the top of the crook. But not at the knees.

She caught it down by her calves.

With her head above the rooftops and her legs clinging to the pole, Jo felt like a worm in the beak of a bird. Refusing to become breakfast, she put everything into her legs. She willed them to become bands of steel.

The upward force pulled the cold coil hard against her diaphragm, restricting her breath and raising her panic.

She pressed the panic back down while refusing to release her ankles. She might suffocate or be ripped in half, but she vowed to fight up to that point. She vowed not to give. She stared up at the mechanical beast with a defiant stare and drew energy from her rage.

That was when she first noticed it. A familiar rectangular barrel with a yellow tip, a muzzle turning in her direction. A taser.

Her heart sank.

Her tears started flowing.

There was nothing she could do.

She had no shield, no place to hide. Just locking her legs demanded all the might she could muster. She wanted to shout "That's not fair!" but couldn't spare the breath.

Staring back at the beast above, Jo swore she would not yield.

ABOUT THE AUTHOR

Tim began his career in Soviet Counterintelligence with the US Army Special Forces, the Green Berets. With the fall of the Berlin Wall, Tim switched from espionage to arbitrage and moved to Moscow in the midst of Perestroika. In Russia, he led prominent multinational medical companies, worked with cosmonauts on the MIR Space Station (from Earth, alas), and chaired the Association of International Pharmaceutical Manufacturers.

Moving to Brussels during the formation of the EU, Tim ran Europe, Middle East, and Africa for a Johnson & Johnson company and traveled like a character in a Robert Ludlum novel. He eventually landed in Silicon Valley, where he launched new medical technologies as a startup CEO.

Tim began writing thrillers in 1996 from an apartment overlooking Moscow's Gorky Park. Twenty years later, he's still writing. His home office now overlooks a vineyard in Northern California, where he lives with his wife Elena and their two daughters.

Tim grew up in the Midwest. He earned a BA in Philosophy and Mathematics from Hanover College, and then an MBA in Finance and a MA in International Studies from the University of Pennsylvania's Wharton School and Lauder Institute.

Made in the USA
Middletown, DE
10 December 2019